SAILOR & LULA
the complete novels

SAILOR & LULA

the complete novels

BARRY GIFFORD

Seven Stories Press

NEW YORK

Perdita Durango first published in 1992 by Vintage Books as "59° and Raining: The Story of Perdita Durango" in *Sailor's Holiday,* which was originally published in somewhat different form by Random House, Inc., New York, in 1991. First Grove Press edition published in 1996.

The Wild Life of Sailor and Lula first published as *Sailor's Holiday* by Vintage Contemporaries, a division of Random House, Inc., in 1992. Originally published in a somewhat different form in hardcover by Random House, Inc., New York, in 1991. First Grove Press edition published in 1996.

Grateful acknowledgment is made to Hill and Wang, a division of Farrar, Straus and Giroux, Inc., for permission to reprint excerpts from *Empire of Signs* by Roland Barthes. Translation © 1982 by Farrar, Straus and Giroux, Inc. Reprinted by permission of Hill and Wang, a division of Farrar, Straus and Giroux, Inc.

The Imagination of the Heart first published in 2009 by Seven Stories Press, New York.

A Seven Stories Press First Edition

Seven Stories Press
140 Watts Street
New York, NY 10013
www.sevenstories.com

In Canada: Publishers Group Canada, 559 College Street, Suite 402, Toronto, ON M6G 1A9

In the UK: Turnaround Publisher Services Ltd., Unit 3, Olympia Trading Estate, Coburg Road, Wood Green, London N22 6TZ

In Australia: Palgrave Macmillan, 15–19 Claremont Street, South Yarra, VIC 3141

College professors may order examination copies of Seven Stories Press titles for a free six-month trial period. To order, visit http://www.sevenstories.com/textbook or send a fax on school letterhead to (212) 226-1411.

Book design by Jon Gilbert

Library of Congress Cataloging-in-Publication Data

Gifford, Barry, 1946-
    Sailor & Lula : the complete novels / Barry Gifford. -- A Seven Stories Press 1st ed.
        p. cm.
    ISBN 978-1-58322-910-1 (pbk.)
    I. Title.
    PS3557.I283S24 2010
    813'.54--dc22
                                                2010008181

Printed in the United States

9 8 7 6 5 4 3 2 1

CONTENTS

WILD AT HEART

THE STORY OF SAILOR AND LULA

This book is dedicated to the memory of Charles Willeford

You need a man to go to hell with.
—Tuesday Weld

CONTENTS

Wild at Heart: The Story of Sailor and Lula

GIRL TALK

Lula and her friend Beany Thorn sat at a table in the Raindrop Club drinking rum Co-Colas while watching and listening to a white blues band called The Bleach Boys. The group segued smoothly from Elmore James's "Dust My Broom" into Robert Johnson's "Me and the Devil" and Beany let out a snort.

"I can't stand this singer," she said.

"He ain't so bad," said Lula. "Carries a tune."

"Not that, just he's so ugly. Guys with beards and beer guts ain't quite my type."

Lula giggled. "Seein's how you're about thick as a used string of unwaxed dental floss, don't know how you can criticize."

"Yeah, well, if he says all that flab turns into dick at midnight, he's a liar."

Lula and Beany laughed and swallowed some of their drinks.

"So Sailor's gettin' out soon, I hear," said Beany. "You gonna see him?"

Lula nodded and crushed an ice cube with her back teeth and chewed it.

"Meetin' him at the gate," she said.

"I didn't hate men so much," said Beany, "I'd feel better wishin' you luck."

"Can't all husbands be perfect," Lula said. "And Elmo prob'ly would-n'ta ever got that second one pregnant you hadn't kicked his ass out."

Beany twisted her blond bangs into a knot on her forehead.

"Shoulda put a thirty-eight long in his groin, what I shoulda done."

The Bleach Boys kicked into some kind of Professor Longhair swamp mambo and Beany grabbed a waitress.

"Bring us a couple more double-shot rum Co-Colas, 'kay?" she said. "Damn, Lula, look at that bitch wiggle."

"You mean the waitress?"

"Uh huh. Bet if I had a butt like hers Elmo wouldn'ta stuck his dick in every other keyhole this side of the Tangipahoa."

"Hard to say for sure," said Lula.

Beany's eyes watered up. "I guess," she said. "Only I'd give up plenty—Valiums even, maybe—just to have me some kind of a butt anyway, you know?"

Sailor and Lula lay on the bed in the Cape Fear Hotel listening to the ceiling fan creak. From their window they could see the river as it entered the Atlantic Ocean and watch the fishing boats navigate the narrow channel. It was late June but there was a mild wind that kept them "not uncomfortable," as Lula liked to say.

Lula's mother, Marietta Pace Fortune, had forbidden her to see Sailor Ripley ever again, but Lula had no intention of following that order. After all, Lula reasoned, Sailor had paid his debt to society, if that's what it was. She couldn't really understand how going to prison for killing someone who had been trying to kill him could be considered payment of a debt to society.

Society, such as it was, thought Lula, was certainly no worse off with Bob Ray Lemon eliminated from it. In her mind, Sailor had performed a service beneficial in the short as well as the long run to mankind and should have received some greater reward than two years in the Pee Dee River work camp for second-degree manslaughter. Something like an all-expenses-paid trip for Sailor with the companion of his choice—Lula, of course—to New Orleans or Hilton Head for a couple of weeks. A top hotel and a rental car, like a snazzy new Chrysler LeBaron convertible. That would have made sense. Instead, poor Sailor has to clear brush from the side of the road, dodge snakes and eat bad fried food for two years. Because Sailor was a shade more sudden than that creep Bob Ray Lemon he gets punished for it. The world is really wild at heart and weird on top, Lula thought. Anyway, Sailor was out now and he was still the best kisser she'd ever known, and what Mrs. Marietta Pace Fortune didn't find out about wasn't about to hurt her, was it?

"Speakin' of findin' out?" Lula said to Sailor. "Did I write to you about my findin' Grandaddy's letters in the attic bureau?"

Sailor sat up on his elbows. "Were we speakin'?" he said. "And no."

Lula clucked her tongue twice. "I was thinkin' we'd been but I been wrong before. Sometimes I get like that now. I think somethin' and then later think I've said it out loud to someone?"

"I really did miss your mind while I was out at Pee Dee, honey," said Sailor. "The rest of you, too, of course. But the way your head works is God's own private mystery. Now what about some letters?"

Lula sat up and fixed a pillow behind her back. Her long black hair, which she usually wore tied back and partly wrapped like a racehorse's tail, fanned out behind her on the powder blue pillowcase like a raven's wings. Her large grey eyes fascinated Sailor. When he was on the road gang he had thought about Lula's eyes, swum in them as if they were great cool, grey lakes with small violet islands in the middle. They kept him sane.

"I always wondered about my grandaddy. About why Mama never chose to speak about her daddy? All I ever knew was that he was livin' with his mama when he died."

"My daddy was livin' with his mama when he died," said Sailor. "Did you know that?"

Lula shook her head. "I surely did not," she said. "What were the circumstances?"

"He was broke, as usual," Sailor said. "My mama was already dead by then from the lung cancer."

"What brand did she smoke?" asked Lula.

"Camels. Same as me."

Lula half rolled her big grey eyes. "My mama smokes Marlboros now," she said. "Used to be she smoked Kools? I stole 'em from her beginnin' in about sixth grade. When I got old enough to buy my own I bought those. Now I've just about settled on Mores, as you probably noticed? They're longer."

"My daddy was lookin' for work and got run over by a gravel truck on the Dixie Guano Road off Seventy-four," said Sailor. "Cops said he was drunk—daddy, not the truck driver—but I figure they just wanted to bury the case. I was fourteen at the time."

"Gee, Sailor, I'm sorry, honey. I never would have guessed it."

"It's okay. I hardly used to see him anyway. I didn't have much parental guiding. The public defender kept sayin' that at my parole hearin'."

"Well, anyway," said Lula, "turns out my mama's daddy embezzled some money from the bank he was clerkin' in? And got caught. He did it to help out his brother who had TB and was a wreck and couldn't work. Grandaddy got four years in Statesville and his brother died. He wrote Grandmama a letter almost every day, tellin' her how much he loved her? But she divorced him while he was in the pen and never talked about him to anyone again. She just refused to suffer his name. But she kept all his letters! Can you believe it? I read every one of 'em, and I tell you that man loved that woman. It must have broke him apart when she refused to stand by him. Once a Pace woman makes up her mind there's no discussin' it."

Sailor lit a Camel and handed it to Lula. She took it, inhaled hard, blew the smoke out and half rolled her eyes again.

"I'd stand by you, Sailor," Lula said. "If you were an embezzler."

"Hell, peanut," Sailor said, "you stuck with me after I'd planted Bob Ray Lemon. A man can't ask for more than that."

Lula pulled Sailor over to her and kissed him soft on the mouth. "You move me, Sailor, you really do," she said. "You mark me the deepest."

Sailor pulled down the sheet, exposing Lula's breasts. "You're perfect for me, too," he said.

"You remind me of my daddy, you know?" said Lula. "Mama told me he liked skinny women whose breasts were just a bit too big for their bodies. He had a long nose, too, like yours. Did I ever tell you how he died?"

"No, sugar, you didn't that I recall."

"He got lead-poisoned from cleanin' the old paint off our house without usin' a mask. Mama said his brain just fell apart in pieces. Started he couldn't remember things? Got real violent? Finally in the middle of one night he poured kerosene over himself and lit a match. Near burned down the house with me and Mama asleep upstairs. We got out just in time. It was a year before I met you."

Sailor took the cigarette out of Lula's hand and put it into the ashtray by the bed. He put his hands on her small, nicely muscled shoulders and kneaded them.

"How'd you get such good shoulders?" Sailor asked.

"Swimmin', I guess," said Lula. "Even as a child I loved to swim."

Sailor pulled Lula to him and kissed her throat.

"You got such a pretty, long neck, like a swan," he said.

"Grandmama Pace had a long, smooth white neck," said Lula. "It was like on a statue it was so white? I like the sun too much to be white like that."

Sailor and Lula made love, and afterward, while Sailor slept, Lula stood at the window and smoked one of Sailor's Camels while she stared at the tail of the Cape Fear River. It was a little spooky, she thought, to be at the absolute end of a body of water. Lula looked over at Sailor stretched out on his back on the bed. It was odd that a boy like Sailor didn't have any tattoos, she thought. His type usually had a bunch. Sailor snorted in his sleep and turned onto his side, showing Lula his long, narrow back and flat butt. She took one more puff and threw the cigarette out the window into the river.

UNCLE POOCH

"Five years ago?" Lula said. "When I was fifteen? Mama told me that when I started thinkin' about sex I should talk to her before I did anything about it."

"But honey," said Sailor, "I thought you told me your Uncle Pooch raped you when you were thirteen."

Lula nodded. She was standing in the bathroom of their room at the Cape Fear Hotel fooling with her hair in front of the mirror. Sailor could see her through the doorway from where he lay on the bed.

"That's true," Lula said. "Uncle Pooch wasn't really an uncle. Not a blood uncle, I mean. He was a business partner of my daddy's? And my mama never knew nothin' about me and him for damn sure. His real name was somethin' kind of European, like Pucinski. But everyone just called him Pooch. He came around the house sometimes when Daddy was away. I always figured he was sweet on Mama so when he cornered me one afternoon I was surprised more than a little."

"How'd it happen, peanut?" Sailor asked. "He just pull out the old toad and let it croak?"

Lula brushed away her bangs and frowned. She took a cigarette from the pack on the sink and lit it, then let it dangle from her lips while she teased her hair.

"You're terrible crude sometimes, Sailor, you know?" Lula said.

"I can't hardly understand you when you talk with one of them Mores in your mouth," said Sailor.

Lula took a long slow drag on her More and set it down on the edge of the sink.

"I said you can be too crude sometimes. I don't think I care for it."

"Sorry, sugar," Sailor said. "Go on and tell me how old Pooch done the deed."

"Well, Mama was at the Busy Bee havin' her hair dyed? And I was alone in the house. Uncle Pooch come in the side door through the porch, you know? Where I was makin' a jelly and banana sandwich? I remember I had my hair in curlers 'cause I was goin' that night with

Vicky and Cherry Ann, the DeSoto sisters, to see Van Halen at the Charlotte Coliseum. Uncle Pooch must have known nobody but me was home 'cause he come right in and put both his hands on my butt and sorta shoved me up against the counter."

"Didn't he say somethin'?" said Sailor.

Lula shook her head and started brushing the teases out of her hair. She picked up her cigarette, took a puff and threw it into the toilet. The hot end had burned a brown stain on the porcelain of the sink and Lula licked the tip of her right index finger and rubbed it but the stain wouldn't come off.

"Not really," she said. "Least not so I recall now."

Lula flushed the toilet and watched the More come apart as it swirled down the hole.

"What'd he do next?" asked Sailor.

"Stuck his hand down my blouse in front."

"What'd you do?"

"Spilled the jelly on the floor. I remember thinkin' then that Mama'd be upset if she saw it. I bent down to wipe it up and that got Uncle Pooch's hand out of my shirt. He let me clean up the jelly and throw the dirty napkin I used in the trash before doin' anything else."

"Were you scared?" Sailor asked.

"I don't know," said Lula. "I mean, it was Uncle Pooch. I'd known him since I was seven? I kind of didn't believe it was really happenin'."

"So how'd he finally nail you? Right there in the kitchen?"

"No, he picked me up. He was short but powerful. With hairy arms? He had a sort of Errol Flynn mustache, kind of a few narrow hairs on the rim of his upper lip. Anyway, he carried me into the maid's dayroom, which nobody used since Mama lost Abilene a couple years before when she run off to marry Sally Wilby's driver Harlan and went to live down in Tupelo? We did it there on Abilene's old bed."

" 'We' did it?" said Sailor. "What do you mean? Didn't he force you?"

"Well, sure," said Lula. "But he was super gentle, you know? I mean he raped me and all, but I guess there's all different kinds of rapes. I didn't exactly want him to do it but I suppose once it started it didn't seem all that terrible."

"Did it feel good?"

Lula put down her hairbrush and looked in at Sailor. He was lying there naked and he had an erection.

"Does my tellin' you about this get you off?" she said. "Is that why you want to hear it?"

Sailor laughed. "I can't help it happenin', sweetheart. Did he do it more than once?"

"No, it was over pretty quick. I didn't feel much. I'd broke my own cherry by accident when I was twelve? When I came down hard on a water ski at Lake Lanier in Flowery Branch, Georgia. So there wasn't any blood or nothin'. Uncle Pooch just stood and pulled up his trousers and left me there. I stayed in Abilene's bed till I heard him drive off. That was the bad part, lyin' there listenin' to him leave."

"What'd you do then?"

"Went back in the kitchen and finished makin' my sandwich, I guess. I probably took a pee in between or somethin'."

"And you never told nobody about it?"

"Just you," Lula said. "Uncle Pooch never acted strange or different after. And he never did anything else to me. I always got a nice present from him at Christmas, like a coat or jewelry? He died in a car crash three years later while he was holidayin' in Myrtle Beach. They still got way too much traffic there for my taste."

Sailor stretched an arm toward Lula. "Come on over to me," he said.

Lula went and sat on the edge of the bed. Sailor's erection had reduced itself by half and she took it in her left hand.

"You don't have to do nothin' for me, baby," said Sailor. "I'm okay."

Lula smoothed back her hair with her right hand.

"Damn it, Sailor," she said, "it's not always you I'm thinkin' of."

Lula sat still for a minute and then she began to cry. Sailor sat up and held her in his arms and rocked her and didn't say anything until she stopped.

"I knew this would happen. Soon as that piece of filth got out of Pee Dee I knew there'd be trouble. He's just got some kind of *in*fluence over her I can't decipher. There's somethin' wild in Lula I don't know *where* it come from. You gotta find 'em, Johnnie, and shoot that boy. Just kill him and dump the body in a swamp. Eliminate the problem once and *for* all."

Johnnie Farragut grinned and shook his head.

"Now, Marietta, you know I can't kill Sailor."

"Why in blazes not? He killed a man, didn't he? That Somethin' Somethin' Lemon person?"

"And he served his time for it. Another thing: If Lula is with him of her own volition—willingly, that is—there ain't much can be done about it."

"Don't talk down to me, Johnnie Farragut. I know what *volition* means, and that's why I want Sailor Ripley off the planet! He's pure slime and it's leakin' all over my baby. You could push him into makin' some kinda move and then shoot him dead. You'd only be defendin' yourself and with his record nobody'd fuss."

Johnnie poured himself another tumblerful of Walker Black Label. He held the bottle out toward Marietta but she shook her head no and put a hand over the top of her glass.

"I'll locate Lula, Marietta, and if she's with the Ripley boy I'll give him a talkin'-to and try to convince her to come back with me. That's about all I can do." He took a long swallow from the tumbler.

Marietta began to cry. She blubbered for a few seconds and then stopped as abruptly as she'd started. Her grey eyes glazed over and turned slightly purple.

"Then I'll hire a hit man," she said. "If you won't help me, I'll call Marcello Santos. He and Clyde were always close."

"Now, Marietta, I *am* goin' to help you. And don't be gettin' carried away. You don't want to be bringin' Santos and his people into it. Besides, he and Clyde weren't gettin' along so well there toward the end."

"It was the lead paint killed Clyde, Johnnie, not Marcello. You know that. And anyway, Marcello Santos has been sweet on me from before I married Clyde. My mama didn't want me to have nothin' to do with him, so I just always kept it polite. Prob'ly I shouldn'ta listened to her. Look at Lula. *She* don't pay me no nevermind."

"Times is different now, Marietta."

"Manners ain't. Might be kids nowadays got it on their mind the world could blow up any second, but seems hardly any of 'em care or know how to act proper anymore."

"I've noticed," said Johnnie. He took a big sip of scotch, leaned all the way back in Clyde Fortune's old Niagara chair, and closed his eyes.

"Lula included," Marietta said. "And mostly it's my own fault. After Clyde died, I tended to indulge Lula more'n I should have, I suppose."

"Yours was not an uncommon reaction, Marietta."

"I understand that, but this obsession she has with this murderer I *don't* understand."

Johnnie belched softly and opened his eyes.

"He ain't a murderer. You got to get off that kick," said Johnnie. "And far's I can tell Sailor was entire clean prior to that event involved Lula. Even there he was protectin' her. Just got too forceful is all."

"Maybe I oughta take a trip, Johnnie. Go to Cairo or Spain or Singapore on one of them tours the Diners Club is always sendin' me brochures about. Think Lula'd go with me?"

"I believe you'd best take things one step at a time, Marietta."

HEAT WAVE

"I used to like the heat, Sailor, I really did," said Lula. "But right now I don't care how good it is for my skin. I could use a cool breeze."

Sailor Ripley and Lula Pace Fortune were sitting next to each other in lawn chairs on the porch of the Cape Fear Hotel. It was early evening but the temperature was still in the nineties, down from the high of a hundred and six that had been reached at just past three o'clock in the afternoon.

"Who told you that the heat does anything good for skin?" asked Sailor.

"Magazines, honey. The ones for women? Like you get in the Winn-Dixie by the checkout."

Lula was wearing her yellow one-piece and Sailor was naked except for his blue boxer shorts with white polka dots on them. She stroked his arm nearest her, the left.

"You've got beautiful skin, Sailor. It's so smooth. I just love to trace my fingertips down your arm or back without thinkin', you know? It reminds me of a skier slidin' through perfect white snow."

"It's 'cause I don't go out in no hot sun," said Sailor. "I don't get fried up like you."

"Oh, I know," Lula said. "There's lots of articles now about how many people, kids even, are gettin' skin cancer? 'Cause the ozone layer is disappearin'. Seems to me the government could do somethin' about it."

"How's that?" asked Sailor.

"Keepin' us separated from outer space and all," said Lula. "One of these mornin's the sun'll come up and burn a hole clean through the planet like a X ray."

Sailor laughed. "That ain't never will happen, honey," he said. "Least not in our lifetime."

"It's the future I'm thinkin' of, Sailor. What if we have children and they have children? You mean you wouldn't be upset if some big ol' fireball loosed itself on your grandkids?"

"Peanut, by that time they'll be drivin' Buicks to the moon."

Lula stared out at the water. Now that the sun had completely gone, a beacon from the Cape Fear River pilot's tower, which was a hundred yards or so south of the hotel, lit up a path along the channel. Neither Sailor nor Lula spoke for several minutes. Down the row on another porch a woman laughed. It was a kind of wild, crazy laugh, and for the few seconds it lasted Lula squeezed Sailor's arm as tightly as she could.

"You okay, honey?" Sailor asked, rubbing his arm where she'd squeezed it.

"I guess so," she said. "I'm sorry I grabbed you so hard but that woman's laugh creeped me out. It sounded like a hyena or somethin', didn't it?"

"Never heard one," said Sailor.

"Oh, you know, like on the *National Geographic* TV?"

"Just sounded like an old gal havin' a good time to me."

"Of all the movie stars?" Lula said. "Susan Hayward had the best laugh. She was all throaty and husky soundin'. You ever see that old picture on the late movie she was the woman went to the electric chair or the gas chamber, I forget which?"

"Nope," said Sailor.

"She was married to this dope addict who beat her up? And she was friends with these robbers and there's a killin' and she's mostly innocent but she ends up with the death sentence anyway. Well, she got to laugh a lot in that one."

"Until they croaked her," Sailor said.

Lula nodded. "Uh huh. But Miss Susan Hayward didn't get cheated on her laugh."

"You hungry yet?" Sailor asked.

"I could eat, probably," said Lula. "But I need me a kiss first, honey. Just one?"

SOUTHERN STYLE

Lula put on her favorite pink shortie nightgown and snuggled up next to Sailor, who was lying on his stomach with only his undershorts on watching *The Dating Game* on the television.

"What you want to watch this silliness for?" Lula asked. "Ain't one of those people have a real thought in their brain."

"That so?" said Sailor. He kept his gaze on the TV. "You want to tell me what if any real thoughts you had lately?"

"What you have to get personal about so quick?" said Lula. "All I mean is you could possibly read a book or somethin'. I hate the way people look and act on TV? They're like puffed-up dolls? And sick lookin', especially in color. People are better off in black-and-white."

Sailor grunted.

"What's that, honey?" said Lula.

"We didn't have no TV up at Pee Dee, baby, you know? They don't make no special A-number-one effort to keep county farm inmates entertained. You kind of have to make do with what you got."

Lula slid her head up and kissed Sailor on the cheek. "I'm sorry, sweetie," she said. "I forget some moments where-all you been the last two years."

"Twenty-three months, eighteen days is all," Sailor said. "Don't need to make more of it than it was."

"While you were away?" said Lula. "Mama insisted on throwin' this dinner party for the Armisteads, some acquaintances of hers from Mississippi. They'd drove up to deliver their daughter, Drusilla, to the college? Sue and Bobby Breckenridge was there also, and Bobby's mother, Alma. Alma must be eighty-six or eighty-seven years old now? She just sat in a corner chair and didn't move or say a syllable. She must be deaf because she never reacted to anythin' anybody said all evenin'. You listenin', Sailor?"

"I been trained to do more'n one thing at a time, peanut, you know that."

"Just checkin', so I know I ain't talkin' for no good reason. Well, Eddie

Armistead is just one very tall anteater of a man? Runs a drugstore in Oxford, where he was born and raised. And Mama has all these books by William Faulkner, you know, the writer? Paul Newman was in a old movie of one of 'em? And Lee Remick when she was so young and beautiful? Now she's old and beautiful, of course. So Mama went to visit William Faulkner's house once in Oxford, 'cause it's a museum now I guess, and wound up meetin' the Armisteads."

"What about the wife?" asked Sailor.

"Mrs. Armistead?" said Lula. "Oh, well, she didn't say very much. Elvie, I think that's her name? The anteater did all the talkin'. He said stuff like when he was a boy Mister Bill—that's what he called William Faulkner?—would scold him for runnin' through the tulip beds of his plantation. Rowan Oak, I think it's named. 'You must run around the flowers, Eddie,' the anteater said William Faulkner told him. 'Yes, sir, Mister Bill,' the anteater said he'd say, before runnin' off over William Faulkner's tulip beds again. For some reason my mama thought this was someway humorous.

"Anyway, Sailor, what I wanted to tell you was about the dinner. That was the best part. Drusilla? The daughter? Why, she looked like somethin' you drink through a straw. And when Mama was fillin' her plate for her Drusilla shouted out—so far, like old Alma Breckenridge, she hadn't said a thing all evenin' either—not to let the potatoes touch the meat? Bobby and I just looked at each other and laughed. 'What'd you say?' he asked Drusilla. 'I just couldn't eat at all if they were touchin',' she said. Don't you think that's about the strangest thing you ever heard?"

"Heard stranger," said Sailor. "But she's a case."

Lula clucked her tongue. "And then, later on? After the Armisteads had left? Bobby said Drusilla was the first real Mississippi belle he'd ever met."

On *The Dating Game* a cute blond girl in a short white dress was standing and giggling and hugging a tall cute guy who had lots of dark hair.

"So what's happenin'?" Lula asked.

"This couple's goin' on a date to Hawaii," said Sailor. "The girl chose him over two other guys."

"Don't the reject guys get anythin'?"

"Gift certificates to Kentucky Fried Chicken," Sailor said.

"That don't seem fair," said Lula.

"Hell, why should *The Datin' Game* be different from real life?" asked Sailor. "At least them boys is gonna get somethin' to eat."

THE DIFFERENCE

"I'm not sure what to do about Mama."

Lula was sitting on the edge of the bathtub smoking a More while Sailor stood in front of the sink, shaving.

"What can you do?" said Sailor. "She's been your mama for twenty years and change now. You know she ain't about to change her ways at this late date."

Lula was looking up at the back of Sailor's head, admiring his curly chestnut hair.

"Honey?" she said. "I sure am glad that prison haircut is on its way to growin' out. Gives me somethin' to grab hold of while we're makin' love."

Sailor laughed. "When I was twelve there was a girl lived next door named Bunny Sweet who was a couple or three years older than me. Bunny loved an old hit record, 'Party Doll' by Buddy Knox, and she used to go around singin' it all the time, especially the part where he says, 'run my fingers through your har.' That's how he says it, 'har' not 'hair.' One day Bunny and two friends of hers came up to me and asked if they could run their fingers through my har, like in the song. They liked that it was so long and wavy. These girls were kind of the bad girls in the neighborhood. Hung out with the local hard asses, guys older than them. They were real sexy, you know? So, sure, I told 'em, go ahead. They formed a circle around me and Bunny slid her long, purple nails into my hair, and then her friends did it, too."

"What'd they say when they did it?"

"Somethin' like, 'Ooh, baby, it's so soft!' I remember the tobacco stains on their fingers, the way they smelled from Florida Water and cigarettes. I thought about their hands, that they'd jacked guys off and stuck 'em in their own pussies. I had a hard time standin' still. When they finished they sniffed their fingers, rubbed 'em together and wiped 'em off on their skirts. It got me real excited."

"You never done nothin' more with 'em?" asked Lula. She flicked the ash off her cigarette into the tub.

"Not with those girls, I didn't," said Sailor. "It wasn't much after that time, though, that I went with a buddy to a party at some girl's house I didn't know. We got into a game of spin the bottle and I wound up goin' into a back room with a very proper-lookin', pretty little blond girl wearin' a blue-checked dress. We were supposed to just kiss once and come back out, but it didn't happen that way at all. She had shiny red bee lips and we really got into it, takin' our time and usin' our tongues."

Lula laughed. "That's hell o' raw for twelve years old," she said.

"It was a surprise, too," said Sailor. "For me, anyway. 'Specially from this straight-lookin' chick I ain't never seen before. So after about three or four minutes we hear the kids in the other room hootin' and hollerin' and whistlin'. Both this girl and I were hot, right? And like I say, real surprised by it. 'I guess we better go out now,' she says to me. We were in a kind of storage room, with pieces of furniture all stacked around us, in some dim red light, and her eyes and lips looked huge. She put her hand on the side of my head and real slowly brushed her fingers through my hair. I tried to kiss her again but she dodged it and ran out. I heard the kids hoot and shout even louder when she came back in the other room. I remember startin' to wipe her lipstick off with the back of my hand, but I stopped and decided to leave it there. Then I followed her out."

Lula tossed her More into the toilet. "You know, there's somethin' I ain't never told you about, Sailor. When I was almost sixteen I got pregnant."

Sailor rinsed his face and toweled himself off. He turned around and leaned back against the washbasin.

"You tell your mama?" he asked.

Lula nodded. "She got me an abortion in Miami from some old Jewish doctor with the hairiest nostrils and ears I ever seen. He told me after I'd be able to have kids no problem. He did it in a hotel room on the beach and when we were goin' down in the elevator? And I was almost passin' out and cryin' with my mouth closed? Mama says, 'I hope you appreciate my spendin' six hundred dollars, not countin' what it cost us to get here and back, on Dr. Goldman. He's the finest abortionist in the South.'"

"You tell the boy who knocked you up?"

"It was my cousin, Dell, done it. His folks used to visit with us summers."

"What happened to him?"

"Oh, nothin'. I never let on to Mama about Dell bein' the one. I just flat refused to tell her who the daddy was? I didn't tell Dell, neither. He was back home in Chattanooga by then anyhow, and I didn't see the point. Somethin' terrible happened to him, though. Six months ago."

"What's that, peanut?"

"Dell disappeared. He'd started behavin' weird? Like comin' up to people every fifteen minutes and askin' how they were doin'? And just seemin' real spacey and actin' funny."

"Actin' funny how?" said Sailor.

"Well, like Mama told me Aunt Rootie—Dell's mama?—she found Dell up in the black of night all dressed and makin' sandwiches in the kitchen. Aunt Rootie asked him what he was doin' and Dell told her he was makin' his lunch and goin' to work. He's a welder? And she made him go back to bed. Then he'd carry on about the weather? Talk about how rainfall's controlled by aliens livin' on earth sent as spies from another planet. Also how men wearin' black leather gloves 'cause they got metal hands are followin' him around."

"Prob'ly the rain boys from outer space," Sailor said.

"It ain't so funny now, though," said Lula. "December, before Christmas? Dell disappeared and Aunt Rootie hired a private eye to find him. He was missin' for almost a month before he wandered back in the house one mornin'. Said he'd been drivin' to work and the next thing he knew he was in Sarasota, Florida, on a beautiful beach, so he decided to stay for a while. The private eye cost Aunt Rootie over a thousand dollars? Then a little while later Dell run off again to someplace and nobody seen him since."

"He don't sound so crazy to me," said Sailor. "Probably just he needed to make a change is all."

"One thing about Dell?" Lula said.

"What's that?"

"When he was about seventeen he started losin' his hair."

"So?"

"He's twenty-four now. A year older than you? And he's about bald."

"There's worse things can happen to a man, honey," said Sailor.

"Yeah, I suppose," said Lula. "Hair does make a difference, though."

DIXIE PEACH

Sailor and Lula sat at a corner table next to the window in the Forget-Me-Not Cafe sipping their drinks. Lula had an iced tea with three sugars and Sailor had a High Life, which he drank straight from the bottle. They'd both ordered fried oysters and cole slaw and were enjoying the view. There was a nail paring of a moon and the sky was dark grey with streaks of red and yellow and beneath it the black ocean lay flat on its back.

"That water reminds me of Buddy Favre's bathtub," said Sailor.

"How's that?" Lula asked.

"My daddy's duck-huntin' partner, Buddy Favre, used to take a bath ever' evenin'. Buddy was a stumpy guy with a mustache and goatee and kinda slanty eyes so he looked like a devil but he was a regular guy. He was a truck mechanic, worked on big rigs, eighteen-wheelers, and he got awful filthy doin' it. So nights when he got home he soaked himself in a tub full of Twenty Mule Team Borax and the water turned a kind of thick grey and black, like the way the ocean looks tonight. My daddy would go over to Buddy's and sit in a chair in the bathroom and sip I. W. Harper while Buddy bathed, and sometimes he took me with him. Buddy smoked a joint ever' night while he was in the tub. He'd offer it to Daddy but he stuck to the whisky. Buddy said the reefer come from Panama and that he was gonna end up there one day."

"Did he?"

"I don't know, honey. I lost track of him after Daddy died, but Buddy was a pretty determined type of man, so I imagine he'll make it eventually if he ain't already."

"Where'd you get high first, Sailor? You remember?"

Sailor took a long swig of his High Life. "Sure do. I was fifteen and Bobby Tebbetts and Gene Toy—my half-Chinaman friend I told you about?—we was drivin' Bobby's '55 Packard Caribbean to Ciudad Juarez so we could get laid. Bobby'd been down there before when he'd been visitin' some family in El Paso, and he and a cousin of his went over to Juarez and got their peckers wet for the first time. Gene Toy and I got

Bobby to talkin' about it one night and we just decided on the spot to get up and go get it done."

"That's an awful long way to go," said Lula, "just to get some pussy."

"We was only—let's see, I was fifteen and Tebbetts was seventeen and a half and Gene Toy was sixteen. I had my first taste on that trip. At that age you still got a lot of energy."

"You still got plenty energy for me, baby. When's the first time you done it with a girl who wasn't hookin'?"

"Maybe two, three months after Juarez," said Sailor. "I was visitin' my cousin, Junior Train, in Savannah, and we were at some kid's house whose parents were out of town. I remember there were kids swimmin' in a indoor pool and some of 'em was standin' around in the yard or the kitchen drinkin' beer. A girl come up to me that was real tall, taller than me, and she had a real creamy complexion but there was a interestin' star-shaped scar on her nose."

"Was it big?"

"No. About thumbnail size, like a tattoo almost."

"So she come up to you?"

"Yeah." Sailor laughed. "She asked me who I was with and I said nobody, just Junior. She asked me did I want a beer and I held up the one I was holdin'. She asked me did I live in Savannah and I said no, I was visitin' family."

"She know them?"

"No. She looked right at me and run her tongue over her lips and put her hand on my arm. Her name was Irma."

"What'd you say to her then?"

"Told her my name. Then she said somethin' like, 'It's so noisy down here. Why don't we go upstairs so we can hear ourselves?' She turned around and led the way. When she got almost to the top step I stuck my hand between her legs from behind."

"Oh, baby," said Lula. "What a bad boy you are!"

Sailor laughed. "That's just what she said. I went to kiss her but she broke off laughin' and ran down the hallway. I found her lyin' on a bed in a room. She was a wild chick. She was wearin' bright orange pants with kind of Spanish-lookin' lacy black stripes down the sides. You know, them kind that doesn't go all the way down your leg?"

"You mean like Capri pants?" said Lula.

"I guess. She just rolled over onto her stomach and stuck her ass up in the air. I slid my hand between her legs again and she closed her thighs on it."

"You're excitin' me, honey. What'd she do?"

"Her face was half pushed into the pillow, and she looked back over her shoulder at me and said, 'I won't suck you. Don't ask me to suck you.'"

"Poor baby," said Lula. "She don't know what she missed. What color hair she have?"

"Sorta brown, blond, I guess. But dig this, sweetie. Then she turns over, peels off them orange pants, and spreads her legs real wide and says to me, 'Take a bite of peach.'"

Lula howled. "Jesus, honey! You more than sorta got what you come for."

The waitress brought their oysters and slaw.

"Y'all want somethin' more to drink?" she asked.

Sailor swallowed the last of his High Life and handed the bottle to the waitress.

"Why not?" he said.

"I'll drop Mama a postcard from somewhere," said Lula. "I mean, I don't want her to worry no more than necessary."

"What do you mean by necessary?" said Sailor. "She's prob'ly already called the cops, my parole officer, her p.i. boyfriend—What's his name? Jimmy Fatgut or somethin'?"

"Farragut. Johnnie Farragut. I suppose so. She knew I was bound to see you soon as you was sprung, but I don't figure she counted on us takin' off together like this."

Sailor was at the wheel of Lula's white '75 Bonneville convertible. He kept it steady at sixty with the top up to avoid attracting attention. They were twenty miles north of Hattiesburg, headed for Biloxi, where they planned to spend the night.

"I guess this means you're breakin' parole, then?" said Lula.

"You guess," Sailor said. "My parole was broke two hundred miles back when we burnt Portagee County."

"What'll it be like in California, Sailor, do you think? I hear it don't rain much there."

"Considerin' we make it, you mean."

"We got through two and a half states already without no problem."

Sailor laughed. "Reminds me of a story I heard at Pee Dee about a guy had been workin' derrick on the Atchafalaya. He hooked up with a prostitute in New Iberia and they robbed a armored car together, killed the driver and the guard, got away with it. The woman done the shootin', too. She planned the whole thing, she told this guy, only she was followin' a plan laid out by her boyfriend who was doin' a stretch for armed robbery up at Angola.

"They were headed for Colorado and had gone north through Arkansas and then over through Oklahoma and were around Enid when who bushwhacks 'em but the boyfriend from Angola. He'd gone over the wall, went lookin' for his old squeeze, and learned about the armored-car robbery. It'd made all the papers because it was so darin' and ingenious. It couldn't have been nobody but her, he figured, 'cause of the way it'd been pulled off, and he'd told her the best route to take to Colorado where the cash could be hid out in a old mine he knew about. He never counted on her attemptin' to pull this gig on her own, of course. It was the score he'd reckoned on makin', maybe usin' her, when he got out of Angola. Anyway, he caught up with 'em before the feds did, and blew 'em both away."

"Nice story, honey," said Lula. "What on earth made you think of it?"

"They'd made it through two and a half states, too, before the road ended."

"What happened to the hardcase from Angola?"

"He got caught by the FBI in Denver and sent back to Louisiana to finish his time on the robbery beef. He's supposed to've stashed the armored-car loot in the Colorado mine. The bodies ain't never turned up."

"Maybe they're buried in the mine, too," said Lula.

"Could be. I heard this from a guy'd done time in Angola. You hear lots of stories in the slam, babe, ain't many of which float. But I buy this one."

Lula lit up a cigarette.

"That don't smell like a More," said Sailor.

"It ain't," said Lula. "I picked me up a pack of Vantages before we left the Cape?"

"They sure do stink."

"Yeah, I guess, but they ain't supposed to be so bad for you."

"You ain't gonna begin worryin' about what's bad for you at this hour, are you, sugar? I mean, here you are crossin' state lines with a A-number-one certified murderer."

"Manslaughterer, honey, not murderer. Don't exaggerate."

"Okay, manslaughterer who's broke his parole and got in mind nothin' but immoral purposes far's you're concerned."

"Thank the Lord. Well, you ain't let me down yet, Sailor. That's more'n I can say for the rest of the world?"

Sailor laughed and shot the Pontiac up to seventy.

"You please me, too, peanut," he said.

ON THE GULF COAST

"Life is a bitch and then you marry one."

"What kinda trash talk is that?" said Lula.

Sailor laughed. "What it says on the bumper sticker up front. On that pickup."

"That's disgustin'. Those kinda sentiments shouldn't be allowed out in public. Is this Biloxi yet?"

"Almost. I figure we should find us a place to stay and then go eat."

"Got anyplace special in mind?"

"We oughta stay somewhere outa the way. Not in no Holidays or Ramadas or Motel Six. If Johnnie Farragut's on our trail he'll check those first."

They passed the Biloxi City Limits sign.

"How about that one?" said Lula. "The Host of the Old South Hotel."

"Looks more like the Ghost of the Old South," said Sailor. "We'll try her."

The lobby smelled of fried-chicken grease and there were three old men sitting on straight-backed chairs under the giant ceiling fan watching *The Oprah Winfrey Show* on a big black-and-white television. All three of them looked up at Sailor and Lula when they walked in. There was a giant leafy potted plant that looked like marijuana next to the TV.

"When I was a kid," Sailor whispered to Lula, "my grandaddy showed me a photo of his daddy at a reunion of veterans of the Confederate army. These old geezers over here remind me of that picture. If one or two of 'em had long white beards, they'd look just like them old soldiers in Grandaddy's album. According to Grandaddy, by the time that picture was taken just about all the survivors had promoted theirselfs to general."

The room was small but cheap, sixteen dollars. The plaster on the walls and ceiling was cracked and there was an ancient Motorola TV with rabbit ears hulking in a corner. There was a card table with four plastic glasses and a pink ceramic pitcher on it. In another corner was a decrepit brown bureau and in the middle of the room was an enormous bed with a chipped black headboard. Lula stripped off the dishwater grey bedspread, tossed it over by the bureau and stretched out on the bed.

"I hate hotel bedspreads," she said. "They don't hardly never get washed, and I don't like the idea of lyin' on other people's dirt."

"Come look at this," said Sailor.

Lula got up from the bed and looked out the window. She noticed that the lower left pane was cracked in two places.

"What, honey?" she said.

"There ain't no water in the swimmin' pool. Just a dead tree fell in, prob'ly from bein' struck by lightnin'."

"It's huge. This musta been a grand old place at one time."

Cars zoomed by on the beachfront highway that ran in front of the hotel.

"Lots of servicemen here," said Lula.

"Let's get fed, sweetheart. The light's fadin' fast."

After dinner, Sailor and Lula went for a walk on the beach. The full moon bleached the sand stark white and turned the Gulf a wrinkled magenta. Lula took off her shoes.

"You really figure Mama got Johnnie Farragut after us?" she said.

"If anyone, it'd be him, honey."

A headless wave rolled up to Lula and she allowed it to wash over her feet. They walked along without talking for a few minutes. The only sounds other than the waves breaking on the beach were cars and trucks honking and racing up on the road.

"You think he'll run us down?" asked Lula.

"Who? Johnnie?"

"Yeah."

"Might. Then again, he'd maybe have better luck findin' Elvis."

"You don't believe Elvis is still alive, do you?" said Lula.

Sailor laughed. "No more'n James Dean is a wrinkled, twisted-up vegetable shut away in a Indiana rest home."

"But you gotta consider all them strange facts. Like the corpse was shorter and weighed less than Elvis?"

"That's just stuff to sell more magazines, sweetheart."

"Well, I wouldn't blame Elvis, though. If he was alive and just wanted to lie low?"

"He's lyin' low okay," said Sailor. "About six feet lower'n we do. Don't concern yourself with it."

Lula clucked her tongue twice. "I heard somethin' awful on the radio the other day," she said. "About this old rock 'n' roll guitarist, he was forty-seven? He got arrested for bein' drunk in Virginia and hanged himself in his cell. Left a wife and seven children. Radio said his daddy was a Pentecostal preacher."

"Guy up at Pee Dee, when he found out a old cell buddy of his got blown away by the son of a bitch his wife took up with while he was servin' time, said, 'Another derailment on life's railway to heaven.' I don't know, peanut, if maybe we won't get a little lucky."

ORDINARY COMPANIONS

Johnnie's first meal, whenever he was in New Orleans, was always at The Acme. He got right in the lunch line and ordered rice and beans with sausages and an oyster sandwich. After he paid for the food, he set his tray down on a table by the window and went over to the bar, where he asked for a Dixie, got it, refused a glass, paid for the beer and walked back with it to his table.

Johnnie ate half of the oyster sandwich before he took a man-sized pull off the Dixie. Still the sweetest beer in the South, he thought, as he swallowed. The polluted river water gave it that special taste, and no doubt if a body drank enough of it he would begin to glow in the dark. That stretch of the Mississippi from Baton Rouge to New Orleans isn't called the Cancer Corridor for no good reason. But it sure tasted good on a ninety-eight-degree day in the Big Easy.

As he ate, Johnnie thought about where, other than New Orleans, Lula and Sailor might have gone. N.O. seemed the most likely place, since they could find work for which they could get paid under the table and fit in more easily than in Atlanta or Houston. Besides, Lula always liked New Orleans. She'd stayed there many times with Marietta, mostly at the Royal Sonesta, whenever Marietta needed to get away on an antiques-shopping trip. Of course, they could be most anywhere by now: New York, Miami, even on their way to California. But N.O. was a good enough guess for now.

"Do you mind if I share this table?"

Johnnie looked up and saw a large, chocolate-colored man in his late forties or early fifties, wearing a powder blue porkpie hat and holding a tray filled with plates of food, smiling at him.

"The others," said the man, "they are *ocupado*."

"By all means," said Johnnie. "Make yourself to home."

"*Muchas gracias,*" the man said, sitting down. He extended his well-developed right forearm and offered Johnnie a big hand to shake. "My name is Reginald San Pedro Sula. But please do call me Reggie."

Johnnie wiped off his right hand on his napkin and shook.

"Johnnie Farragut," he said. "Pleased to meet ya."

Reggie did not remove his porkpie hat and began eating ferociously, finishing half of his meal before saying anything more.

"You are from New Orleans, Señor Farragut?"

"Johnnie, please. Nope. Charlotte, North Carolina. Here on business."

Reggie smiled broadly, revealing numerous tall, gold teeth. "I am from Honduras. Originally from the Cayman Islands, but now for many years in Honduras. Do you know Honduras, Johnnie?"

"Only that it's supposed to be a pretty poor sight since the hurricane come through last year."

"Yes, that's so. But there is not much to destroy. No big buildings like in New Orleans. Not where I live in the Bay Islands."

"Where is that?"

"North of the mainland. On the island of Utila. We have a certain sovereignty in the islands, you know, since the United States forced the British to give them up over a century ago."

"What do you do there?"

"Oh, many things." Reggie laughed. "I have an appliance shop. But I am also with the government."

Johnnie took a bite of the oyster sandwich.

"In what capacity?" he asked.

"In many capacities. Mostly with the secret service."

Reggie reached into his back pocket and took out his wallet. He handed a card to Johnnie.

"'General Osvaldo Tamarindo y Ramirez,'" Johnnie read aloud. "'Teléfono 666.'"

"He is my sponsor," said Reggie. "The general is the head of the secret police of Honduras. I am one of his operatives."

Johnnie handed the card back to Reggie and Reggie gave him a small piece of paper, folded once. Johnnie unfolded it. The printing was in Spanish.

"That is my *permiso*," Reggie said. "My permit to kill. Only if necessary, of course, and only in my own country." He laughed.

"Of course," said Johnnie, refolding the piece of paper and handing it over to Reggie.

"I am authorized to carry a forty-five, also," said Reggie. "United

States Marine issue, before they made the unfortunate switch to the less dependable nine millimeters. I have it here, in my briefcase."

Reggie held up his stainless-steel briefcase and then replaced it on the floor beneath his chair.

"Why are you in New Orleans?" asked Johnnie. "If you don't mind my askin'."

Reggie laughed. He took off his hat and scratched furiously at his completely bald head for a few seconds, wiped the sweat off his scalp with his napkin and put his hat back on.

"Certainly not," Reggie said. "I am here only briefly, in fact, until this evening, when I fly to Austin, Texas, to visit a friend of mine who is an agent for the CIA. He wants to take me bass fishing. He comes to Utila and goes fishing with me. We are in the same businesses and also we are fishermen."

Johnnie swallowed the last of his beer. He'd eaten all he could and stood up to leave. This fellow Reginald San Pedro Sula, Johnnie thought, was undoubtedly telling the truth, but Johnnie had no desire to get into it any deeper.

"It's been a real pleasure, Reggie," he said, extending his hand. "I wish you *buena suerte* wherever you go."

Reggie stood up. He was at least six feet six. He shook Johnnie's hand.

"The same to you," he said. "If you are in Honduras, come to the Bay Islands and visit me. The Hondurans are great friends of the American people. But I have a joke for you before you go. If a liberal, a socialist and a communist all jumped off the roof of the Empire State Building at the same time, which one of them would hit the ground first?"

"I couldn't say," said Johnnie. "Which one?"

"Who cares?" said Reggie, grinning.

Johnnie walked down Iberville Street toward the river. He was eager to get back to his hotel room and read more of Robert Burton's *The Anatomy of Melancholy.* Burton's book, the first treatise on the subject written by a layman, had been published originally in 1621 and was still relevant today. As Johnnie turned the corner and headed north on Decatur, he repeated to himself Burton's definition of melancholy: "A kind of dotage without a fever, having for his ordinary companions fear and sadness, without any apparent occasion."

He'd read for a little while, Johnnie thought, then take a nap. It was more likely he'd run onto Sailor and Lula, if they were here, at night, anyway.

"Hear now how leeches is comin' back into style," said Sailor.

"Say what?" said Lula. "Honestly, sugar, you can talk more shit some-times?" She took out a cigarette the length and width of a Dixon Ticonderoga No. 2 pencil and lit it.

"Got you a pack of Mores again, huh?"

"Yeah, it's a real problem for me, Sailor, you know. When I went in that drugstore by the restaurant in Biloxi? For the Kotex? I saw 'em by the register and had the girl throw 'em in. I'm not big on resistin'. So what about a leech?"

"Heard on the radio how doctors is usin' leeches again, like in old times. You know, when even barbers used 'em?"

Lula shuddered. "Got one on me at Lake Lanier. Lifeguard poured salt on it and it dropped off. Felt awful. He was a cute boy, though, so it was almost worth it."

Sailor laughed. "Radio said back in the 1920s a I-talian doctor figured out that if, say, a fella got his nose mostly bit off in a barfight or some-thin', and he needed a skin transplant there, they'd sew one of his forearms to his nose for a few weeks, and when they took it off they'd slap a couple leeches where the new skin attached from his arm to keep the blood movin' so the skin'd stick."

Lula rolled down her window on the passenger side of the front seat of the Bonneville. They were on the outskirts of New Orleans.

"Sailor? You expect me to believe a man'd be goin' around with a arm sewed to his nose? For *weeks*?!"

Sailor nodded. "How they used to do it," he said. "Course they got more sophisticated ways now. Radio said the Chinese, I think it is, fig-ured a better idea is by insertin' a balloon in the forehead and lettin' it hang down on the nose."

Lula shrieked. "Sailor Ripley! You stop! You're makin' this shit up and I ain't gonna sit for it!"

"Honest, Lula," Sailor said. "I prob'ly ain't precisely got all the facts straight, but it's about what they said."

"Honey, here we are in N.O.," said Lula, "and it's time to change the subject."

Sailor pulled off the road into a Gulf gas station mini-mart.

"We're about dry bones, sweetheart," he said, stopping the car next to a self-serve pump. A sign on the top of it said PLEASE PAY INSIDE BEFORE FUELING.

"Get me a Mounds?" Lula shouted to Sailor as he went into the store.

A tall black man about thirty-five years old, wearing a torn green Tulane tee shirt, grease-stained brown slacks, no socks, ripped tennis shoes and a dirty orange Saints baseball cap, was piling items on the counter by the cash register. In the pile were four ready-made, plastic-wrapped sandwiches, two tuna salad and two cotto salami; six Twinkies; a package of Chips Ahoy chocolate chip cookies; four Slice sodas; two Barq's root beers; and a large package of fried pork rinds, extra salted.

"Sorry, gentlemen," the man said to Sailor and another guy who'd come in right behind Sailor and was also waiting to pay for gas, "I'm 'most finished on my shoppin' here."

"This be it?" the old guy behind the counter said.

"Y'all take American Express?" asked the man.

"Yessir," said the old guy. He had on a green Red Man chewing tobacco cap and a faded blue, short-sleeved attendant's work shirt with the name Erv sewn in black cursive above the chest pocket.

"Then lemme throw in a couple more things," said the man.

Sailor and the man in line behind him watched as the black man gathered up several more packages of Twinkies along with a few cupcakes and half a dozen cans of Pretty Kitty cat food, three liver and three chicken dinner portions, and tossed them on his pile.

"Pussycats gotta eat, too," he said to Sailor, smiling. He had no upper teeth that were visible.

He handed an American Express card to the clerk, who ran it through the verifier. The card checked out okay and the old guy prepared a charge slip, had the man sign it and bagged the purchases.

"I'd just soon have a paper bag rather than a plastic one, if it's same to you," the man said to the clerk.

"We don't have no paper bags," the old guy said, shoving the plastic bag he'd filled toward the man.

"Thanks for waitin', gentlemen," the man said to Sailor and the other patron, picked up his bag and walked out.

"All I want's ten bucks regular," Sailor said to the old guy. "Oh yeah, and a Mounds bar." He took one off the candy and gum rack next to the register and handed the clerk a twenty-dollar bill.

"I ain't got my American Express card with me," he said, "so I got to use cash. Hope that's okay."

Sailor smiled at the old guy but the clerk kept a poker face and just gave him his change. The guy in line behind Sailor shook his head and grinned.

"That took long enough," Lula said when Sailor got back to the car. "You forget my Mounds?"

Sailor tossed her the candy bar.

"I think the country done changed just a little while I was away, peanut," he said.

Lula sank her small white teeth into the chocolate-covered coconut.

"You got to keep an eye on it," she said as she chewed. "That's sure."

By the time Sailor finished pumping the gas, Lula had polished off both sections of the Mounds bar.

"Hope you don't mind I didn't save none for you," Lula said as Sailor climbed back into the driver's seat. "I was dyin'?"

BIRDS DO IT

"I love it when your eyes get wild, honey. They light up all blue almost and spin like pinwheels and little white parachutes pop out of 'em."

Sailor and Lula had just finished making love in their room at the Hotel Brazil on Frenchmen Street.

"Oh, Sailor, you're so *aware* of what goes on with me? I mean, you pay *attention*. And I swear, you got the sweetest cock. Sometimes it's like it's talkin' to me when you're inside? Like it's got a voice all its own. You get right *on* me."

Lula lit a cigarette and got up from the bed and walked over to the window. She stuck her head outside and craned her neck around but she couldn't quite see the river. Lula sat naked on the end of the table under the open window, staring out and smoking.

"Enjoyin' the view?" Sailor said.

"I was just thinkin' about how people oughta fuck more in the daytime. I don't think there'd be so much trouble about it if they did."

"What kinda trouble?"

"Oh, I don't know. Just seems like people make more of a big deal out of it at night? Get all sorts of exotic expectations, I guess, and things go strange in 'em. It checks out simpler in daylight's what I think."

"You're prob'ly right, sweetie," said Sailor. He yawned, then threw off the sheet that had been covering him and stood up. "Let's go down and get somethin' to eat, okay? Otherwise, I won't make it past dark."

Sailor and Lula sat at the counter in Ronnie's Nothin' Fancy Cafe on Esplanade, drinking double-size cups of Community coffee. Lula picked apart a giant jelly doughnut, licking the powdered sugar off her fingers. A man on the stool next to Sailor lit up a rum-soaked crook.

Sailor said to him, "My grandaddy used to smoke crooks. Wolf Brothers."

"Used to cost seven cents apiece," the man said. "Now they're five for a buck. Buck and a half some places. Want one?"

"No, thanks," said Sailor, "not while I'm eatin'."

"George Kovich," said the man, extending a gnarled, liver-spotted hand, the knuckles of which looked as if they'd been broken more than once. "You mighta heard of me."

Sailor shook his hand. "Sailor Ripley. This woman is Lula Pace Fortune."

Lula nodded and smiled at George Kovich.

"Pleased to meet you, young lady," Kovich said.

"Don't know that I have," said Sailor. "Should I know about you for anything in particular?"

"Was in all the papers a while back. Two—no, three years now. I'm seventy-six, was only seventy-three then. Had a business in Buffalo, New York, called Rats With Wings. Killed pigeons for anyone who wanted 'em killed. Did *hand*somely, *real* handsomely, for three or four months, till I got shut down."

"Why were you killin' pigeons, Mr. Kovich?" asked Lula. "Were you in the exterminatin' business?"

"No, ma'am, I was a housepainter, in the union forty-one years. I'm retired now, livin' with my sister, Ida. Ida moved down here twenty-five years ago, married an oil man named Smoltz, Ed Smoltz. He's dead now, so it's just me and Ida. I sold my house and moved down after the city of Buffalo put me out of business. Hell, RWW was doin' them a service, and they charged me with endangerin' the public."

"Tell us about the pigeons, Mr. Kovich," said Lula.

"They're useless pests. I've shot hundreds of 'em. My neighbors hired me to get rid of the pigeons that gathered on their roofs and porches and made noise and left droppings all over. I was doin' a job, a good one. Shot a hundred ten of them flyin' rodents just on my own in a couple of days. Neighbors asked me how come the spotted bastards didn't light on my house or my brother Earl's anymore, and I told 'em the truth. I shot 'em. Earl's gone now. Heart attack six months ago. His widow, Mildred, she still lives in the house next to mine. She's stone deaf but the racket the pigeons made drove Earl crazy. He could hear 'em even with the TV on. He owned a bar thirty years, the Boilermaker, on Wyoming Street. Earl's roof was a favorite spot for pigeons. They lit there day and night. I wanted to toss a grenade up there."

"If your neighbors didn't mind," said Sailor, "how'd you get put out of business?"

"Woman drivin' down the street spotted me on a roof with my rifle. She called the police and they came out and arrested me. Thought I was a sniper! Seventy-three years old! Boys at the VFW loved that one. Cops didn't understand about the pigeons, the damage they do to personal property. I used to complain to the city but they never lifted a finger. I was gonna put out poison, but I was afraid somebody's cat would eat it. Hell, I had six cats myself. So I used the twenty-two because it didn't make much noise and the ammo was cheap."

"What happened on the charges?" asked Sailor.

"Guilty on a reduced charge. Hundred-dollar fine and ordered to desist. Pigeons carry diseases and muss up the place. You seen it. Plain filth."

Kovich stood up and put some money on the counter. He was a large man, six two even though he was slightly stoop shouldered. For a man in his seventies he exuded a surprisingly powerful presence. He looked strong.

"It's a serious situation," he said. "Not like the Turks and the Armenians, maybe, or the Arabs and the Jews, but I want people to remember me and what I've done and pick up where I left off. Somebody had to make a move. It was nice meetin' you folks. Ida's expectin' me."

After George Kovich had gone, Lula ordered another jelly doughnut and more coffee.

"Once in the Variety Do-Nut?" she said to Sailor. "I saw a big ol' roach crawl across a creme-fill I was gonna take? When I told the girl workin' there about it she said she was sorry, but even though she wanted to, she just couldn't charge me any less for that one. If Mr. Kovich'd been there he prob'ly woulda just taken out his gun and drilled that bug on the spot."

" 'I don't locomote no more.' "

"What's that?" said Sailor. "You don't what?"

"I'm just readin' here? In the *Times-Picayune*?" said Lula. "About Little Eva, who sung that song 'The Locomotion' that was a hit before we was even born?"

"Still a good one," Sailor said. "What's it say?"

" 'Little Eva's doin' a brand-new dance now,' " Lula read. " " "I don't locomote no more," said Eva Boyd as she wiped the counter at Hanzies Grill, a soul food restaurant in Kingston, N.C. It's been twenty-five years since Boyd, as teen-aged Little Eva, hit the top of the charts with "The Locomotion." "I ain't into singin' over chicken," the forty-three-year-old Boyd said in a recent interview. She still sings with a gospel group from her church and is considerin' makin' a record. "She sounds beautiful," said waitress Loraine Jackson.' "

"Good to know she ain't quit singin'," said Sailor. "It's a gift."

Sailor and Lula were sitting on a bench by the Mississippi watching the barges and freighters glide by. It was late evening but the sky was plum colored, soft and light.

"I don't think we should hang around too long in N.O.," Sailor said. "This is likely the first place they'll come lookin'."

Lula folded the newspaper and put it down next to her on the bench.

"I don't see what Mama can do about us," she said. "Seems to me unless she has me kidnapped, there's no way I'm goin' back without you. And you'd just get popped for violatin' parole if you do. So, there ain't much choice now."

"You know Dimwit Taylor, guy hangs around front of Fatty's Dollar-Saver?"

"Sure. He don't have no teeth and's always smilin' so ugly and sayin', 'Man ain't lonesome long's he got a dog.' Only he ain't got no dog?"

"The one."

"What about him?"

"You ever sit down and talk with him?"

"Not hardly. Always looks like he just crawled out of a pit. Smells it, too."

"He used to be a ballplayer, professional, mostly on barnstormin' teams around the South. Told me once in Alabama, like forty years ago, he was playin' in a game against a black team from Birmin'ham had an amazin' young center fielder could grab anythin' hit his way. There wasn't no outfield fence at the field they was playin' at, so nobody on Dimwit's team could put the ball over this kid's head. He'd just spin, run out from under his cap and take it out of the air like a piece of dust. After the game, Dimwit talks to the boy, turns out he's only fifteen years old."

"What's this got to do with us bein' on the run?"

"That's just it," said Sailor. "Dimwit asked the kid how'd he know just where to head soon's the ball's hit, so he'd snatch it before it touched the ground. And the kid said, 'I got the range and the speed to change.' Dimwit said the kid had it exactly right, and he made it to the big leagues, too."

"So you figure you got the range, huh?"

Sailor laughed. "I do, peanut. I just got to trust myself, is all. And I got speed to burn."

Lula pushed herself right up against Sailor and rested her head on his chest.

"I like how you talk, Sailor. And you know what? I believe you, I really, really do."

LOCUS CERULEUS

On his first night in New Orleans, Johnnie Farragut sat on a stool in Snug Harbor watching the Braves lose again on TV, this time to the St. Louis Cardinals. A guy down the bar was complaining loudly about the ineptitude of the Atlanta team.

"The Cards ain't got a guy on the team can poke a ball past the infield, and the Braves still can't beat 'em," the man shouted. "Murphy must be a saint, stickin' with this outfit. He could be playin' in New York, L.A., anywhere, makin' his two million on a winnin' club."

"Maybe he likes the weather in Atlanta," said someone else.

"Yeah, and Mother Teresa is carryin' her and Bishop Tutu's love child," said the bartender.

Johnnie ordered his second double Black Label on the rocks and took out his pen and spiral notebook. He'd always wanted to be a writer, especially for television shows like *The Twilight Zone*, *The Outer Limits* or *One Step Beyond*, programs that, unfortunately, were no longer on the air. Whenever he had an idea for a story, he wrote it down. Just now Johnnie felt a ripple in his locus ceruleus, the area of the brain from which dreams emanate. Johnnie had read about this, and he believed that the locus ceruleus was his center of creativity. He never ignored the signal. Johnnie took his drink and notebook and moved to a booth so that he could concentrate. Finding Sailor and Lula would have to wait.

A GOOD CONNECTION
by Johnnie Farragut

Harry Newman sat on a corner stool in Barney's Tavern, watching the ballgame on TV. An error by the Braves shortstop in the bottom of the ninth gave the game to St. Louis and Harry swore under his breath. He'd put a couple of Jacksons on Atlanta this morning on the long end of five to two; a good bet, he'd figured. Lousy luck was all it was, he thought. All the guy had to do was keep his glove down, flip the ball to second for the force, and that was it. Instead, the ball goes through, all the way to the wall, two runners score, and that's the name of that tune.

Harry swallowed the last of his beer and slid off the stool. Barney came over behind the bar. "Tough luck, Harry," he said. "You oughta know better. The Braves never have no good luck in St. Louis." "Yeah, and I never have no good luck anyplace," said Harry, as he headed out the door. "That guy," Barney said to the customer who'd been sitting at the bar next to Harry, "he just don't know how to bet, is all. Loses ten times for every one he wins." "Some guys are like that," said the customer. "They never learn."

Harry walked downtown, shuffling along, not sure of where he was headed. He almost bumped into someone, excused himself, looked up, and that's when he saw it: a bright yellow 1957 Buick convertible. It was cherry, in perfect condition, sitting in the front row of Al Carson's used-car lot. Harry went right to it and ran his hand over the right front fender, then stroked up and along the top. It was the most gorgeous automobile he'd ever seen.

"She's somethin', ain't she, Harry?" said Al Carson, who'd come up behind him. Harry didn't even turn around to look at the wizened little car dealer. He just couldn't take his eyes off the old Buick. "She sure is," said Harry. "It looks brand-new." "Just about," said Al. "Only a fraction more than 15,000 miles on her in thirty years. A little old lady kept it in her garage. Only drove it to church on Sundays and to see her sister across town twice a month. Hard to believe, I know, but true." "How much, Al?" asked Harry. "How much do you want for her?" "Three grand," said Al. "But for you, Harry, make it twenty-seven fifty." "I've got about forty bucks on me now, Al," said Harry. "How about if you take that and I'll pay you a hundred a month?" "I don't know, Harry," Al said, shaking his tiny bald head. "Your credit ain't been at the top of the list lately." "Oh, come on, Al. I'll pay you. I will. I've just got to have this beauty."

Harry walked around the car, opened the driver's side door

and got in. "Hey, what's this?" he said. "A telephone? They didn't have telephones in many cars over thirty years ago!" "Doesn't work, of course," said Al. "Don't know that it ever did. Doesn't appear it was ever really hooked up to nothing. I bought the car from the old woman's son and he couldn't tell me about it, either. Just said he always thought it was odd, too. What'd the old lady need a phone in her car for, anyway?" Al laughed. "I guess I should charge you extra for it!"

Harry slid back out and handed his two twenties to Al. "Come on, Al. You can trust me for it. You know me. I ain't gonna go run nowhere and hide." "You don't ever have enough dough to go nowhere!" said Al. "But I guess I can let you take it. Come on in the office and sign the paper and you can drive it out right now. She runs real good."

Harry drove his cherry 1957 Buick all over town that day, showing it off to everybody, proud as could be. After cruising around the neighborhood a few times he decided to take it out into the country for a real spin, to cut it loose and see what she could do on the open road. Not far past the city limits it began to rain. Harry put on the windshield wipers and they worked just fine, humming away as they cleared the water from view. Harry gave the Buick the gun, hurtling along the highway like a yellow flame. Rounding a curve, however, the tires hit a slick spot and the Buick spun out of Harry's control. He fought to keep the car on the road but it wobbled, slid and finally flew off the side into a ditch. The impact knocked Harry out.

"This is the operator. How may I help you? Hello, this is the operator speaking. How may I be of assistance?" Harry came to slowly, awakened by the sound of a voice. Someone was speaking to him. But who? He shook his head, opened his eyes, and saw that the telephone receiver had fallen off the hook. "Hello? Hello? This is the operator. What number do you want?" The voice was coming from the car phone. Harry shook his head again. He thought this must be his imagination, that his head was full of cobwebs from the crash. But no, it was the operator talking.

Harry picked up the receiver. "Hello," he said. "Operator? I'm sorry, I...I've just been in an accident and I'm stuck in a ditch. I mean my car is stuck. I must have lost control in the storm and gone off the road. Yes, I'm all right, I think," he told her. "Where am I?" Harry struggled around in the seat to look out the window. The rain had stopped. "About fifteen miles past the city limits, I guess. On the old Valley Road. Could you call a tow truck for me? Yes, certainly, Operator. I'll hold on." Harry shook his head again and felt his shoulder, his legs. He seemed to be in one piece, not seriously hurt. Another voice came on the line. "Bud's Service Station? Right, yes, well, I've had an accident. She told you? Twenty minutes? Great, great. No, I guess I'll be here all right." Harry hung up the telephone and stared at it.

Twenty minutes later a truck pulled up. The lettering on the sides of the doors of the cab said BUD'S TOW 24 HOURS. A large man, about fifty years old, with a two-day growth of beard and an unlit cigar stub stuck in his mouth, climbed down out of the cab and came over to where Harry was standing beside the Buick. The man wore a dark blue work shirt with the sleeves rolled partway up each meaty forearm. The name Bud was emblazoned above the left front pocket.

"They don't make these new buggies like the old ones," Bud said, as he looked the Buick over. Harry laughed. "That's pretty good," said Harry. "She was holding the road pretty well until that curve back there." Bud grunted and bent down to look at the right front wheel that was twisted halfway around. Bud grunted again as he raised himself back up. "Yeah, I keep my daddy's old '36 Packard runnin'," he said. "Now that's an automobile that won't let you down so long as you take care of it. They just churn these babies out now in too much of a hurry. They don't make 'em to last. Well, let's see if we can get her out of this," said Bud, as he walked back to the tow truck.

Bud had the Buick up and out of the ditch in ten minutes. "Hop up in the cab," he told Harry. "We'll take her back to the station and get that wheel straightened out." Harry and Bud climbed into the truck and Bud started off toward town. He reached over and snapped on the radio. "Say," he said, "I noticed that telephone in the car. You rig that up yourself? What is it, shortwave?" Harry nodded, confused. "No, er . . . yes, yeah, that's it."

The truck radio buzzed as it warmed up and Bud fiddled with the dial as he drove. "Got to hear the game. Who're you bettin' on? The Braves or the Yanks?" "What?" asked Harry. "In the Series, it starts today, you know. I like Milwaukee myself. Spahn and Burdette are gonna be tough to beat in a short Series," said Bud. "But I'm afraid of that crafty little lefty, Ford. I'm pretty sure of one thing, though." "What's that?" asked Harry, still trying to figure out what was going on. "That bum Larsen won't pitch another perfect game like he did last year." Bud laughed. "I'd bet the station on that!"

"But Larsen pitched his perfect game in the '56 Series!" said Harry. "That's right, pal," Bud answered. "Like I said, last year. Probably nobody'll do that again in our lifetime, I'll bet." Just then the radio kicked in, and the voice of Mel Allen, the New York Yankees' announcer, filled the cab of the truck. "Welcome to the broadcast of the World Series," said Mel Allen in his unmistakable, mellifluous drawl. "It's a beautiful afternoon here on October second, nineteen hundred and fifty-seven, as the Milwaukee Braves and the New York Yankees prepare to do battle in the House that Ruth Built."

Harry rubbed his head, unable to speak. Then he relaxed and began to smile, suddenly comfortable with the situation. "So whaddaya think?" asked Bud. "The Braves'll win it in seven games," Harry said. "You can bet on it." "That's what I wanted to hear!" said Bud, pounding a fist on the steering wheel. Harry just grinned and watched the road. As the truck passed the City Limits sign, Harry said, "I might put a few bucks down on the Braves myself. Yeah, I think I'll do just that."

ANIMAL LIFE

"Did you know that my mama was a runner-up for Miss Georgia Chick in 1963?" asked Lula.

"No, sweetheart, I didn't. But I thought you had to be from Georgia to be in a contest like that," said Sailor.

"She was livin' in Valdosta then, with my Great-Aunt Eudora, Aunt Rootie's mama. You remember Rootie, she's Cousin Dell's mama? Dell went crazy and disappeared a while back? Anyways, this is from the time before she married Daddy, which wasn't until 1968. Every year there's this beauty pageant in Gainesville, Georgia. Used to be, anyhow. And Eudora's dear friend, Addie Mae Audubon? Who was a descendant of the man who invented bird watchin'? She got Mama into it. I got the sterlin' silver bracelet the judges give her in my jewelry box back home. Says on it, 'Miss Georgia Chick Contest, 1963,' engraved."

"What'd the winner get?"

"Prob'ly a car or somethin'. Trip to Miami Beach, maybe? When I asked her about it, Mama said she didn't win 'cause her tits wasn't big enough for the one-piece bathin' suit she wore. But she had the best teeth, she said. The girl that won? Mama told me her teeth were almost as big as her tits. I saw a photo of the contest with Miss Georgia Chick holdin' a box of baby roosters. Mama was standin' right beside her."

"You know what they do with 'em?" asked Sailor.

"With what? The baby roosters?"

"Uh huh. Grind 'em up for fertilizer. Only hens make good fryers."

Lula made a face. "Oh, Sailor, that's so sad. Killin' all them babies like that."

"What they do, though," said Sailor.

"Well, Mama said the place stunk terrible. The whole town of Gainesville. From the chicken business? She never has forgot it. The next year Mama moved back up home."

Sailor and Lula hadn't gone to sleep yet, though it was almost four o'clock in the morning. They were lying in bed in their room at the Hotel Brazil, holding hands. A blue snake of light from the streetlamp curled in under the window shade and stretched across their bodies.

"Sailor?"

"Honey?"

"Ever imagine what it'd be like to get eaten alive by a wild beast?"

"Mean a tiger?"

"Yeah. Sometimes I think it'd be the biggest thrill?"

Sailor laughed. "It better be, darlin', 'cause it'd be the last."

"Ripped apart by a gorilla, maybe," said Lula.

"How about bein' squeezed to death by a python?"

Lula shook her head. "I don't think so. That might be way too slow? And you'd feel your ribs crackin' and insides oozin' out. I'd rather get grabbed sudden and pulled apart quick by a real powerful animal."

"Lula, sometimes I gotta admit you come up with some weird thoughts."

"Anythin' interestin' in the world come out of somebody's weird thoughts, Sailor. Couldn't have been no simple soul dreamed up voodoo, for an instance."

"Voodoo?"

"Sure. How else you explain stickin' pins in dolls to make a person squirm or have a heart attack? Or cookin' someone's fingernail clippin's to make 'em vomit till they ain't got nothin' left inside and drop dead. You tell me, Sailor, who could come up with shit like that ain't super weird?"

"You got me, peanut."

"You certain?"

"I ain't never met anyone come close to you, sugar."

Lula rolled over on top of Sailor.

"Take a bite of Lula," she said.

"He's here," said Lula. "Johnnie Farragut? I seen him."

"Where?" asked Sailor.

"Over at the Cafe du Monde. He was sittin' at a table outside, eatin' doughnuts."

"He see you?"

"I don't think so. I was comin' out of the praline shop across the street? And I spotted him and come right back here to the hotel. I guess this means we'd best scoot, huh, Sailor?"

"I s'pose, sugar. Come sit next to me a minute."

Lula set her box of pralines on the dresser and sat down on the bed by Sailor.

"We'll be okay, honey. I'll go down do a oil change and we'll hit it."

"Sailor?"

"Uh huh?"

"Recall the time we was sittin' one night behind the Confederate soldier? Leanin' against it. And you took my hand and put it on your heart and you said, 'You feel it beatin' in there Lula get used to it 'cause it belongs to you now.' D'you recall that?"

"I do."

Lula put her head down in Sailor's lap and he stroked her smooth black hair.

"I was hopin' you would. I know that night by heart. Sometimes, honey? I think it's the best night of my life. Really."

"We didn't do nothin' special I can remember. Just talked, is all."

"Talkin's good. Long as you got the other? I'm a big believer in talkin', case you ain't noticed."

"I had a dream while you were gone," said Sailor. "It's strange, but when I was up at Pee Dee I didn't hardly dream. Maybe a couple or three times, and then nothin' I could remember. About girls, I guess, like ever'body is in."

"You remember this one?"

"Real clear. It wasn't no fun, Lula. I was in a big city, like New York, though you know I ain't never been there. It was winter, with ice and snow all over. I was stayin' in some little ol' rathole with my mama. She was real sick and I had to score some medicine for her, only I didn't have no money. But I told her anyway I'd go get the pills she needed. So I was out in the streets and there was about ten million people comin' and goin' in all directions, and it was impossible for me to keep walkin' straight, to get to wherever it was I was goin'. The wind was blowin' super hard and I wasn't dressed warm. Only instead of freezin', I was sweatin', sweatin' strong. The water was rollin' off me. And I was dirty, too, like I hadn't had no bath in a long time, so the sweat was black almost."

"Boy, sweetie, this is weird okay."

"I know. I kept walkin', even though I didn't have no money for the medicine or a good idea of where to go. People kept pushin' me and knockin' into me, and they was all dressed up for the cold weather. I guess they figured me for a bum or head case, seein' as how I was so filthy and dressed wrong. Then I thought of you and headed for your house. Only it wasn't your house really, it was in this cold, dark New York City, and it was a long way there.

"I was strugglin' ever' step of the way. Pushin' through the crowds. There was more and more people and the sky seemed like it was daytime, only it was dark, too. You were livin' in some big buildin' and I had to go up lots of stairs, but finally I found where it was. You let me in only you weren't real pleased to see me. You kept sayin', 'Why'd you come to see me now? Why now?' Like it'd been a long time since we seen each other."

"Oh, baby, what an idea. I'd always be happy to see you, no matter what."

"I know, peanut. But it wasn't all like you were so unhappy I was there, just you were upset. My bein' there was upsettin' to you. You had short hair, too, and chopped off in front. You had some kids there, little kids, and I guess you'd got married and your husband was comin' home any minute. I tell you, Lula, I was shakin' wet. All this black sweat was pourin' off me, and I knew I was scarin' you, so I took off. And then I woke up, sweatin', and a couple minutes later you come in."

Lula slid her head up to Sailor's chest and put her arms around him. "Sometimes dreams just don't mean nothin'? What I think, anyway.

Stuff come into your mind you don't got no control over, you know? It just come in there and ain't nobody knows for sure why. Like I dreamed once a man stole me and locked me in a room in a tower with one tiny window and there was nothin' but water outside? When I told Mama about it she said it was somethin' I remembered from a story I heard as a child."

"Well, I ain't upset about it, darlin'," said Sailor. "Just give me a odd feelin' there a minute is all."

Lula lifted her head and kissed Sailor under his left ear.

"Dreams ain't no odder than real life," she said. "Sometimes not by half."

THE POLISH FATHER

Johnnie Farragut sat on a bench in Jackson Square watching a pair of tourists take photos of one another. The couple spoke a language Johnnie did not recognize. Croatian, maybe, he thought, although he didn't know what Croatian sounded like. The man and woman were short and stout, probably in their thirties, though they looked older. Their clothes hung loosely from their bodies, obviously not having been tailored to order. After several turns each of posing and shooting, which entailed a considerable amount of heated discussion and dramatic gesticulation, the couple left the park.

As they waddled away, arguing in their grumbling language, Johnnie was reminded of a man who had lived down the street from him for a while when he was a boy. The man, whose name Johnnie could not remember, was Polish, and he had two sons, both round-faced, straw-haired kids a few years younger than Johnnie. There was no mother with the family, just a nice old grandmother who spoke only Polish. She and Johnnie would always nod and smile to each other whenever they passed on the street. The father was also round and fat, and he was bald and wore small, wire-rimmed glasses. His kids' faces were always dirty and it seemed as if they were always eating something: apples, cake, candy bars.

The Polish father was building a boat in his yard. Every evening Johnnie heard the man pounding nails into the frame. Many of the neighbors complained about the noise, but the construction continued without respite during the year and a half or so that the Polish family lived there. In his room late at night, Johnnie could hear the hammering and sawing. From what he'd seen of it, Johnnie thought it was to be a sailboat. At about this time, Johnnie remembered, he'd begun to read books at the library such as *Kon-Tiki* and *Clipper Ship Days*. It wasn't until much later that he discovered the novels of Joseph Conrad, who was Polish, and whose real name was Jozef Teodor Konrad Nalecz Korzeniowski, and Herman Melville.

The Polish boat builder stimulated Johnnie's interest in the sea. He wondered where the man intended to sail once he finished his boat.

Johnnie asked the man's sons, but they didn't know. They just shrugged their shoulders, sucked in their pudgy cheeks and blew snot from their dirt-covered noses straight to the ground. Since Johnnie's mother always snarled, "There he goes again," whenever she heard the hammering, he never discussed it with her.

One early-fall morning Johnnie was passing the Polish family's house and he stopped to look at the boat. It was out in the yard inverted on two homemade horses and was about thirty feet long. The man was planing the sides. He nodded to Johnnie and continued planing. His bald head was covered with sweat and he was humming a fast, foreign-sounding tune.

"Where are you going to sail her?" Johnnie asked him. The man stopped for a moment and stared blankly at Johnnie, as if he hadn't understood the question. Johnnie considered asking him again, but then thought that perhaps the man did not speak English very well, so he waited. Finally the man shrugged, gave a vague grunt, shoved his small pair of glasses up the bridge of his short, fat nose, they slid back down again, and he continued to plane. Johnnie watched him for a few minutes and then walked away.

The following spring the Polish family left town. The boat was moved on a flatbed truck, strapped down with heavy rope. The man and his two sons and the grandmother drove away in a car behind the truck. Johnnie couldn't remember who was driving the truck, but he recalled that when he went into his house and told his mother that the boat and the Polish family were gone, his mother said, "Thank Jesus, we won't have to listen to that awful poundin' no more."

ROAD KID

Outside Baton Rouge, Sailor said to Lula, "Sweetheart, keep your panties up. We're in Jimmy Swaggart country."

Lula giggled. "Jimmy's just another of them cheapskate preachers? Wantin' somethin' for nothin', is how I see it."

"At Pee Dee I heard about a guy named Top Hat Robichaux lives around here. Real name's Clarence, I think, but he's from the town of Top Hat, which is just north a ways, so that's what they called him."

"What's he do?"

"Used to be a safecracker. Now he's got his own country church up in Top Hat, Louisiana. He started it at Pee Dee, called the Holy Roller Rebel Raiders."

"Sounds like a football team," said Lula. "*Two* football teams."

Sailor and Lula both laughed. They were buzzing west on Interstate 10 in the Bonneville with the top down. Sailor kept on right past the capital city but slowed to a stop a mile or so beyond the western boundary to pick up a hitchhiker.

"Sure you want to do this?" asked Lula. "Might be a way they could track us."

"He's just a kid, honey. Look at him."

The hitchhiker was a boy of about fifteen or sixteen with a pack on his back, and he was carrying a large, covered cardboard box that he placed gently on the back seat next to him. His face was covered with freckles and acne. There wasn't a clear spot on it other than the whites of his eyes, which were a washed-out blue. His long brown hair was straggly, uncombed, and looked as if it hadn't been shampooed for weeks, if not months. He wore an old green army field jacket with the name MENDOZA sewn in capital letters on a white strip above the left breast pocket. The boy had an uneven smile on his face that exposed his jagged, yellow teeth.

"Thanks a lot," the boy said as he settled into the car, stowing his pack on the floor between his feet. "I been standin' out there off and on for two hours, ha-ha! Since noon about, ha-ha! Cops catch ya hitchin' on a interstate around here they throw ya on a county road crew for a week, 'less you can pay the ticket, ha-ha! Which I ain't got, ha-ha!"

"My name's Sailor, and this here's Lula. What's yours?"

"Marvin DeLoach," said the boy. "But ever'body calls me Roach, ha-ha! Roach DeLoach, ha-ha!"

"You always make that strange little funny laugh when you talk?" asked Lula.

"Ain't laughin', ha-ha!" said Roach.

"What you got in the box?" asked Sailor.

"My dogs, ha-ha!"

Roach slid the top off and tilted the box slightly toward the front. Inside were six small husky pups that couldn't have been more than two weeks old.

"I'm headed to Alaska, ha-ha!" said Roach. "These dogs is gonna be my sled team, ha-ha!"

"This kid's crazy," Lula said to Sailor.

"Where you from, Roach?" Sailor asked.

"If you mean where was I born, it was Belzoni, Missi'ppi, ha-ha! But I been brought up in Baton Rouge."

"Why you goin' to Alaska?" said Lula. "And where'd you get them puppies? They look sick."

Roach stared down into the box at the baby huskies and stroked each of them twice with a religiously unwashed hand. The dogs whimpered and licked his dirty fingers.

"I saw this movie on the TV, ha-ha! *The Call of the Wild*. I ain't never seen snow, ha-ha! I got these dogs at the pound. Nobody wanted 'em, ha-ha! Ever'body here got theirself pit bulls or some kinda hounds. I'm gonna feed these boys good so they'll be big and powerful and they can pull me real fast through the snow, ha-ha!"

Roach pulled a piece of raw cow's liver out of one of the pockets of the field jacket and began ripping little bits off it and feeding them to the dogs.

"Sailor!" Lula screeched when she saw this. "Stop! Stop the car now!"

Sailor pulled off the road onto the shoulder of the highway and stopped. Lula opened her door and jumped out.

"I'm sorry, but I can't take this," she said. "Roach, or whatever your name is, you come out of there with them dogs this instant!"

Roach stuck the liver back in his pocket and pulled his pack and the box of tiny canines after him. Once he and his belongings were deposited on the roadside, Lula hopped back into the car and slammed the door.

"I'm truly sorry? I'm truly sorry, Roach," she said. "But you ain't gonna make it to Alaska? Least not any part of the way with us. You'd best find a party to take care of those dogs proper, before they all die? And, if you don't mind my sayin' so? You could most certainly use some serious lookin' after yourself, startin' with a bath! Bye!"

Lula took a pair of sunglasses off the dashboard and put them on. "Drive," she said to Sailor.

Once they were rolling again, Sailor said to Lula, "You don't feel you was a little hard on the boy, honey?"

"I know you're thinkin' that I got more'n some of my mama in me? Well, I couldn't help it, Sailor, I really couldn't. I'm sorry for that boy, but when he pulled that drippin' hunk of awful-smellin' meat out of his pocket? I near barfed. And them poor diseased puppies!"

Sailor laughed. "Just part of life on the road, peanut."

"Do me a favor, Sailor? Don't pick up no more hitchers, okay?"

TALK PRETTY TO ME

"Know what I like best, honey?" said Lula, as Sailor guided the Bonneville out of Lafayette toward Lake Charles.

"What's that, peanut?"

"When you talk pretty to me."

Sailor laughed. "That's easy enough. I mean, it don't come hard. Back at Pee Dee all I had to do to cheer myself up was think about you. Your big grey eyes, of course, but mostly your skinny legs."

"You think my legs is too skinny?"

"For some, maybe, but not for me they ain't."

"A girl ain't perfect, you know, except in them magazines."

"I been makin' do."

"Can't see where it's harmed you none."

"I ain't complainin', sweetheart, you know that."

"I think most men, if not all, is missin' an element, anyways."

"What's that mean?"

"Men got a kind of automatic shutoff valve in their head? Like, you're talkin' to one and just gettin' to the part where you're gonna say what you really been wantin' to say, and then you say it and you look at him and he ain't even heard it. Not like it's too complicated or somethin', just he ain't about to really listen. One might lie sometime and tell ya he knows just what you mean, but I ain't buyin'. 'Cause later you say somethin' else he woulda got if he'd understood you in the first place, only he don't, and you know you been talkin' for no good reason. It's frustratin'."

"You think I been lyin' to you, Lula?"

Lula stayed quiet for a full minute, listening to the heavy hum of the V-8.

"Lula? You there?"

"Yeah, I'm here."

"You upset with me?"

"No, Sailor, darlin', I ain't upset. Just it's shockin' sometimes when what you think turns out to not be what you think at all."

"It's why I don't think no more'n necessary."

"You know, I had this awful, long dream last night? Tell me what you think of it. I'm out walkin' and I come to this field. This is all in bright color? And there's all these bodies of dead horses and dead children lyin' all around. I'm sad, but I'm not really sad. It's like I know they're all gone to a better place. Then a old woman comes up to me and tells me I got to bleed the bodies so they can be made into mummies. She shows me how to make a cut at the sides of the mouths of the corpses to drain 'em. Then I'm supposed to carry the bodies over a bridge across a real beautiful river into an old barn.

"Everything's really peaceful and lovely where I am, with green grass and big trees at the edge of the field. I'm not sure I got the strength to drag the bodies of the horses all that way. I'm frightened but I'm ready to do it anyway. And I'm sorta cryin' but not really sad? I can't explain the feelin' exactly. So I walk to the rear of this huge grey horse. I go around to his mouth and start to cut him. As soon as I touch him with the knife he wakes up and attacks me. The horse is furious. He gets up and chases me across the bridge and into and through the old barn. Then I woke up. You were sleepin' hard. And I just laid there and thought about how even if you love someone it isn't always possible to have it change your life."

"I don't know what your dream means, sweetheart," said Sailor, "but once I heard my mama ask my daddy if he loved her. They were yellin' at each other, like usual, and he told her the only thing he ever loved was the movie *Bad Men of Missouri*, which he said he seen sixteen times."

"What I mean about men," said Lula.

SURVIVORS

"No, Marietta, I haven't found 'em."

"Maybe they ain't *in* N.O., Johnnie. They could be dead in a ditch in Pascagoula, Missi'ppi, by now. Or possibly Lula's barefoot and pregnant in Pine Bluff, Arkansas, and that horrible Sailor person's pumpin' gas in a fillin' station for two dollars an hour."

"Calm down, Marietta. If there'd been an accident we woulda known about it by now. There ain't no use your gettin' exercised prematurely."

"Prematurely! Don't toss feathers at me, Johnnie Farragut. My only child been kidnapped by a dangerous criminal and you keep tellin' me to be calm!"

"I'll handle it, Marietta. Like I told you, there ain't no evidence Lula done nothin' against her will."

"Well, you better get a move on, Johnnie, before that boy got her holdin' down a Memphis street corner and shootin' dope up her arms."

"Really, Marietta, you got more scenarios swimmin' around in your brain than Carter got pills. Try to take it easy. Go over to Myrtle Beach for a few days."

"I'm stayin' right here by the phone until you find Lula, then I'm comin' to get her."

"Just hold tight, woman. I'll call you again in a couple days whether I got a lead or not."

"You just got to locate Lula, Johnnie. This is the kinda mistake can take a Hindu's lifetime to unfix. I got to attend a meetin' of the Daughters of the Confederacy from two to four tomorrow afternoon, otherwise I'll be at home. You call soon's you got somethin', even if it's three in the A.M."

"I will, Marietta. Goodbye now."

Johnnie hung up and sat in the telephone booth, thinking about Marietta Pace Fortune. She was still a goodlooking woman but she was getting more peculiar than ever. Marietta had always been nervous and demanding. Why he was still sweet on her after all these years Johnnie couldn't quite figure. Marrying her was out of the question, it just wasn't something Marietta would do. She wasn't cut out for a December romance, she said. The woman wouldn't be fifty for two or three years yet and she acted like life forgot her address. Except when it came to Lula, that is.

At the far end of Inez's Fais-Dodo Bar on Toulouse Street, Reginald San Pedro Sula, wearing his porkpie hat and a green seersucker leisure suit, sat on a stool drinking a martini. He spotted Johnnie walking toward the door.

"*Hola!* Señor Farragut!" Reggie shouted. "We meet again."

Johnnie went over to Reggie and shook hands.

"I thought you were in Austin, Texas. Or Takès-us, as they say in these parts."

"I was. Now I am on my way back to Utila, in the morning. Would you like to enjoy a martini with me?"

"Why not?" said Johnnie, hoisting himself onto the stool to Reggie's right. "How was the fishin'?"

"I think they are too serious, these American fishermen. In Honduras we are not so concerned with the method."

Reggie ordered a martini for Johnnie and another for himself.

"So," said Johnnie, "it's back to the islands."

"Yes. I spoke yesterday to my son, Archibald Leach San Pedro Sula, who is named after Cary Grant, and he told me there was a shooting. Teddy Roosevelt, one of the local shrimp boat captains, was on a picnic with King George Blanco and King George's wife, Colombia, and there was, apparently, a disagreement of some kind, during which King George and Colombia were killed. Teddy Roosevelt is in jail now. These people are all friends of mine, so I must return and find out what happened."

"This island of yours sounds like a kind of unpredictable place."

Reggie laughed. "It has its moments of uncertainty. But how are you finding New Orleans, Señor Farragut?"

"Call me Johnnie. N.O. always been a good town to sit around in."

"I can tell you are an intelligent man, Johnnie. One difference between your country and mine is that in the islands it does not pay to reveal one's intelligence. I am reminded of the time I saw a blue heron walking next to a river. He looked like a Chinese gentleman in a blue coat wobbling along the rocks. He appeared extremely vulnerable and defenseless, yet he was undoubtedly a survivor. That is our duty, Johnnie, as intelligent men, to survive."

Reggie raised his glass to Johnnie's. *"Hasta siempre,"* he said.

"Hasta siempre," said Johnnie.

"Do you know how it came about that copper wire was invented in Scotland?" Reggie asked.

"How's that?"

"Two Scotsmen were fighting over a penny."

Johnnie finished off his martini.

"I got to admit, Reggie," he said, sliding off the stool, "you're one in a dozen."

OLD NOISE

"You didn't raise a fool, Marietta. Lula got too much Pace in her to throw her life away on trash. My guess is she's havin' herself a time, is all."

Marietta and Dalceda Delahoussaye were sitting on the side porch of Marietta's house drinking Martini & Rossi sweet vermouth over crushed ice with a lemon slice. Dalceda had been best friends with Marietta for close to thirty years, ever since they boarded together at Miss Cook's School in Beaufort. They'd never lived further apart in that period than a ten-minute walk.

"Remember Vernon Landis? The man owned a Hispano-Suiza he kept in Royce Womble's garage all those years before he sold it for twenty-five thousand dollars to the movie company in Wilmington? His wife, Althea, ran off with a wholesale butcher from Hayti, Missouri. The man gave her a diamond ring big enough to stuff a turkey and guess what? She was back with Vernon in six weeks."

"Dal? Just *what*, you tell me, has Althea Landis's inability to control herself have to do with my baby Lula's bein' stole by this awful demented man?"

"Marietta! Sailor Ripley prob'ly ain't no more or less demented than anyone we know."

"Oh, Dal, he's lowlife. He's what we been avoidin' all our lives, and now my only child's at his mercy."

"You always been one to panic, Marietta. When Enos Dodge didn't ask you right off to go with him to the Beau Regard Country Club cotillion in 1959, you panicked. Threatened to kill yourself or accept an invitation from Biff Bethune. And what happened? Enos Dodge'd been in Fayetteville with his daddy and asked you soon as he got back two days later. This ain't a moment to panic, lovey. You're gonna have to quit spittin' and ride it on out."

"You're always such a comfort to me, Dal."

"I give you what you need, is all. A talkin'-to."

"What I need is Lula safe at home."

"Safe? Safe? Ain't that a stitch! Ain't nobody nowhere never been safe a second of their life."

Dalceda drained the last drop of vermouth from her glass.

"You got any more of this red vinegar in the house?" she asked.

Marietta rose and went into the pantry and came out carrying a sealed bottle. She unscrewed the cap and poured Dalceda a drink and freshened her own before sitting back down.

"And what about you?" said Dalceda.

"What about me?"

"When's the last time you been out with a man? Let alone been to bed with one."

Marietta clucked her tongue twice before answering.

"I plain ain't interested," she said, and took a long sip from her glass.

Dalceda laughed. "What was it you used to tell me about how Clyde carried on when you and him made love? About his gruntin' that come from way down inside sounded so ancient? Old noise, you called it. Told me you felt like you was bein' devoured by a unstoppable beast, and it was the most thrillin' thing ever happened to you."

"Dal, I swear I hate talkin' to you. You remember too much."

"Hate hearin' the truth is what it is. You're just shit scared Lula feels the same way about Sailor as you did with Clyde."

"Oh, Dal, how could she? I mean, do you think she does? This Sailor ain't nothin' like Clyde."

"How do you know, Marietta? You ever tried the boy on for size?"

Dalceda laughed. Marietta drank.

"And Mr. Dogface Farragut comes mopin' and sniffin' around you regular," said Dalceda. "You could start with him. Or how about that old gangster, Marcello 'Crazy Eyes' Santos, used to proposition you when you was married to Clyde?"

Marietta snorted. "He stopped askin' after Clyde died. My bein' too available musta thrown him off the scent."

"That's most certainly the case with Louis Delahoussaye the Third," said Dalceda. "I don't think he's asked for it more'n twice in six months for a grand total of a not so grand eight and one-half minutes."

"Dal? You think I oughta keep dyein' my hair or let it go white?"

"Marietta, what I think is we both need another drink."

NIGHT LIFE

"I wouldn't mind a little night life," said Lula. "How about you?"

Sailor cruised the Bonneville slowly along Napoleon Avenue, casing the neighborhood. It was nine o'clock at night and they were in the town of Nuñez, on the Louisiana side of the Louisiana-Texas border.

"Hard to tell what's shakin' in a place like this, honey," said Sailor. "You don't want to be walkin' in the wrong door."

"Maybe there's a place we could hear some music. I feel like dancin'. We could ask somewhere," Lula said.

Sailor turned left into Lafitte Road and spotted a Red Devil gas station that still had its lights on.

"Someone up here might know somethin'," he said, and pulled the car over.

A skinny, pimply-faced guy of about eighteen, wearing dirty yellow coveralls and a crumpled black baseball cap with a red felt *N* on it, walked over to them.

"Gas?" he said.

"Got enough, thanks," said Sailor. "We're lookin' for a place has some music, where we can maybe get somethin' to eat, too. Anything like that around here?"

"Cornbread's," said the attendant. "They got western. No food, though, 'cept bar nibbles."

Lula slid over in the front seat and leaned across Sailor.

"How about rock 'n' roll?" she asked.

"There's a boogie joint just about a mile straight out Lafitte here. But that's a black place mostly."

"What's the name of it?" asked Sailor.

"Club Zanzibar."

"You say it's straight ahead a mile?"

"About. Where Lafitte crosses over Galvez Highway. State Road 86."

"Thanks," said Sailor.

The Club Zanzibar was in a white wood building on the left-hand side of the road. A string of multicolored lights was hung over the front. Sailor parked the Bonneville across from the club and cut the engine.

"You ready for this?" he asked.

"We'll find out in a hurry," said Lula.

When they walked in, a band was playing a slow blues and three or four couples were swaying on the dance floor. There were a dozen tables and a long bar in the room. Eight of the tables were occupied and six or seven men sat or stood at the bar. Everyone in the place was black except for one white woman, who was sitting alone at a table smoking a cigarette and drinking Pearl straight from the bottle.

"Come on," said Lula, taking Sailor by the hand and leading him onto the dance floor.

The tune was John Lee Hooker's "Sugar Mama," and Lula insinuated her body into Sailor's and left it there. After that the band picked up the beat. Sailor and Lula danced for twenty minutes before Sailor begged off and dragged Lula over to the bar and ordered two Lone Star beers. The bartender, a tall, heavyset man in his early fifties, served the beers, took Sailor's money and gave him his change with a big smile.

"This is a friendly place, son," said the bartender. "You folks just relax and have a nice time."

"No problem," said Lula. "You got a real fine band here."

The bartender smiled again and moved on down the bar.

"You notice that woman when we come in?" Lula said to Sailor. "The white woman sittin' by herself?"

"Uh huh," said Sailor.

"Well, she ain't talked to nobody and ain't nobody spoke to her that I could tell. What you make of that?"

"Honey, we bein' strangers here and all, this is the kinda place we don't want to make nothin' of nothin'."

"You think she's pretty?"

Sailor looked at the woman. She lit a new cigarette off a butt, then squashed the butt in an ashtray. She was thirty years old, maybe more. Shoulder-length bleached blond hair, black at the roots. Clear skin, green eyes. Long, straight nose with a small bump on it. She was wearing a low-cut lavender dress that would have emphasized her breasts had she not been so flat chested. Slender.

"I tend to like 'em with a little more meat on the bones," said Sailor. "Face ain't bad, though."

Lula got quiet and sucked on her beer bottle.

"What's wrong, sweetheart? Somethin' botherin' you?"

"Aw, it's just Mama. I been thinkin' about her. She's prob'ly worried to death by now."

"More than likely."

"I want to call her and tell her I'm okay. That *we're* okay."

"I ain't so sure it's a great idea, but that's up to you. Just don't tell her where we are."

"Pardon me?" Lula said to the bartender. "Y'all got a phone here I can use?"

"Straight back by the gents'."

"Back in a bit," she said to Sailor, and kissed him on the nose.

Marietta answered the telephone on the second ring.

"I have a collect call from Lula Fortune," said the operator. "Will you accept?"

"Of course!" said Marietta. "Lula? Where *are* you? You all right?"

"I'm fine, Mama. I just wanted to tell you not to worry."

"Why, how *could* I not worry? Not knowin' what's happenin' to you or where you are? Are you with that boy?"

"If you mean Sailor, Mama, yes I am."

"Are you comin' home soon, Lula? I need you here."

"Need me for what, Mama? I'm perfectly fine, and safe, too."

"You in a dance hall or somethin'? I can hear music behind you."

"Just a place."

"Really, Lula, this ain't right!"

"Right?! Mama, was it right for you to sic Johnnie Farragut on us? How could you *do* that?"

"Did you run into Johnnie in New Orleans? Lula, are you in New Orleans?"

"No, Mama, I'm in Mexico, and we're about to get on a airplane to Argentina!"

"Argentina! Lula, you're outa your mind. Now you just tell me where you are and I'll come for you. I won't say nothin' to the police about Sailor, I promise. He can do what he wants, I don't care."

"Mama, I'm hangin' up this phone now."

"No, baby, don't! Can I send you somethin'? You runnin' low on money? I'll wire you some money if you tell me where you are."

"I ain't that dumb, Mama. Sailor and I been on a crime spree? Knockin' off convenience stores all across the South? Ain't you read about it?"

Marietta was crying. "Lula? I love you, baby. I just want you to be all right."

"I am all right, Mama. That's why I called, to let you know. I gotta go."

"Call me again soon? I'll be waitin' by the phone."

"Don't be crazy, Mama. Take care of yourself."

Lula hung up.

Sailor and the bleached blond in the lavender dress were together on the dance floor. Lula saw them, went over to the bar, picked up a beer bottle and threw it at Sailor. The bottle bounced off his back and clanged to the floor, bouncing but not breaking. He turned around and looked at Lula. Nobody else in the place gave any sign that they'd seen what had happened. Lula ran out.

Sailor found her sitting on the ground, leaning against the passenger side of the Bonneville. Lula's eyes were red and wet but she wasn't crying. Sailor knelt down next to her.

"I was just wastin' time, peanut, till you come back."

"It's me who's wastin' time, Sailor, bein' with you."

"Honey, I'm sorry. It wasn't nothin'. Come on and get up and we'll take off."

"Leave me be for a minute? Mama gets all insane and then I see you dancin' with some oil town tramp. How you figure I'm gonna feel?"

"Told you not to call her."

Sailor stood and leaned against the hood of the car until Lula got up and climbed inside. He got in and started it up. Lula took Sailor's blue canvas jacket from the back seat and put it on. She kissed Sailor on the cheek, put her head down sideways on his lap and went to sleep. Sailor drove.

"Johnnie! At last! I thought you was never gonna call."

"I got some news, Marietta. Lula and Sailor been here. They checked out of the Hotel Brazil on Frenchmen Street two days ago."

"Listen, Johnnie, Lula called me last night. She knew you were in N.O., so they left the city."

"Did she tell you where she was callin' from?"

"No, but my guess is they're headed west, so prob'ly Texas. Could be Houston. Their money must be runnin' low. I don't think Sailor had much to begin with, if any, and Lula took the six hundred she had saved in the Cherokee Thrift."

"How'd she sound? Was she doin' okay?"

"How could she be doin' okay, Johnnie? She's tryin' to prove somethin' to me, that's all. Lula ain't doin' no more'n showin' off, defyin' me."

"Marietta, she's tryin' to grow up, is all. It don't have everything to do with you. I don't mean to insult you or nothin', but Lula got to get shut of you somehow, and this is how she's chose to do it. I understand how painful it is for you."

"How *could* you understand? She's the only flesh and blood I got left I care anything about. Lula's my *daughter*, Johnnie. I'm comin' to New Orleans."

"Hold on, Marietta. There ain't no good you can do here until I get a line on which way they went. Could be they're halfway to Chicago."

"They're headed west, Johnnie, I know it. Prob'ly to California. Lula always has wanted to go there. I'll be in on the Piedmont flight at seven tomorrow night. Meet me at the airport and we can get goin' right away."

"I'll meet you, Marietta, if that's what you want, but I'm against it."

"Seven tomorrow evenin'. We can eat at Galatoire's. Fix it."

Marietta hung up.

Johnnie hung up the hotel phone and walked out onto the balcony overhanging Barracks Street. It was one in the morning and the air was warm but misty. He could hear a recording of Babs Gonzales singing "Ornithology" in his froggy voice coming from a radio or stereo. "All the cats are standin' on the corner," Babs Gonzales sang, "waitin' for the chicks to finish their slave." Johnnie lit up a Hoyo de Monterrey cigar and tossed the match into the street.

In 1950, Elia Kazan had filmed *Panic in the Streets* here, staging a shooting on the Barracks Street Wharf. Johnnie had read somewhere that it was the actor Jack Palance's first movie. Palance, with his face resculpted following a car wreck into a wicked Mongol mask, portrayed Blackie, the perfect, unrepentant killer. Palance could convey cruelty more convincingly than anyone in those days, Johnnie thought. It takes a certain amount of desperation to do that. "I'm not a desperate person," Johnnie said aloud. He blew smoke from his cigar into the night mist. If a man is no good at convincing himself of something, he thought, then there isn't much chance he'll do a very good job of convincing anyone else.

"Ornithology" segued into King Pleasure and Betty Carter's "Little Red Top." "You really got me spinning," they sang. Johnnie stayed on the balcony until the song ended before he went back inside. He had an idea for a story about a man with a terrible disease that robs him of his ability to remember anything unless he mutilates himself.

DAL'S SECRET

"Dal? I'm goin' to N.O."

"You hear somethin' from Johnnie?"

"Just that they left the hotel they was stayin' in. Firetrap called the Brazil? Johnnie don't know no more."

"Marietta, I'm dead against it. Leave Lula be. It'll take years to undo what you're doin'."

"I can't help it, Dal. I can't just sit around waitin'."

"I might as well tell you now about Clyde."

"What *about* Clyde?"

"One time he come to me."

"One time he come to you? Dal, did you and him have an affair?"

"Not nearly. No, he come to ask me about you. Before Lula was born."

"What *about* me?"

"Thought maybe you was too high-strung to have children, and wanted my opinion."

"Go on."

"Told him I thought it was a good idea, your havin' a child. That he shouldn't fret."

"Swell of you, Dal. How come you never told me before?"

"Clyde asked me not to."

"Clyde been dead for years."

"I promised him, Marietta."

"So why confess now?"

"It ain't a confession."

"Why bring it up then?"

"'Cause I think you're makin' a mistake, what you're doin' now. Clyde wouldn't want it."

"Clyde ain't gonna know about it, Dalceda. Unless you got some way of communicatin' with him I ain't heard about."

"You have a safe trip, Marietta. If you need me to do somethin' for you here, give a shout. And give my love to Lula, if you find her."

"Dal, I know you think I'm wrong on this, but I mean well."

"I know you do, Marietta. Bye."

"Bye, Dal."

After she hung up, Marietta started to cry. She cried for a full ten minutes, until the phone rang. By the fourth ring Marietta had composed herself sufficiently to pick it up.

"Marietta? It's Dal. You stop cryin' yet?"

"Just now. Almost."

"Stop it now, hear? Pull yourself together and go do what you have to. Maybe I'm the one is wrong."

"You ain't wrong, Dal. Not for you, anyway. You're the only one knows me."

"Love you, Marietta."

"Love you, Dal."

"Bye again."

"Bye."

BAD IDEAS

"Sometimes I feel just like one of Dracula's wives. You know, those skinny women in see-through robes with long hair and fingernails who follow the Count around and do what he says?"

Lula was sitting on the edge of the motel bed filing her nails while Sailor did his daily fifty fingertip push-ups.

"Sure," said Sailor, "I seen the movie. But why?"

"I get so low down. It's as if someone's sucked all the blood out of my body."

"We all get that way once in a while, honey," Sailor said between push-ups. "As my grandaddy used to say, ain't no one person got a monopoly on grief."

"Oh, I know," said Lula. "I'm not even feelin' particularly sorry for myself. It's just I'd like it sometime that Daddy hadn't died on me so soon? And that Mama wasn't such a crazy bitch more'n twice a month? And that she didn't hold it against you about havin' to kill Bob Ray Lemon? Lots and lots."

Sailor finished the last of his fingertips and sat up with his back against the bed.

"My grandaddy used to read the obituaries every Friday mornin' at breakfast," Sailor said. "He'd get the newspaper and commence to tell me who died and what of and all about their lives and relatives left behind. Grandaddy'd shake his head and laugh and wonder about why poor departed Cleve Sumpter married his first wife, Irma Sykes, had three children and went into the millinery business in Aiken, divorced Irma, got hitched to Edna Mae Raley, quit makin' hats, opened up a barbecue restaurant in McCall, and twenty years later died of emphysema while listenin' to the Braves ball game on the front porch of a old-people's home in Asheville."

"Sounds morbid to me," said Lula. "Readin' the obits? I never look at 'em. And why'd he do it just on Fridays?"

"I don't know," said Sailor. "But I enjoyed listenin' to Grandaddy talk about the people as if he knew each and every one of 'em personal."

"What'd they write about your grandaddy when he died?" asked Lula. "Or is he still livin'?"

"He died when I was up at Pee Dee," Sailor said. "They wouldn't let me out to go to the funeral, of course. Grandaddy was my best friend when I was a kid. Family give him some shit, I guess, 'cause he wasn't no great shakes in business, and he done some hard time early on for assaultin' an officer when he was in the service. I never read his obituary notice, if there was one, but that's fair enough. Prob'ly they didn't have much in there about his teachin' me to hunt and fish or cook biscuits."

"Sailor?"

"Yeah?"

"Wouldn't it be fabulous if we someway stayed in love for the rest of our lives?"

Sailor laughed. "You think of the weirdest damn things to say sometimes, peanut. Ain't we been doin' a pretty fair job this far?"

Lula reached down with both of her arms and put them around Sailor's neck. She dropped her emery board on the floor.

"Oh, you know what I mean, don't you, honey? It'd make everything so simple."

"At Pee Dee all you think about is the future, you know?" said Sailor. "Gettin' out? And what you'll do when you're on the outside again. But I'm out now and I don't know what to think about yet."

"I just think about things as they come up," said Lula. "I never been much of a planner."

"It ain't altogether terrible just to let things go along sometimes," Sailor said. "My grandaddy once read me the obituary of a man who'd owned a big manufacturin' company of some kind and run for U.S. senator four times and lost every time. 'Imagine all them bastards that man had to pretend to like,' Grandaddy said, 'and all for nothin'.' I ain't gonna do nothin' for no good reason, Lula. All I know for sure is there's already more'n a few bad ideas runnin' around loose out there."

Lula reached over and turned on the radio that was on the table next to the bed.

"If I could but win your heart, little girl, then I would have treasure untold." It was Jimmie Rodgers, the Singing Brakeman.

"I love these old yodelly country songs," said Lula. "They're all so corny but sweet, too."

Sailor nodded. "My grandaddy told me that when Jimmie Rodgers died, he went down to the depot to watch the train that was carryin' his body back to Meridian, Mississippi, go by. Jimmie had the TB so bad they kept a cot in the recordin' studio so that he could lay down and rest after doin' a tune."

"Musta been a lot of people loved him," said Lula. "That must be a great feelin'. To know there's all these strangers out there think so much of you?"

"My experience, the more people get to know each other the less they get along," said Sailor. "It's best to keep people to bein' strangers. That way they don't get disappointed so easy."

"How much we got left, honey?"

"Under a hundred," said Sailor.

Sailor and Lula were in a Shell station in Houston. Sailor had just filled the Bonneville with regular and checked the oil and water.

"You want to stick around here, Sailor? See if we can get some work?"

"Not in Houston. This is where they'd expect us to stop. We'll be better off in some place more out of the way."

"You want me to drive for a stretch? Give you a chance to rest."

"That'd be good, Lula."

Sailor kissed her and climbed into the back seat and lay down. Lula slid behind the wheel and lit up a More. She wheeled the car back into traffic and toward the entrance to the interstate, following the loop around Houston headed for San Antonio. She clicked on the radio. Perez Prado's band, playing "Cherry Pink and Apple Blossom White," came on. "Another damn oldies station," Lula muttered, and turned the dial. She found a nationwide call-in talk show and left it there.

"Come in, Montgomery, Alabama," said the host, a man with a gruff Brooklyn accent.

"Artie? That you, Artie?" said the caller, an elderly-sounding woman.

"Yes, ma'am. What's on your almost-perfect mind this evening?"

"How ya feelin', Artie? I heard you wasn't doin' too well recent."

"I'm fine, thank you. I had a cardiac infarction but I'm on a new diet and exercising regularly. I've never felt better."

"Well, that's so good to hear, Artie. You know some of us depend on you down this way. You're so entertainin' and you get so many interestin' guests."

"Thank you. It's listeners such as yourself who made me want to get up out of that hospital bed and back into the studio as fast as I could."

"Just remember, Artie, it's the Good Lord you got to thank for everything. He's watchin' over us."

"Thanks for the call, ma'am. San Francisco, California, hello."

"Hello, Artie? This is Manny Wolf in San Francisco."

"Mark Twain said the coldest winter he ever spent was a summer in San Francisco. How you doin', Manny?"

"Oh, pretty good, Artie. Heard you had a heart attack."

"Yeah, but I'm okay now."

"Well, Bill Beaumont did a bang-up job while you were out."

"He's number one, isn't he? What's on your almost-perfect mind tonight, Manny?"

"The Giants, Artie. They sure did a nosedive, didn't they?"

"Injuries, Manny. You can't win ball games if half the pitching staff goes down, including three starters. I look for 'em to be back in it next year."

"They coulda made some deals, Artie."

"With what? Nobody wants damaged goods."   .

"They coulda made some deals they woulda tried."

"Wait till next year. Thanks for callin', Manny. Boston, Massachusetts, you're on the air with Artie Mayer."

"Jesus!" said Lula, attacking the dial. "How can anyone listen to this crap?"

She settled on an all-news station. Sailor was snoring. Lula took a last puff of her More and tossed it out the window.

"An alleged child prostitution ring that provided young girls for businessmen in Houston, Dallas, Fort Worth and other cities has been broken up by Houston police," said the radio. "Investigators theorized that the ring, which operated out of a redbrick warehouse building on the north side of downtown Houston near Buffalo Bayou, may be part of a larger operation run out of Los Angeles and New Orleans by Vietnamese citizens."

"Wow, this is good," said Lula. She turned up the volume.

"The ring's activities were revealed yesterday after a fifty-five-year-old Houston pai-gow dealer was arrested for allegedly having sex with a twelve-year-old girl at an Airport Loop motel Tuesday night. Chick Go, who works at Lucky Guy's card parlor, was apprehended in a raid on the Nighty-Night Motel. He was arraigned yesterday on charges of engaging in sex acts with a child and contributing to the delinquency of a minor. He was released on ten thousand dollars' bail. More arrests are expected.

"The young prostitutes' customers, said a police spokesman, were carefully selected, primarily successful businessmen who had something to lose if they ever informed authorities about the child sex ring. Most of the prostitutes are apparently runaways who need a place to live in exchange for sexual favors. Police said they have identified and questioned at least four girls, all Asians twelve to fifteen years old, who have been living in the North Houston warehouse with a Vietnamese pimp since February. The girls are being treated as victims, said police sergeant Amos Milburn. 'These are really just children,' he said, 'but they've been exposed to a lot already.'"

"I'll bet," said Lula, lighting up another cigarette.

"In international news, India plans to release crocodiles in the Ganges, the holy Hindu river in which millions of people bathe annually, to scavenge for corpses, authorities said. One hundred fifty crocodiles reared at a state-owned farm in southern Kerala state will be dumped in the river near cities where corpse pollution levels are the highest. The reptiles were supposed to be of a docile species, said a senior government official, but it seems the breeders bungled and reared attack crocodiles."

"Damn!" said Lula.

"The Indian official who supplied this information did so only on condition of anonymity. The *Crocodilus palustris* species, he said, has a reputation for killing and breeding quickly. Some one hundred thousand corpses are cremated on the banks of the Ganges in Varanasi every year, while millions of Hindus bathe in the river in the belief that the water will purify the soul and absolve them of sins. The government plans to cleanse the Ganges first at Varanasi, the holiest Hindu city. The Uttar Pradesh state authorities last October released five hundred turtles in the Ganges near Varanasi to try and reduce human pollution and now plan to put in the crocodiles to devour floating corpses dumped by Hindus too poor to pay for cremation."

"Holy shit!" said Lula. "It's the night of the livin' fuckin' dead!"

"What's that, peanut?" said Sailor, kissing her on the ear from behind.

"I can't take no more of this radio," she said, and switched it off. "I ain't never heard so much concentrated weirdness in my life. I know the news ain't always accurate, but the world's gettin' worse, I think, Sailor. And it don't sound like there's much we can do about it, neither."

"This ain't news, sweetheart. I hate to tell ya."

Johnnie chewed his trout slowly and carefully. He was listening to Marietta while trying to avoid swallowing the bones.

"She's all I have, Johnnie. If I didn't go after Lula now, I'd never forgive myself."

"I understand how you feel, Marietta, it's just I can't see you're helpin' matters. Lula ain't a baby, she got a mind of her own. There comes a point you gotta let go."

Marietta put down her knife and fork, sat back in her chair and stared hard at Johnnie.

"You sound like some textbook on child rearin'," she said, "which is interestin', considerin' you never raised no children."

They sat in silence throughout the rest of their meal, and Marietta paid the check with cash, since Galatoire's did not accept credit cards.

Once they were outside on Bourbon Street, Johnnie said, "You want to spend the night in town or get on the road? Either way's solid with me."

"I can sleep in the car," said Marietta. "Let's head for Houston and see if we can pick up the trail."

Marietta settled back in the front passenger seat of Johnnie's 1987 candy-apple-red Cadillac Seville. She closed her eyes and thought about what Dalceda Delahoussaye had said about Clyde's coming to her with his worry over Marietta's nervous nature. She'd done a good job, she thought, raising Lula. This situation with the Ripley boy was just a freak occurrence, something Marietta knew she could talk Lula out of face-to-face. She prayed that Lula wasn't pregnant again.

As soon as Johnnie was certain that Marietta had fallen asleep, he rolled down his window partway and lit up a Hoyo. He had committed himself to her, so he'd stick with the chase, but he didn't like the feel of it now. He had a foreboding about the whole deal. Johnnie kept the Cadillac at a steady seventy-five. Marietta's head was tilted back and to the side away from him. Her mouth was half open and her chest was rising and falling in a regular rhythm. He turned on the radio, keeping the sound low.

"Finally, a sad item in the sports news," said the radio. "Eligio Sardinias, a leading boxer in the 1930s who fought under the name Kid Chocolate, died today in Havana, the Cuban state radio reported. He was seventy-eight years old. The Cuban-born boxer was elected to the Boxing Hall of Fame in 1959. As Kid Chocolate, he won the world junior lightweight title in 1931, and followed that up by winning the New York featherweight title, then considered a major championship, in 1932, by beating Lew Feldman with a twelfth-round knockout. He fought for the world featherweight title in 1930, losing a fifteen-round decision to Battling Battalino. The next year he lost a bid for the world lightweight title against Tony Canzoneri, also in a fifteen-round decision. Kid Chocolate's professional record was a hundred thirty-two wins, ten losses and six draws, with fifty KOs."

Lew Feldman, thought Johnnie, must have been a Jewish fighter. There were lots of them in the old days. Barney Ross, of course, and Benny Leonard, both champions. Many who fought under Irish or Italian names. Maybe there was a story in this, Johnnie thought. A Jewish kid, just off the boat before the war, goes into the army, where he learns how to box from an old sergeant whose own pro career was cut short due to an injury. The kid takes the sergeant's name, Jack O'Leary. He fights his way close to the top, only to be prevented from getting a shot at the title by an anti-Semitic promoter who finds out the kid's a Jew.

The kid can win the title and the promoter knows it. The only way he'll let the kid in the ring, however, is if the kid agrees to take a dive so the promoter and his mob cronies can make a bundle betting against him. A real 1940s-style melodrama, Johnnie thought. Sergeant O'Leary is on his deathbed, wounded and dying. He gets wind of the tank job and sends word to the kid before the fight to win the title for him, to not disgrace the name Jack O'Leary. John Garfield could have played the kid in the movie, with Harry Carey as the sergeant, Eduardo Ciannelli as the crooked promoter, Arthur Kennedy as the kid's manager-trainer, Juano Hernandez as the corner man, and Priscilla Lane as the girlfriend.

Johnnie ran the movie over and over in his mind as he drove, reinventing the scenes. The title would be *Don't Die for Me*. Nothing in real life, thought Johnnie, ever seemed quite as honest as this.

THE MIDDLE OF THINGS

In San Antonio, Lula said, "You know about the Alamo?"

"Talked about it in school, I remember," said Sailor. "And I seen the old John Wayne movie where mostly nothin' happens till the Mexicans overrun the place."

Sailor and Lula were in La Estrella Negra eating birria con arroz y frijoles and drinking Tecate with wedges of lime.

"Guess it's a pretty big deal here," said Lula. "Noticed drivin' in how ever'thing's named after it. Alamo Road, Alamo Street, Alamo Square, Alamo Buildin', Hotel Alamo. They ain't forgettin' it in a hurry."

"Pretty place, though, San Antone," said Sailor.

"So what we gonna do, hon? About money, I mean."

"I ain't worried. Figure we'll stop somewhere between here and El Paso and find some work."

"When you was a boy?"

"Uh huh."

"What'd you think about doin' when you grew up?"

"Pilot. Always wanted to be a airline pilot."

"Like for TWA or Delta, you mean?"

"Yeah. Thought that'd be cool, you know, wearin' a captain's hat and takin' them big birds up over the ocean. Hang out with stews in Rome and L.A."

"Why didn't you do it?"

Sailor laughed. "Never really got the chance, did I? Wasn't nobody about to help me toward it, you know? Not bein' much of a student, always gettin' in trouble one way or another, I kinda lost sight of it."

"You coulda joined the air force, learned to fly."

"Tried once. They didn't want me 'cause of my record. Too many scrapes. I never even been in a plane."

"Shoot, Sail, we oughta take a long flight when we got some money to waste. Fly to Paris."

"I'd go for that."

As soon as they'd finished eating, Sailor said, "Let's keep movin', Lula. Big towns is where they'll look."

Sailor drove with Lula curled up on the seat next to him. Patsy Cline was on the radio, singing "I Fall to Pieces."

"I wish I'd been born when Patsy Cline was singin'," said Lula.

"What's the difference?" Sailor asked. "You can still listen to her records."

"I coulda seen her maybe. She got the biggest voice? Like if Aretha Franklin woulda been a country singer all those years ago. That's what I always wanted to do, Sailor, be a singer. I ever tell you that?"

"Not that I recall."

"When I was little, eight or nine? Mama took me to Charlotte and put me in a talent show. It was at a big movie theater, and there was all these kids lined up on the stage. Each of us had to perform when our name was called. Kids tap-danced, played instruments or sang, mostly. One boy did magic tricks. Another boy juggled balls and stood on his head while he whistled 'Dixie' or somethin'."

"What'd you do?"

"Sang 'Stand By Your Man,' the Tammy Wynette tune? Mama thought it'd be extra cute, havin' me sing such a grown-up number."

"How'd it go?"

"Not too bad. Course I couldn't hit most of the high notes, and all the other kids on stage was talkin' and makin' noises durin' my turn."

"You win?"

"No. Some boy played 'Stars Fell on Alabama' on a harmonica did."

"Why'd you quit singin'?"

"Mama decided I didn't have no talent. Said she didn't wanta waste no more money on lessons. This was when I was thirteen? Prob'ly she was right. No sense playin' at it. You got a voice like Patsy's, you ain't got no hesitation about where you're headed."

"Ain't easy when you're kinda in the middle of things," said Sailor.

"Like us, you mean," said Lula. "That's where we are, and I don't mean in the middle of southwest Texas."

"There's worse places."

"If you say so, honey."

"Trust me on it."

"I do trust you, Sailor. Like I ain't never trusted nobody before. It's scary sometimes. You ain't got much maybe or might in you."

Sailor laughed, and put his arm over Lula, brushing her cheek with his hand.

"Maybe and might are my little brothers," he said. "I gotta set 'em a good example, is all."

"It ain't really them worries me, it's those cousins, never and ever, make me shake."

"We'll be all right, peanut, long as we got room to move."

Lula clucked her tongue twice.

"Know what?" she said.

"Uh?"

"I don't know that I completely enjoy you callin' me peanut so much."

Sailor laughed. "Why's that?"

"Puts me so far down on the food chain?"

Sailor looked at her.

"Really, Sail. I know how you mean it to be sweet, but I was thinkin' how everything can eat a peanut and a peanut don't eat nothin'. Makes me sound so tiny, is all."

"How you want, honey," he said.

WELCOME TO BIG TUNA

Big Tuna, Texas, pop. 305, sits 125 miles west of Biarritz, 125 miles east of Iraaq, and 100 miles north of the Mexican border on the south fork of the Esperanza trickle. Sailor cruised the Bonneville through the streets of Big Tuna, eyeballing the place.

"This looks like a lucky spot, sweetheart," he said. "Whattaya think?"

"Not bad," said Lula. "Long as you're not large on cool breezes. Must be a hundred and ten and it ain't even noon yet."

"Hundred twelve, to be exact. What it said on the Iguana County Bank buildin' back there. And that's prob'ly two degrees or more shy of the actual temp. Chamber of commerce don't like to discourage visitors, so they set it low."

"I can understand that, Sail. After all, there's a big difference between a hundred twelve and a hundred fourteen."

Sailor circled back and stopped the car in front of the Iguana Hotel, a two-story, whitewashed wooden building with the Texas state flag draped over the single porch above the entrance.

"This'll do," he said.

The second-floor room Sailor and Lula rented was simple: double bed, dresser, mirror, chair, sink, toilet, bathtub (no shower), electric fan, window overlooking the street.

"Not bad for eleven dollars a day," said Sailor.

"No radio or TV," said Lula. She stripped off the spread, tossed it in a corner and sat down on the bed. "And no AC."

"Fan works."

"Now what?"

"Let's go down to the drugstore and get a sandwich. Find out about where to look for work."

"Sailor?"

"Yeah?"

"This ain't exactly my most thrillin' notion of startin' a new life."

They ordered bologna and American cheese on white with Cokes at the counter of Bottomley's Drug.

"Pretty empty today," Sailor said to the waitress, whose plastic name tag had KATY printed on it.

"Ever'body's over to the funeral," Katy said. "This is kind of a sad day around here."

"We just got into town," said Lula. "What happened?"

"Buzz Dokes, who run a farm here for twenty years, died somethin' horrible. Only forty-four."

"How'd he go?" asked Sailor.

"Bumblebees got him. Buzz was on his tractor Monday mornin' when a swarm of bees lit on his head and knocked him off his seat. He fell underneath the mower and the blades chopped him up in four unequal parts. Run over a bee mound and they just rose up and attacked him. Poor Buzz. Tractor trampled him and kept goin', went through a fence and smacked into the side of a Messican's house. Took it clean off the foundation."

"That's about the most unpleasant incident I heard of lately," said Lula.

"There's always some strange thing or other happenin' in Big Tuna," Katy said. "I've lived here all my life, forty-one years, except for two years in Beaumont, and I could put together some book about this town. It wouldn't all be pretty, I tell you. But it's a sight better than bein' in a place like Beaumont, where people come down the street you don't know 'em and never will. I like bein' in a place where I know who I'm gonna see every day. What are you kids doin' here?"

"Lookin' for work," said Sailor.

"Any kind in particular?"

"I'm pretty fair with cars, trucks. Never done no ranchin', though, or farmin'."

"You might talk to Red Lynch. He's got a garage just two blocks up the street here, 'cross from the high school. Called Red's. He might have somethin', seein' as how the boys he usually hires don't last too long before they take off for Dallas or Houston. Not enough goin' on to keep 'em here. Red oughta be back from Buzz's funeral in a half hour or so."

"Thanks, Katy, I'll check it out. Tell me, why's this town named Big Tuna? There ain't no body of water around here woulda ever had no tuna in it."

Katy laughed. "That's for sure. All we got's wells and what falls from the sky, which ain't been a whole heck of a lot lately. The Esperanza's dry half the year. No, it's named after an oilman, Earl 'Big Tuna' Bink, who bought up most of Iguana County back in the twenties. Used to be called Esperanza Spring, only there ain't no spring, just like there ain't no tuna. Bink'd go off on fishin' trips to California, Hawaii and Australia and such, and have these big mounted fish shipped back here to his ranch. He died when I was ten. The whole county went to his funeral. Ever'body called him Big Tuna. There's a oil portrait of him hangin' in the Iguana County Bank, which he owned. Where you-all from?"

"Florida," said Sailor. "Orlando, Florida."

"Boy, my grandkids'd sure love to go to that Disney World. You been there plenty, I guess."

"Lots of times."

Lula sucked on the straw in her Coke and stared at Sailor. He turned and smiled at her, then went back to making conversation with Katy. Lula suddenly felt sick to her stomach.

"I'm gonna go back up to the room and lie down, Sailor," she said. "This heat makes me tired."

"Okay, honey, I'll see you later."

"Bye," Lula said to Katy.

"Have a nice *siesta*, dear," said Katy.

Outside everything looked cooked, like the white of a fried egg, with brown edges. Lula walked very slowly the half block to the Iguana Hotel and barely made it up the stairs into the room before she threw up.

"You Red?"

Sailor was talking to the sweaty, grimy back of a stocky, shirtless man whose shoulders, arms and head were buried under the hood of a brown 1983 Buick Regal.

"No," the man grunted, without extricating himself. "Inside."

Sailor stood in what looked to be a junkyard. Greasy or rusting automobile parts, bottles, cans, torn-up couches, seatless or one-legged chairs, discarded screws, nails, springs, empty cartons, crushed cardboard boxes and other assorted garbage were strewn on the ground in front of Red's Garage. A fat red dog of indeterminate breed with only one ear slept by the entrance. A tall, skinny man in his early thirties with wild, uncombed hair the color of a pomegranate, wearing a grease-smeared white-and-red Hook-'em-Horns tee shirt and dark grey work pants, walked out of the corrugated-metal Butler building.

"You lookin' for me?" he said.

"If you're Red."

"Well, I ain't Blackie," said Red, with a smile.

Sailor held out his right hand to shake.

"Name's Sailor Ripley. Katy over at the drugstore thought you might maybe have some work I could do."

Red extended his own oil-blackened right hand and shook.

"Business ain't like the weather," he said.

"Meanin'?"

"Ain't real hot right now. Rex there, though," said Red, nodding toward the half-naked man burrowed into the Buick, "is about to relocate to San Angelo. I might could use a man when he does."

"When'd that be?"

"Week, ten days. Hey, Rex, how long till you head for Angelo?"

Rex pulled his head out from beneath the hood. He wiped his face with a crusty black rag and spat tobacco juice on the ground next to the sleeping red dog. The dog didn't twitch. Rex had a blue, quarter-inch-width scar across his nose.

"Susie's ma says we can have the trailer middle of next week," he said.

"You good with engines?" Red asked Sailor.

"I ain't no Enzo Ferrari, but they used to call me Wrench when I was a kid. Raced C Stock."

"We'll see how she goes then when Rex takes off. Check back."

Two men, both about forty, walked up to Red. One of them wore a grey baseball cap with a Confederate flag on it and the other had on an LBJ straw Stetson.

"How's it look?" said the man in the Stetson.

"Reckon the head's cracked, like I thought."

"Shit, that's what I was afraid of. It'll take some time then."

Red nodded. "It will," he said.

The man wearing the Rebel cap knelt down next to the fat red dog and scratched behind the dog's remaining ear.

"How you doin', Elvis?" he said to the dog. "Don't look like Elvis ever missed a meal, Red."

"He's always been regular," said Red.

Elvis didn't move. A dozen flies rested on his face.

"Anybody need a beer?" asked Rex, taking a six-pack of Bud from a small Kelvinator set up on blocks just inside the garage. He handed one to each man, kept a can for himself, tore the plastic ring off and tossed it on the ground and put one beer back in the refrigerator.

"I'm Buddy," said the man with the cap to Sailor, "and this here's Sparky."

Sailor introduced himself to Sparky and Buddy and Rex. They all shook hands or nodded and moved out of the sun to drink their beers.

"You fellas live here?" Sailor asked Sparky and Buddy.

Buddy laughed. "Feels like it now, don't it, Spark?"

"Car broke down," said Sparky. "The Buick over there. We been here a week while Red and Rex been troubleshootin' it."

"Where you headed?"

"California," said Buddy. "We live in San Bruno, south of San Francisco. Sparky's a plumber and I drive a produce delivery truck."

"Shoot, how'd y'all end up down here?"

"Deep in the Big Nowhere, you mean?" said Sparky. "Long story." He took a swig from his can.

"Short version is that Spark's dad died in Tampa," said Buddy, "left him his car. Spark and I flew down for the funeral and afterward packed up the stuff Spark wanted to keep, loaded it into the Buick. Made it far as Seguin, just the other side of San Antonio, before the car started actin' up. Tuned it there and thought we was okay, but around Kerrville the damn thing overheated somethin' fierce. Clicked off the AC and pushed it too far, I guess. Twenty-four miles west of Big Tuna it stuttered and boiled up. I was drivin' and pulled off on a dirt access road. There was nothin' around but dust and snakes and it was about a hundred and twenty with no hope of shade."

Sparky laughed. "This pickup comes along and Buddy throws himself in front of it, wavin' his arms like a weighted-down vulture tryin' to take off."

"No shit," said Buddy. "We woulda died out there. So the guy in the pickup used his towrope to pull us back to the Big Tuna here, where we've placed our fate in the unhygienic but supposedly automotively capable hands of Inman 'Don't Call Me Inman' Red Lynch. How about yourself?"

"My girl and I are lookin' for a place to settle," said Sailor. "We're bunked down at the Iguana Hotel."

"So are we," said Sparky. "It's the only hotel in Big Tuna. Have you met Bobby 'Just Like the Country' Peru yet?"

"No, we just got in a hour and a half ago."

"You will," Buddy said. "He's the Mr. Fix-it at the Iguana. His truck broke down here a couple of months ago."

"Escaped con," said Rex. "Man got some serious prison tattoos."

"Ever'body got a past," said Red.

"Just some got more future in 'em than others," Buddy said.

"That ain't no lie," said Rex.

Sailor finished his beer, stood it on the ground and stepped on it, crushing it flat.

"Been nice meetin' y'all," he said. " 'Preciate the beer. I'll be seein' y'all soon."

"Very soon," said Buddy.

"One thing about bein' in Big Tuna," said Sparky, "you don't have much choice about who you see and who you don't."

Sailor found Lula asleep on the bed. There was a terrible odor in the room and a big damp spot on the rug near the door.

"That you, Sail, honey?"

"The only one."

Lula opened her eyes and looked at Sailor.

"You see Red?"

"Uh huh. Met him and a bunch of boys. What's that smell?"

"I barfed. Tried to clean it with Ivory and water but it didn't do much good."

"You sick?"

"A little, I think. Darlin'?"

"Yeah?"

"Come sit by me."

Sailor went over and sat on the bed.

"I don't know that this is the right place for us."

Sailor stroked Lula's head.

"It ain't gonna be forever, peanut."

Lula closed her eyes.

"I know, Sailor. Nothin' is."

ONE NIGHT IN NACOGDOCHES

"Too late for the riot, Johnnie boy, as usual."

Johnnie and Marietta were having dinner with Johnnie's friend Eddie Guidry in Joe R's Steak 'n' Shrimp in Nacogdoches, Texas.

"Kinda riot, Eddie?"

"Cops killed a black kid who'd stuck up a 7-Eleven, durin' the process of which he'd coldcocked a seventy-eight-year-old white woman with a pistol. She died. Kid got away but cops in Bossier City caught him, shipped him back to Nacogdoches, where some fool deputy beat him to death. Boy was fifteen. One of the local black attorneys, woman named Rosetta Coates, who's very powerful around here, graduated top of her class at Austin, made a speech about it got the whole town excited. Result was thirteen dead, eleven of 'em blacks. Stores burned, looted. Regular Mardi Gras, Texas-style."

"Johnnie tells me you're a writer, Mr. Guidry," said Marietta.

"Yes, ma'am."

"May I inquire as to what type of writin' you do?"

"Adventure novels, action stuff. Doubt you'd be much interested in 'em."

"Would I have heard of any?"

"Had a pretty near best-seller three, four years ago, called *Death Chopper*. Did damn good in convenience stores."

"That's interestin', Mr. Guidry. I wasn't aware books were sold in those places."

"Hell, yes. Ain't no bookstores left, practically. Buy you a toothbrush, quart of low-fat, double A batteries, pack of Trojan-enz, *TV Guide* and a paperback best-seller all in the same run."

"Eddie and I met in the service, Marietta," said Johnnie. "We were together at Fort Jackson, then again in Nam."

"Do you write much about your experiences in Vietnam, Mr. Guidry?"

"No, ma'am, not really. In order for 'em to sell they gotta be like comic books. I ain't what you'd classify as a *serious* writer, unless you're talkin' money only, and *that's* sure as shit serious! No, Johnnie's the literary one. You ever read any of his stories?"

"Why, Johnnie," said Marietta, "why ain't you ever showed your writin' to me?"

Johnnie just shook his head and cut into his steak.

"He's got the ideas, this old boy," said Eddie. "Wish I had 'em."

From her room at the Ramada Inn after dinner, Marietta called Dalceda Delahoussaye.

"Dal? How you, honey?"

"Marietta? Where are you?"

"Nacogdoches, Texas, of all places. Johnnie wanted to stop by and see a old friend of his named Eddie Guidry. You ever heard of him? Says he writes war novels."

"Louis read one of 'em. *Chopped to Death,* I think it was. Man's a multimillionaire, Marietta. He single?"

"Divorced with four children. Lives with a Mexican girl, Johnnie told me. Daughter of the fam'ly maid. Prob'ly all of fourteen years old."

Dal laughed. "Nothin' we can do about them young ones, Marietta. They just keep on comin'."

"Mr. Guidry ain't my type. Man's got hair, Dal, I swear! Hairline's down on the bridge of his nose and hair's stickin' out on him from ever'where, 'specially his ears. Pretty disgustin'."

"What about Lula?"

"Johnnie's got a guy in San Antonio checkin' around. We know they're runnin' low on money, so they'll have to stop someplace and work. Johnnie's ninety percent positive they're headed west. His associate in San Antone's makin' calls. Cover more ground with a telephone than you can in a car, Johnnie says."

"Sounds smart. You sleepin' with him, Marietta?"

"Oh, Dal, hush. We got separate rooms at the Ramada."

"Last night I come in the bedroom and Louis is sleepin', but he's got this big ol' hard-on. Well, big for Louis, anyway. So I climb over him real careful and take it out of his pajama bottoms and stick it in me."

"Dal!" Marietta squealed. "You're lyin'!"

"How else am I gonna get him to do it? Anyway, he woke up quick and come quicker, so it was nothin' to write home about. I tell you,

Marietta, we oughta go down to Old Mexico and get us a couple maraca-playin' beach boys like Ava Gardner had in that movie? We ain't dead or dried up yet but it won't be long. I'm *serious,* Marietta."

"I'm tired, Dal. I'll let you know soon's I find out somethin'."

"Think about what I'm sayin' now, okay? Love you, Marietta. You take care."

"I will, Dal. Bye."

READER'S STORY

"You ever see that Errol Flynn movie, *Objective, Burma!*?" Sailor asked.

Lula was sitting in a chair, painting her toenails.

"Not that I recall," she said.

"Flynn and a group of soldiers is about to jump from an airplane into the jungle near Mandalay or somewhere during World War Two," said Sailor, "and one of the guys asks Flynn, 'What if my chute doesn't open?' And Flynn says, 'Well, you'll be the first on the ground.'"

Lula laughed. "He was awful handsome," she said, "even if he did have a mustache? I never have cared for facial hair on a guy unless he was so ugly it covered him up."

Sailor got up from the bed and began putting on his clothes.

"Let's go have some dinner, peanut," he said. "I'm ready."

"My toenails gotta dry first, Sailor. Tell me a story while we're waitin'."

"What kinda story, darlin'?"

"Anythin' you got to say interests me," said Lula. "You know that."

"You really are dangerously cute, honey," Sailor said. "I gotta admit it."

Lula giggled and stretched out on the bed, dangling her feet over the edge.

Sailor sat down in a chair by the window. He could see the heat waves roll down the street.

"Up at Pee Dee I met a guy named Reader O'Day," he said. "Reader was in for doin' in his common-law wife. Got seventeen to life for second-degree murder."

"What kinda name is Reader?" asked Lula.

"He's called that on account of he reads a lot. I never heard his Christian name that I can recall. He's always readin' some book that his people send him. Reader went to college. He's about forty-six now and he still reads books."

"That's amazin'," said Lula. "I mean, it's probably pretty rare for a criminal of any kind."

"For a long time he was readin' books by a dead French guy. Reader

told me all this guy's books were parts of what was called *Rememberin'
Things Past.* I think that's the name. Anyway, accordin' to Reader, the
author got the idea for writin' down all this stuff just after he ate a
cookie."

"A cookie?"

"Yeah. The French guy bit into a cookie and a whole flood of things
he remembered filled up his brain and he wrote 'em down. Reader said
the guy was sick a lot and he was still writin' when he died, right up to
the last second."

Lula clucked her tongue a couple of times.

"Why'd Reader clock his old lady?" she asked.

Sailor shook his head and whistled softly through his teeth.

"That's a whole story," he said. "Seems they had a daughter that didn't
get along too good with the mother, and Reader stuck it out for the kid's
sake. According to him, the woman acted pretty violent toward the little
girl and toward Reader, too. Reader said once she attacked him with a
hot iron and another time with a chain saw."

"Sounds like that movie I wouldn't go see," said Lula.

"Reader figured he ought to stay around to protect his daughter. For
a while they lived down around Morgan City and he worked in the oil
fields. When the oil business went belly-up he moved back to the Piedmont and worked the tobacco. The woman worked once in a while as a
helper in a hospital. Reader said she was just Alabama trash and he'd
picked up with her in the first place at a time when he wasn't feelin' none
too high on himself neither. After the daughter was born, though, he
kinda changed his ways."

"He must come from good people?" said Lula. "After all, he did go to
college."

"I believe he said his daddy was a doctor," Sailor said. "So prob'ly he
was a disappointment to his folks, out kickin' around the oil fields and
doin' jobs anybody could be doin'. Anyhow, the woman kept buggin'
him to marry her and make their daughter legitimate. Reader didn't want
to get hitched to this woman and told her he was only still with her
'cause of the kid. This went on for some time, I guess, her after him to
marry her and him refusin'. One day when the daughter, who was about
ten years old at the time, was at school or somewhere, Reader's old lady

come at him with a rifle and threatened to kill him unless he married her. When he told her to back off, she fired the gun and just missed him. He said the bullet grazed his left ear and smacked into the wall behind him. He grabbed the rifle away from her and went a little crazy."

"You mean he shot her?" said Lula.

"Five or six times," said Sailor. "Guess he got so mad he just stood over her and kept cockin' the rifle and firin' till it was empty. Then he made a real mistake."

"As if pluggin' half a dozen slugs into the lady wasn't enough," Lula said.

"Instead of callin' the cops," said Sailor, "and pleadin' self-defense or justifiable homicide and bein' driven out of his mind, he wrapped up her body in a shower curtain and buried it underneath the house."

"What'd he tell his daughter?"

"Just that her mother'd gone away for a vacation or somethin'. Reader dropped her with his folks and took off. Went to New York, Chicago, Las Vegas, all over. He got caught when he tried to sneak back and see his daughter."

"How'd the police find the body?"

"That's the good part," Sailor said. "They didn't. At least not until Reader told 'em where he'd stashed it. They went ahead and prosecuted him based on circumstantial evidence. In the middle of the trial, with Reader thinkin' he was gonna walk, they subpoenaed his mama, and when she refused to testify they popped her in the slam. She's a older woman in poor health, so she can't take more'n a week. When she gets out she admits that Reader told her about the shootin'. Reader testifies that his common-law wife attacked him first and that she got shot by accident while they was strugglin' for the weapon. He tells 'em where the body's buried, they dig it up, and find her full of holes fired point-blank. Put together with his havin' hit the road, this don't do Reader no good. The jury just wasn't about to buy his side of the matter. He told me most of the jurors was women, and when he said in court that his common-law wife used to get riled up regular whenever she got on the rag, they looked about set to lynch him right now. Reader was prob'ly the nicest fella I met at Pee Dee. Your toes dry yet, peanut?"

NIGHT AND DAY AT THE IGUANA HOTEL

"How do you get sixteen Haitians into a Dixie cup?" said Sparky.

"How?" asked Lula.

"Tell 'em it floats."

Sailor, Lula, Sparky and Buddy were sitting in the lobby of the Iguana Hotel at ten P.M., sharing Sparky's fifth of Ezra Brooks and shooting the shit.

"Sparky's big on Florida jokes," said Buddy.

"You need a active sense of humor to survive in the Big Tuna," said Sparky.

Bobby Peru walked in and came over.

"Hey, everybody," he said.

"Sailor, Lula, this here's the man himself," said Buddy. "Bobby, this is Sailor and Lula, the most recent strandees, economic variety."

Bobby nodded to Lula and offered a hand to Sailor.

"Bobby Peru, just like the country."

Sparky and Buddy laughed.

"Accordin' to Red and Rex," said Buddy, "Bobby's the most excitin' item to hit Big Tuna since the '86 cyclone sheared the roof off the high school."

"Only in town two months and there ain't a young thing around don't know how that cobra tattoo works, right, Bob?" Sparky said.

Bobby laughed. He had a lopsided grin that exposed only three brownish front teeth on the upper right side of his mouth. He had dark, wavy hair and a small, thin nose that bent slightly left. His eyebrows were long and tapered and looked as if they'd been drawn on. What frightened Lula about Bobby Peru were his eyes: flat black, they reflected no light. They were like heavy shades, she thought, that prevented people from seeing inside. Lula guessed that he was about the same age as Sparky and Buddy, but Bobby was the kind of person who would look the same when he was forty-five as he did when he was twenty.

"You from Texas, Mr. Peru?" Lula asked.

Bobby pulled up a chair and poured himself a shot glass full of whisky.

"I'm from all over," he said. "Born in Tulsa, raised in Arkansas, Illinois, Indiana, lived in Oregon, South Dakota, Virginia. Got people in Pasadena, California, who I was headin' to see when my Dodge busted a rod. Still meanin' to get out there."

"You was in the marines, huh?" said Sailor, noticing a USMC tattoo on Bobby's right hand.

Bobby looked down at his hand, flexed it.

"Four years," he said.

"Bobby was at Cao Ben," said Sparky.

"What's Cao Ben?" asked Lula.

"How old are you?" Buddy asked her.

"Twenty."

"Bunch of civilians got killed," said Bobby. "March 1968. We torched a village and the government made a big deal out of it. Politicians tryin' to get attention. Put the commandin' officer on trial for murder. Only problem was, there weren't no such persons as civilians in that war."

"Lotta women and kids and old people died at Cao Ben," said Buddy.

Bobby sipped the whisky and closed his eyes for several seconds before reopening them and looking at Buddy.

"You was on a ship, pardner. Hard to make contact with the people when you're off floatin' in the Gulf of Tonkin. It weren't simple."

"Saw Perdita this afternoon," said Sparky. "Came by Red's lookin' for you."

"Had some business over by Iraaq," said Bobby. "I'm just about to go check on her now."

He stood up and set the shot glass on his chair.

"Good meetin' you," Bobby said to Sailor and Lula. "*Adiós*, boys."

He walked out.

After Bobby was gone, Lula said, "Somethin' in that man scares me."

"Bobby's got a way," said Buddy.

"Can't shake that institution odor," Sparky said, and poured himself another shot.

Lula put a hand on Sailor's leg.

"Darlin', I still ain't feelin' so well," she said. "I'm goin' to bed."

"I'll come along," said Sailor.

They said good night to Sparky and Buddy and went upstairs.

In the room, Sailor said, "Man, that barf smell don't fade fast."

"I'll get some white vinegar to rub on it tomorrow, honey, take care of it."

Lula went into the bathroom and stayed there for a long time. When she came out, Sailor asked if there was anything he could do for her.

"No, I don't think so, Sail. I just need to lie down."

Lula listened to Sailor brush his teeth, then urinate into the toilet and flush it.

"Sailor?" she said as he climbed into bed. "You know what?"

"I know you ain't particularly pleased bein' here."

"Not that. Might be I'm pregnant."

Sailor rolled over and looked into Lula's eyes.

"It's okay by me, peanut."

"Well, nothin' personal, but I ain't so sure it's okay by me."

Sailor lay down on his back.

"Really, Sailor, it ain't nothin' against you. I love you."

"Love you, too."

"I know. Just I'm sorta uncomfortable about the way some things is goin', and this don't help soothe me."

Sailor got out of bed and went over by the window. He sat down in the chair and looked out. Bobby Peru and a Mexican woman with black hair longer than Lula's were parked across the street in a maroon 1971 Eldorado convertible with the top down. Sailor watched as the woman pulled a knife out of her purse and tried to stick Bobby with it. He took the knife away from her and tossed it. She got out of the car and ran. Bobby fired up the Eldo and drove after her.

"I know this ain't easy, Lula," Sailor said, "but I ain't gonna let things get no worse, I promise."

"I've always been fascinated by the ways people do business, Marietta. When they discuss large sums of money they lower their voices, they whisper. It don't matter whether the sonofabitch'll be dead or too old to spend the money he might make eventually from a deal, it's the *thought* of it that counts. The reverence, the absolute reverence some people have for money amazes me. For the mere mention of large sums, as if the money would disappear if they referred to it in less than the most respectful terms. I tell ya, Marietta, the only two things anybody seems to be interested in anymore are money and losin' weight."

Johnnie and Marietta were drinking coffee in a booth in the Bad Bull truckstop diner in Biarritz.

"Johnnie, all I care about right now is Lula."

A waitress came over and refilled Johnnie's cup. Marietta covered hers with her right hand.

"I'm fine, honey," she said to the waitress, who was about seventeen years old. "Don't she remind you of Lula?" Marietta asked Johnnie. "She got the same buttery skin."

The waitress smiled and put their check on the table and walked away.

"Listen, Marietta, there really ain't no point in your hangin' out on the road like this. I 'preciate the fact you enjoy my company and all, but until I got some more concrete information to go on, you're just wastin' your time."

"I'd go crazy sittin' home. Least this way I'm *doin'* somethin'."

Johnnie sighed and sipped his coffee.

"Truth is," he said, "I'm gonna give this squirrel hunt about another couple days, is all. Week, maybe. I got work waitin' on me in Charlotte. Maceo in San Antonio can keep after it and I'll be callin' people around the country might be able to help out. You can bet Sailor's parole officer's reported him missin', too."

Marietta's eyes filled with tears and her nose began to run.

"Marietta, you're drippin' in your coffee."

Johnnie handed her a napkin. Marietta took it and wiped her eyes and blew her nose.

"I hate feelin' helpless, Johnnie. I hate it worse'n anything. Dal was against my comin', too."

"We'll hang in a touch longer, like I said. Maybe we'll run onto a lead right quick."

"I got to use the ladies' room."

Johnnie took his notebook out of his pocket and looked over what he'd written the night before in the motel. He'd decided to write about his childhood, beginning with his earliest sexual memories.

MY EARLY YEARS
by *Johnnie Farragut*

When I was very young, three or four years old, I would imagine that I was a leopard, a panther, crawling around on the floor, from which vantage point I would attempt to look under women's dresses. Once our maid caught me doing this to her. She wore stockings and I could see up to where they were fastened onto her garter belt and the large black area between her legs. She squeezed my head between her knees and laughed.

"Sniff it, baby," she said. "Sniff it good. You won't ever get enough."

I panicked, I was frightened and tried to pull my head loose, but it was stuck. She had me firmly between her thighs. The only direction I could move was up, so I pushed higher under her dress until my face was against the soft wet cotton of her panties. She started to move so that my nose rubbed against her clitoris, making her pants wetter, then harder over my mouth and chin. I was choking, I could barely breathe, but the iron grip of her legs held me helpless.

All I could see was black and my face was sticky. The smell was overpowering, like in a stable. At first I thought it was like that, like piles of horse manure, but then I knew it was different, like nothing I'd smelled before. I thought I was dying, I was suffocating, and she spread her legs slightly and held my head into her as she breathed faster and made more horrible sounds, rubbing herself back and forth over my hair. Finally she released me. I didn't die, I fell back on the floor and opened my eyes. I looked up at her and she was grinning.

"Come on, baby," she said, holding a hand down to me. "We better go wash your face."

Marietta came back and sat down.

"When you gonna let me read your writin', Johnnie?"

Johnnie closed his notebook and put it back in his coat.

"One day soon, maybe. When I got somethin' I think'll interest you."

"Prob'ly more things interest me than you think."

"I ain't never sold you short, Marietta, you know that."

Marietta smiled. "I know, Johnnie," she said. "I most certainly do."

MOSQUITOES

Sailor was changing the oil in the Bonneville when Bobby Peru pulled up in the maroon Eldo.

"Need a hand?"

"Thanks, Bobby, about done."

Sailor slid the pan of dirty oil out from underneath the Bonneville.

"Where's the best place to dump this?"

"Around back. Come on, I'll show ya."

Sailor picked up the pan and followed Bobby down the side of the Iguana Hotel.

"Empty it right in them weeds. Ain't nobody comes back here anyway. You about ready for a beer?"

"Sure, Bobby, that'd be fine."

"Let's go by Rosarita's. You been there yet?"

"No, haven't heard of it."

"Thought maybe Sparky and Buddy'd taken ya. Come on, I'll drive."

They got into the Cadillac and Bobby guided it slowly along Travis Street, Big Tuna's main drag.

"This your car?" Sailor asked.

Bobby laughed. "Hell no, belongs to Tony Durango. I been datin' his sister, Perdita, lately. Tony's up in Fort Worth with his wife's family for a couple weeks, so he's lettin' me use it. Where's that pretty little lady of yours today?"

"Restin' in our room. She ain't been feelin' well."

"Sorry to hear it. Women are always havin' some kinda physical problem. Been my experience with 'em."

Bobby turned off Travis onto Ruidoso Road and gunned the Eldo up to seventy. He rodded it for five minutes until they came to a closed-down filling station, where Bobby slowed down and circled around behind the building. A half dozen pickup trucks and three or four cars were parked in a row and Bobby wedged the Cad in between a tan Ford Ranger and a white Ranchero.

"Used to be this was a Mobil," said Bobby as they got out of the car.

"Man converted it into a private club and named it after his wife. She left him and he shot himself. The wife owns it now."

They entered a long, dark room where a dozen men, most of them wearing cowboy hats, sat on stools at a bar drinking beer out of frosted mugs.

"No hard liquor here," Bobby told Sailor. "Just beer."

They claimed two stools and Bobby said, "Coupla Stars, Jimmy."

The bartender, who was no taller than five feet five or six and weighed at least two hundred and forty pounds, brought over two bottles and two mugs.

"How ya be, Bobby?" he said. "Who's your *amigo*?"

"Sailor, meet Jimmy, otherwise known as Mr. Four-by-Four. He's always lookin' out for the patrons' welfare. Won't let ya drink no more'n forty, fifty beers, 'less you ain't drivin'."

"Howdy, Sailor," said Jimmy. "Enjoy yourself."

He walked back toward the other end of the bar.

"Thought you said this was a private club," Sailor said to Bobby. "How come I'm allowed in without bein' a member?"

"You black?"

"No."

"You an Indian?"

"No."

"Then you're a member."

"I've Got a Tiger by the Tail" by Buck Owens was playing on the jukebox, and Bobby kept time rapping his knuckles on the bar.

"Three or four millionaires in here right now," he said.

Sailor looked around at the other customers. All of them were modestly dressed.

"They look like a bunch of good ol' boys to me," said Sailor. "I guess it's oil money, huh?"

"Oil, gas, cattle, farmin'. Ain't nobody shows off around here. Iguana County's one of the richest in Texas."

"Wouldn'ta guessed it, that's sure."

"Ready for another?"

"Why not?"

When they were on their fifth round, Bobby went over to the jukebox and dropped in some quarters.

"Q-seven," he said, climbing back onto his stool, "three times. Pee Wee King's 'Waltz of Regret,' my favorite tune."

Pee Wee's steel guitar rippled through the cigarette haze and buzzed around Sailor's head. His reflection wobbled in the long mirror behind the bar.

"I been studyin' a situation over in Iraaq," said Bobby. "Take two men to handle it."

"What's that?"

"Feed store keeps up to five K in their safe. Need me a good boy for backup. Even split. You interested?"

Sailor knew he was slightly drunk. He rotated his head on his shoulders and flexed his back muscles. He stared at Bobby and worked hard to focus his eyes.

"Be easy, Sailor. There's two employees. I take one in the back to open the safe, you keep the other'n covered. You ain't plannin' on raisin' a fam'ly in Big Tuna, are ya?"

"Lula tell you she's pregnant?"

Bobby grinned, showing those three brown teeth.

"Couple grand or more'd give you two a leg up. Get you to the West Coast, Mexico, most anyplace, with a few dollars in your jeans. I got it figured good, Sailor. Simple's best."

"I ain't sure, Bobby. I got to consider this careful."

"I respect you for it, Sailor. Don't do a man no good to go in on a deal with less'n a full tank. You had enough?"

Sailor finished his beer and nodded. "Have now."

"Come on outside, I got somethin' to show ya."

Bobby looked around before he opened the trunk of the Eldorado. He peeled back a brown army blanket and said, "That's a double-barreled, sawed-off Ithaca shotgun with a carved pistol grip stock wrapped with adhesive tape. Next to it's a cold Smith and Wesson thirty-two handgun with a six-inch barrel. These'll do 'er."

Bobby covered the weapons with the blanket and closed the trunk. He and Sailor got into the car. The sky was dark pink. Bobby turned on the radio as they drove, fiddling with the dial until it landed on a classical music station out of San Antonio playing Gottschalk's *Night in the Tropics*.

"I sometimes listen to this serious stuff," said Bobby. "Kills off the mosquitoes in my brain."

Sailor bent over the bed and kissed Lula's hair above her left ear.

"Hi, hon," she said. "You been drinkin', huh?"

"Few beers is all. Feelin' any better?"

Lula rolled onto her back, stretched her arms in the air and yawned.

"Can't tell yet. Where'd you go?"

"Smell's mostly gone. That vinegar really done the job."

"Buddy and Sparky come by earlier."

"How they doin'?"

"Okay, I guess. Sparky said Red's promised to have 'em out of here by the weekend."

"Oughta make 'em happy."

"So where'd you say you was?"

"Went with Bobby."

Sailor went into the bathroom and washed his face. Lula came in and sat on the toilet to pee.

"Hope you don't mind, Sail, I couldn't wait. What's Mr. Peru Like the Country up to?"

"Not much."

"Don't think he ever been up to much good his whole life."

Sailor laughed. "Maybe not."

"Sail?"

"Uh huh?"

"Let's leave here."

"We're goin' to, Lula, real soon."

"I mean tomorrow."

"We got about forty bucks, sweetheart. That'd get us to El Paso."

"Rather be in El Paso than Big Tuna."

Sailor walked out of the bathroom, took off his clothes and got into bed. Lula flushed the toilet, rinsed her face and hands, then came out and picked up her pack of cigarettes from the dresser.

"You shouldn't be smokin' if you're pregnant," said Sailor. "Ain't smart."

Lula stuck a More between her lips and lit it. She took a deep drag, blew out the smoke and stared at Sailor.

"Who says I'm smart?" she said. "You up to somethin' with Bobby Peru, Sailor?"

"What could I be up to, Lula?"

"He's a stone fuckin' criminal, honey, and you ain't."

Sailor laughed. "I killed Bob Ray Lemon, didn't I?"

"That was a accident. I bet both our asses Bobby Peru done murdered all kinds of people, and meant it, too."

"That was in Vietnam."

"He's the kind liked it."

"Lula, I got to get some sleep."

"Buddy told me about that thing at Cao Ben?"

"What?"

"Was a massacre. Soldiers there murdered old folks, women and babies, and dumped 'em in a trench. Bobby Peru prob'ly killed the most."

"Lula, he mighta did, I don't know. But it don't matter now. Lotta guys go outa control in a war and it ain't their fault."

Lula puffed hard on her cigarette.

"I sure enjoy smokin', Sailor. I hate that it's bad for you."

Sailor turned on his side, away from Lula, and pulled a pillow over his head.

"That Mexican woman, Perdita Durango, who's been goin' around with Bobby Peru? Did you know she drowned her own baby? Katy at the drugstore told me when I was out gettin' the vinegar."

"Anything else people told you today you ain't mentioned yet?"

"That man's a black angel, Sailor. You hook up with him, you'll regret it. If you live to."

"Thanks, darlin', I know you got my best interest in mind, and I 'preciate it sincerely. I love you, but I gotta sleep now."

Lula lit a second More off the first and stubbed out the butt on the dresser top.

"Shit," she said, softly. "Shit, shit, shit."

THE MEANING OF LIFE

"Okay, Spark, here it is," Buddy said, putting his pen down on the counter. "My all-time top ten, in no particular order. 'Lucille' by Little Richard, 'Lonely Nights' by The Hearts, 'He's So Fine' by The Chiffons, 'Be My Baby' by The Ronettes, 'Sea of Love' by Phil Phillips, 'High Blood Pressure' by Huey 'Piano' Smith and The Clowns, 'It's Rainin'' by Irma Thomas, 'You're No Good' by Betty Everett, 'I'd Rather Go Blind' by Etta James, and 'Sittin' on the Dock of the Bay' by Otis Redding. What do you think?"

"I've always been partial to 'Sea of Love' myself," said Sparky. "But where's 'My Pretty Quadroon' by Jerry Lee Lewis? Just kiddin'. But how about 'Breathless,' at least? Where's Sam Cooke? Elvis? Chuck Berry? 'Just One Look' by Doris Troy? 'Stay' by Maurice Williams? 'I'm a King Bee' by Slim Harpo? Or 'Little Darlin'' by The Gladiolas? 'If You Lose Me, You'll Lose a Good Thing' by Barbara Lynn? Marvin Gaye? Little Miss Cornshucks? Sugar Pie DeSanto? The Beatles? The Stones?"

"Can't all be in the top ten. Those are the ones I'd take. Not meant to please anyone but myself. Besides, makin' lists helps pass the time."

Buddy and Sparky were sitting in Bottomley's Drug, drinking 7-Ups. The temperature outside was 115 degrees.

"Well, will you look at this," said Katy, who was standing behind the counter reading yesterday's *San Antonio Light*. "Knew someday somethin' like it would happen to him."

"Who you talkin' about?" Buddy asked.

"Joe Don Looney, the football player. Greatest halfback in Texas high school history. Here, take a look."

She handed the newspaper to Buddy.

" 'Joe Don Looney Dies In Crash,' " Buddy read aloud. " 'Joe Don Looney, a former college and pro football player known as a rebel both on and off the gridiron, died Saturday in a motorcycle accident in southwest Texas, officials said. Looney, forty-five, was killed when he failed to make a curve on State Highway 118, according to the Department of

Public Safety. Looney was thrown clear of the motorcycle and hit a wire fence, reports said.' "

"Just like Lawrence of Arabia," said Sparky.

"Ain't never heard of no Arabia, Texas," said Katy.

" 'The accident occurred around eight-thirty A.M. about nine miles north of the town of Study Butte in rural Brewster County. He was pronounced dead at the scene. Looney attended Texas Christian briefly before enrolling and starring for Cameron Junior College in Oklahoma.' "

"Boy's life was never the same after he left Texas," Katy said.

" 'He made the All-Junior College All-Star team and was recruited by then–Oklahoma coach Bud Wilkinson. In 1962, Looney rushed for 852 yards and was named to the All-Big Eight Conference team, but Wilkinson asked him to leave the Sooners because of discipline problems. Looney appealed to Wilkinson and was allowed to stay. But Looney was thrown off the team the next year when he decked an O.U. coach.' "

"He was one wild-ass kid, all right," said Katy.

" 'In the 1963 NFL draft, Looney was selected in the first round by the New York Giants. He played for three more pro teams, Baltimore, Detroit and Washington, before retiring.' "

Buddy folded the paper and put it down on the counter.

"Joe Don was a legend when I was a girl," said Katy. "Handsome, too. But he went off the deep end somewhere."

"He went to India," Buddy said, "and studied with a guru and became a vegetarian. I remember seein' a TV program not too long ago, like *The NFL Today,* that did a short feature on Looney. He'd taken a lot of drugs in the sixties, like most of us, and in the seventies went to India, found a teacher and changed his lifestyle. After a few years, he came back to Texas and built a ten-sided house in the desert. Each wall inside had a picture of his guru on it. He lived alone and spent most of his day prayin'. He prepared his own special food, was celibate and didn't take drugs or medicines of any kind. He told the TV reporter that everything he'd been taught as a kid, to be a tough, football-playin' chicken fried steak eater, was wrong. That's why he'd always had such a hard time, he said, because he'd never really believed it was what he was meant to be doin'.' "

"He was right," said Sparky. "At least he got to find out before he died of a heart attack from eatin' all that meat and pumpin' his body full of steroids."

"That boy was marked for an early death," said Katy, "however it happened. Findin' out the meanin' of life and all is fine, far as it goes, but dead's dead, you know what I mean?"

FRIENDS

"Nice of you to drop by," said Perdita.

Bobby let the screen door bang shut behind him as he came in.

"Told you I would."

Perdita sat down on the couch, shook a Marlboro from the pack on the coffee table and lit it with a red Bic. Bobby roamed around the living room. The taps on the heels and toes of his boots clacked loudly against the hardwood floor.

"You still riled?" asked Bobby.

Perdita laughed. "You still screwin' sixteen-year-olds in the ass?"

Bobby smiled and kept circling.

"Ain't never had no teenaged girl pull a blade on me."

"Wish I'd cut you up good."

"Heard from Tony?"

"Juana called. They're stayin' another week."

Bobby stopped walking and stared at a family photograph on the wall.

"Stayin' a few extra days in the cow town, huh? This you?"

Perdita turned her head and looked, then turned back.

"Yes."

"How old were you? Twelve?"

"Almost. Eleven and a half. Ten years ago in Corpus."

"Mm, mm. What a tasty thing you musta been."

"Nobody was tastin'."

"Shame."

Bobby turned around and leaned down and put his face next to Perdita's from behind.

"The cobra's waitin' to strike, *chica,*" he said.

Perdita crossed her legs and smoked. Bobby lowered his hands into the front of her blouse and cupped her small breasts. Perdita pretended not to care. He rubbed her nipples with the tips of his fingers, making them become rigid. She burned the back of his left wrist with her cigarette.

Bobby jumped back, then grabbed Perdita's hair and pulled her over the couch onto the floor. Neither of them spoke. She tried to stand up but Bobby kept his right foot on her chest while he blew on the back of his wounded wrist. Perdita shoved his leg to one side and rolled away. She stood up and spit at him.

Bobby grinned. "I knew we could be friends again," he said.

ONE STEP BEYOND

Lula read a magazine article about Evel Knievel, the man who'd tried to jump a rocket-shaped motorcycle across the mile-wide, 600-foot-deep Snake River Canyon; over 150-foot-tall fountains in front of a Las Vegas hotel-casino; a baker's dozen double-decker buses in London, England; a shark-filled pool in the Chicago stockyards; and made several other remarkable attempts at vehicular glory. At the Snake River, Knievel had crashed against the side of a mountain. In all, he'd broken at least forty bones, including both arms and his pelvis, and endured numerous brain concussions. Knievel had more than a dozen steel plates in his body, the article said, and now walked with the use of a gold-knobbed sword-cane since an operation had left one of his legs a half-inch shorter than the other.

Patsy Cline got killed in some kind of wreck when she was real young, Lula remembered. Patsy used that slow curve in her voice to talk about one kind of crazy. This daredevil idea, though, went way beyond natural.

BOBBY'S BAD DAY

"Take one of these," Bobby Peru said, handing a plastic-wrapped package to Sailor.

"What is it?"

"Panty hose. Work better'n stockin's. Pull one of the legs down over your face and let the other leg trail behind your head."

They were in the Eldorado, about two blocks away from the Ramos Feed Store in Iraaq. Perdita was at the wheel, Bobby was next to her and Sailor rode in back. The top was up.

"Here's the pistol," said Bobby, taking the Smith and Wesson out of his belt and passing it to Sailor. "Remember, soon as we get inside you keep that bad boy up where those hicks can see it. Once they notice the Ithaca and the Smith, they'll know we ain't foolin' with 'em."

Perdita tossed her cigarette out the window and immediately took out another and lit it with the dashboard lighter.

"Comin' up on it now, Bobby," she said.

Bobby slipped the panty hose over his head and adjusted it. His face looked crooked, distorted and flat, the lips pancaked across the lower half and his hair plastered down over his forehead like broken teeth on a comb.

"Come on!" Bobby stage-whispered, his head snapping toward Sailor like a striking asp's. "Get that mask on!"

Sailor ripped open the package and pulled a nylon leg over his head, stretching the calf part to fit.

Perdita pulled up in front of the store. The street was deserted.

"Keep it revved, Chiquita. We won't be long," Bobby said.

It was two o'clock in the afternoon and the sun took up the entire sky. As Sailor got out of the car, he felt the intense heat of the day for the first time. Until that moment, he'd been numb. Sailor had passed the preceding hours in a kind of trance, unaware of the temperature or anything other than the time. Fourteen hours, Bobby had said, that's when they'd go in. They'd be out at fourteen-oh-three and thirty seconds, he promised, with something in the neighborhood of five thousand dollars.

Bobby went in first, carrying a black canvas Sundog shoulder bag in his left hand. He raised the sawed-off shotgun with his right and in a firm voice said to the two men behind the counter, "Move into the back room, both of you. Now!"

They moved. Both in their mid-fifties, portly, with wire-rim glasses and crown-bald heads, the men looked like brothers.

"Stay here," Bobby told Sailor as he followed them. "Keep an eye on the door. If anyone comes in, herd 'em on back, quick."

Sailor held the Smith up high, where Bobby could see it if he looked. Behind him, Sailor could hear Bobby instructing one of the men to open the safe. Neither of the men, so far as Sailor could tell, had said a word.

An Iguana County deputy sheriff cruised up in a patrol car and parked it on an angle in front of the idling Eldo. The deputy got out of his car and walked over to the driver's side of the Cadillac. He looked at Perdita through his aviator-style reflector Ray-Bans, smiled, and placed both of his hands on the rag top.

"Waitin' for somebody, miss?" he said.

"*Mi esposo,*" said Perdita. "He's in the feed store picking up some supplies."

"You'd best be careful of that cigarette, ma'am. It's about to burn down between your fingers."

Perdita stubbed out her Marlboro in the ashtray.

"*Gracias,* officer."

Bobby came out of the store in a hurry, still wearing the panty hose on his head, carrying the shoulder bag and the shotgun. Perdita jammed the gearshift into reverse and peeled out, knocking the deputy down. She floored the Eldo for fifty yards, braked hard, yanked it into drive and spun a mean yo-yo, fishtailing viciously but managing to keep the car under control. Perdita hit the accelerator again as hard as she could and never looked back.

The deputy came up on one knee with his revolver clasped in both hands. He fired his first shot into Bobby's right thigh and his second into Bobby's left hip. The shock of the initial slug caused Bobby to drop the bag. The impact of the second forced Bobby's right hand to twist sideways so that both barrels of the shotgun wedged under his chin. The Ithaca went off, blowing Bobby backwards through the RAMOS on the plate-glass window of the feed store.

Sailor had been right behind Bobby until he saw Perdita hightail it. As soon as he spotted the deputy, Sailor hit the ground, losing the Smith as he fell. He put his hands over his hosieried head and kept his face in the dirt until the deputy ordered him to stand up.

"Hello, Mace, it's Johnnie."

"Glad you called, boy. You still east of El Paso?"

"We're at the Best Western in Fort Stockton."

"Oughta take you about two hours to get to Lula. Just heard on the news that Sailor Ripley and another guy tried to stick up a feed store in Iraaq. They're holdin' Ripley in the Iguana County jail in Big Tuna. Deputy sheriff shot and killed the other one."

"'Preciate it, Maceo. Be talkin' to ya."

"Anytime."

Lula was sitting on a bench in the waiting room of the Iguana County Courthouse when Johnnie and Marietta walked in. As soon as she saw Lula, Marietta ran over, sat down next to her and hugged and kissed her.

"Oh, baby, I was beginnin' to think I was never gonna see you again."

Tears were pouring down Marietta's cheeks. She held Lula to her and Lula did not resist.

"Sweetheart, I'm so sorry about all this. I know you think I'm a crazy old woman, but I was so worried!"

"You ain't old, Mama. Hello, Johnnie."

"Hello, Lula. How you holdin'?"

"I'm tired, just real, honest-to-Jesus dog-tired."

"You're comin' home, precious," said Marietta. "Johnnie's gonna drive us to the San Antonio airport."

"Mama, Sailor's in deep trouble here. I can't just leave him."

Marietta took Lula by the shoulders and looked straight at her. Lula's eyes were bloodshot, her hair was greasy and stringy, and her cheeks were pale.

"Oh, yes, you can," Marietta said.

LETTER FROM LULA

Sailor Ripley
#461208
Walls Unit
Huntsville, Texas 77340

Dearest Sailor Darling,

The first thing youll want to know is Im keeping the baby. Mama wasnt for it in the beginning but I think shes looking forward to it. Im gonna name it Pace no matter if its a boy or a girl. Pace Ripley sounds good dont it? Its kind of hard to believe that Pace will be ten years old when you get out.

What else can I tell you? Im feeling fine its not so terrible being with mama cause shes calmed down a lot. I think our running off that way scared her plenty and she has more respect for me now. She doesn't even speak poorly of you no more at least not so often. I explained to her how you was worried about us not having money and the idea of a baby and all and how of course it was no excuse for committing an armed robbery but there it is.

I hope its not too horrible for you inside the walls again I know how much you hate being confined. Is it different in a Texas prison than it was at Pee Dee? I bet it aint as pretty. The doctor here says I got to stay at home while Im pregnant. Theres something wrong with the way Im carrying the baby but if I keep still and dont smoke and eat right which mama and her friend Dalceda Delahoussaye are seeing to he says I should be just fine. It sure is hard not to smoke. I miss my Mores!!! I feel like Im kind of in prison too but I know in six months itll be over and Ill have a son or daughter to show for it. Our child!!

I hope you know it hurts me to not be able to visit you all I can do is write letters which is OK I like writing. Did you know that Johnnie Farragut is a writer? Mama told me he showed her some stories and things he wrote and that she liked them. She says he has an interesting imagination.

Did Perdita Durango ever get caught? Ill bet shes in Mexico now or somewhere out of the authorities reach. I have to confess it dont bother me one little bit about Bobby Peru being shot dead. He was one of them types you could feel it was coming and he killed his share as we know. Remember once I called him a black angel well hes not in heaven Ill guarantee. If he is then I never want to go <u>there</u>!!!

It was excellent of you to give yourself up the way you did and not try to shoot it out youd be dead too and never have got to see your child Pace. I hope this name is all right with you Sailor if its not tell me and Ill think it over some more but I love it and certainly hope you do.

Im going to take a nap now. Your probably thinking about how I was always sleeping at the end there in the Iguana Hotel and now I still am but the doctor says sometimes being pregnant makes the mother be that way and Im one of them. I love you Sailor. I dont know how much or what it means though I miss you an awful bunch sometimes I know your thinking about me cause I can feel it. I miss your not being around to call me peanut nobody else ever called me that.

Like I said I have to rest again. Its not really so simple to write like this at least not like it was before when you was at Pee Dee cause that was for only two years not ten. Time dont really fly honey does it?

Love,
your Lula

LETTER FROM SAILOR

Lula P. Fortune
127 Reeves Avenue
Bay St. Clement, N.C. 28352

Dear Lula,

It is fine with me about the baby as you already know. And Pace being your family name and all is just right. What about a middle name if it is a boy after my grandaddy Roscoe? He would be proud I know though he is long passed. Pace Roscoe Ripley does not sound so bad do you think? If it is a girl instead choose whatever name you want for a middle I do not care. Leaving it be is OK without a middle or you might want to put in your mother Marietta. Anyway is good. Just you stay healthy.

Your right this place is not so pretty as Pee Dee. Not pretty at all. There are boys inside these walls meaner than Peru you can bet. There is a Death House. I am getting along. The only thing is not thinking about the future. Your right there 10 years is not 2. The baby will be 10 but I will be 33. There is always a chance of early parole though the rap back home and the fact I busted parole there probably cancels that. I am not there idea of a good risk.

I really got no idea what happened to Perdita. She disappeared as you figured. She is a strange person and I did not know her well. Tell your mama I am dreadful sorry about each and everything that has happened and the last thing ever in my mind is to see you harmed. You are her daughter but I would like to marry you if you would consent while I am inside. This can be arranged because I asked. The preacher would do it but I know you cannot leave home. Maybe after you have the baby you would come here.

Write often peanut. I am in the laundry at 5. There are car magazines and TV. Other than that is mail.

I love you. It is hard to end this letter. If I stop writing your gone. There is not a lot more to say though. Vaya con dios mi amor.

Sailor

RITARDANDO

"I'm goin', Mama. No way I can't go."

"You ain't takin' Pace, though."

"Course I am, Mama."

Marietta sighed. "What time's Sailor's bus get in?"

"Six."

Neither Marietta nor Lula said anything for at least half a minute. Finally, Marietta asked, "Got any plans?"

"Figure we'll go have supper someplace. Maybe get some barbecue out by Stateline. Sailor always liked that Havana Brown's Pig Pickin'."

"Well, you be careful with that boy, Lula."

"Sailor ain't a boy no more, Mama. He's thirty-three years old."

"Don't mean him," said Marietta. "It's Pace concerns me."

"Really, Mama, I gotta go."

"I'll be at Dal's, honey, you need me."

"Hi and all to Dal. We'll talk later."

"Bye, Lula. Love you."

"Love you."

Marietta hung up first. Lula was relieved that Marietta hadn't told her a second time to be careful.

"Pace? You ready, honey?"

The boy walked into the front room from the kitchen, eating a chocolate bar. Lula got up from the couch and looked in the wall mirror.

"Shouldn't be eatin' no candy now, darlin'."

"Just a Mounds, Mama."

Lula finished fixing her hair, picked up her purse and headed for the door.

"Come, baby," she said.

From the back seat of the car, Pace said, "How'll we know what he looks like?"

Lula made a wide left turn onto Jeff Davis Highway without signaling, causing the driver of a white Thunderbird headed across the intersection to jam on his brakes in order to avoid a collision. The T-bird driver sat on his horn and shouted at Lula.

"Mama, you almost crashed us."

Lula steadied the steering wheel of her Camaro with her left elbow while she struck a match and lit up a More. She threw the match out the window and took possession of the wheel with both hands, the cigarette clamped in her teeth.

"Don't give me no trouble now, Pace, please. This ain't my easiest day in a long time. And what do you mean how we gonna know what your daddy looks like? You seen his photo."

"How'll he know what we look like? He seen our photo?"

Lula puffed furiously several times on her More before she took it out of her mouth and dropped it.

"Damn it, child! Now look what you made me do."

"What I make you do, Mama?"

Lula felt around on the floor with one hand until she found the cigarette.

"Nothin', honey," Lula said, stubbing it out in the ashtray. "Mama's just actin' strange."

"You ain't actin', Mama."

"Why, Pace Roscoe Ripley, ain't you got the cute mouth tonight."

"It's Grandmama does the actin'."

Lula didn't know whether to laugh or pretend to be angry.

"Who'd you hear that from?"

"Uncle Johnnie."

Lula laughed. "Then it must be true," she said.

"I still ain't sure what my daddy looks like."

"Like you, sweetheart. You and your daddy got the same mouth, eyes, ears and nose. Only difference is your color hair is black, like mine."

It started to rain, so Lula turned on the wipers, rolled up her window and flipped on the AC.

"My daddy ain't never killed nobody, has he, Mama?"

"Course he ain't never killed nobody. Why'd you say that, Pace?"

"Heard Uncle Johnnie and Grandmama talkin'."

"And?"

"Grandmama said how Sailor murdered a man."

"Wrong, baby. Your daddy never committed no murder. Musta been you didn't hear Grandmama proper. He made some mistakes, is all. Your daddy ain't always been so lucky."

Pace leaned over on the passenger side of the front seat and rolled down the window, letting the rain in.

"Pace, you close that. The seat's gettin' wet."

"I like the rain, Mama, it's steamin'."

Lula reached across and rolled the window back up.

"We're almost at the depot, honey. Sit back a minute."

Lula pulled the Camaro into a stall in the Trailways parking lot and cut the motor. She sat and watched as the blinking blue-and-white neon BUS sign gnawed its way through the grainy grey sky and sprawled across the windshield.

"Why we sittin' here, Mama?"

"Thinkin' a second, baby. Somethin' just now reminded me of a place me and your daddy stayed once."

"Where?"

"In a old hotel by the end of a river."

Lula shuddered and without thinking slid her right hand inside her shirt and caressed her left breast.

"Mama, it's hot."

Lula opened her door and she and Pace climbed out. They held hands as they walked through the warm rain toward the station. The big clock on the side of the building showed ten minutes past six.

"I'm scared, Mama."

"Why, honey?"

"Case Daddy don't like me. What if he don't like that I got black hair?"

"Pace, your daddy'd love you even if you didn't have no hair at all."

Lula saw Sailor as soon as she opened the door. He was sitting in an orange plastic chair against the opposite wall, smoking a cigarette.

"Still partial to Camels, huh?" Lula said to him.

Sailor smiled. "First pack of tailor-mades I had in a while," he said.

He stood up and looked down at Pace, who was still holding hands with Lula. Sailor put out his right hand.

"You must be my son," he said.

"Shake hands with your daddy," said Lula.

Pace released Lula's hand and put his own in Sailor's. Sailor gripped it gently but firmly, pumped once, then let go.

"Pleasure to meet you, Pace. I read a lot about you."

Sailor looked at Lula. Her eyes were full of tears and she let them loose.

"Good thing it's rainin'," she said, smiling. "Nobody'll know the difference."

"Nobody'd care but me," said Sailor.

Lula forced a laugh. "You hungry? Pace and I ain't had dinner yet."

"Lead the way."

Sailor picked up his black metal suitcase and followed them outside.

"No rag top, huh?" said Sailor as Lula drove.

Lula started to reply, then stopped. She stared straight ahead, gripping the wheel hard. Suddenly, she pulled over to the side of the road, killed the engine and got out of the car.

"What's wrong, Mama?" said Pace.

"Don't worry, son," Sailor said, turning to him and patting Pace's head. "Just stay here."

Sailor got out and went over to Lula, who was leaning back against the hood.

"I'm sorry, Sailor. I just can't help it. Give me a minute and I'll quit."

"Boy's frightened, Lula. This ain't no good."

"Really, Sail, I'll be okay. Look, it's just the rain now."

"It's a mistake, honey. You two go on. I'll walk back to the depot."

"What're you talkin' about? That's your son in there."

Sailor smiled. "He ain't never known me, Lula, so there ain't much for him to forget. Not seein' each other for ten years makes it next best to simple for us, too."

"How can you say that, Sailor?"

"What makes sense, is all."

Sailor went around to the driver's side, reached in and pulled the keys out of the ignition. He unlocked the trunk, removed his suitcase and closed the lid.

"Don't do this, Sailor, please," said Lula.

Sailor slipped the keys in her shirt pocket and leaned his head into the car.

"*Oiga, amigo,*" he said to Pace. "If ever somethin' don't feel right to you, remember what Pancho said to the Cisco Kid: 'Let's went, before we are dancing at the end of a rope, without music.'"

Sailor stood up and looked at Lula. Her long black hair was matted from the rain and her eye makeup ran in dark streaks down her face.

"You been doin' fine without me, peanut. There ain't no need to make life tougher'n it has to be."

He picked up his suitcase, kissed Lula lightly on the lips and walked away. She let him go.

PERDITA DURANGO

This book is dedicated to the memory of Larry Lee
1942–1990

Pleasure which vanishes vanishes for good. . . . Other
pleasures come, which replace nothing.
—Roland Barthes

CONTENTS
Perdita Durango

FAST FORWARD

Perdita met Manny Flynn in the San Antonio airport restaurant and bar. He was gobbling chicken fajitas and she was smoking a cigarette, an empty glass in front of her on the table, which was next to his.

"You wanna 'nother one?" Manny asked.

Perdita looked at him. Fat but neat. He wiped his thin lavender lips with a napkin. A waitress came over.

"Sweetheart, bring me another Bud and give that girl there whatever she wants."

"Wish somebody'd make me an offer like that," said the waitress. "What'll it be, honey?"

Perdita took a long drag on her Marlboro, blew out the smoke and killed it in an ashtray.

"Coke," she said.

"Diet?"

"Not hardly."

The waitress looked hard at Perdita for a moment, then wrote on Manny Flynn's check.

"One Bud, one Coke," she said, and hurried away.

Manny forked down the last bite of fajita, wiped his mouth again with the napkin, stood up and redeposited himself at Perdita's table.

"You live in San Antone?" he asked.

"Not really."

"You sure do have beautiful black hair. See my reflection in it just about."

Perdita withdrew another Marlboro from the pack on the table and lit it with a pink and black zebra-striped Bic.

"You catchin' or waitin' on one?" asked Manny.

"One what?"

"A plane. You headin' out somewhere?"

"My flight's been cancelled."

"Where you lookin' to go?"

"Nowhere now. About yourself?"

"Phoenix. Four-day computer convention. I sell software. By the way, my name is Manny Flynn. Half Jewish, half Irish. What's yours?"

The waitress brought their drinks, set them down quickly on the table without looking at Perdita, and left.

"Perdita Durango. Half Tex, half Mex."

Manny laughed, picked up his beer and drank straight from the bottle.

"Pretty name for a pretty Miss. It *is* Miss, isn't it?"

Perdita looked directly into Manny Flynn's eyes and said, "You want me to come to Phoenix with you? You pay my way, buy my meals, bring me back. I'll keep your dick hard for four days. While you're at the convention, I'll do some business, too. Plenty of guys at the hotel, right? Fifty bucks a pop for showin' tit and milkin' the cow. Quick and clean. You take half off each trick. How about it?"

Manny put the bottle back down on the table, then picked it up again and took a swig. Perdita turned away and puffed on her cigarette.

"I gotta go," Manny said. He threw several bills on the table. "That'll cover mine and yours."

He stood and picked up a briefcase and walked away. The waitress came over.

"I'm goin' off duty now," she said to Perdita. "You finished here?"

Perdita looked at her. The waitress was about forty-five, tall and skinny with bad teeth and phony red hair that was all kinked up so that it resembled a Brillo pad. She wore one ring, a black cameo with an ivory scorpion on the third finger of her right hand. Perdita wondered what her tattoos looked like.

"Just about," said Perdita.

The waitress scooped up Manny Flynn's money. Perdita nodded at it.

"Gentleman said for you to keep the change."

"Obliged," said the waitress.

Perdita sat and smoked her Marlboro until the ash was down almost to the filter.

"Dumb cocksucker," she said, and dropped the butt into the Coke.

"Mummy says he has more money than he knows what to do with."

"Why does he work, then? He still works, doesn't he?"

"Oh, he's just so greedy, that's why. Mummy says he needs to work just to have something to do, which doesn't make any sense at all. At least not to me. I mean, he has all kinds of stocks and everything, lots of property all over the country. He's just so cheap I can't stand it, and neither can Mummy."

"So why does she go out with him?"

"It's just someone, I suppose, until she can find a man she really likes. Could be he's hung like an Australian crocodile, for all I know. Mummy's always had a weakness for big cocks. She told me."

"She *told* you that? My mother's always acted like babies come from a stork."

"You mean like dropped down a chimney?"

"Yeah, I guess."

Both girls laughed.

"She'd never talk to me about sex. Once I asked her if they had Tampons when she was a girl and she said, 'When the time comes, young lady, we'll discuss all that sort of thing.' Then, when I got my period in March, remember? The week before my birthday?"

"I remember."

"She gave me a box of Kotex sanitary napkins and a can of cunt spray and said, 'More of each of these will be on the second shelf of your bathroom closet.'"

"So she never discussed anything?"

"Get real. My mother would drop dead if she knew half of what I've done."

"Mine, too, probably, even though she's such a slut herself."

"Come on, I need to get some boots to go with that cowgirl skirt Kristin gave me."

"Sounds good. Oh, do you have your credit cards? Mummy took mine away for a month and I might see something I like."

"Yeah, no prob."

Perdita watched the two girls as they walked out of the coffee shop. Neither of them was more than twelve years old. Both had long blond hair, wore tight, short, black skirts, expensive-looking blouses and large gold hoop earrings. Perdita felt for a moment like stabbing them each in the back and chest and throat dozens of times. She imagined their blood running black, dripping down their smooth golden legs. Just as suddenly the feeling passed, and she forgot about them.

That evening, when Perdita was driving along Tres Sueños, she saw two little girls, eight or nine years old, sitting on the lowered tailgate of a parked pickup truck, petting a fuzzy brown puppy. One of the little girls had long, dark hair cut into bangs in front; she reminded Perdita of herself when she was that age. This sight made Perdita sad because it made her think also of her twin sister, Juana, who was dead. Juana had been shot and killed by her husband, Tony, who was drunk, during an argument. Tony had then murdered his and Juana's two daughters before putting the gun in his own mouth and blowing off the top of his own skull. Perdita missed Juana, and her nieces, Consuelo and Concha, too. She guessed she might forever. Tony she always could have lived without.

THE NAME OF SCIENCE

When Perdita first saw Romeo Dolorosa she thought he was very ugly. He was drinking a papaya milkshake at an outdoor fruitstand on Magazine Street in New Orleans. She ordered a large orange juice and avoided looking at him, staring across the street at a Shoetown. When she turned back to pay, the fruitstand operator, a bent-backed, dark gray man of indeterminate age or race, said, "The gentleman there already done, sweet thing."

"It's your lucky day, señorita," said Romeo. "And mine, perhaps, too."

"What's that supposed to mean?" asked Perdita. "I don't need a new friend."

Romeo laughed. "Oh, but you do," he said, and laughed again. "What a charming manner you have, Señorita Spitfire. Are you the daughter of Lupe Velez? My name is Romeo Dolorosa."

Perdita looked more closely at Romeo. He was really quite handsome, she realized, with long, wavy black hair, deep brown skin and blue eyes; perhaps an inch under six feet tall, but substantial looking. He had beautifully shaped, very muscular arms that tapered gracefully down from the short sleeves of his blue and red Hawaiian shirt. It was odd, Perdita thought, that her first impression of him was so unflattering. She wondered what she had seen in Romeo to have made him appear that way.

"I don't know what you're talking about," she said. "Thank you for the orange juice. My name is Perdita Durango. Who is Lupe Velez?"

"Better, much better. Lupe Velez was an actress, a movie star from Mexico sixty years ago, who was famous for her hot temper."

"Why should I have reminded you of her? You don't know me."

"I am trying to make a beginning. Please, I apologize for my presumptuous behavior. Do you live in New Orleans, Perdita?"

"I've only arrived this afternoon. I'm looking around."

Romeo nodded and smiled broadly. He had very large white teeth.

"If you will allow me to buy you dinner," he said. "I'll be happy to show you the town."

As Perdita sipped the orange juice through a straw, she raised her 8-ball black eyes to Romeo's, smiled, and nodded slowly.

"Now we're getting somewhere," he said.

At Mosca's that evening, Romeo asked Perdita if she knew what a "resurrection man" was. She shook her head no.

"A hundred years ago and more," said Romeo, "doctors at medical colleges paid men to rob graves, mostly in nigger cemeteries, and deliver the corpses to them to be used for dissection by students. The doctors soaked the bodies in whisky to preserve them. It wasn't until almost the twentieth century that laws were changed to permit dissection of humans."

"Why you tellin' me this?" asked Perdita, licking salad dressing off her fork.

Romeo grinned. "Science is everything," he said. "The most important thing, anyway. Often it's necessary to go against what is the popular thinking to achieve discoveries. I think about things this way, scientifically. There's nothing I would not do for science."

"About those people saw the Virgin Mary at Tickfaw?" asked Perdita. "And the woman in Lubbock took the photo of St. Peter at the gates of heaven? How's science deal with that?"

"Need funds to research," Romeo said. "Like the $1,925 some fundraiser withdrew without permission this morning from the First National Bank of St. Bernard's Parish on Friscoville Street in Arabi. Science needs money, just like everything else."

"You tellin' me you're a grave robber or a bank robber? I ain't totally clear."

Romeo laughed and stuck a fork into his stuffed catfish.

"Scientists gotta eat, too," he said.

THE GOOD LIFE

"I knew a guy once named Bobby Peru," said Perdita. "You know, like the country? Thought he was a bad dude, and he was, kinda. Coulda helped us out here, I think, but he got himself killed."

"Know what soothes me?" Romeo said.

Perdita laughed. "Yeah, I sure do."

"That, too," said Romeo. "But I like to read the weather reports in the newspaper. Like for other places than where I am. 'Ten below with snow flurries in Kankakee.' 'Fifty-nine and raining in Tupelo.' Never fails. Calms me."

Perdita Durango and Romeo Dolorosa were sitting facing each other in a bathtub filled with smoky gray warm water in the Del Rio Ramada. Romeo was fondling an H. Upmann New Yorker and flicking the ash into the bathwater.

"Wish you wouldn't do that," said Perdita.

Romeo laughed. "Why not? Keeps away the evil spirits, don't it?" He laughed again, showing off his perfect Burt Lancaster teeth.

"How long you suppose these guys are gonna go for this voodoo shit, Romeo? They ain't all all the way stupid."

"Makes you say that? Could they might be. Besides, it ain't voodoo, neither. *Santería, chiquita.* That's hocus-pocus, Latin-style. But you're right, we gotta do somethin's gonna make 'em pay better attention."

"I know what'll do it," Perdita said.

"Yeah?"

Perdita nodded, her thin black eyebrows uncoiling like cobras.

"Kill somebody and eat him."

"You mean like cannibals."

"Sure," she said. "Nothin' can be more horrible than that. It'll stick in their brain."

Romeo laughed and puffed on his cigar.

"You bet it will, okay," he said. "Stick to their ribs, too."

Perdita smiled and tickled Romeo's penis under the water with the big toe of her right foot. The cobras on her forehead flattened out like reptiles on a rock in the sun.

"You know how to help a man in both mind *and* body, *mi corazón*. What I like about you. It's the good life, okay."

"Let's do it tomorrow," Perdita said.

NIGHT THOUGHTS

At three-thirty in the morning Romeo woke up and lit the half of the cigar he'd left in the ashtray on the table next to the bed. The smoke woke Perdita up.

"What's the matter, hon?" she said. "Can't sleep?"

"Thinkin'."

"Anything in particular?"

Perdita had her eyes closed; her long black hair was strewn across her face.

"Once read about how just before the Civil War ended, rebel soldiers buried the treasury of the Confederacy within one hundred paces of the railroad tracks between McLeansville and Burlington, North Carolina."

"How come nobody's dug it up?"

"Good question. It was all gold coins kept in iron cooking pots. Some farmer found one of 'em, but there's supposed to be about fifty million dollars worth still in the ground there. Somethin' to think about."

"For after we get done here, maybe."

Perdita fell back asleep. Romeo finished off most of the Upmann, imagining himself overseeing a crew of his disciples digging up pots of gold along a stretch of railroad tracks next to a tobacco field. The disciples could then be shot and buried in the holes. This was not impossible, he decided.

NEW MORNING

Perdita woke up and turned on the radio. She lay in bed listening to the news with her eyes closed.

"Finally," said the broadcaster, "from China today comes the announcement that seventeen convicted felons were sentenced to death and executed before a crowd of thirty thousand people at a stadium in the southern city of Guangzhou. The public trials and executions were carried out, according to the *Legal Daily* newspaper, 'in order to allow the masses to celebrate a stable Chinese Lunar New Year.' How's that for Southern justice, folks?"

Perdita switched it off. She looked over at Romeo, who was still asleep. His mouth was open and his mustache drooped over his upper lip, the long black hairs fluttering as he snored. Romeo might be part Chinese, thought Perdita. The way his face hairs hung so limp, not like on Mexicans. Or Spanish, she reminded herself. Romeo insisted on identifying himself as Spanish, no belly-crawling Indian blood in *his* veins. Perdita snickered. No matter what Romeo said, he didn't look like no white man. He even talked like a Chinaman sometimes, so fast you couldn't follow what he was saying.

They were heading back to the ranch today, which was good. She needed to build a new altar for the sacrifice. This would be something different, really special. Not like with the chickens and goats or dogs. Romeo was a good organizer, he knew how to get the shit across the border, how to get the money. Perdita smiled, thinking about the one time Romeo had tried to smoke marijuana himself. He'd gotten dizzy and had to lie down until his head cleared. Wouldn't touch the stuff for nothing now. That was cool, though, she figured. The dope didn't get in the way of doing business. Perdita made a mental note to buy more candles, they were almost out. Also some grain alcohol. They could use a new sledgehammer, too.

Perdita stuck the index finger of her right hand into Romeo's mouth and pushed down on his tongue. He gagged, coughed hard, and sat up.

"What!? What the fuck?" he said, and worked at clearing his throat.

"Vamonos," said Perdita. "We got lots to do today."

LETTER FROM CARIBE

Caribe 2.14.1989

Hello Romeo.

Jest these few lines to let you know that everything at your house is fine. Well Mr Dolorosa sir there is a tolk out in Caribe that you wants to sell your house. People had been asking me about the sale on the house but all I can do is to gave them your phone number so that they can call you and talk with you about it. Well I hope that you will bee back some day jest so that the people wood stop tolking so much shit. Mr Romeo this time I had seed some bad days because in December my dorie brook down cood not even get out to fish can't fine no woor here and most of the time I wood only eat one male per day. So last month the lady at Caribe Keys that bys the fish seant me up her boat so that I can make some money but the first week out fishing was good but the monny was so small. She gets half of the monny an the other half is in between me and another. Look the first 4 days we sold 1,500 Caribe dollar and so far we cant get out for the winds the winds has been from 10 to 20 knots from the eastnortheast an from east for allmost two months that my boddy can get out to fish. I had been a little sick the last pass few week so I went to an Amarican docter here an he told me that my boddy was ran down a lot so he put me on some toneck a madacen and I feale a little better these last few days. But Nelmy had been on an off with her Hedakes. Well yesterday school open for the kids but Alix had healp us a lot with them gatten them most of what they need. Kenny want even come down so that I can get a few days woor with him I jest dont know watt I will do if this wind dont stop I needs to get out fishing for atlest one more week before you gets here. Mr Rome Nelmy sent to say hello an she hopes that you is fine an she wants you to tell Perdi hello for her. And not to forget her T-V. Mr Dolorosa sir I dont know for shore but some people was saying that Rocky James was senten to jail for 20 years an if Reggie San Pedro Sula ever came back to Caribe he wood go to jail for 15 years. Well the people was at first was saying that you and Mr San Pedro Sula wood go to jail when you ever all got back from the USA but

Mr Reggie was here about a week ago and he did not have any problem at all. Mr Romeo if I was you I wood keep away from Reggie San Pedro Sula ontell everything is normal again. Virgil Fredrex is a little up set because Woody Hall took all of his stuff out of the room on the hill an carid it down to his house that is about all for know ontell another Mr Rome take good care Love from my hole fam Nelmy Danito Chonge Nansy Branny and my sister an brothers mom & dad Your good fren

Danny Mestiza

TRAVEL PLANS

"Do you think some people are born wanting to travel?" Romeo asked. "Or do you figure it's a kind of thing comes over you?"

"You mean like in the blood," said Perdita.

"Sorta, yeah."

They were bouncing along in the Cherokee on the dirt road between Zopilote and Rancho Negrita Infante. Perdita had purchased everything she required in the hardware store in Del Rio and she was excited. Romeo's babbling usually made her uneasy but today she didn't mind listening, giving him the feedback he needed to process his thoughts.

"When I was a kid in Caribe, you know," he said, "my family used to go to the harbor when my Uncle Roberto went to sea. I was seven years old the first time I remember it clearly. There was a big gray boat tied up at the dock. *'Margarita Cansino'* was the ship's name, in giant black letters. And underneath that was painted the port of origin, *'Panama.'* We were there to hug Tio Roberto and wish him a safe journey, which, of course, I did. But I was so impressed by the size of the ship and the thought of it sailing out into the ocean beyond the Gulf, beyond the Caribbean, that the idea of traveling entered my dreams. From that moment I knew I would voyage out far into the world beyond Caribe."

Perdita, who was driving, did her best to avoid the ruts and large rocks in the road. She lit a Marlboro with the dash lighter.

"But yet here you are," she said, "still not so very far from there."

"I've come back, of course. After all, this is my home. I told you about when I lived in New York, in Paris, in Los Angeles. I was in Buenos Aires and Montevideo, too. In Caracas, Miami, La Paz. One day I'll go to Egypt, to China, to Madagascar to see the fabulous monkeys. I am already twenty-seven years old, but I have plenty of time to travel. Soon there will be enough money for us to travel whenever and to wherever we want."

"It makes me happy to have you include me in your plans," said Perdita.

Romeo laughed. "And why not? You're the proper one for me. Four years younger, beautiful, smart, strong. Someday we'll have children."

"You'll inform me, of course, when the time for that is appropriate."

"Of course, *mi amor*. You'll be the first other than me to know."

"*Bueno, jefe*. And what other plans do you have for us?"

"It's enough for now to finish this business we have."

"I've been thinking about it, Romeo. I think what we have to do is take someone off the street. An Anglo."

Romeo looked at Perdita through his brown-lensed Body Glove glasses.

"An Anglo?" he said.

"That would make the most impression."

Romeo turned his head and stared out the open window at the desert. The hot breeze caused by the Jeep's passage plastered his black hair to his forehead.

"Kidnapping," he said.

"What?" said Perdita. "I couldn't hear you."

Romeo gritted his teeth and let the wind hit his face. Believe it, he told himself. Life with this woman will be without apologies.

LOCAL COLOR

Perdita stopped the Cherokee at the entrance to the Rancho Negrita Infante. She cut the engine and got out, leaving the driver's door open. A few feet from the Jeep she squatted, coiled her skirt around her and urinated on the sand. Romeo watched Perdita from the passenger seat and grinned.

"Always liked it that you don't never wear panties," he said, as Perdita climbed back in.

"Easier that way," she said. "Used to I wore 'em, but one day I just left 'em off. Now I don't think I own a pair."

Perdita started the Jeep up and proceeded toward the complex. She liked this drive, the dust and white sun. It was like being on another planet.

"You know I never asked you," Perdita said, "about how the ranch was named."

"Story is some local woman got pregnant by a black American soldier, and when the child was born it was black, too, a baby girl. So some of the villagers—they're called *'Los Zarrapastrosos,'* the ragged ones—took the baby and killed her and buried the body out this way in an unmarked grave."

"Why'd they do that?"

Romeo shrugged. "Ashamed, I guess. Surprised they didn't kill the mother also and bury them together."

Perdita wiped the sweat from above her upper lip and pulled the hair out of her eyes.

"Jesus but I hate that kind of ignorant shit," she said.

THE CAUSE

There was a main house, a large shack, really, about twenty-five feet by thirty feet, made of tarpaper and wood. The windows were rough squares cut to accommodate removable boards, but they were nailed shut. There was a smokehole above a black cauldron that at the moment contained a boiled hog brain, a turtle shell, a horseshoe, the spinal column of a goat, and dried blood. On the otherwise bare walls were cheap representations of Our Lady of Guadalupe and Jesus Christ. On the floor next to the crudely built altar was a *Book of Rites* from La Iglesia Lukumi Babalu-Aye.

"Leave the door open, honey," Romeo said to Perdita. "Get some of the stink out."

"We have to clean this place up, Romeo. Get your boys in here with some brooms. Dump the garbage. They leave their goddam empty bottles and cans everywhere."

"*Sí,* señorita. I will see to it immediately."

Romeo laughed and grabbed Perdita, pulling her to him and kissing her. She shoved him away and began emptying her bags of candles.

"Hey, *santero*, let's do this, okay?"

Romeo and Perdita cleaned up the house themselves, and then Romeo hauled the debris away in the Jeep. He dumped it in a trench his men had dug about a mile away. Gray shit swirled in the brown air. It reminded Romeo of the August day he came back to Tampa after completing the year he'd been stationed in Lebanon with the Marines. Maria-Jose, his grandmother, had asked him, "They let you visit the Garden of Eden?"

Adolfo Robles drove up in his 1950 Dodge pickup and leaned out the window.

"What we up to, Romeo?" he asked. "We got something going later?"

Romeo took a black kerchief from his back pocket and wiped the sweat and dirt from his face and neck.

"Something big, Adolfo. Meet me back at the house."

Adolfo nodded and grinned, jammed the Dodge into gear and drove slowly away. Romeo kicked some dirt into the trench. He'd been one of the lucky ones, having survived the bombing of his Marine barracks in Beirut. More than two hundred sleeping men had died and Romeo had been barely roused by the noise of the explosion. Standing and sweating next to a garbage pit in Mexico, he was convinced there was a noble reason he'd been spared. Romeo pulled out his cock and pissed into the pit. He stood there after he'd finished, fondling himself, watching the steam rise. The air smelled burned.

THE HAND

"The island of Petit Caribe, where I was raised," said Romeo, "is approximately one mile long and three miles wide. There were only two automobiles on Petit Caribe back then and of course one day they collided with each other."

Adolfo laughed. "But how could that happen?" he asked.

"How everything happens, Adolfo. It was in fact impossible for it *not* to happen. This is the working of the world."

Romeo and Adolfo were sitting on the bottom step of the porch drinking Tecates. Perdita was inside arranging the chairs and candles.

"Look, here is a letter I just received from Caribe, from my cousin, Reggie, who takes care of the old family property."

Romeo took an envelope out of his back pocket, opened it and removed a piece of paper. "Listen," he said.

"*'Dear Cousin Romeo. I hope this Letter finds you doing the verry bes for your self. I talked to your Lawer on how much it would cost to bring the people to move the two men on the land and he Said 3000 Caribe dollar he mus be out of his mind I then call the Aterny Generald office to my fren Teresa. She is the secon to the Boss. Teresa said nothing can be done so I took the mater in my owne hand and the problem is solve. The only thing is to tell you the sharks are have a feaste day. So Good News.'*

"*'The weather gets good now I hope we are now in our third week of Bad Weather Romeo. Can you send som monie for fishing wire and the wood turnin lathe an som tools an som buckets also sheet rock screws. I am try to buy a mud Hog pump too for workin the Swamp Land joining the North Line by Rockys property. My daughter Halcyan almos drown in the Lagoon las week but she is fon now. All we here wish you well an you send us som thing now Okay? Your cousin an pal—Reggie.'*

"There are constant difficulties on the island," said Romeo, "the same as anywhere. There is no more sense made there than here. You must control your own hand, Adolfo, remember! The rest is unimportant."

Adolfo nodded and studied his left hand. After a few seconds he drained the Tecate and, with his right hand, tossed the can as far as he could.

DESPERADO

"I had a friend in Tampa a few years ago," Romeo told Adolfo as they rode in the Dodge truck toward the border. "Eddie Reyes, a Cuban from Marianao. He lived for a while with my family, even after I left there. I don't know where he is now. Eddie had been a cop but quit the force and was going to law school at night when I met him. He worked during the day in a meat packing plant.

"This Eddie would take several showers each day, very long showers during which he would scrub himself all over many times and use great quantities of soap and shampoo. Then he would spend an equal amount of time drying himself. Eddie had much hair on his body and lots of curly black hair on his head, and of course he had a beard. I do not exaggerate when I tell you that this bathing and drying process took up most of his time."

Alfonso, who was driving, shook his head and laughed.

"He sounds like a crazy man," he said.

"Yes, he was probably a little crazy," said Romeo, "but let me tell you why. One night when Eddie was a cop he was sent to investigate a burglary in progress and a junkie got the drop on him. The junkie made Eddie lie down on the ground on his back and stuck the dangerous end of a forty-five automatic between his eyes. The junkie told Eddie he was going to kill him and pulled the trigger. Eddie shit and pissed in his pants and the gun jammed. The backup cops arrived and the junkie panicked, dropped the forty-five on Eddie's chest and tried to run but the other cops caught him.

"The junkie never went to jail. He gave the cops some information they needed about some other scam and he was allowed to plead guilty to a charge of firing a weapon in a public place. Even though the gun never went off! He got away with a suspended sentence. When Eddie heard about it he quit the force and got the job in the meat packing plant. Eventually he started taking law courses. I always figured all the washing he did was connected to the junkie trying to shoot him. It made Eddie a little strange, I guess, still trying to clean off the shit and piss."

"Maybe it would have been better if the gun had not jammed," said Alfonso. "It must be difficult to live in such a desperate way."

Romeo stared out the window at the passing desert. There was nothing moving other than the heat waves.

"Maybe," he said, "but still, it's better to be desperate than dead."

PIGEONS

Perdita and Romeo watched the people pass. They sat at a table behind the front window of the South Texas Barbecue, drinking Lone Star. Perdita's idea was to identify a likely prospect, follow him and in some way lure him back to the Rancho Negrita Infante.

"What are you gonna say, honey?" asked Romeo. "Come with me to the Casbah?" He laughed. "We ain't exactly Charles Boyer and Hedy Lamarr, you know. Or, I tell you everything you ever want to know about Lukumi Babalu-Aye? Introduce yourself as a Python Priestess of *Palo Mayombé* and you'd appreciate his allowin' Adolfo to lop off his head with a machete so's we can drain the blood from his body, then hack it apart, cook it up and serve him at the Zombie Jamboree?"

Perdita puffed desultorily at a Marlboro.

"Better you point, I'll follow, club him down, dump him in the Jeep and take off. No tricks."

"That's a nice one," said Perdita, pointing to a young guy crossing the street toward them. "Blond, tan, good shoulders."

"You gonna fuck him or eat him?"

Perdita raised a cobra eyebrow. "Both, maybe."

"He's not alone," said Romeo. "There's a girl with him."

"Could be we'll both get lucky, *macho*. Let's go."

Romeo and Perdita got into the Cherokee and cruised slowly along the Boulevard Botánica, keeping a close eye on the young couple, who were taking in the tacky bordertown sights.

"College kids," Romeo said. "Down from Austin, or maybe just Southmost."

The couple went into a bar and Romeo parked the Cherokee in front of it. When the couple didn't come out after ten minutes, Perdita said, "Let's go inside."

The place was called El Loco's Round-Up, and the young couple, along with several other people, were gathered around a tall, white-haired gringo who was leaning against the bar and talking. Romeo and Perdita went over to listen.

"Everybody who becomes involved with the movie business learns about it the hard way," said the man. He looked familiar to Romeo, but he couldn't quite place him. "When I went out to Hollywood I was fresh from my daddy's insurance company," the man continued, punctuating his speech with sips of J.W. Dant. "I didn't hardly know which hole a woman peed out of. Pardon me, ladies," he said, smiling, "but that's the truth."

"Who is this guy?" Perdita whispered.

"Ssshh," said Romeo. "I know I seen him somewhere."

"I was a good-lookin' kid in those days, though, the kind they were after, like Coop, McCrea, Johnny Mack, Randy Scott. Didn't matter I was out of a Boston insurance office. I looked the part, so they stuck me on a horse and I fit. I did all right, saved my money and didn't forget everything they taught me at Harvard, just the things I never could remember. Trained me to talk like I was bred to take my meals from a Montana Hereford. Some of the others, though, didn't do so well. Lash was makin' pornos last I heard. At his age it's more a credit than a discredit. And Sunset's a doorman at the Thunderbird in Vegas. Saw him there myself. Duke, of course, you all know what he did. Licked everyone and everything except the Big C. And Randy didn't die broke. Only real mistakes I made was to marry a couple of American women. Shoulda stuck to Mexican and Japanese, or somethin'."

When the man paused to pour himself a fresh shot and knock it down, Romeo said to Perdita, "Happy Pard, Protector of the Pecos! That's who he is. Man's a legend."

"I heard you, pardner," Hap said, nodding his head at Romeo. "You're dead right. Made over one hundred westerns before I got my own TV series. They just churned 'em out over at Republic and Monogram. Started the series when I was forty-five, and it ran nine years. Still on in parts of Asia and South America. My real name is Winston Frost, but everybody's called me Hap for so long I finally had it changed legal. The wiseguys even made me sign my IOUs that way!" He laughed. "That was a mean road for me, folks, that gamblin'. For years I'd bet on anything. Why, I'd wager on which cube of sugar a fly'd land on. I tell you, that Russian sonofabitch, Fyodor Dostoyevsky, had it pegged natural. Just read that story of his, 'The Gambler,' and you'll see what I'm gettin' at. Man was the greatest writer ever lived. Had himself the same problem as me."

"What's he talkin' about?" Perdita whispered.

"Don't matter," said Romeo. "There go your pigeons."

The boy and girl, neither of whom were more than nineteen or twenty, walked out of El Loco's followed closely by Perdita and Romeo. Perdita caught up to the boy on the street and put her arm through his. Romeo came up next to the girl and showed both of them the nose of his .38.

"Amigos," he said, "we're goin' for a little ride."

FACES

"So what is this? Where are you takin' us?"

"Relax, amigo," Romeo said. "Just a ride in the country. And hey, *mil gracias*, by the way, for not makin' a fuss back at the border."

"Said you'd shoot us if we did," said the girl.

"Now, sweetheart, I might've, that's right. You can't never be certain a man means what he says, but I've always made sure there's plenty of meanin' in my life. Ain't that right, honey?"

Perdita rode shotgun. She didn't answer, remaining stonefaced, thinking about how best to get the job done. Better to kill them before they got to the ranch. But the boy was cute. She could use him, maybe, then kill him. Romeo'd stick his thing in a keyhole if he thought it'd feel good. He could jump the little white whore if he wanted.

"We'll just be *compañeros* now for a while, if it's okay," said Romeo. "Now, my name is Romeo and the mystery woman here is Perdita. What can we call you?"

"Don't say anything," said the girl.

Perdita stuck her head out the window and let the wind blow through her hair. This is the right girl, she thought. They'd snatched them the perfect platinum bitch. Be easy to smack her, that's for sure.

Romeo laughed. "Better to be friendly, little lady. Easier all the way around."

"Why should we make anything go easy for you?" the girl said.

"You figurin' on ransomin' us?" the boy asked. "If you are, my folks don't have much money. Dad manages a Luby's in El Paso. My mom's a typist for a real estate office. Estelle's folks ain't any better off."

"Estelle?" said Romeo. "Is that your name, princess? Estelle. Almost like Estrellita, little star. I like that better, much better. Estrellita! That's what we'll call you. You like that, Perdita?" He laughed. "And now you, boy. *Cómo se llama?*"

"It's Duane."

"Okay, okay," said Romeo. "I'll take it. Regular name for a regular guy. You look like a regular guy, Duane. You *are* regular, aren't you?"

"I guess."

Romeo smiled his big smile. "Now, yeah! We all know each other's names, and that's a step. Duane and Estrellita. Romeo and Perdita. Mix 'em any way you choose. Duane and Perdita. Estrellita and Romeo. How about Estrellita and Perdita? There's a pair. Or Romeo and Duane. Ha! There they go, hand in hand, the good little boys. We could do this one up right, use some brainpower."

"Where are you taking us?" asked Estelle.

"Show you where the people live, Little Star. Be a place to tell about, you get the chance the next family picnic, all the little Estrellitas and Duanes and things are there, drinkin' bug juice, eatin' pie, honeydews. Fourth of July, could be."

"Only it won't," said Perdita, not turning around.

Romeo laughed. "Oh, Duane and Estrellita, you've heard of 'voices'? You know, like, from the air, not from a person."

"Like disembodied?" Duane asked.

"I think so," said Romeo. "Not a body, just a voice. Like from God."

"Yeah?"

"You're gonna hear it." Romeo turned quickly, looking around at the boy and girl tied up in the back seat.

"Won't be no Fourth of July, baby," said Perdita. "No Thanksgivin', neither."

"How about *Cinco de Mayo*?" Romeo asked.

Perdita smiled at him, showing an even dozen of her tiny white teeth. "What you think of Christmas in hell, Chico? Think your honeycunt here can handle that?"

Romeo banged the steering wheel with both hands, howled and rocked back and forth as he drove.

"Holiday in hell!" he shouted. "Happy fuckin'-A holiday! Whew! You make it right, sugar. Make it fuckin'-A, hard-as-a-rock, crazy-baby okay!"

Perdita laughed. "Well, I guess I love you, too," she said.

A FEW GOOD MEN

Tyrone "Rip" Ford had been born and raised in Susie, Texas, and in the forty-three years of his existence had never, excepting his time in the service, lived beyond plain sight of the Rio Grande. Rip became a deputy sheriff of Larry Lee County when he was twenty-one, three years out of high school and three weeks out of the U.S. Army. He became sheriff of Larry Lee County ten years later and had held the job ever since.

Rip Ford's father, Royal Ford, had nicknamed his son after his own paternal grandfather, Colonel Rip Ford, an early member of the Texas Rangers. After rising to the rank of captain in the Rangers, Rip Ford, elevating himself to colonel, had subsequently recruited a fugitive company of men from South Texas to fight under his command during the War Between the States. Composed mostly of wanted men and men considered too old or too young to be conscripted by the Confederate Army, Ford's irregulars united primarily for the purpose of resisting an expected invasion of South Texas by a Union brigade of Negro soldiers.

Colonel Ford's raggedy group maintained a peripatetic camp along the Mexican side of the border, dodging hostile Kickapoos and Apaches and staging supply raids on isolated settlements on both sides of the river. Declared an outlaw by General Robert E. Lee, his followers branded as criminals and lowlifes, the original Rip Ford attempted to construct a deal just prior to the surrender at Appomattox whereby his company would have switched their allegiance to the North and assisted the Union in a campaign against Mexico. This realignment did not come to pass, but Colonel Ford did succeed in acting as agent between Yankee merchant ship owners and Southern cotton growers, convincing the shipping magnates to place their boats under Mexican registry and transport cotton to the fleet of European ships, mainly English, sitting in the Gulf of Mexico and the Caribbean Sea.

Royal Ford had always admired his grandfather's resourcefulness, and hoped his son—whose Christian name, Tyrone, was given him by the boy's mother, Louise, an ardent admirer of the movie star Tyrone Power—would exhibit a similar tenacity and sense of purpose. Royal was

Perdita Durango

killed during a robbery at the Gulf gas station he'd owned and operated in Susie since his discharge from the army following World War II. A drifter named Ulysses Neck had shot Royal Ford in the back of the head while Royal lay face down on the floor of the office of his Gulf station. Ulysses Neck had exactly thirty-two dollars and eight cents in his possession when he was apprehended by two Texas Rangers an hour later less than ten miles away in the town of Fort Dudgeon. Neck took his own life that night by hanging himself by a belt from the high bars of his cell in the Larry Lee County jail, the same jail that Royal's son, Rip Ford, now commanded.

Rip had never married. His life was his work; no citizen of Larry Lee County could question Sheriff Ford's dedication. From Fort Dudgeon to Susie to Madre Island, Rip Ford was well-known and, at the very least, grudgingly respected by Anglos and Hispanics alike. Throughout its century-long history, there never had been a permanent black resident of Larry Lee County. Those Negro Yankee troops so feared by Louise Ford's son Tyrone's great-grandfather never did materialize.

The moment Rip Ford learned of the disappearance of the two college students, Duane Orel King and Estelle Kenedy Satisfy, he felt a sharp pain in his lower back.

"What's wrong, Rip?" asked First Deputy Federal Ray Phillips, noticing the sheriff's grimace.

"Like as somethin' just poked me with a pitchfork above the right buttock, Fed," said Rip. "Never felt nothin' like it before."

"Better hope ain't nobody down in the Mud Huts stickin' no pins in a doll got your name on it," said Federal.

Both men laughed.

"Nothin's happenin'. *Yet!*"

Fed Phillips looked over at the man who said this and I.D.'ed him. It was Ramon Montana, one of the county's more prominent drunks.

"You can hear me, Señor Fed! You know I mean what I'm sayin' when I say somethin'. I *said*, nothin's happenin'. *Yet!*"

"Heard you, Ramon. Havin' a good weekend already, I can tell."

Ramon Montana staggered to the curb where he fell on his knees and regurgitated into the gutter. He shook himself like a wet dog, got up, cleared his throat, threw back his shoulders, put one foot in the air as if he were about to climb a flight of stairs, listed to starboard and toppled to the sidewalk.

"C'mon, there, Ramon," said Fed, helping him back to his feet. "Let's see we can get you home before you get so scarred up your sister can't recognize you."

"Ain't *goin'* home!" Ramon shouted. "Can't make me. My sister's dead, anyhow."

"Better'n takin' you to jail."

Ramon grumbled but allowed Fed Phillips to escort him the half-block to his rooming house, where Fed led Ramon up the stairs and in the door.

"On your own, now, *amigo*. Sleep tight."

"Tell you, Señor Fed, some strange shit goin' on. You see I ain't talkin'. They gonna kill them kids, them *gringos*, the *gringa*. You hear about it, 'member I tell you firs'. Man got the evil eye. Evil eye."

Fed closed the door and went back to the street. Who's gonna kill what kids? he thought. Fed headed toward El Loco's to see what he could find out.

Over at the jail, Rip Ford sat in his office looking at the picture of Ava Gardner he kept in a plastic frame on his desk. It was a full-face photo taken in 1954 by a Frenchman, Philippe Halsman. Rip knew this because the photographer's name and the date were printed on the back of the picture. It was a postcard, really, but set into the frame like it was made it look proper, as if it were his wife or fiancée. In the picture, Ava Gardner's tousled black hair obscured her right eye, and her full, closed lips were pulled slightly to the right, resulting in something less than a smile. They looked as if they'd been smeared shut with red paint, though the photo was in black and white. It wasn't so much a fuck-me face as a I've-been-there-and-back look, the kind of expression you see only on the most expensive whores. This was Ava at her best, right after *Mogambo*, which Rip had seen as a boy from the balcony of the Joy Rio in El Paso. It was ten o'clock on Saturday night and he stared at Ava Gardner's immutable face, the face of a lifetime a lifetime ago. Rip let the telephone ring for thirty seconds before he picked it up.

BAD ROAD

As Romeo drove, Estelle Satisfy thought about her mother, Glory Ann Blue Satisfy, and wondered whether she'd ever see her again. Glory Ann had been born and raised in Divine Water, Oklahoma, a place she dearly loved and wished she'd never left. The house on Worth Avenue in Dallas, where Estelle had grown up, never pleased Glory Ann, nor did Dallas. Glory Ann never stopped complaining about the city. "When I wake up in the mornin'," she'd say to Estelle, "I like to know who I'm goin' to see that day. There's too many surprises here in the Big D."

Glory Ann weighed three hundred pounds now. Her husband, Estelle's daddy, Ernest Tubb Satisfy, who'd been named after the famous singer, stood five-feet four and weighed one-hundred-ninety-five. He drove a 7-Up delivery truck and smoked Larks but took only three puffs of each one before putting it out. Ernest Tubb claimed the Larks lost their taste after the first two drags. He took the third one, he said, just to keep proving it to himself.

Estelle remembered her dog, Gopher, who died after he ate an entire extra large anchovy and onion pizza when she was in the seventh grade. Ernest Tubb buried Gopher under the plum tree in the backyard and Estelle still placed flowers on the grave every year on the anniversary of Gopher's death, April fifth. Estelle thought about these and other things that had happened in her life as the Cherokee bounced down a bad road to only the devil knew where.

Romeo, if that really is his name, looks like the devil, thought Estelle. And that Perdita woman looks weird and dangerous, too. I just hope they're not going to kill us, not before I've even got my cherry popped. That'd be a slap and a half, for sure, after all I've done to preserve my chastity. I should have left it to Stubby Marble. Grace Jane says the Marble boys, Eugene and Stubby, do it better than anyone, and I guess to hell she knows. Stubby kept after me the better part of a month before he gave up. Duane now, he acts like he don't care. I don't know, maybe he don't. I wish I knew what's goin' on here, really. I'm just a college girl with a lot of potential in the field of commercial art who ain't never even got laid yet. I know life ain't fair or even supposed to be, but this is somethin' different.

Duane pretended to be asleep. He kept his head down and tried hard not to think, but he couldn't help it, the thoughts just kept on coming. This wasn't the end of a good time, it was the beginning of a bad one. If Estelle hadn't insisted on goin' out for a beer, Duane thought, we'd be in our hotel room now and maybe she'd be lettin' me. Be a shame to die havin' been with only one girl, and her just Grace Jane Bobble, who the Marbles nicknamed "The Wide Missouri" not for no good reason. This gal Perdita is a picture, though. Reminds me of that poisonous snake from South America in the reptile and amphibian book we used in biology, one with the triangle-pointed, yellow-red face and orange ice eyes. She's the type'll bite and once the teeth are sunk you'd have to chop off the head with a hatchet to pry loose.

Duane opened his eyes and looked at Estelle. She had her eyes shut and was biting her lower lip and crying. Duane felt like crying, too, but he didn't. He wouldn't stop himself if he started, but no tears came. Maybe I can figure a way out of this, Duane thought. Estelle would be grateful, I bet, and let me do it. I wonder who done it to her other than the Marbles. They said she was some sweet meat. This life's sure got question marks scattered around like dogshit in a empty lot, the way Daddy says. I guess I ain't been steppin' careful enough.

HEROES

"Tell you who my heroes are, Duane. That way you get a better idea of who I am."

Romeo and Duane were sitting in chairs on the porch of the main house at Rancho Negrita Infante. Estrellita, as Rome insisted Estelle be called, was asleep in a locked bedroom. It was almost midnight.

"I on purpose am leavin' your legs free, Duane. Sorry about your hands, though. You tell me if the wire's too tight."

"No, it ain't."

"*Bueno, bueno.* We got to keep the blood circulatin'. So here's my list: James Ruppert, George Banks, Howard Unruh, Pat Sherrill, Charles Whitman, R. Gene Simmons, Sr., James Oliver Huberty, and Joseph Wesbecker. Know every name by heart. Recognize any?"

"Don't think so."

"Not even Whitman?"

Duane shook his head no.

Romeo laughed. "Guess you don't do so good in history class."

"Got a B."

"Maybe they didn't cover this part yet. Here's what these men done. Ruppert killed eleven people, eight of 'em kids, at a Easter Sunday dinner in Ohio. Banks took out twelve, includin' five kids, in Pennsylvania. Unruh shot thirteen people in twelve minutes in Camden, New Jersey. He was somethin' else, too. Said, 'I'd've killed a thousand if I'd had enough bullets.'

"Sherrill murdered fourteen at a post office in Oklahoma. Simmons, Senior, got fourteen, too, all family members, in Arkansas. Buried a dozen under his house. Huberty slaughtered twenty-one at a McDonald's in San Diego, I believe. Wesbecker shot seven and wounded a bunch in a printing plant in Kentucky. And Whitman, of course, cut down sixteen from the tower on the campus of the University of Texas in Austin. Surprised you ain't heard of him."

"When did he do it?"

"About 1966, around in there."

"Before my time."

"Hell, boy, so was Hitler, and you can't tell me you ain't heard of him!"

"I heard of him."

"How about Attila the Hun? You heard of him?"

"I guess so. He was some kind of Turk or somethin'."

"Well, I don't include those guys had armies or other people doin' their killin' for 'em. I just rate the ones take it into their own hands. Also, I don't count the serial murderers, the ones done it over a long, drawn out period of time. It's only the ones just all of a sudden know they can't take no shit no longer and just explode on the world! There's more than those I mentioned but those are right off the top of my head. This kind of thing is a particular study of mine."

Perdita came out on the porch and rubbed her left thigh against Duane's right arm. She put her left hand into his thick blond hair and rubbed it around.

"You been tellin' the boy a bedtime story, Romeo?" she said.

"Just fillin' in a few holes in Duane's education."

Perdita smiled. "I got one or two need fillin', too. You two intellectuals feel like helpin' a lady out?"

THE BAT

Romeo unlocked the door to the bedroom and entered. He stood still for a full minute, listening to Estrellita's breathing. There was a shrill, brief whistle each time she exhaled. Romeo closed the door, bolted it, and put the key in his right front pants pocket. He walked to the bed and sat down on the edge. Estrellita had long, honey-brown hair, and Romeo stroked it slowly and softly with his left hand. She stirred slightly and he stopped, allowing her to roll over on her back, her head turned to the right. Her eyelids fluttered and she pursed her full lips, then relaxed again, whistling softly.

"Hey, Little Star," Romeo whispered. "Come, Estrellita, *niña*. Romeo *es aqui*."

She didn't move, and her breathing seemed to cease altogether. Romeo smiled. He knew she had to be awake.

"Little Star, don't pretend," Romeo said, in a normal voice. "You can open your eyes. All you'll see is me."

A rivulet of moonlight squeezed into the room through a crack in the second to the highest board covering the window. Estrellita did not move other than to barely open her left eye. She saw Romeo's face in purple shadow, then closed it again.

"You think I come to harm you, huh?" he said. "Why would you think so? Your friend, Duane, he's not bein' harmed. He's getting happy, probably, by now."

"Where is he?" asked Estrellita. "Is he dead?"

Romeo laughed. "No, of course not, señorita. He's assisting a damsel in distress. Another fair lady, such as yourself."

Estrellita turned her face to Romeo and opened both of her eyes. He looked like a giant bat.

"You mean Perdita's got him?" she said.

"Yeah, I suppose that's a good way of puttin' it."

"She reminds me of a kind of snake."

Romeo smiled. "A pretty snake, though."

"She looks cold."

Romeo moved closer over Estrellita's body and touched her left cheek with his right hand.

"Estrellita, *mi flora blanca de la noche. Tu es la luz de mi vida.*"

She moved her head and shoulders slightly to the right, away from Romeo's touch.

"Don't be afraid, Little Star. You're safe with me."

Estrellita started to laugh, then suddenly stopped and began to cry. Romeo watched the tears stream out of Estrellita's eyes and roll down the sides of her face into the pillow. Slowly he bent his head and with his tongue licked the tears from her cheeks. Estrellita couldn't move. It was as if Romeo's gesture paralyzed her and his saliva made her face numb. She'd never felt this way before.

"Close your eyes again, Estrellita, *bonita*," Romeo said, and kissed her left ear, her honey-colored hair, her left eyebrow, the tip of her nose. "Romeo is going to take care of you."

PLEASURES

"Well, which one is it gonna be?" asked Romeo. "You think maybe the boy?"

Perdita kicked at the dirt with one of her rattlesnake-skin boots. A soft wind was blowing from the south and it flicked at the ends of her loose black hair.

"*No sé*, baby. This is a tough one."

"You sweet on him, huh?"

"Be more fun to keep him around for a while, anyway. How about your little vaca, Estrellita?"

Romeo took off his straw Stetson and wiped his thick red-black hair with his left hand. He was sitting on the top rail of the corral fence next to the ceremonial hut. The sun was very strong, as usual, but there was a threat of rain in the air. Perdita leaned against the fence, looking east at the scabrous brown hills.

"She was the real thing, chica, *una virgen*. Bled hot and plenty, like *crème de caramel.*"

Perdita laughed. "Too bad we didn't know it before. To sacrifice a virgin would have made us some serious *mayombérias.*"

"Maybe better to use a local, is what I'm thinkin' now," said Romeo. "Get a kid from Zopilote. Duane and Estrellita might come in handy down the line."

"Tell Adolfo to be sure to have enough garlic this time."

Romeo laughed. "You should have seen his face when I told him how when Satan walked out of the Garden of Eden, garlic sprouted from wherever his left foot hit the ground. Adolfo crossed himself and said, '*Madre de dios, es verdad?*'"

Perdita felt an itch between her legs, reached down with her right hand, balled it into a fist, and rubbed her clit hard.

"You know, Rome," she said, "the only two real pleasures left to man on this earth are fucking and killing. When those are gone, *guapito*, so are we."

BEAUTIES

Rip Ford was in bed with a prostitute named Lupita Luján when Federal Phillips called.

"Sheriff, I'm down here at El Loco's Round-Up. A couple of the boys recognized Romeo Dolorosa, that snake-priest dope dealer from Zopilote, and his girlfriend, The Priestess. Apparently they had a beer or two and suddenly disappeared. Nobody noticed they were gone until they were."

"That it?"

"So far. Gonna check it out further, see if I can get a fix on if the bastard's runnin' anything through here. Be kinda surprised if he is, seein's how he didn't attempt no disguise or nothin'. And, oh yeah, that old drunk Ramon Montana's talkin' some shit about people killin' a couple Anglos. Might be somethin' to do with Dolorosa since Ramon was carryin' on about a dude with a evil eye. That's *santería* talk."

"Call me back you hear more."

"You got it."

Rip hung up and returned his attentions to Lupita.

"Oh, ho-ney," she said, "where you get this scar from on your shoulder?"

"Oil spilt from Psyche's lamp."

Lupita frowned. "How a lamp can do this to you?"

"Just teasin', sweetheart. Old bullet wound from Nam. Guess you never heard about how Psyche woke up Cupid the middle of one night when a drop of oil burned his shoulder, and how his mama, Venus, made the poor girl's life a misery."

Lupita shrugged, rolled over and pulled the sheet up over her short plump body.

"I don't hear about nothin' stuck in this pisshole. Who was this bitch?"

"Psyche?"

"Yeah."

"The most beautiful female mortal on earth. Stole away her mother-in-law's admirers."

Lupita snorted. "No wonder she hated the girl. You know her pretty well, huh?"

"We never exactly met."

"Then how come you so interested? You lookin' to nail her ass, hey?"

Rip got up and pulled on his pants.

"Time to separate reality from myth, Lupita. *Vamonos.*"

Lupita threw back the sheet and stretched. High on her right thigh was a tattoo of a black scorpion with a red stinger poised to strike, sitting on a purple rose. Written on a blue banner beneath it were the words MALA CHICA.

"She have any kids, this *perfecta*?" asked Lupita.

"Matter of fact, yeah," Rip said. "A daughter, named Pleasure."

Lupita laughed. "She ever hit the street, she don't need to change it, *es seguro!*"

IL AFFARE

Romeo listened to the train whistles in the distance. They sounded like wheezes from an organ with a mouse running across the keys. He sat in the driver's seat of the Cherokee, smoking, the windows rolled down, waiting for his cousin, Reggie San Pedro Sula, and Marcello "Crazy Eyes" Santos. It was almost two o'clock in the morning. The crescent moon lit the desert landscape partially, giving it the feel of a bombsite, twenty years after, the only residents rodents, insects and reptiles.

The deal sounded strange, thought Romeo, but if Santos was involved it would, of necessity, be very profitable. Reggie had worked for Santos before, several times, usually as a shooter. He'd do the job, pick up his money and go back to the islands. The money lasted quite a while in Caribe, but sooner or later he'd need another jolt, and as long as Santos survived there would be work for Reginald San Pedro Sula. Romeo was agreeable to the meet, although this was a slightly unusual procedure in a couple of ways. First, Reggie rarely was involved at the top of a deal; and two, Santos seldom ventured out of his hometown of New Orleans. But Romeo was prepared to listen. He knew when and how to be patient.

Romeo heard the car coming. He tossed away his cigarette and waited, listening for half a minute as the engine noise grew louder. The long, black car pulled off the highway across from Romeo and came to a dusty stop. The motor idled and Reggie got out of the back seat, closed the door behind him, and walked over to Romeo.

"*Hola, primo,*" Reggie said. "*Que tal?*"

"You tell me," said Romeo, as they shook hands.

Reggie was very tall, at least four or five inches over six feet, and heavyset. He was about fifty years old, his skin was the color of milk chocolate, and he wore a lavender leisure suit. His bald head reflected the moonlight. It was odd, Romeo thought, for Reggie not to be wearing a porkpie rain hat. In fact, Romeo could not recall a time he'd seen Reggie without a hat, other than when he went to sleep, since he'd lost most of his hair.

"I think I let the man, Señor Santos, tell you himself," said Reggie. "It's a good deal, a fair arrangement, you'll see."

Reggie smiled broadly, revealing his numerous gold teeth.

"There must be some danger in it, though," said Romeo, "for him to get you off the island."

Reggie gave a brief laugh. "There is usually some danger involved, is there not?" he said. "Though the man needs me for another matter, for where we are heading from here."

"I see. And how is everyone back home? Danny Mestiza wrote to me that Rocky James got a double sawbuck in the joint."

"Oh, yes, but he's out now again. I think for good. There was some irregularity but Señor Santos was able to clear it up for him. Halcyan an' Rigoberto is fine an' healthy. The money you sent helped out very good. I talk very strong about you to Señor Santos so he would consider you for this job."

"What is the job?"

"You come to the car an' he tell it himself. Remember you don't call him 'Crazy Eyes.' He don't like it when he see it in the newspaper, how they do just to annoy him."

Romeo climbed down, walked across the road and got into the back seat of the Mercedes-Benz limousine. Reggie closed the door and stood outside. A soft light was on inside the car. Marcello Santos had a drink in his right hand, three fingers of his favorite single malt Scotch whisky, Glenmorangie. He was wearing a dark gray suit with a blue shirt and a red tie; a pair of black Cole-Haan loafers, with tassels, and red, blue and yellow argyle socks; two-dollar drugstore sunglasses with bright yellow frames; and a large gold or diamond ring on each finger of both hands, excluding his thumbs, one of which was missing. He had a brownish-black, curly toupee glued to his head; some mucilage had trickled onto his forehead and dried there. Santos was sixty-eight years old and had ruled organized crime in the southern and southwestern United States for a quarter-century without ever having been convicted of either a felony or a misdemeanor.

"*Buona notte*, Mr. Dolorosa. Romeo," said Santos, extending his left hand, the one minus a thumb, as would the Pope or a princess. "Good to see you again."

Romeo squeezed the fingers.

"It is always my pleasure," he said.

"This is somewhat of an unusual place to meet, I know, Romeo, but as we are on our way to another meeting, and I hate to fly, I thought it would be the most expedient. I'm glad you could come."

"It's no problem, Marcello, in any case."

"*Bene.* Your cousin, Reginald, speaks well of you, you know. He tells me you take care of your family and friends back on the island. It's commendable of you."

"I do what I can."

Santos nodded and sipped his Scotch whisky.

"Would you like a drink, Romeo?"

"No, thank you. I am driving, and it's very late."

"Yes, all right. Here is my proposal. It is very simple. There will be a truck here at this spot forty-eight hours from now, a refrigerated truck, accompanied by a car. The truck will be loaded with human placentas to be used in the cosmetics industry. They are blended in skin creams that some people think can keep them looking young. Maybe it does, maybe not. I don't know. This load must be delivered as soon as possible to a private laboratory in Los Angeles. I would like you to drive the truck there for me. That way I know the shipment will be in good hands. The driver of the truck will turn it over to you, should you decide to do this, and leave in the accompanying automobile. All you have to do is deliver it to the address in Los Angeles that this man will give you. I have ten thousand dollars for you now, in old bills, fifties and hundreds. When you arrive safely in L.A., your cousin, Reggie, will be there to give you another ten thousand dollars, also in old bills, and in similar denominations."

"Why don't you just have Reggie drive the truck?"

"I need him with me for a situation between now and when the delivery must be made. He'll fly to California as soon as this other business is finished. Can you do this?"

Romeo nodded. "Certainly, Marcello. I am glad to help you however I can."

Santos took off the cheap yellow sunglasses and looked at Romeo. His eyes were grayish-green with large red pupils that jumped and shimmied like flames. Crazy eyes. Despite himself, Romeo shivered.

"*Bene! Molto bene!*" said Santos, patting Romeo on the knee with the four fingers on his left hand. He put the sunglasses back on and drank the remainder of his whisky.

Santos flipped open a panel in the floor and took out a package and held it out to Romeo.

"*Buona fortuna, amico mio,*" said Santos. "Remember always that God and I, we both are with you."

Romeo accepted the package.

"I won't forget," he said.

THE HOUSE OF DREAMS

When Adolfo unlocked the shed door, the boy, even though he was blindfolded, looked up, his head cocked toward the noise. His mouth was gagged with a black rag, his hands tied behind his back and his feet bound together with heavy clothesline. He made no sound.

"Tiene años?" asked Romeo.

"Diez," said Adolfo. "Perdita made the choice."

"What do you know of his family?"

Adolfo shrugged. "A poor one, like most of those in Zopilote. He is one of four brothers, I think. Maybe two or three sisters. Perdita said it must be a boy. Maybe they don't even miss him."

"Is Perdita here?"

Adolfo nodded. "Preparing for the ceremony."

"Have you notified the others?"

"Everyone will assemble at ten o'clock. Carlos and Teresa are coming from Mexico City."

"What about the DeLeon family? And the Acostas?"

"No word from Jorgé Acosta, but all of them are notified."

Romeo turned to go, then looked back at the boy.

"Do you know his name?" he asked.

"He is nothing special. His name is Juan."

"Oiga, Juanito," said Romeo. "At ten o'clock tonight you will become immortal. Do you know what that means?"

The boy did not move. Romeo noticed the dark stain that ran all the way down the boy's left pantsleg. In the dirt next to his bare left foot was a wet spot the size of a dinner plate.

"It is no matter," Romeo said.

"This is something an ordinary man can never know. You will enter the House of Dreams, Juanito, where you will live forever. Your mother and father and sisters and brothers, your grandparents, aunts, uncles, cousins, all you will greet in their dreams. And only you, among them, will be safe."

Romeo went out and Adolfo followed, closed the door and locked it.

QUIET TIME AT THE RANCHO NEGRITA INFANTE

"So, it's agreed, then. After this we drive to L.A. for Santos."

"I always wanted to see California," said Perdita.

"Duane and I can take turns drivin' the truck, and you and Estrellita can handle the Cherokee."

"How soon does Santos want it there?"

"Fast as possible. He's not paying me twenty thousand dollars to stop and take a donkey ride through the Grand Canyon. Get what things you want to take together now and put 'em in the Jeep. I want to be ready to go."

Perdita was painting her toenails shocking pink. Her cunt itched but she knew Romeo wouldn't fuck her, never before a big show. That's how she thought of it, as a performance, like in the circus. She'd only seen a circus once, when she was six years old in Corpus. It was a small troupe, about a half-dozen wagons; one tent, one ring. They'd had an unusual attraction: an albino tiger. Perdita and her older sister, Juana, had stood in front of the cage and watched the beautiful white beast pace back and forth without stopping. Every thirty seconds or so, the tiger would utter a low growl, a lugubrious, slow rumble that seemed to unravel as it hit the air. This noise, Perdita felt, came from extremely deep within the animal, that he was just waiting for the proper moment to release his real feelings, his frustration and wounded pride. At that time his roar would be so deafening, so powerful that the people within aural reach would be paralyzed by fear, and the giant white cat would pounce on them and eat them up.

For weeks after the circus left town, Perdita had dreamed about the tiger. He would stand over her, straddling her lithe girl's body, then pin her to the ground with his paws, his saliva dripping down on her face, before slowly, carefully taking her head into his huge mouth and crushing it with one big bite. This dream did not frighten Perdita. It gave her a warm feeling. The tiger's mouth, she imagined, would be hot and wet, the enormous teeth, gleaming like polished swords, piercing her skin and bones cleanly, painlessly. And then the tiger would chew her, separating Perdita into smaller and smaller parts, until finally, when the beast had swallowed everything, she would wake up.

Perdita had told this dream to only one person in her life, an old man named Pea Ridge Day, who pumped gas in the Green Ace filling station in Corpus. Perdita and Juana would go there to buy grape NeHi sodas from the machine, and Pea Ridge, who was usually just sitting in his red flamingo chair, would talk to them. He told the girls that people called him Pea Ridge because he'd been born in Pea Ridge, Arkansas, but that his Christian names were Clyde and Henry. He said that when he'd been a younger man he'd pitched in the National League for St. Louis, Cincinnati, and Brooklyn, whenever they were. Pea Ridge claimed he'd left a note to his wife and kids thirty years before, saying that he was going off into the Ozarks to commit suicide, but instead he hitchhiked down to Texas, where, as Perdita and Juana could plainly see, he was still very much alive. After Perdita told Pea Ridge Day her dream, he stopped talking to her as much, and one morning, when she and Juana went to the Green Ace station for a grape Nehi, he was gone. Perdita decided that Pea Ridge had probably gone back to Arkansas to see his family before he really died. She never absolutely believed that his disappearance was connected in any way to her having told him her dream, but Perdita decided then and there not to tell anyone else about it just the same.

"That sound all right to you, honey?" Romeo asked.

Perdita blew on her toes.

"You know me, baby. I travel light."

THE OTHER SIDE OF THE RIVER

"We live on one side of the river, the side of the Great Light. On the other side of the river, the side of the Great Night, is where we must go. We must cross over the river into the Great Night so that we may gain power to live. We must cross over and cross back. We must replenish our power over others, over our enemies, over the ones who would keep us in pain, in sorrow, in misery. This is the Truth, the one Known Truth, and it will keep us alive, keep us strong, enable us to devour our enemy before he devours us."

Romeo stood alone in the middle of the room, his eyes closed, his head tilted back. In front of him was an altar surrounded by flickering candles, the only light in the room. On the floor around the circle of light were strewn dozens of crosses, costume jewelry, framed pictures of the saints, dog, cat, cattle and chicken bones, bird feathers, strips of black material, balls of hair, safety pins, saucers filled with milk, silver and gold coins, and pieces of paper with names written on them.

There were approximately sixty people crowded into the room, staring at Romeo or sitting still with their eyes closed, concentrating, listening. Closest to the altar, seated on the floor, were Perdita, Estrellita and Duane. Perdita embraced herself and swayed gently, slowly. Estrellita and Duane held hands level with their waists, their upper arms bound tight to their bodies by clothesline, their eyelids taped open so that they were unable even to blink.

Adolfo sat to the left and slightly to the rear of Romeo, keeping a steady beat with his hands on both sides of an hourglass drum. Romeo shuddered, his body quivering, then undulating, twisting and turning snakelike, and he began to moan. As he moaned louder and his movements became more spasmodic, others in the room moaned and moved their bodies, gyrating and jerking uncontrollably. The temperature in the already close room became hellish. Sweat poured off the faces of the witnesses, as it did down the forehead and cheeks and bare arms of Romeo Dolorosa, the *nanigo*, the *santero*, the magician, the High Priest of the Goat Without Horns Ceremony.

Romeo opened his eyes and looked around the room. His eyes grew large, then very large, the pupils dilating so that they filled the iris. He began to tremble, to shake more violently now, his eyes bugging out, swelling hideously, seemingly about to burst from his head. His body puffed up like a gigantic mosquito sucking blood from a baby. Adolfo beat harder on the drum, humming and moaning tunelessly, as did most of the witnesses.

The door to the outside opened and two men, wearing white shirts, black pants and black hoods over their heads, entered, carrying the boy, Juan, on a litter, which they placed on the altar. Juan lay perfectly still as the men withdrew into the audience, his eyes closed. He was completely naked and his body had been painted white and covered with sweet-smelling oil and garlic. Romeo bent over the boy and vomited on his chest. Juan's eyes remained closed. Romeo picked up a large knife from the altar and held it over Juan's neck.

"Shango!" Romeo shouted, and suddenly slit the boy's throat.

Blood spurted straight up from the wound like black oil from an uncapped well. It poured out over Romeo, and as he shook himself the blood spattered those closest to him. Juan's legs and arms kicked and flailed and Romeo jumped and danced, groaning and shouting, "Shango! Shango!" Everyone in the room watched now as Romeo returned to the body and plunged the knife deep into little Juan's chest, sawing and hacking until he had pried loose the boy's heart. Romeo dropped the knife and lifted the bloody, pulsating heart and drank from it, his face, hands, arms and chest shimmering red in the puce light.

Romeo went to the body once more, reached in with both hands, the heart having been discarded on the altar, and pulled out the dripping viscera. He stepped out of the circle, Juan's innards dangling from Romeo's fists, and passed among the observers, many of whom made shrill, shrieking sounds as the possessed *babalao* wiped his soiled hands on their lips and foreheads, smearing them with the sacrificial flesh and blood. Romeo returned to the circle and collapsed. Adolfo ceased his drumming. The people rose and left the room as quickly as possible, pushing together into the night, avoiding each other's eyes.

Only Perdita, Estrellita, Duane and Adolfo remained with Romeo and Juan's mutilated corpse. Perdita and Adolfo both lay down on the floor and fell into a heavy sleep. Estrellita and Duane, their eyes taped open, sat motionlessly, fingers locked, minds frozen. A small calico cat with green eyes came in the open door, walked slowly over to one of the saucers filled with milk, and drank.

GOOD EYE

"You talk to the girl's parents, too," Rip asked, "or just the boy's?"

"I only could get hold of Mrs. Satisfy," said Fed. "Glory Ann. She says the FBI's already on the job. They got some kind of deal with the Drug Enforcement agents who been after this Romeo Dolorosa for a time now. Apparently the DEA had him set up at Del Rio, but he got away. Now that there's a probable double kidnap across the border, the FBI's buttin' in."

Rip got up from his desk and walked over to the window. Because of the heat, Calle Brazo was practically deserted at three P.M.

"Don't underrate those boys, Fed. Them and us always has got along good."

"You gonna follow up on Ramon's tip about a dropoff at Junction?"

"Have to. Figure to camp out on the highway there tonight."

"Want company?"

"Come if you want, Fed, though I doubt there'll be anything movin' but the usual, wetbacks and coyotes."

"There is, we'll be on 'em like a king snake on a pegleg rat."

Rip and Fed headed toward Junction, which was at the extreme southern end of Larry Lee County, fifty miles south of Susie, at nine o'clock that night. Before he'd become a drunk, Ramon Montana had been a lawyer, a successful one, and as such had kept up on most of the significant doings in South Texas. The bottle claimed him now, but Ramon still listened carefully to what people said and how they said it, and he managed to remember about half of what he heard. When he eavesdropped on the Castillo brothers, Eddie and Lou, at the bar in El Loco's, and caught the name Marcello Santos, Ramon, even though he was half in the bag, paid particular attention. One of the Castillos' cousins, Pete Armendariz, was a soldier in the Santos family. Armendariz had recently called the Castillos and talked about having to deliver a truckload of goods down at the junction highway, after which he intended to drop in on Eddie and Lou. The Castillos were looking forward to Pete's visit.

"With soldiers like Armendariz," Fed Phillips told Rip, "ain't no call for Santos to hire a publicity agent."

Rip laughed. "Pete ain't exactly the genius in the group," he said, as they tooled along in the unmarked white Ford Crown Victoria.

At junction, which was nothing more than a crossroads leading north to McAllen, south to Reynosa, northwest to Laredo, and east to Brownsville and Matamoros, Rip pulled off the road and drove a few hundred yards into the scrub. When he was far enough from the highway not to be spotted, Rip cut the engine and he and Fed got out.

"We'll hike back over and find us some cover," Rip said. "Grab that thermos from the back seat. I made fresh coffee. Be interestin' to see if this is gonna turn out to be anything. Just hope it ain't somethin' Ramon overheard in Wild Turkey town. What else you know about this black magic dope-runnin' cult operatin' out of Cándido Aguilar or Zopilote, or wherever it is?"

"Just that the dude runnin' the show, Dolorosa, is supposed to be some kinda supernatural freak can change into a snake or a jaguar. Least that's what the Mexicans say."

"Nagual."

"What's that?"

"Nagual's got the body of a jaguar and head of a man. Indians believe only a *brujo* can transform himself like that."

"Well, whatever he is, he's sure got all the peons between Corpus and Tampico spooked proper. Whole state of Tamaulipas is afraid of this cat and his bunch. Keeps the power over 'em, that's for certain."

"Religion's about the most powerful force there is, Fed. It's just sex by another name. Think about all the damage been done throughout history in the name of some religion or other. Every blamed war been a so-called holy war. Not much you can do to persuade a person's dead convinced they got God on their side other than get 'em down and make sure they can't get up again."

"My daddy, Federal Lee Phillips, before he died, used to say, 'If God had any mercy in Him, he'd keep me clean.'"

"Man had a conscience, Fed. That's somethin' to take refuge in."

"Just couldn't abide bein' a sinner and not bein' able to do nothin' to prevent it. Finally, he stuck a forty-four in his right ear, the deaf one. You know that Blackhawk I got at the office in the left side bottom desk drawer with the *Hustlers*? That's the weapon he done it with."

Rip stopped walking.

"This here's prob'ly the best brush for us to hide behind," he said. "Got a good view of the crossroads."

"Rip?"

"Yes, Fed?"

"You reckon there really is a man can change into a jaguar?"

"Doubt it, but I suppose in these times anything's possible."

"Dolorosa would have to be the devil himself then, Rip, loosed upon the land, not no ordinary human."

Rip took out his Smith & Wesson .357 revolver, checked to see that it was fully loaded, and replaced it in the holster.

"Like I say, Fed, it wouldn't take more than a little to surprise me. Meantime, all we can do is keep our good eye on the road."

TOUGH BOYS

Perdita did not like the idea of having to drive all the way to Los Angeles with Estrellita.

"Why can't I drive Duane and you take Estrellita in the truck?" she said.

"What if he overpowers you and steals the Cherokee?" asked Romeo.

"We'll tie him up."

"Bad idea, *mi amor*. Someone sees the kid, it's trouble. I figure you can handle Estrellita better. She's scared shitless of you, anyway. She won't try anything. And Duane will be under my control. Trust me, *chica*."

"You know," said Perdita, as she lit a Marlboro, "I never like it when you call me '*chica.*' Maybe because that guy I used to know I told you about, Bobby Peru, he called me that. He's dead now, of course, and it don't really matter, but I'd just same rather you didn't."

Romeo closed the back of the Jeep, took out a red and white kerchief from his back pocket and wiped the dust from the tops and toes of his steel-tipped purple and black lizard-skin boots. He replaced the kerchief in his pocket and smiled his movie actor smile at Perdita. Romeo's large white teeth shone in the moonlight. Perdita looked at him. Romeo's teeth were a lot nicer than Bobby's, she thought.

"Didn't realize you were so sensitive, sweetheart," Romeo said. "Still got that tough boy in your mind, huh?"

Perdita took a deep drag on her Marlboro, blew out the smoke in a fast, thin pink stream, and flicked the butt off a cactus.

"I ever tell you how he was killed?"

"Not that I remember."

"He was attemptin' to rob a feed store in West Texas and a patrolman shot him."

"You saw this happen?"

"No. I heard about it later, on the radio."

Romeo shrugged his shoulders and dropped his smile.

"Life goes bad that way sometimes," he said. "And you move with it from there. You felt something sincere, then, for this Peru."

"He wasn't no real friendly person. It's not easy to say just what there was between us. I ain't particularly upset he's dead, if that's what you mean."

"What if I were killed, Perdita, would you mourn?"

Perdita studied Romeo's face hard for a moment, then looked away. She thought about Tony, Juana's husband, and how he'd once tried to force her to suck his cock while Juana was taking a shower. Perdita would have bit it hard if Tony had been able to pry open her mouth but he hadn't. She'd told Juana about it as soon as she came out of the bathroom, and Juana had grabbed a kitchen knife and stuck it into the thigh of Tony's left leg. Perdita could still remember the way Tony's face twisted up with pain and how he staggered out the front door to his Eldorado and drove off to the hospital with the black knife handle sticking up out of his leg. She and Juana had laughed a lot over that one, both then and at later times when one of them would mention it. The thought of Tony hopping to the car made Perdita laugh now. Juana and Tony were dead so there was nobody left but herself to remember what happened and laugh about it.

"Ain't it time we got goin'?" she said.

BON VOYAGE

Pete Armendariz was a pill lover. He didn't care what kind of drug or vitamin he ingested, he just enjoyed the act itself, feeling the tablets, big or small, on his tongue, and then the exquisite infusion of water or whisky that washed the round or oblong things down his throat. Tonight Pete had taken six bumblebees, enough speed to keep even a big man like him—six-four, two-seventy—going for up to forty-eight hours, along with his usual evening complement of twelve thousand milligrams of vitamin C; two dozen Stresstabs with zinc, calcium and magnesium; twenty-two Super Hy-Vite time-release multivitamins with twenty-eight nutrients coated with natural alfalfa juice concentrate; and sixteen Giant E-ze with 3-rivers oyster extract to keep his libido bopping. Pete prided himself on his enormous capacity for fucking, fighting and eating. He credited the vitamins with keeping him fit and looking younger than his twenty-nine years.

As he guided the truck closer to Junction, Pete grew more and more excited by the thought of partying with his cousins, Eddie and Lou. It had been no little while since the three of them had done some serious shitkicking together. Pete enjoyed his size, his muscle, his overwhelming appetites. He'd played offensive tackle at Baylor University in Waco for a year, but got kicked off the team for beating up an assistant coach who suggested too strenuously that Pete quit calling the quarterback "Cunt Lips." Pete hated quarterbacks, believing they got all the glory while the linemen, such as himself, did all the real work. He played part of another year for the Red Raiders of Texas Tech at Lubbock, but got expelled for sexually assaulting a student nurse who was attempting to prevent Pete from stealing a vial of Darvocet at the university medical center. After college, Pete went to New Orleans, where he tended bar in three or four places until he went to work for the Santos family.

Pete pulled the truck over on the northwest side of the highway, turned off the ignition and jumped down from the cab. Dede Peralta came up right behind the truck in the Lincoln Town Car. Pete walked over to the driver's side of the Lincoln and Dede rolled down his window.

"We're a little early," said Dede. "You were really barrelin' that baby."

Pete grinned, causing his *bandido* mustache to curl up slightly at the ends.

"Got some people to see," he said. "Hopin' you could drive me up to Susie, about forty-five minutes from here. I'll get back to N.O. on my own."

Dede nodded. "Don't see why not."

Romeo and Perdita, accompanied by Duane and Estrellita in the back seat, drove up in the Cherokee and stopped behind the Lincoln. Romeo got out and walked up to Pete.

"I am Romeo Dolorosa."

"You're right bang on time, Mr. Dolorosa," said Pete. "Mr. Santos appreciates it. Mr. Peralta, in the car here, has got your instructions."

Dede handed a nine-by-twelve-inch manila envelope to Romeo.

"The directions to the delivery location in Los Angeles are very clear," Dede said. "If you encounter any difficulties along the way, or once you are in L.A., that you are unable to take care of yourself, there is a number to call. Mr. San Pedro Sula will meet you at your destination, as you know. Mr. Santos says he has great confidence in you, Mr. Dolorosa. I know you will justify his faith."

Romeo saw Rip Ford and Federal Ray Phillips jump out from the dark, guns drawn, just before the sheriff shouted, "Hands up, *amigos!* Hang 'em on your ears!"

Pete dived to his left and rolled behind the truck before Rip or Fed could squeeze off a shot. Romeo hit the deck and Dede pulled a nine-millimeter Heckler & Koch semi-auto loaded with hot Israeli ammo from his crotch, turned toward the cops and got a bullet between his eyes. The index finger of his right hand locked on the trigger and fired seven rounds through the roof of the Town Car after he was already dead.

Pete crawled under the truck, took out his .45 Browning automatic and blasted away. Romeo heard one of the cops cry out, followed by several more shots, then nothing. He lay on the ground behind the Lincoln, waiting for a voice, a noise. From where he lay, Romeo could not see inside the Cherokee. He shifted his position and looked under the truck, but Pete wasn't there. Romeo waited for thirty seconds before he crawled around the rear of the Town Car. He looked up at the front window of the Cherokee but no faces were visible. He figured that Perdita and the others were on the floor, keeping their mouths shut.

He peered around the end of the car and saw both cops lying perfectly still on the ground. Romeo crawled toward Rip and Fed on his hands and knees, made sure that they were dead, then looked over by the side of the truck for Pete. He was lying on his back, his head toward Romeo, the .45 still in his right hand. Romeo stood up and walked over to him. There was a hole in Pete's chest the size of a silver dollar. He was dead, too. Romeo took the gun out of Pete's hand, then went back over to the cops and took their guns and ammunition belts. He carried the guns and belts to the Cherokee and tapped on the window of the passenger side. Perdita raised her head from the seat.

"Take these and stick them in the lock box," Romeo said. "Everyone else is dead. Duane, you come with me in the truck. We'd better get started. It's a long way to go and no tellin' what other fun and games the gods got in store for us."

Perdita lit a Marlboro. Estrellita was curled up on the back seat, shaking and crying.

"I tell you, Romeo," said Perdita, "this bitch of yours don't straighten up, she ain't gonna make it to no California."

GHOULS

Estrellita watched Perdita smoke. Perdita kept both hands on the steering wheel of the Cherokee and controlled the cigarette with her lips and teeth. She puffed on the Marlboro while it was between her lips and held it in her teeth when she exhaled. Perdita's long, loose black hair rested on the shoulders of her magenta tee shirt. She was wearing black cotton trousers and huaraches. Hidden by her hair were large silver hoop earrings, to each of which was attached a thin strip of red ribbon. Romeo had told her that a piece of red or brown material worn on the body neutralized the power of one's enemies, drained it from them like a grounding wire pulling electricity into the earth.

"How long you been smoking?" Estrellita asked.

Perdita did not respond. She did not really dislike Estrellita; she cared nothing about her.

"I only tried it twice," said Estrellita. "The first was in the summer before high school. I was with Thelma Acker at her house when her parents were gone. Her mother had an opened pack of Pall Malls in a kitchen drawer, so we smoked one. Only about half of one, really. I took about three puffs and coughed like crazy every time. Then around a month ago at a Sig Chi party I tried a Sherman. You ever have one of those? They're black. Kind of sweet tastin', too. Didn't care for it, either, though I didn't cough so much as with the Pall Mall."

Perdita took a final drag on her Marlboro and put it out in the ashtray.

"I know I'm just talkin' about nothin', and that you hate me," said Estrellita, "but I'm so scared I don't know what to do. I always talk a lot when I'm nervous. Do you talk a lot when you're nervous? Are you ever nervous? Are you ever gonna talk to me?"

Perdita looked quickly at Estrellita, then back at the road.

"You're gonna murder us, too, eventually," Estrellita said. "Isn't that right? Duane isn't very smart, really. I hope you know that. I mean, he's okay so far as pullin' on his pants one leg at a time, but he can't understand you people."

Perdita grinned slightly. "Do you?" she asked.

"I think you and Romeo are incredibly deranged individuals with no morals. You're the most evil creatures on the planet. I know you'll kill me soon so I'm sayin' it. My only hope is in the next life, which is what my Aunt Crystal Rae Satisfy always says. Now I know she's been absolutely correct all this time, that it's literal truth. There's too much ugliness on this earth, seein' how it's crawlin' with soulless ghouls."

"What's a ghoul?" said Perdita.

"What you and Romeo are. The worst kind of evil person. A person who'd violate a corpse."

Estrellita bit her lower lip but didn't cry.

"Whoever gave you the notion you was God's perfect child?" Perdita said. "Does Romeo call you *Santa* Estrellita when you go down on him? He always likes the religious angle. Tell you straight, Miss Satisfy, honey, you're right. It was up to just me, you'd be buried by now out in that desert along with them others. Your blond pussy's what's keepin' you alive, so you'd best make use of it for all it's worth. Girls like you got a kind of sickness, the only way to cure it is to kill it. Always talkin' about love and what's good, that shit, when you're same as me, just no particular piece of trash."

"You really think that? That we're the same kind of person?"

"Ain't seen no evidence to doubt it."

"Well, you're plenty wrong, I don't mind tellin' you. God may create people equal, but after that they're on their own."

Perdita laughed. She shook another Marlboro from the pack on the dash, stuck it between her lips and punched in the lighter. She kept her eyes on the jittery red taillights of the truck.

"A person don't never know who they are till someone knows better tells 'em," said Perdita. "A person won't listen might never know, they never stop to hear. Romeo's good at figurin' out people."

The lighter popped out and Perdita took it and lit her cigarette.

"He's a kind of fake, 'course," she said, "but he's got a unlimited way of seein' things. He's got the power to make people believe him."

"He's horrible," said Estrellita. "You're both so horrible I bet God don't even believe it."

Perdita laughed as she spit out the smoke.

"God don't take everything so serious, *gringa*. You see pretty soon how much He cares about you."

Romeo turned up the radio. Ernest Tubb was singing "When a Soldier Knocks and Finds Nobody Home."

"This is one of my daddy's favorites," said Duane. "It's real sad. He used to sing it to us when my brother Herschel Roy and I were small. It and Jimmie Rodgers tunes like 'Why Should I Be Lonely' and 'Somewhere Down Below the Dixon Line.'"

Romeo kept the truck headed west at a safe speed.

"One I always enjoyed was 'My Darlin' Clementine,'" Romeo said. "I seen that old movie, too, where the sheriff, Wyatt Earp, says, 'Sure is a hard town for a fella to have a quiet game of poker in,' after Doc Holliday runs off a cheater in the Tombstone saloon. The best line, though, is from Walter Brennan, who plays Pa Clanton, father of the meanest boys in the territory. After Earp busts up the sons' tormentin' of a travelin' actor, Brennan comes in and horsewhips 'em, then says, 'When you *pull* a gun, kill a man.' That's beautiful, Duane.

"Also, when Saint Henry Fonda, who's Wyatt Earp, walks out of the hotel into pourin' rain at three in the mornin' on the night his youngest brother's been killed, he walks alone away from the camera along the plank-covered street, and everything's gray and black streaks, like real life."

Duane was silent, watching the shadows jump past as the refrigerated truck, carrying two thousand-plus pounds of female detritus, stuck East Texas in its back pocket.

"Man, I remember when I was in Tampa, Florida," said Romeo, "seventeen years old, at my grandmother's house, and I saw the movie *Vera Cruz* on television. It changed my life, the way Saint Burt Lancaster looked and talked. He had about 108 giant gleaming teeth, and wore a dusty black outfit and black drawstring hat, a black leather wristband and a silver-studded black gunbelt with a pearl-handled revolver strapped to his right thigh. You ever see that one, Duane?"

Duane shook his head no and stared out the window. The desert at night looked like a tigerskin rug.

"Saint Burt is an outlaw," Romeo continued, "operating in Maxim-

Perdita Durango

ilian's Mexico, who hooks up with Saint Gary Cooper, playing a former Confederate colonel from Louisiana who has no desire to live under Yankee rule. Saint Coop's idea is to score enough loot to refinance the Rebel cause. Saint Burt is the greatest gunslinger alive. He can shoot equally well with either hand, and even backhanded! He and Saint Coop and their gang join up with Maximilian rather than Juarez because the Emperor pays better. They agree to help escort a French countess and her carriage to Vera Cruz. The trick, of course, is that a load of gold is hidden in the carriage, and everybody wants it. One of Juarez's generals, Ramirez, pulls a superb stunt when he surrounds Saint Burt and his men on the walls of a town square. Burt rotates his lion's head as dozen after dozen of Ramirez's peasant army appear, and when our Black Saint sees he's trapped, he unleashes his magnificent grin and the world stops, blinded by the glare. The scene resembles a painting by Velasquez.

"Saint Burt's name is Joe Erin; Saint Coop is Ben Train. Joe is slick, crude, flashy, schooled by old Ace Hannah, the man who gunned down Joe's father. And Joe makes a point of telling Ben how and when Joe paid Ace back. Ben Train is elegant, older, gentler. It's sincerely wonderful when Joe says of Ben, 'I don't trust him. He likes people; you can never count on a man like that.' Joe spills wine on himself when he drinks from a glass. Ben speaks French and charms the countess, much to Joe's dismay. They make a great pair.

"Joe Erin is the kind of man I wanted to be: fierce, daring and dangerous, combined with the elegance of Ben Train. The Great Burt approaches that at the end of *Vera Cruz*, when he and Saint Coop have their showdown. Saint Burt twirls his pistol one last time into his holster before collapsing, grinning more brilliantly than ever as the reluctant but superior shooter Ben Train's bullet takes his life. It is a dramatic ending, Duane, the most perfect ending for a man. It's the path to sainthood."

"You gonna shoot us, Mr. Dolorosa," said Duane, turning toward Romeo, "after we get to the West Coast, maybe. Ain't that right?"

Romeo whistled softly, gritted his teeth and grinned.

"We ain't got to that part yet," he said. "There's no script, like for a movie. Be best to work things out as we go along, *amigo*, don't you think?"

"I'd appreciate it."

"Thought you would."

COMMUNION

"When I was twelve years old," said Estrellita, "my mama and I and my friend Daisy Samples and her cousin Cutie Lewis were sitting on our front porch one summer evenin' talkin', when here come the preacher and his wife, and couple or three children and a pair or more other poor relations, to find out why it was our family hadn't been to church lately.

"'Evenin', Mrs. Satisfy,' the preacher said. 'Evenin', Estelle. Evenin' all of you.' We're Baptists, sort of. What I mean by that is none of us is really much on churchgoin' anymore. When I was real small we went more, maybe two or three times a month. But it was around the time I'm talkin' about, I guess, that we began to really slack off.

"Anyway, the preacher's talkin' about how terrible wet the air is, and how that brings out the mosquitoes, and so on, and his dumb kids are scratchin' and kickin' at each other, fightin', bored out of their skulls, the mother's shushin' 'em, and the couple of dumb souls are startin' to wander off in different directions. So the preacher asks mama why we ain't been around in church lately, and she tells him things has been shaky with her and Ernest Tubb, but we'll be back in by and by, the next Sunday, prob'ly.

"Then he asks Daisy Samples if she'd be interested in comin' on Sunday, too, and Daisy says, 'Not me, preacher, I'm a Catholic.' Well, this takes the preacher back, 'cause you know how bad the Baptists hate the Catholics. He keeps up his smile, though, and turns to Daisy's cousin, Cutie, but before he can ask her, my mama, Glory Ann, says, 'Don't think you'll be wantin' her, either, seein' how Cutie's half a Catholic and half a Jew.'

"Whew! Hearin' that word, *Jew,* just stunned the man, and he begun herdin' his people back to the car, tippin' his beat-up gray slouch hat with the sweat stripe around the middle, and tellin' mama and me he'd see us in church. I don't recall whether we went that week or not."

Perdita kept her eyes on the road.

"We were Catholics," she said.

"Did you go to church a lot?"

"When I was young, I did. Didn't impress me much, though, not like it did my sister, Juana. She was sold on it for a bit, until our neighbor, Cruz Fierro, told her about how the nuns ate their own babies."

Estrellita looked at Perdita, then out the passenger side window. Blue shark's teeth nibbled at the black curtain.

"What do you mean, ate their babies?"

"To get rid of the evidence, so nobody'd find 'em. Better than buryin' bodies could be dug up. Cruz was a hustler up in Houston, and a junkie, but he wasn't a liar. The dope killed him. He made it with a priest, who told him that a nun who had a baby was made to eat it herself, as a punishment. That turned Juana off from wantin' to be a bride of God. She married that fucker Tony instead."

Perdita laughed. "Juana woulda done better," she said, "even if she'd had to eat her own kid. Might be she'd still be alive."

THE WORLD AND EVERYTHING IN IT

Woody Dumas, special agent in charge of the United States Drug Enforcement Administration's regional office in Dallas, leaned back in his chair and put his feet up on his desk. He tore open a jumbo bag of salted peanuts and cracked and ate them as he spoke.

"I'm hearin' you, Doyle, loud and clear," Woody said into the telephone cradled between his left cheek and shoulder, "no need to shout. Don't take no whiz kid to figure out Santos is involved at the top of the deck, either. This the first you FBI geniuses heard of him? Okay, okay, Mr. Cathcart, sir! Soon as I got a bead on these tree squirrels, you'll know about it. My guess is they got some *maquila* around El Paso, but could be they're movin' the goods all the way to the West Coast. I got my best bird dogs on hunt, so don't take a header. You bet, Doyle, good buddy. *Adios* for now, huh?"

Woody hung up, cracked open another peanut and popped it into his mouth. He'd turned fifty the day before but looked ten years younger. He still had a full head of thick, sandy brown hair and a mostly unwrinkled face. Woody Dumas had never married and never been tempted to. At six-two and one-eighty-five, he moved at a leisurely pace, took a multivitamin pill daily with his orange juice, didn't eat sweets or drink coffee, worked out three times a week on a LifeCycle and with weights at the Downtown Health Club, and got at least six hours of sleep each night. His favorite reading material was the sports section of the newspaper. Woody did not believe in cluttering up his mind with a lot of unnecessary information. Life was complicated enough, he felt, without mixing in a bunch of half-baked ideas.

Woody knew that Crazy Eyes Santos was behind the skin business, just as he was behind virtually every other major illegal enterprise across the South and Southwest. The Mexicans had tied him to most of the cocaine and marijuana being smuggled across the border, and Doyle Cathcart, the special agent in charge of the Federal Bureau of Investigation office in Houston, was certain that Santos was using his dope network to transport experimental cosmetic materials. There was some ugly shit going on down around the border, too, that Woody had been hearing about, all kinds of so-called religious garbage, including animal and even human sacrifice.

At precisely four-thirty P.M., Woody Dumas swung his maroon and white Tony Lama boots to the floor, tossed the bag of peanuts on the desk and stood up. He brushed himself off, picked his white Stetson from the hatrack and placed it firmly on his head. There was more sickness in the world today, Woody believed, than at any time in history. Walking out of the Federal Building he thought of an incident he'd read about in the *Morning News,* something that had taken place in San Francisco shortly after the recent earthquake there. A man named DeSota Barker had been directing traffic at a busy intersection after the city-wide power failure knocked out the spotlights, and an impatient, probably cracked-out motorist had shot and killed him. Barker was subsequently listed among the victims of the earthquake.

"The more things there are to figure," Woody thought, "the more things there are get figured wrong."

He climbed behind the wheel of his brown 1978 Malibu Classic and cranked it up. Woody sat in the car, letting the engine idle, thinking about Salty Dog, the Airedale he'd had when he was a boy. When Woody was fourteen and the dog was four, Salty had bitten two old ladies—one while she was watering her lawn, the other as she was walking up the steps to her house—within a week. He'd never bitten anyone before that, but the county took Salty away and put him to sleep. Woody didn't understand why he thought about Salty Dog almost every day at this time. It had been thirty-six years since they'd gassed Salty, Woody realized, and the world just hadn't been right since.

THE BIG DAY

"Didn't you tell me you used to live out here?" Romeo asked Perdita.

They were at the Rim City Truck-o-Rama, fueling up. It was not quite six o'clock of a new day. Perdita looked around. A sharp wind came up and blew sand into her face. She put on her sunglasses.

"Not too far," Perdita said.

She pulled a Marlboro out of the pack she'd stuck in the front of her Wranglers and put it between her lips but did not try to light it. Perdita walked over to where a dozen Macks and Peterbilts dozed, night sweat sparkling on their metallic hides. She kicked at a wad of red mud caked on one of the giant tires.

"How you doin'?"

Perdita turned around. It was Duane. She still had the unlit cigarette in her mouth, so Duane took a book of matches from his pocket and fired it. He watched Perdita's straight black hair fly back from her Chiricahua cheekbones like a quarter horse's tail in deep stretch at Ruidoso Downs. The weak sun brushed red streaks on it.

"We gonna drive straight through, you think," Duane asked, "or what?"

"Romeo'll likely want to sleep during the day and drive at night. You figure you and Little Miss Poison maybe could slip out on us?"

Duane half-laughed. "I don't guess," he said.

Perdita leaned back against the tire she'd kicked.

"You ever think that someone might be watchin' us?" she asked.

"Who someone?"

Perdita took a hard drag on her Marlboro, then flicked it away.

"I mean some kind of super intelligent bein'. Somethin' invisible, like a ghost. Someone who knows everything's goin' on."

"Guess it's possible. Sounds like you're talkin' about God, though."

Perdita shook her head. "This ain't no god."

"Why can't we see him then?"

"He'll step in on his own sweet time. When the big day comes, and it's comin' quick."

"What'll happen on the big day?"

"Snakes and spiders, rainin' on the people."

"Heard that after the hurricane in South Carolina last month, snakes was everywhere. Moccasins, copperheads, all kinds, blown out of the swamps."

"This'll be worse. He knows what we're doin', all of us. There ain't nobody innocent, not you, not me, not Estrellita."

"Or Romeo."

Perdita nodded. "Sky'll fall on him, too. Maybe especially on him."

The sun stood up and chopped the chill in two.

"Hey, you two lovebirds!" Romeo shouted from where he was pumping gas. "Let's go inside the cafe here and get some breakfast."

The four of them sat in a booth. Bill Monroe was singing "A Fallen Star" on the jukebox. After they'd ordered, Romeo went over to the cashier's stand, bought a *San Antonio Light*, came back and sat down.

"Now here's a good one," he announced, "about a guy named Bubba Ray Billy, a con in Angola, Louisiana, who got fried yesterday. Seems this Billy, who was twenty-six, raped and murdered by stabbing seventeen times an eighteen-year-old girl named Lucy Fay Feydaux. Bubba Ray had picked up Lucy Fay, it says, in his 1954 blue and white Oldsmobile Holiday on a country road outside Opelousas one night four years ago. 'He must of took her against her will,' said the girl's mother, Irma. Mr. Archie Bob Feydaux, Lucy Fay's father, attended the execution and told reporters that he and his wife supported the death penalty and had been waiting four years for Billy to die."

Their food had begun to arrive while Romeo was reading, and he gulped down his orange juice and half a cup of coffee before continuing to paraphrase and quote from the paper. Perdita kept her dark glasses on and smoked her way through the meal while Duane and Estrellita kept their heads down as they ate their eggs, toast, sausages and grits.

"So the good old boys over to Angola strapped Bubba Ray Billy into Gruesome Gertie," Romeo said, "the big oak electric chair, and ended Archie Bob and Irma Feydaux's vigil. Billy was one mean cat, according to this. He'd had a Grim Reaper tattooed on his chest while in the Death House and confessed to at least two other killings in addition to the kidnapping and attempted murder of a Poplarville, Louisiana, teenager and the rape of the boy's girlfriend.

"'I don't run from nothing,' Billy said. 'People say I'm an animal, but they wouldn't say it to my face. I wouldn't say I'm an animal,' he told reporters, 'but I am a cold person.' Boy was a regular case, wouldn't you say, Perdita, honey? Get this: his daddy, Guinn 'Boss' Billy, spent twenty-eight of his fifty-five years in the slam for cattle theft, aggravated battery and manslaughter. When queried by the press as to his reaction to Bubba Ray's impending execution, Boss Billy just told them that he would sleep through it and said his son deserved to die."

Romeo whistled long and softly through his teeth.

"Man, the boy's daddy's an even harder case. This last part's the best. Bubba Ray apparently didn't talk much during the big day. He ate a last supper of fried oysters and shrimp, even though, as he said, he didn't feel much like eating. When a reporter commented to him that he'd nevertheless cleaned his plate, Billy smiled a little and said, 'I guess some old habits is just tough to break.'"

Romeo put down the newspaper, stabbed a pat of butter with his knife and stuck it in his bowl of oatmeal, poured half a glass of milk over it, and signaled for the waitress, who was an elderly, lame Mexican woman with one half-shut eye.

"Señora," he said, when she limped over, "I sure would appreciate it if you could scare up some molasses for me to sweeten up this cereal. Oatmeal just don't taste the same without it."

A VISIT TO SPARKY & BUDDY'S

"You want the usual, Mr. Dumas?"

"Maybe a little extra ice, Sherry Louise, if you don't mind. It's a warm one."

Woody loosened his tie and arched his back. He didn't like sitting on stools but tonight, for some reason, he felt unusually tired. Ordinarily, he stood at the bar. It was a slow evening at Sparky & Buddy's; there were only two other customers in the place.

"There you go, Mr. Dumas, cranberry juice and soda with a slice of orange, two maraschino cherries and extra ice, in a chimney."

"Sherry Louise, you take good care of me and I want you to know that I appreciate it."

Woody slid a five dollar bill to her across the black mahogany.

"This is yours," he said.

"It's my pleasure, Mr. Dumas. Always is."

Woody watched Sherry Louise walk back to the other end of the bar. She undulated, like a giraffe. She must be a half-inch or so over six feet tall, Woody figured, in the green and white New Balance running shoes she wore while she was on duty. Her bright red hair was piled up on her head, adding a good three or four inches of height. Tall and *mucho* skinny, too skinny for his taste, Woody decided. Sherry Louise looked like a section of two-inch pipe stood on end with a bird's nest set on top. She was extra sweet, though, and Sparky said she was the most dependable and honest bartender they'd ever had. Her husband, Eddie Dean Zernial, a former stock car driver, was a carpet layer. Sherry Louise was always going on about how messed up Eddie Dean's back and knees were, both from collisions and rug tacking, but one night she'd told Woody that didn't interfere with their sex life any, since she preferred riding high to lying low. Woody had a difficult time imagining what it would be like to make love to Sherry Louise. It was better that way, he thought; one less thing to have to think about.

A short, stout man of about forty came in and sat down two stools to Woody's left. He was perspiring heavily and used a bar napkin to wipe the sweat from his mostly bald head. Sherry Louise smiled at Woody as she passed him.

"What can I do you for, handsome?" she asked the man.

He held up his right hand and horizontally extended three fingers.

"Wild Turkey," the man said, "straight. Water chaser, with plenty of ice."

"Appears all you gentlemen need coolin' down this evenin'," said Sherry Louise. "Ain't all that hot, I don't think."

She poured the whisky into a double shot glass, filled another with ice and tap water and set them both in front of the customer. He put his money on the bar, Sherry Louise took it, walked to the cash register, made change and brought it back.

"Just shout, you need me," she told him, and smiled again at Woody. "You all right for now, Mr. Dumas?"

Woody smiled at her. "Just fine, Sherry Louise."

"Sons of bitches ain't never gonna find her," said the short, bald man.

Woody turned toward him.

"Come again?"

"Go over that border don't expect no favors, what I always say."

"Woody Dumas," said Woody, offering his right hand to the man.

"Ernest Tubb Satisfy," he said, giving Woody's hand a quick, wet shake, after which Ernest Tubb picked up the shot glass and sipped noisily.

"What border you mean?" Woody asked.

"Messican, 'course. Chink counterfeiters makin' Rolexes, computer innards, that shit, government'll go after like cockstarved banshees. Let it be some poor little Texas gal gets grabbed off the street and they can't figure their asshole wipes north or south. Yesterday on the Blaupunkt in my Mark IV, I heard about G-men bustin' a Hong Kong ring of fake soy sauce manufacturers. Seized more than one hundred thousand bottles of bogus soy along with the perpetrators. Economics is what it is, pure smilin' simple. That's what I say."

Ernest Tubb swallowed the rest of his three fingers, gave it a fast chase and cracked an ice cube with his back teeth.

"Goin' after 'em myself," he said. "Glory Ann, she thinks I'll get myself killed, but a man's gotta do what he feels deepest in his heart is the right thing. That's what I say. So I'm goin' after Estelle. She's my baby."

Ernest Tubb hopped down from his stool.

"Good talkin' to ya," he said to Woody, and walked out.

Sherry Louise came over.

"What was Elmer Fudd there so fired up about?" she asked.

"Man's on a mission of some kind," said Woody. "No doubt about it."

"Ain't much left in this lonesome world got no doubt in it," Sherry Louise said.

Woody laughed. "No real comfort in knowin' that, either, I suppose."

Sherry Louise cleared away Ernest Tubb Satisfy's glasses and wiped the bar clean.

"Seems like sometimes bein' even a little intelligent just don't pay, Mr. Dumas. You know what I mean?"

CRITICS

"Thought it'd be a good idea to see a movie," said Romeo. "Might relax everybody a little bit."

Romeo, Perdita, Duane and Estrellita were in a room at the Orbit Motel in Buck's Bend, New Mexico, halfway between El Paso and Las Cruces. It was four o'clock in the afternoon; they'd slept eight hours.

"We can get back on the highway right after it's over, when it's dark. Noticed on the way into town one of them multi-theater complexes out at the shopping center. What kind of pictures you like, Estrellita, honey?"

Estrellita sneezed and coughed.

"You catchin' cold?" asked Romeo.

"I'm okay," said Estrellita. "I don't care much what show we see."

"What about you, Duane?"

"Don't care."

"Hey, c'mon everybody! Cheer up!" said Romeo. "After all, I'm buyin'."

Perdita did not comment.

Romeo herded everyone into the Cherokee, leaving the truck parked under the Orbit sign, which was an orange neon planet with a purple spaceship, connected on one side by a metal spoke. Several yellow-white stars twinkled on and off around the planet, and a few that didn't work buzzed and hissed.

At the movie complex, Romeo said, "This *Shocker* sounds like fun. Accordin' to the poster here, a mass murderer gets sentenced to the electric chair, only instead of it killin' him, he feeds on the juice and becomes crazier and more powerful. Let's go."

Romeo bought the tickets and they went inside. The movie turned out to be even more bizarre than the advertising promised. An insane, sadistic killer, who'd worked as a television repairman and with other electronic devices, is scheduled to die, and his last request in the prison is for a TV set. He hooks his hands up to the television tubes with jumper cables and transfuses himself with electrical current. The guards rush in and disconnect him, and in the ensuing struggle he practically bites off one's lower lip and breaks another's fingers. When they finally give him the big jolt, the chair and the entire penitentiary power system shorts out, and the killer's electrified self, in the form of phantom particles, escapes and wreaks havoc all over again. The film moves back and forth between dreams and reality, and the monster manages to plug himself into a satellite and transmit his ens through television all across the country. He runs rampant among cable and network landscapes until he's programmed into oblivion by the hero, who's been chasing him over the airwaves.

"Man, I'll bet that con in Louisiana," Romeo said when they were all back outside after the movie, "Bubba Somethin', who got singed the other day, woulda asked for a TV set, too, instead of shrimp and oysters, if he'd seen this picture first."

"It was kinda interestin'," said Duane.

"I enjoyed the hell out of it," said Romeo. "Just shows how capital punishment don't really make much of a difference, after all. What'd you girls think?"

"It was disgusting," Estrellita said. "These kinds of movies are for morons."

"Hear that, Duane?" laughed Romeo. "Your sweetheart here's callin' you a moron."

"Least he's got company," said Perdita, lighting up a Marlboro.

"Well, Duane, *amigo,* there you go," Romeo said. "Everyone's a critic. No wonder now, is it, why the world's in such a mess. Can't nobody agree on nothin'."

THE CHOICE

Marcello Santos was unhappy. Dede Peralta had been a long-time associate of his, a friend in a business where few men could truly consider themselves friends. Dede was dead, as was his soldier Pete Armendariz, and Crazy Eyes was upset. He had called a meeting to be held in the farmhouse of his six thousand acre property west of New Orleans. Set in the middle of a swamp, with only one heavily guarded road leading in and out, it was the only place Santos felt totally safe. He had named this haven "*Il Giardino d'Infanzia*," the nursery. It was as The Nursery that Santos and others, including federal and local police agencies, referred to it in conversation. A small handpainted sign hanging over the entrance to the house read, "Three can keep a secret if two are dead."

Present at the meeting, called for eight o'clock on a Tuesday night, were Santos; Alfonse "Tiger Johnny" Ragusa, the crime boss of Houston and El Paso; Beniamino "Jimmie Hunchback" Calabrese, a capo in the Gambino family, from New York; Nicky "Bigfoot" DeAngelis, the Alabama and West Florida drug king; Reggie San Pedro Sula, who stood by Marcello; and the bodyguards for each of the others: "Papaya Phil" Romo, with Ragusa; Provino "The Fist" Momo, with Calabrese; and Vincent "Pit Bull" Deserio, with DeAngelis.

The air conditioning was fighting a losing battle against the ninety-five-degree heat and ninety-nine-percent humidity of the Southern Louisiana night. Santos took off his jacket and mopped his forehead with a black silk handkerchief.

"Thank you, gentlemen," he said, "for coming to The Nursery. You all know how this tragedy of Dede has hit me so hard. I have been in mourning since the news reached me. The reason for calling you together is that we have a problem, a most serious problem, that, if we are going to be able to continue what has been so far a profitable participation in the cosmetics trade, we must solve.

"The problem is this Dumas, who is, of course, the special agent of the Drug Enforcement Agency in Dallas. Our friend from Dallas, Joseph

Poca, whom you all know as 'Joe Polkadots,' is, unfortunately, at the present time in prison. Therefore, we are empowered, with the permission of Joe Polkadots, that I have very recently obtained, to act on our own behalf concerning special agent Dumas. I call for suggestions."

"Marcello," said Tiger Johnny, "I'll be happy to take care of this creep. He is, after all, in Texas, which is my state. I can arrange for a pipe bomb to be placed in the man's car, and it will be done. Allow me this privilege."

"A thought," said Jimmie Hunchback. "It might be wiser to have an outside representative handle the job. Why not I leave The Fist here go up to Dallas to take care of it himself? Killing a federal agent is a thing the government won't forget, but in this case I don't think they'd suspect someone from my part of the country."

"Nicky Bigfoot," said Santos, "what do you feel is the correct thing?"

At seventy-nine, Nicky DeAngelis was the oldest of the group. He had ruled the Florida Gulf Coast area for forty years, and Marcello sincerely respected his opinion. Like Santos, Nicky Bigfoot, who earned his nickname because he'd made a large and lasting impression in the course of his career, wore dark glasses most of the time. Unlike Santos, who wore them to cover up his strange eyes, Nicky used them so that he could catnap without anyone knowing he was dozing off. His bodyguard, Pit Bull Deserio, was fiercely protective of his boss, and listened closely to everything that was said in his presence in case Nicky needed him to whisper into his ear any information the old man had missed. Deserio did this now, and it took several moments before Nicky responded to Santos's question.

"I go with Jimmie the Hunch," said Bigfoot. "You understand that's how come he's called Jimmie Hunchback. Not because he's got a crippled back, which, as you can see, he don't. If he says his man will do the job right, we should honor his judgment. With all respect to you, Johnny Ragusa, it should be a hitter from someplace out of Texas."

Santos held up his left hand, the one minus a thumb.

"It's settled, then," he said. "Jimmie's man, Provino Momo, will take care of the agent Dumas. Now we can relax and play some serious pinochle! Reggie, give Signore DeAngelis another cup espresso so he can't say he's asleep when I beat him with the cards. Everyone, have more wine, whisky, whatever you want. There is plenty food, also, spaghetti and oysters. You know we like to eat in Louisiana!"

Santos held up a glass filled with wine in his right hand.

"To you, *Il Pugno*, our blessing. And to us all, *salute!*"

"Thanks, especially, for sending up the files on Dolorosa and Durango, Doyle. They're quite a pair."

Woody Dumas had been reading the FBI reports on the skin-business smugglers that Doyle Cathcart had faxed to him overnight, and Doyle had just telephoned to make sure the information had arrived.

"Didn't recall who she was right away," Woody said, "but that name, Perdita Durango, was stuck in my head from someplace."

"She was hooked up with that feed store holdup awhile back in Iraaq," said Doyle. "Remember? One of the stickup men got his head blown off and the other one was captured and sent to Huntsville. The Durango gal was the getaway driver, and danged if she didn't get clean away."

"So now you figure she's mixed up with this barefootin' dope dealer."

"Right. He's also some kind of *santería* priest. They apparently murdered a boy in a ceremony, and the Mexicans want 'em."

"Well, I'm about to saddle up, buddy, and get on the trail. Word is the target is in Los Angeles, so I'm headin' west."

"Just watch your tail, fella. They shoot horses, don't they? They'll sure as shit shoot you, too."

Woody laughed. "'Preciate your concern, son. You take care, too, now. Hear?" he said, and hung up.

Jimmie Hunchback's best boy, Provino Momo, sat in a rented dark gray Ford Thunderbird across the street from the Federal Building. The Fist was an expert at sitting and waiting. As a child, he'd had tuberculosis and had to spend nearly two years resting. During those two years, from the age of eleven until he was thirteen, The Fist mostly slept and read comic books. An only son, he was not allowed to play at all with other children during his illness, and was kept on a strict low-fat, salt-free diet. He didn't realize how angry he had become during this hiatus until five years later when, during a disagreement in a poolhall in the Red Hook section of Brooklyn, the now fully-grown Provino Momo beat a forty-year-old man to death with his hands. It was from this incident that his nickname derived. Word got around about this big, tough, quiet kid with the grip of steel—he was six-four, two-fifty at eighteen—and The Fist went to work as a soldier for the Gambinos, New York's largest organized crime family. Eventually, he earned the confidence of Jimmie Hunchback, and became the capo's right-hand man.

Now, as The Fist sat in the rented T-bird, watching for the Drug Enforcement agent whose photograph he had next to him on the front seat, he thought about the various men and women he had personally whacked on behalf of the business. Usually, The Fist avoided this kind of rumination, but for some reason, perhaps because he would turn forty years old tomorrow, the same age as his first victim had been, he allowed himself to review this side of his life. Altogether, The Fist figured, he had murdered at least twenty people, most of them without any weapons other than his own hands. That wasn't so many, he thought, not in twenty-two years. He didn't know whether to be pleased or not by this, but his reverie ended a moment later, as soon as he spotted Woody Dumas walking out of the building.

Woody's Malibu was parked directly across from The Fist's T-bird. The agent unlocked his car, got in, started it up and drove away. Didn't even check for a bomb, The Fist thought, as he followed him, wondering why anyone who made a halfway decent living would drive such a crummy-looking car. Maybe these federal guys didn't get paid so well. In any case, he figured, Dumas could drive a better short than this turd-colored piece of junk. It looked too much like a cop car to even be a cop car. The Fist owned an identical pair of white '88 Cadillac Sedan de Villes. He drove them on alternate days, and when one of them was in the repair shop he always had the twin to use. Even though it was too small for a man his size, he didn't mind driving this T-bird. It had pretty good pickup and held the road okay. He wouldn't hesitate to rent another one.

Woody drove slowly through the downtown traffic headed toward his athletic club, which was in the newly gentrified warehouse district. He wanted to get in a good workout before the trip to L.A. After parking his car in the alley behind the club, Woody opened the trunk to get his gear. As he bent over to take out his gym bag, the trunk lid came down hard on his back, causing his legs to collapse. Woody fell to the ground. All he could see were two large, brightly polished brown Cordovans.

Woody reached his right hand down to his left ankle and pulled from its holster his Charter Arms Bulldog Pug .44 long snub-nose revolver. He felt himself being lifted and squeezed at the same time. Suddenly, he found it very difficult to breathe and realized he was being crushed to death by an enormously powerful person. Woody brought his backup gun as close to his own head as he could and just as he was about to lose consciousness glimpsed the face of his attacker. He squeezed the trigger, hoping the business end was pointed in the right direction.

The Fist fell backward, his gigantic fingers still gripping the agent's arms, so that when Woody again opened his eyes he saw that he was lying on top of a huge man without a nose. The gun had discharged point blank into The Fist's face and the Glazer safety slug had ripped apart his nostrils, leaving an ugly, large red hole above his upper lip and between his two bloodshot eyes, both of which were wide open and staring up emptily at Woody.

A vision of Salty Dog came immediately to Woody's mind, and he closed his eyes and rolled off The Fist onto his back. Salty was chasing an old woman who was wearing a black raincoat, the tail of which the bounding Airedale held tightly in his teeth.

"Get her, Salty," Woody said. "Get her, boy!"

Mona came up for air and Santos barked at her, "No, no, *cara mia*, don't stop! I'm almost there!"

"I need a break, Marcello, please. My mouth gets tired, and besides, look, it's *fiacco*."

Santos groaned heavily. "Everything is difficult these days. Life is *una pioggia continua*."

Mona got up off her knees and went over to the bar, put a teaspoonful of sugar in a glass, half-filled it with Bombay Sapphire, stirred it with a red swizzle stick that had the words RIZZO'S SOCIAL CLUB • NEW ORLEANS lettered on it in gold, and took a healthy swallow.

"Relax, Marcello," she said. "I'm gonna take a bath."

Crazy Eyes Santos watched his mistress of ten years, Mona Costatroppo, walk out of the room. He listened to the water run into the bathtub. Mona was thirty-one years old, still beautiful, Santos thought, but no longer slim-figured. When he'd first seen her, working as a teller in Grimaldi's bank in Gretna, she looked like Claudia Cardinale, only skinnier. The big dark-brown eyes, long mouth with thick red lips, perfect uptilted breasts. Mona ate too many syrup-filled chocolates now, and drank too much of that fancy gin. Two more years of this, Santos figured, and she'd look exactly like his wife, Lina. At least Lina had provided him with four children.

"Marcello," Mona called from the bathroom. "Be a *costata di agnello* and bring me another drink, would you?"

Santos stood, stuffed his penis inside his pants, and zipped them up. He walked out of the apartment and closed the door softly behind him.

"Marcello!" Mona shouted. "Marcello, are you coming? And don't forget the sugar!"

DETOUR

A few miles east of Tucson, Romeo turned south off the interstate. He checked his sideview to make sure that Perdita had made the unexpected turnoff in the twilight. "One thing about our little Apache princess there, Duane boy," Romeo said, "she can handle a vehicle good as any man, better than most."

"Why we takin' this two-lane all of a sudden?"

"There's an *hombre* I'd like to see in Nogales, on the Mexico side, long as we're so close by. Man owes me. Name's Amaury 'Big Chief' Catalina. Calls himself Big Chief because he claims he's a direct descendant of some Aztec king. Hell, we're all descendants of one kind of king or other. Runs a restaurant called La Florida. Pretty sure he'll be there, unless he's dead, which he should be. Man shouldn't get used to owin', Duane. It's unhealthy."

In the Cherokee, Perdita pulled on the lights.

"What's our hero up to now?" she asked herself, following the large white refrigeration truck down Arizona State Highway 82.

"What did you say?" said Estrellita, who was about half awake.

Perdita looked quickly at her, then fastened her eyes back on the narrow, darkening road. She hated the girl's bright blond hair.

"Sonoita? Patagonia? Where are we?" Estrellita asked, reading a distance sign.

Perdita punched in the dash lighter, put a cigarette between her teeth, and as soon as the lighter popped back pulled it out and lit up.

"You sure smoke a hell of a lot," Estrellita said.

"Won't be botherin' you too much longer, I got anything to say about it. Don't you worry."

They rode in silence until Romeo rolled through the crossroads that was Sonoita and headed for Patagonia. Perdita had no choice but to follow the white truck.

"Must be he's goin' to see someone owes him money," she said. "Just another detour on our way to nowhere."

At Patagonia, a one-street town about twenty miles north of the border, Romeo pulled the truck over and stopped. Perdita slid the Cherokee to a halt right behind him. Romeo hopped down and came over to Perdita's window, which she lowered all the way.

"Bet you're wonderin' what I'm up to, huh, ladies? Well, there's a kind of spooky gentleman in Nogales, on the Mex side, I mean to pay a quick call on, see if I can shake some of what he owes me out of his jeans. We'll be on our way to L.A. again in no time. Perdita, sweet thing, in Nogales I'll park this rig on the U.S. side, in the Safeway foodstore lot. We'll leave both vehicles there and walk across the border. I think Estrellita, here, and our good buddy Duane will behave proper, don't you? Now I'm just gonna make a phone call from the booth over there next to the old railway depot. Shouldn't take long."

In the telephone booth Romeo opened the manila envelope Dede Peralta had given him. He found the sheet of paper he was looking for and held it up to read the number as he dialed. Romeo dropped in the necessary coins, and after the third ring someone answered.

A man's voice said, very softly, "Bayou Enterprises."

"This is Romeo Dolorosa. I'd like to speak with Mr. Santos, please."

"Mr. Santos is out of town. What's this about?"

"I just wanted to tell him that I'll be a little late to the party. I'm having car trouble, but it's being fixed. Can you please convey this information to Mr. Santos when you speak to him?"

"Sure, he keeps in touch. That it?"

"Yes, that's all. Tell him I'll be there as soon as I can."

"I'm sure you will," the man said, and hung up.

Romeo hung up on his end and walked back over to Perdita. He smiled at her and leaned forward with one hand on either side of the door.

"Santos isn't a man to fuck with, Romeo," she said. "I hope you're not fucking with him."

"I can handle it, Perdita, darlin'. You know me."

Her eyebrows twitched, the snakes coiling, but Perdita said nothing as she watched Romeo walk to the truck and climb back in.

"Bet you wish sometimes you didn't," said Estrellita.

Perdita started up the Cherokee and followed along. A half hour later she parked behind Romeo in the Safeway lot in Nogales. All of them got out.

"You kids do what I say and you'll be all right," Romeo told Duane and Estrellita. "If either of you say anything to the customs, I'll shoot you both on the spot, and the customs officer, too. Okay, *vamonos*."

The four of them filed through the turnstile into Mexico. Romeo led them past rows of beggars and through a maze of hustlers and shills, down a comparatively deserted sidestreet and into a courtyard. A white neon sign that said BILLARES blinked and sputtered over one of two doors. Over the other was a dull yellow globe with LA FLORIDA painted on it in black script.

"My memory's not so bad," laughed Romeo. "It's been four or five years since I've been here. Come on, let's go in."

There was a long bar to the right of the entrance, and perhaps a dozen tables to the left in front of a small stage. Several men sat at the bar; none of them were well-dressed. Only two of the tables were occupied. A man in a shabby black tuxedo with a red cummerbund came up to Romeo and asked if the four of them were there for dinner.

"Possibly," said Romeo. "We'll see."

The host smiled and showed them to a table.

"Señor Catalina esta aqui?" asked Romeo, as they were seated.

"He will arrive in perhaps ten minutes," said the host, who gave each of them a menu. "Are you a friend of his?"

"Oh yes," said Romeo, "a very old one."

"I will tell him you are here when he comes in. What is your name?"

"Dolorosa. Just say Dolorosa."

The host kept his smile and said, "As you wish. Your waiter will be with you in a moment."

When the waiter came, Romeo ordered margarita all around. He'd drunk half of his when he saw Amaury Catalina approaching, weaving sharklike through the other tables. The Big Chief was not smiling.

"Romeo, *amigo! Que tal?* What a marvelous surprise to see you!" Catalina exclaimed, smiling now with every part of his round brown face except the eyes, which were hard and dull, motionless black pellets.

Romeo rose and embraced him.

"I thought it might be," Romeo said, also smiling a smile without mirth.

Big Chief Catalina was topheavy, carrying well over two hundred pounds on his medium-large five-foot ten-inch frame. With his caterpillar mustache and thinning black hair greased straight back on his wide, flat head, Catalina looked ten years older than his thirty-four.

"Say, Chief, why don't we go someplace and talk?"

"Of course, of course. We can use my office."

"Be back shortly, Perdita," said Romeo. "You keep an eye on the kids. Make sure they eat their vegetables."

Catalina signaled to the waiter, who came over immediately.

"See that these people have anything they want," said the Big Chief, "without charge."

Catalina's office was an eight-by-eight windowless box, with a desk, two chairs, and a filing cabinet. On the wall to one side of the desk was a postcard photo of Pancho Villa on his horse in front of his army in 1914. Catalina took a bottle of Gusano Rojo mezcal and two glasses from a drawer and put them on top of the desk, then poured double doses for Romeo and himself.

"Before you ask me about the money, *amigo,* we have a drink, yes? This is good mezcal, from Oaxaca."

"Cómo no?"

"To your health!"

They swallowed the shots of mezcal and set the glasses back on the desk.

"Now, Señor Pain, you can ask me about the money."

"Do you have it?"

"No. I have money, but not for you, unfortunately."

"Do you mean that you do not have it for me now, or that you will never have it for me?"

Catalina laughed abruptly but did not smile.

"This is a choice you are welcome to make. Choose the answer that makes you most comfortable."

"May I have another drink?"

"Of course, help yourself."

Romeo stood, picked up the bottle of Gusano Rojo and pushed it with all of his strength into the Big Chief's face. The glass shattered and cut into Catalina's nose, cheeks, and chin. Romeo picked up the largest piece and stabbed both of the man's eyes, then jammed the jagged edge into his throat and tore it open. Blood gushed out of the Big Chief's face and neck, but he made no noise other than a slight gurgle before collapsing to the floor behind his desk. Romeo leaned over him and saw the mezcal worm lying on the floor. He picked up the worm and dropped it into Catalina's mouth.

"There you go, *macho*," Romeo said. "You've proved your manhood now."

"We're not staying for dinner," Romeo said as he took Estrellita's arm and lifted her to her feet. "Come on, Perdita, Duane. I just heard the food here's not so good."

FLIGHT

Due to the powder burns, Woody Dumas had most of the left side of his head covered with a gauze bandage. Firing the gun so close to his face had left him at least temporarily deaf in his left ear. Woody was on a plane to Los Angeles, slumped in a window seat sipping orange juice, thinking about his life, which had almost been squeezed out of him by Provino "The Fist" Momo in a Dallas alley.

It wasn't really so terrible, he figured. Look at the situation in Eastern Europe, where so many people are desperate to escape to the West, leaving behind them possessions, parents, even children in their feverish rush to freedom. Or in China, with the soldiers shooting students down like dogs in Tiananmen Square. The government here had done that, too, of course, back in the sixties, and the Mexicans murdered dozens in '68 before the Olympics. Person-to-person violence is never as horrifying as faceless, wholesale slaughter, Woody decided, not ultimately. As gruesome and senseless as some individual murders are, he thought, the impersonality of mass maiming and killing is sordid and perverse beyond belief.

Woody remembered an old guy named Buzzard who used to hang around the neighborhood when Woody was a kid. Buzzard was almost a bum, but not quite. He fixed zippers and did some sewing for people, so Woody figured he must have been a tailor at one time in his life. Buzzard always had about ten days' growth of whiskers sticking out of his long, mule-like face, and he walked around flapping his arms as if they were wings, which was why everyone called him Buzzard. He wore a red-and-black-checkered lumberjack coat that obviously had never been cleaned, and a blue peaked cap with earmuff flaps tied together on top. His eyes, Woody recalled, were clear green with black specks in them. Nobody knew where Buzzard slept until he was found poisoned to death in an unused trash bin behind the public library. He'd been drinking black liquid Shinola shoe polish, using a slice of Wonder bread as a filter, pouring the Shinola through the bread into a coffee can. The only other thing in the trash bin with Buzzard's body was a dog-eared hardcover copy of the 1914 A. L. Burt Company edition of *Tarzan of the Apes* by Edgar Rice Burroughs, which was tucked like a pillow under Buzzard's head.

A stewardess came by with a cart and said something to Woody. He turned his head so that he could listen with the good ear and asked her what she'd said.

"May I bring you another orange juice?" she asked.

"Sure, sure, I'd like that," Woody said, handing her his plastic cup. Then he had another thought. "Oh, miss? Could you please make this one a screwdriver?"

She nodded, refilled the cup with juice, and gave it back to Woody along with a miniature bottle of Wolfschmidt. He paid her, unscrewed the cap and poured the contents into the orange juice, mixing it around with the index finger of his right hand. Woody had not drunk an alcoholic beverage in nearly a decade and he wasn't certain why he'd decided to do so now; it just seemed like the right thing to do. Woody lifted the cup.

"For Buzzard," he said.

SALAMANDERS

Perdita didn't like what was happening. She was pleased to be going to Los Angeles, but she knew already that it was over between her and Romeo. She wouldn't say anything yet, just let the deal go down and pick her spot to split. Maybe take care of this Estrellita bitch before then.

"What's on your indecent little mind tonight, honey?" asked Romeo. "You been awful quiet lately."

Romeo and Perdita were at the Round-up Drive-in in Yuma, waiting at the take-away counter for their order. They'd left Duane and Estrellita tied up together back in the motel room.

"Nothin' much, tell the truth. Just appreciatin' the beautiful evenin'."

Cars and trucks zoomed by on the street in front of the drive-in. The air was sickly warm and sticky and stank of burnt oil. A grayish haze hung like a soiled sheet across the sky. The breeze kicked at a corner of it now and again, wrinkling the gray just long enough to permit a peek at the twinkling platinum dots decorating the furious fuchsia. A tall, lean, cowboy-looking guy in his late twenties walked up to the take-out window.

"How you people doin' tonight?" he said.

"Not bad," said Romeo. "Yourself?"

The cowboy took off his black Stetson, reached into it and took out a half-empty pack of unfiltered Luckies. He offered it to Romeo and Perdita, both of whom declined, then shook one between his lips, flipped the pack back in and replaced the hat over his thick, tangled dark-brown hair.

"Can't complain," he said, and pulled a book of matches from the left breast pocket of his maroon pearl-buttoned shirt and lit the cigarette. He bent down a little and looked in the window.

"Hey, Betsy!" he called. "How about a couple double-cheeseburgers and a side of chili and slaw."

"Be a few minutes, Cal," a woman shouted from within. "You want any fries with that?"

"Why not?" said Cal. "I'll take whatever you got to give, Betsy."

The woman laughed and yelled back, "Oh, hush! You know that bar talk don't cut it with me."

Cal smiled and straightened up. He stood off to the side of the window away from Romeo and Perdita and puffed on the Lucky Strike.

"So what's doin' in Yuma these days?" asked Romeo.

Cal looked at him and said, "That your Cherokee there, with the Texas plates?"

"That's right."

"You all from Texas, then?"

"Right again."

"Passin' through, I suppose."

"You got it."

"Headed for California, I bet. L.A."

"You're on the money tonight, cowboy."

Cal laughed, took a last drag, and tossed away the butt.

"Not a whole lot to keep people here, I don't guess," he said. "It ain't the most excitin' city in the world."

"Nothin' wrong with peace and quiet, that's what you want."

"Ain't much of that here, either. Heat gets people mean, fries their brains and makes 'em dangerous. Tough on every livin' thing except salamanders."

"Salamanders?" said Perdita.

"Yeah," said Cal, "you know, them lizards can withstand fire."

An eighteen-wheeler downshifted and belched as it passed by, spewing a brown cloud of diesel smoke over the drive-in. Perdita coughed and turned away.

"Here's your order, sir," Betsy said to Romeo from the window, shoving it through. "Be $17.25."

Betsy was a middle-aged Asian woman with badly bleached blond hair.

Romeo put a twenty down on the counter, picked up the bag, and said, "Change is yours."

"'Preciate it and come back now. Yours is comin' up, handsome," she said to Cal.

"I ain't goin' nowhere."

"No kiddin'," she said, and laughed.

"You folks take care now," Cal said to Romeo and Perdita.

"Do our best," said Romeo. "You, too."

Driving back to the motel, Perdita said, "You get a good look at that gal back there?"

"You mean Betsy?"

"Woman had the worst hair, Jesus. Never saw no Oriental person with blond hair before."

"Plenty more surprises where we're headed, Perdita. Just you wait. I got big plans for us."

She turned and stared at Romeo. He was grinning, confident, full of himself.

"Don't make me no promises you can't keep," Perdita said. "There ain't nothin' worse for a woman than a man punks out on her. That happens, no tellin' what she'll do."

"I'll keep this in mind, sweet thing," said Romeo, nodding and grinning, "I surely will."

HISTORY LESSON

"E. T. Satisfy, is it? Hometown, Dallas."

"Right the first time."

The clerk looked up from the registration card across the desk and down at Ernest Tubb.

"How you mean to pay for this?"

"Cash," said Ernest Tubb, handing the clerk a hundred dollar bill.

The clerk took it, examined both sides, went into another room for a minute, then came back and gave Ernest Tubb his change plus a receipt and a room key.

"You got 237. Upstairs and around to the right. Ice and soda pop machines by the staircase. Need more you holler."

"I'm obliged."

In the room the first thing he did was phone home.

"Glory Ann? It's me, Ernest Tubb."

"Just where in Judas's country are you?" she asked. "I been worried crazy!"

"Easy, woman. I'm at the Holiday on Madre Island. Got a lead in Larry Lee County that Estelle and Duane Orel mighta come down here. College kids on break partyin' both sides of the border. Heard about two were kidnapped a week ago. Might be them. I'm headed for Mextown soon's I hang up."

"Kidnapped! Save Jesus! Rita Louise Samples is here with me now, and Marfa Acker's comin' back later. They been my cross and crutch since you disappeared on me."

"I ain't disappeared. I told you, I'm huntin' for Estelle."

"If I lose you, too, don't know what I'll do."

"You ain't lost nothin', Glory, includin' weight. You stickin' to that lima bean diet Dr. Breaux put you on?"

"Ernest Tubb, be serious! Who can think about dietin' at a time like this?"

"I am serious, Glory Ann. You keep eatin' like a herd of javelinas cut loose in a Arby's and you'll flat explode! Rita Louise and Marfa be scrapin' your guts off the kitchen walls and collectin' 'em in a box to bury. You keep clear of them coffeecakes, hear?"

Glory Ann began to cry.

"Oh, Ernest Tubb, you're just a mean tiny man."

"Lima beans, Glory Ann, Lima beans," he said, and hung up.

Ernest Tubb backed his Continental out of the parking space, drove to the motel lot exit and turned right. He was thinking about the last time he and Glory Ann had made love. She'd insisted on being on top and just about squashed him. He'd felt like he imagined those people in their cars felt when that freeway fell on them during the big quake in California.

It was several seconds before Ernest Tubb realized that he'd turned his Mark IV in the wrong direction on a one-way thoroughfare. By the time he saw the nose of the White Freightliner and heard the horn blast it was too late for him to do anything about it.

"Oh, Glory!" Ernest Tubb said, and then he was history.

BACK AT THE NURSERY

"You understand what has to be done?"

"I do."

"You have no problem about it?"

Reggie hesitated, then shook his head no.

"Good."

Santos poured more Glenmorangie into his glass, swirled the brown liquid around and stared down into it.

"You and your cousin have been close friends, have you not?"

"We were raised together as boys, but then Romeo and his mother left Caribe. Since then we are in touch."

Santos took off his yellow-framed sunglasses and set them on the table. He rubbed his eyes with his abbreviated left hand, then smoothed back his hair. He looked at Reginald San Pedro Sula, who wanted to turn away from the two small darting animals imprisoned in Marcello's face, but Reggie steeled himself and did not flinch. Santos's eyes were the color of Christmas trees on fire.

"It's not that there is anything personal in this," Santos said, "but Romeo has done some terrible things, things so terrible that not even the Mexican authorities can allow him to operate there any longer. I have sent some people in to take care of the situation in Zopilote. From now on we will handle the business. It was necessary to remove your cousin from the area in order to effect the change. In the meantime, he does us the favor of transporting other goods for us, for which he is fairly compensated. After the delivery is secured, you will pay him the remainder of what we have agreed, and then you will kill him."

Santos lifted his glass with the fingers and opposing digit of his right hand and drank most of the Scotch in it.

"After Romeo is dead, of course," he said, "the money is no good to him, so you will take it as payment for doing me this favor."

"That is most generous of you," said Reggie.

Santos closed his eyes and shook his head.

"Not generous, Reggie—just. There is a difference."

He reopened his eyes and put his sunglasses back on. Reggie relaxed, taking off his powder-blue porkpie hat and wiping the sweat from his bald head with a lime-green handkerchief.

"Deception is merely a tool of resourcefulness," said Santos. "Have you ever heard of Captain Philippe Legorjus?"

"I don't believe so, sir."

"Well, he is the commander of France's elite anti-terrorist forces. Not long ago he was sent by his government to New Caledonia, which is in the South Pacific, to quell an uprising by the Kanak rebels on the island of Ouvea. New Caledonia is part of the French Overseas Territories, and so it was necessary to protect the French citizens who live there. It is also the place from which the French conduct their nuclear tests.

"In any case, Captain Legorjus was kidnapped by the rebels, along with twenty-two others. The leader of the Kanak Socialist National Liberation Front, I believe it was called, was something of a religious fanatic, and had been trained for guerilla warfare in Libya by Khadafy. This man vowed to maintain a state of permanent insecurity in the French South Pacific Territory if the separatists' demands for independence were not met. A familiar story. I remember a newspaper photograph of him, wearing a hood and holding a rifle, the pockets of his field jacket stuffed with cartridges. He threatened to kill a white person a day so long as the French government occupied Noumea, the capital of New Caledonia.

"While the Kanak leader carried on making speeches to the press, Legorjus organized the hostages and not only led them to freedom but took control of the separatist stronghold, disarmed the rebel soldiers, and captured their leader, enabling several hundred French naval infantrymen to swarm in and restore order. Upon his return to Paris, Legorjus was accorded a parade down the Champs d'Elysées and declared a national hero."

Santos paused and looked at Reggie, who smiled and said, "He must be a brave man, this captain."

Santos nodded. "Brave and cunning, Reggie. I make a point of studying these kinds of extraordinary men. There is much to be learned from their behavior. My firm belief is that life must be lived according to a man's own terms, or else it is probably not worth living."

"I am sure you are right, Mr. Santos."

Marcello licked the stub on his left hand where his thumb had been.

"I know you will do a good job for me," he said, walking over to the window and looking out at the sky.

"Ah, *si sta facendo scuro*," Santos said. "It's getting dark. You know, Reggie, I am almost seventy years old, and despite all I know, there is still nothing I can do about that."

WAVES

Woody looked out at the swimming pool. There were three kids and a dog in it, a golden retriever. Apparently the motel people didn't mind that the dog was swimming. He'd been in there for at least fifteen minutes and nobody had said anything about it. California was a different world, anyway, Woody thought. Maybe the animal rights group had successfully lobbied for legislation allowing dogs to use motel pools.

The Wild Palms Motel, where Woody Dumas was staying, was in the middle of Hollywood, one block south of Sunset. It was not the kind of place Woody thought he could ever get used to, let alone like. The weather was good enough, he supposed, but the people in L.A. had a way of talking that put him off. It was as if they were convinced everything they said either had a deeper meaning or meant something other than what Woody thought they were saying. Maybe it was the spectre of the film industry that made everyone want to feel as if they belonged in it, like a club, and were therefore integral to the machinery of the place. He couldn't quite put his finger on it, but whatever it was, Woody didn't get it.

Not that it mattered, anyway. Woody was in town to do a job, and tonight he would be staked out across the street from a warehouse on Ivar just off Hollywood Boulevard, a few blocks from the Wild Palms, awaiting the arrival of a shipment of illicit skin. According to the best information available to the various authorities, Crazy Eyes Santos was operating cosmetics factories on the West Coast, using wetbacks to do most of the work. Seizing a delivery of the proportion expected tonight or tomorrow would be a major step in cracking the operation.

Woody decided to have lunch and then come back to the motel and take a nap. He walked past the swimming pool on the way to his car and noticed a beautiful young woman sitting in a lounge chair dedicatedly applying suntan lotion to herself. She had long blond hair, a slender figure and very long legs. She wore an orange, tiger-striped bikini and oversized blue sunglasses, the frames of which were shaped like butterfly wings. The golden retriever had his paws up on the side of the pool in front of the young woman and was barking excitedly in her direction. A terrifically fat man wearing a pair of lavender Bermuda shorts and nothing else to cover his vast, very pale expanse of skin, came out and jumped into the pool, displacing no small amount of water, most of which splashed on the young woman, disturbing her ministrations.

"Marv, you fat piece of pigshit!" she screamed, jumping up. "Did you have to do that?!"

The golden retriever clambered out of the pool and shook himself furiously right next to her.

"Goddammit!" she said, throwing her plastic bottle of lotion at the dog, somehow missing him by a good six feet. "This is going to be a great fucking time!"

Woody continued to the parking lot, unlocked the government K-car, got in and started it. He decided to drive out to Santa Monica, to the ocean. It might be nice, Woody thought, to buy a sandwich and sit and look at the water for a while.

He'd eaten half of a BLT and was sipping from a can of Canada Dry ginger ale through a straw, when a tall, gaunt-faced man who looked to be in his mid-forties, sat down on the bench next to Woody. The tall man, Woody thought, resembled the actor John Carradine, but a beaten-down, hard-luck version; more the way Carradine looked as the ex-preacher in the movie of *The Grapes of Wrath*. The man's clothes were shabby, worn-out, and he needed a shave, but he held himself erect and gave the appearance of being at ease.

"Do you mind if I speak to you?" the man said.

"No," said Woody.

The man stared at Woody and examined the gauze bandages. His eyes were black, without light. When he spoke, Woody noticed that several of his teeth were missing.

"You've been injured."

"Burned," Woody said.

"I hope you're not too uncomfortable."

"I'm doing fine, thanks."

The man turned his face back toward the ocean.

"Waves are the heartbeat of the earth," he said.

"That's not bad," said Woody. "I like that."

"I used to be a poet. A singer, too, in nightclubs. I sang the songs I wrote. But no longer."

"Why'd you stop?"

"You probably think I'm an alcoholic, or a drug addict, but I'm not. I like to have a martini now and then, of course, and I've sampled drugs, but they're not to blame for my condition, which, as you can see, is less than glamorous. I just lost interest in life, that's what happened. There's nobody to blame, not even myself. I'm not crazy, either. At least I don't think I am. One day the carriage stopped for me and I waved it on."

"Are you hungry?" Woody asked. "You can have this half of my sandwich, if you like."

The man took the sandwich from Woody and held it in his lap.

"You're very gracious," he said. "Are you a religious person?"

"Not really, no."

"Neither am I, never have been. Organized religion is unseemly."

"Here, you can have the rest of this, too," said Woody, handing the man the can of ginger ale.

Woody stood up. "I've got to go."

"I know, your carriage is here."

Woody laughed. "I suppose it is."

"You understand," said the man, "it's not as if I had no choice."

"I believe you," Woody said, watching the man bite into the sandwich.

CAMISADO

"Hey, buddy, it's been a long time!"

"Too long, I guess."

Doug Fakaofo and Romeo hugged each other and smiled.

"I was glad to hear you were comin' out," said Doug. "What brings you?"

"Business, what else these days, huh? Not that we can't put in some good party time, too, of course," laughed Romeo.

"That's great, man!"

"But I got a favor to ask you, Doug. I got some people with me and I want to leave 'em here while I take care of something. It shouldn't take long, maybe only a couple of hours. We're just in off the road and they'll prob'ly sleep for a while anyway."

"Hey, you know it's no problem. They'll be safe here. Bring 'em into the house."

"Thanks, man. I knew I could count on you."

"Any time."

Romeo had spoken to Lily Fakaofo, Doug's wife, from a pay phone in El Centro. Doug was out at the time, but Lily had told Romeo they'd be happy to see him. The Fakaofos lived in Hacienda Heights, a largely Samoan-American section of Los Angeles. The Samoan community was a tight one, distrustful of mainstream America; they kept mostly to themselves. Not even the police knew much about the people there, and Romeo figured it would be a perfect place to stash Estrellita and Duane while he and Perdita delivered the shipment to Reggie in Hollywood.

Doug "Big Brown" Fakaofo had been in the Marines with Romeo, and they'd kept in touch. The Fakaofos were heavy reefer users and they greatly appreciated the kilos Romeo sent them via UPS from Texas on their birthdays and at Christmastime. Both Doug and Lily were large individuals, Doug going about two-eighty and Lily a nifty two-ten or so. Lily's brother, Tutu Nukuono, whom Romeo had met only once, weighed well over three hundred pounds. Tutu had worked as a plumber with Doug until a few months before, when he beat a cop to death with a chain during a brawl in the parking lot of the Moonlight Lagoon, a local bar that catered mainly to Pacific islanders. Tutu was now serving a life sentence without possibility of parole at Folsom.

"I sure was sorry to hear about your brother, Lily," Romeo said. "He's a good kid."

Lily shrugged. "He shoulda known better than to stomp a uniform. Him and a bunch of his biker buddies got carried away wailin' on some Devil's Dragons, I guess it was, who'd strayed into the neighborhood."

"White boys lookin' for strange-colored pussy," said Doug. "They got into it with Tutu's gang, the cops come, one of the blues tangled with Tutu, and that was it. Only reason he didn't get the gas was there weren't no way they could prove premeditation."

"Well, I know Folsom ain't no picnic," said Romeo.

Doug nodded. "Yeah, but Tutu already got himself some friends inside. Anybody can handle it, he will. Let's go get your people."

Lily told Romeo she'd feed Duane and Estrellita, then lock them in the back bedroom, the one Tutu had used. Doug volunteered to ride shotgun for Romeo in the truck; Perdita would follow them in the Cherokee and they'd all drive back together to Hacienda Heights.

"She's some tough, sexy-lookin' lady, that Perdita," Dough said to Romeo as they headed off to deliver the goods.

Romeo grinned. "Think she's a keeper, do ya?"

Doug laughed. "Guess I could keep her occupied for a hour or few, I concentrated hard enough," he said.

"Never doubted you for a minute, Big Brown. Perdita Durango's somethin' all right. Picked her up at a fruitshake stand in New Orleans. The creature's got a mind of her own, though, you know?"

"Just have to be sure she don't stay awake longer'n you do, she's angry about somethin'. Some women you need to watch like that. Lily's on my side all the way, always has been."

"You're a lucky fellow, Doug. Stay that way."

"Tryin' to. What you plan to do with those kids?"

"It's a good question. Think we've squeezed just about all the use out of 'em. They've seen too much to cut loose. I'll deal with that pretty quick, soon as this is finished."

Romeo kept checking in the sideview for Perdita. She stayed right behind them all the way. When Romeo brought the truck to a stop in front of the warehouse on Ivar, Perdita drove the Cherokee past it and parked a half-block up the street. Doug and Romeo got out and Romeo walked over and knocked on the side door of the building.

"*Hola, primo!* You made it okay, I see," said Reggie, after opening the door. "Come on in."

"I have a friend with me. This is Doug Fakaofo. You remember I told you about him, Reggie. 'Big Brown.' He was with me in Beirut."

"Of course," Reggie said, shaking hands with Doug. "Come in."

As soon as the door closed, Woody Dumas got out of the K-car and motioned with his right arm to the men on the roof of the building next to the warehouse. At that moment, a dozen vehicles, carrying both federal and local law enforcement personnel, converged on the street, entering from either end. Two men used a battering ram on the door, which easily gave way, and most of the rest of them, led by Woody Dumas, ran in single file.

Woody saw Reginald San Pedro Sula, dressed in a blue denim leisure suit and wearing a Los Angeles Dodgers baseball cap, fire two rounds from a .45 automatic; the first into the forehead of Romeo Dolorosa, the second into the left temple of Doug Fakaofo, killing each of them instantly.

"Federal agents!" Woody shouted, as the men surrounded the shooter.

Reggie dropped the gun and raised his hands. He started to smile, but before he could complete it several men grabbed him and threw him to the ground, causing his head to bang against the concrete floor. Woody knelt by the men who had been shot, verifying that they were dead. The forehead wound in the smaller of the two looked large enough for a decent-sized sewer rat to crawl through. The man's mouth was open and Woody could not help but be impressed by his extraordinarily large, perfectly formed teeth that even in death radiated a powerful white light.

AFTER HOURS

Lily Fakaofo was up late, sitting at the kitchen table reading the newspaper, listening to the 24-hour news station on the radio, smoking a cigarette and working her way through the second box of Nilla Wafers she'd eaten since Doug, Romeo, and Perdita had left two and a half hours before. Estrellita and Duane were asleep in Tutu's room.

"From Harare, Zimbabwe, comes this story," said the radio. "The Zimbabwe Football Association banned four players for life yesterday for publicly urinating on the field at a Harare soccer stadium. Association chairman Nelson Chirwa said the organization was appalled by the behavior last Sunday of the four players of the southern Tongogara team. 'It is a public indecency for a player to openly urinate on the football pitch,' Chirwa said. 'We all know that it is all superstition and that the belief in juju that almost all the clubs have taken to believe in is strongly deplored by the association.' He said the four were advised to urinate on the field by witch doctors, who said it would ensure a victory. It didn't. Tongogara lost, two to nothing."

Lily laughed and took a puff on her Bel-Air Menthol Slim. Doug had told her that he thought Romeo Dolorosa was mixed up with some kind of voodoo cult down in Mexico or Texas, but she didn't want to know about it. There was enough real mysterious shit going down in the world, Lily thought, without getting sucked into that phony black magic crap. Take this strange business in Russia she was reading about.

A forty-two-year-old French-Armenian multimillionaire art dealer, who was also a well-known poet, had disappeared in Moscow five months ago. He'd been having a meeting with three Soviet business associates in his hotel room near Red Square when he received a telephone call. He spoke briefly to the caller, hung up, and told his associates to wait there, that he had to go out but would return within the hour. They saw him get into a black Zhiguli limousine and speed away, and that's the last anyone had seen or heard of him, including his family in Paris.

Police, KGB agents, and the Soviet government, specifically the Visual Arts Department of the Cultural Affairs Ministry, with whom he'd had dealings for several years, were pursuing the case. Speculation was that with the restructuring of the Soviet society and increasing entrepreneurial climate, the art dealer had engaged in unlawful export of Russian Orthodox icons and other art items in league with the various crime organizations operating throughout the Soviet Union. Authorities in Moscow were paying particularly close attention to the case because of their feeling that it could lead to the exposure of a homegrown Mafia.

According to an official in the Department of Cultural Affairs, this art dealer was a clever man who spoke several languages fluently, had a wide variety of friends in many countries, was very confident and thought there was nothing he couldn't handle. He had made his millions in a very short period of time, a decade or so, having started out with next to nothing in a small Paris gallery. His family were convinced that he had no dealings with gangsters.

Those involved in the investigation theorized that the art dealer had become enmeshed in a power struggle among the seven major Moscow Mafia families, and found himself in a situation he could not handle; or, that he had simply been double-crossed and disposed of. Another rumor circulating in Armenia and Paris held that he had been selling artworks to the Soviet government itself, that a number of the items were revealed to be forgeries, and he had been killed by the KGB, who dumped his body in a forest outside Moscow. This version maintained that the body had been discovered five days after his disappearance, and the family was fostering the pretense that they had heard nothing from or about him in an effort not to discredit the gallery or his reputation. It was, therefore, a mystery that might never be solved.

"Ha!" said Lily, turning the page. "Another hotshot too smart for his own good."

Lily wolfed down another Nilla Wafer and stretched her back. She figured Doug might stay out partying with Romeo and Perdita after they'd delivered whatever it was they had, and she was thinking that she might just as well go to bed, when the radio brought her up short.

"In Hollywood tonight, a gun battle left two men dead and resulted in the capture of another by federal drug agents, the FBI and the Los Angeles County Sheriff's Department. An illegal cosmetics factory, specializing in the use of unauthorized products and operated in central

Hollywood by organized crime, was raided at midnight during a delivery of approximately one solid ton of human placentas. Authorities identified the dead men as Romeo Dolorosa, of Tampa, Florida, and Douglas Fakaofo, of Los Angeles. The man taken into custody was identified as Reginald San Pedro Sula, a citizen of the Central American republic of Caribe. All of the men are suspected members of the crime family headed by Marcello 'Crazy Eyes' Santos, which is based in New Orleans, Louisiana, and Dallas, Texas. According to Drug Enforcement Special Agent Woodrow W. Dumas, who led the raid, seizure of the two thousand pound shipment of placentas, used in the manufacture of anti-aging skin creams, and discovery of the illegal plant is a major breakthrough. More arrests are expected. Well, folks, that's another kind of Hollywood skin factory, isn't it?"

Lily dropped both her cigarette and the cookie she'd just taken from the box and stood up, knocking over her chair. She rushed to the rear bedroom, unlocked the door and flipped on the light.

"Get up! Get up now!" she screamed at Estrellita and Duane, who were huddled together on the bed. "Get up and get out! Get out of the house! Go, go!"

Estrellita and Duane ran out into the night, taking off down the street as fast as they could. Lily collapsed on the floor of Tutu's room.

"Doug!" she cried. "Doug, you big brown dummy! You poor, big, beautiful, dead dummy! What's your ugly old Samoan mama Lily gonna do now?"

LATE DATE

As soon as Frankie Toro spotted the woman he pulled his metallic cherry Lexus to the curb, leaned over and lowered the window on the passenger side. She was leaning against a mud-encrusted black Jeep parked in the space closest to the street in the lot of an Oki-Dog on Santa Monica Boulevard, holding a soft drink cup and smoking a cigarette.

This was easily the hottest-looking chick Frankie Toro had seen that night. Twenty-two or three, he figured, about five-six, a hundred and ten, hard body, shiny black hair almost to her ass, skin like *café con leche*. A genuine *chicana* doll. She reminded Frankie of Tura Sultana, that steel-cheekboned, *nagual*-eyed, Japanese-Cherokee leather bitch he'd seen in Russ Meyer's desert chase tit movie, *Faster Pussycat, Kill! Kill!*

"Hey, *guapita*," Frankie yelled to her, "you want a date?"

Perdita picked up her bag and slung it over her left shoulder, then walked slowly to the Lexus and looked at the grinning, eager idiot. She smiled at him, stretching the cobras. Frankie pushed open the door.

"Been dyin' for you to ask," she said, and slid in.

LIGHT IN THE FOREST

"Mama?"

"Estelle? Is that you? This is Rita Louise."

"Oh, Mrs. Samples. Is my mama there?"

"No, honey, no, she's down at the funeral home, makin' the arrangements. She's been out of her mind worried about you. Where've you been? Are you all right?"

"What arrangements, Mrs. Samples? Why's she at a funeral home?"

"Oh, my word, Estelle. Of course, you wouldn't know."

"Know what? What wouldn't I know?"

"Your daddy, Estelle, honey. Ernest Tubb. He got kilt in a car crash on Madre Island. The body just arrived today."

"Car crash? Daddy's gone?"

Estelle dropped the phone, fell to the floor of the booth and fainted dead away.

"Estelle? Estelle, are you there?" Rita Louise's voice jumped out of the dangling receiver.

Duane half-lifted Estelle with his right arm and put the telephone to his left ear.

"Mrs. Samples? It's Duane Orel. Estelle's sorta passed out here. Just tell Glory Ann we're safe now, we got away, and if she could to please wire us the airfare to come home."

"I will, Duane, of course, but where are you?"

"Los Angeles, California, ma'am. Western Union downtown'll do. We'll head there soon as Estelle comes to. We been hidin' in the bushes all night."

"Goodness, Duane, isn't life a mess sometimes."

"Yes, ma'am. You'll pardon me sayin' this, but shit happens."

Santos hung up but kept his right hand on the telephone. He groaned and pressed his lips tightly together.

"Bad news, huh, Marcello?"

He sat back in a leather armchair and looked through his dark glasses across the room at Mona Costatroppo, who was perched on a white satin loveseat, her freshly shaved and lotioned legs tucked back under her spreading rump. She had on a low-cut black dress and a single strand of pearls that Santos had bought for her at Cartier in New York. They had cost him nine thousand dollars, Marcello recalled. Mona had a drink in one hand, an unlit black cigarette in the other. She always had a drink in her hand, Santos thought.

"*Una pioggia continua*," he said.

"What now?"

"What now? Now is as before. All fucked up. First, it was Dede. Then *Il Pugno*, The Fist, who we send to hit and who himself gets hit. Now, Reggie, along with the West Coast factory."

"Who Reggie? You mean the *tutsun* from Puerto Rico?"

"Caribe, not Puerto Rico. Caribe."

Mona swallowed a mouthful of gin.

"You drink too much," said Santos. "You're getting fat, too."

"Like Lina, you mean," Mona said. "You got a fat wife, you don't want a fat girlfriend, too, huh? You gonna dump me, Marcello? Is that what you want to do?"

Santos removed his hand from the phone, formed it like a gun, with the third finger and pinkie folded back, the thumb up, and the index and second fingers pointed at Mona. She froze.

"Bang," he said.

"Hear you had a good trip."

"Don't know about good, Doyle. Successful, anyway. We got what we went for. That L.A. is a whole other state of mind, though."

"Didn't lose anyone, either, they tell me."

"No white hats, but I woulda preferred to've brought in the delivery boys. Santos's trigger man took 'em both out before we got there."

"Why you suppose they whacked Dolorosa?"

"Santos set him up. Crazy Eyes controls the border and Dolorosa got the area freaked out with his *santería* routine. Killing the boy was the last straw far as Santos was concerned."

"Kidnapped two college kids, too. They turned up in L.A., you know that?"

"Only heard about it after I got back to Dallas. What'd they have to say about Perdita Durango?"

"Didn't want to talk about her much, just said she's plenty weird and dangerous. They're pretty shook. The girl's father was killed in a car wreck while she was gone, which doesn't help. Happened while he was out huntin' for her, apparently."

"That's rough, all right. What's her name?"

"Satisfy. Estelle Kenedy Satisfy. His is Duane Orel King."

"That Satisfy sounds familiar, but I can't place it just now."

"Well, Woodrow, I got to run. Hell of a job, bud."

"*Gracias,* señor."

"Oh, by the way, how's your hearing?"

"Back in stereo."

"*Bueno.* Be talkin' to ya."

59° AND RAINING IN TUPELO

Tattooed on the biceps of Shorty's left arm were the words ONE LIFE ONE WIFE and tattooed on his right biceps was the name CHERRY ANN.

"That her?" Perdita asked him.

"Who?" said Shorty.

"Cherry Ann your wife's name?"

"Was."

"She change it?"

Shorty laughed and shook his head no.

"Changed wives," he said.

"Kinda puts the lie to your other arm, don't it?"

Shorty yawned and closed his eyes. He opened them and picked up his glass and took a long swallow of Pearl.

"Ain't nothin' stays similar, sweetheart, let alone the same. Or ain't you figured that out yet?"

Perdita Durango and Shorty Dee were sitting on adjacent stools at the bar of Dottie's Tupelo Lounge. It was eight-thirty on Friday night, December thirtieth. Oklahoma State was playing Wyoming in the Sea World Holiday Bowl football game on the television set above the bar.

"Know what I like to watch more than anything else?" Shorty said.

"Not knowin' you any better than I do, which is not at all practically," said Perdita, "I'd be afraid to ask."

"Punt returns."

"That so."

"Yeah. Some people it's triples. Me it's punt returns. I like any kind of runbacks: kickoffs, interceptions, fumbles. But there's somethin' special about a little jack-rabbit of a guy takin' a tall ball and turnin' on his jets."

Shorty took another sip of beer.

"You been in town long?" he asked.

"Few days."

"How's it goin' so far?"

"Been rainin' since I got here. Weather always like this?"

"Time of year it is. Fifty-nine and rainin' sounds about right for Christmas."

"What else Tupelo got to offer?"

"Other than bein' the birthplace of Elvis Presley, you mean?"

Perdita laughed. She swept back her long, straight black hair with one hand and picked up her glass with the other.

"Didn't know about Elvis bein' born in Miss'ippi," she said, and took a sip of beer.

"Where you from?" asked Shorty.

"Here and there. Texas, mostly."

"Brings you this way?"

"Lookin' for somethin', I guess."

Shorty offered his right hand.

"Shorty Dee. Glad to be of service if I can."

She squeezed his fingers.

"Perdita Durango. Pleased to meet you, Shorty. You still married?"

Shorty laughed. "Thought we was beginnin' a conversation here."

Perdita smiled. "How about buyin' me a new beer?"

"Now you're talkin', honey," he said, signaling for another round. "Got any more potentially embarrassin' questions you want to get out of the way?"

"You rich?"

The bartender set two more bottles on the bar in front of them.

Shorty laughed again. "Nigger rich, maybe," he said.

"Bein' nigger rich is all right, I guess," said Perdita, "long as a body got enough friends is rich for damn sure."

They picked up the fresh bottles of beer and tapped them together.

"There you go," said Shorty.

Perdita smiled. "Here I go," she said.

SAILOR'S HOLIDAY

A woman in a red dress came in the door unsteadily. "Whoopee," she said, "so long, Red. He'll be in hell before I could even reach Little Rock."
—William Faulkner, *Sanctuary*

CONTENTS
Sailor's Holiday

LULA CALLS

"Mama, I do appreciate all you been doin' for me, you know that."

"Listen, Lula, you can't go on workin' in a 7-Eleven like this. You're too smart to be wastin' your time sellin' Slurpees to high school kids and cans of King Cobra to drunks. I don't mind supplementin' your income, 'specially where Pace is concerned, long as I got it to give. But you can do somethin' better with your life."

Marietta Fortune took a big sip of Martini & Rossi sweet vermouth and raised her eyebrows as she looked at her friend Dalceda Delahoussaye, who sat across from her at the patio table sipping the same. Marietta wanted Dal to know how exasperated she was by her daughter's seeming dearth of ambition.

"Well, Pace'll be out of school next week," said Lula, "and I gotta figure out what to do with him for the summer. I can't very well start on a new career with a ten year old trailin' after me."

"*New?* You ain't never had one career yet, Lula, and here you are thirty years old."

"Twenty-nine and a half, Mama. Keep it accurate."

Marietta took another sip. "You could get married."

Dal frowned at Marietta and shook her head side to side in disapproval.

"Okay, Mama, I can see where this conversation's headin', and I ain't goin' along with it. Far as that's concerned, you might be considerin' it yourself. Johnnie's still willin'."

"Lula, we're not discussin' me. It's your life got to be lived."

Lula laughed. "Mama, you ain't fifty till tomorrow and you talk like you got one foot and four toes in the grave. Look, I gotta go pick up Pace. We'll be over around noon for your birthday. Say hi to Dal if she's still there. Bye."

Marietta hung up and sighed.

"You and that girl don't never give each other a smidge of space," said Dal. "Why don't you just pretend to be the mature one and back off a spell, let Lula work her life out her own way."

"Oh, she's done great this far, Dal, ain't she? Lula's approachin' middle-age and all she's got's an illegitimate child can't sit still for more'n two minutes 'cause he ain't never had no man around, and no prospects of any kind I can tell. I'm supposed to be comfortable with that?"

"Marietta, you're in a state for nothin'."

The telephone rang and Marietta picked up the receiver.

"Yes?"

As soon as Marietta heard who it was she sat up straighter in her chair and her face lost most of its wrinkles.

"Why, Marcello, what a surprise. Uh huh, I think so. I certainly don't see why not. Around twelve-thirty would be fine. I'm already lookin' forward to it. Thank you for thinkin' of me. Oh, you're awful sweet. Bye, now."

Marietta hung up.

"Don't tell me that old gangster Crazy Eyes Santos is comin' here?" said Dalceda.

Marietta nodded. "Tomorrow afternoon, for my birthday. He remembered."

"I just don't plain believe this!" Dal said, setting down her glass on the table. "I thought he'd done a fade after Clyde died."

"He did. I guess he's just sentimental now we're gettin' older."

"Man's a killer, Marietta. He's been runnin' the rackets down here since we was girls together at Miss Cook's in Beaufort. He's married, too, of course. And besides, Johnnie Farragut's comin' tomorrow, ain't he?"

Marietta relaxed, sinking down in her chair and closing her eyes.

"Won't matter."

"The hell it won't. I wouldn't miss this party for the world."

"One thing about the rest of the world, Dal, they don't give a fig about us and they never have. That's why we got to stick together."

MARIETTA'S PARTY

Saturday morning it rained. By noon the rain had mostly stopped but the sky stayed grainy and the air was unseasonably cold. Marietta hated birthdays, especially her own. She'd learned, however, that there was no use denying them, so now she accepted the attention at these little gatherings if only for her grandson's sake. Like most children, Pace just loved birthday parties, and since Lula kept him and events under control, Marietta more or less sat back and endured the goings-on in relatively good humor.

As expected, Pace and Lula were the first to arrive.

"Happy birthday, Marietta!" Pace shouted, as soon as the door opened.

He gave her a hug and Marietta offered him her right cheek to kiss, which he did, and not ungladly, as he sincerely liked his grandmother, the only one he had.

"That's one of the nicest improvements about this boy, Lula, that he don't call me 'Grandmama' any more."

"Why's that, Mama? I thought you liked bein' considered old and put to pasture."

Lula kissed Marietta on the other cheek and handed her a small package wrapped in red and green Christmas paper.

"Sorry about the inappropriate wrappin's," she said, "but it's all I had. Got ten rolls of it for a dollar at the 7-11, left over from last year. Tell me, you want any."

"Open it now, Marietta!" Pace said. "Before anybody else gets here."

"All right, Pace, I'll just do that."

Marietta carefully unwrapped the gift, handing Lula the ribbon and paper to discard.

"Well, my goodness," Marietta said, holding up a matching teacup and saucer. "This is a lovely surprise."

"It's real old, Grandmama—Marietta, I mean. Mama found it in a junk shop."

"Lady said it's two hundred years old, Mama, but it's real pretty, I think."

"Certainly it is. Just look at the gold edges. It's fine China, I can tell. I hope you didn't spend too much on this, Lula. I hear 7-11 wages ain't all that generous."

"Enjoy it, Mama. I'll go see about the cake."

The doorbell rang and Pace said, "I'll get it!"

"Why, hello, honey," Dal said, coming in. "Don't you look handsome today."

"Mama scrubbed me brand clean, Auntie Dal. She says it makes a difference."

Dal laughed. "It can indeed. Hello, Marietta," she said, giving her a hug. "I won't say happy birthday because of your complex."

"What's a complex?" asked Pace.

"A foolishness that's recognized for what it is," said Dal.

"Mama says I'm foolish lots of times."

"That's different, dear," Dal said, "everyone is. You ain't old enough for the other thing yet."

"I ain't old enough for much. When'll I be old enough for a complex?"

"For some it's all too soon and never too late."

"Dal, hush," said Marietta. "Leave the boy be. Pace, you go on in the back, see you can help your mama with things."

Pace walked toward the kitchen and the doorbell rang again. Dal opened the door.

"Afternoon, Dalceda. Am I early or late?"

It was Johnnie Farragut, the private investigator from Charlotte who'd been sweet on Marietta for thirty years.

"You're plumb on time, Johnnie," said Dal. "Marietta's right here."

Johnnie gave Marietta a kiss on the cheek and handed her an envelope.

"Marietta, I ain't much of a shopper, as you know," he said, "but this is a certificate for a subscription to a ladies' magazine I thought you might like to look at while your hair's dryin' or somethin'."

Marietta opened the envelope, took out the certificate and read it.

"*Spiffy*, 'The Magazine for the New Woman.'"

Dal giggled. "See, Marietta, it ain't for *old* women."

"Sounds like the name of a peanut butter," said Lula, coming up to Johnnie and kissing him. "That's so sweet of you, Johnnie. I'm sure Mama'll love readin' it."

"Sure I will," said Marietta, taking one of Johnnie's hands. "It's real thoughtful."

"Prob'ly be a few weeks before the first issue arrives," Johnnie said.

"That won't bother Mama. You're familiar with her gift for patience."

There was a knock on the door and Lula opened it. A short, wide, impeccably dressed man who looked to be about sixty, wearing a black toupee and yellow-framed sunglasses, stood in the doorway holding a large box with both hands. Lula noticed that his left thumb was missing.

"This is the home of Marietta Pace Fortune," he said. It was not a question.

"Yes," said Lula. "Won't you come in?"

The man entered, saw Marietta and went to her.

"Marietta," he said, balancing the box on one knee and bending forward to take in his own and kiss the hand she'd just held Johnnie's in, "you're still a gorgeous woman. Your Clyde, *era nato colla camicia*. He was born lucky to have had you for a wife. But now, of course, he is dead and we are living."

"Clyde been gone a whole lotta years, Marcello," said Marietta. "Why don't you set down that box?"

"Thank you," he said, putting the box on the floor.

Pace came running up.

"Can I open it, Grand—Marietta?"

"In a moment, perhaps," said Marietta. "Marcello, this is my daughter's boy, Pace Roscoe Ripley. And this here's his mama, my precious Lula. This is my oldest and dearest friend, Dalceda Delahoussaye, whom you might remember. And here's Johnnie Farragut, who's in law enforcement over in Charlotte, an old pal of Clyde's. Everyone, this is Mr. Santos."

Santos nodded and smiled at all of them without removing his dark glasses.

"Mr. Santos?" said Pace.

Santos turned to him, smiling.

"Yes, boy?"

"What happened to your thumb?"

Lula almost said something but held her tongue. She wanted to know what had happened to it, too. Marietta, she figured, already knew.

"You really want to know, hey, boy?" said Santos.

Pace looked up at Santos's large, flat red nose and blue lips and nodded.

"Marcello, you don't have to," Marietta said.

He held up the four digits remaining on his left hand.

"When I was only a few years older than you are now," Santos said to Pace, "I worked in a slaughterhouse, where animals are killed and carved up and their body parts packaged to be sold in stores to be eaten. An older man attacked me because he did not like some things I had said about his work. I had said that he was lazy and a bad worker because he was drunk much of the time, and because of this the rest of us in the slaughterhouse had to work even harder at what already was hard work. The man became enraged and with a hatchet crusted with blood from the animals tried to chop off my left hand. Before he could do it I pulled my hand back and all he got was the thumb."

"I bet you were real angry at him," said Pace.

Santos nodded. "Yes, I was. I was so angry, that even though this man was older and bigger and stronger than I was, I took the hatchet away from him with my other hand and hit him with it between his eyes."

"With the blade part?" asked Pace.

"Yes, boy, with the blade."

"Did you kill him?"

"He died," said Santos. "It was his own foolishness that killed him."

"Oh, I know about that," Pace said. "He musta had a complex."

Dal laughed and then quickly covered her mouth with her hands.

"Marietta," Santos said, "I regret that I am unable to stay longer, but there are people waiting for me. I will call you soon, if I may."

"Please do, Marcello," she said. "And thanks so much for my present."

Santos smiled. "The present, yes. Well, it's a little something."

He turned to the others.

"It's been a pleasure," he said, and went out.

All of the adults gathered in the doorway and watched Santos climb into the backseat of a black Mercedes-Benz limousine and be driven off.

"Look, Marietta, look!" Pace shouted.

Everyone turned from the door and looked at Pace. He had opened the box Santos had brought and was holding up a huge purple silk robe with black velvet lapels.

"There's writin' on it," said Pace, showing them.

Across the back of the robe in bright gold capital letters were the words SANTOS BOXING CLUB, and underneath, in slightly smaller, silver letters, it said, BILOXI & N.O.

"Can I put it on, Marietta? Can I?" Pace asked.

"Yes, child, put it on."

"What a strange man," said Lula.

"Everybody got their way," said Marietta.

"Santos is someone used to gettin' *his* way most all the time, is my guess," said Dal.

"So that was Crazy Eyes Santos himself," said Johnnie.

"Well, come on now, Lula," said Marietta, "this is my birthday party. Let's get these folks some cake!"

THE THEORY OF RELATIVITY REVISITED

All of the urinals were occupied, so Sailor Ripley used one of the stall toilets to relieve himself. As he did, he read the graffito someone had scrawled with a black felt-tipped pen on the wall container of Protecto toilet seat covers: IRANIAN DINNER JACKETS. Sailor snickered, zipped his jeans, picked up his suitcase and went back out into the Greyhound terminal. His bus to New Orleans was not scheduled to depart for another hour, so he bought a Jackson *Clarion-Ledger* from a vending box and sat down to read it on one of the hardwood benches.

ATLANTA'S BLACK MAYOR VISITS 'REDNECK BAR' caught his eye right away. The mayor of Atlanta, seeking white votes in his effort to become Georgia's first black governor, had gone to a Cobb County bar and defended the owner's right to put racist records on the jukebox. The candidate said, "I'll go anywhere to talk to anybody about the future of Georgia," and had brought with him a couple of records to give the owner, one by Ray Charles and one by Hank Williams, Jr. The bar owner told reporters that to avoid embarrassing the mayor he had removed two records from the jukebox: "Alabama Nigger" and "She Ran Off With A Nigger." He intended to put them back, he said, after the visit.

"Life don't get no less stupefyin', that's certain," Sailor whispered to himself, and turned the page.

Sailor had been working as a truck loader in a lumberyard out toward Petal, Mississippi, "The Checkers Capital of America," for six months, living alone in a crummy transient hotel in Hattiesburg, drinking too much, and thinking hard about Lula and their son, Pace. He hadn't known how awful it would be not to see them at all, especially Pace. During the almost ten years he'd spent in prison on the armed robbery conviction he'd kept alive the idea that when he got out they'd all be together and life could continue from there. Once he'd seen Pace and Lula, however, he'd panicked and run. The time since then had been hell for him. Sailor hated his life in Hattiesburg, where he'd gone for no reason other than he'd once heard a fellow inmate talk about how beautiful Hattiesburg was in the spring when the magnolias blossomed. The magnolias blossomed all right, but their beauty did not improve Sailor's mood. He needed a change, and New Orleans, where he and Lula had been happy for a few days a decade ago, was an easy target.

Sailor was thirty-two and a half years old, but he felt a lot older. The hard time in Huntsville had changed him, he knew that. Very little that he observed about the workings of the world made sense. Without the hope of ever again seeing the only two people he cared anything about, there didn't seem much point to life. *His* life, anyway. The hour passed and Sailor rose when he heard the passenger page for the bus to New Orleans.

He stowed his suitcase in the overhead rack and took a seat next to a window. Just as the bus turned down the street toward Interstate 59, Sailor saw a woman get out of a new blue BMW convertible, a cigarette stuck between her teeth, and toss her long black hair back over the collar of her suede jacket. Perdita Durango looked the same as she had ten years earlier, Sailor thought, when she'd dropped off him and her boyfriend Bobby Peru in front of the Ramos Feed Store in Iraaq, Texas. Five minutes later Bobby was dead, Sailor was caught red-handed and Perdita was to hell and gone in the getaway car. Suddenly life seemed a whole lot shorter to Sailor than it had the moment before.

PLAN A

"You're goin' where?"

"New Orleans, Mama, to visit Beany. You remember, Beany Thorn? She wrote invitin' me and Pace, soon as school's out."

"How could I ever forget that wild-ass child? She give away two, or was it three fatherless babies before she was seventeen?"

"One, Mama, and the boy woulda married her only Beany wouldn't. He was gonna be a dogcatcher like his daddy. Other two she had done away with early."

"Cracked up Lord knows how many automobiles, too. And it was her lawyer daddy, Tapping Reeve Thorn, bribed a federal judge and got caught and both he and the judge did three years at some country club in Alabama. Then her mother, Darlette, drank herself brainless and had to be shipped out to a zombie camp up in the Smoky Mountains. After servin' his time, Tap threw himself away on a topless dancer in Charlotte and bought her a condominium. Last I heard he was racin' stock cars at the speedway and there was talk of him bein' indicted again for some junk bond scam. Them Thorns ain't exactly simple to forget, Lula. What's the trashy daughter up to in New Orleans? Hookin'?"

"She's married now, to a good man named Bob Lee Boyle, owns a alligator repellent manufacturin' company. They got a son, Lance, who's six years old; and a new baby girl, Madonna Kim. They live in a fabulous big house in Metairie, over in Jefferson Parish, and Beany says there's plenty of room for Pace and me to stay as long as we want. Plan A is to give my notice at the 7-Eleven."

"Well, that's somethin'."

"Mama, be honest. You got more than a little to be thankful for."

"I'm late for the Daughters, Lula. Let's talk later."

"I'm sure the memory of the Confederacy'd live on without you, Mama, but okay."

"Bye, precious. Love you."

"Love you, too."

"Most gators go for gars. Not often one tackles somethin' much larger, like a human."

"Bob Lee knows more about alligators than anyone, almost," said Beany. "Least more about 'em than anyone I ever knew, not that I ever knew anybody before *cared*."

Lula, Beany, and Bob Lee were sitting at the dining room table in the Boyle house in Metairie. Lula and Pace had flown in late in the afternoon, and they had just finished dinner. Pace and Lance were upstairs in Lance's room watching TV, and Madonna Kim, the baby, was asleep.

"It sounds fascinatin', Bob Lee," Lula said, fiddling with the spoon next to her coffee cup. "How'd you get started on gators?"

"Grew up around 'em in Chacahoula, where my daddy's folks're from. I spent considerable time there as a boy. We lived in Raceland, and my mama's people come from Crozier and Bayou Cane, near Houma. Later I worked for Wildlife Management at Barataria. Started workin' on my own mix after a biology professor from Texas A&M came by askin' questions. Told me a man could make a fortune if he figured out how to keep crocs from devourin' folks live on the Nile River in Africa, for instance, and in India and Malaysia. Crocs and gators react about the same to stimuli. Secret to it's in their secretions, called pheromones. They got glands near the tail, emit scents for matin' purposes. Other ones around their throat mark territory. Beasts use the sense of smell to communicate."

"Lula and I've known a few pussy-sniffin' beasts ourselves," said Beany, making them all laugh.

"If that's true, Lula," said Bob Lee, "then you know what I'm talkin' about. Same thing goes for these reptiles."

"What do y'all call your product?"

"'Gator Gone.' Got it trademarked for worldwide distribution now. Warehouse is in Algiers and the office is on Gentilly, near the Fair Grounds. Come around some time. Right now, though, I gotta go make some phone calls, you ladies don't mind."

"We got lots to talk about," Beany said. "You go on."

Bob Lee got up and went out of the room.

"He's a swell man, Beany. You're fortunate to have him."

"Only man I ever met didn't mind my bony ass!"

They laughed.

"And he don't beg me to give him head all the time, neither. Not that I ever cared particularly one way or the other about it, but it's a change. Only thing is the name, Beany Boyle. Sounds like a hobo stew."

"You look like you-all're doin' just fine."

"Pace sure is a sharpie. Image of his daddy."

"Ain't he? Breaks my heart, too."

"You and Sailor ain't in touch, I take it."

Lula shook her short black hair like a nervous filly in the starting gate.

"Haven't heard from him since he got out of prison over six months ago. We met that one time for about fifteen minutes at the Trailways, and then he just walked off in the night. Guess it was too much to expect we could work anything out. And I think seein' Pace scared Sailor, made those ten years I never went to visit him jump up in his face. I don't know, Beany, it's hard to figure out how I feel for real. And Mama don't make thinkin' for myself any easier."

"Marietta's a vicious cunt, Lula, face it. She ain't got a life and she's afraid you'll get one. That's why she freaked when you and Sailor run off. I'm surprised she let you come here, knowin' how she hates me."

"She don't hate you, Beany, and she ain't really vicious. Also I'm twenty-nine and a half years old now. She can't exactly tell me what I can or can't do."

"Don't stop her from manipulatin' you every chance. So what's the plan?"

"Thought maybe you could work on one with me. I need help and I know it."

Beany reached across the table and held Lula's hand.

"I'm with you, Lula, same as always. We'll figure out somethin'."

The baby began to cry. Beany smiled, squeezed Lula's hand and stood up.

"There's my Madonna Kim," she said. "Another complainin' female. Let's go get her in on this."

POPPY AND PERDITA

Carmine "Poppy" Papavero put his lime green seer-sucker-jacketed right arm around Juju Taylor's D.J. Jazzy Jeff and the Fresh Prince tee-shirted shoulders and smiled.

"You know, Juju, you keep doin' good like this, I'm gonna have to say somethin' nice about you to Mr. Santos."

"It definitely be a pleasure workin' for you, Mr. Papavero. Tell Mr. Santos can't nobody cover like Juju's Jungle Lovers. We handle however much shit you want. Got Lovers be in Alabama, too, you want to spread it out."

"I'll keep it in mind. Meanwhile, you take care of Mississippi north of the Gulf and we'll see how it goes. What's this I hear about an L.A. gang moving in?"

"They show up here we be all over 'em like smoke on links."

Poppy patted Juju on the back, then squeezed his thick neck.

"Be seeing you soon, Juju."

Poppy walked out of the gang's safehouse and saw Perdita Durango leaning against the blue Beamer. He went over and kissed her forehead, which was on a level with his chin. Poppy went six-three and a hard two-forty. Perdita had never had a steady his size before. Poppy punished her during their lovemaking but never to the point where it became painful. She'd learned to enjoy the weight.

Perdita had met Poppy at Johnny Black's Black & Blue Club in Gulfport, where she'd gone with an acquaintance named Dio Bolivar, a local liquor salesman and small-time hoodlum with a pencil-thin mustache and flashy clothes. Poppy had come over to their table and asked what a beautiful lady like her was doing in a low-rent joint with an unsuccessful pimp. Dio heard this and jumped up like a jack-in-the-box, ready to duke until he saw who'd said it.

"Oh, good evenin', Mr. Papavero," Bolivar said, having recognized Crazy Eyes Santos's chief enforcer on the Gulf Coast. Poppy led her away, and that was the last Perdita ever saw of Dio Bolivar.

She had told Poppy about her childhood in Corpus Christi; how her sister, Juana, had been murdered by her husband, Tony, who had also murdered both of his and Juana's daughters before shooting himself, but not much else. She didn't want him to know about the jams she'd been in in Texas and Mexico and California. It was a good idea, Perdita thought, to start fresh, keep her mouth shut and let this big man pay the bills. He didn't seem to mind so long as she kept herself pretty and available. It wasn't hard work and Papavero wasn't nearly as moody as most of the other guys she'd known. Besides, Perdita felt grown up with Poppy, respectable, like a regular woman rather than a piece of Tex-Mex trash. She decided that this was a gig worth holding on to.

"These Jungle guys are turning out better than I thought," Poppy said to Perdita as he drove them away. "They force people to buy shit even if they're not users, just to stay healthy. Not even Santos thought of that!"

Perdita sat in the passenger seat with her body turned toward Poppy, making sure that her tight black skirt rode halfway up her thighs. Poppy looked over at her and stroked her legs with his hairy right hand.

"You really do please me, Perdita," he said. "I never told you, but I was married once. It didn't last too long, about five years. It ended, let's see now, when I was thirty, fifteen years ago. Her name was Dolores, but everybody called her Dolly. She worked in the Maison Blanche on Canal Street when I met her, in the women's apparel department. I went there to buy a birthday present for another girl. I saw Dolly and forgot all about the girl. She had big tits, a big nose and a flat ass. There was something about her, though, that got me, aside from her tits. Dolly had a way of looking at you that made you think she knew all about you, who you really were deep inside. It sounds dumb, I know, but if you'd met her you'd understand."

"It don't sound dumb. I've known people like that. One guy, especially, who was a kind of strange, religious person. He's dead now."

"Yeah? You have? Well, Dolly's the only one I've ever known had that look, like she knew every rotten or good thing you'd ever done in your entire life. It was spooky."

"So what happened to her and you?"

"I married her, like I said. It was going along good enough, I guess, but she didn't like not knowing what I did every day, where I went, and that sometimes I was out until five or six in the morning or took off without telling her for a few days."

Poppy shook his head, remembering.

"No, she didn't like what I was doing. Dolly knew I was moving up in the organization, bringing home more money, which was okay because I'd made her quit her job at the Maison Blanche. But then she wanted a child and no matter what we did, she couldn't get pregnant. We went to a couple of doctors and they both said it was because of some defect she had in her system, and there was no way to correct it. They suggested we adopt, which Dolly didn't want to do. I wouldn't have minded. There's plenty of orphans need homes and that way she could have a kid, but for some reason she didn't want one unless it was her own. Her parents and grandparents were all dead, she didn't have any family but me."

"What color hair did she have?" asked Perdita, lighting up a Marlboro.

"Kind of reddish-blond. Her mother was Polish, she told me, and her father was Czech. She kept pictures of them on the bedroom dresser. I came home one night late, about four A.M., from the Egyptian Sho-Bar on Napoleon Avenue that I was running then, and Dolly wasn't there. At first I thought maybe she'd gone down to the all-night pharmacy on Esplanade for something, but when she wasn't back by five I knew that wasn't it. I looked at the dresser, and the pictures of her parents were gone. Dolly walked out on me. No note, no phone call, nothing. I was upset at first, of course, but after a week I didn't care. I just hoped she was happier wherever she was, and I went on with my life."

Perdita didn't say anything as Poppy sped them south on 59 toward New Orleans. They passed a Greyhound and Perdita thought how much better it was to be traveling in a new BMW than on a bus. She lowered the tinted window a crack and tossed out her cigarette butt. Sailor Ripley saw the blue car zoom by and a cigarette fly out and bounce off the side of the bus just below where he was sitting.

"What do you think, Perdita?" asked Poppy. "Is that a sad story or not?"

"Heard lots sadder," she said.

Poppy Papavero laughed and grabbed her left thigh.

"So have I, pussycat. So have I."

"She left when?"

"Yesterday. I tell you, Dal, this is just another way for Lula to avoid facin' the future, if she's ever gonna have one's worth a thing."

"Marietta, it don't matter how much or how little you fuss. Lula's gonna find herself or not and you can't do nothin' about it."

"Okay, Dal, I believe you, but that still don't make me feel any better. And why is it in the back of my mind I got this sneakin' notion Sailor Ripley ain't out of the picture?"

"He is the boy's father, after all. And it's plain Lula ain't yet resolved her feelin's about him."

"But, Dal, it's been more'n ten years she's had to figure it out."

"That ain't nothin' where love's concerned, Marietta, you know that. And Lula feels guilty as get-out over not havin' gone to see Sailor all that time he was shut away from society. You didn't have no little to do with that, either."

"Dal, I swear on my grandmama Eudora Pace's grave I never told Lula not to visit Sailor. She was just busy bringin' up her son by herself and couldn't never get away."

"This ain't worth our arguin' now, is it? You and I know well enough how much influence you keep over that girl."

"I got to. Look at the fix Lula got herself in the last time she ran off. Mixed up with a bunch of deranged criminals in a West Texas desert, people gettin' shot and killed all around, and her pregnant besides. If Johnnie and I hadn't tracked Lula down in that Big Tuna hellhole who knows where she'd be today? Prob'ly'd have two or three more illegitimate children and be lost out in some godforsaken place like California, surrounded by a hundred kinds of drug-crazed devil worshipers."

"Marietta, how you can carry on. Lula's just in New Orleans visitin' an old friend. It'll be good for her, gettin' away for a bit. By the way, you heard any more from Santos?"

"Two dozen red roses arrived this mornin', with a card."

"I'll be. What'd it say?"

"Oh, somethin' like, 'To Marietta, who always deserves the best, from Marcello.'"

"Natalie Suarez knows someone in N.O. knows Mona Costatroppo, the woman your playmate Crazy Eyes been keepin' down there the last few years."

"So?"

"Natalie says this friend of hers heard from Mona Costatroppo that Santos cut her off flat about a month back, threatened to kill her if she made a fuss."

"Now, Dal, do you believe that? People're always tryin' to find somethin' ugly to talk about. Here you are, always settin' yourself up as the voice of reason far as me and Lula's concerned, and you fall for this silly third-hand gossip out the mouth of a woman we both know don't have the brain of a peacock on mood pills."

"I ain't fell for nothin'. I'm just tellin' you what I hear concerns Santos, is all. It may or may not be true, but it's out there in the air and I thought you deserved to know. Apparently the Costatroppo woman sold some of the jewelry and furniture Santos had given her and moved to New York or Chicago, afraid for her life."

"I'd be more afraid for my life in one of those places than I would down here anywhere. And anyway, how do we know what this Troppo person done to Marcello riled him in the first place, if in fact there's any truth to the story at all?"

"Natalie Suarez claims he just got tired of her after she got a little fat and sloppy. Her friend said she'd developed a drinkin' problem."

"There you are, then! Who wants to be around a drunk?"

"And of course there's his wife, Lina, who pretends ain't a thing wrong."

"Maybe there ain't, Dal, you ever consider that? Marcello's a man knows his own mind, always has. Clyde didn't never have a bad word to say about him when he was alive, and I don't either. I vote we end this part of the conversation right now."

"Fine with me, Marietta. Sorry I couldn't get to Tuesday's meetin' of the Daughters. Louis made me go with him to visit his mama in the nursin' home in Asheville. Don't make no sense draggin' me, I told him, she's so gaga. But I guess it helps him, me bein' there. What'd I miss?"

"Oh, Dal, you won't believe what Esther Pickens heard about Ruby Werlhi and Denise Sue Hilton's son-in-law. You know, Walker French-Jones, the tennis pro?"

BRIGHT LIGHTS, BIG CITY

As soon as Sailor got off the bus he headed toward the Hotel Brazil. He didn't know if it was still there but he didn't bother to check a city directory, figuring he'd find something similar in the neighborhood if necessary. From Elysian Fields he cut across the park, surprised to see so many homeless people camped out and sleeping on benches. He turned left on Frenchmen Street and there it was, the Brazil, looking as dilapidated as it had ten or more years before, but still standing. He entered, asked the elderly white male desk clerk for a room overlooking the street, paid thirty dollars for two days in advance, took his key and hiked up the stairs to the third floor. Sailor could not remember which room he and Lula had stayed in, but this one was pretty close. He opened the window, leaned out and looked east. There was the river, huge and green, with a gray Yugoslav freighter, flanked by black tugs, pushing past the Bienville Wharf.

He lay down on the bed and lit up an unfiltered Camel. The hint of a breeze blew into the room, startling Sailor for a moment. It was unexpected and caused him to shiver, despite the intense heat and high humidity. The Hotel Brazil did not provide room-cooling except during winter, when there was no heat. A strange sensation came over him, as if an invisible, gauzy-feeling substance had intruded on the finger of fresh air and draped itself around his body. Sailor's cigarette burned down steadily between the index and second fingers of his right hand, its ash building but remaining attached due to his immobility.

"Lula's here," Sailor said. He trembled and the ash fell off the cigarette onto the floor.

Sailor swung his legs off the bed, stood up and went back over to the window. He took a swift drag on the Camel and flicked it out into the street. Directly below, two old men, one black the other white, were struggling over a half-pint bottle of Old Crow.

"That's mine!" the black man shouted.

"Hell it is!" said the white man.

"I bought it, I'mo drink it!"

"Bullshit! Half's my money! Give it!"

"I knock yo teef out, ugly mufuck, you had 'ny."

The white man lurched toward the black man, fell to his knees and wrapped his arms around the black man's legs.

"Let go, fo I smack yo bleach head!"

"Mine, mine!" screeched the white man, who was crying now.

The black man raised the bottle to his mouth and took a long swig. People walking along the sidewalk avoided them. The black man staggered to the curb, dragging the white man, who clung stubbornly to his legs. The black man stopped and took another long drink, killing the bottle.

"Here go, mufuck," he said, bringing the dark brown bottle down hard on the white man's head.

The glass shattered, cutting into the bald, freckled skull of the genuflecting man, the pieces scattering over the sidewalk. The white man did not release his hold on the black man's legs. He remained attached, sobbing loudly, his body heaving, the top of his head a puddle of blood and broken glass. The black man balanced himself with his hands on the hood of a dirty beige '81 Cutlass parked by the curb and kicked loose his legs, leaving the white man slumped on the ground as he stumbled away.

Sailor looked down at the crying, bleeding man whom passersby continued to ignore. A New Orleans police car pulled up in front of the hotel and two cops got out. They lifted the injured man, holding him under each arm, deposited him in the backseat and drove off. The black man, Sailor noticed, was sitting on the ground, leaning against a shabby white building on the opposite side of the street. Above the man's head, in faded black paint, were the words JESUS DIED FOR THE UNGODLY. The man's eyes were closed and there were splotches of bright red, undoubtedly the other man's blood, on the front of his short-sleeved white shirt.

Sailor went back to the bed and lay down on his back. He had no idea where to begin looking for Lula, and he did not want to contact Marietta. A picture of Perdita Durango standing on the street in Hattiesburg flashed in his brain. Lula used to say the world was weird on top, he thought. She sure was right there. Sailor rolled over into a fetal position and closed his eyes.

SAVING GRACE

Elmer Désespéré put his railroad engineer's cap over his stringy yellow-white hair and went out. At the foot of the stairs of his rooming house he stopped and took a packet of Red Man chewing tobacco from the back pocket of his Ben Davis overalls, scooped a wad with the thumb and index finger of his right hand and planted it between his teeth and cheek in the left side of his mouth. Elmer replaced the packet in his pocket and strolled down Claiborne toward Canal Street. The night air felt thick and greasy, and the sidewalk was crawling with people sweating, laughing, fighting, drinking. Police cars, their revolving red and blue lights flashing, prowled up and down both sides of the road. Trucks rumbled like stampeding dinosaurs on the overhead highway, expelling a nauseating stream of diesel mist.

Elmer loved it all. He loved being in the city of New Orleans, away from the farm forever, away from his daddy, Hershel Burt, and his older brother, Emile; though they'd never bother a soul again, since Elmer had destroyed the both of them as surely as they had destroyed his mama, Alma Ann. He had chopped his daddy and brother into a total of exactly one hundred pieces and buried one piece per acre on the land Hershel Burt owned in Evangeline Parish by the Bayou Nezpique. After doing what he had to, Elmer had walked clear to Mamou and visited Alma Ann's grave, told her she could rest easy, then hitchhiked into N.O.

Alma Ann had died ten years ago, when Elmer was nine, on November 22d, the birthday of her favorite singer, Hoagy Carmichael. Alma Ann's greatest pleasure in life, she had told Elmer, was listening to the collection of Hoagy Carmichael 78s her daddy, Bugle Lugubre, had left her. Her favorite tunes had been "Old Man Harlem," "Ole Buttermilk Sky," and Bugle's own favorite, "Memphis in June." But after Alma Ann was worked to death by Hershel Burt and Emile, Hershel Burt had busted up all the records and dumped the pieces in the Crooked Creek Reservoir. Now Elmer had buried Hershel Burt just like he'd buried Bugle Lugubre's Hoagy Carmichael records. It made Elmer happy to think that the records could be replaced and that Hoagy Carmichael would live on forever through them. Alma Ann would live on as well, by virtue of Hoagy's music and Elmer's memory, but Hershel Burt and Emile were wiped away clean as bugs off a windshield in a downpour.

The only thing Elmer needed now was a friend. He'd taken the two-thousand-four-hundred-eighty-eight dollars his daddy had kept in Alma Ann's cloisonné button box, so Elmer figured he had enough money for quite a little while to come. Walking along Claiborne, watching the people carry on, Elmer felt as if he were a visitor to an insane asylum, the only one with a pass to the outside. When he reached Canal, Elmer turned down toward the river. He was looking for a tattoo parlor to have his mama's name written over his heart. A friend would know immediately what kind of person Elmer was, he thought, as soon as he saw ALMA ANN burned into Elmer's left breast. The friend would understand the depth of Elmer's loyalty and sincerity and never betray or leave him, this Elmer knew.

The pain was gone, too. The constant headache Elmer had suffered for so many years had vanished as he'd knelt next to Alma Ann's grave in Mamou. She soothed her truest son in death as she had in life. Jesus was bunk, Elmer had decided. He'd prayed to Jesus after Alma Ann had gone, but he had not been delivered. There had been no saving grace for Elmer until he'd destroyed the two marauding angels and pacified himself in the name of Alma Ann. It was he who shone, not Jesus. Jesus was dead and he, Elmer, was alive. He would carry Alma Ann's name on his body and his friend would understand and love him for it.

"Say, ma'am," Elmer said to a middle-aged woman headed in the opposite direction, "there a place near here a sober man can buy himself a expert tattoo?"

"I suppose there must be," she said, "farther along closer to the port."

"Alma Ann blesses you, ma'am," said Elmer, walking on, spitting tobacco juice on the sidewalk.

The woman stared after him and was surprised to see that he was barefoot.

HEART TALK

"Speakin' of abuse?" said Beany, as she fed Madonna Kim her bottle of formula. "I didn't know that's what Elmo was doin' until I saw them women on Oprah's show talkin' about how their husbands, mostly ex now, 'course, like Elmo and me, used to take all kinds of advantages. Worst is the ones beat 'em up, which Elmo only done once to me, when he was stewed and I threw a pet rock at him after I'd found out from Mimsy Bavard the baby Etta Foy was havin' was his."

It was nine A.M. and Beany and Lula were sitting on the front porch swing of the house in Metairie, discussing men. Pace and Lance were on the lawn shooting rubber-tipped arrows at a target, trading off turns with the only bow.

"Bob Lee wouldn't never hit me, even if he thought he had a reason to. He takes off, he's angry enough. Comes back about two hours later and raids the refrigerator."

"Where's he go?"

"Oh, mostly he'll drive around, or maybe go to a movie at the mall. One time he come home with this really strange look on his face. I asked him, 'You still mad at me, Bob Lee?' I don't recall now what it was set him off in the first place. I think somethin' to do with my lettin' Lance cry too long. Bob Lee's a real softie it comes to babies cryin', he'll just run and pick 'em up. I told him you got to let 'em settle down on their own or they just get so damned spoiled they're always fussin'. Anyway, he come in lookin' like a wild dog just bit the head off his favorite cat. And Lord knows, Bob Lee loves cats."

"How come you ain't got any then?"

"Lergic. Me and Lance both. Bugs Bob Lee, but nothin' we can do about it. I tell him he's got his gators to pet."

"So what weirded him out?"

"I'm tellin' you, this movie he seen, called *Blue Velvet.* You seen it?"

"No. Ain't heard of it."

"After he seen it, Bob Lee couldn't even eat. He wouldn't let me go see it, though I wanted to. I woulda gone anyway, of course, but with Lance bein' a baby then I didn't get a chance. Bob Lee told me he coulda never imagined the awful behavior went on in that movie. He did say there was a couple pretty women in it."

"Was it a porno?"

"Don't think so. Bob Lee don't care for 'em, though I don't mind 'em once in awhile if there's some laughs in it. Sorta horrifies Bob Lee I can take sex less than serious sometimes. This *Blue Velvet*, though, must be somethin' else entirely. He said it made his brain shut down, like all the fuses blew."

"We oughta rent it for the VCR."

"Good idea. Watch it while Bob Lee's at work."

Pace came up on the porch and sat on the top step. Lance was still busy shooting arrows.

"What we gonna do today, Mama?" Pace asked.

"Thought maybe we'd go swimmin'. You like that idea?"

"I suppose."

"C'mon, Pace!" Lance shouted. "It's your turn!"

"Comin'!" Pace shouted back. He looked at Beany and said, "Lance ain't a bad kid, but he goes bugshit you leave him alone a minute. You notice that, Aunt Beany?"

Pace got up and resumed playing with Lance.

"That boy is a natural, Lula," said Beany. "Don't know where you got him."

"Got him from Sailor is where."

"He ever hit you?"

"Sail? You jokin'? Sailor Ripley wouldn't raise a hand to me or nobody."

"Hold it, Lula. He killed a man. Bob Ray Lemon. Remember?"

"That was different. He thought Bob Ray was tryin' to harm me. Imagine it still's eatin' at him, what he done."

"Bet he misses seein' his boy."

Lula watched Pace pull back the bowstring and send an arrow into the very heart of the target. Tears burst from her eyes and Beany handed her one of Madonna Kim's spit-up towels.

"He's just so beautiful and precious to me, Beany," Lula said, wiping her face, "just like Lance and Madonna Kim are to you. But he's really all

I got in the world. If anything bad happened to Pace, I don't know what I'd do. Shoot myself, prob'ly."

Madonna Kim coughed and knocked the bottle away. Beany put her over her shoulder and patted the baby's back.

"Stop talkin' foolish, Lula. Ain't nothin' but good gonna ride that boy."

Madonna Kim let out a burp so loud that it startled Beany and Lula, and they laughed.

"Oh, Beany, I'm so glad I come to see you. It really means a lot to me, your takin' us in this way."

"Hush. Means a lot to me, too."

They looked at their boys playing on the grass in the morning sun, wrestling now, rolling around and laughing, Pace allowing the weaker, smaller Lance to pin him. They jumped up and ran over to the porch.

"Mama?" said Lance. "Pace says we're goin' swimmin'. Is it time yet?"

"Carmine, *come va?*"

"I am fine, Marcello. I know you are, too."

"And how is that?"

"The other night I ran into the Calabrese, Jimmie Hunchback, at Broussard's. I asked him about you, and he said, *'Il vecchio porta bene gli anni.'* "

Papavero heard Santos chuckle at the other end of the line.

"Old man, he calls me," said Santos. "I should call him up and tell him this old man still knows how *tenere il coltello dalla parte del manico.*"

Poppy laughed. "Nobody will ever doubt that you know how to hold the knife, Marcello, or that you would use it if you had to. *Non ho notizie di te da molto tempo.* What can I do for you?"

"I wanted you to know that I'm coming in two days. The thing with Mona has caused some trouble there I must take care of myself."

"*La Signora Costatroppo ha fatto parlare di sé.* The lady has caused much talk."

Santos sighed. "She knows too much, Carmine. *Il passato non si distrugge.* The past cannot be undone, but *non si sa mai quando può succedere una disgrazia.* One never knows when an accident might happen."

"One would think that after all you've done for her, given her, she would be more respectful."

"My friend, *a chi tutto, a chi niente.* Who can say what is enough or not enough for anyone? *Non fa niente,* it doesn't matter. I know where she hides and soon I can tell you, *mi sono liberato di un incomodo.*"

"Your life is long, Marcello. There is much to look forward to."

"Mona was once a morsel to be savored, Carmine, but *un pranzo comprende molte pietanze.* A meal consists of many dishes. Already *la ferita si sta cicatrizzando.* The wound heals as we speak. I have sent *un colpo di vento,* a gust of wind, to blow away the problem."

"I will be glad to see you, Marcello. I'll be here."

"*Bene.* I may need your help on a couple of matters. The business goes well with the *tutsuns?*"

"*Molto bene*, better than I expected."

"You are a smart man, Carmine. You earn my respect. *Ciao*."

"*Ciao*, Marcello. *Buon viaggio*."

A WALK IN THE PARK

The air seemed cooler in Audubon Park. Lula and Beany, who was carrying Madonna Kim in a pouch strapped to her chest, strolled slowly beneath the magnolia trees as Pace and Lance ran ahead, playing tag. Lula and the boys had swum most of the morning, and then they had all gone to the Camellia Grill and eaten a large, wonderful lunch which they were now walking—in the boys' case, running—off.

"I can't believe how safe and fine I feel," said Lula, "just bein' here. It ain't nearly so hot as I thought it'd be."

"Wish you lived nearby, Lula. It'd be great to be able to hang out together like this whenever we wanted to. And the kids are gettin' along so good."

Lula watched the boys circle a tree and take off at breakneck speed toward the lake, Lance chasing the fleeter Pace.

"Pace!" she shouted. "You take care Lance don't fall in!"

"I will, Mama!" Pace yelled, just before he and his pursuer disappeared behind a boathouse.

"I gotta admit, Beany, Sailor been on my mind a whole lot lately, more than I'm comfortable about. I mean, he ain't never been off it entire since we met when I was sixteen. It's amazin', but that's almost half my life."

"No point in fightin' it either, sweetie. Some things just meant to be. Guess it was destiny you and him'd be matched. But you don't even know where he might be, huh?"

Lula shook her head no, reached back with her right hand and wiped the sweat off the back of her neck.

"Don't know that I even want to see Sailor, really," she said. "Truth is, though, no guy I been out with before or since ever thrilled me like Sailor. I mean, really *thrilled* me, Beany, you know?"

"Not sure I do, Lula."

"Like I would always, *always,* get excited that Sailor was comin' to get me, or I was goin' to meet him. Even when things between us wasn't so smooth. Didn't ever seem to matter what kinda problems we were havin', or what else was goin' on, I'd get a actual *thrill* thinkin' about him. That never's happened with another man, Beany, not like that. There's been moments I been happy, of course, and thought I was doin' all right. But I made love enough with other boys to know there can't never be anyone but him makes a difference in my soul."

Lula stopped walking and Beany stopped, too. Lula put her forehead against the back of Beany's right shoulder and let the tears come. She was shaking, and Beany started to turn around, but Lula held her still.

"Wait, Beany, just let me rest my head on you like this. I'll be fine in a minute and I don't want you to look at me until I am."

Beany didn't move.

"There," Lula said, raising her head and smiling, giving her hair a shake, wiping her eyes with the backs of her hands, "I'm better. Guess that's what they mean, havin' a shoulder to cry on," she laughed. "Never took it for real quite the same way before."

Beany looked into her friend's red, watery, large gray eyes.

"You always got me to cry on, Lula," she said, "just like I hope I always got you."

Lula hugged Beany, being careful not to squeeze too tightly and crush Madonna Kim between them.

"You got me, Miss Beany, forever."

They disengaged and began walking again. Madonna Kim snoozed peacefully.

"Hey, where'd them boys go?" said Lula.

"Prob'ly runnin' around the lake. We'll find 'em. Lance been here lots of times. They won't get lost."

Just then Lance appeared from behind the opposite side of the boat-house and ran over to Beany and Lula.

"I can't find Pace," he said. "He must be hidin' on me."

Lula shivered. "Where'd you see him last?" she asked.

"I tagged him and run on ahead, and when he didn't catch up I turned around and Pace wasn't nowhere. Mama, can I get a ice cream?"

Lula took off running toward the lake. She followed the path around the water but did not see Pace. She stopped to rest and think, and Lance came running up behind her.

"Aunt Lula, Mama says come quick. A lady saw Pace go off with some man."

"Oh, shit. Oh, shit," Lula kept saying, as she and Lance ran back toward Beany.

Beany and a thin, gray-haired woman of about fifty, wearing yellow shorts, a red tank top and green Nike running shoes, with a Sony Walkman headset radio hanging around her neck, were standing next to the boathouse.

"Lula, listen," said Beany. "This woman says she saw a boy looked like Pace walk away with a man."

"The boy was about ten or eleven, with black hair," the woman said. "He was wearin' blue jeans and a blue tee shirt said 'Tarheels' on it in white block letters."

"Oh, shit," said Lula. "That's him, that's Pace!"

"Well, when I saw him I was joggin' into the park on the north path there, and this boy was holdin' hands with a young man not much more than a boy himself, maybe eighteen, nineteen. Was an odd-lookin' young man, too. Real slight build, wearin' overalls and a kind of railroad engineer's cap, with long, dirty-blond-lookin' curly hair hangin' down under it."

"Pace wouldn't just go off with some stranger!" Lula said.

"Are you sure this guy in the overalls wasn't pullin' Pace along with him?" Beany asked the woman.

"He mighta been, I don't know. I just ran past 'em, goin' kinda slow, of course, so I got a good look at 'em both."

Lula ran to the north path and followed it out of the park to the street. She stood there, breathing hard, looking each way, but there was nobody else around. Lula ran down the street to where it intersected a main thoroughfare. Cars whizzed by in both directions.

Lula grabbed a young black woman who was walking by and yelled at her, "Did you see my son? He's ten years old and has black hair and he's wearin' a Carolina Tarheels tee shirt. A white man wearin' overalls just kidnapped him!"

"No, lady," said the young woman, "I ain't seen him."

Lula let go and fell to her knees.

"Oh, shit! Oh, shit! Oh, shit!" she cried. "Sailor, Sailor, I need you now!"

ONE NEVER KNOWS

Mona Costatroppo looked out the window of her room in the Drake Hotel in Chicago. Lake Michigan, she thought, staring at it, was as big as an ocean.

"What's the name again, this beach here?" she asked Federal Agents Sandy Sandusky and Morton Martin, both of whom were seated on the couch under a hideous oil painting of a tropical sunset.

"Oak Street," Sandusky said. "That's Oak Street beach."

"About a billion bodies on it," said Mona, "look like flies on dogshit." She turned away from the window.

"So, you'll guarantee if I tell you all I know about Santos's organization you'll set me up someplace with a new identity?"

"Federal Witness Protection Program," said Martin. "Even Europe, you want to go there."

Mona nodded. "Okay, you bums get outta here now, let me think this over."

The agents rose together and Sandusky said, "We'll be here tomorrow morning at ten o'clock, Ms. Costatroppo."

"Never figured anybody'd be callin' me Miz, 'less slavery got legal again. You be here what time you want. But now, get out."

The agents left and Mona poured a healthy dose of Bombay Sapphire into a glass and drank it fast. She poured some more into the glass, emptying the fifth she'd bought that morning, and was about to swallow it when there was a knock at the door.

"Who's there?" she asked.

"Valet. I have your laundry."

Mona walked over, the glass in her left hand, and turned the doorknob with her right.

"Put it on the bed," she said, walking toward the window, not bothering to see who it was coming through the door.

As Mona lifted the glass to her lips and opened her mouth, she heard a loud pop. She dropped the glass and started to turn around, but before she could there was another loud pop, which she did not hear. Mona sat down suddenly on the floor, her head banging hard against the window that overlooked Oak Street beach and Lake Michigan, but she didn't feel a thing.

NIGHT AND FOG

Sailor was awakened in his room at the Hotel Brazil by a series of shrieks coming from the hallway. He jumped out of bed and stubbed the big toe on his left foot on the leg of the table next to the door, opened the door and limped into the hall. Two women of indeterminate age, one blond, one red-haired, were rolling on the carpet in front of the staircase attempting to mutilate each other in any way possible. They were screaming and cursing at the top of their voices. Sailor stood by the door to his room rubbing his sore toe and watching the women wrestle. He looked at his watch: it was a couple of ticks shy of six A.M. The more heavyset of the women, the blonde, stood and grabbed the redhead and dragged her to her feet, then ran her into the wall, knocking the red-haired wrestler stupid and busting her nose. Blood spurted on the wall, the floor and the blond bruiser, further infuriating her. She yelled, "You cunt!" and practically picked up the bleeder and threw her down the stairs. The blonde stood in the hallway panting hard, wiped her face with her meaty right forearm, and spotted Sailor standing there in his underwear with his left leg resting on his right knee, holding his toe.

"What the fuck you lookin' at, buster?" she said.

Sailor lowered his leg and looked behind him. He was the only spectator. He turned back to the woman.

"Thanks for the wake-up," he said, and went back inside his room.

The screaming ceased and Sailor limped over to the washbasin, where he rinsed his face, brushed his teeth and combed his hair. He pulled on his clothes and went out. There was no sign of the battling women, only a neck-high smear of blood on the wall.

The morning air was warm and foggy. Sailor headed for Rod's, a 24-hour cafe on Ursulines Street just off Decatur in the Quarter. He bought an early edition of the *Times-Picayune* from a machine, thinking he'd check out the job opportunities. Sitting at the counter in Rod's, Sailor ordered chicory coffee and a Spanish omelette. He lit up his first Camel of the day and opened the paper. There on the lower right of the front page was the heading, BOY VISITING CITY IS KIDNAPPED. Sailor read the article that followed.

> A ten-year-old boy, Pace Roscoe Ripley, visiting the city with his mother, Lula Pace Fortune, of Bay St. Clement, N.C., was kidnapped in broad daylight yesterday afternoon while on an outing with friends in Audubon Park. A woman who apparently witnessed the abduction while she was jogging in the park described the kidnapper as being approximately eighteen or nineteen years old, with long blond hair, wearing striped overalls and a railroad engineer's cap. Pace Ripley was described by his mother's friend, Mrs. Beany Thorn Boyle, of Metairie, as under five feet tall, black hair, wearing blue jeans, a blue and white tee shirt with the word "Tarheels" on it, and white sneakers. Anyone with relevant information should contact the New Orleans Police Department. Tel. 555-0099.

"You got a directory here?" Sailor asked the fry cook.

"On the floor behind you," he said, without turning around. "Under the phone."

Sailor flipped to the section listing residents of Metairie, and found BOYLE BOB LEE AND BEANY . . . 833 CHARITY . . . 555-4956. He put in a coin and dialed.

"Hello?" said Bob Lee.

"This is Sailor Ripley, Pace's daddy. Is Lula there?"

"Hold the phone."

Sailor dropped his cigarette and stepped on it.

"Sailor?! Is it really you?"

"Oh, peanut, yes! It's me! I'm in N.O. I just read about Pace in the paper."

"Please come here now, Sail. I don't know what to do."

"Don't do nothin', honey. I'm comin', your Sailor's comin'!"

Sailor hung up and ran out of the cafe. The fry cook heard the screen door slam, scooped up the half-done omelette from the grill and tossed it in the trash.

"Mrs. Fortune?"

"Speakin'."

"This is Beany Boyle, in New Orleans? Lula's friend. Used to be I was Beany Thorn?"

"I remember you. Why are you callin' me? Has somethin' happened to Lula?"

"No, ma'am, not to Lula, but I got some terrible news."

"Go on."

"Pace been kidnapped, Mrs. Fortune. We was all takin' a walk in the park and the boys, Pace and my son, Lance, took off outta Lula's and my sight—I was carryin' my baby, Madonna Kim?—and someone snatched Pace."

"I knew somethin' awful'd happen if Lula left home! Put her on the line!"

"She's kinda out of it right now, Mrs. Fortune. She asked me to call you."

"You put Lula on the line right now, dammit!"

"I really can't, she's too broke up to talk to you. The police are handlin' it and Sailor's here."

"*He's* there?! Satan takes a holiday!"

Marietta hung up.

"Mrs. Fortune? Mrs. Fortune, are you there?"

Beany hung up.

As soon as she'd cut Beany off, Marietta dialed Santos's private number. A man answered on the third ring.

"Bayou Enterprises."

"This is Marietta Pace Fortune, Clyde Fortune's widow. I got to speak to Marcello Santos right away! It's urgent!"

"Wait," the man said.

Two minutes later, Santos came on the line.

"Yes, Marietta. How pleasant to hear from you."

"Marcello, somethin' real *un*pleasant's happened. My grandboy,

Pace—you met him at my birthday party. Remember, he asked you about your thumb?"

"I do."

"He's been kidnapped, in New Orleans!"

"When did this happen?"

"Yesterday, I believe. I just got the call. You gotta help find him! Lula's there and that horrible Sailor Ripley's with her. I'm gonna be about flat outta my mind in a New York minute!"

"Calm yourself, Marietta. I will do everything I can, of course. As it happens, I am about to leave very shortly for New Orleans. Before I go, I will contact people there who may be able to help. I will call you from Louisiana as soon as I have any information."

"He's my only grandchild, Marcello! Lula knew how to raise him, this wouldn'ta happened."

"Do you know how the kidnap occurred?"

"Someone stole Pace out of a park is all I know."

"The police have been notified?"

"I suppose, yes. But you gotta get him back for me, Marcello, please!"

"I will make a call right away. Do you want me to send someone to stay with you?"

"No, no, I'll get Dal. You need the number where Lula's at?"

"It won't be necessary. Goodbye, Marietta. We will talk again very soon."

"I appreciate this, Marcello. I wouldn't ask if it wasn't so important."

"I know, Marietta, I understand. Goodbye."

Marietta called Dal next.

"Dal? Pace been kidnapped in New Orleans by God knows who and Sailor's there reattachin' himself to Lula! Can you believe my life?! Who'd I kill, Dal? I ask you! What'd I do to deserve this?"

"Slow down a sec, peach. You're sayin' Pace been kidnapped and Sailor'n Lula're back together in N.O.?"

"That's it! That's the package."

"What's bein' done?"

"I just now got off the phone with Santos. He's goin' there himself today. That slut friend of Lula's, Tap Thorn's daughter, called me, said they got the police workin' on it."

"What'd Lula say?"

"She didn't. The Thorn girl wouldn't let her come to the phone. Said Lula was in a faint, or somethin'."

"Wouldn't doubt it. I'll be over in a minute, Marietta. Is the back door unlocked?"

"Good, Dal, yes. Bye!"

Marietta dialed the number of Johnnie Farragut's office in Charlotte.

"JF Investigations. Farragut talkin'."

"Crazed animal stole Pace in N.O. and Lula's back with Sailor!"

"Marietta? What?"

"Pace been kidnapped! Lula and him went to N.O. to visit Tap Thorn's most irresponsible child, the one married a alligator wrestler, and now Sailor's there, too!"

"Have they called the police?"

" 'Course they have. I called Santos soon as I heard, and he's sendin' in the troops. Johnnie, I tell you, it's another trial! Clyde burned to death, Lula run off with a robber and killer, now my precious grandbaby been taken!"

"I'm comin', Marietta. Take me two and a half hours. You call Dal yet?"

"She's on her way."

"Good. I'm leavin' now."

Marietta hung up, staggered into the front room, where only a few days before Pace had unwrapped her birthday presents, and collapsed into Clyde's worn old leather armchair. She heard the back door open and close.

"Marietta? Where are you?"

"In here, Dal."

Dalceda Delahoussaye came in, dropped to the floor, and hugged Marietta's knees.

"Oh, Marietta, I'm so sorry. This is a nightmare."

"I ain't certain there's a God, Dal, I never been convinced. But one thing I do know, there's a Devil, and he don't never quit."

BROTHERS

Elmer's room was ten feet by ten feet. There were two windows, both of which were half-boarded over and nailed shut; a sink; a single bed; one cane armchair; a small dresser with a mirror attached; and a writing table with a green-shaded eagle-shaped lamp on it. The one closet was empty because Elmer had no clothes other than the ones he wore. He had been meaning to buy some new pants and shirts, but he kept forgetting. Elmer foreswore shoes; they interfered with the electrical power he absorbed from the earth through his feet. In one corner was a pile about two feet high of canned food, mostly Campbell's Pork and Beans and Denison's Chili. On the dresser were two half-gallon plastic containers of spring water and a Swiss Army knife that contained all of the necessary eating untensils plus a can opener. There was no garbage in the room, no empty cans or bottles. Elmer disliked refuse; as soon as he had finished with something, he got rid of it, depositing it in a container on the street.

Pace slept on the bed. Elmer sat in the cane armchair, twirling his hat on the toes of his left foot and looking at the illustrations in his favorite book, *The Five Chinese Brothers*. His mother, Alma Ann, had read this story to him countless times and Elmer knew every word of it by heart. This was fortunate, because Elmer could not read. He'd tried, both in the two years he'd attended school and with Alma Ann, but for some reason he found it impossible to recognize the letters of the alphabet in combination with each other. Elmer had no difficulty identifying them individually, but set up together the way they were in books and newspapers and on signs and other things confused him. He had taken *The Five Chinese Brothers* with him from the farm and he looked at the pictures in it while reciting the story to himself several times a day. Elmer was anxious to show the book to his friend, but he would wait until he was certain Pace was really his friend. Alma Ann had told Elmer that sharing something, even a book, was the greatest gift one human being could bestow upon another. It was very important, she said, to have complete and utter faith in the sharer, to know that he or she would share in return. Elmer was not yet sure of this friend, since he had never had one other than Alma Ann, though he hoped that he and Pace would become perfect companions.

The five Chinese brothers were identical to one another, and they lived with their mother. They had no father. One brother could swallow the sea; another had an iron neck; another could stretch his legs an unlimited distance; another could not be burned; and another could hold his breath forever. Elmer recited the story softly to himself as he looked at the pictures, twirling his engineer's cap for a few minutes on one foot, then switching it to the other. The Chinese brother who could swallow the sea went fishing one morning with a little boy who had begged to accompany him. The Chinese brother allowed the boy to come along on the condition that he obey the brother's orders promptly. The boy promised to do so. At the shore, the Chinese brother swallowed the sea and gathered some fish while holding the water in his mouth. The boy ran out and picked up as many interesting objects that had been buried under the sea as he could. The Chinese brother signaled for his companion to return but the boy did not pay attention to him, continuing to hunt for treasures. The Chinese brother motioned frantically for him to come back, but his little friend did not respond. Finally the Chinese brother knew he would burst unless he released the sea, so he let it go and the boy disappeared. At this point in the story, Alma Ann had always stopped to tell Elmer that this boy had proven not to be the Chinese brother's perfect friend.

The Chinese brother was arrested and condemned to have his head severed. On the day of the execution he asked the judge if he could be allowed to go home briefly and say goodbye to his mother. The judge said, "It is only fair," and the Chinese brother who could swallow the sea went home. The brother who returned was the brother with an iron neck. All of the people in the town gathered in the square to see the sentence carried out, but when the executioner brought down his sword, it bent, and the Chinese brother's head remained on his shoulders. The crowd became angry and decided that he should be drowned. On the day of his execution the Chinese brother asked the judge if he could go home and bid his mother farewell, which the judge allowed. The brother who returned was the one who was capable of stretching his legs. When he was thrown overboard in the middle of the ocean, he rested his feet on the bottom and kept his head above water. The people again became angry and decided that he should be burned.

On the day of the execution, the Chinese brother asked the judge for permission to go home to say goodbye to his mother. The judge said, "It is only fair." The brother who returned was the one who could not catch on fire. He was tied to a stake and surrounded by stacks of wood that caught fire when lit, but the Chinese brother remained unscathed. The people became so infuriated that they decided he should be smothered to death. On the day of his execution, the Chinese brother requested that he be allowed to go home to see his mother. The judge said, "It is only fair," and of course the brother who returned was the one who could hold his breath indefinitely. He was shoveled into a brick oven filled with whipped cream and the door was locked tight until the next morning. When the door was opened and the Chinese brother emerged unharmed, the judge declared that since they had attempted to execute him four different ways, all to no avail, then he must be innocent, and ordered the Chinese brother released, a decision supported by the people. He then went home to his mother with whom he and his brothers lived happily ever after.

Elmer knew that he and Alma Ann could have lived happily ever after had she not been worked to death by Hershel Burt and Emile, who would have also worked him to death had Elmer not executed them. He hoped with all of his might that this boy Pace would be worthy of his friendship and not be like the boy who accompanied the Chinese brother to the sea. Elmer put down *The Five Chinese Brothers* and looked at Pace. The boy's eyes were open. Elmer stopped twirling his foot.

"You gonna let me go home to my mama?" Pace asked.

Elmer remembered what the judge had said to the Chinese brothers. "It's only fair," he said.

Pace sat up. "Can I go right now?"

"Problem is," said Elmer, "I don't know I can trust you yet."

"Trust me how?"

"To come back."

Pace stared at Elmer's pale blue eyes.

"You're crazy, mister," he said.

"Alma Ann said I weren't, and she knows better'n you."

Pace looked around the room.

"Guess the door's locked, huh?"

Elmer nodded. "I don't guess."

"So I'm a prisoner."

Elmer started twirling his cap on his right foot.

"You'n me is gonna be perfect friends."

"Holy Jesus," said Pace.

Elmer shook his head. "Jesus is bunk."

"I just couldn't handle it, peanut, seein' you and Pace so sudden after all them years livin' on nothin' 'cept hope. Reality's a killer, Lula, you know? That's why I run from you like I done. Been six months now, though, and I'm gettin' used to bein' outside the walls. Might be I'm more ready to deal with things the way they are, includin' you'n Pace."

"If we ever find him."

"We'll find him sweetheart. Ain't no kidnapper gonna keep our fam'ly apart. After all, we're together again, even though the circumstances is rotten."

It was nine A.M. and Sailor and Lula were sitting at the kitchen table in Beany and Bob Lee's house having coffee. They'd been awake most of the night, not talking very much, mostly just holding and looking at one another and crying. They'd finally fallen asleep in each other's arms, fully clothed, emotionally exhausted, on the living-room floor. Lance had awakened them about an hour ago, shaking Lula, saying, "Y'all can use my bed, Aunt Lula. I'm up." The telephone rang and Beany came into the kitchen from the laundry room and answered it.

"Boyle home."

She listened for a few seconds, then handed the phone to Lula.

"Police, for you."

"This is Lula Fortune. Yes, Detective Fange, of course we can. My boy's daddy's here now, he'll be comin' with us. Soon as possible, I understand. Bye."

She handed the phone back to Beany, who hung it up.

"Detective Fange wants us to come down to the police station, Beany, see if we can recognize any faces in their suspect books we mighta noticed in the park."

"I'll go next door right now, make sure Tandy Flowers can watch the kids."

A half hour later Sailor, Lula, and Beany were on their way to New Orleans police headquarters in Beany's red 1988 Toyota Cressida station wagon. Sailor and Lula sat in the backseat, holding hands and not talking, while Beany drove. She took Bonnabel Boulevard to Metairie Road, turned left and followed it west into Orleans Parish until they hit the Interstate, which she seldom used, preferring to drive on surface streets; but today was different, they were in a hurry, so Beany braved the truck traffic and headed downtown on Highway 10.

"You don't have to come in, Sailor, you don't want to," Lula said, after Beany had parked the wagon and they were walking across the street to the station. "No need for you to be uncomfortable."

"It's okay, Lula. These kinda cops ain't much compared to them old boys at Huntsville. In there you blink more'n twice a hour and the man figures that's one too many, he'll lay your head open quicker'n grain goes through a pigeon. I'll be fine, honey, thanks for thinkin' of it."

Detective Fange gave Beany and Lula several large books of mug shots to look through. Sailor sat next to them at the table, thinking that he might recognize one or two men he'd known in North Carolina or Texas prisons. Fange was a short, stout, dark-haired man in his mid-forties. He had a deep triangular crease in the center of his forehead that twitched every few seconds, and he had a habit of smiling briefly after he spoke a sentence.

"You even think you seen one of these fellas in Audubon Park, you holler, right?" said Fange, punctuating this order by exposing his tobacco-stained teeth for a half-second.

The two women nodded.

"I'll be in my office, two doors down, you need me."

After Fange had gone, Beany said, "That triangle on his forehead? That's right where the third eye is."

"Third eye?" said Lula. "What are you talkin' about?"

"It's the mystical one allows a person to see into the soul. Read about it when I was pregnant with Madonna Kim."

"Beany, I just ain't up for that strange shit right now. Let's go over these faces."

Beany and Lula looked carefully at each photo, full-face and profile of every man and a few women, but recognized none of them. Sailor didn't see anyone he knew until they were halfway through the final book.

"I know him," he said, pointing to a particularly ugly white man who looked a lot like former President of the United States Lyndon Baines

Johnson. "He bunked in Walls Unit at Huntsville, same as me. Afton Abercrombie, that's him. Everybody called him LBJ, 'cause of the resemblance. He hated bein' called that since he was convinced it was LBJ allowed the Mafia to assassinate John F. Kennedy in Texas. Claimed Johnson was in cahoots with the Dallas organized crime people who done it. Abercrombie's kind of a nut about the subject, reads all the books come out concernin' the case. Says Crazy Eyes Santos had a lot to do with it, too."

"What was he in for?" Beany asked, pointing to Abercrombie's picture.

"Multiple rape and attempted murder, I believe. Liked to screw old ladies, *real* old ladies, like in their eighties. He'd get jobs as a janitor or nurse's aide in nursin' homes and attack old women couldn't defend theirselves. Said most of 'em didn't complain, half of 'em bein' senile and not knowin' what was goin' on, and the other half thankful for the attention. What done Abercrombie in was rapin' a dyin' woman hooked up to some breathin' device. Tubes come loose durin' the assault that set off a signal and the nurses caught him in the act."

"One real sick puppy," said Beany.

"No doubt about it," Sailor said. "Abercrombie jacked off a dozen times a day, dreamin' about old ladies. Good poker player, though."

After they'd finished looking through the books, Beany and Lula stopped into Detective Fange's office. He looked up from his desk and the triangle on his forehead twitched.

"No luck, hey, ladies?" he said.

Lula shook her head no.

"What now?" she asked.

"We got bulletins out about the boy, and officers showin' copies of the photo of him you give us. Any information turns up, I'll let you know."

"We're gonna keep searchin' ourselves," said Sailor.

"Expect you would," said Fange. "Let's hope Pace just walks in the door tonight askin' what's for supper. Happens sometimes."

Detective Fange gave a quick smile and returned his attention to the papers on his desk. Sailor took Lula and Beany by the arm and led them to the elevator.

Perdita Durango was sitting in Poppy Papavero's blue BMW in front of the building when Sailor and the two women came out. She was waiting for Poppy, who had told her he had to drop into the police station for a minute in order to renew his hunting license. Poppy had laughed after he said this, and told her to leave the motor running. Perdita dipped her head as soon as she spotted Sailor, hoping he wouldn't look in her direction. He guided his female companions across the street without turning toward Perdita, and she relaxed as she watched him climb into the backseat of a red station wagon and drive away. She wanted to follow Sailor and find out where he was staying. He was the only person alive who could link her to the robbery attempt more than ten years before in Texas. Perdita thought about this while she waited for Poppy. There was only one thing to do, she decided, and that was to kill Sailor.

"Thanks for waiting, sugar," said Poppy, as he got into the car. "Eddie Fange's one serious coonass, but he's dependable as trouble. He sure is upset about this kidnapping case, though, I can tell."

Poppy steered the BMW into traffic.

"What case is that?"

"A ten-year-old boy was kidnapped out of Audubon Park. Here, Eddie gave me a photograph."

Poppy took the picture out of the left breast pocket of his jacket and handed it to Perdita.

"Boy's name and address are on the back," he said. "Some Short Eyes got him, I bet. Those are the scum of the planet. They ought to be shot on the spot and their bodies fed to the gators."

Perdita read the name, Pace Roscoe Ripley, and the address, 833 Charity Street, Metairie, Louisiana. She memorized the address and handed the photo back to Poppy.

"Yes," she said, "that's terrible."

THE CUBAN EMERALD

"You partial at all to hummin'birds?" asked Elmer.

"What you mean, 'partial'?" said Pace.

Elmer Désespéré sat in the cane chair twirling his engineer's cap on the toes of his city-dirt-blackened right foot.

"Mean, do you like 'em."

Pace rested on his elbows, dangling his legs over the edge of the narrow bed.

"Ain't seen many, but I suppose. They just birds."

Elmer bared his mossy teeth. "One time Alma Ann and me spotted a Cuban Emerald," he said, and shifted the cap to his equally soiled left foot. "Alma Ann had her a bird book said that kinda hummin'bird don't naturally get no further north'n South Florida. But we seen it hoverin' over a red lily at Solange Creek. Alma Ann said it musta been brought up by someone to Louisiana 'cause it was too far for it to've strayed."

"What color was it?"

"Green, mostly, like a emerald, and gold."

"You ever seen a emerald?"

"No, but they's green, I guess, which is why the bird's called that."

"What's Cuban about it?"

Elmer frowned and let the hat fall off his foot.

"This'n's special, Alma Ann said. Ain't no other bird like it over the world."

"My mama and me had us a bird, but it died."

Elmer's eyes opened wide. "What kind?"

"Parakeet. It was blue with a white patch on the head. His name was Pablo."

"How'd he die?"

Pace shrugged. "We just found him one mornin' lyin' on his side on the floor of his cage. I took him out and looked in his mouth."

"Why'd you do that?"

"What the doctor always does to me when I'm sick, so I done it to Pablo."

"See anythin'?"

"Not real much. Pulled out his tongue with my mama's eyebrow tweezer. It was pink."

"You bury him?"

"Uh-uh. Mama wrapped Pablo in a ripped-up dishtowel and put him in the freezer."

"Why'd she do that?"

"We was gonna burn him later, but we forgot. Mama says throwin' a body on a fire's the only way to purify it and set free the soul. The kind of Indians they got in India do it, Mama says. But we just forgot Pablo was in the freezer till a bunch of time later when Mama was cleanin' it out and found the dishtowel all iced up. She run hot water over it and unrolled it and there was Pablo, blue as always."

"What'd she do?"

"Stuffed him down the disposal and ground him up."

Elmer whistled through his green teeth. "Don't guess that done heck for his soul."

Pace lay back on the bed and crossed his arms over his chest.

"I reckon his soul had pretty well froze solid by then," he said.

"If I ever had a Cuban Emerald died on me, I wouldn't burn it, or stuff it in no disposal, neither. I'd eat it."

Pace closed his eyes. "The beak, too? Bird beaks is awful sharp."

"Yes, I believe I would. I'd swallow it beak and all, so my insides'd glow emerald green."

"Don't know how I ever coulda thought you was crazy, Elmer. I apologize."

Elmer nodded. " 'Preciate it."

Santos looked in the mirror over the washbasin in the restroom of his office on the top floor of the Bayou Enterprises building on Airline Highway in Kenner and adjusted his hairpiece. He used a wet tissue to scrub off the excess mucilage that had trickled down and dried on his forehead. Santos took off his yellow-framed dark glasses and stared at himself. He hated the nickname Crazy Eyes, but he had to agree with the old Don, Pietro Pericolo, who had given it to him when he was the Don's driver, that his eyes were indeed very strange. The red pupils spun and danced inside the green irises, which were surrounded by yellow sparks. Santos put his sunglasses back on. The old Don had been dead for many years now, and Marcello still missed him. Don Pericolo had kept his word and made certain that Santos was in position to take over the organization when the stomach cancer claimed him. On his deathbed, the old Don had motioned for Santos to come closer, and whispered in his ear, "*Che cosa viene appresso,* Marcello?" Then Don Pericolo had died, his last taste of life softly settling on Santos's face.

"What comes next, Don Pericolo?" Santos said to his own reflection.

He went into his office and sat down behind the gigantic oak desk that had been built in Palermo more than one hundred years before for Lupo Sanguefreddo, Don Pericolo's predecessor. Santos pressed a button that was on the underside of the right top drawer and the door to an outer room opened, admitting Carmine Papavero.

"Marcello, you look *meraviglioso!*" said Carmine.

"Sit," Santos said, motioning with his right hand to a chair on the opposite side of the desk. "There is a serious matter that I would appreciate your trying to do something about. A young boy has been kidnapped here in New Orleans, the grandson of an old friend of mine. I want you to find him, if possible."

"Marcello, I know of this situation already. I have a photograph of the boy."

Carmine took the photo out of his pocket and put it on Santos's desk. "Is this the grandson of your friend?" he asked.

"It is. How did you get this?"

"From Eddie Fange, the detective who takes care of the Orleans Parish payoffs. It's his case."

"Very good, Carmine. My friend is very worried about the boy, as you can imagine."

"Of course, Marcello. It's a horrible thing, the theft of a child."

"*Tutto ciò mi preoccupa.* The way the world is today worries me. With all these *pazzi* running loose, nobody is safe, not even a small boy."

Carmine nodded. "I have a description of the kidnapper. He was *scalzo,* barefoot. An insane person."

Santos sighed deeply. "I must call the child's grandmother now and comfort her. Go and find out what you can."

Carmine stood, picked up the photo and replaced it in his coat pocket.

"Please convey to her my sympathies," he said, and left the room.

Santos nodded and began dialing Marietta's number. She answered before the second ring had ended.

"Lula?" Marietta shouted.

"It is I, Marietta, Marcello."

"Oh, Marcello, I'm frantic. There ain't been no word yet."

"I just wanted to inform you that my people are doing everything they can."

"Dal and Johnnie are helpin' me get through this. They're lambs."

"Marietta, you know I think a great deal of you. Had it not been for my respect for Clyde, things could have been different."

"Let's not talk about that kind of thing now. I'm way too upset to consider mighta-beens. I appreciate your efforts on behalf of my family. I'm in your debt."

"No, Marietta, where we are concerned there is no debt, only friendship."

"Marcello, if some maniacal creature's harmed my beautiful grandboy I'll just die!"

"It is at such moments that my old friend Don Pericolo would say, *non bisogna abbattersi così facilmente.* One should not get discouraged so easily. You must remain strong."

"Yes, Marcello, you're right, of course."

"We will speak soon, Marietta. Goodbye."

"Bye."

Marietta hung up and wiped the tears from her eyes with a vermilion silk handkerchief that had belonged to her grandmother, Eudora Pace.

"The gangster got a line on the case yet?" Johnnie asked.

Marietta stared hard at him, then said, "Who ain't a gangster these days, Johnnie Farragut? The whole world's nothin' but a big racket, with one murderin', thievin' bunch tryin' to horn in on another. Least Santos is on our side, and I'm glad we got him."

"Amen," said Dalceda. "Anybody ready for another cocktail?"

NIGHT IN THE CITY

"My daddy murdered a man once," Pace said. "I heard my grandmama talkin' about it with her friend Johnnie, who's a private investigator and carries a gun. Mama thinks I don't know Sailor really killed Bob Ray Lemon, but I do. He'll get you, too, soon as he finds out what's happened and where I am, which'll be any minute. Him or Crazy Eyes Santos, Grandmama's other man friend, who's a big gangster and kills people all the time. Won't bother him a bit to twist your puny chicken head clean off the neck. You'd best just let me go and run for it, or you'll be fish scum, you'll see."

Elmer Désespéré was beginning to realize his mistake. He had grabbed an unworthy boy, someone not suited to be his perfect friend, and he was in a fix over what to do about it.

"I done murdered *two* men," said Elmer, who was sitting in the cane armchair across from where Pace sat on the floor next to the bed. Elmer had tied Pace's hands together behind his back after the boy had attempted to put out Elmer's eyes with the fork part of the Swiss Army knife. "And prob'ly I'll have to murder a mess more before I'm through, includin' you, it looks like."

"Let me go and you won't have to kill me. I won't tell anyone where you live. You don't let me go, they'll find us and kill you sure. Least right now you got a choice."

Elmer stood up. "I got to go out, get some fresh water. I'll figure out later what I'm gonna do, when I talk to Alma Ann. She'll guide my hand."

Elmer took hold of Pace, dragged him into the empty closet and shut the door.

"I wouldn't be surprised she instructs me to twist *your* puny chicken head," Elmer shouted. "Clean off the neck!"

He went out into the street and headed for the Circle K convenience store. This child was a puzzlement, Elmer thought. He would have to be more careful of who he snatched next. Follow him for a while, maybe, see if he acted right. This one weren't no good at all and likely never would be. Can't trust a pretty face, ain't *that* the truth!

Elmer had been thinking so hard about Pace that he did not realize he'd turned the wrong way off Claiborne. Somehow he had wandered onto a street called St. Claude and he was lost. It was very late at night and Elmer missed Alma Ann. He wished she were here and he was tucked into bed with her reading to him. He saw some men gathered up ahead at the corner and he walked toward them. Before Elmer had gone halfway, he noticed that three men were walking toward him, so he stopped where he was and waited, figuring if the direction he needed to go in was behind him then he wouldn't need to cover the same ground. The three men, all of whom were black and no older, perhaps even younger, than Elmer, surrounded and stared at him.

"Come you ain't got no shoes on?" asked one.

"Don't make no connection otherwise," said Elmer.

"Feet's black as us," said another of the men.

"You heard of the Jungle Lovers?" the third man asked.

Elmer shook his head no.

"We them," said the first man. "And this our street."

"You a farm boy?" asked the second.

Elmer nodded. "From by Mamou," he said. "Road forks close the sign say, 'If It Swim I Got It.'"

"Where that?"

"Evangeline Parish."

The three men, each of whom was wearing at least one gold rope around his neck, began moving around Elmer, circling him, glancing at one another. Elmer stood absolutely still, unsure of what to do.

"You got any money, hog caller?" said one of the men.

"No," said Elmer.

The man behind Elmer pulled out a Buck knife with a six-inch blade, reached his right arm around Elmer and slit his throat completely across, making certain the cut was deep enough to sever the jugular. Elmer dropped to his knees and stuck all four fingers of his left hand into the wound. He sat there, resting back on his heels, blood cascading down the front of his overalls and on the sidewalk, for what seemed to him like a very long time. Elmer looked up into the dark eyes of one of the men and tried to speak. He was asking the man to tell Alma Ann he was sorry to have failed her, but the man did not try to listen. Instead, he took out a small handgun, stuck its snub nose all the way into Elmer's mouth and pulled the trigger.

"Don't worry about it, Sailor," said Bob Lee, "I can afford to take the day off. This ain't no small matter, after all, and the police can't be expected to exercise a whole lot of manpower over one more stole child."

"Want you to know I 'preciate it, Bob Lee," Sailor said, "extra much. What you and Beany's doin' for me and Lula's special. I mean, you got your own two kids and a new business to worry about. I ain't about to forget it."

Sailor and Bob Lee were preparing to hit the streets together and search for Pace.

"Just let me kiss Beany goodbye and we can get movin'."

Sailor waited for Bob Lee in the living room. Lula was still asleep, having taken a medication Beany's doctor had prescribed to help her relax. How he, Sailor, could have been so selfish, so stupid, so cowardly, astounded him. Had he acted like a man six months ago, Sailor thought, this wouldn't have happened. It had been his opportunity, after wasting the dime, to take care of Pace and try to make things up to Lula. They were his responsibility and he'd failed them and himself as well. Sailor prayed now for another chance. Ten years in the joint had proven to him that it wasn't every man who had a choice in life. The fact that he'd blown it twice before with Lula ate at Sailor. It was his fault, he'd decided, that their precious son was in this unholy circumstance. If anything terrible happened to Pace, Sailor knew he would be unable to go on living.

In Huntsville, Sailor had come in contact with the most hard-luck boys he ever could have imagined. Most of them were murderers or had been involved, as he'd been, in the commission of crimes during which one or more persons had died. One fellow, Spook Strickland, a tough nut from Anniston, Alabama, where he'd been a Grand Dragon or Imperial Wizard in the Ku Klux Klan, had told Sailor his belief that God's message was that nobody *deserved* to live. The gospel according to Spook Strickland maintained that staying alive was an option not available to everyone, and that's why people like him existed, to destroy the least worthy among them. Sailor had asked him why God had created billions of people in the first place, and why He continued to produce more, a question that gave Spook Strickland a good, long laugh. After he'd settled down, Spook had told Sailor that most human beings were provided for target practice. Those people were slaves, Spook said, disposable and without redeeming value. Organizations such as the Klan and the Great Whites, the prison gang Spook led at Huntsville, were placed on earth as reminders of the true nature of homo sapiens, and to maintain a necessary order. Each member of the Great Whites had on the underside of their upper right arm a tattoo of a shark with the words ORDER AT THE BORDER OF HELL etched around it. Spook Strickland had tried to get Sailor to join but Sailor resisted, even though things might have gone easier for him while he was inside, since Spook's gang controlled many of the more worthwhile and profitable functions in the prison, including drugs, cigarettes, and the machine shop. Sailor had hung out with the Great Whites, though, more for protection from the Mexican Mafia and Uhuru Black Nation than out of subscription to their ideas. He had needed to stay alive, that's all. He had, and now it was up to him to act right.

"Ready to roll, fella," said Bob Lee, putting a hand on Sailor's right shoulder. "Beany'll make sure Lula's all right while we're gone. Told her we'd call in a couple of hours or so."

Perdita Durango had parked a few houses away behind a silver Plymouth Voyager. She watched Sailor get into the passenger side of Bob Lee's black and tan Lincoln Town Car, and started the engine of Poppy's BMW as Bob Lee backed down the driveway into the street. She followed the Lincoln onto Veterans Memorial Boulevard and headed east two cars behind, turning right on Pontchartrain, then going east again on 610. Bob Lee got off the Interstate at Gentilly Boulevard and backtracked to St. Bernard Avenue, where he pulled into a shopping center and parked in front of a storefront office that had the words GATOR GONE, INC. stenciled on the tinted window glass. Perdita brought the BMW over near the shopping center entrance and kept the engine idling. Bob Lee got out of the Town Car and went into the office of Gator Gone, Inc. Sailor stayed in the car.

Perdita picked up the Smith & Wesson .357 Magnum from the floor between her feet, shifted the BMW out of neutral into first gear and glided toward the black and tan Lincoln. She pulled into the parking space to the right of Bob Lee's car, shifted the BMW into reverse, keeping the clutch and brake depressed, and lowered her window. Sailor was staring straight ahead as Perdita raised the gun with both hands and aimed at his right ear. The instant she pulled the trigger Sailor leaned forward to pull his left pantsleg over his boot. The bullet went behind Sailor's head through the Lincoln's windows into the roof of a pink Acura parked on the other side, ricocheted off the Acura and to the right into the yellow wood facing of the building. Sailor hit the deck and kept his head covered with his arms while Perdita peeled the BMW backward out of the parking space, spun a one-eighty, braked hard, shifted furiously into first and floored the gem of Bavarian engineering, fishtailing her way out of the shopping center. Sailor opened his door, rolled on the pavement and looked up in time to see its blue butt with the words PAPA UNO on the license plate streak away.

Bob Lee came running out of Gator Gone, Inc., saw Sailor stretched out on the ground, and yelled, "Ripley! You all right?"

Sailor rolled over on his back, saw the frightened look in Bob Lee Boyle's big brown eyes, and closed his own.

"I'm fine, Bob Lee," he said, and grinned, feeling the sun on his face. "Just never know what part of your life's liable to open up again at any particular time."

Sailor opened his eyes and saw the crowd of people gathering around him. He scrambled to his feet and brushed himself off.

"Come on, Bob Lee," he said, "let's go find my boy."

OUT OF THIS WORLD

Guadalupe DelParaiso had lived at the same address all of her life, which was seven months more than eighty-six years. She had never married, and had outlived each of her sixteen siblings—nine brothers, seven sisters—as well as many of her nephews and nieces, and even several of their children. Guadalupe lived alone in the downstairs portion of the house her father, Nuncio DelParaiso, and his brother, Negruzco, had built on Claiborne Avenue across the street from Our Lady of the Holy Phantoms church in New Orleans. The neighborhood had undergone numerous vicissitudes since Nuncio and Negruzco had settled there. At one time the area had been home to some of the Crescent City's most prominent citizens, but now Our Lady of the Holy Phantoms, where the DelParaiso family had worshiped for forty years, and where Guadalupe and her sisters and brothers had attended school, was closed down, and the street was littered with transient hotels, beer and shot bars, pool halls, and the drunks, junkies and whores who populated and patronized these establishments.

Guadalupe rented the upstairs rooms in her house by the week. She made sure to get the money in advance and kept a chart on the wall in her kitchen listing the dates the rent was due for each room. Guadalupe would rent to singles only, and not to women or blacks under the age of fifty. She had not left the house in four years, depending on her bachelor nephew, Fortunato Rivera, her sister Romana's youngest son, who was now fifty-two years old, to bring her groceries and other supplies twice a week. She paid Fortunato for what he brought her on Wednesdays and Sundays, and gave him a shopping list for the next delivery. Guadalupe had not been sick since the scarlet fever epidemic of 1906. The doctor who attended her at that time told her mother, Blanca, and Nuncio, that Guadalupe's heart had been severely damaged by the fever and that he did not expect her to live beyond thirty. It was Guadalupe's oldest sister, Parsimonia, however, who succumbed to a weak heart at the age of twenty-nine. As the years passed, Guadalupe only became stronger in both body and mind.

Guadalupe was making up her list for Fortunato, who would be coming the next day, Wednesday, when she heard a pounding noise, like the stamping of feet, coming from the room above the kitchen. She had rented the room almost a week before to a soft-spoken, polite but bedraggled-looking young man whom, she believed, worked for the railroad. The young man had seen the ROOM FOR RENT sign in the front window and had taken what had once been her brothers Rubio, Martin, and Danilo's room immediately. He paid Guadalupe a month's advance because, he told her, it looked like the kind of a place his mama, Alma Ann, would have been pleased to occupy. Guadalupe had not seen the young man since the day he'd rented it.

This pounding disturbed Guadalupe; she could not concentrate on her grocery list. She went into the pantry, picked up her broom, brought it back with her to the kitchen and bumped the end of the handle several times against the ceiling.

"You stop!" she shouted. "No noise in Nuncio's house or you get out!"

The pounding did not stop, so Guadalupe put down the broom, left her part of the house and walked slowly up the stairs. She stopped at the door to the young railroad worker's room and listened. She could not hear the pounding as distinctly from the hallway as she could in her kitchen, but she heard it and knocked as hard as she could on the door with her left fist.

"You stop! You stop or leave Nuncio and Blanca's house!"

The pounding continued and Guadalupe removed her keychain from the right front pocket of her faded rose-colored chenille robe and unlocked the door. The single overhead sixty-watt bulb was burning, but there was nobody in the room. The noise was coming from the closet, so she opened it. A body hurtled past Guadalupe so fast she did not see who or what it was, and by the time she turned around, it was gone. Guadalupe had been tremendously startled; suddenly she felt faint, and staggered to the cane armchair. She sat down and attempted to calm herself, but she was frightened, thinking that the shadow that had rushed out of the room had been the ghost of her severely disturbed brother Morboso, the one who had hanged himself in that closet. It had been Parsimonia who discovered Morboso swinging there, and it was this incident, Nuncio and Blanca believed, that had damaged Parsimonia's heart and led to her premature death. The ghost of Morboso DelParaiso was loose, Guadalupe thought. Perhaps he had driven away the young railroad man, or even murdered him as he had the pretty young nun, Sister Panacea, whose body Nuncio and Negruzco and Father Vito had secretly buried after midnight on October 21, 1928, in the garden of Our Lady of the Phantoms. Guadalupe rested and remembered, seeing again what she could not prevent herself from seeing.

Pace ran down the stairs and managed to turn the big gold knob on the front door by holding it between the bottom of his chin and his neck. He ran a block down the street before he stopped in front of an old Indian-looking guy who was leaning against the side of a building sipping from a short dog in a brown paper bag.

"Untie me, mister!" Pace shouted at him. "Get my hands loose, please!"

The Indian's eyes were blurry and he seemed confused.

"A crazy man kidnapped me and tied me up!" Pace yelled. "I just ran away! Help me out, willya?"

The Indian held out his half-pint of wine, as if he didn't know what to do with it if he assisted Pace.

"Put your bottle down on the ground and undo this here knot," said Pace, turning around and showing the Indian his hands.

The old guy bent over and carefully deposited his sack on the sidewalk, then straightened up and tugged on Pace's hands until they were freed.

"Thanks a lot, mister," said Pace, tossing away the strip of bedsheet Elmer had used to bind him. He reached down and picked up the Indian's short dog and handed it to him. "Don't know if God loves ya," Pace shouted, "but I do!"

Pace ran along Claiborne until he saw a police car parked at the curb. He went over to the car and stuck his head in the open window on the passenger side.

"Evenin', officer," Pace said to the policeman sitting behind the steering wheel. "I'm Pace Roscoe Ripley, the boy got kidnapped in the park the other day? Are you lookin' for me?"

THE OVERCOAT

Federal Bureau of Investigation agents Sandy Sandusky and Morton Martin stopped into the Lakeshore Tap, a tavern on Lincoln Avenue about a mile from Wrigley Field. In another hour or so, when the Cubs game ended, the place would be packed; at the moment, the two agents were the only customers. They sat on adjoining stools, ordered drafts of Old Style, and drained half of their beers before Sandusky said, "Is there a field office in North Dakota?"

"Where in North Dakota?" asked Martin.

"Anywhere."

"Why do you ask?"

"Because that's where we're going to be transferred to unless we can nail whoever ordered the hit on Mona Costatroppo, that's why."

Both men took another swig of beer.

"We know it was Santos," Martin said.

"The man hasn't had a rap pinned on him once. Never done time, Morty, never had a speeding ticket."

"If we can locate the shooter, we got a chance."

"He's in the sports book at Caesar's Palace right now, a hooker on each arm, betting trifectas at Santa Anita with the fee."

"So what do we do, Sandy?"

"Buy bigger overcoats."

Sandusky swallowed the last of his draft and climbed down from his stool.

"Order me one more, Morty. I'll call the office."

Sandusky came back five minutes later, a big grin on his ruddy face, and slapped Morton Martin on the back.

"Give us a couple shots of Chivas," Sandusky said to the bartender.

"What's up?" asked Martin. "Santos turn himself in?"

"Not quite, but Detroit picked up the hammer."

"No kiddin'. I thought you told me he was in Vegas juggling bimbos."

"Where I'd be."

The bartender brought two Scotches and Sandusky slapped down a ten.

"Keep the change," he said. "Looks like I won't need a new overcoat, after all."

Sandusky handed a glass to Morton Martin, tapped it with his own, and said, "To Tyrone Hardaway, a.k.a. Master Slick, resident of Chandler Heights, Detroit, Michigan, product of the Detroit public school system, who just couldn't keep his mouth shut or the blood money in his pocket for more than twenty-five minutes."

Sandusky and Martin knocked down the Chivas.

"Apparently, this Hardaway was letting all of his homeboys know what a big man he was, working for the guineas. He was buying gold chains, leather jackets and primo drugs for everyone in the neighborhood while bragging about the fresh job he'd done in Chicago for the famous Mr. Crazy Eyes. Somebody snitched on him, of course, and the Bureau brought him in no more than an hour ago. They say he told them that Santos's people forced him to whack the broad; otherwise, Tyrone said, the organization was going to move him off his turf and let another gang handle the crack trade."

"I know J. Edgar Hoover always said there was no such thing as organized crime in this country, but I'd bet Tyrone is telling the truth."

Sandusky laughed, and motioned to the bartender. After both men had refills, Sandusky held up his glass and admired its amber contents.

"To the truth!" he said.

"Yes, Mama, he's here with us now, and he's doin' fine."

"Put the boy on the line, Lula."

Lula handed the phone to Pace.

"Hi, Grandmama. Marietta, I mean. How you?"

"Pace, darlin', you call me Grandmama all you want. We been so worried! Your Auntie Dal and Uncle Johnnie been with me the whole time, waitin' for news. Your mama says you ain't got a hair out of place. Tell me what happened."

"I escaped, is all. The man left me tied up in a closet and when someone opened the door I ran out of there fast as I could. Bo Jackson couldn'ta caught me. I was flyin'!"

"Who was this man? Did he harm you?"

"Crazy kid, not too much older'n me, really. Name was Elmer Désper-somethin'. He was searchin' for a friend, he told me. His mama died on their farm and after he didn't get along with his daddy and brother, so Elmer killed 'em. Least that's what Sailor said. Elmer's dead, too. Found him this mornin' with his head blowed off. He didn't really hurt me none, only tied up my hands when he put me in the closet. I got a wino to undo me after I escaped."

"What a terrible time for you! Is Sailor intendin' to stay with y'all for a while?"

"I hope so, Grandmama. He's my daddy."

"I'm just so pleased you're safe, sweetie pie. I'll see you real soon. Let me have your mama again. Love you."

"Love you, Grandmama."

Lula took the phone.

"Mama, I want you to know Sailor and I've decided to try to stay together. We got a lot of talkin' to do and things to work out, we know, but we both think it'd be best for us and Pace if we can be a fam'ly."

"Lula, you know I only want what's best for you and my grandboy, so I hope you know what you're doin'. This ain't the proper moment for us to get into this, what with Pace just bein' found and all, but I got a strong opinion on the matter, as you could imagine."

"Yes, Mama, I can. We're all gonna stay here with Beany and Bob Lee while Sailor and I figure out what to do. Bob Lee's offered Sail a job at the alligator repellent factory, and Beany'd like me to take care of Madonna Kim and Lance when she enrolls in the St. John the Baptist College of Cosmetology in Arabi. There's plenty of room here, and if things work out between me'n Sailor, we'll find our own place."

"Well, Lula, I've promised Dal I'd hold my tongue until we're all calmed down from the kidnappin', so I will."

"Mama, it *is my* life."

"Johnnie got some business to attend in N.O. next week and he's asked me to come with him. You can't believe what a rock Johnnie's been for me these last few days."

"You oughta marry him, Mama, before you get too old to enjoy yourself."

"Lula, hush. I expect we'll be stayin' at the Sonesta."

"Separate rooms?"

"'Course, separate rooms. Listen, Lula, I'm thinkin' I'll attend the Daughters meetin' this afternoon, now we got Pace safe, so I'll say bye. I'll let you know when Johnnie and I'll be in."

"Okay, Mama."

"Keep a eye on my grandboy, now. Love you, Lula."

"Love you."

Marietta was hanging up when Dalceda Delahoussaye came in through the back door like a fireball.

"Marietta! I been dialin' you like mad!"

"I was talkin' to Lula, honey, and Pace. He ain't hurt and he sounds fine. Man who took him's dead."

"Lula told us he was fine last night!" Dal shouted as she raced through the kitchen into the front room.

"Needed to hear his precious voice. Dal, what are you doin'?"

Dal had switched on Marietta's nineteen-inch Sony Trinitron and was flipping the dial.

"What I was callin' you about was Santos. What number's that all-news channel?"

"Eleven, I believe. What about Santos?"

"He's been arrested! Look, here it is."

"Arrested? What are you ravin' about?"

"Hush and listen!"

"In New Orleans this morning," said the television news reader, "federal agents took into custody reputed organized crime king Marcello Santos on charges of conspiracy to commit murder and murder of his alleged mistress, Mona Costatroppo, in Chicago last week."

Videotape came onscreen showing Santos, his hands cuffed in front of him, being taken out of the backseat of a black car and led by FBI men up the steps of a courthouse. His sunglasses were askew, as was his toupee. He was obviously shouting something at the reporters following him, but it was impossible to hear what he said. The news reader continued:

"Santos, known as 'Crazy Eyes' because of an unusual congenital opthalmic condition that causes his eyes to frequently change color and appear unstable, became the head of the Pericolo crime family following the death of Pietro 'The Sicilian Salmon' Pericolo in 1962. According to noted organized crime authority Hieronymous Bernstein, author of the best-selling book, *From Fear to Uncertainty: Behind the Breakdown of the Mafia*, the Pericolo family, which controls rackets across the southern United States, especially along the Gulf Coast, had its foundation in Palermo under the leadership of the legendary gangster Lupo Sanguefreddo, who was assassinated while having a shave in the barbershop of the Egyptian Gardens Hotel in Miami Beach in 1939. Sanguefreddo was fighting a deportation order at the time of his death."

Marietta turned off the set.

"Don't know how they can get away with sayin' all that stuff about a man never been convicted of a thing!" she said. "Do you believe he done it, Dal?"

"You mean had Mona Costatroppo killed?"

Marietta nodded.

"Hard to say. That kind of woman digs her own grave."

The telephone rang and Dal picked it up.

"Hello, Johnnie. Yes, we just watched it on the news. She's all right. Yes, I will. She talked to Pace and he's fine. Yes, okay. Bye."

Dal hung up and said, "Johnnie wanted to know if you'd heard about Santos. Says he'll be back around six. I'm goin' to the Daughters at two. You comin'?"

"Might as well. They'll all want to know about Pace."

"Don't be worryin' too much about your old buddy Marcello. He'll find a way out, like always."

"Ain't it somethin', though, Dal, how it's just one weird thing happens after another?"

"Stay tuned," said Dal, opening the front door. "I got a powerful hunch there ain't never gonna be a end to it."

"It's the terrible truth, Jimmie. They are transferring Santos to Chicago tomorrow for the arraignment. No bail is being allowed until after the charges are brought. And even then, who knows? Our attorney here in New Orleans, Irving Bocca, says there is no guarantee the Chicago judge will grant bail, no matter what amount. The government wants him bad, and they figure this is their best shot. I don't blame them, either, for thinking that. You know Marcello wanted to take care of this business himself, and I believe he acted too hastily, though I know nothing of the details."

"Who is handling the case in Chicago for him?"

"Louis Trifoglio. The father, not the son."

"Good. So, you know how to proceed?"

"*Conte pure su di me.* Jimmie, you can count on me."

"You have my blessing, Carmine. Have you settled things yet with Tiger Johnny?"

"Yes. *Ci comprendiamo.* I am certain we understand each other."

"You know, as far as I am concerned, *è un buon' a nulla.* He is good for nothing, like all of the Ragusas."

"*C'è voluto del bello e del buono per convincerlo.* It took some convincing, but things will be all right."

"If you say it, it must be so. *Ciao*, then, Carmine. You will keep me informed of Marcello's circumstances."

"Of course, Jimmie. I will. I am grateful for your blessing. *Ciao.*"

Both Jimmie Hunchback, in New York, and Poppy Papavero, who was sitting in Santos's chair in the office of Bayou Enterprises, hung up. Poppy had been entrusted to run the organization in Marcello's absence, regardless of how long that might be, and he was pleased with the knowledge that Santos's associates had agreed without debate about his capability. He picked up the receiver again and dialed Perdita's number.

"Yes?"

"Perdita, my pet, things are good, under control. While Marcello is away, I am in charge. Now listen, I've been thinking about us, what we should do."

"Do about what?"

"I think we should get married. What do you think of that idea?"

"Heard worse."

Poppy laughed. "Does that mean you say yes?"

"Sure, it's what you want."

"It is. I know of a good house to buy, in a good place; a modest yet spacious house in a convenient location. It belongs now to Irving Bocca, who is willing to sell."

"Where's this house?"

"Metairie. It will be perfect, Perdita. We won't know anybody there, and nobody will know us."

EVIDENCE

After an unusually late supper, Bob Lee excused himself and said he had to go back to the office to take care of the paperwork he'd ignored during the excitement of the last few days, and Beany took Lance and Madonna Kim upstairs to put them to bed, leaving Lula, Pace, and Sailor at the dining-room table. Lula had told Beany not to worry about the dirty dishes, she'd heated up more of the Community coffee Sailor had taken such a liking to, and poured them each another cup. During the time Lula had gone into the kitchen for the coffee and come back, Pace had put his head down on the table and dozed off. Lula sat next to Sailor and together they watched their son sleep.

"Well, peanut, I'd like to believe we got us a fightin' chance."

"You'd best believe it, Sail. Look at that little boy breathin' there. If he ain't worth the effort won't never nothin' will be. Pace and us both just come through the worst scare we've ever had, and I guess to hell we've had a few in our short lives. It's one thing your gettin' yourself in deep shit with bad actors like Bob Ray Lemon in North Carolina and Bobby Peru in Texas, but now you got a fast-growin' son needs you. Reverend Willie Thursday back home in Bay St. Clement says a boy without a father's a lost soul sailin' on a ghost ship through the sea of life."

"It ain't my intention to let you and Pace down, and I won't be playin' no chump's game again, neither. Speakin' of the past, though, I seen Perdita Durango."

"Here in New Orleans?"

Sailor nodded. "Didn't figure on tellin' you this, but someone took a potshot at me in the shoppin' center by the Gator Gone office the other day. I'm pretty sure it was Perdita. I made Bob Lee swear he wouldn't say nothin' about it."

"But, Sail, why would she want to shoot you?"

"Maybe she thinks I'm out to get her for runnin' out on me and Peru. I'm the only one could I.D. her for the caper. I also spotted her on the street last week when I was leavin' Hattiesburg. She was with the same blue BMW squealed away from the shootin' in the shoppin' center."

"Sweet Jesus, honey. What're we gonna do about this?"

"Don't panic, peanut. I'll just have to keep the eyes in the back of my head open. Prob'ly Perdita was aimin' to warn, not kill, makin' sure I knew it was her had the drop on me. I wouldn't say nothin' to the cops, anyway."

"Sail, this unpredictable scary behavior don't almost improve my peace of mind."

"I know it, but you're my baby Lula, and at least we're in it together again. You, me, and Pace, that is. Reverend Willie Thursday won't be preachin' no ghost ship sermon concernin' our son."

Lula leaned over and kissed Sailor below his left ear.

"I love you, Sailor Ripley. I always figured we'd find our way."

Sailor grinned and put his left arm around Lula, pulling her closer to him.

"Peanut, it was just inevitable."

SULTANS
OF AFRICA

Piero Aldobrandi, unhelmeted, was wearing the black cuirass and the red commander's scarf and carrying the baton which linked him forever to this scene of carnage. But the figure, turning its back to the spectacle, relegated it to the mere status of landscape, and the face, strained by a secret vision, was the emblem of a supernatural detachment.
—Julien Gracq, *Le Rivage des Syrtes*

CONTENTS
Sultans of Africa

"The best thing you can hope for in this life is that the rest of the world'll forget all about ya."

Coot Veal shifted his shotgun from right to left and checked the fake Rolex on his right wrist. Buford Dufour had bought the watch for forty bucks in Bangkok when he was in the air force and sold it later to Coot for fifty.

"Half past four," he said. " 'Bout time to give it up, I'd say."

Pace Ripley pulled a brown leather-coated flask from the left hip pocket of his army surplus field jacket, unscrewed and flipped open the top and took a swift swig of Black Bush that he'd filched from his daddy's bottle.

"Want 'ny?" he asked Coot, holding out the flask.

"Naw. I'll get mine shortly."

Pace recapped the flask and put it back in his pocket.

"What you mean, Coot, hopin' you get forgot?"

Coot Veal, who was fifty-eight years old and had never been farther away from South Louisiana than Houston, Texas, to the west; Mobile, Alabama, to the east; and Monroe, Louisiana, to the north; who never had married or lived with a woman other than his mother, Culebra Suazo Veal, who had died when Coot was forty-nine; grinned at the fifteen-year-old boy, his friend Sailor Ripley's son, and then laughed.

"Mean it's not in a man's interest to let anyone interfere with or interrupt what's there for him to do."

Coot pulled out a pistol from his hip holster and held it up.

"This here's a single-shot Thompson Contender loaded with .223 rounds. Not the biggest gun in the world, not the best, either, but it suits me. Read about a Seminole brought down a panther with one in the Everglades."

Coot replaced the pistol in its holster.

"Zanzibar slavers over a century ago called the gun the Sultan of Africa. The world's still ruled by weapons, Pace. They're what separates the operators from the pretenders."

Pace looked out over the marsh. He and Coot hadn't had a fair crack at a duck all day. Water had somehow leaked into his high rubber boots and soaked his woollen socks.

"Okay, Coot," he said, "let's hit it. Gettin' skunked like this is insultin'."

BACKFIRE

Pace and Coot were riding in Coot's 1982 Dodge Ram pickup, headed home to New Orleans.

"You think I should go to a hooker, Coot? I mean, before I start in on regular girls. To have me some experience."

Coot laughed and spit out his open window. Pace uncorked the flask and swallowed some Bush.

"Tough call, kid," said Coot. "Only time I used one I was about your age, maybe a year older. My daddy, Duke Veal, had fashioned me a shoulder holster to wear when I was playin' Chicago gangster. I had a old Chinese target pistol was missin' the firin' pin and stuck it in the shoulder holster. Put on my Sunday suit coat over it and marched down to Rampart Street. Wanted to take off the coat in front of a woman, impress her, so she'd think I was a real racket boy.

"I found me a big, tall red-headed gal and followed her upstairs to her crib. Price was three dollars, plus one or two for the room. Four or five dollars altogether. It was about all the dough I had at the time, but I was convinced this was my best idea to date and I was goin' through with it, hell or high water. Made damn sure she saw me take off my jacket, but she was a seasoned whore. Didn't bat an eye or laugh at me, neither one. Just laid there on the bed with no kind of look at all on her face. I left the holster on, only took off my pants. Did the deed, stood up, put my pants and coat back on and got out of there. Woman never said a word about the gun or nothin' after I give her my money. Haw! How's that for a backfire?"

"You ever tell your daddy 'bout it?"

"Duke? Hell, no. I had, he woulda kicked my sorry ass to Memphis. Duke Veal didn't take kindly to throwin' away good money on bad women."

"Guess you're sayin' I oughta save mine."

Coot nodded and turned on the headlights.

"Might be best," he said. "But I think I still got that old shoulder holster around someplace, you decide you need it."

"That you, Sail?" Lula shouted.

Sailor Ripley let the screen door slam shut behind him.

"No," he said. "It's Manuel Noriega."

Lula came into the front room from the kitchen and saw Sailor slump down into the oversized, foam-filled purple chair that Beany and Bob Lee Boyle had given them last Christmas.

"Who'd you say? Barry Manilow?"

"No. Manuel Noriega, the deposed president of Panama."

"Uh-uh, you ain't him. You got too good a complexion."

Lula went over and kissed Sailor on the top of his head.

"Long day, huh, Sail?"

"You know it, peanut. Gator Gone's goin' great guns since the envir'mentalists got that new reptile protection law passed. Ever' fisherman in the state of Louisiana needs it now. You up to fetchin' me a cold Dixie?"

"No hay problema, esposo," Lula said, heading toward the kitchen. "Bet even Bob Lee never figured his gator repellent'd go this good."

"Yep. That one ol' formula 'bout to make him a rich man. He's talkin' about settin' up a Gator Gone Foundation that'll make funds available to poor folks been victims of gator and croc attacks who're in need of ongoin' medical treatment."

Lula returned with the beer and handed it to Sailor, who drank half of it right away.

"Thanks, honey," he said. "Sure build up a thirst overseein' that shippin' department. You know we're gonna build us our own warehouse in Gretna?"

Lula sat down on the zebra-striped hideaway.

"First I heard. Beany ain't said nothin' about it."

"Yeah, the Algiers location can't hold us, and besides, makes more sense to own than rent."

"Best thing we coulda done is settle here, Sail. New Orleans give us a whole bunch more opportunity than we ever coulda got back in North Carolina."

Sailor took another swig of Dixie.

"Not the least of which is bein' a thousand miles away from your mama. We never woulda had a chance in Bay St. Clement, peanut. Not with Marietta on my case."

"She's calmed down now, darlin', since she seen how swell a daddy you been to Pace. Also your workin' so hard for Bob Lee and everythin'."

"Wouldn'ta made it this far is all I know."

The telephone on the front hall table rang. Lula got up and answered it.

"Ripley home. Hi, Beany. Uh huh, Sail too. God don't make men the way He used to, like Mama says. Madonna Kim got over her cold yet? Uh huh. Suppose I might could. Lemme ask God's almost-best piece of work."

Lula tucked the receiver into her breast and turned toward Sailor.

"Honey? Beany'd like me to 'comp'ny her to Raquel Lou Dinkins's house for about a hour? See her brand new baby, Farrah Sue. You-all be able to survive without me that long?"

Sailor tipped the bottle and drained the last bit of beer, then nodded.

"Hell, yes. Me'n Pace'll get us a pizza or somethin'. Where is that boy, anyway?"

"Went huntin' this mornin' with Coot Veal, your buddy married his mama."

Lula put the phone back to her mouth and left ear.

"Want me to drive?" she asked Beany. "Uh huh. See ya in a minute."

Lula hung up, picked up her purse and car keys from the table, went over to Sailor and kissed him again on the top of his head.

"Sweetheart, you know what?" she said.

"What's that?"

"You losin' some hair right about there."

"Where?"

"Kinda in the middle toward the back."

Sailor felt around on his head with the fingers of his right hand.

"I can't feel nothin' missin', Lula. Anyway, it can't be. Nobody in my fam'ly went bald. Not my daddy or his daddy or my mama's daddy."

"None of 'em lived long enough to go bald, darlin'. Don't worry about it, just a small patch is all. I gotta go."

Sailor jumped up and dropped the beer bottle on the floor.

"Goddammit, Lula! You just gonna run out and leave me after tellin' me I'm goin' bald?"

"Bye! Back soon!"

Sailor watched Lula go out the front door, heard her open and close the door of her new Toyota Cressida station wagon and start the engine. He went over to the hall mirror and leaned his head forward while attempting to look up into the glass, but he couldn't see the top of his head. He turned sideways, tilted his head toward the mirror and rolled his eyes all the way over, but that didn't work, either. The front door slammed and Pace came in.

"What you doin', Daddy?" he said. "And where's Mama goin'? What're you all twisted around for?"

Sailor bent forward toward the mirror again, angling off slightly to the right.

"Take a look, son. Am I losin' my hair?"

Pace stared at Sailor, then shook his head slowly.

"More likely you're losin' your mind, Daddy. We gettin' a pizza for supper?"

RATTLERS

The Rattler brothers, Smokey Joe and Lefty Grove, non-identical sixteen year old twins who were named by their daddy, Tyrus Raymond Rattler, after the two men his daddy, Pie Traynor Rattler, considered to have been the two best pitchers in major league history, tooled through Gulfport along Old Pass Christian Road in their Jimmy, trading swigs off a fifth of J. W. Dant. They were headed back to New Orleans from Biloxi, where they had gone to pay their respects to the memory of Jefferson Davis on his birthday. Smokey Joe and Lefty Grove had taken advantage of the school holiday to visit Beauvoir, the last home of the Confederate president. The federal holiday officially honored the birth of the Reverend Martin Luther King, Jr., who happened to have been born on the same day as Jeff Davis, a convenience appreciated by the Rattlers.

Their mother, Mary Full-of-Grace, had been institutionalized for the past six years in Miss Napoleon's Paradise for the Lord's Disturbed Daughters in Oktibbeha County, Mississippi, and the Rattler boys had considered visiting her but decided the drive was too far for the short time they had. Besides, Lefty Grove reasoned, she wouldn't recognize them for who they were. The last time they'd gone up with their daddy, six months before, she'd called them the apostles James and John, sons of Zebedee. Sometime during the twins' seventh year, Mary-Full-of-Grace became convinced that she was in fact the Holy Virgin, mother of Jesus. She'd insisted that the people about her were not who they pretended to be and that every man she encountered desired to sleep with her. Tyrus Raymond took her to several doctors during the following two years, but her condition worsened, resulting finally in the diagnosis of a breakdown of a schizoid personality, with the recommendation that she be institutionalized as a hopeless case.

"What you think about Mama?" Lefty Grove asked Smokey Joe, who was behind the wheel.

"What you mean, what I think?" said Smokey Joe, reaching out his right hand for the bottle.

"Mean, you got a notion she ever gonna recover her mind?"

"Ain't 'xactly likely, how Daddy claims."

Smokey Joe took a quick swallow of Dant and handed the fifth back to his brother.

"You finish it, Lef'. I be dam see the road."

"Want me to drive? I feel good."

"Feelin' good and drivin' good ain't the same. I'll handle her home."

Lefty Grove put his red and yellow L.A. Gear high tops up on the dashboard and sucked on the bottle.

"'Bout Ripley?" said Smokey Joe. "Figure to trust him?"

"You mean on the deal, or just keep his mouth shut?"

"Either."

"Need a third, Smoke, you know? Pace a good boy."

"Mama's boy, you mean."

"Least he got him a almost sane one."

Smokey Joe snorted. "What you mean, almost sane?"

"Like Daddy said when he come home after deliverin' Mama to Miss Napolcon's, 'Ain't one of the Lord's daughters got a firm grip on life.' He put a extra pint of fear in their blood, makes 'em more uneasy than men."

"Daddy ain't naturally wrong."

"Uh-uh," said Lefty Grove. "He's a Rattler, by God."

IN BED WITH THE RATTLERS

Pace stared out the window of his room at the maple tree in the backyard. A blue shape flashed from branch to branch. Pace raised his right hand, formed his fingers into a gun and pointed the barrel at the flitting patch of blue.

"Bam!" he said, bouncing the tip of his index finger off the glass. "You done bought the farm, Mister Jay."

Pace lowered his hand and relaxed his fingers. He heard the downstairs telephone ring.

"Son!" Sailor shouted. "Phone for you!"

"Comin', Daddy!"

Pace stood up, pushed his feet into a pair of thongs, walked downstairs and picked up the telephone receiver from the hall table.

"Pace Ripley speakin'."

"Hey, boy, how you?" said Lefty Grove Rattler. "What you been up to?"

"Oh, hi, Lefty. Nothin' special. Went duck huntin'."

"Got you a few birds, huh?"

"Naw. Weren't a good day."

"Been thinkin' 'bout what we discussed?"

"Haven't had time, tell the truth."

"You still like the idea, though, don't ya? Better'n workin' at Popeye's."

"Know that, Lefty Grove. I like it, sure. Mean I'm in, I suppose."

"Knew we could count on you, Pace. Smokey Joe'll be glad to hear it."

"Thought he don't like me."

Lefty Grove laughed. "He don't like nobody much, even me. Ain't to worry."

"I guess I won't, then."

"There you go. Meet us at Nestor's Sandwich City on Magazine, tomorrow evenin' at six."

"'Cross from Jim Russell's Record Shop?"

"Got it right and tight tonight, Pace Roscoe."

"How you know my middle name's Roscoe?"

"Us Rattlers is straight from the gate to the plate, boy. Got to know who you're dealin' to, well as with. Abyssinia."

Lefty Grove hung up and Pace stood in the hallway holding the phone to his left ear.

"You still on the line, son?" Sailor shouted from the kitchen.

Pace put the receiver back in the cradle.

"All through, Daddy."

"Come on in, then," said Sailor, "have a piece of your mama's pecan pie. You been lookin' skinny."

Pace massaged the back of his neck with his right hand. His head ached and he needed a drink.

"Back in a minute, Daddy," he said, and went out the front door.

Pace sat down on the bottom step and rested his head and arms on his knees. The Rattlers were dangerous, sly boys, all right, and now he was about to climb into bed with them. At first Pace had thought they were joking when they proposed that he join them in knocking off the shakedown drop in the Quarter. Lefty Grove explained to him how each Thursday afternoon at three o'clock the weekly protection money from the businesses in the French Quarter was delivered to an idle caboose on a sidetrack near the Bienville Wharf. The collection remained there, cared for by two men, until approximately three forty-five, when a private armored car came to fetch it. Pace was both scared and excited by the idea of committing a crime. Something inside him wouldn't allow Pace to resist the promise of the thrill.

A cousin of the Rattlers, Junior Broussard, had worked for Carmine "Poppy" Papavero, the Gulf Coast rackets boss, for four years until Junior's death a couple of months back. Junior's wife, Manuela, had shot him, Lefty Grove said, during an argument about Junior's friendship with a woman named Jaloux Marron, a hostess at one of Papavero's nightclubs. Until then Junior had been in charge of the protection haul. Lefty Grove and Smokey Joe had overheard their cousin talking about the setup with their daddy, Tyrus Raymond, and decided to snatch the cash if they could. Junior being out of the way made things easier, Lefty Grove explained, because they wouldn't have to kill their own cousin if they were forced to. Three guns were better than two, the Rattler brothers figured, and Lefty Grove had tapped Pace to complete the trio. The deal was set to go down next Thursday. Today was Sunday. Pace had four days to make up his mind.

"What you doin' sittin' out here?" Sailor asked from behind the screen door.

Pace lifted his head. "Just thinkin', Daddy." He stood up. "Guess I'm a little tired. Me and Coot got out early this mornin'."

"Well, come have some pie. Your mama'll be insulted we don't make a major dent in it."

DOWN TIME

"Daddy?"

"Yes, son?"

"You never have talked much about the time you done in prison."

Sailor sliced into his wedge of pecan pie with one side of his fork, scooped up the piece, delivered it to his mouth, chewed and swallowed. Pace sat across the table from him, holding a fork in his right hand, ignoring his own piece of pie.

"Not much to say, I guess, Pace. Jail time is down time far's I'm concerned. You don't come out any different than how you went in, 'cept older. That's if you come out at all."

"How many times you been in, Daddy?"

"Twice."

"Once for manslaughter and the other for armed robbery, that right?"

"Correct. Didn't mean for the first to happen. Just a bar fight with a slime-bucket named Bob Ray Lemon was botherin' your mama. I was nineteen years old and didn't know no better'n to knock the sorry son of a bitch cold. He didn't get up and they stuck me in a work camp up on the Pee Dee River for two years. I'd had me any kind of lawyer I wouldn'ta done a minute."

"What happened the other time?"

Sailor put down his fork and shook his head.

"That was my mistake. Lucky I'm even here to talk about it. Your mama and me was tryin' to get to California from North Carolina, runnin' from your grandmama, Marietta, and her detective friend, Johnnie Farragut, who she'd signed on to track us down. Marietta didn't like the idea of her fine and only daughter takin' up with a ex-con such as myself. Lula met me at the gate the day I got my walkin' papers from Pee Dee, and we took off in her old white Bonneville convertible. Made it as far as West Texas when we about run out of funds. That's where I went over the line."

Sailor stood up and walked over to the refrigerator, opened it, took out two bottles of Dixie beer, shut the door, came back over to the table, handed one to Pace and sat back down. He popped his open and took a long swallow.

"How you mean 'over the line,' Daddy?"

"Your mama was pregnant with you and we was stuck like bugs in a bottle, stranded in a podunk town called Big Tuna. Met a mean fella there named Bobby Peru. Lula said he was a black angel and told me I should stay away from him, but of course I didn't pay no attention and got hooked in on a plan to rob a feed store over to the county seat, Iraaq. We went ahead and done it and Bobby got his head blowed off. I got caught, of course, and Peru's girlfriend, a strange Tex-Mex gal named Perdita Durango, who was drivin' the getaway car, escaped. They sent me to Huntsville, where I put in ten years down to the hour."

"Whatever happened to Perdita Durango?"

Sailor smiled, lifted the brown bottle to his lips and took a sip.

"Oh, she's around somewhere, I suspect. A Grade-A piece of work like her don't just fade away."

"What was it like inside the walls, Daddy? How'd you get by?"

"Remindin' myself every minute of every day how stupid I was to end up there in the first place. Knew if I was still alive when I got out I'd do anything, any kind of straight job, not to go back again. And I thought about your mama and you, how you-all were gettin' along. Figured you both were better off without me, the way I'd been goin', but knew if I had the chance to change, I would. Until I could prove it to myself, though, it wouldn't do to make you and your mama suffer my ignorance. That's why it took a little while after I got sprung for us to get back together. I had me some serious readjustin' to do."

"Bet there's some lost souls behind them bars."

"The lostest, son. Now eat your pie and drink that beer and we'll get us some rest. Tomorrow's already feelin' like it's gonna be longer'n today."

AFTER HOURS

Sailor flopped down into the Niagara, levered the footrest chest high, fingered the space command and flipped on the new RCA 24-inch he'd bought at Shongaloo's Entertainment Center right after his recent raise from Gator Gone. He dotted the i across cable country until it hit channel 62, when the sound of CCR's "Bad Moon Risin'" stopped him. It was past one o'clock in the morning. Pace was asleep upstairs and Lula was at Beany's, baking cakes for the Church of Reason, Redemption and Resistance to God's Detractors fundraiser. Sailor ticked the volume up a couple of notches. Suddenly the music faded out and a man's face in close-up came on the screen. The man was about forty years old, he had blond, crew-cut hair, a big nose that looked like it had been sloppily puttied on, and a dark brown goatee.

"Howdy, folks!" said the man, his duckegg-blue eyes blazing out of the set like laser beams. "I'm Sparky!"

The camera pulled back to reveal Sparky standing in front of an old-fashioned drugstore display case. Behind the counter and just to the side of Sparky's left shoulder was another man of the same approximate age but four inches taller. This man had thick, bushy black hair with a severe widow's peak and a discernibly penciled-in mustache under a long, sharply pointed nose.

"This asparagus-shaped fella behind me's my partner, Buddy," Sparky said, and Buddy nodded. "We'd like to welcome you-all to Sparky and Buddy's House of Santería, the store that has everything can make that special ceremony just right."

The words SPARKY & BUDDY S HOUSE OF SANTERIA 1617 EARL LONG CAUSEWAY WAGGAMAN, LOUISIANA flashed on the screen in giant red letters superimposed over the two men. The letters stopped flashing and Sailor sat up and took a closer look. Blood root suspended from the ceiling and dozens of jars filled with herbs, votive candles in a variety of colors, and various unidentifiable objects lined the rows of shelves behind Sparky and Buddy. Sparky raised his arms like Richard Nixon used to, the fingers of each hand formed in a V.

"We've got the needs for the deeds, ladies and gentlemen. We've got the voodoo for you! Oh, yes! We've got the voodoo, hoodoo, Bonpo tonic, Druid fluid, Satan-ratin', Rosicrucian solution, Upper Nile stylin', Lower Nile bile'n Amon-Ra hexes, Tao of all sexes, White Goddess juice'll kick Kundalini loose, the Chung-Wa potion'n ev'ry santería notion!"

Sparky lowered his arms, walked forward past the camera eye, then returned carrying two twisting snakes in each hand.

"Get a load of the size of these rattles, Pentecostals!" he shouted, raising his right arm, the one draped with a pair of diamondbacks. "And ladies, check out these elegant coachwhips!" Sparky raised his left arm to show them off. "Hey, Buddy! Tell the good folks what else we got!"

Sparky walked off-camera again and Buddy leaned forward over the counter, pointing to the floor with his right hand.

"Take a good look here, people," he said, and the camera eye dipped down, closing in on a one-hundred-ten-pound brindled pit bull stretched out on the floor, his head resting between his front paws, a seeing-eye harness strapped to his barrel chest. Next to his enormous head was a black water bowl with the name ELVIS stenciled on it in raised white letters. "We got a good selection of man's best friends, too."

Sparky's legs came back into view and the camera panned back up. "Mullahs, mullahs, mullahs!" Sparky intoned. "You got trouble with the Christian Militia? Come on down! And hey, troops! Them mullahs makin' you a cardiac case? Those Ayatollah rollers got you grittin' your bicuspids? You-all come on down, too! We are a hundred and five percent bona fide non-sectarian here at Sparky and Buddy's!"

Again the giant red letters spelling out SPARKY & BUDDY S HOUSE OF SANTERIA 1617 EARL LONG CAUSEWAY WAGGAMAN, LOUISIANA flashed on the screen.

"Right, Buddy?" Sparky said, and the flashing letters blinked off.

"Affirmative, Sparky!"

"And, Buddy, we got a special I ain't even told my mama about! This week only we discountin' mojos. Mojos for luck, love, recedin' hairlines, bald spots, money honey and—my own favorite, works like a charm—irregularity. This one's guaranteed to get you goin' and flowin'!"

Sailor watched as from behind the counter Buddy lifted up two wine glasses filled to the brim with amber liquid. He handed one to Sparky and together they raised the glasses high.

"Well, Buddy, as our old pal Manuel used to say in Tampa many years ago, *salud* and happy days! This is the four-hundred-sixty-sixth appearance we've made for Sparky and Buddy's House of Santería. Remember, we're at 1617 Earl Long Causeway, in the community of Waggaman, servicin' all of south Louisiana. Y'all come on down!"

"Bad Moon Risin'" started up again and the giant red letters reappeared for several seconds before the station segued into the video of L.L. Cool J's "Big Ole Butt." Sailor pressed the OFF button on his space command. He sat still for a minute, then lifted his left arm and with his fingers explored the crown area of his head where Lula had told him his hair was thinning. He got up and went over to the hall table, picked up the pencil and pad next to the telephone and wrote down Sparky and Buddy's address.

SNAKES IN THE FOREST

"They do it different now, Lula. Ain't hardly no cuttin' to speak of. Drop a line in through the navel and reel the creature out. Stick a Band-Aid on it. Make two tiny incisions on the sides, is all."

"But, Mama, you gotta stay in the hospital least one night. The doctor told you that."

"Don't know why. I might could take off right out of there, I feel good enough."

"Doctor says if there's a stone they gonna have to cut it out the regular way. That happens, you'll be in there three, four days."

"There ain't no stone and I ain't lettin' 'em run no tubes through me."

"You'll let 'em do what's necessary, Mama. This is your gall bladder we're discussin' now, not no perm job. I'll be into Charlotte tomorrow at noon, so I'll see you about one-thirty, all goes well. Dal's pickin' me up."

"You already talked to her?"

"Of course, Mama. We got it worked out how to take care of you."

"You're still the one needs takin' care of, Lula. How's my grandboy doin', anyway?"

"Pace is just fine, and so's Sailor. He got him a raise a couple weeks back. Bob Lee's Gator Gone repellent's sellin' better'n ever."

"Sailor throw the new money away on a TV or a truck?"

"Oh, Mama, you ain't never gonna give him a chance to redeem himself, are you?"

"Guess you're still attendin' that crackpot church, else you wouldn't be usin' that word."

"The Church of Reason, Redemption and Resistance to God's Detractors ain't no kinda crackpot outfit, Mama, and you know it."

"Know nothin' of the kind. Saw where that preacher of yours got arrested for havin' a video camera hid in the ladies' restroom at the church buildin'."

"It wasn't Reverend Plenty put it there, Mama. There's always snakes in the forest."

"With that type of weird individual leadin' the flock, Lula, you can't expect no better. Reverend Willie Thursday spoke here in Bay St. Clement last Sunday about false prophets like Goodin Plenty, sayin' how the world depends on them to save it. That's stupid talk, Lula. No way the world's welfare revolves around any one person. You'd best get shut of that nut case soon as now."

"The Three R's is right thinkin', Mama. Goodin Plenty just got a different way of gettin' his point across."

"Such as when he run off to Barbados with his twelve-and-a-half-year-old stepdaughter and she said after how he made her do them disgustin' things with chicken parts!"

"Mama, Rima Dot Duguid done long since been committed. And you tellin' me now you believe what you read in the *National Enquirer*?"

"If she's in the bin, it's no thanks to that perverted sinner."

"Mama, let's stop this. You gotta get your mind right for the comin ordeal. I'll see you tomorrow."

"Just as well. Here's Dalceda now, comin' in the back door."

"Bye, Mama. Love you."

"Love you, Lula. Dal says for me to assure you she'll be at the airport on time. That is if Monty, her new Lhasa apso, don't play sick again."

"I'm sure everything'll be fine, Mama. Bye."

GOOD ENOUGH

Pace got up late. He didn't want to go to school. He lay in his bed, listening for noises in the house. Lula had delivered her cakes to the church and then had Beany drive her to the airport. Sailor was at the Gator Gone warehouse. Pace opened the drawer of his bedside table, took out a pack of Camels and shook one loose. He reached back into the drawer and found a book of matches that had the words WHATEVER HAPPENED TO SEAN FLYNN? printed on it, struck one and lit up the cigarette.

He thought about this deal with the Rattler brothers, and the more he thought about it the less he liked it. Now that he knew the score, however, there would be no easy way to back out. The Rattlers, Smokey Joe in particular, would not take kindly to the idea of Pace's walking around with this information in his head. Either they'd have to alter their plans and choose another target, or do something about Pace, and Pace figured the Rattlers didn't take full possession of more than one idea at a time.

The other night Pace had watched a movie on TV with Sailor called *Bring Me the Head of Alfredo Garcia*. It was about an out-of-luck American piano player in Mexico who searches for the body of a guy who'd impregnated the daughter of a wealthy *patrón*. The American must cut off the corpse's head and bring it to the *patrón* in order to earn a reward. The movie, Pace remembered, got progressively weirder and wackier, with the American doublecrossing and being doublecrossed by everyone he meets. There was a lot of killing, so much killing that the movie became kind of a comedy, with mutilation upon mutilation. The last part was the best, he thought, when the American has the head in a sack covered with flies as he drives his battered old convertible through the sun-baked, scabrous Mexican countryside, swatting away the flies that threaten to engulf him. Pace wondered why the American didn't just put the head in the trunk of the car.

The Rattlers weren't about to let him beg off. Better to tough it out, Pace decided. Lefty Grove and Smokey Joe didn't fool around, and *Bring Me the Head of Pace Roscoe Ripley* was one movie Marietta Fortune's only grandboy was insufficiently prepared to appreciate. Pace lolled around the house most of the day, reading around in one schoolbook and another without retaining much of anything. He didn't so much dislike school as he disliked having to show up there every weekday. If attendance were voluntary, he thought, then school wouldn't be so bad. He could quit in another year, when he turned sixteen, but he knew that his parents wouldn't like it. Sailor hadn't finished grammar school, so of course he expected Pace to go to college and go on to become president of the United States or something. Pace wondered how many presidents had been the son of a twice-convicted felon.

At four o'clock the telephone rang and Pace answered it.

"Pace, honey, that you?"

"Yes, Mama. You at Grandmama's?"

"I am. Just wanted you and Daddy to know I made it safe and sound. Auntie Dal picked me up at the Charlotte airport and we drove through a absolute terror of a rainstorm all the way to Bay St. Clement. Started pourin' the instant our plane landed and it's still comin' down like a shower of Pygmy darts on a safari. Lightnin', too. Sky's blood red. How's it there?"

Pace looked out a window.

"Nothin' special. Sorta gray."

"How was school today?"

"Same as ever."

"Okay, sweetie pie. You need somethin' and Daddy ain't around, go to Beany, you hear?"

"I'll be fine, Mama. Tell Grandmama hello and hope she comes through."

"Hush, 'course she will. Take care now, Pace. Love you."

"Love you, Mama."

"Be home soon's I can."

"Bye, Mama."

"Bye."

Pace hung up and checked his pockets to make sure he had some money, then left the house and headed for Nestor's Sandwich City to meet the Rattlers. He took a bus to the corner of Canal and St. Charles, got off, walked one block down Canal to Magazine, turned right and continued walking. At the northeast corner of Felicity and Magazine, an obese black woman with the largest bosom Pace had ever seen was sitting on the curb with her legs in the street, singing "Give Me That Old-Time Religion."

"It was good for the Baby Jesus," she sang, "it was good for the Baby Jesus. It was good for the Baby Jesus and it's good enough for me!"

Pace kept walking, wondering how in the world a woman's breasts could grow that large, and he picked up the tune. He began singing, half to himself, half out loud, inventing verses as he headed to the rendezvous.

"It was good for Elvis Presley," Pace sang, "it was good for Elvis Presley. It was good enough for Elvis Presley but it weren't good enough for me."

Pace used Stonewall Jackson, Jimmy Swaggart, Paula Abdul, Magic Johnson, Jimmie Rodgers, and the Ninja Turtles in his altered version of the hymn before he reached Nestor's. He entered Sandwich City and stopped singing when he saw Lefty Grove and Smokey Joe sitting on stools at the counter eating fried oyster po'boys.

"Isn't that Pace goin' into Nestor's?" Beany Boyle asked her son, Lance, as she turned right off Napoleon Avenue into Magazine.

Lance leaned forward over the front passenger seat of his mother's Taurus station wagon and took a look.

"Yeah, that's Pace," he said, and flopped down on the backseat next to his sister, Madonna Kim.

"That Nestor's supposed to be some kinda drug den, ain't it?" said Beany.

"I guess," Lance said. "The Rattlers hang out there, I know."

"The who?"

"Rattlers, Mama. They're brothers."

"Them the ones their daddy set fire to the high school in Cut Off after they quit teachin' Creationism? And the mama's stuck away in some Mississippi home for the depraved?"

"Think so. They're mean ol' boys."

"Wonder if Sailor and Lula know where their boy's spendin' his time."

BLACK PLANET

On his way home from Nestor's, Pace stopped to read a handbill posted on a telephone pole in front of Panther Burn Items.

A CHALLENGE TO WHITE PEOPLE

ARE YOU TIRED OF . . .

Affirmative action quotas that discriminate against Whites in hiring, promotion, and admission to colleges?

A non-enforced immigration policy that has flooded our country with millions of scab-laborers and welfare parasites?

The brain-washing, by the schools and the media, of White Youth with racial self-hatred and genocidal race-mixing propaganda?

A non-White crime wave which makes our cities unsafe for our families?

Sham elections that allow only the lying toadies of the criminal ruling class to enter the halls of government?

The turning of this once-great White Nation into an impoverished banana republic ruled by traitors and criminals, owned by foreign corporations and populated by mongreloids?

If so, why not join with the thousands of your White kinsmen and kinswomen of the Third Position who are fighting for White survival?

JOIN THE WHITE ARMED RESISTANCE! IF YOU ARE INTERESTED IN OUR IDEAS PLEASE WRITE OR CALL . . .

WAR, P.O. Box 2222, New Orleans, LA 70115

Recorded Message (555)MAKE-WAR

When he'd finished reading and turned to go, Pace was startled to see a tall, thin, red-faced man in his mid-thirties wearing a yellow straw cowboy hat, plain long-sleeved white shirt with the cuffs and collar buttoned, and sharply creased black slacks standing directly behind him reading the same handbill over his right shoulder.

"Knew a fella worked derrick with told me his wife started complainin' once, ridin' in the car," said the man. "'Life with you's just terrible,' she said to him, and threatened to throw herself right out of the car onto the road. 'Hold on just a minute,' this fella told her, 'let me see I can get up some speed.' He guns it up toward eighty, then cuts the wheel hard into a hundred-eighty degree spin, car rolls over four times and somehow they both survive without even one broken bone between 'em. Fella said after that whenever they was drivin' and he started goin' a little too fast, she just quit talkin' and clamped on her seat belt."

Pace slid away from between the pole and the man, nodded at him and walked off without feeling compelled to reply.

KILLERS

"It's awful what's goin' on in the world, Lula, and it ain't about to stop until the worst. Am I right, Dal?"

Marietta was lying in her hospital bed, reading the Charlotte *Observer*, and talking to Lula and Dalceda Delahoussaye, each of whom were seated on chairs on opposite sides of the bed. They were waiting for the doctor to stop by before having Marietta taken to the operating room.

"Looks it," said Dal. She and Marietta had been friends since their days together at Miss Cook's in Beaufort, more than forty years before. Since that time they had never lived farther apart than a ten-minute walk.

"Whole planet's come unhinged," said Marietta. "Look at this: 'Uniformed Gunmen Kill 8 at Cockfight.' That's the headline. 'Men in military uniforms sprayed gunfire at a group of people attending a cockfight in central Colombia late Saturday, killing eight people, local news accounts said yesterday. The private Radio Cadena Nacional and the domestic news agency Colprensa said the gunmen killed eight people and wounded four in Yacopi in Cundinamarca state, 60 miles north of the capital of Bogota.' Dal, ain't that where Louis used to do business, Bogota?"

"No, Marietta, it was La Paz, Bolivia, but it weren't no better there. Had them a brewery Louis sold 'em parts for. The company needed their own army to protect it and the workers. Louis stayed down there three months once, settin' it up and makin' sure it run right. You remember, Marietta, that's the time I took advantage of his absence to redecorate the livin' and dinin' rooms? He come back and didn't even notice."

"Some husbands is like that, Dal."

"*Some* husband is right."

"Mama, did you take that yella pill the nurse give you?"

"Yes, Lula, dear, I took the yella pill."

"Suppose to calm you."

"I'm calm."

The doctor came in, followed by a nurse.

"How we doin', Mrs. Fortune?" he said. "You ready?"

Marietta folded the newspaper and handed it to Lula.

"Been ready for two hours, Dr. Bonney. Been borin' Mrs. Delahoussaye here and my daughter to death. Don't think you know Lula, do you? Lula, this is Dr. Bonney, a descendant of Billy the Kid. Don't he have the most beautiful wavy black hair and blue eyes? Doctor, this is my favorite daughter, Lula Pace Fortune."

"Lula Ripley, now," Lula said, extending her right hand to the doctor. "How do you do?"

They shook hands.

"You live in New Orleans, your mother's told me."

"Yes, with my husband and son. He's fifteen."

"It's my grandboy's fifteen," Marietta said. "And his daddy that acts like it."

"Mama, stop! Sailor's providin', and he ain't been in no trouble for years."

"Mrs. Fortune," said Dr. Bonney, "I'm gonna let Nurse Conti here prepare you for surgery, if you don't mind. Ladies, I'm afraid you'll have to leave now."

Dal stood up and kissed Marietta on the cheek.

"You be fine, love," said Dal. "I'll talk to you tonight."

Lula leaned over and kissed her mother on the forehead.

"Be tough, Mama."

"Ain't it strange how I always think of your daddy at moments like this?" said Marietta. "Clyde's face slides right into focus whenever I have a serious situation to consider."

"Don't worry, Mrs. Fortune," Dr. Bonney said. "You won't hardly be able to tell we touched you."

"Didn't think Billy the Kid fathered any children," said Lula.

"I'm not a direct descendant of his, Mrs. Ripley, but we are of the same stock."

"Every family's got its killers, Doctor," said Marietta, staring straight at Lula. Then she turned and smiled at Dr. Bonney. "It ain't as if there's anything you could do about it."

"Pace, buddy? Bob Lee mentioned to me today that Beany told him she saw you goin' into Nestor's Sandwich City yesterday down on Magazine. That right?"

Pace looked at Sailor, then away. They were in the kitchen and Pace was eating a bowl of cereal. The Wheaties box with a picture of Michael Jordan on it was on the table between them.

"I guess."

"What you mean, you guess? Either it was you Beany seen or it wasn't. Which?"

"Mean I guess it was me, she says so."

"So what's happenin' in Nestor's these days other'n dope deals?"

Pace scooped up a tablespoonful of Wheaties and crammed it into his mouth. He couldn't answer while he chewed. The telephone rang and Sailor picked it up.

"Ripley home, Sailor speakin'. Hi, peanut, how you? That's good. Told you she'd pull through. Your mama's like a big dog on a red ant. How long you figure? Uh huh. Well, do what's needed. I know. Oh yeah, we're fine. Pace is sittin' here wolfin' his Wheaties like any other All-American pup. We're busier'n blazes at the factory. Okay, I will. Love you, too, peanut. Bye now. Uh huh. You bet. Bye."

Sailor hung up.

"Mama says to tell you she loves you and that both Grandmama and Auntie Dal send their love. Mama's got to stay with your grandmama for several days, until the doctor says Marietta can get around on her own. Now, what's news at Nestor's?"

"Nothin', really, Daddy. Met up with some boys there, is all."

"You in any kinda fix, son?"

"No, Daddy, I ain't."

"You'd tell me, you was, wouldn't you?"

" 'Course."

"Come to me anytime 'bout anything, you understand? Ain't nothin' can upset me 'less you're less'n straight about it."

"I hear you, Daddy. Thanks."

There was a knock on the back door and then it opened. Coot Veal came in.

"Hey, Sail!" Coot said. "Hey, Pace!"

"Hello, Coot," said Sailor. *"Que paso?"*

Coot had on a yellow and blue LSU baseball cap with a drawing of a tiger on it and a white tee shirt with the words BUBBA'S BILOXI PORK BAR printed on the front and WE MIGHT BE CLOSED BUT YOU'D NEVER KNOW IT on the back. He took a clean bowl and a spoon out of the dish tray, sat down at the table and poured himself some Wheaties.

"I was a kid," Coot said, "they had Bob Richards on the box. Bet you don't know who Bob Richards was," he said to Pace.

"Right again," said Pace.

"O-lympic pole vault champ, I believe. And a good Christian. Hollywood even made a movie about him. Or was that Bob Matthias? Maybe they made movies about both of 'em. Matthias was a O-lympic athlete, too. And prob'ly not a bad Christian, either, though I don't know for sure. What I do know for sure is I ain't partial to this new deer dog law they're tryin' to put through in Mississippi. The rich folks there get it in and next week the sonsabitches in Baton Rouge be hollerin', too."

"What law's this?" asked Sailor.

"Seems the Miss'ippi Property Rights Association's lookin' to outlaw huntin' with dogs, only allow still-huntin'."

"They can't do that," Pace said.

"Hell, they can't!" said Coot. "Look what they done about abortion and taxes. Ask your daddy, he knows. Landowners want the territory to themselves, and there ain't much open territory left. No more road huntin' at all, they say, from trucks or standin'. Wanna do away with dogs altogether. You 'magine not allowin' blue ticks or runnin' walkers in the woods? Only place you'll be able to see 'em is up in the Madison Square Garden prancin' around with a tube pushed up their asshole."

"Why they doin' this?" Pace asked.

"What begun it was a old boy in Petal, I think it was, got shot by a hunter after he chained up the hunter's dogs runnin' loose on his property."

"I used to work over in Petal," said Sailor.

"Didn't know that," said Coot.

"For a short time, in a lumberyard. After I weren't required by the Texas state prison system to stay close to home no more."

"Some bad apples, no question, could ruin the sport for ev'ryone. Let their hounds run wild, kill people's pet ducks, scare children. But it ain't most of us can't control our dogs. Hell, a man's dogs is part of his fam'ly. Problem is the landowners who do their huntin' in private clubs. They buy up all the land in the first place and don't leave nothin' for the common man. People should be let to hunt the way they like to hunt. Miss'ippi state legislature done already passed a bill bans huntin' from within one hundred feet of the center line of a road. Now they mean to regulate firearms, too."

"It don't sound good," said Sailor.

"Pretty quick this whole country'll be nothin' but a suburb of Tokyo, anyway. We're lucky, they'll let us out on Sunday to take a leak. Other six days we'll be too worried or busy bendin' over to risk it."

Sailor laughed. "Got a point there, Coot."

Coot stood up. "Gotta take a leak, too," he said, "while I still got the chance. How you doin', Pace? Stayin' out of trouble?"

"Mostly."

"All a man can do," said Coot.

JALOUX

Inez's Fais-Dodo Bar had been a fixture on Toulouse Street in the Quarter for more than thirty years. The original owner, Inez Engracia, had been shot to death by a jealous lover six months after the place opened. Inez's heir, her sister Lurma, sold out to Marcello "Crazy Eyes" Santos, the organized crime king of the Deep South, who was now serving a life sentence in the Federal Correctional Institution at Texarkana for conspiracy to commit murder and the murder of his mistress, Mona Costatroppo. Mona had been killed in a hotel room in Chicago, where she was waiting to testify against Santos as part of her participation in the Federal Witness Protection Program. The Crazy Eyes Gang and its holdings, legitimized as Bayou Enterprises, were being overseen in Santos's absence by Carmine "Poppy" Papavero. Papavero had invited Bob Lee Boyle to have a drink with him at Inez's to discuss the possibility of Bayou Enterprises becoming involved in the distribution of Bob Lee's Gator Gone repellent and related products. Bob Lee knew better than to reject outright Papavero's overture, so he accepted the meeting and asked Sailor to accompany him.

"You know more about this kind of thing than I do, Sail, that's why I wanted you to come along."

Bob Lee and Sailor were walking along Toulouse toward Inez's at nine o'clock in the evening. They'd left Bob Lee's Grand Prix in the parking lot of Le Richelieu on Barracks Street, where Sailor knew the attendant, Fudge Clay. Fudge's brother, Black Henry, had been at Huntsville with Sailor for two years until another inmate had carved up Black Henry in the shower room, the result of miscommunication concerning a sexual question.

"What the hell I know, Bob Lee? Only thing is to listen to the man, hear what he has to say and take it or don't take it from there."

The two Gator Gone representatives turned into the Fais-Dodo and Sailor immediately spotted Carmine Papavero. The Gulf Coast mob boss, wearing his signature burgundy blazer, was seated at a large corner table with three other men. Papavero's photograph had appeared often enough in the local newspapers and on television since he'd replaced Marcello Santos that even Bob Lee, who made no effort to keep up on current events, recognized him. As Sailor and Bob Lee approached his table, Papavero rose to greet them. He was a large man, his belly strained at the single-buttoned sports coat, and he wore a wide yellow tie decorated by a hand-painted pink flamingo.

"Mr. Boyle, I believe," said Carmine Papavero, reaching his thick right hand toward Bob Lee, who took it quickly into his own and participated in a solid shake.

"Yes, sir," said Bob Lee. "And this is my colleague, Mr. Sailor Ripley."

Papavero withdrew his right hand from Bob Lee's and thrust it at Sailor, who reciprocated.

"A pleasure, Mr. Ripley. Please, sit down both of you."

Two of the men who had been seated at Papavero's table got up and walked away, allowing Bob Lee and Sailor to take their chairs. Papavero did not bother to introduce the man who remained, an extremely thin, blue-skinned individual with a pinhead and creaseless ears the size and shape of dieffenbachia leaves. Bob Lee looked once at the man and did not look at him again. Sailor recognized the man instantly as the former inmate at Huntsville who had stabbed Black Henry Clay, Fudge Clay's brother, to death in the shower room. He was not certain if the man, whose name was Zero Diplopappus, recognized him.

"You fellas need drinks," Papavero said, and signaled a waitress who stood near the table, her only duty while it was occupied by Carmine and his group.

"Dixie," said Bob Lee.

"Two," said Sailor.

"Two Dixies," said the waitress. "Anybody else need anything?"

Zero Diplopappus's ears waved once, as if a sudden breeze had sliced through the room, but he did not speak. Papavero did not reply and the waitress walked away.

"Mr. Papavero, sir," said Bob Lee.

"Please, call me Poppy. All of my friends do."

"I just want you to know, sir, that I agreed to meet with you out of respect, not because I'm interested in changing my arrangements for product distribution."

"That's fine, Mr. Boyle—Bob Lee—I understand, and I appreciate your candor. But I am in a position to make you an offer, a generous offer, on behalf of Bayou Enterprises for fifty-one percent of the Gator Gone Corporation. You would be retained, of course, as director of the company. Name your price."

"Can't do it, Mr. Papavero."

"Poppy, please."

"I just don't want to sell Gator Gone. It's all I have. I invented the repellent and started by manufacturing it and shipping it out of my garage. I worked real hard, along with Sailor here, to build up the business. We just now got it goin' good, and I ain't ready to give it up. Don't know that I'll ever be."

The waitress brought the two beers, placed them on the table along with two glasses and left.

"Mr. Ripley, is it?" Papavero said to Sailor.

"Yes, sir."

"Why don't you take your beer over to the bar and drink it there. I'd like to discuss this business in more detail with Bob Lee here, a little more privately, if you don't mind."

"I don't mind," said Sailor. "Okay with you, Bob Lee?"

Bob Lee nodded and Sailor stood up, picked up his Dixie and went over to the bar. Zero stayed in his seat.

"You a friend of Poppy's?"

Sailor turned around and saw a young woman, no more than twenty-two, with short, white-blond hair, wearing long purple and pink parrot earrings. Her small cat's eyes were clear green.

"Just met him."

"I'm Jaloux Marron. How about you?"

Sailor smiled. "I'm nothin' of the kind. But my name's Sailor."

Jaloux Marron smiled, showing uneven, very white teeth.

"Hey, Sailor, buy me a drink?"

"Buy you a beer's about it. I ain't rich."

"Good enough."

Jaloux gave the high sign to the bartender, caught his eye and pointed to Sailor's bottle, then at herself. The bartender nodded, cracked open a cold Dixie and set it in front of her.

"How you like N.O.?" she asked Sailor.

"Pretty much. I live here."

"No kiddin'? You look too decent."

"First time anybody accused me of that."

"Guess there's more to you than meets the eye."

"You meet my eye just fine, Miss Marron."

"Just Jaloux'll do."

"Everybody's damn informal around here."

"It's that kinda place. You want to go someplace else, get some room service?"

Sailor laughed. "Can't do it."

"Guess you really are decent."

"Really married, anyhow. You know Papavero?"

"Sorta. I work for him, just like everyone else."

"I don't."

"Yeah, you-all're too decent."

Bob Lee came over and touched Sailor's arm.

"Let's go, Sail," he said, and headed for the door.

Sailor took a long drink of Dixie, then said, "Been swell meetin' ya, Jaloux. You're a good-lookin' lady, if you don't mind my sayin' so."

"Don't never mind that kinda talk, Sailor. Be nice to see you again, especially when you ain't feelin' so decent."

Jaloux took a card from a small sequined handbag and held it out to Sailor.

"Don't lose this, okay?" she said.

He took the card and read it. The words NIGHT TALK and a telephone number were printed on it. Sailor looked into her little green eyes.

"Try not to," he said, and walked out of the bar.

"What d'ya think?" Sailor asked Bob Lee as they headed toward Barracks Street.

"Think it's time to go home, watch 'Fishin' Hole' on ESPN."

At the parking lot, Sailor decided not to say anything to Fudge Clay about seeing Black Henry's slayer in the Fais-Dodo, and he didn't exactly know why.

"We ain't gonna need no masks," said Smokey Joe, "because they ain't gonna be nobody left over to identify us."

"Don't mention that little fact to Ripley, brother. Might could weird him out."

Lefty Grove and Smokey Joe Rattler were sitting in their Jimmy, which was parked on Decatur Street near the corner of Esplanade, waiting for Pace. Lefty Grove zipped open the green Tulane Wave athletic bag that was on the floor between his feet, removed a Black Magic sheath-sprung switchblade and put it into his pants pocket. He took out two Colt Pythons, stuck one in his belt and handed the other to Smokey Joe.

"Where'd ya find these nifty partners?" Smokey Joe asked.

"Skeeter McCovery brung 'em back from Mobile last month. Skeeter says there's more weapons per square mile in Alabama than there are wanted men in Florida, which is sayin' somethin'."

"Well, he ain't no liar and he done a job or two. You figure on Ripley packin'?"

"Don't see a need for it. We got enough to put out all the lights."

The Rattler brothers sat and smoked Marlboros. Lefty Grove was wearing a powder blue tank top with the words HAVE YOU HUGGED A COONASS TODAY? stenciled on the front, black Levi's with the bottoms rolled twice, and a pair of brand new Head tennis shoes without socks. Smokey Joe wore a black tee shirt emblazoned with a rubberized image of Michael Jordan executing a reverse dunk, the rubber part of Jordan's dangling tongue torn off, faded Lee Riders ripped at both knees, and green Converse high tops without socks. Both boys planned to wear red and white cotton handkerchiefs tied around their heads to cover their hair. Tyrus Raymond, their daddy, had told them that people are more easily identified by their hair, both color and style, and by whether or not they have any, than by any other common characteristic.

"How many years Daddy been considered dead now?" asked Smokey Joe.

"'Bout twenty, I believe. Why?"

"Don't know. Just thinkin' how his name bein' engraved on that Vietnam Memorial in Washin'ton is kinda spooky."

"Daddy don't mind. Far's the government knows he's long gone, so he don't have to pay no taxes or nothin' forever. Pay for ever'thin with cash the way he does, use out-of-state driver's licenses and not registerin' nothin' in his name means he's about free as any man can be. Bein' declared legally dead has all the advantages of bein' really dead without none of the drawbacks, such as *bein'* dead. Long as you're alive, you ain't got nothin' to worry about."

"Seems to me, only way a man got nothin' to worry about is if he *is* dead. Long as you're alive you got problems, Lef', even if all the governments of the world got your account cancelled. Devil got your name down's a differ'nt story."

"How's that?"

"That ol' boy make you wish you was back on earth payin' your neighbor's taxes, I'm right convinced."

"Ain't wise makin' reference to no devil around Daddy, you know. He'll think it's Mama's blood talkin'. There's Pace Ripley comin' now."

Pace walked up to the passenger side and nodded.

"Nice afternoon for a armed robbery, Ripley, don't ya think?" said Lefty Grove.

"Cloudy day like any other."

The Rattlers wrapped the red and white kerchiefs around their heads, knotted them at the back and got out of the truck. Pace had on a plain white tee shirt, an unzipped beige windbreaker, blue Wranglers and red Air Jordans with tube socks.

"You carry this," said Smokey Joe, handing Pace a canvas mail sack. "Just do what we talked over and one day we'll three be eatin' Big Macs on Mars."

Lefty Grove slapped a black Baltimore Orioles baseball cap on Pace's head.

"Wear this," Lefty Grove said, "so they can't see your hair."

The Rattlers carried the Pythons stuffed into the front of their pants with their shirts over them. Pace followed behind as they made their way across the railroad tracks by the wharf. It was three-twenty-five on a

Thursday afternoon when they boarded the discarded brown caboose. Zero Diplopappus saw them first, but there was no conversation. Smokey Joe shot Zero in the head at point-blank range and didn't wait for him to go down before facing the other protector of the take and holding the Python in front of his eyes. The money was on a table in large, brown paper shopping bags. Pace shook the contents of each bag into the canvas mail sack while Lefty Grove guarded the door. Nobody spoke. When all of the money had been collected, Pace slung the sack over his right shoulder and exited the caboose with Lefty Grove. Smokey Joe grinned at the man he had covered.

"You're all dead," croaked the man, whose name was Dewayne Culp. Dewayne Culp's skin was yellow and heavily wrinkled, and he had an enormous Adam's apple that ascended and descended inside his thin, withered neck like a rickety elevator in a decrepit hotel.

"Uh-uh," said Smokey Joe, before he pulled the trigger again, "you are."

The three boys were in the Jimmy headed east on Chef Menteur Highway when the two armored car guards entered the caboose. One of them bent over Dewayne Culp, took one look and stood up. The other guard helped Zero Diplopappus to his feet and handed him a handkerchief, which Zero used to wipe away the blood on his face from where he'd been grazed by Smokey Joe's bullet.

"It was them two punk cousins of Junior's," said Zero, "the Rattlers, with another kid. They thought I was dead."

Zero's massive ears flapped a couple of times, then he laughed.

"Third kid was the likeness of a fella I run into the other day," he said, "an ex-con I done time with in Texas, name of Sailor Ripley. Would be somethin' if it turned out to be his boy, wouldn't it?"

HOMAGE TO PROMETHEUS

"Know why the Good Lord created women?"

"Why's that?"

"Sheep couldn't do the dishes."

The Rattler brothers both laughed hard. They were sitting in the pickup cab. Pace was riding in the back of the truck, his black cap pulled down as far as it would go. The plan was to hide out in Mississippi for a spell, close to Miss Napoleon's Paradise, so Smokey Joe headed the Jimmy north on Interstate 59 toward Meridian, where they'd connect to Highway 45 and shoot straight into Lookout World. Nobody would figure on their being with the Lord's Disturbed Daughters, the Rattlers thought, and this way they could spend some time with Mary Full-of-Grace.

"We'll stash the money with Mama," said Lefty Grove. "It'll be safe there."

"You sure, Lef?" said Smokey Joe. "She finds out, she'll just give it away."

"I'll make sure she don't know she even has it. Hide it when she ain't lookin' in that old trunk from Grammy Yerma ain't been taken out from under her bed since she come there."

Pace watched the Sportsman's Paradise roll away from under him. He considered the situation, not quite comprehending the fact that he and his semi-moronic compañeros were now officially fugitives from Gulf Coast Criminal Central. Pace had gotten into the deal in the first place based on his notoriety as the son of Sailor Ripley, the Texas killer and bandit. That was a sure-enough hoot, seeing as how Sailor had been caught during his first attempted robbery and the only killing he'd done had been an accident in North Carolina. Pace's daddy had never gotten away with a thing, but his reputation as a hard case, false though it was, had tainted his boy and pressured Pace into acting stupid. Maybe that was it, Pace thought, us Ripleys is simply dumb as they come. No good reason I should be speedin' away with these backyard chicken fuckers. Ought to be life weren't always more ornery a animal.

Pace wished he'd taken along his flask. A healthy hit of Black Bush would drop him over the edge just now. WELCOME TO LOUISIANA flashed by and Pace knew they'd crossed into Mississippi. Suddenly the sun faded and Pace looked up. Black clouds formed like Mike Tyson's fists were about to batter the planet. He pulled his windbreaker up over his head and closed his eyes. Is this what it felt like to you, Daddy, Pace whispered, when you were in the deep shit?

TALK TURKEY TO ME

Poppy Papavero and Zero Diplopappus sat in the front seat of Poppy's powder blue BMW, which was parked next to the curb outside ARRIVALS at the New Orleans International Airport. Zero's head had a white bandage wrapped around it that pinned back his elephantine ears so that he looked like Chuck Connors as Geronimo in the movie based on the life of the Apache chief. Both Connors and the gangster had blue eyes, however, rendering any actual resemblance to Geronimo extremely dubious. Poppy puffed on a Monte Christo while they waited for his wife, Perdita, to arrive on a connecting flight from New York. She had been in Europe for three weeks, shopping and sightseeing.

"Don't worry, Poppy," said Zero, "we'll find these guys and get the money back. I got a good idea where they are."

"Yeah? Where's that?"

"Up by Starkville. The Rattler mother's a crazy, been locked up in some home there for years."

"What makes you think that's where they've gone?"

"They're kids. If they ain't with the papa, which they ain't—'cause we checked, and that guy's plenty crazy, too—then they're with the mama. My guess is they go see her before goin' anywhere else."

"Ah, they could be in Memphis by now, or Chicago."

"I'll get 'em, Poppy, believe me."

Poppy looked at Zero, took the cigar out of his mouth and grinned.

"I do, Zero, I believe you." He tossed what was left of the Monte Christo out the window.

Zero's eyes narrowed and half closed.

"I'm gonna fillet all three of 'em," he said.

"Mm, mm," said Poppy. "I can smell that deep-fried boy cookin' right now."

At his house in Metairie, Sailor put the card Jaloux Marron had given him on the table by the telephone and dialed the number printed on it. Someone picked up after three rings.

"Night Talk. This is Cindy speakin'. Call me Cin. And what do you want to talk about?"

"Hello," Sailor said, "I'd like to speak to Jaloux, please."

"She's on another line at the moment. Would you like to talk to me, or would you prefer to wait? I'm sure I can tell you whatever it is you need to hear."

"I'm sure you can, but I need to speak with her."

"Hang on, then, honey."

A radio station came over the line while Sailor was on hold.

"In other news, the state of Nevada has six hundred to seven hundred fifty new residents who are multiplying rapidly, but many of them may not live out the year. The Nevada Department of Wildlife has transplanted wild turkeys to western and southern parts of the state to establish the birds, which are not native to Nevada, in an effort to increase the population for hunting, a biologist involved with the project said today.

" 'The population is growing so fast I expect we might have a hunt by next year,' he said. 'We'll probably set up isolated hunts. In the meantime, the birds are relatively visible and are tremendously spectacular to watch, especially during mating. When the male turkey struts, his tail feathers fan out with very colorful displays. And they're darn fast birds, too,' he added, 'able to run as fast as a horse and fly as rapidly as smaller ducks.'

"According to this report, the transplanted turkeys are mostly of the Rio Grande variety, and they thrive on river bottom lands instead of the forests the birds usually enjoy. Most of these turkeys came from Amarillo, Texas.

"Nationwide, the turkey population has grown to four million after a low of thirty thousand at the turn of the century, when unregulated hunting, clearing and burning of native hardwood habitat and human encroachment threatened the species. By all accounts, the wild turkey has made quite a North American comeback.

"From New York City, where the only Wild Turkey you can find is in a bottle, comes another kind of news. A twenty-three-year-old woman, who was raped and robbed when she was trapped between a subway revolving-gate exit and a locked fence blocking the stairs to the street, won the right to sue the Transit Authority for negligence. The woman, a television makeup artist, was on her way home at ten P.M. last July nineteenth, when she left the station through a one-way revolving turnstile and found the stairs to the street barred and locked. A man she asked for help came through the turnstile, produced a knife, and robbed and raped her. It is not clear how he got out, but police believe he had a key or squeezed over the gate."

"Hi, this is Jaloux. We can talk now."

Sailor was startled by the sudden switch from the radio to reality.

"Uh, hello, Jaloux. This is Sailor Ripley. We met the other evenin' in Inez's Fais-Dodo Bar and you give me your card."

"Uh huh. What you want to talk about, Sailor?"

"I need some information, Jaloux, about my son, and I thought you might could help me get it."

"What's his name?"

"Pace. Pace Roscoe Ripley. He's fifteen and I found out from a note he left me that he was involved in a robbery of funds belongin' to your boss, Mr. Papavero. I was hopin' to find out where Pace is now, if Papavero and his bunch got it figured out yet."

"Honey, this is somethin' I *can't* talk about. I'm sure you understand."

"'Course. I was just hopin' we could make a date to meet somewhere—anywhere, anytime—long as it's soon."

"Give me your number, Sailor. I'll ask around and call you back."

"Fine. It's 555-8543. I was thinkin' about callin' you anyway, Jaloux, you know? I mean, I had you on my mind."

"Talk to you later, Sailor Ripley. You can tell me what I had on when you had me on your mind. Bye."

She hung up before he could say, "Thanks, Jaloux."

SCOOBA'S

The boys stopped at Scooba's Cafe in Lookout World, population 444, to have something to eat after a long night on the road and before visiting Miss Napoleon's Paradise. Lookout World had been named by the daughter of Fractious Carter, Metamorphia, after his death in 1962 at the age of 101. Until then, the town was called Carter, having been owned, operated and maintained by him since its incorporation. Metamorphia was fifty-nine years old when her father died and she was his sole heir. She'd never married and had waited all of her life to get away. Before taking off, Metamorphia changed the town's name to what she shouted out at Fractious's funeral. "Look out, world!" Metamorphia cried as she walked away from the grave. "I ain't sixty yet!"

Nobody in Lookout World had heard from her for forty years, except for a picture postcard of the Halliday Hotel, Ohio and 2d streets, "Grant Stayed Here," postmarked Cairo, Illinois, and dated October 2, 1969, which was received by Leander Many, Fractious Carter's lawyer, who was at that time ninety-four and about to be a terminal victim of emphysema, brought on, Many believed, by his lifelong penchant for the practice of onanistic asphyxia. Metamorphia wrote: "Bet you Bastards think I am Beyond Hope. Maybe your Right. Lester says I got a Head Start to Satan." Neither Leander Many nor anyone else in Lookout World knew who Lester was.

Lefty Grove and Smokey Joe each automatically ordered hotcakes, grits with gravy, and chicory coffee, the same meal Tyrus Raymond Rattler ate every morning of his life since his sons could recall. Pace stared at the counter girl. She was about his age, under five feet tall, too skinny to lie on, with messy mud-red hair and bad acne. She looked like he felt.

"Come, boy," she said, "already sunup in Lowndes County."

"Grits 'n' gravy, is all," Pace said. "And a Coke, you got one."

"Got it."

She went off to put in their order and Pace picked up a day old *Delta Democrat-Times* that was lying on the stool next to him. Sailor had told Pace how it had been his own daddy's practice to turn to the Obituaries page first thing; it had become Sailor's habit, too, and now Pace searched for the death column. It was always interesting to read about other people's lives, Sailor said. It took your mind off your own.

JOE SEWELL, 91, HALL OF FAMER TOUGHEST TO STRIKE OUT was the top line. "Joseph Wheeler Sewell, the eagle-eyed batter who struck out only 114 times during a fourteen-year major league career, died on Tuesday at his home in Mobile, Alabama," Pace read. "He was elected to the Baseball Hall of Fame in 1977 and was ninety-one years old when he died. Over eleven seasons with the Cleveland Indians and three with the New York Yankees, from 1920 to 1933, Joe Sewell struck out only three times in two seasons and only four times in two others. Umpires deferred to his judgment to the point where if he chose not to swing at a pitch, they would virtually always call it a ball.

"Mr. Sewell, who was born in the town of Titus on October 9, 1898, said that he developed his batting skills as a youngster in rural Alabama by repeatedly tossing rocks and lumps of coal into the air and belting them with a broomstick. No one in major league history who played as much struck out less, and Mr. Sewell played a lot. He entered the American League as a twenty-one-year-old replacement for Ray Chapman, the Indian shortstop who became the only big-leaguer to die in a game when he was struck in the head by a pitch thrown by Carl Mays of the Yankees. From September 7, 1920 until May 2, 1930, when he was kept in bed with a brain fever, Mr. Sewell played in 1,103 consecutive games.

"At five feet, six-and-a-half inches tall and 155 pounds, Joe Sewell compiled a career batting average of .312, including a high of .353 in 1923 and nine other .300 seasons. Most of his 2,226 hits were singles, but none was of the broken-bat variety. Aside from his record of 115 straight games without striking out in 1929, the most compelling evidence of Mr. Sewell's uncanny ability to put wood solidly onto the ball was that *he used only one bat during his entire major league career.* It was a thirty-five-inch, forty-ounce Ty Cobb model Louisville Slugger he kept in condition by seasoning it with chewing tobacco and stroking it with a Coca-Cola bottle.

"Mr. Sewell was a star football and baseball player for the University of Alabama, and led the school baseball team to four conference titles before joining the minor league New Orleans Pelicans in 1920. Before that summer ended, he was on a World Series championship team as Cleveland beat the Brooklyn Dodgers.

"After his career ended, Mr. Sewell worked for a dairy and was a major league scout. In 1964, at the age of sixty-six, he became the Alabama baseball coach, winning 114 games and losing ninety-nine in seven seasons. His two younger brothers, Tommy and Luke, both of whom are dead, also played in the major leagues. Mr. Sewell is survived by a son, Dr. James W. Sewell of Mobile, a daughter, L.C. Parnell of Birmingham, ten grandchildren and fourteen great-grandchildren."

The waitress brought the boys' breakfasts and set the plates down on the puce Formica counter.

"Need anythin' else, y'all holler," she said.

"What's your name?" asked Smokey Joe.

"Hissy. Mama's Missy, sister's Sissy."

"What's your daddy's?"

"Ever'body calls him Bird-Dog, but his real name's Buster. Buster Soso."

Pace put down the newspaper and picked up the can of Coke Hissy Soso had brought him and studied it.

"What you eyeballin' that can for?" asked Lefty Grove.

"Wouldn't do to rub a old wood ball bat with this, would it?" said Pace.

LULA'S PLANS

"Hi, Sail, sweetie. How're my boys?"

"Oh, Lula, it's you."

"Who were you expectin' to call? Ann-Margret, maybe?"

"No, honey, I thought it might be Pace. How's Marietta?"

"Mama's recoverin' faster'n they'd like, as if we couldn'ta guessed she would. Dal and I can't no more keep her down than Imelda Marcos could quit buyin' shoes. I'm thinkin' I might stay another couple days, though, just to make certain her heart don't start flutterin', like after she had that bad fall last summer."

"Whatever's best, peanut."

"Then, of course, Reverend Plenty's appearin' in Rock Hill on Monday? I'm also thinkin' it could be a excitin' deal to go hear him at the openin' sermon of the first South Carolina branch of the Church of the Three R's. I could stay over in Charlotte with Bunny Thorn, Beany's first cousin once or twice removed? The one lost her left arm, most of it anyway, in a car wreck at the beach in Swansboro when she was eighteen? You remember my tellin' you about her? I ain't seen Bunny in years. She owns a laundromat out by the Speedway. Wonder if Bunny'd go hear Goodin Plenty with me."

"Sounds all right to me, Lula. Stay as long as you need."

"How's Pace? He gettin' to school on time and eatin' proper?"

"He's been keepin' busy."

"You got a eye on him, Sail, don't you?"

"Don't be worryin' about us Ripley males, honey. We're survivors."

"Glad to hear it. Sailor?"

"Yes, ma'am?"

"You love your Lula?"

"I do, peanut. Always will, too."

"*Hasta siempre.* darlin'."

"*Hasta siempre.*"

"Glad you could make it, Coot," said Sailor. "This'd be a tough one to face alone."

"Got plenty of food, weapons and ammo and the Ram's gassed to the gills. Figure we can work the give-and-go, you'n me's all we got, like them Shinin' Path people in Peru. You heard of 'em, haven't ya? The Cocaine Commies? Good Chinese-style guerilla fighters, though. What's your idea on the procedure?"

Coot Veal was decked out in his best cammies, black lace-up Red Wings, green Semper Fi hat, and double-reflector wraparounds. He took a small black leather pouch containing an Urban Skinner out of a pocket of his field jacket, clipped it on to his belt and twisted it front to back. The telephone rang and Sailor lifted the receiver.

"Ripley."

"Sailor, I got bad news." It was Bob Lee Boyle.

"What now?"

"Bomb blew out the front door and some windows of the new warehouse."

"When'd this happen?"

"About a half hour ago. Guess Papavero don't take no like a man."

"Not many do."

"I ain't changin' my mind, though, Sail. I mean, Gator Gone's *mine*."

"I'll back you, Bob Lee, whatever you decide."

"'Preciate that, Sailor Ripley. Knew you would. I'm goin' over to assess the damage now. Comin'?"

"Can't, Bob Lee. Pace is in some trouble and I got to attend to it first. I'm sorry but it's priority."

"Understand. Anything I can do?"

"Make sure you don't say nothin' to Beany or it'll likely get back to Lula. Coot Veal's here. Think we can handle it, thanks the same."

"Okay, good buddy. Let's each check in later."

"You got it, Bob Lee. *Cuidado,* hear?"

"I'll try."

"And give me a holler you hear direct from them boys."

"Sail?"

"Uh huh?"

"This what's called a hostile takeover bid?"

Sailor hung up and told Coot what had happened.

"This said ol' life's becomin' a tougher proposition all the time," Coot said. "I had me a terminal disease no tellin' what I'd do. As it is my short list is gettin' longer all the time."

"Figure it'll be any better in the next?"

"You turnin' Hindu?"

"Heard a piece on the news earlier about a sixteen-year-old boy, not much older'n Pace, escaped from Cuba on a surfboard."

"A surfboard?"

"Yeah. Seems a East German tourist bought the kid a windsurfin' board and he took off for Florida. Made it thirty miles before the boom broke, which he managed to re-rig somehow, well enough to go another thirty miles when the thing give out for good. Got picked up by a Bahamian freighter crewed by Koreans couldn't speak Spanish or English. They notified the U.S. Coast Guard, who took the boy the last thirty-mile stretch into Key West. Kid said he was goin' to live with relatives in Miami. Didn't seem to think what he done was so remarkable. Just wanted to be free, is all."

"Desperate people do all kinds of incredible things."

Sailor nodded. "Made me wonder about Pace. What made him so damn desperate that he'd do this fool thing with them worthless Rattlers?"

Coot shook his head and said nothing, just took off his shades, checked them for smudges and put them back on. The doorbell rang and Sailor answered it.

"Hi, Sailor man."

"Thanks for comin' by, Jaloux. You find out anything?"

Sailor let her in.

"Poppy's wife—sometimes I go shoppin' with her?—she told me they figure the boys is headed north into Mississippi."

"What's there?"

"Rattler brothers got a insane mama locked up in a place called Miss

Napoleon's Paradise for the Lord's Disturbed Daughters. Perdita says Zero, Poppy's top gun, is goin' after 'em with some pistols. Zero was wounded durin' the takedown and he won't be lookin' to take no prisoners."

"You say Perdita?"

"Yeah. Poppy's wife. Why?"

"She a Tex-Mex woman, last name of Durango?"

"Don't know that I ever heard her own last name, but yeah, she's from Texas and looks Mexican, all right. You know her?"

Sailor nodded. "I did. Listen, Jaloux, you been a big help. Anything I can do for y'all, let me know."

"There is, Sailor man. Definitely is somethin' you can help me with."

"I got to get goin' now, Jaloux. My boy's in tough and I got to find him before this Zero does."

"I'm goin' with you, then."

"Really, Jaloux, you don't want to get mixed up in this, 'specially as how you're an employee of Mr. Papavero's. Me and my pal Coot here can handle it, I hope."

"I'm comin' along, Sailor. I know right where Miss Napoleon's is, 'count of I used to live nearby in Starkville for two years when my mama was married to her third husband, man named Dub Buck owned a Buick dealership. Had him a string of signs on old Highway 82 from Eupora to Mayhew said, 'Buy Buck's Buicks.' Dub had did some small piece of time before Mama met him, for exposin' his self in a public park up in Greenville. I liked him, though. Dub died of food poison in Nogales one weekend when I was fourteen. Least that's what Mama said when she come home without him. She and me moved to N.O. right after."

"Coot, this here's Jaloux Marron," said Sailor. "She's gonna show us the way."

"Semper Fi, Miss Marron," said Coot, tipping his cap.

"Can't say the same, Mr. Veal."

BACK TO BUDDHALAND

Smokey Joe pulled the Jimmy up to the premium pump at the self-serve Conoco in Meridian and cut the engine.

"Be right back," he said to Lefty Grove, as he got out and headed for the pay-in-advance window.

As he approached the pay window, Smokey Joe could see that there was a problem. A medium-sized black man in his thirties, with long, slanted, razor-shaped sideburns, wearing a camel hair sportcoat, was arguing with the Vietnamese kid behind the bulletproof pane.

"Pay for cigarettes!" said the Vietnamese kid, nodding his head quickly, causing his lank, black forelock of hair to flop forward almost to the tip of his nose.

"I paid you for 'em, motherfucker!" the black man shouted. "You already got my money!"

"No, no! Pay now! You pay for cigarettes!"

Standing off to one side, about eight feet from the man, was a young black woman wearing a beige skirt that ended mid-thigh of her extraordinarily skinny legs, and a short brown jacket that she held tightly around her shivering body despite the intense heat.

"Pay him or let's go!" she shouted. "I ain't wastin' street time on no cigarettes!"

"Keep the damn cigarettes, then, chump monkey!" the man yelled at the kid, throwing a pack of Winstons at the window. The pack bounced off and fell on the ground. "And go back to Buddhaland! Leave America to us Americans!"

The man turned away from the window and saw Smokey Joe approaching.

"Hey, man," he said, "you familiar with this area?"

"Why?" asked Smokey Joe.

"My wife and me got a problem with our car, see, and we need—"

"Sorry," Smokey Joe said, "I don't have any money to give away today."

"No, man, I don't want no money. All we need is a ride. We got to get our car towed."

"Call a tow truck."

"That's the problem, see, we don't know our way around here and we got to get the car fixed."

There was a large sign next to the garage door in the station that said MECHANIC ON DUTY 24 HOURS. Smokey Joe pointed to it.

"There's a mechanic right here," he told the man.

"Wouldn't let no chump monkey from Buddhaland touch it!"

"Come on!" shouted the woman, her thin naked knees shaking. "Turn loose, Chester. It ain't happenin'!"

Smokey Joe saw the man's eyebrows twitch and his face contort, twisting up on the left side, his nostrils flaring. The man hesitated for a moment and Smokey Joe braced himself, thinking that the man might attack him. But the man turned his back to Smokey Joe and followed the woman into the coffee shop of a motel next door.

"Ten bucks premium," Smokey Joe said to the kid, sliding a bill on the metal plate beneath the window.

As Smokey Joe pumped the gas, a well-dressed, overweight, middle-aged black woman, who had just finished fueling her late-model Toyota sedan, said, "Shouldn't be treatin' nobody like that. Ain't no way to be treatin' people here. This ain't no Asia."

She got into her car and drove away. One of the Vietnamese attendants, dressed in a clean, crisp blue uniform, walked out of the garage and over to Smokey Joe.

"This is bad neighborhood," he said, shaking his head. He took the fuel hose from Smokey Joe, who had drained his ten dollars' worth, and replaced it on the pump.

Smokey Joe slid behind the steering wheel of the Jimmy and started it up.

"You hear any of that?" he asked Lefty Grove.

Lefty Grove nodded and said, "Even gettin' gas nowadays reminds me of what Ray L. Menninger, the veterinarian-taxidermist, who Daddy said was the most honest man in Iguana County, Texas, used to say: 'With me, one way or the other, you get your dog back.'"

THE PARADISE

Nell Blaine Napoleon had moved into The Paradise eighty-two years ago, when she was four and a half years old. Her father, Colonel St. Jude Napoleon, a career army man, and her mother, Fanny Rose Bravo, had designed and had the twenty-six-room Paradise house built for them, and they had both lived and died there. Nell was their only child. By the age of twelve, Nell had decided to devote her life to the well-being of others. She was initially and forever inspired by a local black woman called Sister Domino, who spent each day administering to the sick and needy. Sister Domino allowed the young Nell to accompany her on her rounds of mercy, and taught her basic nursing skills, which Sister Domino had acquired at the Louise French Academy in Baltimore, where she had lived for eighteen years before returning to her Mississippi birthplace. Sister Domino's ambition had been to assist Dr. Albert Schweitzer at Lambarene, in Africa, and she read everything she could about him and his work, constantly telling Nell what a great man Schweitzer was and how there could be no higher aspiration in life than to work to alleviate the suffering of those persons less fortunate than themselves. The "Veritable Myriad" Sister Domino called the world's population.

Nell's parents never attempted to dissuade their daughter from her passion, or to turn her away from Sister Domino. Both St. Jude Napoleon and Fanny Rose Bravo were great believers in self-determination, and if this was the path Nell chose to follow, it was her business and no one else's. Their feeling was that there were certainly worse directions a life could take, and they let her be. The only time Nell had unwillingly had to separate herself from Sister Domino was the period during which she was required by her parents to attend Madame Petunia's School for Young Women in Oriole, between the ages of fourteen and seventeen. During her holidays, however, Nell would be back at Sister Domino's side, going from home to home among the poorest residents of Oktibbhea, Lowndes, Choctaw, Webster, Clay, Chickasaw, and Monroe counties. Following graduation from Madame Petunia's, Nell never wavered, dedicating herself fully to Sister Domino's work, which became her vocation also.

After her parents were killed by a falling tree that had been struck by a double bolt of ground lightning during a late-August electrical storm, Nell, who was then twenty-four, inherited The Paradise and invited Sister Domino to live there with her, which offer Sister Domino accepted. Eventually, Sister Domino and Miss Napoleon, as Nell came to be called, succeeded in converting the house into a combination hospital and retreat for those individuals incapable of dealing on a mutually acceptable basis with the outside world. Sister Domino's mandate, however, held that those residents of The Paradise be *serious* Christians. No blasphemy was tolerated and no waffling of faith. This policy, though, extended only to The Paradise; those persons she and Nell treated outside the house were not required to adhere to Christian tenets, the Lord's beneficence being available to the Veritable Myriad.

Sister Domino never did get to the Congo to assist Dr. Schweitzer, though Nell offered to pay her way. There was always too much work to be done at home, Sister Domino said, and when news of Dr. Schweitzer's death reached her, Sister Domino merely knelt, recited a brief, silent prayer, arose and continued scraping the back of a woman whose skin was inflamed and encrusted by eczema. Sister Domino died three years later, leaving Nell to carry on alone. As the years passed, however, Nell limited her ministrations to women, preferring their company to that of men, whom, Nell concluded, tended toward selfishness in their philosophy, which displeased her. Once made, Nell's decision was irreversible, and her devotion was further refined by her increasing acceptance of nonviolent, mentally disturbed women. A decade after Sister Domino's death, Nell officially registered her home with the county as Miss Napoleon's Paradise for the Lord's Disturbed Daughters. A large oil portrait of Sister Domino, painted from memory by Nell, hung on the wall opposite the front door so that the first sight anyone had upon entering was that of Miss Napoleon's own patron saint.

Mary Full-of-Grace Crowley Rattler fit in perfectly at The Paradise. As the mother of Jesus Christ, it was simply a matter of being acknowledged as such that contented her. At no time during her stay had Mary Full-of-Grace caused Miss Napoleon the slightest difficulty, not even when another woman, Boadicea Booker, who also believed she was the mother of the Christ child, lived at The Paradise. Boadicea had died within three months of her coming, so it was possible, Miss Napoleon believed, that Mary Full-of-Grace had no knowledge of her existence. When Tyrus Raymond Rattler and his sons came to visit Mary Full-of-Grace, Miss Napoleon was pleased to welcome them, as they were unfailingly polite and well-behaved. Even when Lefty Grove and Smokey Joe were small children, Miss Napoleon noticed, they had minded their father precisely and comported themselves properly in the presence of their mother. Therefore, when Mary Full-of-Grace's sons and another boy appeared on the front porch of The Paradise one windy afternoon, Miss Napoleon welcomed them inside.

"Afternoon, L.G.," she said. "Afternoon, S.J. Your mother will be pleased to see you. And who is this young gentleman?"

"Hello, Miss Napoleon," said Lefty Grove. "This is our friend, Pace Ripley."

Pace set down the sack he'd been carrying and nodded to the old woman, who was barely more than four feet tall. Pace figured her weight at about seventy-five pounds. His daddy could lift her off the ground with one hand, he figured, dangle her by her ankles with his arm stretched straight out.

"Hello, ma'am," Pace said. "Beautiful place you got here."

"My parents, Colonel St. Jude and Fanny Rose Bravo, built it and left it in my care so that I might care for others. You boys can go right up, if you like. Mary Full-of-Grace is in her room. She never leaves it until dark."

"Thank you, Miss Napoleon," said Smokey Joe. "We 'preciate all you done for Mama."

"The Lord prevails and I provide," said Miss Napoleon, as the Rattler brothers, followed by Pace, who carried the sack, filed up the stairs.

Mary Full-of-Grace was sitting perfectly still in a high-backed wing chair next to the windows when the boys entered her room. Her long, silver-blue hair hung in two braids, one on either side of her V-shaped head. She wore a white, gauzy robe with a golden sash tied at the waist. Pace noticed that she had almost no nose, only two air holes, and hugely dilated brown eyes. She kept her long, thin hands folded in her lap. Her fingers looked to Pace as if they were made of tissue paper.

"Hello, Mama," said Lefty Grove, who kissed her forehead.

"Hello, Mama," said Smokey Joe, who followed suit.

The brief, soft touch of their lips left dark marks on her skin.

"This boy here's our associate, Pace Ripley," Lefty Grove said.

"Hello, Mrs. Rattler," said Pace, trying to smile.

Both brothers looked quickly and hard at Pace.

"This here's the mother of Baby Jesus," said Smokey Joe.

Mary Full-of-Grace stared out the window to her left.

"My son is soon in Galilee," she said. "I keep the vigil."

Smokey Joe motioned to Pace and Pace slid the sack containing most of the money from the robbery under the light maple four-poster bed.

"Well, Mama, we don't mean to disturb you none," said Lefty Grove. "We'll just come back by and by."

Smokey Joe headed out the door and Pace followed.

"By and by," said Mary Full-of-Grace. "He will be by, by and by." She continued to stare out the window.

"So long, Mama," said Lefty Grove, closing the door behind him.

They did not see Miss Napoleon on their way out but Pace spotted the portrait of Sister Domino.

"Who's that?" he asked, walking over to take a closer look. "And what does this mean?" he said, reading the words carved into the bottom of the frame. "God's Gift to the Veritable Myriad."

"Must be was Miss Napoleon's mammy," said Smokey Joe. "What the hell you think?"

Pace trailed the Rattlers out of The Paradise, wondering about those words carved into the frame. A hunchbacked old woman was coming carefully up the steps of the porch, holding a large, blue plastic fly swatter.

"Suck cock!" she spat at them. "Suck cock! Suck cock! Suck cock!"

"You won't regret goin', Bunny. Reverend Plenty puts on a show and a half."

"I'm lookin' forward to it, Lula. Been needin' to get away from the laundromat anyway. More'n even a two-armed woman can handle there."

Lula and Bunny Thorn were riding in Lula's rented T-bird from Charlotte to Rock Hill to witness Reverend Goodin Plenty's first-ever sermon in South Carolina. His Church of Reason, Redemption and Resistance to God's Detractors had been running ads in every newspaper within two-hundred-fifty miles of Rock Hill for a month.

"How's your sex life, Lula? You don't mind my askin'."

Lula laughed, looked quickly at Bunny, then back at the road.

"Well, okay, I guess," she said, and with her right hand shook a More from an opened pack on the seat next to her, stuck it between her lips and punched in the dashboard lighter. "How's yours?"

"Lousy, you don't mind my complainin'. Guys'll do it once with a one-armed woman, just for a kick, 'cause it's kinda unusual, you know. That's it, though. They don't come lookin' for seconds. I been wed to a rubberized dick for a year now. Least it don't quit till my arm give out. I'm considerin' joinin' some women's group just to meet some queer gals. Maybe they won't mind a two-hundred-twenty-pound washerwoman with one musclebound arm. And I almost lost it, too, tryin' to unjam a Speed Queen the other day."

The lighter popped out and Lula lit her cigarette, took a couple of powerful puffs and laughed again.

"Bunny, you're somethin' fresh, I tell you. Sailor'd love you to death."

"Yeah? Think I oughta come visit, stay at your house? Maybe get Sailor to give me a workout or two?"

Lula coughed hard and tossed the More out the window.

"Just jokin', hon'. Tried to get Beany to ask Bob Lee if he'd do it, but she didn't go for the idea. And she's my cousin! Guess I'll have to stick with Big Bill."

The parking lot at the Rock Hill church site was full by the time Lula and Bunny arrived, so Lula parked the T-bird across the road. Since groundbreaking for the church building had not yet commenced, a giant tent had been set up and filled with folding chairs. Lula and Bunny managed to find two together at the rear. The tent was filled to capacity by the time Reverend Goodin Plenty, dressed in a tan Palm Beach suit with a black handkerchief flared out of the breast pocket, walked in and strode down the center aisle, hopped up on the platform, grabbed a microphone and faced the audience.

"My goodness!" Goodin Plenty said as he smiled broadly and sized up the crowd. "Ain't this just somethin' spectacular! My, my! Not a empty seat in the Lord's house tonight. Ain't it grand to be alive and holdin' His hand!"

"Yes, sir, Reverend!" someone shouted.

"Tell us about it, Reverend!" said another.

Reverend Plenty smoothed back his full head of prematurely white hair with both hands, making the microphone squeal, then raised up his arms as if he were a football referee signaling that a touchdown had been scored.

"I am gonna give you somethin' tonight, people! The Church of Reason, Redemption and Resistance to God's Detractors is here in the great state of South Carolina, first to secede from the Union, to stay!"

"Maybe so," shouted a tall, skinny, bald-headed man wearing a blue-white Hawaiian shirt with red and yellow flowers on it, who jumped up from the front row, "but *you* ain't!"

The skinny man held out a Ruger Redhawk .44 revolver with a seven-and-one-half-inch scoped barrel and pointed it straight at the Reverend's chest.

"This is for Marie!" the man yelled, as he held the gun with both hands and pulled the trigger, releasing a hardball round directly into Goodin Plenty's left temple as he attempted to dodge the bullet. The shell exploded inside the Reverend's brain and tore away half of the right side of his head as it passed through.

A riot broke out and Lula and Bunny got down on their knees and crawled out of the tent through a side flap. As soon as they were outside, they stood up and ran for the car.

"Holy shit!" said Bunny, as Lula cranked the engine and sped away. "That was better than the Hagler-Hearns fight! Only thing, it didn't last as long."

Lula put the pedal down and drove as fast as she dared.

"Uh-uh-uh," Bunny uttered. "That Marie must be some *serious* piece of ass!"

SHAKE, RATTLE & ROLL

Wendell Shake watched the Jimmy's oversized tires crawl through the mud ruts toward his farmhouse. He lifted the .30-06 semi-automatic rifle to his right shoulder and sighted down the four-power Tasco scope. At his feet, propped on end under the window, was a loaded eleven-and-three-quarter inch, forty-pound draw Ninja pistol crossbow with a die cast aluminum body and contoured grips. Wendell had come home to Mississippi and the Shake family farm two months before, after the fifth severed head had been found in a garbage can in the Bronx. That was the last of them, Wendell decided, one for each borough of New York City, to show the Jews, Catholics, and coloreds what he thought of their so-called civilization. Armageddon was about to commence, Wendell believed, and he was an operative of the avant-garde. It was his Great Day in the Morning, as he liked to call it, at last, after forty-eight years of silent suffering, witnessing the slaughter of the innocents. Now, however, the rest of the avenging angels were poised to strike, and the message Wendell had delivered was being read and discussed. Perhaps, Wendell thought, as he watched the Rattler brothers and Pace disembark from their vehicle, he was about to receive an acknowledgment of his effort.

"This place been abandoned for years," Lefty Grove said to Pace, as the three boys walked up the path to the house. "Daddy and us used it lots of times when we come up to visit Mama. Been about three, four months since we been here, I guess. Right, Smoke?"

" 'Bout that, Lef. You remember this gate bein' wired shut like this?"

Smokey Joe placed his left hand on the post and vaulted himself up in the air.

Before Smokey Joe had cleared the top rail, a bullet smacked into the center of his forehead, knocking him backward, so that his legs looped over the front of the rail by the backs of his knees, leaving the upper half of his body dangling upside down on the opposite side.

Lefty Grove and Pace both hit the ground and covered their heads. They heard the screen door of the house open and slam shut, footsteps coming down the porch steps and then on the path toward them. Neither of the boys dared to move. The footsteps stopped at the gate.

"Charity, gentlemen," said Wendell Shake, "ain't got nothin' to do with mercy. Even in a foreign land."

Lefty Grove raised his head and saw a middle-aged man about six feet tall and two-hundred pounds, wearing a red and gray flannel shirt, red suspenders, black pants and low-cut, steel-toed, brown work shoes. His hair was almost completely gray, with dark patches at the front, worn very long, touching his shoulders. It was difficult to see the man's face because of his heavy red beard and the way his head was pressed down close to the rifle. The man's eye sockets seemed devoid of white.

"Suppose you say somethin'," Wendell said to Lefty Grove, "and they ain't the right words?"

Wendell rested the rifle barrel on Smokey Joe's right knee, keeping the business end directed at Lefty Grove's head.

"Could be there'd be repercussions."

Pace looked up and saw Wendell standing at the gate. A light rain was falling.

"Both you boys stand up," Wendell ordered, and they obeyed.

Wendell flipped Smokey Joe's legs up with the barrel, causing the corpse's head to hit the ground before the rest of it pretzeled over. Lefty Grove and Pace got to their feet.

"Come in, gentlemen," said Wendell, unfastening and opening the gate to admit them.

Wendell marched the boys up the steps into the house, where he motioned with the gun to a wooden bench against a wall of the front room.

"Sit yourselves down there, gentlemen, and tell me what's brought you this far."

Pace sat down and Lefty Grove remained standing.

"Look, mister," said Lefty Grove, and Wendell shot him through the heart.

The last Rattler brother collapsed on the floor next to Pace's feet, made one slight lurch after he was down, then lay perfectly still. Pace closed his eyes.

"Didn't exactly sit, did he?" said Wendell, looking down at Lefty

Grove's body, then up at Pace. "That's a rhetorical question, son. You needn't answer. Open your eyes."

Pace looked at the man. Wendell Shake had mud puddles where his eyes ought to have been, and he was grinning, exposing gums that matched his suspenders and a dozen crowded, yellow teeth.

"We'll wait together, son," Wendell said. "There are terrible things soon to be revealed, and man craves company. That's but one flaw in the design. Do you love the Lord, boy?"

Pace said nothing.

"Please answer."

"I do, sir," said Pace. "I surely do love the Lord."

"Then the Lord loves you."

Wendell pulled up a goose-neck rocker and sat down, resting his 30-06 across his knees. He began to sing.

"I'm goin' to take a trip in that old gospel ship, I'm goin' far beyond the sky. I'm gonna shout and sing, till the heavens ring, when I kiss this world goodbye."

Pace saw the pistol crossbow lying on the floor beneath a window on the other side of the room.

They decided to take two vehicles, Coot riding alone in his red Dodge pickup and Sailor with Jaloux in her metallic blue Chevrolet Lumina.

"All the top stock racers back home use these," said Sailor, as Jaloux drove, following four car lengths behind Coot Veal's Ram.

"These what?" Jaloux asked. "And where's back home?"

"North Carolina, born and raised. Luminas, they all run 'em. Quick, light, and powerful."

"Kinda like me," said Jaloux, laughing, "only you don't know it yet."

Sailor looked over at her. Jaloux was short, about five-three, with a sweet little figure that tempted Sailor to suck on her like he would a piece of hard candy, rub her smooth with his tongue until she disappeared. It wouldn't happen, though. There was no way Sailor wanted to risk breaking the bond between him and Lula. All he needed from Jaloux Marron was her help in finding his and Lula's son. This wasn't the time to get complicated.

"Mama's second husband, he was a welder," said Jaloux. "Kind of a criminal, though."

"Yeah, what kind?"

"All I know's what Mama says, but Terrell—his name was Terrell Vick—he'd need somethin' extra, Terrell'd just go out at night and knock somebody over the head and take it. Never nothin' big, I guess, small-time. Maybe that's what prompted Mama to get rid of him."

"What about your own daddy?"

"He was French. Not Cajun, real French, from France. Belgium, really, which is a place close to France. His family was all from there. Marcel Marron. *Marron* means chestnut, you know."

"I didn't."

"Yeah, he was livin' in Antwerp before he come to the States. Started sellin' hosiery for some New York company and wound up in New Orleans at a convention, where he met Mama. She was on her own by then, nineteen years old, and was sorta hard up for cash, I guess, workin' as a party hostess for this bunch of conventioneers at the Monteleone.

'Course all them boys, they just after a quick dip, and why not? That's how Mama met Marcel Marron and he got her pregnant, married her, and hung around N.O. until about two months after I was born, then run off. Mama says she never knew where to, and ain't never heard. Maybe back to New York, or Antwerp. Least I'm legal."

"You mean legitimate."

"Can't have it both ways, huh?"

"How'd you get started at the Fais-Dodo?"

"After high school, which I went three years, only work I could find was fast food places or checkin' in grocery stores. That weren't no decent money, so a guy I knew, Jim-Baby Fitch, tended bar at Inez's for a while, introduced me to the manager, Blackie Caddo, happens to be from Plain Dealin', where Mama grew up partly. He hired me and there you go."

"Strange how them things turn out."

Sailor switched on the radio and they listened to Eddie Floyd sing "Knock on Wood" before the news on the hour.

"In Baton Rouge today, a man who two days ago shot and killed another man who had just shot and killed a woman in a shopping mall, turned himself over to the police.

"Enos Swope said he acted on impulse after seeing Kirkland Ray kill his former fiancée, Yvette Vance. Lieutenant Frank LeRoi, of the Baton Rouge police department, said, 'Ray murdered this woman. She's down, she's wounded, and he goes and shoots her in the head again after she's down.'

"Swope said that as he pulled into the mall's parking lot he saw Ray chase Yvette Vance, waving a revolver in the air. Swope took out his own gun, a forty-four caliber pistol, and shot at the back of Ray's car as Ray was pulling away, hoping to disable it. His second shot penetrated the door and struck the fleeing man, who slumped down in his seat. Ray's car went out of control and crashed into a light pole, toppling it over onto the top of a 1958 Cadillac Coupe De Ville, trapping seventy-eight-year-old Johnson Buckeye inside. Both Buckeye and Kirkland Ray were taken by ambulance to a hospital, where Buckeye is listed in stable condition. Kirkland Ray was pronounced dead on arrival.

"'I didn't want to kill him,' said Enos Swope, a twenty-five-year-old washing machine repairman. 'I was just trying to help a lady.'

"Swope fled the scene, he told police, because he was afraid of being treated like a criminal. After reading in the newspaper that police were searching for a third person believed to have been involved in the incident, he came forward.

"'My life is a mess now,' Swope said today. 'I could lose my job, everything I own. I don't want to lose my gun. I paid dearly for it. I don't want my gun marked up. It's such a pretty gun. I love that gun.'

"Police have decided not to file charges against Enos Swope, pending a grand jury's review of the case."

Jaloux followed Coot Veal off the highway to a Short Stop convenience store.

"Hey, Sailor," Coot said, before they went in for a coffee break, "forget what I was sayin' before about them Shinin' Path people in Peru."

"Why's that, Coot?"

"Well, I was just listenin' to the radio news?"

"Yeah, so was we."

"Had a report that them guerrillas shot and killed nineteen peasants, nearly all of 'em women and children, in a small village up in the Andes. These peasants went there to escape the rebel attacks down below. Said some of the kids weren't no more'n two or three years old. Just like Nam."

A young black woman, no more than fifteen years old, a bright yellow scarf wrapped around her head, holding an infant with one arm and a bag of groceries with the other, was coming out of the Short Stop. Sailor held the door open for her.

"Thanks, mister," she said, passing Sailor without looking at him.

"No problem," said Sailor.

WORKING IN THE GOLD MINE

Carmine Papavero and Zero Diplopappus left the office of Bayou Enterprises at seven-forty-five A.M. Poppy slid behind the wheel of his powder blue BMW and punched up his home number on the cellular phone as he pulled into the commuter traffic on Airline Highway.

"H'lo."

"*Buona mattina*, Perdita *mia*. I wake you up?"

"Uh huh."

"Sorry, sweetheart, but I figured if I didn't call now I might not get another chance until late."

"Got a busy day, huh?"

"Zero and I are going to Mississippi today, after we make a stop in town. We might not be back until tomorrow, tomorrow night."

"I'm still pretty beat from all that flyin', honey, so I'll be sleepin' mostly. That Europe's okay, but it's too damn far away. Think from now on I'll just stick to Dallas or Palm Beach, I need somethin' special."

"Whatever pleases you, honey. Get your rest and we'll have some fun when I return."

"Hold ya to it."

Poppy laughed. "Sleep tight, baby," he said, and hung up.

"You ought to get married, Zero. Change your outlook."

"Only one I'm lookin' out for is me. Besides, I was married once."

"Oh yeah? What happened?"

"Back in Tarpon Springs, when I was eighteen. A local girl, Flora Greco. She drowned on our honeymoon in Mexico."

"I'm sorry, Zero. I didn't know."

"I don't look back. Where we stoppin'?"

"Sonny Nevers needs a visit. We'll catch him at his jewelry store right when he opens at eight."

Poppy guided the Beamer off Interstate 10 onto Claiborne and turned down Elysian Fields. He pulled in front of the Gold Mine and parked. He and Zero waited until Sonny Nevers pulled up the doorshade, then they got out and rang the bell next to the store entrance. Nevers recognized Zero and Poppy and buzzed them in.

"Don't even say it!" said Sonny, edging his five-feet four-inch, three-hundred-pound body around from behind the counter to greet the two men. "I'll have it tomorrow, no problem."

Poppy accepted Sonny's handshake and waved away the smoke from what was already the jewelry salesman's second Partagas Topper of the day.

"Wasn't expecting there'd be one," said Poppy. "You've always been a man of your word, Sonny."

"Had a small cash flow difficulty here, just straightened it out. You can count on it. Want a cigar?"

"I know I can. No, thanks."

The doorbell rang. Sonny looked out and saw two men in blue sports coats carrying briefcases.

"Salesmen," said Sonny, who went back behind the counter and pressed the buzzer.

"What can I do for you gentlemen?" he asked, after they'd entered.

Both men were more than six feet tall, well-built, had blond hair and wore Carrera sunglasses. Each man pulled a .45 automatic from his briefcase and pointed it at Sonny and Poppy and Zero.

"We'll kill all three of you," said the slightly taller of the two men in a calm voice, "unless you give us what you've got in the safe."

Nobody said a word as the taller man followed Sonny into the rear of the store. The other man kept Poppy and Zero covered while he pulled down the doorshade and reversed the OPEN sign to CLOSED. In less than five minutes, the taller man emerged from the back, carrying a large black satchel filled mostly with twenty-four-karat gold used for the manufacture of gold chain.

Sonny ran out and hurled his huge body at the man with the satchel. The other blond man turned and shot Sonny in the face, the slug going in under the nose, lifting off the top of the fat man's head. Sonny's corpse belly-flopped on the floor as an umbrella of blood spread around him. Zero and Poppy plastered themselves against the wall. The taller blond man turned toward them and fired twice. One round entered Poppy's open mouth, killing him instantly. Zero dropped to his knees, so the man's first shot missed entirely, shattering the plaster above his head. The second shot, however, was on target, gouging a large opening in the left side of Zero's neck, causing his oversized ears to flap furiously as he crumpled over on the cool, black-and-white-tiled floor.

The two blond men put their guns into the briefcases and left the store, the shorter man making certain that the door was closed securely behind them. The men walked swiftly to a new black Cadillac Fleetwood, put the satchel, containing nearly seventy-five pounds of gold worth three quarters of a million dollars, and the briefcases into the trunk, locked it, got into the car and drove away at a moderate speed. Inside The Gold Mine, Zero Diplopappus watched a ribbon of sunlight wriggle slowly through the front window and settle on what was left of Sonny Nevers's face. Zero did not live long enough to close his eyes.

"You don't have to be afraid to talk to me, boy," Wendell Shake said to Pace. "Got somethin' to say, say it."

"I ain't," said Pace.

"This world's an awful cruel place, son. Worst place I ever been."

"You remind me of a person I met once, named Elmer Désespéré," said Pace, "hailed from Mamou. He weren't so crazy for it, neither."

"There's a few of us is sensitive to more'n the weather. Where's this Elmer now?"

"He was killed on the street in New Orleans."

"Mighta guessed. It's the good go young, like they say. But there'll be one Great Day in the Mornin' before it's finished, I guarantee."

"Sir?"

"Yes, son?"

"What is it exactly gripes you, you don't mind my askin'."

Wendell grinned. "Ain't worth explainin'. Best repeat what Samuel Johnson said: 'Depend upon it that if a man talks of his misfortunes there is something in them that is not disagreeable to him; for where there is nothing but pure misery there never is any recourse to the mention of it.'"

Pace stared at Wendell, who sat stroking his red beard.

Wendell stood up and said, "Time to tend the garden. You'll stay put, won't ya?"

Pace nodded and watched Wendell walk out of the room. As soon as the madman was out of sight, he scrambled to his feet, ran over to the pistol crossbow and picked it up. Pace heard Wendell relieving himself in what he assumed was the toilet. He crouched under the window and waited. When Wendell reentered the room, Pace pressed the trigger that released a black dart into his captor's left eye. Wendell fell down and Pace dropped the crossbow and ran out of the house, headed on foot the four miles to Miss Napoleon's Paradise.

Wendell Shake carried no identification of any kind, and when his body was found, along with those of the Rattler brothers, the only item discovered in his pockets by police was a personal ad torn from a news-paper.

> If any open-minded, good-humored men of any race wish to write, I'm here and waiting. BF doing a 60-year term for something that just came out bad.
> Lamarra Chaney #1213 P-17
> Women's Correctional Facility
> Box 30014, Draper, UT 84020

Miss Napoleon, Jaloux, and Sailor were sitting in rocking chairs on the front porch at The Paradise, drinking iced tea. Coot had driven into Starkville to see if he could dig up any information on the whereabouts of Pace and the Rattler brothers. It was late afternoon, siesta time for the Lord's disturbed daughters, and things were quiet.

"It's the kind of thing happens if you hold the faith," said Miss Napoleon. "Tell the truth, I was worried about paying the bills for the first time in my life. We live modestly here at The Paradise, as Sister Domino insisted, but even so we had begun to struggle. When Mary Full-of-Grace came down those stairs last night and delivered into my hands that money, it was the answer to our prayers. Now we'll be able to continue as we've always done, and provide for more than just ourselves. I've thought about opening a haven for the homeless, which until last night didn't seem possible. The Lord has plans for us we cannot even imagine."

"You always been the kind of woman make God or any man do for, Miss Napoleon," said Jaloux.

"Child, don't you know the Lord's not a man? He's all things to all manner of people, and He provides best for those who provide for others. In this case, Mary Full-of-Grace was His instrument of mercy. Praise be."

Just then, Coot Veal's Ram came tearing up the drive, and Sailor could see that Coot had a passenger with him. The truck stopped and Pace jumped out. Sailor dropped his iced tea, hopped down off the porch and embraced him.

"Boy was runnin' down the road, Sail," said Coot, coming around the front of the truck. "Couldn't believe it myself when I saw who it was. And you won't believe this, neither. Heard on the radio that Papavero and his henchman, Zero the Greek, been shot and killed in N.O. under mysterious circumstances. Their bodies was found in a jewelry store on Elysian Fields."

"The Rattlers is dead, too," said Pace. "We was gonna hide out at a abandoned farmhouse—least the Rattlers thought it was abandoned—

and turned out a crazy man with a red beard was there. He shot both Lefty Grove and Smokey Joe. I was gonna be next, but he got to talkin' with me, all kindsa strange talk, and when he went to the head I got the drop on him with a pistol crossbow and let him have it. Then I run outta there fast as I could. Daddy, it was worse than what happened to me that time with the wild boy from Mamou."

Sailor and Pace stood and hugged each other.

"It's okay now, son," said Sailor. "Looks like the Lord done pulled off another one."

Miss Napoleon nodded and smiled and rocked in her chair.

"Come on up here, you two," she said to Coot and Pace, "and have a cold glass of tea."

"Guess this means whatever's between us is gonna have to wait," said Jaloux.

Coot and Pace were waiting in the truck while Sailor said goodbye to Jaloux in front of Inez's Fais-Dodo Bar.

Sailor grinned and brushed back his silvery black hair with both hands. Jaloux reached her right hand under the left sleeve of his white tee shirt and traced the large vein in his bicep with her index finger.

"Guess it'll have to, Jaloux. You been a giant help to me and my boy, and I ain't forgettin' it. I know I owe you."

"Rather have it be voluntary, you know what I mean."

Sailor laughed, leaned forward and kissed her above her left eyebrow.

"I do," he said.

Coot drove the Ripleys home and they were surprised to see Lula's red Cressida wagon in the driveway.

"Jesus, Mama's home," said Pace.

They got out of Coot's truck, and Pace ran into the house.

"Comin' in, Coot?" Sailor asked.

"No, Sail, thanks. I'm pretty well bushed, all this drivin'. Talk to y'all later'd be best."

"Thanks, buddy. Couldn'ta done it without ya."

Coot grinned, saluted and drove off.

"Sailor, honey!" Lula shouted, as soon as he walked in the door. "You won't believe what happened! Reverend Plenty got assassinated in Rock Hill and Bunny and I barely escaped with our own lives! I been tryin' to call you-all but there ain't been no answer. I been wild!"

Lula rushed into Sailor's arms and held him tight. Pace was lying on the couch with his eyes closed.

"Sail," Lula said, "I'm afraid the devil got this world by the tail and he ain't lettin' go."

Sailor smiled and kissed the top of Lula's left ear.

"Maybe so, peanut, but I ain't lettin' go of you, either."

Lula almost swooned. "Oh, Sail, that's what I needed to hear."

CONSUELO'S
KISS

There are two kinds of women: those who move to make room when you sit on the bed and those who remain where they are even when you have only a narrow edge.
—Edmund Wilson

CONTENTS
Consuelo's Kiss

CONSUELO'S KISS

Consuelo Whynot licked idly at her wild cherry-flavored Tootsie Pop while she watched highway patrolmen and firefighters pull bodies from the wreckage. The Amtrak Crescent, on its way from New Orleans to New York, had collided with a tractor-trailer rig in Meridian, hard by the Torch Truckstop, where Consuelo had stopped in to buy a sweet. The eight train cars had accordioned on impact and the semi, which had been carrying a half-ton load of Big Chief Sweet 'n' Sour Cajun-Q Potato Chips, simply exploded.

"The train's whistle was blowin' the whole time and, Lord, it sounded like a bomb had went off when they hit," said Patti Fay McNair, a waitress at the Torch, to a rubbernecker who'd asked if she'd seen what happened.

Consuelo Whynot, who was sixteen years old and a dead ringer for the actress Tuesday Weld at the same age, stared dispassionately at the carnage. The truck driver, a man named Oh-Boy Wilson from Guntown, near Tupelo, had been burned so badly over every inch of his body that the firemen just let him smolder on the spot where he'd landed after the explosion. His crumpled, crispy corpse reminded Consuelo of the first time she'd tried to make Roman Meal toast in the broiler pan of her cousin Vashti Dale's Vulcan the summer before last at the beach cottage in Ocean Springs. She never could figure out if she and Vashti Dale were once or twice removed. That was a result, Consuelo decided, of her unremarkable education. Venus Tishomingo would fix that, too, though, and the thought almost made Consuelo smile.

Four hospital types dressed in white and wearing plastic gloves slid Oh-Boy Wilson into a green body bag, zipped it up, tossed it into a van, and headed over to the wrecked Crescent, which had passenger parts sticking out of broken windows and crushed feet, hands, and heads visible beneath the overturned cars. Consuelo didn't think there'd be anything more very interesting to see, so she turned away and walked back to the truckstop.

"You goin' north?" she asked a man coming out of the diner.

The man looked at the petite young thing wearing a red-and-white polkadot poorboy that was stretched tightly over her apple-sized breasts, black jean cutoffs, yellow hair chopped down around her head like somebody had given it the once-over with a broken-bladed lawn mower, red tongue still lazily lapping at the Tootsie Pop, and said, "How old're you?"

"I been pregnant," Consuelo lied, "if that's what you mean."

The man grinned. He had a three-day beard, one slow blue-green eye and a baby beer gut. Consuelo pegged him at thirty.

"West," he said, "to Jackson. You can come, you want."

She followed him to a black Duster with mags, bright orange racing stripes, Moon eyes and a pale blue 43 painted on each side. She got in.

"My name's Wesley Nisbet," he said, and started the car. The ignition sounded like thunder at three A.M. "What's yours?"

"Consuelo Whynot."

Wesley laughed. "Your people the ones own Whynot, Mississippi? Town twenty miles east of here by the Alabama line?"

"Sixteen, be exact. You musta passed Geography."

Wesley whistled softly and idled the Duster toward Interstate 20.

"Where you headed, Consuelo?"

"Oxford."

"You got a boyfriend there?"

"Better. I'm goin' to see the woman of my dreams."

Wesley checked the traffic, then knifed into the highway and went from zero to sixty in under eight without fishtailing.

"This a 273?" Consuelo asked.

"Dropped in a 383 last week. You into ladies, huh?"

"One. What's the '43' for?"

"Number my idol, Richard Petty, ran with. Lots a man can do for ya a chick can't."

Consuelo bit down hard on the outer layer of her Tootsie Pop and sank her big teeth deep into the soft, dark brown core. She sucked on it for a minute, then opened her mouth and drooled down the front of her polkadot poorboy. Wesley wolfed a look at Consuelo, grinned, and gunned the Duster past ninety before feathering back down to a steady seventy-five.

"You ain't met Venus," she said.

"Who's gonna watch the worms?"

"Already taken care of, Sail, honey. Beany'll do it."

"She's gonna be helpin' out at Gator Gone, too, you know, fillin' in for me."

"Beany can handle more'n one thing at a time, darlin'. She can't get by one time, Madonna Kim will. She ain't doin' much between marriages."

"Can't believe that girl, peanut. Only seventeen and put two men in the grave."

"Bad luck is all it is, Sailor. Madonna Kim ain't no spider woman. Mean, Beany and Bob Lee raised her right."

"Just glad Pace ain't never got hooked up with her."

"How could he, bein' off in Nepal since before Madonna Kim got her first period?"

"We heard from the boy lately?"

"Month ago's the most recent. He was preparin' to leave Katmandu for the place in India the tea comes from?"

"Darjeelin'."

"That's it. Was gonna be a long trek, he said, three months or so. Wanted to know when we was comin' over and go on a hike with him. Says he ain't gonna be doin' it forever."

"I seen that Abominable Snowman movie more than enough times to know I ain't ever goin' near no Tibet, and Nepal's near it."

"Don't know how Pace can take bein' in such a cold climate. Bad enough when it snows here in New Orleans once in the blue moon. Place just shuts down."

"You know 'bout blue moons, peanut? I mean, what one is, really?"

"No, what? Just sometimes the way the sky is makes the moon look blue."

"Uh-uh. It's when there's two full moons in the same month. Second one's the blue moon."

"Where'd you hear this?"

"Woman named Jaloux Marron, used to work for Poppy Papavero, told me, long time ago."

Sailor and Lula Ripley were eating breakfast in the Florida room of their house in Metairie. Sailor was on his second cup of Community and third Quik-Do raisin-nut muffin, and Lula was halfway finished with a peach, which was all she could handle before about noon. It was seven-forty-five A.M.

"Papavero was that gangster got shot in a jewelry store, right? Dozen years ago?"

"That's right, peanut."

"And who was this Jealous woman?"

"Jaloux. Gal worked the bar at Inez's Fais-Dodo before it was shut down. Believe it's a fish place now. No, antique store, that's it."

"So how'd you know her?"

Sailor sipped his coffee and looked out the sliding glass doors at the bird feeder.

"How come there ain't no seed in the feeder?" he asked.

"'Cause there ain't no birds around."

"Might be if there was somethin' for 'em to eat."

"Didn't realize you was such a bird lover. Who was she, Sailor?"

"Told you, Lula. Girl worked for Papavero. Met her once I was at Inez's. Weren't nothin' more to it. I ain't seen her for twelve years."

Lula popped a small slice of peach into her mouth and swallowed it without chewing. She sucked on her tongue and stared blankly at a photo of Ava Gardner wearing a low-cut dress that Sailor had clipped out of the *Times-Picayune* and tacked to the wall the day her obituary had appeared in the newspaper. Ava was a homegirl, one of North Carolina's finest.

"Don't seem possible I'll be fifty years old next week, does it, peanut? Never figured on lastin' this long. Might just last a while longer, now I come this far. What do you think?"

"Might could, you will," said Lula. "Dependin'."

"Dependin'? Dependin' on what?"

"Dependin' on your keepin' the love of a certain good woman."

Sailor laughed, put down his cup, and reached his right hand across the table toward Lula.

"I ain't about to mess with true love, Lula, you know it. I never have."

She accepted Sailor's hairless hand into her own and smiled at him.

"I know that, darlin'. Just sometimes, even at forty-seven and a half years old, that ol' bug gets to squirmin' in my brain and knocks a wire loose. I love you, baby. Always have, always will. We're it, you know?"

Sailor nodded and squeezed Lula's slim left hand with the ruby ring on the third finger that she'd worn ever since Sailor had given it to her when she was sixteen years, six months and eighteen days old.

"I do know, peanut. Don't need no remindin', though it's okay you do it now and again."

The telephone rang and Lula reached over with her free hand and picked up the receiver.

"Oh, hello, Mama."

"You busy?"

"No, me'n my true love're just about to take off on a little trip to celebrate his first half-century on the planet."

"He takin' you to the Bahamas again on one of them gamblin' junkets just so's he can piss away your home improvement savin's?"

Lula laughed. "We're takin' a car trip, Mama, up to Memphis. Sailor always did want to visit Graceland, so we're goin' now. Be gone about a week."

"What about your worms?"

"Beany and Madonna Kim'll keep an eye on 'em."

"That Madonna ain't got the brains or morals of a worm. Didn't her last husband shoot himself after he come in on her screwin' his daddy?"

"That was the first one, Mama. Lonnie Wick? The Wick Wallpaper people? Second one hanged himself. Jimmy Modesta, had a beverage distribution company in Slidell. Used to get us all that Barq's and Dr Pepper for nothin'? That one weren't really all Madonna Kim's fault."

"What you mean, Lula? I recall now she shamed him with a homeless person."

"Man ran a shelter, Mama, there's a big difference. Anyway, them Modestas has a family history of chronic depression. Jimmy's brother, mother and a couple or three others took their own life before him."

"No loss to this earth, I'm positive," said Marietta Pace Fortune. "Look, Lula, I'm glad I caught you on your way out the door because I want you to know I got a houseguest."

"You call from North Carolina just to tell me you got a visitor? This another of your and Dalceda Delahoussaye's destitute Daughters of the Confederacy? Why can't Dal take in this one?"

"No, Lula, it's not. It's Marcello Santos."

"Santos?! Mama, ain't he in jail for life?"

"Released him from Texarkana day before yesterday. He's sick, Lula, real sick. Heart's about to quit. Feds figured a sick old man can't cause them no more trouble."

"Yeah, but Mama, Crazy Eyes Santos ain't just anyone. He was the crime king of the Gulf Coast since before I was born. You always said Daddy didn't trust him. What about that company of his he used as a front, Bayou Enterprises?"

"He ain't interested, Lula, really. Besides, no way after all these years the ones runnin' things'd let him back in. And he ain't got no crazy eyes no more, he's got cataracts both sides and can barely see. Your daddy didn't depend on Marcello's word, that's true, but Clyde Fortune didn't trust anyone, tell the truth, even me, probably. Anyway, Marcello had no place to go. Was stayin' at The Registry in Charlotte when he called me. I got him fixed up in my room. I'm usin' the study, had Johnnie Farragut bring over a cot. He and Marcello are in the front room together right now, watchin' 'Wheel of Fortune.' Marcello says it's the favorite show in the joint."

"Life is full of surprises, Mama, ain't it? I thought he and Johnnie hated each other."

"Johnnie been retired from the detective business ten years now, Lula. He's almost seventy-five and all he cares about is raisin' flowers. Dal and I got him comin' twice a week to the There But for the Grace of God Garden Club."

"Mama, I got to hand it to you. Talk about the lion lyin' down with the lamb!"

Marietta cackled. "Ain't no beast so fierce as time, Lula. It's time makes us all lie down in the here and now or the hereafter, one."

"I'll check in with you-all when we get to Memphis. Meantime give my love to Dal and Johnnie. Santos, too, I suppose."

Lula looked at Sailor, who was grinning. His teeth were several shades of brown from thirty-eight years of smoking unfiltered Camels. She figured his lungs must be several shades of black. Maybe if she quit smoking

Mores, Lula thought, Sailor would quit Camels, and they wouldn't die of cancer or, almost worse, emphysema, where a person had to haul a machine around with him and keep tubes stuck up his nostrils so he could breathe.

"Love you, Lula," said Marietta. "You be careful on the road. There's serious enough devils every step of the way. You hear from my grandboy?"

"Pace is fine, Mama. He's off on a trek."

"Don't know why he'd want to hole himself up way behind the Bamboo Curtain like this. Boy got a mind of his own, though, I'll give him that."

"Mama, I'm goin'. I got Sailor Ripley to protect me, so don't worry."

Lula smiled at Sailor and he raised his left arm and flexed the bicep.

"He ain't always done such a spectacular job of it, Lula, or can't you remember?"

"Bye now, Mama. Love you."

Lula hung up.

"I know, peanut," Sailor said, "the world's plenty strange and not about to change."

"Might not be worth gettin' up in the mornin' it was any different, Sail, you know?"

"Your folks know where you're goin'?" asked Wesley Nisbet, as he guided his Duster into the Bienville National Forest.

Consuelo had not looked at Wesley since she'd gotten into the car. She didn't feel like talking, either, but she knew it was part of the price for the ride.

"They ain't known where I'm goin' ever since I been able to reason."

"How long you figure that is?"

"More'n seven years, I guess. Since I was nine, when me'n Venus got brought together in the divine plan."

Wesley slapped his half-leather-gloved right hand hard on top of the sissy wheel.

"Goddam! You mean that woman been havin' her way with you all this time? Hell, that's sexual abuse of a child. How is it your folks didn't get this Venus put away before now?"

"They couldn't prove nothin', so they sent me away to the Mamie Franklin Institute in Birmin'ham. I escaped twice, once when I was eleven and got caught quick, and then two years ago I stayed gone three whole months."

"Where'd you go?"

"Venus and me was shacked up in the swampy woods outside Increase. Didn't have no money, only guns, ammo and fishin' tackle. We ate good, too. Venus is about pure-blood Chickasaw. She can live off the land without askin'."

"How'd you get found out?"

Consuelo snorted. "Simon and Sapphire—those are my parents—hired about a hundred and one detectives. Still took 'em ninety days. Venus found us a pretty fair hideout that time."

"What's she doin' in Oxford?"

"Got her a full scholarship to study the writin's of William Faulkner, the greatest writer the state of Mississippi ever provided the world. Venus is also a writer, a poet. She says I got the makin's, too."

"You write poetry?"

"Not yet, but Venus says I got the *soul* of a poet, and without that there's no way to begin. It'll come."

"You ever read any books by this fella she's studyin'?"

Consuelo shook her head no. "Venus says it ain't important. 'Course I could, I want."

Wesley kept his ungloved left hand on the steering wheel and placed his right on Consuelo's naked left thigh. She didn't flinch, so Wesley slid his leather-covered palm up toward her crotch.

"You wouldn't know what to do with my clit if I set it up for you on the dashboard like a plastic Jesus."

Wesley's right hand froze at the edge of her cutoffs. He kept it there for another fifteen or twenty seconds, then removed it and grabbed the gear-shift knob, squeezing it hard.

"You're some kinda wise little teaser, ain't you?" he said.

Consuelo turned her head and stared at Wesley's right profile. He had a scar on the side of his nose in the shape of an anchor.

"How'd you get that scar?" asked Consuelo. "Bet you was doin' such a bad job the bitch just clamped her legs closed on it."

Wesley Nisbet grinned and took the Duster up a notch.

"I'm likin' this more and more we go along," he said.

MEN IN CHAIRS

"You two need anything this afternoon? I'm goin' out."

"No, Marietta," said Johnnie, "thanks. Marcello and me's doin' good."

Johnnie Farragut and Marcello Santos were both seated in overstuffed armchairs with their feet up on needle-point footstools in the front room of the Fortune home, watching a talk show on the twenty-four-inch Sony. A practically naked woman was on the screen, her long, slender, tentacle-like legs seemingly about to entwine themselves around the shoulders of the show's male host, who was perched on a step below the chair in which his guest was seated. The fluffy-haired host held the microphone up in front of her dangling breasts, which were delicately contained by a slip of pink cloth.

"Who's she?" asked Marietta. "Some X-rated movie actress?"

"Concert violinist," Santos said. "Just played Brahms's 'Opus 25.' Very nicely, too."

"Never saw no violinist looked like that."

"While back there was a woman played cello in the all-nude," said Johnnie. "'Member her?"

"I don't," said Marietta. "I'll leave the cultural events to you gentlemen, then, you don't mind. Back after the Daughters meetin'. Dal's goin' with me, so you-all're on your own if you spill your milk or need your pants changed."

"Bye, Marietta," said Johnnie.

He and Marcello sat quietly for several minutes, listening to the inane banter between the violinist, whose right breast rested on the microphone, and the unctuous host, waiting for the woman to stand up again so they could watch her parade in her skimpy dress. The show broke for a commercial and when it resumed the female violinist was gone.

"Damn," Johnnie said, "woulda appreciated seein' them stems once more. Only thing better to look at than a cluster of Cecil Brunners."

"You're an amusing man, Johnnie," said Santos, "and a most fortunate one. Before my eyes began giving me such problems, I read a great deal. In the penitentiary, there isn't much else of a savory nature to help pass the time, as you, having been in the law enforcement business, certainly know. I most enjoyed reading the bulletins and studies issued by the Justice Department, which were made available on a regular basis by the prison library. One of the last I read revealed that in the United States approximately 640,000 crimes per year are committed that involve the use of handguns. More than 9,000 people per year are killed in the process, and another 15,000 are wounded. Also committed each year are over 12,000 rapes, 200,000 robberies and 400,000 assaults by individuals possessing guns. Three quarters of the perpetrators of these crimes are strangers to the victims."

"Don't tell me that you, of all people, Marcello Santos, one of the most feared crime bosses of our time, is advocatin' gun control!"

Santos laughed. "I'm boss of nothing any longer, Johnnie. Those days are long passed. Yes, I am against the easy availability of weapons. It's the amateurs that ruin the business. In the proper hands, these kinds of things don't happen. Certainly they do not happen so often."

"There's a lot of guns in the world, but there's only one Johnny Rocco."

"What's that?"

"Line from an old movie. Anyway, you got a point, Marcello. Funny how we end up wheezin' in armchairs like this, in the parlor of a woman we both been chasin' after for decades. Though you, of course, was necessarily out of the runnin' for a spell. And after bein' on opposite sides of the fence, so to speak, in our professional lives. Kinda creeps up on a person that there ain't much he can do to influence his outcome."

Santos sat back in his chair with his eyes closed, his large, thick hands with the left thumb missing folded together in his lap.

"Tell me, Johnnie, have you had a happy life?"

"I guess so, Marcello. My regrets don't amount to much. Only thing is, I never made no mark as a writer, which is somethin' I'd always had in mind."

"Do you believe in an afterlife?"

"You mean, like heaven? Or reincarnation?"

"Call it what you like."

"No. Do you?"

Santos nodded his head slightly.

"I do. I'm looking forward to it. What I feel behind me is only pain."

The two men sat without talking, neither of them really listening to or watching the television. Johnnie thought about a cat he'd had for a while when he was a boy, an orange tom his father had named Kissass. Kissass had been electrocuted one summer evening when a bolt of ribbon lightning struck a power line that lashed down over him as he streaked across the lawn in front of the Farragut house on Stivender Street in Bay St. Clement. That was sixty-five years ago, Johnnie thought. He could remember Kissass's face an instant before the strike, and he stopped his memory right there.

RUNNING INTO DARKNESS

Rather than take 10 into 55 around the lake, the fast way, Sailor decided to drive over the Lake Pontchartrain Causeway and head west just before Covington on Interstate 12, then pick up 55 north of Pontchartrain, which would take them all the way into Memphis. He and Lula had agreed to take their time, and Sailor kept the Sedan de Ville at a respectable sixty as they cruised across twenty-four scenic miles of the most polluted lake south of Erie.

"Ever tell you about the time I seen a corpse floatin' here?" he said.

Lula was adjusting her eye makeup in the visor mirror on the passenger side of the front seat. She'd had her eyelids tinted the day before and she wasn't sure that she liked the effect. They made her eyes look sunken or something, she thought. Lula studied them now and only half paid attention to what Sailor was saying.

"Tell me what, darlin'?"

"Me'n Slim Leake was takin' his nine-year old-nephew, Pharoah Sanders Leake, whose daddy—Slim's brother, Otis Blackwell Leake—teaches wind instruments at LSU, out for a boat ride, and here come a corpse up on the port side, bloated and fumin' like a abcess on a spaniel's belly."

Lula frowned into the mirror, flipped up the visor and put her beauty utensils into her purse.

"Say what about a dog?"

"No, peanut, I'm tellin' you about a dead body we come across on Pontchartrain here one mornin'."

"Whose body?"

"I don't know. Man drowned or was dumped. Looked like a purple balloon with bad air steamin' out all pores. Stank fierce."

"Delightful. What'd y'all do?"

"Went on and rowed around a while, till Pharoah'd had enough, then took it in and told the dockmaster."

"What'd he say?"

Sailor slipped a Camel from the open pack in his left front shirt

Consuelo's Kiss

pocket, stuck it between his lips, pulled out a black book of matches with a white skull-and-crossbones on it under the words PURVIS PETTY'S PIRATE LOUNGE, flipped the cover and lit the cigarette with one hand, tossed the match out the window, inhaled deeply, and dropped the matchbook back into his pocket.

"Said floaters was a regular feature of the lake and there weren't no extra charge. Didn't seem to excite him none, though before we left I noticed he'd uncovered the NO in front of the SWIMMING ALLOWED sign on the dock. Slim Leake—you remember, back then he was the Gator Gone distribution manager in Port Allen? Slim said the pollution level of the lake was checked daily, and dependin' on the readin', swimmin' was allowed or not."

"Wouldn't never get me in this sewer. Whatever happened to Slim Leake, anyway? He reminded me a little of that movie actor, the one looked like a cute bloodhound. Harry Dean Stanton."

"Yeah, I remember him. He's the one in *The Missouri Breaks* is ridin' with some old boys from Montana into Canada when they hear some horrible animal noise they can't I.D., and Harry Dean says, 'The further north you go, the more things eat your horse.' Whoever wrote that line had a real talent. Always thought that was a pretty fair analysis of the human condition, myself."

"So what about Slim Leake?"

"Not real certain. He and Nelda Bea divorced, of course, his work went to hell in a hurry, he was drinkin' a lot and Bob Lee had to let him go. Last I heard he was up north in Ohio, managin' a trailer park."

"Nice man like Slim deserved better'n Nelda Bea. She was one impatient type of woman."

Sailor inhaled and exhaled a stream of smoke from his nostrils without removing the cigarette from his mouth. Lula looked at him and wondered how many thousands of times she'd seen Sailor pull on a Camel.

"Man might be better off without what he ain't been without since he can't recall," Sailor said, "only there ain't no way he can imagine bein' without it."

Lula nodded. "You know, honey, I'm givin' up smokin'. I got a pack of Mores with me but I ain't gonna crack 'em. This trip's a good occasion to quit."

"More power to ya, peanut. You quit forty, fifty times before. It prob'ly ain't impossible."

Lula stared out the window at the water. Thirty years ago she and Sailor had been on the move like this, only then they were running into darkness. She could recall the feeling all too well, and there hadn't really been a day since that she'd been entirely free of the memory. They were rolling in the light today, though, and Lula knew she should be thankful for it, but somehow the thought of that crazy, out of control time shook her in a way nothing else could.

"Feels fine bein' back on the road, peanut, don't it?"

Sailor tossed his half-burned butt out the window.

"Ain't no substitute," said Lula. "Rest of the world other than what's outside the windshield fades right out. Like yesterday? I was readin' in the paper about a ninety-five-year-old man murdered a eighty-eight-year-old woman in her apartment in New York City."

"How'd he do it? Hammer her with his crutch?"

Lula nodded. "Knocked her out with a lead bar he used for therapy."

"Musta been he caught her with a younger man of ninety-two."

"Uh-uh. Said she'd tried to kill him on orders from the ashes of her dead husband, which she kept in a box on her bedroom dresser. Man accused her of poisonin' fifteen people and practicin' voodoo. Said she'd put a curse on him preventin' him from havin' proper sexual relations and causin' his wheelchair to rust."

"Guess there's no guarantee of goin' gentle into the good night, or however that poem says."

Lula looked at Sailor and smiled. "After all these years, Sail, darlin', you're still capable of surprisin' me."

Sailor laughed. "What you mean, sweetheart?"

"Quotin' poetry and all. I like it."

"Well, I like you."

"I know it, Sailor Ripley. I surely do. And I really do think that despite ever'thin's happened to us, we got a charmed life."

Lula reached up and tied her long, gray-black hair back into a ponytail and put on a new pair of fake tortoise-shell Ray-Bans she'd purchased the day before at the Rexall. A huge beige pelican fell out of the sky, bounced off the roof of the car and tumbled over the passenger side into the lake.

EVERY MAN A KING

"Just want to say one thing," said Wesley Nisbet, "before we get to anywhere, and I don't mean for you to get the wrong idea."

"What's exactly a wrong idea?" asked Consuelo.

"Tough enough tellin' right and wrong in doin', here you come with thinkin'. You talkin' 'bout believin' evil?"

Wesley passed a gray-primered Dodge Shadow that had the driver's flabby left arm hanging out the window.

"Only a man can make a real woman out of you, is all."

"You a medical man, I take it."

Wesley shook his head. "Was a woman in Greenville, guess it was, convinced herself the King of Sweden was in love with her. Took to tellin' everyone she met how the King of Sweden was comin' to town soon to take her away with him and they'd live in his snow palace over there in Europe. She wrote to him every day for years, even though she never got no answer. Ever'body figured she was just a harmless person and was pretty well amused by her obsession."

"How you know all this?" Consuelo asked.

"Read it in a book about sexual behavior written by a doctor. So guess what happened? The King of Sweden, she finds out, is comin' to Memphis to visit Graceland durin' a goodwill trip. Turns out he's a big fan of Elvis. The woman tells ever'one she's meetin' the King in Memphis, closes up her house, takes her money out of the bank and drives to Tennessee. On the day the King of Sweden shows up at Graceland, there she is at the gate, waitin' for him. Naturally, he don't notice her and goes right on in."

"She couldn't go back to Greenville after that."

"Sticks by the gate, gettin' crazier by the minute, and when the King comes out, she pulls a gun from her purse and tries to shoot him, only her aim ain't no good and the bullet hits a tourist from France."

"They musta locked her up for good."

"Uh-uh. She beat 'em to it. Put the pistol in her mouth and blew her brains back to Miss'ippi, right in front of the King of Sweden and

422

ever'body. Doctor who wrote the book said someway the woman had developed a strange condition called De Clerambault's Syndrome, meanin' she was way out of line concernin' her object of affection. I copied out the name of her disease and memorized it."

"Why you tellin' me this, Wesley Nisbet?"

"Your feelin's directed toward this Venus ain't normal, either. There's prob'ly a name for it, too."

Wesley sped up and passed a powder blue BMW with California license plates being driven by a woman wearing a blond wig and large, orange-tinted sunglasses. The woman gave Wesley the finger as he went by.

"Nice folks, them California people," he said.

"Why you so concerned about me?" asked Consuelo. "You don't even know me, and you ain't gonna get to, neither."

"It's Venus I'm mostly curious about. I'm thinkin' I'd like to meet her. Maybe we three can have us a party."

"Wesley, you're givin' me a ride and all, which I appreciate, but I got to say you ain't nearly the answer to nobody's dreams."

Wesley laughed. "Just could be we'll find out there's any truth to that, Miss Whynot, honey."

Consuelo arched her back and stretched her arms behind her, which made her nipples perk up under the polkadots. She held the pose long enough for Wesley to notice, then relaxed.

"Death and destruction ain't never more than a kiss away," she said. "Woman shot at the King of Sweden knew that much."

RED BIRD

Sailor and Lula sat in a tan Naugahyde booth in Rebel Billy's Truckstop off 55 near Bogue Chitto, eating bowls of chili and drinking Barq's. Sailor was reading the *Clarion-Ledger* he'd bought from a box out front.

"Guess we been real lucky with Pace, peanut," he said.

Lula looked over the red lumps on her tablespoon at the top of Sailor's head and noticed that the bald spot on his crown was growing larger. Sailor was supersensitive about losing his hair. Whenever Lula said anything about it, like suggesting he get a weave or try Monoxidil, he got upset, so she ignored the urge to reiterate her feelings regarding the situation.

"Why you say that, sweetheart? I mean, you're right and all, but what made you think of it?"

Lula stuck the spoon into her mouth.

"Item here in the Jackson paper. Headline says, 'Sorrow Ends in Death,' and underneath that, 'Boy, 12, Hangs Self after Killing Red Bird.' Story's out of San Antonio."

Lula retracted the spoon. "Nothin' good happens in Texas, I'm convinced."

"Here it is: 'Conscience-stricken after he had shot and killed a red bird, Wyatt Toomey, twelve years old, hanged himself here last night. The body was found by his sister. A signed note addressed to his parents told the motive for the act.' This is what he wrote: 'I killed myself on account of me shooting a red bird. Goodby mother and daddy. I'll see you some day.'"

"Jesus, Sail, that's a terrible story."

Sailor folded the newspaper to another page.

"Hard to know what a kid's really thinkin'," he said. "Pace had himself a few scrapes, of course, but he got clean, thank the Lord."

"Thanks to you, too, Sail. You been a fine daddy. Want you to know I appreciate it."

Sailor smiled, blew Lula a kiss and leaned back in his corner of the booth and lit up a Camel.

"Hope you don't mind my smokin', peanut. I may be a good daddy but I ain't always such a clean liver."

A waitress came over carrying a pot of coffee.

"Need refills?" she asked.

Sailor covered his cup with his left palm.

"I'm peaceful," he said. "Peanut?"

Lula nodded. "Don't mind a drop."

"Folks don't drink so much coffee they used to," said the waitress, as she poured. "Don't smoke, neither."

The waitress carried a good one-hundred-eighty-five pounds on her five-feet two-inches. She was about forty-five, Sailor guessed, and she reeked of alcohol. Sailor figured her for a nighttime cheap gin drinker. Five minutes after she was in her trailer door after work, he imagined, she'd be kicked back in her Barcalounger watching the news, four fingers of Gilbey's over a couple of cubes in a half-frosted chimney in one hand and five inches of menthol in the other.

"My wife's tryin' to quit," he said.

"I got thirty years worth of tar and nicotine in me," said the waitress, "too late to stop. Anyway, I like it. This health thing's gone just about far as it can now, I reckon. What with AIDS and the Big C, not to mention heart disease and drug-related crimes, might as well let yourself go a little and get some pleasure out of life. My son, Orwell, he's twenty-two now, was born deaf and with a withered-up left arm? He won't eat nothin' but raw vegetables, no meat or dairy. Runs three miles ev'ry damn mornin' before seven, then goes to work at the telephone office. In bed by nine-thirty each night. You'd think Orwell'd want to cut loose, 'specially after the cards he been dealt, but he figures he might could live forever he don't smoke or drink liquor and sticks to eatin' greens. What for? That ain't livin', it's runnin' spooked. Can't stand to see it, but half the world's in the coward's way at present. You folks take care now. Highway's full of God's worst mistakes."

She left the check on the table.

"Gimme a drag on that Camel, willya, Sail?"

He handed his cigarette to Lula and watched her suck in Winston-Salem's contribution to the good life.

"Feel better?" Sailor asked, as she exhaled and handed it back to him.

Lula nodded. "It's terrible, but I do love tobacco. Must be it's in our blood, comin' from North Carolina."

" 'Member that woman kept a vigil out front of the Lorraine Motel in Memphis for three years, place where Martin Luther King got shot? She was protestin' it bein' made into a civil rights museum, 'stead of a medical clinic or shelter for the homeless."

"Kinda do, honey. What happened to her?"

"Cops dragged her away, finally. Don't know where she went after."

"Why you askin' now, Sailor? That was a long time back."

"Oh, I'm thinkin' it might be interestin', long as we're in Memphis, go look at the Lorraine, maybe see the spot James Earl Ray aimed from. I mean, it's our history."

"Think James Earl Ray ever shot a bird when he was a boy?"

"He did," said Sailor, "don't guess it bothered his mind none."

BURNING LOVE

"Had me a buddy for four or five years named Felix Perfecto," said Wesley Nisbet, as his Duster finished off Rankin County. "Perfecto family come over to this country from Mariel, Cuba, on the boatlift in '81. Guess they musta settled in Miami or somewhere in Florida for a while before movin' to Miss'ippi, which is where we met, right here in Jackson. Felix was a good-lookin' cat, dark-skinned with blond hair and blue eyes, which he got from his mama, who was of German extraction. Think her grandaddy was a Nazi fled to Cuba end of WW Two. All the girls went for Felix Perfecto. 'Señor Perfect' they called him. Boy had more women than Madonna had push-up bras. That's why what happened to him's such a tragedy."

Consuelo shifted her left leg out from under her and folded in her right. She couldn't wait to get away from Wesley and was relieved to see the Jackson city limits sign, but she relaxed, knowing it wouldn't be long now, and decided to humor him.

"Somethin' bad happened, huh?"

Wesley whistled softly through his front teeth.

"It ain't pretty."

"*Dit-moi.*"

"*D* what?"

"French for tell me. Venus been teachin' me."

"Felix was goin' steady with a girl name of Felicity Tchula. Señor Perfect and Miss Felicity was quite the couple around here for a good while. She was a red-haired beauty, too, full of freckles with big green eyes and a figure like nothin' this side of Sophia Loren when she was young. Ever see her in that movie, *Boy on a Dolphin,* with Alan Ladd, who had to stand on a box to be as tall as her? She don't wear nothin' but a thin, wet shirt, stays plastered to her tits. Hope Alan Ladd had a bite or two on them bullets.

"Anyway, Miss Felicity's parents weren't altogether keen on her hangin' out with Felix Perfecto, since his main source of income come from dealin' dope. Nothin' serious, mind you. Felix sold reefer, is all, and maybe some pills once in a while, but no crack or ice or hard stuff. He started dealin' in high school and just stayed with it afterward, so's he wouldn't have to work for nobody. He was a happy guy, Felix Perfecto, and didn't never hurt people. They was sorta an ideal couple. Felicity was studyin' to be a registered nurse."

"We're almost to where I'm gettin' off," Consuelo said, "so you'd best tell me the terrible part."

"DeSoto Tchula, Felicity's daddy, decided to try and persuade Felix to break-off with his daughter. He went to see Felix with three or four of his employees, construction workers from off one of the Tchula Buildin' Company jobs. Felix told DeSoto to get fucked and the goons broke both of Felix's legs, ruptured his spleen and kicked him so many times in the balls that one of 'em had to be surgically removed. Felix knew it wouldn't do no good to bring charges against the man, seein' as how DeSoto Tchula was so powerful in the town, so he waited until he healed up good as could be expected before he got his revenge."

"What'd Felicity do after her daddy mangled Perfecto?"

"Felicity's mama, Pearl, took her on a long trip to Europe. When they come back, Felix was about fit, and Felicity went to see him. He hadn't wanted to see none of his friends while he was recuperatin', includin' me, and he didn't let Felicity in, neither. Told her to go home, but warned her not to ride in a car with either of her parents."

"I can guess now what happened. Real burnin' love business, like me'n Venus."

"Uh huh. First, Pearl Tchula's T-bird blew up with her in it in the parkin' lot of the Winn-Dixie on Natchez. Couldn't tell her brains from the canteloupe parts. Quarter-hour later, DeSoto Tchula bit metal in his Lincoln Town Car when he started it up to leave a construction site out at the Ross Barnett Reservoir."

"The cops catch Felix Perfecto?"

"He was already gone by the time the bombs went off. Hijacked a private plane from the airfield, a baby Beechcraft belonged to Tchula, and headed for Cuba. He got there, too, at least in the sky over Havana, but the Cubans wouldn't let him land, sayin' they'd shoot him if he did. He told 'em he was runnin' out of fuel, but they didn't care."

"He explain about his bein' born in Cuba, and all?"

"Suppose he tried, but whatever he said apparently didn't do no good, 'cause the Beechcraft went down a few minutes later in Havana harbor. Felix never got out, drowned inside the cockpit."

"What happened to Felicity?"

"Inherited her parents' money, married a banker from Memphis and moved there. Has three kids, includin' a son name of Felix."

"Fittin'," said Consuelo. "You can drop me up here, at the A&W." Wesley pulled into the drive-in and let the engine idle.

"Sure you don't want to hang out a bit, get to know me better?" he asked.

Consuelo opened the door and got out.

"You prob'ly ain't such a bad guy, Wesley, but I got my own agenda, you know? 'Preciate the lift," she said, and walked off.

Wesley leaned over and swung the passenger door closed. Something about the girl made him twitch where it hurt but felt good at the same time, and he made the not-so sudden decision to make sure this one didn't get away.

BANTER AT BODE'S

Marietta Pace Fortune and Dalceda Hopewell Delahoussaye were in the corner nook in Bode's Diner sipping sour Cokes following the Daughters meeting. The nook had been their regular spot at Bode's for more than sixty years, since they were little girls and used to go there with their mothers. The diminutive Misses Pace and Hopewell had been special favorites of W. Saint Louis Bode, the original owner. Saint Lou, as he was popularly known, made it a habit to present a brand-new copper penny to each child who came into his diner to spend in the gumball machine next to the huge old National cash register. Marietta and Dalceda once figured out that during their girlhoods, Saint Lou had gifted them with approximately two thousand pennies apiece.

W. Saint Louis Bode had retired when the girls reached sixteen, and his only son, W. Cleveland Bode, known to the residents of Bay St. Clement as Mister Cleve, had run the place for the next forty years, until his death, fourteen years ago. Mister Cleve, who had discontinued the policy of passing out pennies to kids after Saint Lou's death three years following his retirement, had never married, and following his funeral the diner was sold by his heirs, cousins who lived in Pensacola, Florida, to the P. L. Ginsberg Group, which owned most of the real estate in downtown Bay St. Clement. To the relief of regular patrons, such as Marietta and Dalceda, who despaired at the thought of doing without their sour Cokes and quiet chats in the corner nook three or four after- noons a week, the Ginsberg people decided to keep the place as it always had been, at least for the time being, which, as Marietta pointed out, was the only time one could count on.

"Clyde wouldn't mind, Dal, do you think? I mean about Santos stayin' at the house."

"Ain't worth thinkin' about, Marietta. Clyde's dead too many years now for what he mighta thought to matter. The world changes, don't it? He'd had to change his thinkin', too, along with the rest of us driftin' souls. If Louis Delahoussaye the Third was still alive, he'd have him a firm opinion, I know."

"And what might it have been?"

Dal sucked some sour up through her straw and let it slosh around her bottom teeth before swallowing.

"That you was disgracin' Clyde's mem'ry. But Louis was a fool far's them things go, Marietta. Best parts about him was his earnin' power and love of small animals."

"You don't really miss him, Dal, do you?"

"Like a old rug was always lyin' in the same spot on the floor till it got walked over so many times it needed replacin'."

"You never replaced Louis."

"Turned out the floor looked better uncovered, after all."

Both women laughed and bent to their straws.

"Amazin', though, how well Marcello and Johnnie keep company, Dal, don't you think?"

"Neither of 'em got much teeth left, Marietta. One's a widower and mistress murderer with nothin' but down-time to show for the past couple decades, and the other's a lifelong bachelor who never had the guts to take what he thought he wanted."

"You're a tough enough nut, Dal. Why I always admired you."

"Only been cracked once, which is plenty."

"You mean Truxno Thigpen?"

Dal nodded. "That boy had lived, my life mighta been a whole sight different. I ain't complainin', though. We had our moment."

"You ever visit his grave?"

"Not for fifty years, Marietta, a whole half-century. Ain't that somethin'?"

"Sailor Ripley's gonna be fifty next week. He and Lula are goin' to visit Graceland for the occasion."

"Trux done one thing for me I never will forget."

"What's that, Dal?"

"After my dog, Clark Gable, died—'member him, the golden retriever?—Trux brought one white rose to my house every day for a month and left it in front of the door."

"You never told me that."

Dal's eyes clouded up. "Never told anyone. My mama and daddy didn't even know who done it."

"How'd you know?"

"Didn't, really. I mean, I didn't see him bringin' the flowers, but I guessed it was Truxno. Couldn'ta been nobody else. Meant to ask him if he was the one, but then that bolt of ball lightnin' scorched the life out of him on the par-three golf course used to be over by the dump before Ginsberg built them apartments, and I never had the chance."

"Dal, I'm thinkin' I might marry Marcello. He ain't got long to go."

Dalceda looked at Marietta and smiled. Her eyes sparkled despite the water in them.

"I got just the dress for you," she said.

PICKUP

"I have a collect call for Venus Tishomingo from Consuelo Whynot. Is this Venus Tishomingo?"

"Yes, it is."

"Will you accept the charges?"

"Yes, I certainly will."

"Go ahead, please."

The operator cut out.

"Hi, Venus, I'm on my way."

"Where you, Suelo, sweets?"

"Next to a A&W in Jackson. Just hitched a ride here from a weird dude in a nasty short. No boy wants to believe a girl ain't simply dyin' to lick the lint off his nuts."

"He make a attempt?"

"Not directly. Told him you was my dream woman and I didn't need no further stimulation."

"Sapphire and Simon know you split?"

"Don't think yet. Was a big train wreck in Meridian, I was there. Fireman on the scene said it's the worst in Miss'ippi hist'ry. Rescue squad'll be pullin' people's parts out of that mess for hours. Prob'ly be findin' pieces in the woods around for days."

"I know, it's on the news here. How long you gonna be?"

"Depends on when I can get a lift. I'm gonna have me a root beer and a burger and catch another ride."

"What happened to the hotrod boy?"

"Made him leave me off. He'd been trouble I woulda asked him to take me up to Oxford. Figure I'll make it in by midnight, I'm lucky."

"Okay, precious. I'll be waitin' up. You call again, there's a problem."

"I will, Venus. Love you dearly."

"My heart's thumpin', baby. Be careful, you hear?"

They both hung up and Consuelo left the phone booth, which was on the side of the road, and walked up to the window of the drive-in.

"Cheeseburger and a large root beer, please," she ordered from the fat man behind the glass.

"Ever'thin' on it?" he asked.

"No pickles."

"Three dollars," said the fat man, as he slid a bag through the space in the window.

Consuelo dug a five dollar bill out of her shorts, handed it to him, and he gave her back two dollars, which she folded in half and stuffed into her right front pocket.

"Y'all hurry back," the man said, his gooey, small hazel eyes fixed on her breasts.

Consuelo smiled at him, tossed her blond chop and pulled back her shapely little shoulders and expanded her chest.

"Maybe," she said.

The A&W was only a few hundred yards from the on-ramp to the Interstate, and Consuelo sipped at her root beer as she headed toward it. She took out the cheeseburger, dropped the bag on the ground and ate it as she walked. Next to the on-ramp was a Sun Oil station, and Consuelo spotted Wesley Nisbet's Duster, the hood raised, parked at a gas pump with Wesley bent into it, eyeballing the engine. She hoped he wouldn't see her. She also noticed a road-smudged white Cadillac Sedan de Ville with a man and a woman in it, about to pull away from the pump opposite the one occupied by Wesley's vehicle. Consuelo wolfed down the rest of her burger, wiped her right hand on her black jean cut-offs and stuck out her thumb as the Sedan de Ville rolled her way. The car stopped next to Consuelo and the front passenger window went down.

"Where you goin'?" Lula asked.

"Oxford," said Consuelo. "I'm a student at Ole Miss and I got to get there tonight so's I can make my classes in the mornin'."

"Guess we can take you far's Batesville," said Sailor, leaning over against Lula. "You'll have to catch a ride east from there on route 6."

"Good enough," Consuelo said, and opened the right rear door and climbed in, careful not to spill her root beer.

Sailor accelerated and guided the heavy machine onto 55 North and had it up to sixty-five in twelve seconds. Wesley Nisbet watched the white Cad disappear and snickered. He gently closed the Duster's hood and slid behind the steering wheel. He wouldn't have a problem keeping a tail on that whale, Wesley thought.

"What river's this?" Consuelo asked, as the Sedan de Ville crossed a bridge just before the fairgrounds.

"The Pearl, I believe," said Sailor. "Where you-all from?"

"Alabama," said Consuelo. "I been home on vacation 'cause my grandmama died."

"Sorry to hear it, honey," said Lula, who was turned around in her seat studying the girl.

"Yeah, we was real close, me and my grandmama."

"You didn't take no suitcase with you, huh?" Sailor asked.

"No," Consuelo said, "I only been gone a few days. Don't need much in this close weather."

Lula examined Consuelo, watching her sip her drink, then turned back toward the front. She looked over at Sailor and saw the half-grin on his face.

"You let me know the AC's too strong for you, Miss," said Sailor. "Wouldn't want you to get a chill in that outfit."

"Thanks, I'm fine," Consuelo said. "And my name's Venus."

THE SUITOR

As Wesley Nisbet trailed the white Cadillac by a discreet one eighth of a mile, he thought about his family. It wasn't too often that the Nisbet clan occupied Wesley's mind. Most of them that he'd known were dead now, anyway, buried alongside the Bayou Pierre near Port Gibson. His mother, Althea Dodu, and his father, Husbye, had been killed in a car wreck when Wesley was four years old. They'd been returning from Pine Bluff, Arkansas, where Husbye had robbed a liquor store of four hundred dollars and a fifth of Jack Daniel's. He was sucking on the Jack when the oncoming Pacific Intermountain Express truck, into whose lane Husbye had allowed his and Althea's Mercury Monarch to drift, slammed into them head-on.

Wesley had been raised thereafter by Husbye's maiden sister, Taconey, in Weevil, Mississippi, where Wesley did his best to avoid going to school and church, preferring to spend his time under the hoods of trucks and cars and exploring the nearby woods, shooting at things with his Sears .22 rifle. Aunt Taconey had died when Wesley was seventeen, and he'd left Weevil at that time, traveling first to McComb, where he worked for a few months in a filling station, then to Memphis, where he was arrested for stealing a battery out of a new Mustang. He did ninety days in the city lock-up and, following his release, drifted down to Meridian, where he got a job as a gravedigger at the Oak Grove Cemetery.

Wesley had had an argument the day before with the foreman at Oak Grove, Bagby Beggs. Beggs, whose father, Bagby Beggs, Sr., had been a guard for twenty years at the prison farm at Parchman, had reprimanded Wesley for having left the tool shed door unlocked the previous night. Even though nothing had been stolen, Beggs told Wesley, this kind of oversight went a long way, in his opinion, toward revealing a man's true character. Beggs went on to inform him that there were plenty of able bodies in the state of Mississippi willing to work and properly acquit themselves of the responsibilities attendant to the job if the challenge proved too exacting for this particular Nisbet.

At first Wesley had tried to wriggle out of it by saying that he thought someone else had already locked the shed, but when he looked directly into Bagby Beggs's square red eyes Wesley knew the foreman wasn't about to buy it, so he apologized and promised not to let it happen again. When Wesley drove away from the job after working a half-day on Saturday, Beggs's last words echoed in his cerebrum.

"There's two sides to me, Mr. Nisbet," Beggs had said, "just like there's two sides to ever'body. The side you see's the side you get, 'cause if you don't see that side you won't see any. If I tolerate you, you'll see me. If I don't, you won't."

Wesley decided as he drove that his career as a gravedigger was about done. Not necessarily because of anything Bagby Beggs had said, but because Wesley felt that life had more to offer him than a position as a caretaker of the dead. He'd enjoyed being able to pay his daily respects to Jimmie Rodgers, the Singing Brakeman, whose remains resided in Oak Grove, but it was time to move on. Maybe he could convince this vixen Consuelo Whynot to take off with him to Charlotte, where he'd begin a career at the Speedway as a stock car racer. First, though, he wanted to check out the lesbian Chickasaw. There were plenty of things his Aunt Taconey hadn't known about, and she'd been no worse off for it, he thought.

One of these days, too, Wesley promised himself, he would go back to Meridian, creep up on Bagby Beggs, and bash his head in with a shovel. Then he'd bury the foreman in an unmarked grave, whether Beggs was already dead or not. It would probably be better not to tell Consuelo about this plan, Wesley decided, at least not right away.

CONFESSION

"There's one thing I been meanin' to ask you about, Marcello."

Santos was propped up in the fold-out bed in the study with two fluffy pillows behind his head. Marietta was sitting in her grandmother Pace's straight-backed mahogany chair on his right side. Johnnie had gone home an hour before, after the three of them had eaten dinner and watched a rerun on television of one of the original "Twilight Zone" episodes, the one about the last man left on earth after a nuclear blast.

This story was a favorite of Johnnie's, who at one time in his life had aspired to being a writer of bizarre fiction. In it, the actor Burgess Meredith portrays a Milquetoast bank clerk whose only real passion in life is for reading, an activity for which, due to work and a nagging wife, he never has enough time or peace to enjoy. When the cataclysmic explosion occurs, he is alone in the bank's vault, and he survives. The clerk, who must wear glasses with Coke-bottle-thick lenses, stumbles out into the light and surveys a rubble-filled landscape. After a painstaking search through the city, he realizes he is the only person around. He goes to the library, is overjoyed to find that the books have been spared, and contemplates a leisurely lifetime of reading without disturbance. Reaching for a book, however, his glasses fall off, and in his effort to retrieve them, inadvertently steps on the lenses, crunching them beyond repair. Helpless without his glasses, his future is shattered, too.

Marietta thought the story was just plain mean and didn't want to hear anything Johnnie thought about irony.

"What do you mean, 'irony'?" Marietta said. "Whenever I hear that word, all I can think of is pressin' Clyde's shirts."

After so many years of friendship, Johnnie Farragut knew better than to argue an abstract point with Marietta Fortune, so he laughed it off and said good night. She'd then fixed up Santos's bed and helped him into it. His condition was worsening visibly day by day, and she didn't see how he could get much weaker and continue living at her house. He was one close step away from an I.V. feeder and a breathing machine.

"You mean Mona, yes?" Santos said, his voice no more than a tiny croak.

"I hate to ask," said Marietta, " 'specially considerin' your heart and all, but I just gotta know, Marcello. Did you have Mona Costatroppo killed?"

Santos sighed heavily. He had been sent to prison for arranging the murder of his mistress, Mona Costatroppo, who had threatened to testify against him in a federal court in New Orleans regarding a variety of criminal charges. The Feds were supposed to have given her a new identity in a distant city as part of the government witness protection program, but she had been shot to death in a hotel room in Chicago by a hitter from Detroit.

"You know, Marietta, my wife, Lina, before she died five years ago, wrote me a letter telling me that she forgave me everything, all of my sins against her and the children, none of whom, of course, will now even acknowledge that I am alive, however barely this is so. I wrote her back, informing her that had I desired absolution I would have remained a Catholic and paid a priest to perform this service. Clergy do not work for nothing, you know. The larger the alleged sin, the larger the church's bite in exchange for removing an obstacle on the path to heaven."

"Marcello, honey, I ain't interested in Lina, or any letters she mighta wrote. Far's I know, she died of natural causes culminatin' in cirrhosis of the liver."

Santos nodded slightly. "That's what I was told."

"It's this other business I need to satisfy myself about, we're gonna take a step. Answer me, Marcello."

Santos's eyes, once fiery, unsettling-to-look-into combinations of red and green, now floated on either side of his nose like opaque yolks in viscous, swampy yellow puddles. He blinked them several times, causing the puddles to overflow their containers and streak stickily down the sides of his face. Marietta took a tissue from a pocket of her robe and wiped away the effluent.

"I did, Marietta. I ordered the death of Mona Costatroppo. It was a terrible moment for me, when I realized what I had done, and that it was too late to prevent it. Mona knew it would happen, sooner or later, when she agreed to testify against me. She telephoned me one night, after she had gone into hiding. 'I have always been willing to die for you, Marcello,' she said, 'and now I am willing to die because of you.' Then she hung up. Now that you know, Marietta, what difference can it make?"

"It's the truth matters to me, Marcello. You had your reasons for doin' what you done, or had done for you, and I can live with that. I was just hopin' you wouldn't lie about this, is all. Murder ain't no more or less than a imperfect act of desperation, and ain't none of us is perfect. Nothin' to forgive or forget."

Marietta leaned over and kissed Santos on the forehead. He smiled at her and covered her left hand with the four remaining fingers of his own.

"I am a happy man tonight, Marietta. For the little it is worth, you have won the undying love and respect of an old, dying gangster."

"It's worth plenty, Marcello."

Marietta kissed him again on the forehead, stood up and grinned down at the once mighty Crazy Eyes Santos.

"'Night, killer," she said.

"Wake up, honey," Lula said to Consuelo, "we're about at the Batesville junction."

Consuelo blinked hard a few times and pinched her cheeks. Her mouth tasted dry and sour. She wished she had an ice-cold soft drink.

"Had me a awful strange dream just now," Consuelo said. "I went into my brother Wylie's room in the middle of the night, to check on him and see if he was all right. He was only about six years old in the dream—in real life he's fourteen and a half—and he was sleepin' sound. But then I looked over and there was this other bed kinda perpendicular to Wylie's, a single mattress, maybe, on the floor, and there was my cousin Worth, who drowned in Okatibbee Lake when he was twelve and I was eleven. Worth looked the same as he did then, with his reddish-brown hair cut short on the sides and floppin' on his forehead. He sat up in the bed and looked at me, and I said, 'Worth, that you?' And he said, 'Who do you think it is? 'Course it's me.' And I reached out my right hand and touched him with my fingers. I really felt him, and I jumped back, 'cause it was such a spooky feelin'. Then I woke up. Worth was real as y'all. Too damn weird by half."

"I don't dream so much anymore, now I'm older," said Lula. "Least I don't remember 'em the way I used to. How 'bout you, Sail?"

"Dreamed more in the joint than anywhere," Sailor said. "Prob'ly 'cause I was always catnappin', and my thoughts stayed close to the surface."

Sailor steered the Cadillac off the interstate and stopped at the State Highway 6 intersection.

"Here you go, Miss Venus. Oxford's due east twenty-five miles. Shouldn't have much trouble gettin' a ride to the university from here."

"'Preciate it much. Oh, by the way, my name's really Consuelo. Consuelo Whynot, from Whynot, Miss'ippi. It's my best friend's name is Venus. She's a Chickasaw Indian. Always wanted to know what it'd feel like to have someone call me by her name, not knowin' it wasn't really mine. Anyway, thanks again."

Consuelo got out of the car, closed the door and walked off. As Sailor pulled his Sedan de Ville across the road and headed down the return ramp to the Interstate, Wesley Nisbet's black Duster crept off at the Batesville exit. He spotted Consuelo, drove up alongside her, leaned over and rolled down the passenger side window.

"Don't I know you?" he said. "Them polkadots is difficult to forget."

"What in blazes you doin' here now?" said Consuelo.

"Thought I'd take me a college tour. I ain't never been to one."

"You're followin' me."

"Just goin' the same way, is all. Hop in."

Consuelo stood on the side of the road for a minute and considered the situation, then she opened Wesley's car door.

"It'll be okay, Consuelo," Wesley said. "Y' always burn a few tiles on reentry."

OUT OF BODY

In Memphis, Sailor and Lula checked into the Robert Johnson Regency, where Hilda Rae, Sailor's secretary at the Gator Gone Corporation, had made them a reservation on the recommendation of Sailor's boss, Bob Lee Boyle, who always stayed there on business trips to the city. It wasn't a fancy place, but it was clean and patroled around the clock by visibly armed security guards. A large sign at the registration desk proclaimed, THE MANAGEMENT SUGGESTS THAT GUESTS LOCK THEIR VALUABLES IN THE HOTEL SAFE DURING THEIR STAY.

"Not much of a view," Lula said, looking out the window of their third-floor room. Across the street was a dilapidated row of mostly abandoned brown brick buildings.

"Didn't come to Memphis for the view, peanut," said Sailor. "Just us and Elvis's home place is all we need."

He came up behind Lula, hugged her with his large arms folded across her breasts, and kissed her gently on the nape of her neck.

"Harder, Sail, honey. Bite me there on the neck how I like it."

Sailor gnawed harder on the lower part of Lula's neck and the tops of her shoulders, which made her moan. She bent backward into him, then forward, dipping her head as she lifted her skirt and lowered her panties.

"Stick it in, Sailor," she said. "Find a hole and drill me."

After they'd made love and showered, Sailor and Lula went downstairs to find a restaurant. Sailor was about to ask the desk clerk if he knew of a good place when Lula grabbed his arm and pointed to a man standing just inside the front entrance.

"Do you recognize him?" Lula asked. "Ain't that Sparky? You remember, he and his friend Buddy was stranded with us in Big Tuna, Texas."

"It sure is, Lula. Holy shit. You know, some years back I thought I saw him on the late-night cable TV sellin' hair restorer. Wasn't certain, though."

They walked up behind the man, who was facing the street, and Sailor tapped him on the right shoulder.

"Hey, pardner, you ever been stuck in the Big Tuna?"

Sparky, who was wearing a straw half-Stetson similar to the one he'd worn in Texas almost thirty years before, turned around and grinned broadly when he recognized the couple.

"Well, look at this! It sure is good to know some of us poor white trash has somehow survived the ravages of time."

Sparky and Sailor shook hands and Lula gave him a big hug.

"Sailor Ripley, I presume," said Sparky. "I thought we'd seen the last of you, along with Bobby Peru and Perdita Durango. Got yourself in with a tough twosome down there. Good to see you made it out."

"Barely did, but here I am. Here we are. Me'n Lula been together again almost eighteen years now."

"Lula, you're just as sweet-lookin' a young thing as ever. Still got that real black hair and big gray eyes with violet lakes in 'em I ain't never forgot."

Lula laughed. "I ain't young no more, and the eyes are real, okay. But I kinda have to cheat now and then on the hair, which is threatenin' to go the way of my eyes."

"Me'n Buddy used to handle hair products back when we had the House of Santería in Waggaman, Louisiana. I could still get you some good dye, you want it."

"I thought that was you and Buddy one time doin' a commercial on the TV!" said Sailor.

Sparky smiled. "We did that for a while, till the FDA come after us. Before that we owned a bar in Dallas. Never did make it back to California."

"Where's Buddy?" Lula asked.

"Waitin' for him now. Better standin' inside the Me'n the Devil Motel here than catchin' a stray slug in the street. Memphis is a unpredictable town."

"What are you-all doin' in Memphis?" Sailor asked.

"Got us a new business, prosperin', too."

Sparky took a card out of his Madras sports coat pocket and handed it to Sailor.

"'S&B Organ Retrieval Service,'" Sailor read out loud. "'Only the best parts.'"

"We got a 800 number, you'll notice."

"Organ retrieval?" said Lula. "What in hell's that?"

"Vital body pieces," Sparky said. "Heart, kidneys, eyes, even livers, though real useful ones is difficult to come by, given the Southern disposition toward Rebel Yell and Wild Turkey."

"Sparky, you jokin'?" Lula asked.

"Nope. We got us some steady customers in the private sector. Keep that card, Sailor. Might come in handy. What about you folks? What's been happenin' all these years? And why're you in Memphis?"

"Sailor's vice-president of the Gator Gone Corporation now, produces alligator and crocodile repellent. It's a worldwide operation, even in India."

"Sell a bunch over there, that's the truth," said Sailor.

"We have a house in Metairie," Lula said, "by New Orleans. Our son, Pace, is livin' in Nepal, leadin' expeditions in the Himalaya mountains."

"Man," said Sparky, "life fools me right and left."

"We come up to visit Graceland," said Sailor. "Never been here before."

"Tomorrow's Sailor's birthday, his fiftieth. We're celebratin'."

"Guess you know about what the King's widow and daughter're doin' with mostly all the proceeds from the estate now, don't ya?"

"No," Sailor said, "what's that?"

"All goes to the Church of Myrmidon, that mind-control cult headquartered in San Diego. The widow and the kid're whole hog in the grip of that fake prophet calls himself Myrmidon, claims to have visited Venus and Mars and wrote all them books about out-of-body experiences. Man lives on a three-hundred-foot yacht, cruises the Greek Islands and the French Riviera. Saw in the newspaper where he was at the Cannes Film Festival last week promotin' a movie about his life. Can't set foot on U.S. soil or the Feds'll feed him into the shredder."

"Heard of the Church of Myrmidon," said Sailor, "but I didn't know they was suckin' the blood out the King's afterlife."

"Yeah, the Colonel bled him while he was alive, and now this Phelp Bonfuca, calls himself Myrmidon, drains his heirs."

"You say Phelps Bonfuca?"

"Uh huh. Myrmidon's real handle."

"I was in the joint with him," said Sailor. "At Huntsville. I did a dime standin' up for that stunt with Bobby Peru, and for four of 'em Phelps Bonfuca was in the same cell block. He was in on some bunco beef. Pyramid scam, I think. Milkin' suckers."

"Still at it," said Sparky. "Only on a big-time basis."

Sailor shook his head. "This don't make me feel so good now about goin' to Graceland, knowin' the money's endin' up in Phelps's pockets."

"It don't matter, Sail, sweetheart," said Lula. "Could be worse. The fam'ly might be donatin' the proceeds to the Cath'lic Church, or the Mormons or somethin'. One cult's same as another."

"Kinda disappoints me, is all."

"Don't matter what people do with their money," said Sparky, "long as they spend it, keep it comin' around where the other guy can reach in, he gets the chance, and grab him a fistful. Say, you folks hungry? Here's Buddy now."

Sailor and Lula looked through the glass door and saw a brown Plymouth Voyager pull up in front. The words S&B ORGAN RETRIEVAL SERVICE—ONLY THE BEST PARTS were stenciled in white on the side.

"We was just about to find us a restaurant when we seen you," said Lula.

"Come on, then," said Sparky. "We'll get some ribs. I know a place they take 'em off the body for you!"

PROFESSIONALS

Venus Tishomingo was six feet even and weighed a solid one-hundred-seventy-five pounds. Her hands were each the size of an infielder's glove, and she wore a 12-D shoe. Her hair was chestnut brown and very thick, and hung down loose past her waist. She wore at least one ring on every finger other than her thumbs. They were cheap, colorful rings she'd bought in pawn shops in Memphis. Her eyes were clear, almost colorless stones set deep in her skull. Most people had a difficult time staring into them for very long before becoming uncomfortable and having to look away. At first glance, Venus's eyes resembled pristine pebbles in a gentle, smooth-flowing stream, but then they came alive and darted toward whomever's eyes met hers. She sat in her one-bedroom cottage in a gooseneck rocking chair, wearing only a well-faded pair of Wrangler blue jeans, reading the *Oxford Eagle*, waiting for Consuelo to arrive or call. An item datelined Jackson caught her eye.

"Pearl Buford, of Mockingbird, accused of trying to sell two of her grandchildren in an adoption scam, has pleaded innocent to charges in federal court here. Buford, 34, who told authorities she used to baby-sit professionally, also pleaded innocent to six counts of mail fraud involving solicitation of offers for the children. She is currently unemployed. Her daughter, Fannie Dawn Taylor, 16, a dropout after finishing 8th grade at Mockingbird Junior High, pleaded innocent to one count of mail fraud."

Venus had it in mind to adopt a child that she and Consuelo could raise together. Maybe more than one. It was too bad, Venus thought, that Pearl Buford hadn't contacted her about taking on Fannie Dawn's kids.

Venus massaged her left breast with her right hand, tickling the nipple with the second and third fingers until it stood out taut and long as it would go. She had large breasts that were extremely sensitive to touch, and Consuelo knew perfectly how to suck on and fondle them. Venus dropped the newspaper and slid her left hand down inside the front of her jeans and rubbed her clit. She closed her eyes and thought about a photograph of a cat woman she'd seen in a book in the Ole Miss library that afternoon. It wasn't really a cat woman but two negatives printed simultaneously, one atop the other, of a cat and a woman, so that the face was half-human, half-feline, with long white whiskers, weird red bolts for eyes and perfect black Kewpie doll lips. Venus came quickly, bucking sharply twice before relaxing and slumping down in the chair. She removed her left hand and let it drape over the arm of the rocker. Her right hand rested in her lap. Venus was almost asleep when Consuelo knocked on the door.

Venus jumped up and opened it. Consuelo threw herself forward onto her naked chest.

"I'm starved, Venie," Consuelo said. "I need your lovin'."

"Got it comin', baby," said Venus, stroking Consuelo's wheat-light hair with a large brown hand.

Venus heard a car engine idling, looked over Consuelo's left shoulder out the door and saw the black Duster in front of the house.

"Who's that?" she asked.

"Wesley Nisbet, the one I told you about. He's a pest, but he give me a lift here. Followed the ride I caught outta Jackson, picked me up again in Batesville."

"He truly dangerous?"

"Maybe, like most."

"He figurin' you're gonna invite him in?"

Consuelo swung her right leg backward and the door slammed shut. "Just another mule kickin' in his stall," she said.

When Wesley saw the door close, he shifted the Duster into first and eased his pantherlike machine away. He drove into town, parked on the northwest side of the square in front of a restaurant-bar named The Mansion, got out of the car and went inside.

"J. W. Dant, double," Wesley said to the bartender, as he hopped up on a stool. "One cube, splash water."

A toad-faced man with a greasy strand of gray-yellow hair falling over his forehead sat on the stool to Wesley's left. The man was wearing a wrinkled burgundy blazer with large silver buttons over a wrinkled, dirty white shirt and a wide, green, food-stained tie. He wobbled as he extended his right hand toward Wesley.

"Five Horse Johnson," the man said. "You?"

"That a clever way of tellin' me you got a short dick or's it your name?"

The man laughed once, very loudly, and wiped his right hand on his coat.

"Nickname I got as a boy. Had me a baby five HP outboard on a dinghy, used to go fishin' in Sardis Lake. Can't hardly remember my so-called Christian one, though the G-D gov'ment reminds me once a year. Hit me up for the G-D tax on my soul, they do. Strip a couple pounds a year. Forty-five G-damn years old. Amazed there's any flesh left to cover the nerves. You ain't from Oxford."

"No, ain't."

"Then you prob'ly don't know the local def'nition of the term 'relative humidity.'"

Wesley picked up his drink, which the bartender had just set in front of him, and took a sip.

"What's it?"

"Relative humidity is the trickle of sweat runs down the crack of your sister-in-law's back while you're fuckin' her in the ass."

Five Horse Johnson grinned liplessly, exposing six slimy orange teeth, then fell sideways off his stool to the floor. Wesley finished his whisky and put two dollars on the bar.

"This do it?" he asked the bartender, who nodded.

Wesley unseated himself and stepped over Five Horse Johnson, who was either dead or asleep or in some indeterminate state between the two.

"Professional man, I'll guess."

"Lawyer," said the bartender.

"I known others," Wesley said, and walked out.

SPRINKLE BODIES

Sailor and Lula spent most of their first afternoon in Memphis having lunch with Sparky and Buddy in the Hound Dog Cafe on Elvis Presley Boulevard across the street from Graceland, a place that specialized in Elvis's favorite sandwich, peanut butter and banana on white. The four of them passed on "The White Trash Blue Plate," as Buddy called it, and ate hamburgers as they listened to old Sun 45s by the Killer, the King, Roy Orbison, Charlie Rich and Carl Perkins on the jukebox, and filled each other in on their respective activities over the past quarter of a century and more. After lunch, Sailor and Lula exchanged addresses and telephone numbers with Sparky and Buddy, who went back to work at Organ Retrieval, and then browsed the Elvis souvenir shops.

Sailor was reluctant to tour Graceland now that he knew about the connection to Phelps Bonfuca, alias Myrmidon, and he told Lula he wanted to think it over some more. He was tempted to go through Elvis's private jet, the *Lisa Marie,* which was on display in the Graceland parking lot, but he resisted the urge, since that cost money, too. He did buy a few postcards and two Elvis tee shirts—both decorated with photos from *Jailhouse Rock,* his favorite Elvis movie—at a shop called The Wooden Indian, because he figured Elvis's heirs didn't own it.

Back in their room at the Robert Johnson Regency, Sailor and Lula lay on the king-size bed in their underwear, smoking and talking. Lula had fallen off the cigarette wagon in the Hound Dog Cafe, having fished a More from her purse and fired it up before she'd even realized what she was doing. She puffed happily away and put any thoughts about the possible consequences into a dark corner of her mind.

"Sail, you know, we really been alive a long time now."

"Sometimes it feels long, peanut, other times not much. Why you say that?"

"Oh, thinkin', is all."

Sailor lit a fresh unfiltered Camel off an old one and stubbed out the butt on the letters RJR in a round glass ashtray.

"Bet Robert Johnson never stayed in no hotel fancy as this," Sailor said.

Consuelo's Kiss

"Robert who?"

"Johnson, man this hotel's named for. Blues singer from Miss'ippi died young. Record comp'ny brought him to the city, right off the plantation, I believe. Think Dallas, or San Antone. Cut some tunes then got killed, shot or knifed or somethin', so there ain't much to listen to. What he done was outstandin', though. Kinda spooky, some of it. That's what Sparky was referrin' to when he called this place the Me'n the Devil Motel. 'Me'n the Devil' was one of Robert Johnson's songs. Another good one was 'Hellhound on My Trail.'"

Lula inhaled hard on a More and then blew a big gusher of smoke into the air where it hovered over the bed like a cumulus cloud.

"Shit, Sailor, you know so much more'n me about things? I mean, strange, about unheard of details, like what happened to Robert Johnson."

"Anybody's interested in the music knows about him, honey. Ain't nothin' special."

"Not just this, Sail. You got tons of information tucked away in every part of your brain you never even gonna use. It's a gift."

Sailor laughed. "Ain't the same as bein' smart, though. I'd been smart, never woulda spent a dozen years of my life behind bars. Only real smart thing I ever done was realize you're the best, peanut. I mean that more'n anythin'."

"Sailor?"

"Huh?"

"Don't laugh at me now, okay? When I say what I'm goin' to say?"

"How do I know if I'll laugh or not? What if it's funny?"

"No, you gotta promise or I can't say it."

"Okay, peanut, I promise."

"You think when a person dies, he just fades away? Mean, there ain't really no heaven or even no hell and it's just all over? Tell me the truth now."

"Thought you figured this out back when you was part of the Reverend Goodin Plenty's flock in the Church of Reason, Redemption and Resistance to God's Detractors."

"You know I ain't been to church since Bunny Thorn and I seen Goodin Plenty shot to death in the tent at Rock Hill. His answers didn't hold up, neither."

" 'Member that ol' Buddy Holly tune, 'Not Fade Away'?"

"Yeah?"

"There's your answer."

"Splain yourself."

Sailor raised himself on one elbow and stubbed out his cigarette.

"I'll tell you," he said, "but now you gotta promise not to laugh."

"I do."

"Well, I believe that when folks die all their energy just disperses in the air and flies off like sparks through the universe. Their spirit shoots out of their body and sprinkles back over ever'thin'. That way nobody dies, 'cause their vital self enters into what's left."

"You talkin' 'bout reincarnation, like in India, where a person can come back in another life as a insect? Or you mean that past lives stuff?"

"Uh-uh. Some people in India figure if they live holy enough, next time around they'll be an American. No, just what I said. I call it the 'sprinkle body' theory. Sometimes maybe because of the way the earth's spinnin' or somethin', more of someone gets transferred into a newborn baby or a bee or a rose, but prob'ly that's pretty rare. I figure it's sorta like tossin' a handful of sand into the sky and lettin' the grains blow into eternity."

Lula lay still and didn't say anything.

"Peanut, you think I'm crazy, thinkin' this?"

"No, Sail, I think you're smart, real smart. About some things, I mean. Mostly important things, and this is one. Wasn't totally your fault you went to prison. There's plenty of bright boys locked up for one reason or another."

Sailor lay back on his pillow, picked up his pack of Camels, shook one out and lit it.

"Can't figure it any other way," he said.

"Sprinkle bodies," said Lula.

"Yeah."

"It makes sense, don't it, Sail? It truly does."

The room was almost completely dark, and Sailor stared at the burning end of his cigarette.

"This is the only chance we got to be who we are, Lula, to have all of ourselves in one package."

"I believe you, Sailor. I believe in you, too. But I guess you must know that by now."

Lula turned toward Sailor and fit her head into his right armpit.

"I love you, too, peanut," he said. "And you know what?"

"Huh?"

"Neither of us ain't never had another choice in this world."

Lula nuzzled in even closer.

"Listen, Lula," said Sailor, "I want you to have engraved on my tombstone: 'Dear Peanut, I love you to death,' and underneath just my name."

"Oh, Sail, don't be depressin'. You ain't about to die anytime soon."

"Prob'ly Elvis, even though he was a overweight drug addict, didn't think he was gonna go at forty-two, honey. Just remember, okay?"

"Course I will, sweetheart, it's what you want. Just you remember I love you to death, too."

"Okay, peanut, guess we might just as well do it, even if Phelps gets the money."

"Don't matter anyway, Sail. This bein' your birthday you should do what you want. It'll be fun visitin' Graceland. Elvis didn't die there, did he?"

"Yeah, he O.D.'ed sittin' there on a toilet."

"Prob'ly if he'd always stayed in Memphis, or got him a spread down in that beautiful area around Hernando, Miss'ippi, he'd've lived a whole lot longer. Elvis was outta his true element in California, I believe. Read a Elvis-on-Other-Planets Weight Chart was in a *Enquirer* or somewhere, said that since he weighed 255 when he died, Elvis woulda weighted 648 pounds on Jupiter but only 43 on the moon."

Sailor and Lula had awakened early on the morning of his fiftieth birthday. They'd each gone to the bathroom, peed and brushed their teeth, then gone back to bed and made love. Ordinarily Lula had a hard time coming when they did it so soon after waking, but today she'd been able to get the calf out of the chute so easily that it gave her the giggles.

"What's so funny?" Sailor asked.

"Nothin', honey, just feelin' nice and warm, is all. Look, bring that big bad thing up here where I can treat it right."

Lula grabbed Sailor's cock and pulled him up so that he straddled her chest. She guided him into her mouth, placed her hands on his buttocks and let him move himself forward and back until the hourglass-shaped vein on his penis swelled to bursting and her throat was flooded.

"Still works good, don't it, peanut?" Sailor said, getting off the bed.

"I'm a lucky girl, all right."

Sailor went into the bathroom to take a shower and Lula switched on the TV. The news was on and Lula cranked up the volume in order to hear over the running water.

"In Oxford, Mississippi, last night," the young, African-American woman newscaster said, "a man was shot and killed with his own gun by a half-naked woman, who was then run over and killed by the man's car when it went out of control. Police in Oxford are calling the incident the

'Lesbian Indian Murders.' The killings were apparently the result of a love triangle involving the man, who has been identified as Wesley Nisbet, address unknown, and the woman, Venus Tishomingo, a Chickasaw Indian who was a student at Ole Miss, and a sixteen-year-old girl named Consuelo Whynot, who was present at the scene. Miss Whynot, who was unhurt, is being held in protective custody at the Lafayette County Jail in Oxford."

"Sailor! Sail, come here! You won't believe this!"

Sailor turned off the water and grabbed a towel.

"What is it, peanut?" he said, running in and dripping everywhere.

"You know that girl hitcher we picked up and drove from Jackson to Batesville?"

"Yeah?"

"She's in jail in Oxford. Near as I could make out, a man and a woman were fightin' over her and killed each other. Cops got her in custody."

Sailor ran the towel over his head, under his arms, around his back, down his legs, daubed his feet and tossed it on the bed. He started to put on his clothes.

"Let's get down there, peanut. She might could use some help."

"What could we do for her? Besides, it's your birthday and we're goin' to Graceland."

"Don't matter what day it is. Just think it's what we oughta do. Fuck Graceland, anyway. I re-decided I don't want none of our money filterin' down to no Church of Myrmidon."

Lula got up and began to pack. The telephone rang and Sailor answered it.

"Ripley speakin'."

"Sailor, this is Dalceda Delahoussaye."

"Hello, Mrs. Delahoussaye. Why you callin'? How'd you know we was in Memphis?"

"Marietta told me. Is Lula there?"

"Yeah. You rather speak to her? She's packin' 'cause we're about to leave."

"Don't really matter, I s'pose. Marietta wanted her to know that Marcello Santos had heart palpitations yesterday and is under doctor's care at the Sister Ralph Ricci Convalescent Center here in Bay St. Clement. Marietta's stayin' by his side and won't leave."

"That so? Look, lemme put Lula on."

Sailor handed her the phone.

"Dal? Mama all right?"

"Yes, Lula, Marietta's fine, but Santos is havin' serious chest pains and's in Sister Ralph's. Marietta's there with him, holdin' his hand and readin' him chapters from his favorite book, Eugene Sue's *Mysteries of Paris*."

"That's Mama. He gonna pull through?"

"Don't think he's got long to go, Lula, but he might could hang on, bein' he's one tough Sicilian. There's somethin' else, though."

"What's that?"

"Johnnie Farragut's kidneys just completely quit on him this mornin' early, and he's over at Little Egypt Baptist plugged into a dialysis machine. Marietta don't even know yet. I ain't told her since she's got her hands full with old Crazy Eyes. Doctor at Baptist says unless Johnnie gets a transplant soon he's done."

"Sweet Jesus, Dal, what a phone call."

"Sorry to be the one, Lula, but I thought you'd want to hear the news sooner'n later."

"'Course, Dal, I 'preciate it. Sailor and I are leavin' here now. We got a stop to make in Oxford, then we'll head for home, I guess. I'll call you when we get to Metairie."

"Okay. Take care drivin'."

"We will, Dal. Bye."

"Bye, hon'."

Lula hung up and said, "Shit hits the fan, it splatters."

"You don't care 'bout Santos, do you?"

"Not one way or another, but Dal says Johnnie Farragut's got kidney failure and needs a new one or he's a goner. He's rigged to a device at Little Egypt Baptist."

Sailor picked up the telephone.

"You got that card Sparky give you?" he asked.

Lula found it in her purse and handed it to Sailor, who read the number on it and dialed. A machine answered.

"You've reached S&B Organ Retrieval Service," said Sparky's recorded voice. "Leave a message and we'll do what we can to accommodate your needs. It might cost you some, but at least we won't charge an arm and a leg! Just a little humor there, of course. We stand by our motto: 'Only the best parts!' Be talkin' to ya. Here comes the beep."

"Sparky, Buddy, this is Sailor Ripley speakin'. Listen, Lula's mama's old friend Johnnie Farragut is got kidney failure and's hooked up to a tube or somethin' at Little Egypt Baptist Hospital in Bay St. Clement, North Carolina. He needs a transplant real quick or he's gonna die. If you can help out with this, Lula and I'll find a way to pay you back. We're checkin' out of the hotel now. I'll call you again later."

He hung up, opened his suitcase and threw in his clothes. The phone rang and Sailor answered it.

"Sailor? It's Buddy."

"I just called you."

"I know, we heard the message. We never answer ourselves. Never know who it might be. Anyway, we're on the case. Sparky's contactin' our best retrieval man, John Gray, on the other line. Prob'ly we can get a part on its way to your friend by tonight. And don't worry about the price, it's free of charge. For old times' sake."

"This is awful large of you guys," said Sailor. "Awful large."

Buddy laughed. "Sparky's standin' here talkin' in my other ear now. Hold on, Sailor."

"Sailor? Sparky here."

"'Preciate this, Spark. You guys are beyond outstandin'."

"Anything for veterans of the Big Tuna! You tell Lula's mama not to worry. We gotta run now, we're gonna get this part out."

"We're goin', too. *Adios*, amigo."

"*Ciao!*"

Sailor hung up.

"What'd they say, Sail? Tell me!"

"Boys have it covered, peanut. They're sendin' a new kidney to North Carolina tonight."

"Gonna cost a arm or leg, I bet."

Sailor laughed. "No, sweetheart, it ain't. It's free."

"Them two're somethin' else. Shows you how much good there still is left in the world, Sail. Just gotta know where to look."

"Don't know about good, Lula, but could be Johnnie Farragut'll be able to take a real piss again one of these days."

THE PROPOSAL

" 'When the phantoms cease for a moment to pass and repass on the black veil which I have before my eyes, there are other tortures—there are overwhelming comparisons. I say to myself, if I had remained an honest man, at this moment I should be free, tranquil, happy, loved, and honored by mine own, instead of being blind and chained in this dungeon, at the mercy of my accomplices.'

" 'Alas! the regret of happiness, lost by crime, is the first step toward repentance. And when to this repentance is added an expiation of frightful severity—an expiation which changes life into a long sleep filled with avenging hallucinations of desperate reflections, perhaps then the pardon of man will follow—' "

"Marry me, Marietta," said Santos.

Marietta stopped reading, closed the book and looked up at him. His face was green and puffy and his eyes were closed.

"Marietta Pace, will you marry me?"

She squeezed his right hand, the one with a thumb, with her left.

"Yes, Marcello," said Marietta, "I will."

POISON

"I still ain't sure we're doin' the right thing. I mean, we ain't even relatives."

"Maybe there ain't nothin' we can do, peanut, but I got a feelin' this is a lost girl could use a hand."

Sailor had just turned the Sedan de Ville onto Highway 6 toward Oxford.

"Sail, look how these trees is bein' strangled by kudzu. Them vines strap around 'em like boas on bunnies."

"No stoppin' it, I guess. Kudzu's nature's version of The Blob."

"Wonder if Beany's rememberin' to turn my worms."

Sailor turned up the radio.

"In Miami yesterday," said a newscaster, "a man and a woman died after drinking a six-pack of a Colombian soft drink laced heavily with cocaine. Pony Malta de Bavaria, an imported beverage that has been available for sale in limited quantities in independent grocery stores in the area known as Little Havana, was removed from shelves this morning by order of the Greater Miami Board of Health."

"Used to be Co-Cola had cocaine in it, didn't it, Sailor?"

"Think maybe the first few batches did, till the government figured out a better way to make money off it."

Oxford came up fast and Sailor slowed the Cad as they entered the town. He drove in on Old Taylor Road and followed the signs to the square, where he stopped and asked an old man for directions to the police station.

"They holdin' the 'Last Kiss' girl there, you know," said the man. "I been over but they ain't lettin' nobody in."

The old man was wearing a faded, torn yellow tee shirt that had the words FREE BYRON DE LA BECKWITH on it in black block letters. The man had no hair and no visible teeth, and as he pointed across the square with his left hand, Sailor noticed that the index finger was the only remaining digit on it.

"Lafayette County Jail's just yonder, past the square. Follow around and it'll be on your right. Tickets to view a poison pelt like her'd move faster'n jumper cables at a nigger funeral, I'll guarantee."

Sailor nodded at the man, drove to the jail and parked on the street in front. In the space ahead was a Mercedes-Benz 600 sedan with a Lauderdale County personalized license plate that read WHY NOT.

"Bet that belongs to her parents," said Lula.

"We'll find out," said Sailor, as he opened his door.

As soon as Sailor and Lula entered the station, Consuelo Whynot, who was standing with a well-dressed middle-aged couple and a sheriff, shouted, "They're the ones picked me up in Jackson! They'll tell you 'bout how I was runnin' from that deranged boy!"

"That true?" asked the sheriff, walking toward Sailor and Lula.

"It's true we give her a lift from Jackson to Batesville," said Sailor, "but we don't know nothin' 'bout no boy."

"Why you here?"

"Heard about the incident on the TV news in Memphis, where we was stayin'," said Lula. "Today's my husband's fiftieth birthday, which we was plannin' to celebrate, but he thought it'd be best we drove down and see she needed help."

"You-all sure I didn't tell you 'bout that hor'ble Wesley Nisbet?" asked Consuelo.

"Not that I recall," said Sailor. "You?" he asked Lula.

"Uh-uh."

"I give him one kiss, is all," said Consuelo. "I swear. Said he'd leave me'n Venus be if I did. Had a gun, that boy. Then he told us unless we did a act of love while he watched, he was gonna kidnap me. That's when Venus took after him and the cat caught the chicken. Mama, you got a cigarette?"

The well-dressed woman took a pack of Mores from her purse, removed one and handed it to Consuelo.

"Need a blaze," Consuelo said.

Her mother produced a gold lighter with the initials SOW on it and lit Consuelo's cigarette.

"Sailor, look," said Lula, "she smokes the same brand as me."

"So you folks don't know nothin' 'bout this Nisbet?" asked the sheriff.

"We don't," Sailor said.

"Look, sheriff," said the well-dressed man, "none of this really matters, does it? Consuelo will be with us if you need her. We'll make sure she don't leave home again until this case is cleared up satisfact'rily."

"You can take her," the sheriff said. "Ain't nothin' I can charge her with. It's you and your wife might have a problem, bein' she's a minor."

"Old enough to get married without nobody's permission," said Consuelo. "Though there ain't a man alive can replace Venus in my affections."

"Let's go, Sail," Lula said. "Nobody needs us here."

"Okay, peanut. So long, Consuelo. Good luck."

Consuelo took a deep drag on the More and pushed her free hand back through her brushfire of hair. She pursed her lips and exhaled, then smiled at Sailor.

"Elvis has left the buildin'," she said.

SOLO

John Gray lived, ate and worked alone. He had risen only several minutes prior to the phone call from S&B Organ Retrieval, his best customer. The day had begun well for John Gray, and he hummed the tune of "Just a Closer Walk with Thee" while he shaved. John Gray was forty-five years old, he was slightly more than six-feet three-inches tall, weighed two-hundred-ten well-muscled pounds, wore a bushy black hair weave, and a thick Mexican *bandido*-style mustache that he coated with black Kiwi shoe polish. His eyes were light green, although on a bright afternoon, when he wasn't wearing dark glasses, they turned almost yellow. He wore a three-piece, Wall Street gray Brooks Brothers suit every day, with a red handkerchief in the breast pocket, and black Reebok dress shoes.

John Gray knew where to go for product. He kept his supercharged, midnight blue 5.0-liter Mustang under control as he glided through the Memphis streets. When he arrived at the corner of Murnau and Lewton, he slid to the curb and let the engine idle while he waited. The neighborhood appeared deserted, with abandoned buildings on all sides, but within thirty seconds, two teenaged boys appeared, both wearing Bart Simpson tee shirts, black Levi's and Air Jordans. They came over to the Mustang.

"Got ice, bro'," one of the boys said, as they both leaned their heads toward John Gray, "blow you away."

"No," said John Gray, as he brought up the nine-millimeter machine pistol he'd been holding on his lap, "blow *you* away."

He shot both boys point-blank once each in their foreheads, got out of the car, picked them up, placed them carefully in the trunk and wrapped a heavy brown blanket tightly around the bodies.

As he drove at a modest speed toward the S&B office, John Gray began to sing "Angelo castro e bel" from Donizetti's *Il Duca d'Alba*. Though not a true tenor, John Gray did his best to mimic Caruso's interpretation of the piece, imagining himself as Marcello de Bruges pouring his heart out for Amelia d'Egmont, who is at that moment on her way to meet him.

LIFE AS WE KNOW IT

Sailor and Lula stopped to eat at the Mayflower Cafe on Capitol Street in Jackson on their way home. Most of downtown Jackson had been recently torn down, including the grand old Heidelberg Hotel, and replaced by faceless state government buildings and parking lots. Not that most of the city was that old, Sherman having torched everything that would burn on his march to Atlanta during the unpleasantness known unpopularly as the War Between the States. About the only building left standing after the Yankees left had been the old Capitol. Since the demise of Tom and Woody's Mississippi Diner, the Mayflower was pretty much the end of the line for the downtown restaurant business.

"Same two Greek brothers been operatin' this place since forever," Sailor said to Lula, as they seated themselves in a red leather booth.

He pointed to two ancient-looking, bald-headed, big-nosed men sitting at a Formica table by the cash register. Above the register on the wall was a framed photograph of a man whom both brothers resembled closely.

"That picture's prob'ly of their daddy," said Sailor. "Food's as good here as at the Acme, I recall. Ain't been in since them few months we was apart followin' my release from Huntsville. Those were dark days for me, peanut."

"I know, Sail. They were for me, too."

Sailor shook his head. "Never will forget workin' in that lumberyard in Petal, and livin' in that crummy furnished room over the St. Walburga Thrift Store in Hattiesburg. Whew, that was a bad deal. Come through here and stayed a few days after I left you and Pace in N.O."

"Let's not talk about it, Sailor. Them days is long gone. Look at the good life we created together since then."

Sailor reached across the table and put his hands over Lula's.

"I'm fine, peanut. You don't hear me complainin'. Hate seein' a bad fam'ly situation like the Whynots, is all."

"Won't be no easy road for that Consuelo. Least not for a while."

"She's wild in the country, okay."

A waitress came over and Sailor ordered fried oysters, shrimp, onion rings, fries and two glasses of iced tea.

"That should do it," he said. "What you gonna have, Lula?"

After they'd eaten, Sailor suggested that they not drive all the way home that night, and Lula agreed. They got a room at the Millsaps Buie House on North State Street, a Victorian relic that had originally been the residence of Confederate Major Reuben Webster Millsaps, founder of the local Methodist College, whose house was now operated as an inn. Lula loved the elegant old bed and breakfast place, and she and Sailor slept late the next day, neither of them being in a particular hurry to find out what disastrous occurrence came next.

It was Lula who made the discovery a few minutes after they'd gotten home.

"Sailor! Come see these worms! They're all dead!"

"How could that be, peanut?" Sailor said, running into the backyard, carrying a letter in his right hand. "Thought you told me Beany was watchin' 'em."

"She musta left the hose on the rose bushes too long, and the water seeped into the worm bin and drowned 'em. Sailor, this is the worst!"

"Maybe not, peanut."

He handed Lula the letter.

"It's from Pace," she said.

Sailor nodded. "Go on and read it."

Dear Mama and Daddy,

I am just back from the trek and am writing to tell you the best news of my life. I have met a great girl, a woman I should say, from New York. Actually she is from Brooklyn which is about the same place she says. Her name is Rhoda Gombowicz and yes, she is Jewish. She is about the first Jewish person I have ever known to my knowledge. Rhoda is very beautiful with hair kind of like yours Mama and big brown eyes. Also she is incredibly smart. Sometimes she talks too fast for me and I have to tell her to slow down but she doesn't mind my telling her that. She says everyone in New York talks that way which is one of the reasons she likes me so much she says because I don't. Any way Rhoda and I are in love now and I asked her to marry me when we were on a peak in the Himalayas. She said no woman would say no being proposed to in that spot so she said yes. The one problem is that Rhoda's parents won't let her marry a man who is not Jewish so I have agreed to convert to the Jewish religion. The only religions I know about are Baptist, Buddhist, and Bonpo, so why not? We will leave in a week for New York to meet her family and where I will find out what it takes to become Jewish. I will call or write to you from there. Rhoda says we should live in Brooklyn because that is where her family is. Rhoda is a mental therapist who helps people with their problems by talking to them not a physical therapist who performs rubdowns. You'll like her I know. She is 32 years old five years older than me and never married. Rhoda says if I want I can work in the diamond business with her father and four brothers. I told her I would wait and see about that part. Don't worry about me or anything. The next time you hear from me will be from Brooklyn!

Love, your favorite (and only) son,
Pace Roscoe Ripley

Lula looked up at Sailor but said nothing.

"What you think, peanut?"

"I can't think yet, Sail. I need a minute."

The telephone rang.

"I'll get it," said Lula, who carried Pace's letter with her into the house and held it in one hand while she picked up the receiver with the other.

"Hello?"

"Lula? It's Dal."

"Hi, Dal. How's Santos and Johnnie?"

"It was beautiful, Lula. I wish you coulda been there."

"Been where?"

"At the weddin'. Your mama and Marcello Santos was married this mornin' at three A.M. by a priest at Sister Ralph's. Santos died at ten past three. He was a happy old gangster when his heart quit."

"How about Johnnie?"

"That's the most beautiful part. Johnnie Farragut was the best man. He was strapped down in his bed and taped to a portable piece of equipment moved over from Little Egypt Baptist. After the ceremony, they rushed him back to the hospital where he had a kidney transplant operation. Marietta and I got word from the doctor two hours ago that he thinks it was successful. Doctor said it was a miracle they were able to locate a healthy kidney so quick. Came in on a private jet from Memphis, he said."

"And Mama? How's she holdin' up?"

"Woman's a rock, Lula. You be proud you're her daughter. She's with the mortuary people now, makin' arrangements for Santos's burial. She told me to let you know about ever'thin's gone on and tell you she'll call first chance after she's rested. How's things there?"

"Not quite spectacular as your news, Dal, but other than Beany lettin' the worms die while we was away, the big story is that Pace is gettin' married."

"Well, glory be! Not to one of them Hindu women, I hope."

"No, Dal, to a Jewish girl from Brooklyn, New York. Think she's kind of a doctor. He's movin' there from Nepal."

"You want me to tell Marietta?"

"Better let me do it. Mama's got enough on her mind just now. Give her my and Sailor's love and same to Johnnie Farragut. Thanks for bein' there, Dal. Love you, too."

"Been here all my life, Lula. Bye now."

"Bye. Take care."

After she'd hung up the phone, Lula read Pace's letter again, then put it down on the kitchen table. She looked out through the sliding glass doors into the backyard and saw Sailor standing next to the flooded worm bin smoking a Camel. A huge blue jay landed on the grass about ten feet away from Sailor. He flicked his cigarette at the bird and it screeched and took off.

"Ain't no way human bein's can control their own lives," Lula said out loud, "and ain't no way they ever can stop tryin'."

It suddenly occurred to Lula that she had forgotten to give Sailor a birthday present.

BAD DAY FOR THE LEOPARD MAN

To Monty Montgomery

Maybe what makes life so terribly fatiguing is nothing other
than the enormous effort we make for twenty years, forty years,
and more, to be reasonable, to avoid being simply, profoundly
ourselves, that is, vile, ghastly, absurd.
—Louis-Ferdinand Celine, *Voyage au Bout de la Nuit*

CONTENTS
Bad Day for the Leopard Man

"Lula, you won't believe this."

"Won't believe what, Sail, honey?"

"Article in the *Times-Picayune* I'm readin', says thirty-seven percent of Americans believe in the devil."

"Don't know why that should surprise you none, havin' knowed so many people as you have durin' your sixty-three years on the planet. Count sounds about right to me."

"Peanut, all the trouble this world's seen since the beginnin' of time ain't been the doin' of no devil. It's been the result of two things, organized religion and greed."

"What about sex?"

"Lust I lump with greed."

Sailor Ripley was sitting in his cracked red leather armchair in the front room of the house in Metairie, Louisiana, that he and his wife, Lula Pace Fortune, had lived in for thirty years. Lula, who was three years younger than Sailor, lay on the ecru shag carpet doing stretching exercises. She was still slim-figured at sixty, thanks to what she liked to call "the vain woman's never-endin' struggle against stone-cold nature." Sailor, pot-bellied, mostly bald and slightly arthritic, though otherwise in fair shape, had given up the fight long ago, and not unhappily. He was semi-retired from his vice-presidency of the Gator Gone Corporation, which was now the world's largest manufacturer and distributor of alligator and crocodile repellent. He went into the office in New Orleans two or three times a week to help out his friend Bob Lee Boyle, the company's founder and owner. Sailor read a great deal these days, mostly history and historical fiction, and the newspapers, which were still his greatest source of amusement. He was comfortable in his chair.

"Now here's one, peanut," he said. "Police in Shreveport are mystified, it says, by a series of car bombin's been goin' on over a year. Sixteen people killed the same way and none of the victims seem to be connected. 'Unrelated Murders Stump Cop Braintrust' is the headline." Sailor laughed. "Don't take much, that's sure."

Lula rolled over from her right side to her left and began a scissors motion with her right leg.

"If you was gonna blow up a car, Sail, how'd you do it? Wire a bomb to the ignition? Bet ol' Crazy Eyes Santos done that lotsa times."

"He mighta did, but that's too obvious. Best way is to insert a BB in a gelatin capsule filled with cyanide and drop it in the gas tank. The weight of the BB'll cause it to sink to the bottom of the tank where the small amount of water settled there'll eat away at the capsule. Within a half hour the cyanide'll be released and ignite the gasoline. Boom! There you go."

"Sailor, you're somethin' else, knowin' somethin' 'bout practically ever'thin' the way you do. Where'd you learn that precious piece of information?"

"Same place I picked up most of my practical knowledge, in the pen. Believe it was a fella named Party-Time Partagas, a Marielito, taught me that at Huntsville. He was an old professional killer had been in a Havana prison for years before Castro boatmailed all the Cuban criminals to Key West back in '81. Party was a senior citizen when I knew him. Musta died behind them Texas walls."

"Boy, Sail, that seems so long ago you were inside. Almost like it never happened."

"Wish it hadn't, peanut, but I come through."

"Thank the Lord."

"The Lord ain't always done such a exemplary job, honey. Listen to this: Out in California a guy claimed God told him he could drive his truck through cars, so he drove it into eighteen other vehicles on a freeway durin' the mornin' rush hour. Injured dozens, killed four and stopped traffic for half a day."

Lula switched back to her right side and scissored with her left leg.

"Sounds like more of the devil's doin' there, darlin', not the Lord's."

Sailor laughed. "Guess you're in the thirty-seven percent."

"Old beliefs ain't easy to quit," said Lula. "'Specially when there ain't nothin' better to replace 'em with."

The telephone rang and Lula sprang up like a young girl to answer it. "Hello?"

"Hey, Mama, it's Pace."

"Don't nobody else call me Mama, son. I'd know it's you just by your breathin' anyway. Where you callin' from?"

"Hollywood. I got a job workin' for a director, the fella I told you I met two years ago over in Paris, where I went after me and Rhoda got divorced."

"What exactly are you doin' for this director person?"

"Man's plannin' a new film. He's pretty famous for some horror pictures he made a while back. I'm his factotum."

"His what?"

"Factotum, Mama. Means I'm his chief assistant, right-hand man. I do what's necessary."

"Pace Roscoe Ripley, you're forty years old. Don't you think you oughta be settled in a real job by now?"

"This is a real job, Mama. And didn't I spend eight miserable years in the diamond business in New York with Gombowicz and Sons, or are you forgettin'?"

"That was Rhoda's family's business, son. I mean somethin' of your own."

"Mama, I'm doin' what I want now, like when I was leadin' treks in Nepal. I'm learnin' about the film world."

"Long as you're happy, I guess."

"How're you and Daddy?"

"Oh, we're inchin' by at about the same rate your daddy's hairline's recedin'. His arthritis is caused him to lose some strength in the left arm lately, though. He can't lift nothin' heavier'n a egg with it, and we don't eat eggs 'cause of the cholesterol."

"Reason I'm callin' now, Mama, is to tell you we might be headin' to New Orleans next week to do some research for a screenplay. Wanted to know if you and Daddy were gonna be around."

"Where else we gonna be? Ain't been anyplace in four years but that time Sail insisted on takin' me to Maui the month after your Grandmama Marietta passed away."

Lula's eyes watered at the thought of her mother.

"Mama, you cryin'?"

"No, I ain't. Just hard to believe Mama's gone, is all."

"How's Auntie Dal?"

"Dalceda Delahoussaye got a iron constitution to match her outlook on life. She's hangin' in, far's I know. We spoke day before yesterday and Dal was organizin' the Bay St. Clement chapter of the Daughters of the Confederacy in a protest against a court order bannin' smokin' in restaurants. Can you imagine that? In North Carolina, of all places. Auntie Dal is eighty-five years old and she's still suckin' in a pack a day. Mores, just like me, only I cut down to 'bout half a pack you'll be glad to know."

"I am, Mama. Want to keep you around long as possible. Tell Daddy I'll be home soon."

"You-all want to stay with us?"

"Thanks, Mama, but prob'ly we'll be at a hotel in N.O. That way we won't be disturbin' nobody."

"You ain't no disturbance, Pace, you're our only child. And tell your director friend he's welcome here, too."

"'Preciate it, Mama. Love you."

"Love you, son. Take precautions, you know?"

Pace laughed. "I do. Bye, Mama."

"Bye."

"The boy all right?" asked Sailor, after Lula had hung up.

"Sounds dandy," she said. "He's in L.A., learnin' the movie business. Says he may be here in a week or so with a man he's workin' for."

"You don't sound like you're so happy about it. I mean, his bein' in L.A."

"That Hollywood lifestyle's a long ways short of heaven, Sail, you know?"

Sailor laughed. "Peanut, what ain't?"

BAD DAY FOR THE LEOPARD MAN

The Leopard Man's name was Philip Reál. He was called the Leopard Man behind his back by others in the movie business because of the gothic nature of the films he'd directed and written during the past two decades. Val Lewton, a producer at RKO in the 1940s, had made a series of low-budget horror pictures, including one titled *The Leopard Man*. In a review of Phil Reál's startling first feature, *Mumblemouth*, made when Reál was twenty-three, the Los Angeles *Times* critic had compared the look and feel of the film—heavy shadows and deep suggestions of off-camera hideous goings-on—to Lewton's black-and-white B's that most film historians considered classics of the genre. At the time, it was construed as a compliment, but as the years wore on, and Reál repeated himself with such efforts as *Death Comes Easy, Face of the Phantom, The Slow Torture and Sexual Re-education of Señor Rafferty* and others, culminating in the universally maligned *Dog Parts*, which featured a denouement wherein two Pit Bulls brutally dismember a pregnant Collie bitch and devour her fetus, Phil Reál had become unbankable and persona non grata in Hollywood.

He had gone to Europe, living first for two years in France, then for three in Italy, where he directed and acted in a cheapie called *Il Verme* ("The Worm"), a soft-core pornographic version of the myth of Cadmus, before returning to L.A. Since his return, he had been living alone in a house in the Hollywood hills, working on an original screenplay called *The Cry of the Mute*, based on his own experiences in the industry.

Phil let the telephone ring three times before he picked up.

"Happy birthday, darlin'! How's it feel to be fat and fifty?"

"My birthday was yesterday, Flower, and I'm forty-eight. But thanks, anyway."

"Sorry, sugar. Least you know I'm thinkin' about you."

"I thought you were in Kenya, with Westphal."

"Picture wrapped a month ago, Philly. Where you been keepin' yourself?"

"Right here by my lonesome. I stopped reading the trades and I do my own cooking."

Flower laughed. "You still writin' on that *Moot* script, huh?"

"The word is *Mute,* Flower, and yes, I am. What do you have in the works?"

"Well, you do know me'n Jason got divorced?"

"No, I missed that."

"Yeah, he's livin' with Rita Manoa-noa now, the top whore outta Tahiti that was brought over by Runt Gold to be in the remake of *Captain Cook's Revenge* that never got made? Final decree came through just after I got to Africa. Let me tell you, Philly, they don't call it the dark continent for nothin'. People there're the blackest I ever seen anywhere, includin' Alabama."

"Africa wasn't called the dark continent because of the color of the skin of most of its inhabitants, Flower. It's because it was one of the last places the Europeans got to. 'Dark' referred to unexplored and unknown."

"Phil, you always know about everything."

"That's why I'm such a popular guy."

"Oh, sugar, everyone thinks you're the smartest man in Hollywood."

"As Daffy Duck said, 'Ridicule is the curse of genius.'"

"Anyway, I'm seein' Clark now."

"Westphal? What happened to Suki?"

"He thrown her out before Africa. She's suin' him now, of course. But they weren't never married so he says she can't get much. Clark made her sign a paper while they was livin' together said she couldn't make no claims on him. He done it with all his women."

"I think Clark may be just a tad brighter than I am."

"He sure has more money, Philly, that's the truth. Not as much hair, though."

"He can buy some."

"Don't need to, now the natural look is in. Thinnin' hair is a sign of maturity, you know."

"Spell maturity for me, Flower."

She laughed. "Sugar, ten years ago when I came to California from Mobile, I had me a choice between practicin' spellin' or keepin' my lips over my teeth when I give head. Can't have it both ways in this town.

"Look, I gotta run," Flower said. "Clark's takin' me down to his place in darkest Mexico tonight, the house he bought from Jack Falcon, the famous old director who died last year?"

"I know who Jack Falcon was, Flower."

"Oh, of course you do. Prob'ly you and him went boar huntin' together and everything."

"As a matter of fact, I think I still have my boar rifle around here somewhere."

"I got to go shop now, honey. Happy birthday, even though it's the wrong day. I'll call you when I'm back from Mexico. You still hangin' at Martoni's?"

"Once in a while."

"We'll meet for drinks. Bye!"

Flower hung up, so Phil did, too. He suddenly flashed on the bathtub scene in *Señor Rafferty*, where Flower Reynolds, as the crazed transsexual Shortina Fuse, wearing only a pair of red panties, tosses the sulfuric acid into Rafferty's face. The camera remains fixed on Flower's red triangle while she laughs and Rafferty screams, holding until the final fade. It was Flower's laugh people remembered later, not Rafferty's screams. She had a great laugh. Phil had always regretted not having used it in *Dog Parts*.

Phil had an 11:30 with Arnie Pope at Five Star. The meeting had been set up for him by Bobby Durso, who, during Phil's European hiatus, had become a powerful agent despite his lack of affiliation with an established agency. Bobby operated on his own and specialized in handling writers. Actors, he'd decided, were—with few exceptions—essentially undependable and insecure; dysfunctional people, his shrink called them. Writers, Bobby found, were the hardest-working, most clearly focused and dedicated individuals he'd ever known.

Bobby had been Phil Reál's A.D. on *Death Comes Easy*, then gone back to UCLA, where he'd earned a degree in American history, worked as a bartender for a couple of years, gotten married and begun his present career by representing his wife, Alice, who wrote screenplays. The first script of Alice's that Bobby Durso sold, *Goodbye To Everyone*, wound up grossing over two hundred million for Paramount, and the sequel, *Hello To Nobody*, did equally well. Since then, every producer in town found time to talk to, if not openly court him.

Bobby was not intending to represent Phil Reál, however. At least not in any official capacity. The meet with Arnie Pope had been arranged as a favor, and that's where Bobby wanted to leave it. He hadn't even read Phil's screenplay, if he had one yet, or allowed Phil to describe the story. Phil, Bobby knew, would want to direct the picture himself, and there was no way a studio would allow that. Bobby dealt exclusively with the majors, he didn't touch the independents, and he'd explained his position to Phil, who said that he understood completely.

Arnie Pope was Bobby's brother-in-law—Alice was Arnie's sister—he and Bobby got along all right, and when Bobby asked him to take a meeting with the Leopard Man, no strings attached, he said okay. After all, Arnie figured, the man was a kind of legend in the business, and it could be interesting. Arnie told his assistant, Greta, to reschedule his shiatsu for 11:45.

Phil appeared in Arnie Pope's outer office at 11:29. He did not bring the screenplay with him. Greta buzzed Arnie, who asked her to show in Mr. Reál.

"This is a real pleasure, Mr. Reál," said Arnie, as he stood up and leaned across his desk to shake hands.

"Phil, please."

"Arnie. Sit."

They both sat down.

"This is really great," Arnie said. "I can still remember the first time I saw *Face of the Phantom*. At the Riviera in Chicago, when I was fourteen. Scared the piss out of me. My girlfriend wouldn't even look at the screen. Kept her head buried in my right shoulder the whole time."

Arnie rubbed his right shoulder with his left hand. Phil noticed Arnie's diamond pinkie ring.

"It was great, great," said Arnie.

Arnie smiled and Phil nodded.

"So, what's this Bobby says you've got? Have to tell you, though, that since the Germans bought Five Star, all we've been able to push through are one-namers."

Phil looked puzzled.

"You know: Rheinhold, Dirk, those guys. Muscle men. Put a title underneath, like *Death Driver*, all that's necessary. So, it's 11:31:35. Tell me."

"This is a special picture."

"They're all special, Phil." Arnie again looked quickly at his watch. "Got a title?"

"*The Cry of the Mute.*"

"A mute's someone can't talk, right?"

Phil nodded. "The title is meant to be ironic."

"Ironic, yeah, sure. I got it. So, what happens?"

"It's about a writer-director who was at one time very successful, when he was young, and then his career slipped away from him. He drinks, takes drugs, he travels, and finally returns to make one last picture. Nobody believes in him anymore except for a girl, a woman, who began her acting career in his early films. She's become a big star and gets him a deal, based on her agreement to play the female lead."

"Good. I was waiting for the girl. What does she do?"

"Sells tickets."

"I know. I mean in the story. She helps the guy get back on his feet, cleans him up, marries him, what? Where's the big play come in?"

"He shows he can still pull it off. The picture's both a critical and box office success."

"What about him and her? In the end?"

Phil shook his head. "They don't get together. She marries someone else."

Arnie Pope looked at his watch and stood up.

"When Nick Ray made *In a Lonely Place* he had Bogart," Arnie said.

"Gloria Grahame made the picture work," said Phil.

"Phil," Arnie stuck out his hand as he came around the desk, "I gotta be Japanese in five minutes. Less. Have Bobby send me the script. I promise I'll read it."

Phil stood and let Arnie pinch the fingers of his right hand. Greta appeared.

"Almost time, Arnie," she said.

"Greta," said Arnie, "when Phil's script arrives, read it right away."

Arnie turned and looked directly into Phil's eyes.

"I'll never forget *Face of the Phantom*, Phil. Never. It's a classic."

Arnie nodded and grinned. "Janet Coveleski," he said. "That was her name."

"Whose name, Arnie?" asked Phil.

"The girl I took to see your picture at the Riviera."

Arnie walked out of his office, followed closely by Greta. Phil stood without moving for twenty seconds. He remembered the last frame of *Phantom*, where the man who has never slept with his eyes closed finally closes them, knowing he'll never wake up. Phil closed his eyes.

WRANGLER'S PARADISE

Nobody in Hollywood has a past that matters. What counts is what someone is doing right now or might be doing tomorrow. The film business is open to anyone, and that was the great thing about it, Phil thought, as he drove home from Five Star. A person could be a multiple murderer escapee from prison or a lunatic asylum but if he or she had a bright idea that was considered do-able, and the proper pieces fell together in the right hands at the right time, that person, certifiably depraved or otherwise, could have a three-picture deal in less than the lifetime of a Florida snake doctor.

If one of them is a hit, the escapee could be running a studio within a few months, and as long as the people kept buying tickets the studio lawyers would do everything they could to keep the authorities at bay. A big enough flop, though, and the *wunderkind* would no doubt be back doing laps inside a padded cell before it went to video. Phil loved the strangeness of it, he really did. Hollywood was a wrangler's paradise: the cattle either got to market or they didn't. Rustled, died of thirst, train derailed, didn't matter. No excuses, no prisoners. That was the law of the bottom line.

Driving along La Brea, Phil decided to stop at Pink's. He parked his leased Mustang convertible around the corner on Melrose, got out and joined the line at the outdoor counter. When his turn came, he ordered a double cheeseburger with chili and a black cherry Israeli soda. As he waited for the food, Phil looked across the street. A middle-aged bum had disrobed and begun doing jumping jacks on the sidewalk, his long hair and beard flopping around. Pedestrians passed on either side of him. A swarthy man came out of the convenience store on the corner and walked swiftly toward the naked bum. The swarthy man, who wore a thick black mustache and a square of hair in the center of his chin, pulled a small-caliber revolver from a pocket, pushed the nose of it into the bum's left ear and pulled the trigger. The bum fell down and blood gushed from his head. The swarthy man ran back toward the convenience store.

Phil picked up his cheeseburger and soda, paid the Mexican girl who'd served him, walked to his car, got in and drove away. The bum had looked familiar, Phil thought. He made a mental note to check the newspaper the next day for the story, to see if the bum had been someone he'd known in the old days.

Phil was typing when the telephone rang.

"Pick that up, Pace, will you?" he shouted.

"Philip Reál's line," said Pace.

"Pace, it's Bobby Durso. Phil there?"

"Just a moment, Mr. Durso. Phil, Bobby."

Phil stopped typing and picked up his extension.

"Hey, Bobby."

"How'd it go with Pope?" Bobby asked.

"Thanks for your help but my take is that Five Star wants something I don't have."

"And what's that?"

"A brain-eater."

"A brain-eater? What's a brain-eater?"

"Bobby, I'm about the devil in disguise to Arnie Pope and his people. And it ain't much of a disguise, either."

"Meaning what?"

"Meaning they see right through me the same way I see through them."

"Phil, I love the way you talk but I don't always get the message so easily. I take it you and Arnie didn't get along."

"Oh, on the contrary. Turns out he's had a crush on me forever. But it's one of those two-cars-at-a-stoplight romances. We checked each other out but then he took a right and I was in the left lane."

"So?"

"Light turned green and the cars lined up behind me were honking, so I did the only thing I could."

"Yeah?"

"Drove straight ahead and here I am, same as ever. Not even a fender bender on the way back."

"Well, I tried."

"I appreciate it, Bobby, I really do. You know, I had a dream last night where I was driving an old pickup truck that had 'Al and Popeye's

Hauling Service' painted on the door. I only had one arm, my right, so when I shifted gears I had to be quick about grabbing the steering wheel again. It was hot outside, in the dream, and the breeze through the rolled-down window hit directly on my left armpit, there not being a biceps to block it. I was real cool."

"Phil, you are cool, but I don't know what to tell you."

"Tell me about what, Bob?"

"How you're gonna make it now in this town. If you think I can help, call me."

"Sure thing, Bobby. I'm taking off for a little while but I'll talk to you when I get back. Thanks again."

Phil hung up and closed his eyes. Slowly he raised his left arm until it was entirely vertical and let the air hit his armpit. He reopened his eyes.

"Pace, you make our arrangements for New Orleans?"

"Done, Phil. We leave tomorrow out of LAX at one. Be in N.O. in plenty of time to have dinner at Dooky's. Have Miz Chase make us somethin' special."

"Where are we staying?"

"The Rinaldi, on Gravier, just off the Quarter. Got you a junior suite and me a room."

"Speak to your folks?"

"Mama says they're lookin' forward to meetin' you."

"Maybe they can help me fill in some background for the story. I figure New Orleans is a properly exotic location for *The Cry of the Mute*."

"Spend enough time down there you just might want to change the title to *The Cry of the Mutilated*."

Phil grinned. "I like that, Pace. I like how your rebel brain works. You and your parents have much in common?"

Pace laughed. "Prob'ly more'n necessary, Phil."

THE MUSEUM OF OPINION

Sailor awoke at four A.M. from a vivid dream wherein he had taken a job as curator of the Museum of Opinion in Sweden. Located on a spit of land in the far northern reach of Scandinavia, the museum existed as a sanctuary for certain individuals whose ideas, as expressed either in some public form, such as books, newspapers or via electronic media, or simply by letter to the museum, were deemed by the curator as worthy of recognition and an open-ended invitation to reside in one of the houses maintained by the Foundation of Opinions.

In the dream, Sailor's position as curator entitled him to extend or revoke permits to the society of fellows, as museum residents were called, and to decide all matters of consequence. It was his opinion that counted the most. The only requirement of the fellows was that they regularly post their opinions on the Central Hall bulletin board, so that they could be discussed at mealtimes. Since the breakfasts, lunches and dinners were often—not unexpectedly—volatile affairs, residents were also provided foodstocks in their private rooms. Casual digestion was never a hallmark of the society.

Sailor picked up the pen and notebook he had lately taken to keeping on his bedtable and wrote down the essential belief of the Museum of Opinion as had been dictated to him in the dream: "A man alone is the epitome of conflict."

He lay in bed thinking about the turns his life had taken. It was at such moments, usually in the middle of the night, that he succumbed to a very low opinion of himself. This condition always passed quickly, however, as it did now, and Sailor lay there, listening to Lula's even breathing. He picked up a pack of Camels and the matches that were on the table next to his notebook and lit a cigarette.

He had recently read a biography of Pierre Loti, the nineteenth-century French writer whose real name was Julien Viaud. Loti had dressed himself variously as a bedouin, a pasha and a circus acrobat, had converted to Islam, and conducted countless sexual liaisons with both men and women. "No matter what," Loti wrote, "I am always a déclassé, playing a part."

Sailor thought about what Loti had meant by that. When he was a boy, Sailor had for a time fantasized himself as a character called the Black Phantom, leaping from rooftop to rooftop to rescue persons in distress, then escaping without a word back into the darkness. It was a part he had invented, he realized now, to escape from the constant alcohol-fueled arguments waged nightly by his parents. That had been an ugly time in his life, Sailor thought, almost as ugly as the time he'd spent in prison, away from Lula and Pace.

It was Sailor's opinion that without the ability to escape inside the mind there would be even more murders and suicides than there already were. Hadn't he read somewhere that Sweden had one of the highest suicide rates in the world? Sailor took a hard drag on the Camel, then made a note to look up the meaning of the word *epitome*.

"My mama and Dalceda Delahoussaye used to meet like this at least four afternoons a week at Bode's in Bay St. Clement most all their lives. They was close friends for three quarters of a century, Beany, can you believe that? Even went to boardin' school together. Miss Cook's, in Beaufort."

"Don't look now, Lula, but you and me is creepin' up on bein' friends for *half* a century ourselves."

Lula shook her head. "It's a comfort and frightenin', both, you know."

"I do know," said Beany. "When I think about Madonna Kim turnin' thirty-one next month, it's like, how'd that happen? And Lance is thirty-seven!"

"Which makes Pace forty. Time gotten right out of control, Beany, no doubt about it. We're victims of longevity is what we are. By the way, Pace is comin' home next week."

"To stay?"

"Uh-uh. He's workin' with a director out of Hollywood and they're comin' to N.O. for research, Pace said."

"Pace livin' in L.A. now?"

"I guess."

"That boy been about everywhere, Lula. 'Specially since he and Rhoda busted up."

"Weren't the divorce I minded, it's that they didn't make no family. You know how much I been lookin' forward to havin' grandkids. You're damn lucky, Beany. You got six."

Beany sighed. "Yeah, they're somethin' else, all right. Each of Madonna Kim's four is by a different father, and Lance's two are by his two wives. He's engaged again, did I tell you?"

"No. Who to?"

"Gal named LaDonna, capital L, capital D. She's twenty-two, blonde—natural or not I don't know, since I ain't met her—wants to be a singer of some kind. Lance told me they met in Phoenix two months ago when he was at the computer convention there."

"What's her last name?"

"Flynn. Her daddy's Manny Flynn, guy Lance is thinkin' 'bout goin' to work for. Man built a software empire that's headquartered in Arizona. Lance'd have to move there, which he don't mind, seein's how he's burned out on Atlanta. Only thing, both his ex-wives, Zoe and Charlene Raé, are there, so it'd be tough on him and the kids. Also, don't know if marryin' the boss's daughter's a good idea or not."

"Time'll tell."

Lula and Beany Boyle were lingering over coffee following a salad lunch at Foissoner, their regular Thursday afternoon meetingplace in the French Quarter. The chef and part owner, César Foudre, was the father of Madonna Kim's next-to-last offspring, also named César, and he never allowed the ladies to pay. A tiny man with a thick red whiskbroom-shaped beard, César came out of the kitchen and greeted them.

"Mesdames Boyle and Ripley, a pure *plaisir*," he said, smiling, though his lips were well-hidden, "*comme toujours*. The *repas* was satisfactory?"

"We got most the rabbits beat, César," said Beany. "It was fine."

Lula smiled and nodded her agreement.

"I am teaching Little César how to cook," said César. "It is like swimming, I believe. One is never too young to learn. He is four years old and already he can bake bread. By the time he is six, he will have learned the sauces."

"That's swell, César," said Beany, "maybe he'll teach Madonna Kim how to fry an egg."

César laughed. "For this he will have to first master sorcery, not sauces!"

Beany and Lula laughed, and César excused himself.

"He's not such a bad fella," said Lula, "and he has a good business. Too bad Madonna Kim couldn't settle down with him."

"Lula, there's no use talkin' about my daughter's matin' habits. Soon as César pulled out, she hooked into Roberto Roatan, the jockey got banned for life after fixin' races at Louisiana Downs. Remember him?"

"Madonna Kim always has gone for short ones. You notice that?"

Beany raised her eyebrows and shook her head.

"Asked her about it once. She said little men are more intense."

After they'd finished their coffee, Beany and Lula walked along Burgundy toward the parking lot across Canal, where they'd left Lula's car. At

Iberville Street, a giant black man waving an Israeli flag over his clean-shaven skull strode past them, shouting, "Jews is saved! Jews is saved! Great God Almighty, the Jews is saved!" Following close behind him, carrying short lengths of pipe and sawed-off bats, were a half-dozen skinheads wearing green tanker jackets, leather gloves and combat boots.

"Don't fret," Beany said to Lula, "I don't go no place without a gun."

THAT'S WHAT I LIKE ABOUT THE SOUTH

Pace and Phil were sitting in the lobby of the Rinaldi waiting for Sailor and Lula. It was cold and rainy in New Orleans, early January, so both Pace and Phil wore tan Burberry trenchcoats, cowboy boots and Great White Hunter hats.

"I'll bet you fellas either in oil or from Hollywood."

Pace turned around and saw Sailor's grin.

"Hey, Daddy!" Pace said. He jumped up and they embraced. "This here's Philip Reál, my employer."

Phil stood up and shook hands with Sailor.

"Pleased to meet you, Mr. Reál. Hope Pace is givin' you your money's worth."

"Call me Phil, and if it's all right with you, I'll call you Sailor."

"You bet."

"Pace is rapidly becoming indispensable to me, Sailor. I was very fortunate to have found him."

"Where's Mama?" asked Pace.

"Waitin' in the car. She's dyin' to see you, son."

The three men started together toward the main entrance but before they had gone three steps a shot rang out. Sailor and Pace immediately hit the deck.

"Phil!" Pace yelled. "Get down!"

Sailor grabbed Phil's left arm at the wrist and dragged him to the floor. Several more shots were fired and Sailor looked up just enough to see a tall white man wearing a New Orleans Saints jacket and a black woman in a red dress run across the lobby and out the door. The man and the woman each held a gun in their right hand and a black and white shopping bag in their left. Nobody in the lobby screamed or yelled. Like Sailor, Pace and Phil, they had taken cover and wondered what was going on. There was the sound of a vehicle's tires squealing, a brief roar of an engine, then silence. The inhabitants of the lobby cautiously came out of hiding, stood up and looked around.

"What in blazes was that all about?" asked Phil.

A doorman came running in and shouted, "They got away in a black Cadillac! Had a white woman behind the wheel!"

Sailor ran out, followed closely by Pace and Phil.

Two police cars zoomed into the hotel driveway and four cops got out with their guns drawn. The doorman who had made the announcement came out and repeated what he'd said. A young woman dressed in a dark blue business suit stumbled out after the doorman and collapsed on the top step of the hotel entryway. There was blood in her light brown hair and on the left side of her face. One of the cops kneeled down next to her.

"They took everything from the safe," she said. "All the money and jewelry. Jeffrey's dead, the black girl shot him. The man hit me in the head with his gun."

"Lula!" Sailor shouted at the cops. "They stole my wife! She was in the car!"

Two of the cops grabbed Sailor and shoved him up against a pillar.

"You say your wife was drivin'?" said one.

"I'm tellin' you," said Sailor, "my wife was in the car they drove off in! She been kidnapped!"

"Hold him," one cop said to the other. "I'll check out inside."

"You sure your wife wasn't in on this deal?" asked the cop who was holding Sailor.

"You must be crazy!" yelled Pace. "Why don't you get after them thieves got my mama?!"

More squad cars pulled into the hotel roundabout and a dozen policemen leaped out. Half of them ran over to where Sailor was pinned against the pillar and pointed their weapons at him.

"Look," Phil said to one of the cops, "this man didn't do anything! Some people robbed the hotel and used his car to get away. His wife was in it."

Before Phil could finish his last sentence, the cop had him face down on the ground with a hammerlock on his right arm. Phil's hat fell off and rolled into the roadway.

"This is Philip Réal!" Pace shouted. "The famous director!"

A cop pushed the barrel of his .38 into Pace's stomach and told him to shut up. The left side of Phil's face was pressed into the cold, wet concrete, and it was from this perspective that he watched the right front tire of a New Orleans police car crush his Great White Hunter hat that two days before he had paid $159 for at Banana Republic on Melrose.

THE HORROR

"I hope you understand, Mr. Ripley, and you, too, Mr. Reál, my men were just doin' their job. No harm intended, and you got my sincere-most apology for the rough stuff. What we gotta do now is make sure Mrs. Ripley's returned to you soon and safe as possible."

Police Captain DuMont "Du Du" Dupre, who was in line to become commissioner when the current top gun, Eddie Fange, who had held the office for fifteen years, retired, looked carefully first at Sailor then at Phil, who were seated on folding metal chairs on the other side of the desk from the captain in his office at police headquarters in the new windowless Louis Armstrong City Government Building across from the Superdome on Poydras. Pace stood behind Sailor's chair, his right hand gripping his father's right shoulder. A telephone on the desk rang and Dupre picked it up. The folds of his fat, froglike face alternately contracted and relaxed as he listened and spoke.

"Yeah, Eddie, I heard," said Du Du. "I told them Army boys we wasn't gonna touch it, which they was happy to hear. Shootin' cats in the head to study gunshot wounds don't bother me particular, but I can see how it's bound upset some folks. Uh huh. Let the politicians handle it, I agree. Yeah, Eddie, was about seven hundred felines altogether, 'cordin' our reports. Yes. Yes. They was anethesized, sure. Okay, Eddie, I just goin' refer 'em to the state hereafter. By the way, how your lung doin'? They gonna have to cut it more?"

Du Du winked his liquidy red left eye at Sailor and held up the index finger of his right hand.

"That good," he said, nodding and rolling back his purple upper lip by pushing under it with his lower. "Best to hang on what little we got left so long as possible, I agree. You still got that Enfield .30-06 at Barataria? Right." Du Du laughed. "You know it's same model old Delay Beckwith supposed to used when he shot Medgar Evers. Sure is. You might could get a price for it now. Okay, Eddie, you take care now." Du Du hung up.

"We on this like white on rice, Mr. Ripley," said Du Du, "and there ain't no quit in a case includes murder, armed robbery, kidnappin' and car theft. We'll keep you up on the investigation. Call me personal, any-time."

"I can't just sit still," Sailor said. "There must be somethin' my son and I can do to help."

The creases deepened in Du Du Dupre's rubbery face.

"Don't be gettin' no brave ideas here, Mr. Ripley. We dealin' with people ain't shy 'bout shootin' off more'n their mouth. Best you-all remain at home, let us take care of it."

On the street in front of Louis Armstrong, Pace said, "Daddy, no way I'm waitin' on the blue."

"I'm with you, too, Sailor," said Phil. "Why don't we go back to my suite at the Rinaldi and make a plan?"

"Better to stay at the house," Sailor said, "'case Lula calls, or the kid-nappers. Might be they'll try to ransom her."

"You're right, Daddy. Knowin' Mama, it's possible she could talk her way out of this."

"Anyone can, it's Lula."

The three men got into Phil's rented white Lincoln Town Car. As Pace drove, memories of all the years that he and Lula had spent together whizzed through Sailor's mind. A picture of Lula at seventeen flashed in his brain and he held that image. Lula was sitting on the top rail of the wooden fence that bordered the yard of the Fortune house in Bay St. Clement. Lula wore a checked shirt and a short white skirt, and her thick black hair was tied back with a ribbon. She was smiling and the longer of her large two front teeth was snagged on her lower lip, giving her face a slightly anxious expression. Sailor could picture the indentation line on Lula's lip caused by her overbite and he felt his heart flutter. He knew he would die before he ever stopped looking for Lula.

CAT PEOPLE

Oretta "Kitty Kat" Cross, black female, twenty-five, black hair with two dyed red braids, black eyes—the left with a slight strabismus, or cast—five-five, one hundred ten pounds, no tattoos, rode shotgun.

"Don't see why we had to do this, Kitty Kat. Now we up for kidnappin', too."

Archie Chunk, white male, twenty-eight, sandybrown hair cut short, blue eyes, five-nine, one hundred sixty pounds, broken nose, two-inch horizontal scar middle of forehead, fire-breathing dragon tattoo right biceps, anchor tattoo with snake entwined back of left hand, squirmed around in the back seat of the Cadillac. He kept turning to look out the rear window.

"You prefer we be walkin'?" said Kitty Kat. "The woman be right there. Nobody chasin' us, Arch. Relax."

Archie twisted toward her. "How I gonna relax you shot the dude?"

Kitty Kat vaulted into the back seat, shoved Archie over so that she could sit directly behind Lula, shifted the Colt Python she was holding into her left hand, unzipped Archie's trousers with her right, took out his penis and started jacking him off.

"You stay on 23 to West Pointe à la Hache," Kitty Kat said to Lula, sticking the barrel point into the soft spot at the back of Lula's head, holding it there for several seconds, "then I tell you what to do."

Archie let his head roll back and closed his eyes as Kitty Kat caressed him. She put her thick lips to his left ear and purred like a cat, making a soft, rumbling growl in the back of her throat. Archie's penis, at first touch tiny and flaccid, soon swelled to its full four-and-one-quarter inches and filled with blood so that it resembled a Montecristo Rojo. Kitty Kat growled louder and increased the speed and intensity of her caress. A few seconds later, Archie came, splattering the back of the front seat and dribbling onto his pants. Kitty Kat released her hold on him, reached over and pulled the gold and black leaf-patterned scarf off Lula's neck and used it to wipe up Archie's emission.

"Feelin' better now, peach?" asked Kitty Kat, cleaning her hand with Lula's scarf, then tossing it on the floor.

"Some," Archie said. "Wish I could do for you."

"It okay, I ain' nervous. Seen on *Geraldo* bunch of bitches called they-selfs non-orgastic, or somethin'. They same as me. Ain' like havin' the AIDS or cancer. Bet this old bitch she come easy. Hey, old bitch, you come easy, I bet."

Lula had not said a word since Archie and Kitty Kat had jumped into the car and the woman had put a gun to her head and commanded her to drive fast. She tried to respond but could not.

"Bitch!" shouted Kitty Kat. "Ask you nice does you come!"

Lula nodded. "Yes," she said softly, "I do."

"Easy? It easy comin'?"

"Not always."

Kitty Kat poked the tip of Archie's shrunken penis with the barrel of her Python.

"Zip up, peach," she said. "There ladies present."

"This situation brings back some bad memories," said Sailor, "about the time Pace was kidnapped."

Sailor, Phil and Pace were sitting in the Florida room of the Ripley home in Metairie, drinking Jameson's straight from shot glasses and waiting for the telephone to ring.

"You've never mentioned that episode, Pace," said Phil. "What happened?"

"I was ten years old," Pace said, "and a crazy teenaged boy grabbed me while I was playin' in Audubon Park. He hid me in his room in a boardin' house located in a bad part of New Orleans, told me how he'd been searchin' for the perfect friend, which he hoped I'd be, but I wasn't, of course. He'd murdered his father and brother and cut 'em up in a hundred pieces, then buried their parts on the family farm in Evangeline Parish. I escaped, though."

"Jesus," said Phil, "how'd you get away?"

"Elmer—that was his name, Elmer Désespéré—went out one night after lockin' me in a closet, so I made a fuss, kicked at the door and stomped around, until the landlady, I guess she was, came in and let me out. I hightailed it straight down the stairs and into the street, found a cop and that was the end of the ordeal."

"What happened to this Elmer?"

"Street gang chewed him up," said Sailor. "He wandered into the wrong neighborhood and he got took apart. Tell you, though, the up side to Pace's abduction was that it brought me'n Lula back together."

"How so?" asked Phil.

"I'd done some hard time, ten years to be exact, for armed robbery, durin' the commission of which a man was killed. Pace was born while I was inside, and when I got out things was kinda overwhelmin' for me'n his mama. Lula never did come to visit me durin' my stretch, which didn't much please me, though she did write a lot and send photos of her and Pace."

"I didn't know this, Daddy," Pace said. "I mean, that Mama never once came to see you."

Sailor nodded. "It weren't all her fault, though. See, I was put away at the prison in Huntsville, Texas, and Lula and Pace were in North Carolina, with her mama, Marietta. Marietta never did think real highly of me, and due to the way I was actin' in them days I can't say how I could blame her. I'd done a couple years before that at a work camp in North Carolina for manslaughter, so Marietta pretty much had me pegged as a worthless badass from the get-go."

"But you got nailed unfairly, Daddy, what Mama's always said. You were defendin' her in a bar and the man you hit banged his head on a table or somethin' and died. Man name of Lemon, right?"

"Bob Ray Lemon, right. Anyway, Lula's mama was dead set against her takin' up again with me when I got out, but Lula was eighteen by then and there weren't nothin' really legal Marietta could do about it, though she tried. After my release, Lula met me at the gate and we took off for California, though of course we didn't get more'n half that far. Marietta hired a private detective friend of hers to track us down, but by the time he did I'd pulled the dumb stunt in West Texas that subtracted a decade of my freedom. Marietta pretty much kept Lula prisoner for a while, which weren't too difficult for her to do, seein's how Lula was pregnant at first, and then with Pace bein' an infant it weren't so easy for Lula to travel. After Pace was growed some I guess it was just too hard for Lula to face me behind bars."

"This is a wild story, Sailor," said Phil. "How did Pace's bein' kidnapped figure in your getting back together with Lula?"

"I went to see Lula and Pace soon as I got out, of course, but like I said, we couldn't neither of us handle it. There was too much hard feelin's and pain and all on both sides, though I didn't blame nobody but myself for what'd happened. I took off and went to Mississippi for six months, worked in a lumberyard by Hattiesburg, but I couldn't stop thinkin' about Pace here, and Lula, and how we should all be together. I was in my thirties by then and was finally beginnin' to understand a bit about how the world really works and what a man's gotta do to be a man and find his way. It's one real strange voyage."

"I remember meetin' you, Daddy, with Mama, right after you got out. You just walked away from us."

"I couldn't help myself, Pace. I didn't know what else to do. You didn't know me, weren't used to havin' me around, and I thought maybe you'd be better off without me. I was dead wrong, naturally, and it was just luck that brought me and Lula in contact again. I quit the lumberyard job and took a bus to New Orleans. I got a newspaper to look for a job and there was the article about Pace bein' abducted. Lula had come to N.O. with him to visit her childhood friend, Beany Thorn, whose husband, Bob Lee Boyle, later hired me to work for his company, Gator Gone, which is now the world's largest manufacturer of crocodile and alligator repellent. Wound up workin' for Bob Lee for thirty-ought years."

"So you and Lula found each other again and lived happily ever after," Phil said.

"Couldn'ta guessed you was from Hollywood, Phil," said Sailor. "There been a few detours along the way but we been able to hold our own."

"Quite a romance, Sailor. Like Romeo and Juliet only nobody dies."

"It ain't over, Phil," Sailor said, and swallowed two fingers of Irish whisky. "Lula always used to say the world is wild at heart and weird on top, and sometimes it's tough stayin' out of the way of the weirdness. Kinda like a tornado, you never know where it'll set down or what'll be left in place after it blows through."

"We'll get Mama home safe, Daddy," said Pace.

"You'll pardon me for thinkin' out loud, Sailor," said Phil, "especially at a time of crisis like this, but I think there's a marvelous story here that would make a great film. It's a true romance, Sailor, and there aren't many of those. I came down here to research an incident that took place back in 1957. A black GI shot and killed a prominent white businessman during Mardi Gras and wound up on death row for twenty-five years. Through the efforts of a young white attorney who had never even tried a case, it was finally proven that the victim had provoked the shooting. Witnesses had been suppressed, paid off, and the black man spent more than half of his life in prison for defending himself. The attorney got him out."

"Sorta like you, Daddy, defendin' Mama against Bob Ray Lemon."

"Not quite, son, but maybe if I'd been black they woulda tried to fry me, too. Sounds like a good one, Phil. And you got yourself a happy endin'."

"It's been done before," Phil said, "which doesn't mean the picture shouldn't be made, but you and Lula have something special, Sailor, and I think the world should know about it."

Sailor smiled slightly. "'Preciate your sayin' that, Phil. You want to take a run at it, go ahead. Pace here can help you out on the details. You'll forgive me, though, I don't seem too enthusiastic at the moment, seein's how I'm mostly concerned with gettin' my wife back from the Lord knows who's got her."

Phil poured himself a fresh shot of whisky and took a sip. Flower Reynolds would be perfect for Lula, he thought. That snake Clark Westphal could be a problem, though. He might try to influence Flower against working with him. A movie about the Romeo and Juliet of the Deep South could do it, thought Phil, it could put Philip Reál back on top. What was it Sailor said Lula used to say? The world is wild at heart and weird on top, that's it. *Wild at Heart* would be a great title, all right. Phil nodded to himself as he sipped the Jameson's. Or maybe just *Strange Voyage*. His private title, though, would be *Revenge of the Leopard Man*. It would pave the way for him to make *Cry of the Mute*. Even Arnie Pope, Phil knew, if he was still at Five Star by that time, would be begging to pay for it.

BALL LIGHTNING

Lula looked around the room. Tacked to the walls were pictures severed neatly from magazines, books, calendars and newspapers of different types of lightning. There was one of a rainstorm with a single vertical bolt of cloud-to-ground lightning in a purple sky and a bright pink spot atop the bolt that marked its exit spot; a flame-like ribbon of ball lightning looping through a bloody backdrop; triple ground lightning over Las Vegas that looked like a flaming match head waved over a black bat wing; lightning striking behind a ridge line, its meandering main stem resembling the Mississippi River; an anvil-shaped, violet-tinted storm cloud disclosing a scorpion-like excretion onto a barren landscape; double ground lightning with the secondary channel striking more than five miles away from the primary route; slow-moving air discharge lightning outlining the state of Florida; and double bolts from a monstrous magenta thunderhead.

She sat on a nude, high-backed wooden chair, the only chair in the room, which she guessed to be about fifteen feet by fifteen feet. It was devoid of any other furniture. There were three windows, one in each wall other than the one containing a door, which was closed and, Lula presumed, locked. She was unbound but sat still, waiting for her abductors, to whom she had not spoken excepting the brief exchange with the woman in the car. Lula thought about opening one of the windows and running away, but she was not young anymore, she certainly could not run very fast or very far, and she did not want to antagonize the two captors, who, it seemed to Lula, were unpredictable types. She needed a cigarette. Her Mores were in her purse, which she had last seen on the floor under the front seat of the Cadillac. The door opened.

"You like the pictures, lady?" asked Archie Chunk, walking in. "I love lightnin'. Back in Broken Claw, where I was born and mostly raised—that's in Oklahoma—is the best electrical storms. Come August, I'd stand in the field behind my granny's house and pray for the lightnin' to hit me. Never did, though, even when I held up a five iron."

"Can I have a cigarette?" asked Lula.

Archie took a pack of Marlboros and a book of matches from the breast pocket of his Madras shirt, shook one out to Lula and lit it for her before doing the same for himself.

"Kitty Kat and me don't mean to keep you in suspense," he said, replacing his cigarettes and matches in the same pocket, "but you're a sorta unplanned-on part of the deal, you know? We gotta do one of three things: let you go, kill you, or ransom you. Them're the options."

The black woman came into the room. She was holding a thick, foot-long clear plastic dildo in her right hand and the Colt Python in her left. She walked over to Lula and showed her the dildo, the head of which was smeared generously with some kind of salve.

"You ever use one of these?" Kitty Kat asked.

Lula shook her head no.

"Here," Kitty Kat said to Archie, handing him the gun.

He took it and Kitty Kat hiked her skirt up over her naked crotch, bent her knees slightly as she spread her legs wide enough to admit the instrument into her vagina, then manipulated the dildo with both hands, inserting it slowly, a half inch at a time, until most of it was inside her. Kitty Kat stood directly in front of Lula while she pumped the toy into and partway out of herself. She began to sweat heavily, even though the temperature in the room was only fifty-three degrees. Lula felt the Marlboro burning down between the first and second fingers of her left hand, so she dropped it onto the floor. Archie Chunk stood by, intently watching Kitty Kat work out.

"Master! Master!" cried Kitty Kat. "Master, make me! Make, me, master!" she shouted, plunging the dildo deeper and harder.

Suddenly she stopped and extracted it, breathing hard, her legs quivering. Kitty Kat held the wet tool out to Archie.

"Gimme the gun now," she said, and they exchanged weapons.

Kitty Kat inserted the barrel of the Python into her cunt and massaged herself.

"Got to be gentle with this," said Kitty Kat. "Torn myself before."

Lula remained motionless. Archie Chunk held the slimy stick in his left fist and grinned.

"Wish I could pull the trigger," Kitty Kat whined. "Wish Kitty Kat push it up pussy, pull trigger. Pull pussy trigger. Open pussy, up pussy, pull trigger."

Kitty Kat Cross swayed, shuddered, her mouth open, made a gagging sound and held the stainless blue steel cylinder tight to the left side of her cunt. She trembled and whinnied, then her contractions slowly tapered off until they ceased entirely. Kitty Kat withdrew the Python's nose and stood up straight. She held the gun to her mouth and ran her tongue along the barrel, first one side, then the other, licking it clean.

"Close as Kitty Kat get," she said.

LONG DISTANCE CALL

"You and Mama amaze me, Daddy."

"How's that, son?"

"Way you been able to stay together all these years. Me and Rhoda didn't make it, and same goes for most couples I know or know of. Seems to me you-all're still in love, too. How you manage it, Daddy?"

It was one o'clock in the morning. Phil was asleep on the couch in the front room, a copy of *Obras completas de Federico García Lorca* folded open on his chest, his right thumb over the words, *"En mi pecho se agita sonámbula / una sierpe de besos antiguos."* Pace and Sailor were still in the Florida room, unable and unwilling to sleep, sipping whisky and talking.

"Your mama's a special kind of woman, Pace. She don't hardly ever consider herself first. She's most always been concerned about how other folks around her are feelin' and what they need, not what she wants. That ain't to say she don't know how to please herself or even to get what she wants or needs. She'll take time for her own purposes, but Lula's always been the single most unselfish person I ever have known."

"Grandmama Marietta wasn't that way, though."

Sailor laughed. "Not nearly, though she had her good points, I suppose. She was always lookin' out for Lula."

"How come you and Mama never had no kids after me?"

"Well, when you was born, of course, I was in the joint, and after I got out and Lula and I eventually come back together, there was a whole long time Mama and me just required to get to know each other again. We was in our thirties by then, and I guess my own priority was makin' up for all the time I'd lost with you, too. Tell the truth, we just didn't even give it a thought, plus Lula didn't get pregnant. By the time we mighta had another child we was older'n we woulda liked to be if we were gonna have to look after an infant. It was enough just bein' alive and the three of us bein' together. That's about all I could dream about them years at Huntsville. Sometimes I didn't think it was ever gonna happen."

"I guess me and Rhoda just didn't love each other enough to make our marriage work," said Pace. "Neither of us is as givin' a person as Mama, that's for sure."

"Tough to figure, son. Lovin' and bein' in love is two different things, of course. Best if you can keep both in the house, but it's love that keeps it goin'. People fall in and out of love regular, oftentimes with the same person. Your mama put up with a bunch from me, but I ain't never really lost sight of what it is attracted me to Lula in the first place. I don't mean looks, neither. That means more to some than to others."

"If Rhoda hadn't kept so close to her family, I believe we mighta had a better chance. The Gombowiczes is fine people, Daddy, don't get me wrong, and they was swell to take me into the diamond business with 'em, but between Rhoda's therapy work and havin' to be with her folks so much, it didn't leave hardly no time just for us. Then her bein' spooked about bringin' kids into the world, always talkin' about how there's so many maniacs runnin' around loose and how some sand niggers is gonna get their hands on a nuclear device and blow up the planet anyway, shit. That tore it after too long for me."

Pace poured himself a fresh shot of Jameson's and knocked it back.

"I was sure sorry when it didn't work out, boy, but with you and Rhoda bein' of such diverse heritage and all, can't say as I was entirely surprised. Your mama was surprised it lasted as long as it did, then she was upset about the divorce. You ain't the only victims of the seven year itch."

"Eight, Daddy. We lasted eight years. I still think we'd of had kids it woulda worked out different."

The telephone rang. Sailor and Pace looked at each other and let it ring a second time. Before it rang again, Sailor lifted the receiver.

"Sailor Ripley speakin'."

"Hello, Sailor? This is Rhoda. I'm sorry to be calling so late."

"Rhoda, darlin', how're you? Pace and I just been talkin' about you."

"Is Pace there?"

"Big as life."

"I didn't know where he was, Sailor. We haven't been in touch lately. I was calling you to find out. For some reason all of you have been on my mind the last two days and finally I just decided to call, even if it is past two A.M. here in New York. Is everything all right?"

"As a matter of fact, Rhoda, things ain't all right. Lula been kidnapped durin' a armed robbery. We don't know where she is, so me'n Pace been waitin' by the phone. I thought maybe you was her or the ones got her."

"Oh, Sailor, that's terrible! I'm so sorry."

"Pace is right here. You want to speak with him?"

"If it's all right for a minute. I won't tie up your line."

"It's okay, Rhoda, we got call-waitin' now."

Sailor handed the phone to Pace.

"Hello, Rhoda. How you been doin'?"

"Something made me call, Pace. The feeling was too strong to ignore. I didn't know where you were."

"I'm livin' in L.A. now. Was in N.O. on business when all this happened. Your mental powers ain't diminished none."

"I feel terrible about what's happened to Lula, Pace. I wish there were something I could do to help."

"Don't even know what our move's gonna be yet, Rhoda, but thanks."

"Pace?"

"Uh huh."

"Do you ever think that perhaps our separating was the wrong thing to have done?"

"We ain't just separated, Rhoda, we're divorced. And this ain't precisely the greatest time to be bringin' up this subject, seein' as how my mind's mainly on Mama right now."

"Of course, Pace, certainly. I understand absolutely. I would very much like to talk to you about things, though, when this is all over and Lula's safe. Would you at least consider that?"

" 'Course I will, Rhoda. You okay otherwise?"

"Yes."

"How's the family?"

"There's nothing you need to hear about. Please call me as soon as there's news, all right?"

"Okay, Rhoda."

"Good night, Pace. Give my love to Sailor."

"I will. Good night."

Pace hung up and looked at his father.

"Rhoda says to give you her love."

Sailor nodded and scraped his right hand across his mostly bald head. "Gotta admit, son, the girl has a gift, feelin' somethin' was up."

"Likely just coincidence, Daddy."

"Could be, boy, but keep in mind it don't never pay to underestimate a woman, 'specially one knows your sleepin' habits."

ORIGIN OF THE SPECIES

"Been brought to my attention by Eddie Fange, the commissioner, that felonious crime, kidnappin' in particular, ain't altogether unfamiliar to you, Mr. Ripley."

Sailor had telephoned Du Du Dupre to find out exactly what steps the police were taking to find Lula. It was ten-thirty in the morning.

"What's it got to do with locatin' my wife, Captain Dupre? Past is past."

"You got two convictions of a significant nature, manslaughter in North Carolina, for which you done a deuce, and armed robbery in Texas, includin' a parole violation and a kidnappin' charge was dropped when you went down for a sawbuck on the AR beef. Then a woman you was involved with, a certain Señorita Perdita Durango, drove the getaway vehicle for you and your gun-totin' cohort at the time, Mr. Robert Peru, deceased, durin' this robbery attempt, from which she avoided prosecution, still got a federal warrant out on her for kidnap and torture of two college kids some thirty years back. Mexican authorities wanted her for murder, too."

"I don't know nothin' about any of that."

"Finally, your son, Pace Roscoe Ripley, was his self kidnapped thirty years ago. Five years later he was implicated in a armed robbery and murder right here in New Orleans, and another killin' or two in Miss'ippi, both charges he was cleared of 'count of his bein' held captive and forced to participate. Now your wife been taken prisoner durin' a violent crime. I didn't know better, Mr. Ripley, I'd be mighty tempted to conclude kind of a pattern been developin' here."

"Ever'body's a prisoner of some kind, Dupre. People who learn some correct detail about another person's life are always drawin' conclusions from it ain't accurate, then they start seein' in this one fact an explanation of things ain't got no connection with it at all. A famous dead French author wrote that."

"Can't argue the fact you had plenty time to read, Ripley, all them years you spent behind bars. I ain't been nobody's guest, so I've had to

Bad Day for the Leopard Man

make do with less high-toned material, like newspapers and police bulletins, which I can't hardly get to as it is, bein' that I'm kept pretty busy tryin' to protect citizens from one another."

"I take it you ain't got no line on Lula."

"We're workin' on it, Ripley. I got your number. They contact you, call me right away, let us handle it. Don't do nothin' stupid. I'm hopin' you got quit of that cowboy shit now you're a senior citizen."

Dupre hung up before Sailor did. For some reason, Sailor suddenly remembered the first time he had ever called Lula "peanut," his favorite nickname for her. He had driven over to Bay St. Clement High School in his yellow 1958 Buick Limited, the one his cousin, Jesse Stitch, later totaled in Rocky Mount while Sailor was serving his sentence at Pee Dee, to pick up Lula when classes let out. As soon as she'd spotted his car, Lula ran to it, opened the passenger door and slid into the front seat practically on top of Sailor, where she curled up with her head burrowed hard into his chest.

"Oh, Sail," she had said, closing her eyes and pushing her nose into the black cotton Fruit of the Loom tee shirt that covered his upper body, "I'm so happy you came to get me! You just thrill me to death."

Sailor had laughed, wound Lula's long black ponytail around his right hand and tugged gently on it. Lula was sixteen years old and Sailor sincerely believed that she was the most beautiful creature he had ever seen, a belief he had never come to doubt. Folded up on his lap the way she was had made her seem so small, so fragile.

"Hell, Lula," Sailor had said to her then, "you look like a perfect little peanut."

"I ain't so very little," Lula had said, "but I am your peanut, for now and forever."

That had been forty-four years ago, Sailor calculated. The telephone rang, startling him. His right hand was still on the receiver and he picked it up.

"Sail, is that you? It's Lula!"

"Hello, peanut," he said.

" 'Nough, woman!"

Kitty Kat snatched the telephone from Lula.

"This her old man?" she shouted into it.

"That's my wife you got," said Sailor, "if that's what you mean. You fixin' to turn her loose?"

"Check this out one time, daddio, 'cause I'm gone make it shit simple. Prob'ly she cost you plenty so far an' now she gone cost you some mo'. Ain't sayin' you gots to pay, though. You say no, okay, we put the barrel up her nose, pop go the weasel, then dump in a bayou. You listen?"

"How much?"

"Hun' thou, sma' bill. Put it in a duffel, kind you get in a army surplus. Forty-eight hours from now, this same time, one-thirty, you leave the bag front the gate Judge Perez Park in Arabi. That in St. Bernard Parish, past Tupelo Street. You think you be able find it?"

"It'll be there. What about Lula?"

"Oh, she be turn up theyafter. You leave the money, go 'way. Cops come, y'own posse, anyone, your wife, instead she turn up the *here*after."

The line went dead.

"What's the price, Daddy?" asked Pace.

Sailor hung up the phone.

"A hundred thousand."

"You got that much?"

"Between what we got in the house and what I can borrow from Bob Lee, prob'ly I can raise it."

"You gonna call Dupre?"

"Ain't sure, son. Figure I'll sleep on it and decide in the mornin'."

"Wish our ol' huntin' companion Coot Veal was still alive," Pace said. "He'd help us out. Coot's the one taught me to shoot."

Sailor nodded. "I sure do miss that old boy. Couple others, too, who're no longer around, who I could count on. Sparky and Buddy, friends of your mama's and mine from way back. They was damn resourceful."

"Them the ones located the kidney donor for Uncle Johnnie, weren't they?"

"Uh huh. Just after Lula and I run onto 'em in Memphis. Them two guardian angels kept turnin' up in our lives in some mighty strange circumstances. They both prob'ly passed on by now, though."

"Phil's a stand-up guy, Daddy. Three of us can handle it."

Sailor lowered his head to the table and buried it in his folded arms. Sailor fell asleep and Pace sat there, listening to his father breathe. After a few minutes, Pace leaned over and kissed Sailor on the top of his head.

"I love you, Daddy," Pace said. "Even without Mama you ain't alone in this world."

KITTY KAT TALKS

"I tell you how people like me an' Archie Chunk come up, maybe you get the picture. My mama worked as a aide in a nursin' home, cleanin' after old folks' dirt. Had me an' my two brothers to care for herself after our daddy disappeared. Mama out cleanin' up piss, shit, vomit, wipin' drool off they half-dead faces, proppin' 'em in they wheelchairs for next to no money an' no benefits. She was too proud to take the welfare, she wanted to work. Wouldn't let the state take her kids for no foster homes. She was for keepin' the fam'ly together, even when Daddy gone.

"Mama made us go to school long as we'd mind. We lived in a closed-down motel without no runnin' water or heat. Had us a wood stove but no ice box. Mama got up four ev'ry mornin' fix our clothes, breakfast. She an' me sleep together in one bed, Yusef an' Malcolm in another. We walk with Mama five miles each mornin' in rain an' dark to school. I get sick an' tired walkin' in rain an' dark.

"When Yusef break his arm, fall through a hole in the floor, Mama had to pay cash to fix it, but after his cast come off he never had no pin put in keep the shape, like he suppose to, 'cause Mama ain't had enough money. His arm bent wrong and dangle weird.

"I was twelve a drug dealer hung out around the motel got me pregnant. After I had the baby, I leave it with Mama and go. Malcolm, he drown. Mama, Yusef and my baby, girl name Serpentina, burn to death when the motel catch fire one night.

"Ain't was no diff'rent for Archie. Black or white don't make no diff'rence you down so far. He be on the street since he six, chil' alcoholic. Stealin' all he know, or lettin' some ol' sick fool pinch his peepee fo' a meal at Mickey D.

"I know you scared, lady. Maybe this work out. It don't, least you know there tougher roads than one you been on."

THE BUSINESS

"This is 3099. Any messages?"

Phil was checking in with his answering service in Hollywood.

"Yes, sir. There's one from a Miss Reynolds. She'd like you to call her at your earliest opportunity."

"That's all?"

"Yes, sir."

"Thanks."

Phil direct-dialed Flower's number. She answered on the third ring.

"Philly, where are you?"

"In New Orleans, Flower. What's up? How was Mexico with Westphal?"

"That's what I called you about, Philly. I happened to mention to Clark that you were back in town and he got all excited and started talkin' 'bout how you always been a hero of his and how he'd love to work with you. I just couldn't believe it!"

"I find it a little difficult to believe myself. So?"

"So, he wants to set up a meeting. When y'all comin' back?"

"I'm not sure. We've kind of run into a situation here. Maybe I can talk with Westphal on the phone."

"It'd be a good idea, Philly. I ain't certain Clark got much of an attention span."

"Why do you say that?"

"Just one of my correlations. Attention spans is linked up with sexual habits, I think. Clark comes too quick, so my guess is he got the attention span to match."

"Exactly what did he say, Flower?"

"Just if you had a good idea, he'd listen. You got somethin' beside that *Mute* story?"

"Actually, I do. A love story, like Romeo and Juliet, sort of, only the characters are older."

"Could Clark and I do it together?"

"You two might just be perfect."

Bad Day for the Leopard Man

"Oh, Philly! Do I get to laugh? You know how much I love to laugh."

Phil laughed. "Of course. What would a Flower Reynolds picture be unless you laughed in it?"

"I didn't get to in *Dog Parts*."

"That was a mistake not to be repeated. Give me Clark's number, Flower. I'll call him."

Phil wrote it down and said, "This is nice news, honey. It's a good thing you had such good-looking parents."

"You don't think it's my brain Clark's attracted to, huh?" Flower laughed. "Oh, well, I guess it's just the way the good Lord intended the world should work."

"Wouldn't surprise me. Listen, Flower, if you speak to Clark, tell him I'll call him as soon as I have a chance. There's something going on here that needs to be taken care of first. Tell him I'm a big admirer of his."

"Why lie?" asked Flower.

"Why not?" Phil said.

LONG GONE

DuMont Dupre was fifty-two years old, five-nine and a nose-tackle-thick two-thirty. The lower region of his jaw rolled over on itself twice whenever Du Du looked down. His wife, Lexa Ray, once commented to Commissioner Fange's wife, Floridanna, that nobody had seen the knot in her husband's tie for fifteen years. Du Du had preferred a four-in-hand during their courtship and early years of marriage, Lexa Ray said, but for all she or anyone else knew he could have switched to a half-Windsor by now. Du Du was at his desk in midmorning, lighting up his second Macanudo of the day, when his secretary buzzed him on the intercom. Du Du made sure the entire circumference of his cigar tip was fired and drawing properly prior to responding.

"Yes, Miss Pulse," he said, having depressed the TALK button on his unit.

"Mr. Luneau, the principal at Saint Beverly Carothers High School, is holdin' for you."

"I'll take it."

Du Du punched up line one and said, "*Bonjour*, George, *ça va?*"

"Not very well, I'm afraid, DuMont," said the principal.

"What's the problem?"

"It's your son, Larry Gene."

"L.G.? What's the boy done now?"

"He brought a gun with him to school today, DuMont, pulled it out of his pocket durin' English class and shot himself in the mouth. Back of his head splattered all over Marcy Simmons, girl sittin' directly behind him, but the bullet went past her clean into the blackboard at the rear of the room."

Du Du put the Macanudo into an ashtray and rubbed his free hand over his face a couple of times.

"He's dead, then."

" 'Fraid so, DuMont. Don't understand it, myself. Larry Gene been doin' excellent work this semester, I'm told. Had his grades up to about a C average and he just been named All-Conference tackle."

"L.G. never did care for English. What type firearm he use?"

"Believe Sergeant Hoog mentioned it was a .357-caliber Magnum revolver. The students that seen him do it are pretty shook up, as you could imagine. I'm real stranged out myself. You don't believe how sorry I am to have had to tell you the news, Du Du, but I figured I ought to do it, me bein' the principal."

"Lexa Ray know?"

"Don't believe so. I ain't called her. It's just damn unbelievable. Why on earth he'd do this thing, Du Du? We ain't had no evidence of drug use. You?"

"I suppose I ain't paid close enough attention to L.G. lately to know, George. I 'preciate it was you called."

"Larry Gene was a right decent boy, DuMont. Boy with a future."

"I'm goin' home now, be with Lexa Ray. Where's the body?"

"Police ambulance takin' him to the Orleans Parish morgue."

Du Du hung up and stared at the framed photograph on his desk. In the picture, he and Lexa Ray were seated with Larry Gene and his sister, Taura Beth, standing behind them, each with a hand on one of their parents' shoulders. Du Du inspected the photograph more closely, noticing for the first time that Larry Gene's left ear stuck out almost perpendicular to his head, while the right one was more normally attached. Du Du wondered why this physical peculiarity of L.G.'s had never been apparent to him before.

The police captain slumped back and down in his chair. He unbuttoned his collar and loosened the four-in-hand knot in his tie.

THE UNEXPECTED

Pace heard the front door open and close and he jumped up from the kitchen table, where he'd been sitting with Phil drinking coffee, and hurried toward Sailor.

"Daddy, you okay?" Pace said, seeing his father set down a large canvas bag in the foyer.

"I'm all right, son. Just out collectin' the cash."

"You got it, huh?"

Sailor nodded. "Didn't even have to redo the deal on the house. Bob Lee took the whole hundred K right out the Gator Gone main account."

"I guess to hell he's your friend, Daddy."

"Never have one better. You know how close your mama and Beany been all their lives. She and Bob Lee took us in when you was kidnapped, and it was him give me the opportunity to turn my own life around. Now here they come backin' us up again. They're rare folks, son."

"Made some coffee, Daddy. You want some? Phil's in the kitchen."

Sailor followed Pace back through the house and sat down at the table. Pace filled a cup and placed it in front of him.

"Mornin', Phil. Thanks, son."

"Daddy got the money, Phil."

"I have about ten thousand I can spare, Sailor, if you need it."

"Thanks, Phil, but we're set."

"What about Dupre, Daddy?"

"Called his office from Bob Lee's, but he was out. Apparently there was some family emergency. I'd decided to not bring the cops into it, anyway. Was just gonna check in again with Dupre, pretend I hadn't heard nothin', and ask if he had. Just as well he weren't in."

"Sailor, I want to tell you how much I admire you," said Phil. "Also that I'm with you all the way on this. Just tell me what you'd like me to do."

"That's great, Phil," said Sailor. "I'm workin' up a plan but I ain't got all the pieces in place yet. Think I'll take a nap and dope it out with you-all later. Bob Lee's comin' over this evenin'."

Sailor stood up and walked out of the kitchen.

"Your daddy's a brave man, Pace," said Phil. "He's a cool one."

Pace stared at Sailor's coffee cup, which his father had not touched.

"He been through a bunch, Phil, as you know. Time just don't seem to settle things down, though, the way you'd figure would happen."

The doorbell rang and Pace got up to answer it. He opened the front door and there was Rhoda, his ex-wife, holding a garment bag over her left arm. A suitcase was on the ground next to her.

"Hello, Pace," she said. "I just had to come."

Pace was stunned. He looked at Rhoda, ran his eyes over her dark brown curly hair, down the length of her slender five feet seven inches and then stared directly into her big black eyes, which were shiny and wet.

"Hell, Rhoda, this prob'ly weren't your best idea."

She lifted up her suitcase with her right hand.

"Pace, I'm a psychotherapist. If I didn't act on impulse every once in a while I'd be even more neurotic than I already am. The last unexpected move I made was when I married you. Are you going to invite me in?"

Pace took the suitcase from Rhoda's hand and stepped aside.

A WINTER'S NIGHT IN THE SUB-TROPICS

Lula thought about Sailor. She pictured him lying in their bed, smoking a Camel and staring at the ceiling. When she imagined him this way, Lula realized, Sailor always looked like he had forty years or so before, in the beginning of their time together. Sailor's hair and muscles had dropped away since then, as surely as Lula's looks had begun to fade, her own shiny black hair to turn gray and dull, her large breasts to shrink and sag. All of this was inevitable, Lula knew. No matter how dedicatedly she exercised and avoided bad foods, there was no way she could prevent her body from spreading, her skin from crinkling up like used Reynolds Wrap. Lula recalled the first time she noticed that the curve of her behind had flattened out. She had been trying on a knit skirt at Jaloux, a fancy dress shop in Covington owned by a former call girl who had married a United States senator, and when Lula looked at her profile in the mirror she almost screamed. She felt like the former president did in that old movie when he woke up in a hospital bed after being run over by a train, discovered that his legs were sawed off at the knees and yelled, "Where's the rest of me?!"

Lula felt the same way when she was separated from Sailor for very long. It was almost as if they had become one person named Sailula. She was afraid now, sitting by herself in a darkened room in a strange house somewhere in the swamp, wondering if the two demented creatures that were keeping her from being with Sailor really intended to release her once they had the ransom money. Most of the time, Lula knew, kidnappers killed their hostages whether or not a ransom was paid. Archie Chunk and Kitty Kat Cross had already committed at least one murder, Kitty Kat having gunned down a clerk at the Rinaldi Hotel during the robbery, so one more homicide certainly would not matter. If they were apprehended, the law would demand the death penalty. There was no good reason that they should keep their part of the bargain. The only chance Lula had to stay alive, she figured, would be to talk her way out of it, to somehow convince Archie and Kitty Kat to return her to Sailor.

Rain pelted the roof, leaking through the cracks in the ceiling. Lula refused to cry, keeping her face tight even though she knew the exercise would deepen the creases already established around her eyes.

"Oh, Sail," Lula whispered to herself, "this ain't where I want to be. Shit," she said. "Shit, shit, shit."

Suddenly Lula felt a chill and her entire body shivered. She remembered herself forty years ago, lying pregnant and helpless in a crummy room in the Iguana Hotel in Big Tuna, Texas, just before Sailor Ripley, the only man of her dreams, made the single biggest mistake of his young life. A storm from the Gulf hurled itself desperately at Pointe à la Hache, rattling the walls. Lula watched through the window as a sliver of vertical lightning like in one of Archie Chunk's photos clove in two an oak that stood next to the house, leaving behind a black, electrical sizzle. In another room, Kitty Kat screamed and Lula laughed reflexively, then quickly covered her mouth with her hands. Lula was surprised at herself, unsure of what it meant, of what anything meant. The rain came down harder, blurring everything outside the window.

SAILOR'S PLAN

Sailor, Pace, Rhoda, Phil and Bob Lee Boyle were seated around the din-ingroom table in the Ripley house.

"What about the car, Daddy?"

"They can keep it. Your mama's all I care about."

"So how you figure on playin' this game, Sailor?" asked Bob Lee. "Air strike? Ground assault? Seriously, you want to try somethin' or just leave the money and hope they turn Lula loose?"

"Thought about it real hard, Bob Lee, and I see it this way: Rhoda and I leave the duffel at the Judge Perez gate a half hour early at one A.M., and drive away. I'll leave Rhoda in the car on Tupelo Street and walk back, keepin' out of sight, to a spot where I can conceal myself while keepin' an eye on the gate. Pace and Phil will already be there in place, one on each side of the road. Bob Lee, you'd be doin' us a real favor stickin' by the phone right here."

"Whatever you say, Sailor."

"If they make the pick-up, Pace and Phil will take after 'em in their car. Rhoda, you'll keep an eye out for my black Cad, which the kidnap-pers'll prob'ly be drivin'. If it comes by you headed for the park, creep after it with your lights off and pick me up right after they make the grab. If they come past you from the other direction, after they've made the pick-up, you wait until Phil's car comes by, then follow him. That happens, I'll go with Pace and Phil. If nobody comes to make the pick-up by two A.M., Rhoda, you come get me. If I'm gone, you go home. They might come from the other direction, make the pick-up and turn back the way they come. In that case, it'll just be Phil's car goin' after 'em."

"You aren't going to call in the police, then," said Phil.

"Think we're better off without 'em, Phil."

"We gonna be packin', Daddy?"

"You bet, son. I got enough weapons to go around."

Pace looked at his ex-wife.

"Rhoda," he said, "you don't need to be in on this."

"That's right, sweetheart," said Sailor, "you don't. I can ride with Pace and Phil and you can stay here with Bob Lee, you'd rather."

"Uh-uh," said Rhoda. "I'll be glad to participate in any way you feel is best."

"Bob Lee," Sailor said, "reason I need you here is you'll know what to do if one of us calls."

"You got it."

"Any other questions?" asked Sailor, looking directly at each person in turn around the table. Nobody spoke, so Sailor said, "Okay, then. We'll meet here tomorrow midnight."

"Sailor?" said Phil.

"Uh huh?"

"What do you think of Clark Westphal?"

"You mean the actor? One who done them Filthy Al cop pictures, like *Ripoff* and *Ripoff II*?"

"Right. What would you think of his portraying you in a movie?"

Sailor laughed. "Could do worse, I suppose. Know Lula'd like it."

"I recently saw one of his early films on TV the other night," said Rhoda, "*The Devil's Always Busy*. He certainly was handsome."

"So was Daddy," Pace said. "Mama always told me weren't no man handsomer in her eyes."

"Gray with violet lakes in 'em," said Sailor. "Nobody in the world got eyes to match Lula's."

Rhoda looked at Pace and smiled.

"We'll get her home, Daddy," he said.

SNAKE STORY

"My old man was sixty-one when I was born," Archie Chunk told Lula, while he bound her hands and feet. "Apparently he was pretty proud of the fact, too. We was livin' outside Bartlesville when he died. I was four. His name was Doc. Don't know why. Never heard anyone call him by another, and my ma was dead before I got old enough to ask her. Doc Chunk was a carny man most of his life, but by the time I was born he and my ma were operatin' a travelin' zoo. Had them a couple apes, a camel, black bear and a mess of snakes.

"One mornin' Doc looked in on this giant python that was his feature attraction and saw that he was sheddin' his hide. Way I heard it, my old man went in the cage to clean out the discarded skin and the snake got a whiff of paint thinner was on the old man's hands. Drove that reptile crazy and he locked his self hard around Doc's body. By the time Ma got out there, the python had clumb halfway up a utility pole and Doc Chunk was squoze to death."

"That's a awful way to die, I'd guess," said Lula.

"Yeah, my folks didn't have much luck in the death department," Archie said, as he ran a line from Lula's ankles to her wrists. "My ma was killed two and a half years later in a bar in Festus. Man she was drinkin' with was in a fight and she got in between him and the other guy, who stabbed her in the chest. She bled to death right there on the barroom floor before the ambulance arrived."

"What was her name?"

"Havana Moon. Ain't it pretty? My grandma told me she named her after a song she liked, and named her other daughter, Juella, also after a song. Their unmarried name been Fike. Juella was eleven months younger than Ma, and she died a year to the day but one after her. Juella and her Osage husband, Charlie Chases Weasels, hanged theirselfs after buryin' their infant son what perished in his sleep."

"What are you gonna do with me?"

"Kitty Kat got a place in mind we put you, then go get the cash, I guess. With it and what we scored at the hotel, we might could have us a deluxe trailer home, set it down on a mountain out west somewhere, and never have to work a hard day the rest of our lives."

"Don't sound half bad, Mr. Chunk."

"Archie, to you. Hush now while I tape your mouth. Be more comfort in the closed position."

"Pace, I know what a difficult time this is for you," Rhoda said, "and I hope I'm not complicating things by coming here. I just couldn't help myself, though. The divorce was a terrible mistake, I know that now, and I need to talk to you about it."

Pace and Rhoda were in Pace's boyhood room upstairs at the rear of the Ripley house. Pace was sitting on the edge of the bed and Rhoda was seated in an armchair next to the window overlooking the backyard. Rhoda pulled out a pack of Bel-Air Menthols and a gold lighter from her purse. She extracted a long, white cigarette and lit it. Pace recognized the lighter, with the initials RGR emblazoned on it in mother-of-pearl, that he'd given Rhoda as a gift for her birthday six years before.

"Thought you'd quit," Pace said.

Rhoda took a quick puff and blew out a short cloud of smoke, shook her brown mop and said, "Started up again the day our final decree arrived. I've been very unhappy."

Pace looked out the window, hoping to see some birds. For some reason, the sight of birds in flight never failed to calm him.

"Don't tell me you was happy when I was around," he said. "Least not the last six or eight months."

"I suppose I just didn't realize how difficult it was for you, working for Gombowicz and Sons, how dissatisfied you were. I still don't know why you didn't just quit earlier."

"What was I gonna do in New York, Rhoda? You had your practice, you weren't about to abandon that. At first I didn't mind the diamond business. I mean, it was somethin' completely diff'rent from anythin' I'd ever known. And your fam'ly was great about takin' me in, 'specially your brother, Ethan. It weren't for him I might not of made it at all. Ethan's the one saved my bones on the Irish switch. It was a big change from livin' in Katmandu, sure, and workin' on Forty-seventh Street weren't like leadin' treks in the Himalayas, but it was a new kinda challenge and I loved you and all, so I was willin' to take a shot. Lasted eight years, Rhoda, which ain't 'xactly punkin' out."

"I'd leave New York now if you wanted me to."

Pace shook his head and half-smiled. "Rhoda, you'd really go crazy if you had to be anyplace else longer'n a month, three weeks. It's your place, your fam'ly's there, and like I said, so's your work. You do good up east, I don't."

"I'd give L.A. a try. I could build up a practice there."

"You might could, seein's how there's more sick puppies per square inch in Beverly Hills alone than there are in all five boroughs of New York City. But I don't know how long I'm even gonna stay there, Rhoda. I'm thinkin' 'bout movin' back down south somewhere. Here or Charlotte, maybe."

"What about your work with Phil? Learning the film business and all?"

"We'll see how it goes. I like Phil okay, and he's serious now about makin' a movie based on Mama and Daddy's early life, but tell the truth, L.A. really ain't my kinda town. Besides, Rhoda, geography ain't our only problem."

Rhoda looked around for an ashtray, found a glass one on the bedside table and stubbed out her Bel-Air over the words Stolen from the Hotel Ritz, Paris.

"We could adopt a child, Pace. I think I could handle that now."

"This ain't really what I need to be talkin' about right now," said Pace.

"Are you seeing anyone?" Rhoda asked.

"You mean a girlfriend?"

Rhoda nodded. She kept turning the lighter with the fingers of her right hand until she dropped it on the floor, then picked it up and replaced it in her purse.

"Nobody special. Plenty of good looks in L.A., okay, but there ain't many women willin' to give very much. Never come across such a half-demented herd of vain, selfish folks, female or male."

"Worse than I am, huh?"

"You ain't neither too vain nor the least selfish, Rhoda, not really. You just been brought up a certain way don't entirely mix with the way I am. It ain't your fault."

"You wouldn't have left, Pace, had I been willing to have children. That's the truth, isn't it?"

"Prob'ly woulda been harder for me to go, we had. I'll admit that."

Rhoda stood up. "I'm sorry I came, Pace, I really am. I'm just adding to your problems."

"Don't be sorry, Rhoda. Daddy's glad you're here, and so am I. We're glad to have your help. And Mama'll be happy to see you, too."

Pace stood, put his arms around Rhoda and hugged her to him.

"We can talk some more soon's this mess is finished," he said.

"The air outside felt strange today, Pace, as if nothing were happening. Do you know what I mean?"

"It's tornado weather, sweetheart. Been a while since you've been down here. You just forgot how it feels."

"That's not the only thing I've forgotten how it feels," Rhoda said, and hugged back.

MOVIEGOERS

"Hey, Sailor, look at this," said Phil, handing over the front section of the day's *Times-Picayune,* folded to page sixteen. "There's an article about a kidnapping in Mobile."

Sailor, Phil and Bob Lee had been picking at muffaletas and drinking coffee as they sat at the table in the Florida room.

" 'Kidnapping Victim Back Home in Alabama,' " Sailor read aloud. " 'A Mobile businessman was abducted from in front of his house Tuesday morning when he bent to pick up his morning newspaper. He was returned home safely by taxicab this afternoon after he had been dropped off at a shopping center, said a spokesperson for the Federal Bureau of Investigation. The authorities said they did not know the motive for his abduction or the reason why his kidnappers released him.

" 'The 71-year-old victim, who was taken away by two men, was Alfred Thibodeaux, a soybean and cotton broker who is also a well-known thoroughbred horse breeder. Mr. Thibodeaux assisted in the development of a port shipping terminal and is active in several charities.

" 'Mr. Thibodeaux suffered several cuts on the forehead and cheeks during the ordeal. He apparently engaged in active resistance to his abductors by attempting to beat them with a silver-plated cane he relies on to aid in walking due to his artificial left leg. A neighbor woman, Mrs. Fabrica de Puro, who witnessed his kidnapping, was threatened by one abductor brandishing a handgun, the police reported.

" 'At one P.M. today, however, Mr. Thibodeaux contacted his wife, Antoinetta, from a pay phone next to a Big Gulp root beer stand at the Lurleen Wallace Shoppers Planet. He told his wife he was coming home in a taxicab and that she should have his silver cane, which had been left behind during the initial scuffle, ready for him.

" ' "He seems to be in decent shape, a little tired and stressed out," said Doak Bullard, assistant chief of the FBI office in Mobile. Mr. Bullard would not disclose whether a ransom demand had been made. He said the abductors were not in custody.' "

"Strange, huh, Sailor?" said Phil.

"Yeah," Sailor said, "maybe we'll get lucky with Lula, too."

"Who you got in mind to play Lula in the movie, Phil?" asked Bob Lee.

"Flower Reynolds. She worked for me before."

"Oh yeah, I remember her," said Bob Lee. "Shortina Fuse. She's a southern girl. That scene in *Sexual Re-education* where Señor Rafferty begs Shortina to use the tire tool on his anus is pretty damn unforgettable."

"Didn't know you was such a moviegoer, Bob Lee," said Sailor.

Bob Lee laughed. "You be careful of this fella," he said, pointing at Phil. "He got a awful weird imagination."

FODDER

While Sailor, Pace and Phil crouched in hiding around the entrance to Judge Perez Park, and Rhoda waited in Lula's Crown Victoria station wagon that was parked on Tupelo Street, Archie Chunk was at the wheel of Sailor's Sedan de Ville. Kitty Kat Cross sat in the front passenger seat with the visor down and the interior light on, applying her makeup.

"Man, I in love with this car, Arch," she said. "Got so many nifty convenience, must was design by women."

"I'm glad we didn't kill that old lady," said Archie. "She reminds me of my grandma some."

"Could I'd gone either way with it," Kitty Kat said, as she wielded her blue eyeliner. "Was kinda nice to seen again where my mama worked, though."

"It was the right thing. Never pays to murder folks remind you of loved ones. Now we got fresh plates on the Cad here, and we gonna stop up in Slaughter, get the Barnwell boys to slap on a new paint job, be all set. What color you like it, Kat?"

"This kind classy car, oughta be some type red."

"Sounds good to me."

"You sure you can trust these Barnwells, huh?"

"Oh yeah. Jimmy Dean and Sal Mineo Barnwell been doin' this since they got out of prison, four, five years ago."

"What beef they go down for?"

"Animal cruelty. They was sellin' videos of Rottweilers in leather armor rippin' apart a captured pig. Fish and Wildlife agents busted 'em at a warehouse out in East Feliciana Parish, confiscated four beauty Rotts."

"Shit!" cried Kitty Kat, bending over and looking around the floor. "Dropped my applicator."

Kitty Kat crawled down and wedged her slender body between the seat and the dashboard.

"Hey, Kat, be careful."

"There it is," she said, reaching for the swab.

The car hit a pothole and Kitty Kat fell forward. She attempted to brace herself with her right hand and accidentally depressed Archie's right foot, which was on the accelerator pedal. The black Cadillac swerved out of control directly into the path of an oncoming Mack semi loaded with several hundred 110-pound bags of Dr. Fagin's Organic Fish Fodder.

BROKEN BLOSSOMS

Two old men walked slowly together along the path connecting the main building to the greenhouse. Sparky Plombier and Buddy Rêveur, both of whom were octogenarians, had been friends for seventy years. Now they were residents of Naomi "Hard Cash" Kamil's Just A Closer Walk With Thee Nursing Home in Belle Chasse, Louisiana, a few miles downriver from New Orleans.

The men had been partners in numerous business ventures, including ownership of a bar in Dallas, Texas, Sparky & Buddy's *New* Mystic Knights of the Sea Bar and Health Club in Biloxi, an exotic religious items mail order company in Waggaman, Louisiana, and, most recently, the S&B Organ Retrieval Service, based in Memphis, Tennessee. This last enterprise had proven their most lucrative, and they lived in pleasant circumstances at Closer Walk, as the residents called it, having invested a goodly share of their retirement funds with their old friend Naomi. Known as "Hard Cash" Kamil both for the fact of her having been born in the Delta town of Hard Cash, Mississippi, and for her renown as an astute businessperson, Naomi made certain that Sparky and Buddy had everything they required to make them comfortable during their declining years. Their passion of late was for raising flowers, so Naomi had provided the greenhouse, which Sparky, an avid reader of mystery stories, had christened the Nero Wolfe Memorial Arboretum, in honor of Rex Stout's rotund detective whose own favorite hours were spent tending his Manhattan roof garden.

Buddy hummed the tune to "Stardust" as he shuffled forward, finding himself unable to sustain a whistle of sufficient strength and timbre. He wore a black, hooded Los Angeles Raiders sweatshirt with the hood up, protecting his bald head against the morning chill. Sparky, who at eighty-three maintained a full head of brown hair remarkably absent of gray, went hatless but leaned heavily on a black walnut cane as he proceeded, carefully keeping weight off of his swollen left leg, which limb had been bothersome to him in cold, damp weather ever since his best fighting dog, Meyer Lansky, a red-hued 110-pound Pit Bull Sparky had raised from a pup more than a quarter-century ago, had accidentally locked down on his left knee with almost one ton per square inch of pressure after Sparky's breaking stick, used to pry open a Pit's engaged jaws, had cracked in two and turned the beast's head in the wrong direction during a training session. It broke Sparky's heart to have had to shoot Meyer Lansky through the right eye socket to get him off; he would have almost rather shot himself, but, as Buddy always said, almost is the twin brother of not quite, and even in his pain and near panic of the moment, Sparky knew how to cut his losses, figuring he would be able to acquire another fighting dog a whole lot easier than he could a new left leg.

"Meyer Lansky actin' up, hey, Spark?" asked Buddy.

"Some," said Sparky. "Be okay soon's we get snug in Nero Wolfe."

Buddy held open the door for Sparky, who passed inside and immediately noticed that something was wrong.

"Buddy, either I'm sufferin' from some sudden kind of macabre brain damage or there's a body in the begonias."

Buddy and Sparky moved as quickly as they could on the begonia bed and stared at the woman lying there, her hands and feet tightly bound by synthetic rope, a seven-inch strip of duct tape stretched across her mouth. The woman's big gray eyes glared at the two men, then blinked rapidly several times.

"Spark, either you ain't got no monopoly on geriatric mind disorder or this woman is Lula Ripley."

RADIANCE

JETLINER CRASHES, BURNS AFTER MID-AIR EXPLOSION

SAN ANTONIO, Jan. 18 (SNS)—A Pacific Continental Airways K-711 commercial jetliner en route from New Orleans to Los Angeles crashed and burned yesterday approximately 250 miles west of San Antonio. All 147 passengers aboard are believed to have perished.

Witnesses in the nearby community of Big Tuna, Texas, said that the plane appeared to have exploded in the air, raining metal on the arid land below.

Among the passengers believed to have been aboard were U.S. Senator Rantoul "Bingo" Blaine (D—La.) and Philip Reál, the internationally renowned film director ("Mumblemouth").

A spokesperson for PCA would neither confirm nor deny a Southern News Service report that a note was delivered by an unidentified man to the airline ticket counter at New Orleans International Airport shortly after takeoff that read, "They shall drop from the sky like radiant cherry blossoms."

LETTER TO DAL

Dalceda Delahoussaye
809 Ashmead Drive
Bay St. Clement, N.C. 28352

Dearest Dal,

You are the only person in the world other than maybe Beany who ever really understood me so your the one I need to write this letter to. Thank the Lord Dal your still alive even though you been smoking since before I was born. Mama loved you more than anyone Dal including me probably. I know what a terrible loss it was for you when Mama died and so I feel its OK to tell you not only what has happened here but what Im thinking now about things.

The bad news is Sailor was killed in a wreck. I had to stop just now a minute to catch my breath sometimes it happens I lose control of my breathing and I kind of panic though not so much as I used to when I was a girl. This is Monday when Im writing so last Thursday Sailor was driving home from Bridge City where Gator Gone got there new storage facility and as he was headed on the Huey P. Long Bridge a dumb boy in a Apache pickup cut in front of Sailor from the shoulder and Sailor swerved his car to avoid him but couldnt straighten out in time before he hit the road divider. After smacking into it the car turned over and a transport truck carrying a dozen new Mitsubishi jeeps plowed him half way toward the Old Spanish Trail. Sail probably was already dead by then or knocked out for sure and didnt feel anything else at least its what I hope. The Cadillac with Sailor inside was crushed like it had been squeezed into a metal cube at the junk yard. There was no fire and believe it or not Sailors face was almost unmarked just his body was mashed in a 100 places.

There it is Dal I cant hardly believe it. Pace and me decided to cremate Sailor and we got his ashes here in a box we didnt want no funeral. I got to tell you Dal I feel kind of dead myself. I read once in Readers Digest I think about how often if two people been together a real long time and one of them dies the other dies soon after. Im only 62 and Mama lived into her 80s and youll most probably hit a 100 but I feel like how am I supposed to go on now? I know Mama would say look how she done after Daddy burned himself up so many years ago and didnt she have a long and useful life but you know me Dal and as much as Mama wanted me to be I am not really like her not in the way of strength. I am not exactly a serious religious person either I know that ever since I left the Church of Reason Redemption and Resistance to Gods Detractors. What do I have left Dal I mean it.

Pace is the greatest comfort of course. He and Rhoda tried there for a bit to tie the knot again but as Pace says once the string come unraveled you got to get you a new piece so its off for good. After his boss the movie director was killed in that plane crash Pace went to New York with Rhoda and then to LA to get his possessions and now he dont want to leave me alone so hes at the house. I told him hes 42 just about and I dont want him to end up like Sailors former hunting buddy Coot Veal what never left his mama and didnt make a real life. Pace is different from Coot of course since he been so many places around the world almost but itd be easy for him to stop his life on my account I can tell and I dont want that. He is a Ripley though as well as a Fortune and there aint too much good can be accomplished by arguing. I guess I should feel lucky in that regard to have such a good son and I do but you understand what Im saying.

Thats really about it I dont mean to go on you had plenty enough sorrows through your own life not to need mine. Just I felt you should know what happened to Sailor the way it did. I suppose Ill figure out what happens next for me Dal but if I dont it aint but the end of *my* world nobody elses. It aint either that Im feeling sorry for myself its different. I suppose since Sailor and me come back together thirty some years ago I never even give a thought to our being apart ever again and its the biggest kind of shock to face this knowing Sailor aint in prison this time hes dead and thats the end of that tune like hed say. I cant play no other tune Dal I wont. Remember how the Reverend Willie Thursday used to say a boy without a father is just a lost soul sailing on a ghost ship through the sea of life? Well Im one now a lost soul that is without my man. Sailor Ripley was my man Dal he was the one and Im so glad we found each other the world being as big as it is it was a miracle Im certain. We was never out of love Dal all this time since I was 16 aint that something? I been a fortunate woman I know but I cant believe its over and truth is I guess I might never.

Love you,
Lula

THE
IMAGINATION
OF THE HEART

To the memory of Marshall Clements

At the end of what is necessary, I have come to a place
where there is no road.
—Iris Murdoch

I ain't goin' nowhere.
I been where I'm goin'.
—Amos Milburn

1

My land as Mama used to say tomorrow will be my 80th birthday. Its almost eighteen years since Sailor was killed in a car wreck when that dumb boy in a Apache pickup cut in front of him from the shoulder of the road as Sail was headed on to the Huey P. Long Bridge. All these years and I still cant believe it. Now I walk in the imagination of my heart as spake Jeremiah. Might as well take the time I have left to me on the planet to set down best I can my last thoughts while Im able. Only one interested probably will be Sailors and my one and only child our son Pace Roscoe Ripley. Pace is 58 hard to believe. These days Pace is in NO rebuilding that city after Hurricane Katrina near about totaled it. He got himself a little construction outfit over in Metairie so I dont see him much as Id like. Not too long after Sailor passed I moved from New Orleans back to my home place of Bay St. Clement North Carolina to live with Mamas closest and dearest friend Dalceda Delahoussaye in her big old house had nobody in it but her. We got along great for about ten years then at 92 she fell off a kitchen stool while she was peeling an apple broke her hip and had to stay at the Hattie McDaniel Home for Women of a Certain Age. Dal lasted close on a year there before the Lord called her. I wonder did He hear her last words to me Lula there aint no beast so fierce as a proven woman. I been puzzling over this since Dal said it and I dont guess I got it figured out yet what she exactly meant. Oh well it wont be so very long before Ill get to ask her in person.

2

I will speak that I may be refreshed says Job. I suppose thats why Im writing now. Actually I always been interested in language or languages I should say. I looked it up in Paces old high school encyclopedia and found out there been nine chief language families in the history of the world. They are African Semitic Indo-European or Aryan Indo-Chinese Japanese Ural Austronesian North American Indian and South American Indian. Of course these are divided into many smaller groups the Semitic for instance has Phoenician Hebrew Arabic Aramaic and Ethiopic all languages of the Holy Bible. Im sure in the translating a lot was lost or changed which could be one good reason why so many people take Gods word different. I am only astonished that more than two persons at all get along anywhere any more it sure seems like they mostly dont. For my 80th I stayed in the house and didnt answer the telephone which rang once early in the morning and again late in the afternoon. I figure it was Pace calling from New Orleans but I just didnt feel like talking. Ill call him and tell him I survived thats if I do of course. I hate to say it but if it aint Sailor on the other end of the line I dont care if Im on it or not. I remember when he used to call me from prison after we got off Id cry like there was no tomorrow and now there really aint.

3

Soon after I left NO to live with Dal in Bay St. Clement I drove over to the spot where Sailor and I first declared to one another our absolute undying love. I parked my 1989 Mercury Nightcat next to the Cape Fear light house and took a walk. Just a closer walk with thee I was thinking thee being my own gone gone gone Sailor Ripley. It was in the Cape Fear Hotel that we had reconsummated our love once again after hed been released from the Pee Dee Correctional Facility following the incident resulted in the death of one Bob Ray Lemon. Sailor had only been defending my honor he never was nothing but correct so far as I was concerned so depositing him in Pee Dee was a waste of our time and the resources of the state of North Carolina being as there was nothing in him to correct in the first place. I was sad to see the old Cape Fear Hotel had been closed down. An elderly lady pruning her 'Bama Boy roses across the road told me it happened a couple or more years before things around there were sure more quiet now. I went around back of the hotel to the porch Sail and I sat out on watching the river flow into the Atlantic Ocean as I stood there the tears didnt stop for the longest time. Later I told Dal Id gone there she said honey your mama Marietta thought suffering kept a person from forming too pretty an opinion of their self is how she put it. Nobodys so special the Good Lord dont make them suffer some. How else the heart gets tough enough it dont break completely Dal said otherwise there wouldnt be one person left standing on the planet.

4

Last night I had a dream I was with some people coming from a party in the Quarter walking down Ursulines toward Decatur and here come Sailor in a white Cadillac convertible sitting next to some little blonde driving with the top down looked like Meg Ryan. He had all his hair so it was Sail in his younger days I dont know how old I was. Sailor and the girl sped on by some of us shouted Hey Sailor but he didnt notice or hear. I could hear music blasting from the Cadillac I didnt recognize classical Mozart or something. Must have been what she liked since I never knew Sailor Ripley to listen to anything other than rock or R and B. Thunder and lightning struck just then and rain started coming down hard. It was night but the sky was all lit up with zig zag streaks like vapor trails from jet planes and suddenly they formed together to spell out the words And the children of Israel did evil again in the sight of the Lord. I woke up wet with sweat and called for Dal but then realized she was gone too. I got up and drank half a can of cold Ginger Ale it calmed me down. I went back to bed and read in an old paperback mystery Dal had called The Sailors Rendezvous isnt that strange. Takes place in France.

5

Beanys coming for a visit. Its been nearly 20 years since we actually set blue eyes on one another and being she and I been considering each other best friends for three times that long its a scandal. Beany Thorn never was no favorite of Mamas thats for sure on account of Beanys being so wild and more than most unpredictable. She married first to a man named Elmo Pleasant had a couple kids with him while at the same time he was knocking up highschool girls all over the states of Louisiana and Texas. She tossed his ass out for good just before Sailor got out of jail the first time. Beanys been living in Plain Dealing with her daughter Hedy Lamarr Music and her husband Delivery and their oldest boy Melton who Beany says aint never going to leave home it looks like hes 37 years old. Delivery hes a midget and so is Melton. Delivery and Hedy Lamarrs two other children Spike Jones and Tizane Naureen are normal persons and live in Baton Rouge. Beany says Delivery is a good man and good husband to her daughter who owns a produce stand up on the state highway. There was a time Beany got committed to the nut house at Oriental this was just before her divorce from Elmo. I visited her there and she was so furious at Elmo who had got his lawyer cousin Arafat De Forest the one later got sent up for having sexually molested his own son to file charges Beany abandoned their children for days at a time while she was taking pills that deranged her mind. It was all I could do in my power to keep her from sticking an icepick up Elmos right nostril to disable his motor ability while he was asleep after she got out. Beany got full custody of their kids despite her stretch at Oriental after she proved beyond a doubt Elmo had fathered at least two children by underage girls out of wedlock. Thats a terrible word I think wedlock makes marriage sound like a prison which it is I guess for some though was not for me and my Sailor. Beany arrives tomorrow on the three oclock train and I cant hardly wait.

"Hey, darlin', is that you?"

"What's become of me is what this is."

"Stop it, Lula, you look terrific. It's me who's gone from bein' Miss Grape to Miss Raisin. Let me see if you still got a butt."

Beany Thorn took hold of Lula and turned her around.

"Don't that beat hell, honey, you do!"

Lula giggled. "Hush, Beany, people'll hear."

"Girl, they ought to see! You'd win the Miss Octogenarian of North Carolina contest, if they had one. Do they?"

"Stop it, baby, I'm awful glad to see you, too."

The two women hugged. Beany Thorn picked up her one little fake alligator bag that her daddy, Deacon Don Thorn, had given her on her seventeenth birthday, two days before she'd been packed off to Oriental the first time.

As they began walking away from the train platform, Lula asked, "That all you brought?"

"For a person who might not make it past today, it's enough. As Saint Scarlett O'Hara said, 'Tomorrow is another day, so let's worry about it when and if it gets here.'"

Once they were settled in wicker rockers on the wraparound porch of Dal's house—Lula insisted on calling it that even after Mrs. Delahoussaye's passing—each with a chimney in hand filled with crushed ice, Bombay gin and a teaspoonful of sugar, the two lifelong friends appraised one another more carefully.

"Take a sip, Beany, it'll cool you down."

Beany did, then said, "Lula, you're really more than a friend deserves—you remembered my fondness for Bombay."

"Bought a bottle just because you were comin', though I have to say I don't mind it myself."

"Happy days!" declared Beany, holding up her glass.

"Happy days!" Lula repeated.

"Look at us, Lula, two old biddies no use to nobody."

"At least we ain't pollutin' the planet. Not too much, anyway. We don't drive SUVs or use tampons."

"Lula, you ever think about sex?"

"My land, Beany! Thank the Good Lord, no."

"I must confess, sweetie, I do. Not that I want it, necessarily. After all, I'm dry as a bone. But the thought of havin' a man's big old hairy arms around me comes on now and again. I even have orgasms in my dreams."

Lula gagged on a large swallow of ice cold gin.

"Beany, after all these years you still terrify me."

"Saw a young man in the Wal-Mart the other day—Tuesday, I guess it was—wearin' a sweatstained wifebeater made me tremble. I swear I coulda sucked on him like a Holloway All-Day. Don't tell me you don't have them thoughts even once in a while."

"Beany, I don't want to talk about it. No, in fact. I told you."

Beany ran her tongue over her lips, savoring the flavor of the Bombay gin and sugar, and said, "I got to keep alive in my mind the possibility that I got at least one more romantic episode comin' my way."

"I heard the most terrible thing on the radio last night," said Lula. "You know I can't sleep more than three or four hours, so I listen to the radio in the night."

"I ain't slept more than four hours at a crack since I was twelve, Lula. Ever since I figured out I'd be takin' the Big Dirt Nap someday. Didn't want to miss nothin' before then."

"Heard that the French fella was always explorin' the waters of the world—can't recall his name, somethin' like Crusoe only his first name weren't Robinson, he's dead now—was in a submarine at the bottom of Lake Tahoe in California, and discovered the bodies of a hundred or more Chinese men frozen intact. Turns out these men had been workin' a job out there in about the year 1900 and thought they were bein' taken to the other side of the lake after their job was finished."

"Did the boat go down in a storm?"

"Uh uh. The terrible part is that the bosses didn't want to pay 'em, so they clubbed all them poor little Chinese men and boys and threw their bodies overboard. The lake is super deep and frozen at the bottom, which is why the corpses is all preserved."

"Did the French guy fish out the bodies?"

"Crusoe said it was too horrible and people couldn't deal with it, so he left 'em there. Ain't that the most horrifyin' thing?"

Beany nodded and drank down the contents of her glass.

"Sounds like somethin' Elmo's partner Emilio Zarzoso mighta done. Remember him, Lula? The one who did twenty years for murderin' his wife with a poisonous viper he claimed was an exotic pet escaped from its cage?"

Lula finished off her drink and said, "Time for another sugar gin, Beany, don't you think?"

7

Beanys visit is raising my spirits at least I feel like I got more pep. Theres a word hardly heard much any more. Beany is always agitating about something now its our going off together on a oceanliner cruise to meet rich widowers. I asked her what on earth they would want with us old women and she answered me companionship. These are men cant do for themselves and get lonely not having anything much to do since they retired. They need a woman to get their motor started again. I cant get my own motor started most days so how Im supposed to get him going? Told Beany Id think on it but it seems to me theres a whole lot more widows around than widowers and a man like that needs a young woman to start him up. Beany she wont take no easy so best for me to do is just humor her. Middle of last night I heard noise in the kitchen so I got up went in and theres Beany hitting the gin this time cut with orange juice. She looked at me and said Terrors are turned upon me they pursue my soul as the wind. I recalled from my time with the Church of Reason Redemption and Resistance to Gods Detractors to say My bones are pierced in me in the night season and my sinews take no rest. Beany smiled a good smile she still got almost all her own teeth left and said I know baby I couldnt sleep neither.

8

Beany and Lula were seated outside in the garden of the Lion's Mouth Cafe fingerdipping sardines and Saltines in red salsa and drinking Cosmopolitans. The sun was just about down for the day.

"How you like that Cosmo?" asked Beany. "It's what the twenty and thirty somethin's prefer these days."

Lula took a little sip.

"Ain't too bad. Mite sweet, though. How you heard about 'em?"

"Sex and the City, the TV show? The girls on it are always meetin' up in a outdoor place like this, rushin' in breathless, then suckin' down a Cosmo as they commence complainin'."

"Complainin' about what?"

"Men, 'course. What else?"

"I never seen it."

"I missed it myself, first time around. Now I just catch the late at night reruns. Don't matter, you still got me to listen to."

"Thank goodness."

A waitress came to their table and asked, "You ladies ready for another?"

"Not quite yet," Beany answered. "You, Lula?"

Lula shook her head no.

"But I got a question," said Beany.

"Shoot," the waitress said.

"Why's this place called the Lion's Mouth?"

"Hebrews, 11:33. 'Who through faith subdued kingdoms, wrought righteousness, obtained promises, stopped the mouths of lions.' We're mostly God-fearin' folks around here, but you gotta have a place to let your hair down and this is as close as you get in Bay St. Clement."

The waitress walked away.

"Whew," said Beany, "she sure answered my question, didn't she?"

Lula nodded. "I only been here twice," she said.

Beany leaned forward and took Lula's left hand between both of her own.

"Lula, you know what we gotta do?"

"What?"

"Take a trip together."

"Where? When?"

"Now, tomorrow, or the next day. Don't matter much where. Let's just go to be goin'."

"Oh, Beany, quit. You mean take a sea cruise?"

"Hell, no. Them're for old folks. Anyway, I'd feel like a prisoner on a boat. We can drive."

"I don't know about you, Beany, but I gotta admit I'm feelin' shakey goin' on the interstate."

"Fine, we'll take back roads, go slow."

Beany still colored her hair. In the fading sunlight, Lula noticed, it had a greenish glow.

"Don't think I'm up to travelin', Beany. I'm happy these days just stickin' close to home."

"Lula, we're goin'! I won't let you set in a rockin' chair waitin' on the death ship."

"I'll think on it."

"We just gotta decide which way we're headed: up, down, or out west."

"Beany, I believe this Cosmo is makin' me dizzy. It and the heat."

"Okay, sweetie pie, we'll head back to Dal's, but by tomorrow mornin' we'll have a plan. We need an adventure, baby, bring out our inner girl."

"Beany, you're crazy."

Lula's oldest and best friend left in the world cackled and said, "Board certified by the backwardest state in the entire confederacy."

"I don't know about that, Beany. Louisiana got itself some pretty stiff competition down here in the backwards department."

I guess its time I went back to NO. Pace tells me its a sorry sight since Katrina but this might be my last chance to see the city where I spent most of my life. I suppose I been reluctant to go since Sailor was killed I got so many memories there and hes in almost all. Beanys got my best interest in mind I know and this way Ill get to see my son. By the time Beany and I got back to the house from the Lions Mouth cafe she had pretty much made up my mind for me so I called Pace on his cell phone which as far as I know is the only number hes got. He didnt answer but I left him a message saying Im coming with Beany see you in a few days. I got his address in Metairie and if he aint got room for us to stay there Im sure we can find some hotel dont charge a arm or a leg. Beany herself aint been in NO for years she says and we can go on up to Plain Dealing after so I can see Hedy Lamarr and meet Delivery Music and their son Melton. Beany thinks Melton who dont have nothing better to do would drive me back to Bay St. Clement and then he can take a train back to Plain Dealing. It all sounds fine but I have to confess Im afraid being in NO again without Sail is gonna be tough. I could hardly stand it after he died thank goodness I had Dal to go to. After Mama passed I recalled what she had written to me from beside the deathbed of her old beau Marcello Santos. Marcello may have been a gangster Mama said but it werent all his fault hed done what he done because as it says in Kings he walked in all the way that his father walked in and served the idols that his father served and worshiped them. Santos may have done that which was evil in the sight of the Lord but he was set out on a path not of his choosing and at his very end he asked Mama to forgive him his ways cause he knew God would not. And Mama said she asked Marcello is thine heart right as my heart is with thy heart and he answered her it is so she said give me thine hand and he did and he was taken up into the chariot. Going to NO now might just be best help me conquer some shadows.

First thing this morning Beany and I drove over to Oscaritos Service to have my Mercury Nightcat checked out for the trip. That Oscarito is the nicest boy come up from Mexico about six years back with his brother Jose Pinto whos working now as a plasterer Oscarito tells me in Chicago. Oscarito hired on with old Dip Robinson at Dips Gulf Gas and now hes running the show. Dip is a good man but I aint unhappy he retired as this Oscarito is a ace mechanic. Oscarito says where he come from they couldnt afford to buy new parts so he learned how to make his own from leftovers. Even with all the computer stuff you gotta know now to make a car go he can work miracles with a wrench and a screwdriver. I believe if hed been assisting Doctor Frankenstein the monster would have come out right and never killed that little girl picking flowers. Beany and I left the Mercury with Oscarito walked over to the graveyard and talked about our route. Beany has it figured pretty well already we head for Myrtle Beach then Charleston to Beaufort down to Savannah and cross Georgia through Valdosta to Dothan Alabama and on into Mobile from there through Pascagoula Biloxi Gulfport Pass Christian whats left of it and then NO. Im steadying myself for a fright since Hurricane Katrina kicked ass along the gulf coast too. Beany says shes heard how the planet is getting too hot for humans and anyway pretty soon once all the ice melts up north they already got polar bears eating each other everyone living next to water will be under it. None of this news is easy to swallow maybe itll come down to what Isaiah said about hail sweeping away the refuge of lies and waters overflowing the hiding place because there wont be no place to hide people are either all in this boat together or there aint going to be no boat to be in.

11

"Lula, you about ready?"

"Comin'. I ain't so mobile as I used to be. Might be time for some replacement parts, I could afford 'em."

Lula came down the stairs slowly, keeping one hand on the bannister, carrying a small, brown, weatherbeaten valise in the other.

"That all you bringin', baby?" Beany asked.

Lula reached the bottom of the steps and put the valise down on the floor.

"This is Sailor's old getaway bag," she said. "I thought this's the proper occasion to use it. Holds all I'll need. I believe he'd be happy to know he's goin' back out on the road."

"What you mean 'he'?"

"Feel like Sailor's comin' with me, Beany, you know? Sail never went nowhere far from home he didn't take this valise."

"Elmo always insisted on takin' with him all he could. 'Never can tell when we'll be back, if ever,' he used to say. Man always was lookin' to move on, and that was a sign."

Lula held her tongue. She never had cared for Elmo, even when Beany'd been convinced he was the bee's knees, but she saw no earthly reason to add to her good friend's storehouse of ill thoughts concerning the man. After all, Lula thought, they'd soon be visiting with Elmo Pleasant's blood daughter, Hedy Lamarr, and who knew what memories she had of him. Most certainly Beany had long ago poisoned that well.

"Beany, before we get goin' there's one thing I gotta say."

"What's that, baby?"

"Back in the day Sailor and I were startin' out on a trip, it was his fiftieth birthday, drivin' across Lake Pontchartrain, time we encountered that strange girl, Consuelo Whynot."

"Teenager was mixed up with a lesbian Chickasaw in Miss'ippi, I recall. Killed a fella."

Lula nodded. "Wesley Nisbet, but it was Venus Tishomingo shot him, not Consuelo. Then Nisbet's car run Venus over."

"Sweet Jesus, like in that movie Christine. What about it?"

"Just that when we were on the bridge beginnin' that trip there was a bad sign Sail and I ignored. A big dead pelican fell from the sky and crashed on the roof of our Sedan de Ville. We'd understood it was a omen we would've turned around and gone back to N.O. Never woulda been involved with them crazy folks. Promise me, Beany, we get some kinda sign we stop right there, scoot back to Bay St. Clement."

"Okay, Lula, a dead pelican crashes on us, we'll turn back."

"Not just a pelican. I mean any weird incident could be a warnin'."

Beany stared into Lula's still bright gray eyes and held up her own right hand with the index and second fingers pressed together and the other two held down by her thumb.

"What's that?" asked Lula.

"Indian sign, means I promise. We good to go now?"

"Uh huh. Just I believe we're way too old for that sorta foolishness, Beany, don't you?"

We made pretty good progress today for two old women. We got kind of a late start but arrived in Myrtle Beach just after sunset. As we drove I couldnt help but think about Sailor and how when we were kids going to Myrtle Beach was about the end in the holiday department. Beany insisted on driving most of the way she goes faster than me of course. I called Pace again from a gas station by Calabash but got his message voice and left him one so at least he knows or will know when he listens to it that we really are on the road and headed his way. Beany is half decided to get herself a cell phone finally I guess its a good idea if your stuck on a highway at night with a flat tire or something but I keep resisting getting one as just one more modern piece of business to deal with. I hope I dont regret not having one I know it could be a lifesaver someday. So here we are in Myrtle Beach thank the Lord in off season so it was no trouble finding a place to stay. The Sunrise in Egypt Motel used to be was run by Betty Jane and Delmer Holden he was a distant cousin of the actor William Holden kept a poster of The Wild Bunch movie on the lobby wall. Thats gone now theres new owners but the rooms are clean. Sailor told me once he and a buddy Dodge Johnson whose daddy named him after his favorite car got stuck here for two days in a rainstorm and Dodge Johnson read the New Testament through about ten times out loud because he couldnt read silent and drove Sail almost crazy. Dodge claimed Revelations foretold the New Heaven and the New Earth was on another planet and that to get right with the Lord it was necessary to follow the Pure River and leave behind the dogs sorcerers whoremongers murderers idolators and liars who would all be condemned to dwell in New York City where Satan had reappeared following his thousand years of banishment from Gods Kingdom. Sailor never could stand to listen to anyone preach the New Testament after that but neither did he ever go to New York City.

"Beany, I'm afraid to go to N.O."

Beany was at the wheel and Lula was in the front passenger seat of the Nightcat at ten in the morning of a gray day as they motored slowly south on state highway 17 near Murrells Inlet.

"What're you sayin', baby?" asked Beany. "Afraid of what?"

"What we're gonna see. How wrecked the city is from the hurricane. I lived there forty years and I don't know if I could bear to see the place so torn up."

"You seen it on TV."

"Seein' somethin' on TV ain't the same as in person, Beany, you know that. I'm worried it'll break my heart."

Beany honked the horn at a black Cadillac Escalade in front of them that was moving too slowly and weaving out of its lane and back.

"Take it easy, there'll be a passin' lane in a minute."

"Natural disasters is part of life, Lula, it's why they're called natural. Hell, I'm a natural disaster myself, bein' in and out of mental institutions, mostly destroyin' my children's lives. It ain't difficult to see how the planet woulda been better off without the Good Lord planted me on it."

Tears rolled down Beany's cheeks. She wiped them away as she drove.

"Oh, Beany, darlin', that ain't true. You're one of God's rarest creatures and my dearest friend. Just you had a wild hair, is all, and couldn't always keep it in place."

"Yeah, like the most uncontrollable cowlick in the history of Crowley, Louisiana."

The road widened and Beany stabbed the accelerator pedal and zoomed the Mercury around the lumbering SUV.

"I was right, Lula. Look!"

As they sped by, Lula glimpsed the driver of the Escalade, a big-haired thirty-something holding a cell phone to her left ear.

"Is she smokin', too?" Beany asked.

"Can't tell. Oh, wait. Yep, she surely is. Got a long, thin ciggie between two fingers of her steerin' hand."

"You never smoke no more, Lula?"

"Ever' once in a while I puff on a Viceroy. 'Bout twice a month, maybe."

"Strange," said Beany, "smokin's about the only bad habit I didn't have, you know?"

"What you mean, 'didn't'? You still got time to develop one or two more mean deals before Armageddon."

Beany laughed. Her tears were gone.

"Wish Hedy Lamarr loved me the way you do, Lula, but I guess I get what I deserve. Deliver me from the hand of strange children, it says in Psalms."

"Like that teenager in Little Rock was on the news," Lula said, "decapitated his mother, a dog, and a parakeet."

Beany clucked her tongue. "You're right, Lula, things always could be worse."

14

When Lula took over the wheel at McClellanville, she asked Beany if she could borrow her sunglasses. Beany handed them over.

"Thanks, they're darker than mine," said Lula. "Glare here's bad."

"Amazin' you don't wear glasses 'cept to read," Beany said. "I can't get from the kitchen to the bathroom without mine."

"I got my mama's eyes, I guess. Marietta never wore any type of eye-glasses. I recall her readin' Eugene Sue's *Mysteries of Paris* to Marcello Santos when he was on his deathbed, didn't have on no spectacles."

"You're blessed. I started wearin' 'em when I couldn't read the writin' on the squares on the Monopoly board at Oriental."

"Did I ever tell you about Sailor's recurrin' dream involvin' a kind of board game?"

"No, Lula, what was it?"

"Well, it wasn't really on a board, it was on sand, on the ground. Sailor said the first time he had it he dreamed he was sittin' on the desert floor with a group of Indians, Hopis, perhaps, in the southwest somewhere, Arizona or New Mexico, and there was lines marked out in front of 'em, carved in the sand, creases like, and Sail and these Indians were movin' beads or stones, white rocks, from one place to another. He said they were sittin' on a mesa, all the colors were very bright, tan and beige and blue from the sky.

"After that, the second time he had the dream and the times after, the game was spread out over a much larger distance. There were more lines or creases drawn in the sand, shapes of figures like animals, and the beads or balls now, not stones or rocks, had to travel much further. Sailor told me he and the other players were sittin' with their legs folded underneath 'em on the ground and one of the rules was nobody could stand up to move any of the balls."

"Did he say how they moved?"

"Yes, this is the good part. They transported their pieces by mental telepathy, by the power of their mind. Ain't that somethin'?"

"Never heard nothin' like it. Did Sailor say if he won or not?"

"No, I don't believe winnin' was the object of the game. Every time Sailor had this dream he told me it got more complicated and he couldn't really explain how the game was supposed to go, just the players bein' able to move the pieces with their thoughts was the important thing."

Beany shook her head. "Whew, I never knew Sailor had such a deep mind."

"He used to could surprise me, Beany. There was more to him than most people suspected. Sailor was a special boy."

"I'm glad you told me this, Lula. Puts Sailor in a whole different light."

"Beany, if I remember right, there used to be a good Dairy Queen in Wando we can stop at."

"Okay, baby, I could do with a strawberry double dip."

Sprinkles hit the windshield and Lula turned on the wipers.

"Oh, one more thing about Sailor's dream?"

"Tell, me."

"After he passed, I found a bunch of drawin's in his desk, markin's like the ones he described had been made in the sand in the Indian game."

"I guess he was tryin' to figure it out."

"Uh huh. That dream was a A-Number One mystery."

Beany nodded and said, "Sure as shootin', just like ever'thin' else."

15

After stopping for an ice cream in Wando and gassing up the Merc, Beany took the wheel for the busy stretch into Charleston.

"One night last week I couldn't sleep," said Lula, "so I turned on the TV and there was one of Sailor's favorite old black and white movies, Virginia City, with Errol Flynn and Humphrey Bogart as a Mexican bandit."

"Don't believe I ever seen it," Beany said. "Think I'd remember Bogey as a Mexican."

"He weren't real convincin'. Had a drawed on pencil-thin mustache and a bad accent, was weaselly-lookin'. That Errol Flynn, though, was just about scrumptious as a man could get. Makes all these skinny actors today look sick."

"I'm with you there, Lula. What's the picture about?"

"A Civil War western, where Randolph Scott—who was plenty cute, too, though Sail always said he was a three dollar bill—is with our side and he's sent to Virginia City, Nevada, to get gold to finance the Confederacy. Flynn's a Yankee undercover agent out to stop him. He does, but he likes Scott so doesn't let the Union have the gold, which he buries under a rockslide. Bogart's got a gang of filthy desperadoes ridin' around robbin' everybody. Best part of the movie, though, is when Flynn's double does a header on horseback over a cliff."

"Who's the girl? That simpy, Goody Two-Shoes person always about to faint ever' time Errol noticed her?"

"You mean Olivia de Havilland. No, she was much prettier than this one. This is a dancehall gal workin' for the rebels who's only a half-attractive blonde with doll-baby ringlets, sort of a third-rate American Marlene Dietrich. Had an annoyin' voice, too. I'll bet even Flynn didn't put it to her."

A light rain persisted but Beany kept her window down. "I like feelin' the soft drops while I drive," she said. "It's like they're pokin' me to keep payin' attention to the road."

Lula kept her window cracked slightly just to catch a tiny breeze.

"But Lula? My best guess is ol' Errol had all his leadin' ladies like chickens-in-the-basket. Them actors and actresses are always at it. I read in some magazine years ago a interview with John Derek—one was married to Bo Derek?—where he said he made fifty movies and durin' each one he went to bed with the actress played opposite him. He said it was expected by the director—unless the director was gunnin' her, too—and, most of all, by the actress her own self, made her more confident. 'Course it helped Derek that he was about the prettiest boy when he was young, even more than that French actor looks so queeny now. Read how he goes to Tahiti every couple years for a face lift."

"Yeah, I guess so," said Lula. "But I like to think even in Hollywood there's true romance once in a while."

"You don't think you woulda cheated on Sailor with Errol Flynn?"

"Uh uh, Beany, not a chance. Can't say I wouldn't have appreciated the offer, but I knew Sail was my man since I was sixteen years old. Even when he was sent up for pullin' that feed store holdup in Texas with that devil Bobby Peru, I stayed true. Also when we was separated after. I believed in my heart it was in the stars that we was meant to be together forever."

Beany sighed and said, "Lula, that's so precious. I believe you, I always have. But even if I'd been as lucky with a man as you were with Sailor Ripley, I wouldn'ta passed on Errol Flynn."

16

I been thinking lately about my daddy how my life might have been different had he not died so early in it. No doubt he would not have approved of my marrying Sailor no more than Mama did so Im certain we would have had a powerful disagreement in that department. I like to think on him sitting in his favorite chair the one with the ripped up armrests torn apart by my cat Blue Eyed Jane named after Daddys specialmost Jimmie Rodgers song. He loved to listen to those old records of Jimmies his granddaddy give him he had em all on 78. Nobody did Jimmie right Daddy said so he made this music that would last as long as anyones and then died from TB. Why Should I Be Lonely had the words I preferred the best of all. Why should I be so lonely why should I be sad though another is taking from me the best pal Ive ever had shes taking the sunshine with her leaving the clouds for me but why should I be so lonesome when theres nobody lonesome for me. This describes my feeling for Sailor having fallen into the embrace of Madame Death who Sail said would be my only rival. How could I know when I was a child and listened to those songs with my daddy that Jimmie had already saw Madame standing in the shadows.

17

Beany and I spent the night at the Henry Nimrod B & B in Charleston
and when I woke up this morning Beany had left me a note saying shed
already gone down to breakfast. Imagine my surprise when I found her
sitting at a table with a beautiful boy who looked about sixteen but as it
turns out is twenty three. His name of all things is Epistrophy Trane
Taylor but goes by his initials ET. He was staying at the Nimrod for a
couple of days while exploring Charleston hes from Lake Charles
Louisiana. Told us his mama and daddy are jazz people so named him
after their favorite tune by Monk and middle name after Coltrane. He
was just a little kid when the movie ET come out so it was a natural to
be called that and it stuck. ET has long wavy light brown hair and green
eyes you can imagine looking in em and seeing a jungle lagoon with crocodiles gliding along. You really could get a little lost staring in there I
cant explain it better. Anyway Beany seen him and the breakfast room
was filled so she asked ET if she could sit at the table with him and he
jumped right up and pulled out a chair for her. Turns out ET graduated
college last June now its October and has been traveling around by bus
and thumb for almost four months trying to figure out what he wants
to do with his life. Hes been to the midwest and up and down the east
coast sometimes doing small jobs the usual. His degree from of all places
Daniel Schmutz University in Switzerland is in computer science so ET
could work anywhere with his skills but he says he cant stand the idea of
sitting at a desk in front of a computer screen all day I dont blame him
a bit. We asked how it was he went to school over there in Switzerland
especially being from Lake Charles he said his grandparents live there its
where his mama grew up in those mountains. She met his daddy on a
holiday trip to NO and they run off together got married she was
eighteen and they been living in his daddys home town of Lake Charles
ever since. ETs daddy is a car mechanic with his own garage and a
trumpet player on the side. His mama runs the business and paints pictures of flowers mostly also she plays the cello. Besides English ET speaks
German his mama taught him growing up she didnt speak English

hardly at all when she run into ETs daddy to be. His name is Alastair Taylor his family being originally from Scotland but ET says everybody calls his daddy Duke because of Duke Ellington its the name of the garage Dukes. ET told us hes running real low on money and is hitching his way to Lake Charles so Beany said he could ride with us to NO without asking me not that I would have said no. He accepted and went to get his things from his room just a pack and a guitar. After ET was gone Beany whispered to me not to panic but this boy made her wet at least feel she could be wet then laughed crazy out loud so everybody stared. I been writing this waiting in the car for her and here she is with ET carrying our bags. I got a feeling something out of my control is going on but is it a sign?

/

"I been readin' this book I picked up in Atlanta, Why God Don't Need to Carry a Gun. Says people ought just listen to their inner voice so there can be peace in the world."

"What's this inner voice sayin'?" Beany asked ET. She was driving. Lula was in the front passenger seat and ET was in the back, strumming on his Gibson Hummingbird.

"It's the Lord's message comin' through His angels, is what it is. A person's body is sort of a celestial radio station. You got to get tuned in to His frequency."

"You mean the angels are broadcastin' for Him from inside us?" asked Beany.

"God's disc jockeys," said ET, and strummed a G major chord. "They're pluckin' on your heartstrings like they do on their harps, singin' 'Babylon is fallen, is fallen, the Lord's son is callin', is callin'. He who worships the beast and his image shall carry his mark, and dwell ever after without rest in the dark.'"

"You really believe this, ET?" Lula asked. "What it says in this book?"

"I guess so."

"There ain't no guessin' when it comes to religion," said Lula.

ET sang, accompanying himself on his guitar: "Oh God don't need to carry a gun/ And you know He ain't the only one/ No, you and I can be in His number, too/ Lambs and lions and beasts of burden/ Us creatures commanded by His word and/ Then we'll all be raptured with His son."

"Never heard that hymn before," said Beany.

"I know," said ET, "I wrote it myself. Glad as gravy you gals give me a ride. I knew as soon as I seen you both together that it was a sign."

Lula rolled down her window all the way and let the breeze hit her full in the face.

Somewhere around the turnoff for Edisto Island, Lula drifted off to sleep and dreamed that she was her much younger self alone on a beach at sunset. Suddenly, a big red wave rose up and crashed on the ground in front of her and as the water receded revealed human body parts lying on the sand. Arms, legs, what looked like a neck, even a few heads littered the beach. She was jolted out of this daytime nightmare by a bump.

"Sorry," said Beany, "couldn't dodge some possum remains."

Lula recognized the tune playing on the radio, "Little Rain" by Jimmy Reed. Sailor had always said that this was the slowest blues song ever recorded. "Old Jimmy done gone catatonic on this one," Lula recalled Sailor saying, as the singer slurred the line, "Little rain keep a-fallin' on this here love of mine."

She looked over her left shoulder and saw that ET was sitting with his legs folded, his fingers forming a teepee, and his eyes closed.

"He's meditatin'," Beany told her. "Says he does it twice a day. Told me while you were snoozin' that if ever'body in the world meditated at precisely the same time every day, there wouldn't be no more war."

"He might be right."

Lula reached into the back seat and picked up ET's copy of Why God Don't Need to Carry a Gun. ET did not notice since he was still in a trance.

"Listen here what it says, Beany: 'When the king of Israel was in Samaria, there was a famine and a woman said unto him, "Give thy son, that we may eat him today, and we will eat my son tomorrow." So the king gave up his son and they boiled and ate him. When on the next day the king asked the woman for her son, she hid him. The king of Israel took no vengeance upon this woman, but instead mourned the loss of his son for all to see. Do you think the king of Israel's unselfish act was an inspiration to his people, or do you think he was just stupid to have allowed the woman to trick him? Do you think the woman should have been punished for her deception? Do you believe cruelty born out of desperation is justified? If you were God, would you have acted to rectify the situation?'"

"If I was God, I wouldn'ta done nothin'," said ET, who had emerged from his trance.

"You wouldn'ta restored the king of Israel's son to life?" asked Lula.

"Nope. This way it becomes an act that nobody would forget, and the story told and re-told as it has been on down the line as a lesson of supreme generosity."

"Generosity my ass," said Beany. "Myself, I woulda had that bitch boiled and eaten."

They rode for a few minutes in silence, each absorbed by their thoughts, then Lula said, "My deceased husband, Sailor Ripley, liked to quote the dyin' words of some Spanish general: 'I do not have to forgive my enemies. I have had them all shot.'"

"That'll work," Beany said.

"Mm-mm," said ET, "maybe age got somethin' to do with how a person thinks about things."

20

I clearly can remember how I felt surrounded by Sailors big strong arms. This memory will never leave me. The three times Sail and I got back together namely after he was sprung from Pee Dee after serving his time for manslaughtering Bob Ray Lemon then when he was released after being in Huntsville following the feed store robbery in Texas and finally after we once and for always was reunited during the time Pace was kidnapped in NO on each occasion without talking when he crushed me to his chest I melted into him and no words could ever describe this peaceful feeling. Home for me was in that mans arms and I aint been home since Sailor Ripley left this planet. Now with Beany and the boy ET we are stopped at a service station in Beaufort ET is gassing up the car and Beany is in the restroom. Im looking forward to seeing Pace as I am feeling a little bit low at the moment probably because I am so used to being alone so even though I love Beany dearly and she always means well it tires me out to be so long in her company or I guess anybodys. ET aint no trouble hes just lost as are so many these days. This was true of Sailor and Pace too for some time until they both got it figured out it took a while they had to learn there aint no rules in the game of life. ET told me hes always felt like a stranger loosed upon the world unwanted sent to Switzerland and all and I said Pace and me felt that way after Sailor was taken from us so early and sudden. I quoted scripture cursed be he that perverteth the judgment of the stranger the fatherless and the widow which covers us three dont it you got to follow your heart and dont despair no matter how creepy things get. Here comes Beany.

21

"C'mon, Lula, have some fun!"

"I am havin' fun, Beany. You go on and dance, I just enjoy watchin'."

Lula, Beany, and ET were in Hollywood Del's, a nightclub on the outskirts of Savannah. Beany had been dancing with ET to Felix Mendelssohn and His Sepia Cats, a band that specialized in '60s soul music. Just now they had launched into "Shotgun," the old Junior Walker & the All-Stars tune. ET went to the bar to get himself another beer and Beany plopped down in a chair next to Lula's.

"I like they're playin' oldies, Lula, honey, 'cause I can't get into this hip rap, or rap hop, or whatever they call it. Whew! It's a wonder I can even move out there on the dance floor. You catch me tryin' to do the skate?"

Lula laughed. "You're amusin' and amazin', Beany, you truly are. Somebody'd knock into me, I'd go flyin' and end up in the hospital with a busted hip."

"Lula, I know I'm an old lady, but d'you think it'd offend ET if I asked him to go to bed with me just once?"

It took Lula a few seconds to realize that Beany was deadly serious, then she said, "Hard to say. I know the very thought kinda offends me."

"Why? I ain't expectin' a miracle, only it'd be sorta sweet to have some affection of the intimate type."

"Beany, it might could take a miracle for that boy to get an erection in your presence, and even if he did you'd break apart soon as he squeezed you."

Beany took a swig from her bottle of Pabst Blue Ribbon and shook her head. "It's embarrassin' to be horny at eighty," she said.

"Ladies, meet Jamilla."

Lula and Beany looked up to see ET with a dark-skinned young woman.

"She's from—Where is it you're from again?"

"Nazareth," said Jamilla. "That's in Israel. I'm an Arab Israeli."

"'And Joseph came and dwelt in a city called Nazareth: that it might be fulfilled which was spoken by the prophets. He shall be called a

Nazarene.' That's from Matthew, 'course. Nice to meet you, Jamilla. I'm Lula and my friend here is Beany."

Beany gave Jamilla a tiny wave. "World's oldest teenager."

"We're gonna go dance," said ET, taking the girl by the hand.

"Well, I guess that answers my question," Beany said. "Look at her, she sure is shapely. Shoot, I hate bein' ancient."

"Beany, you gotta try to get comfortable with it or you'll be miserable all the rest of your days."

"What you think of all these female teachers seducin' their boy students lately? Some are even havin' babies by 'em."

As Felix Mendelssohn and His Sepia Cats segued from "Shotgun" into "Green Onions," Lula watched Jamilla and ET take it down a notch and slither easily into scratch 'n' sniff mode.

"I don't think the world is so wild at heart any more, Beany, just weird on top. Probably each generation on its way out thinks what's come after them is missin' a bulb and dimmer for it. Then again, maybe it's just us old folks can't see so good and it hurts us to admit it."

"Lula, stop."

"Stop what?"

"Sayin' 'us old folks.' I plain can't stand it, even I know this is true."

Lula placed one of her hands over one of Beany's on the table. Tears rolled down Beany's cheeks.

"When the angels call and ask me to recall the thrill of them all, then I shall tell them I remember you."

Beany smiled and used her free hand to wipe away the tears.

"What part of the Bible's that from?" she asked.

"Ain't. It's words from an old song Mama and Dal liked."

"Thanks, baby, but it's Sailor you'll tell the angels about, not me."

Beany picked up Lula's hand and kissed it, then looked for ET and Jamilla on the dance floor. They weren't there.

22

At nine o'clock the next morning, Lula and Beany were dressed and ready to get back on the road. They had made coffee on the Mister Coffee machine in their room at The 4 Queens Motel located on the business loop of highway 95, availed themselves of four complimentary powdered doughnuts which Beany had brought back from the lobby, and dialed ET's room twice but had no answer.

"He's probably off somewheres with his Jewess. What you think, Lula?"

"She's an Arab, Beany, not a Jew. Think about what?" Lula was still sipping her second cup of watery Folger's.

"How long should we wait?"

"Hate to say it, but if ET ain't come around by the time we set to roll, he'll have to catch his self another ride."

"What I think, also."

Fifteen minutes later, as the two women were putting their bags into the Merc, the telephone rang in their room. The door was open. Lula went back in.

"Mornin', ET. Yeah, we're on the verge. Guess we could, but no longer. Glad you understand. See you shortly, then."

Beany and Lula were leaning up against the side of the car watching storm clouds form to the east when a metallic green Dodge Dart rumbled into the motel parking lot and stopped next to the Nightcat. Jamilla, wearing blue jean cutoffs clean to the bikini line and a red halter top, got out from the driver's side while ET exited the passenger side.

"Sorry I'm a little late, ladies," he said, "but Jammy and I didn't get to her crib until past four."

Beany took one look at ET and shouted, "Damn, boy! What in creation happened to you?"

With his right hand, ET gingerly fingered the blackened area around his right eye.

"Had a brief scuffle with a former suitor of Jammy's. He followed us to her place from Hollywood Del's and sucker punched me."

Jamilla had on dark glasses with fake rhinestones decorating the frames.

"He hit you, too?" Beany asked.

Jamilla just shook her head no and kept her back to the Dart.

"I'll get my pack and guitar and we can be goin'," said ET, and headed toward his motel room.

"Hope you made it worth his while," Beany said to Jamilla, who remained mute, her hands stuck in the back pockets of her shorts.

"Beany, quit," said Lula.

"You sure got pretty legs, though," Beany said.

"How do you like livin' in Savannah, Jamilla?" Lula asked. "Compared to Israel, I mean."

"They got fightin' here, too," said Beany.

Jamilla did not respond. ET came back, carrying his things, which he set down on the ground next to Lula's car. He went over to Jamilla.

"It's all good, huh, baby?" he said to her. "My eye'll be fine. I'll holler at you from Lake Charles."

ET leaned in to kiss her and Jamilla brought out a push-button stiletto from her left back pocket and shoved the blade hard into ET's abdomen. She kept her hand on it and twisted the knife before he fell, then lost her grip.

Lula and Beany could not believe this had happened. Neither of them made a sound. They stood frozen as Jamilla opened the driver's side door of her car, climbed in, started it up, threw the shiny green machine into reverse and backed away. The two women watched the Dodge Dart fishtail out of the lot and roar onto business 95, then they dropped down and kneeled on either side of ET's prostrate body. His eyes were open and his lips were still puckered up, expecting to be kissed. Lula pushed the tips of the index and middle fingers of her right hand against the carotid artery of ET's neck, held them there for a few seconds, then looked up into Beany's eyes.

"This is worse than weird," said Lula.

23

I been sitting in our room number 8 at The 4 Queens Motel just thinking about everything thats happened and listening to the radio. When I was a girl I listened a lot to the radio it seems like back then it was something more people did just sit and listen and dream and maybe there wasnt no more good news then than there is now but it didnt seem like things was moving so fast that every time a person stepped out the door the world was a different place than when you went inside. Beany has been spending time with Mr and Mrs Taylor ETs parents since they come to get their sons body and take it back to Lake Charles. I guess they are going to have the corpse shipped by railroad they cant take it in their Sedan de Ville. If this had happened to Pace when he was so young as ET I dont know what I would have done probably felt like killing myself but I wouldnt because of Sailor. We gave the Savannah police our eye-witness testimony to the murder and two days later the highway patrol spotted Jamillas car in Fernandina Beach parked at a Steak and Shake and arrested her and a forty year old man named Hamid Khartoum who told the authorities he was Jamillas fiance. This must have been the same one hit ET that night we met her at Hollywood Dels nightclub but Im not certain. Jamilla confessed to the killing her fingerprints was of course on the knife so there aint going to be a trial only a sentence which will likely be for life. Her fiance will get time for being a accessory after the fact for helping her escape. Its all too terrible and reminds me too much of the bad business in Big Tuna all the years ago. The Taylors are good people and devastated. Beany told me Jamilla her last name is Salim said she stabbed poor ET because she says he defiled her body those are the words she used. Beany knows more details but I told her honestly I dont need to hear any. The girl is crazy out of her freaking mind and this Hamid Khartoum is some moron under her thumb. A cute tune I heard on the radio a moment ago is a new version of Put Your Head On My Shoulder the old Paul Anka song done by a group called Blue Mother Tupelo its just the sweetest and sexiest record I believe Sailor would have dug it to death. The girl doing the vocal can really sing too sort of warbly she reminds me a bit of Patsy on I Fall to Pieces mixed with the way Brenda did Heart in Hand both favorites of mine and Sailors. This music is personal as opposed to that stuff could be anybody or nobody just some machine. Sailor said the record companies sometimes produce music they think will be commercial with equipment then hire people to pretend its theirs and have them on a video like actors. I want to hear a real person whispering the song in my ear. Theres the phone. It was Beany saying the police are letting us continue on our way tomorrow they have our written statements its all they need. Thank goodness we wont have to testify in a courtroom. I called Pace yesterday he answered and I told him what happened and he said he never told me but when he was married to Rhoda Gombowicz and living in New York they were attacked one night in front of their building by two men with knives took Paces wallet and Rhodas purse then one of the men stabbed Pace in his left leg on the thigh so he wouldnt run after them. Rhoda took Pace to a hospital they stitched him up and he made Rhoda promise never to tell me and Sailor so we wouldnt worry about him being in New York as if there werent no crime in New Orleans. Matthew says from the days of John the Baptist until now the kingdom of heaven suffereth violence and the violent take it by force. This is a fact of life I been touched so many times by violence what to do but bear it and bless them who are less blessed than others. Pace said to come on hes got a nice little apartment above a courtyard on Orleans Street in the Quarter for Beany and me to stay at and dont pick up no more stray boys on the road. In the newspaper Rashid Salim Jamillas daddy said she only done what was right by their law and that he would have killed ET if she had not. I wonder if Mister Salim ever seen his daughter wearing next to nothing like on the day she stuck ET.

24

"Ain't seen you so quiet since that time I visited you in the bin and you was drugged dumb."

"Tell you, Lula, God's truth, it took all my energy and more just to try accomodatin' and consolin' Duke and Lady Taylor. Their guts is twisted, their hearts are broke and their brains been blasted by a A-bomb."

Lula and Beany were near Willacoochee, Georgia, halfway between Waycross and Tifton. It was a sunny day but colder than normal, not a cloud in the sky.

"That ET's mama's name, Lady?"

"It's really Ladina but Duke calls her Lady, so ever'body else in Lake Charles does, too. Suppose when she's back in Switzerland she's called Ladina."

"Sorry I wasn't more helpful to 'em, Beany, and to you, too, but I just could barely stand it myself. I been through plenty, as you know, but the shock of seein' that girl stick ET right in front of our eyes done somethin' to me I can't rightly describe."

"Made you sick, is what it did. Sure did me. I kept up for ET's folks' sakes, is all. Horrible the way his beautiful green eyes was emptyin' out when he was on the ground, life leakin' like anti-freeze into the earth."

Lula's eyes were fixed steady on state highway 82. She felt Marietta's presence, as if her mama were sitting in the car next to her instead of Beany. Marietta wasn't such a difficult person as most people thought, Lula had decided. She just knew what she wanted and was tough-minded about it. Lula was not so tough, not like that, never had been. She wished that the murdering whore Jamilla Salim had not been wearing dark glasses when she stabbed ET. Lula thought that she would have liked to have seen her eyes at precisely the moment the blade entered ET's body. After Jamilla and Hamid had been taken into custody in Fernandina Beach, Lula had seen her on the TV news sitting in the back seat of a highway patrol car. Jamilla, still wearing dark glasses, had stuck out her tongue at the reporters and photographers and Lula remembered being stunned at how incredibly long it was, the longest tongue by far that she had ever seen.

25

The trip has pretty much been a blur since we left Savannah and now we just got to Dothan Alabama where Sailors daddy lived at one time and worked as a colporteur hawking bibles and other religious items door to door. This was before Sailor was born he told me even before his mama met his daddy. Sailor had some family in this state but he didnt keep in touch and we never visited or wrote. I always had a strong feeling for family but not Sail except for me and Pace of course and as long as he and Mama kept a decent distance from one another they was all right. Just now the song Stars Fell on Alabama come into my head the way Billie Holiday sung it with that crackly wrinkle in her voice My heart beat like a hammer my arms wound around you tight and stars fell on Alabama last night. Sailor used to say she was a sly singer knew right when to put her toe in the water. Beanys been unearthly silent until this evening when she got into it on the telephone with Hedy Lamarr seems Hedy found out her husband Delivery Music been giving free produce from his market to a 18 year old name of Jacey Spikes whos a member of their church Rock Hard Baptist shes the singer for a Christian band called Rock Hard. Delivery says there aint no hanky panky in it hes just helping out a poor girl and her family. Hedy told Beany this Jacey Spikes was responsible for their previous minister having to leave after his wife found nude pictures of Jacey on his computer she was fourteen then now shes five foot eight with platinum blonde hair and titties out to there. Beany asked Hedy if she had any proof of Delivery carrying on behind her back and Hedy said no but that this girl was such an attraction male attendance at their church gone up by more than half since Rock Hard been performing on Sundays. Some of the wives complained to the minister Reverend Swindle who Hedys convinced is a secret morphine addict has a strange close friendship with a local Doctor Caldwell but he told them the collection baskets reflect overwhelming approval of most worshippers end of discussion. Dont ride herd too close on your man Beany said to Hedy or your liable to get a horn in your leg better to let Delivery have his fantasy at his age he aint very likely to start something he most

The Imagination of the Heart

probably cant finish anyway. Out the window of our room at the Hotel Lurleen I can see smokestacks shooting shit high into the dark sky theres gold silver and other colors sparkling in the blackness its beautiful but probably are particles cause cancers lung disease and allergies. Lord it seems everywhere you look theres something to worry about I know what Sailor would say so dont look.

26

Beany had the wheel and following her conversation with Hedy Lamarr
had regained some of her energy. She was doing her best to dismiss from
her thoughts the unfortunate episode in Savannah. She and Lula were
cruising in the Merc past cottonfields on state route 84 in a steady drizzle.

"Once I saw Wilson Pickett, who for my money was the funkiest,
down and flat out dangerous-seemin' soul singer of 'em all," said Beany,
"on a TV show. He was from Alabama and had gone as a young man up
to live in Detroit, where he stayed. The interviewer asked him had he
ever been back to Alabama and Pickett got wicked on the spot, said he'd
been booked to perform in Tuscaloosa, I believe, and was on the way
there from the airport in Birmingham, but when the car started passin'
cottonfields he freaked out, told the driver to turn around and take him
back to the airport. His memories of havin' to pick cotton as a child hit
him harder than he could have imagined, he couldn't take it. 'Ninety-
nine and a half just won't do!' Pickett shouted, like in his song.
'Ninety-nine and a half won't cut it! Gotta be I'm one hundred per cent
or I'm out the game!'"

"Poor man," said Lula. "I can understand not wantin' to go back
somewhere somethin' awful happened to you. For instance, I ain't in all
this time been back to Texas, nor will I ever go."

Rain began falling harder.

"Mind if I cut on the heater?" Beany asked.

"Please do. I just felt a little shiver myself."

"That's what Wilson Pickett was doin' on that TV show, shiverin',
soon as he heard the word Alabama. It'll prob'ly happen to us now, Lula,
whenever someone says Savannah."

Lula could not help but think how beautiful the cottonfields looked
in the rain.

27

I just now switched off the TV in our room at the Chickasaw Motor-In. Beany done most of the driving today so shes been sleeping for a couple hours but Im more restless than usual. Watching and listening to the news dont help calm me it never does but I got to admit its hard not to think the world is in the worst shape probably since WW2 and no doubt worse since now with the kinds of weapons almost anyone can get their hands on it wouldnt take but a few minutes for the entire planet to explode and almost all its creatures to expire. Pace never has had no kids so I dont have any grandbabies to worry about Ive always been a little maybe sometimes more than a little sad about that but now Im thinking Im not because of how theyd have to be living in this messed up time in history. Sailor read to me once a story about how after a nuclear war the people who remain half of them live above the ground and the other half beneath in caves. The ones in the beneath who are ugly and beastly and never see the light of day control the ones above who are all beautiful cause of course they have sunlight and flowers and fresh air and eat fruit and vegetables. The beneath people are really raising the outdoors ones like cattle to eat. Whenever they need to have a feast the beneath creatures turn on a loud siren that hypnotizes the healthy outside ones who all march like zombies toward the place the loud noise is coming from its the entrance to the cave where the beast people are waiting and when enough of the healthy pretty people have gone down that day the siren stops and the cave door closes. Then the beautiful dumb ones come out of their trances and go back to their perfect seeming life like nothing is wrong and they dont miss the ones gone under to be devoured by the beneath people. In the end I think a volcano explodes and covers everything and the beneath folks are cooked below and the up top people are boiled alive by a flood of hot lava. So both groups are wiped out and thats the end of civilization. Now we got a situation where all these different countries think they got the right answer or religion including of course our own and I dont believe nobody does some are more greedy than others and more righteous but a person in a mountain hut in Asia got just as much right to their version of the way things ought to be as one in LA thinks more about her tan line than one who might be starving in a desert covered by flies in Africa. And here at home we got demented men shooting down children in schools and politicians in Washington DC supposed to be our leaders molesting boys and girls its just like Rome was in the long ago I believe. My question now is of those who will be left on this planet after the bombs and missiles go off which ones go beneath and who stays above. I know the presidents and dictators already have underground places with food and guns stashed away to go to so it aint really no big mystery who the beneath people would be. And when their food supply runs out they got the guns and going cannibal aint a stretch. I would choose to be above if I could but not if the beneath could control my mind. Its late and we want to drive from Mobile to NO tomorrow so Ill quit and try to sleep some. Maybe before everything goes forever ass over backwards as crazy old Coot Veal Sailors hunting buddy used to put it about a million years ago people everywhere will come to their senses and stop their feuding and bad behavior but I hate to say I doubt it. I think this version of civilization is already tipped over too far to get right and there aint no way in anyones heaven or hell to keep us poor fools from being ramroded down the chute. In Pauls second letter to the Thessalonians he wrote And to you who are troubled rest with us when the Lord Jesus shall be revealed from heaven with his mighty angels in flaming fire taking vengeance on them that know not God and who shall be punished with everlasting destruction. Well Im troubled but cant rightly rest believing how I do that there aint going to be no selection about who shall be destroyed.

28

Lula made sure that she and Beany got an early start the next day, which was Sunday, October eighth.

"Elmo, he was a big baseball fan," said Beany, "maybe you remember. Anyway, October the eighth is a date I can't forget 'cause it's the anniversary of the day in 1956 Don Larsen of the New York Yankees pitched the only perfect game in the history of the World Series. Elmo'd been a Yankee fan from since he was a boy and that was a big day for him. Used to he'd get in fights with kids all the time around Natchitoches, where he grew up, he told me, because of his likin' the Yankees. Most of the other kids rooted for the Saint Louis Cardinals because back then they were the only team from the South or closest to, bein' that Missouri was a border state. I never was much of a fan myself but those times I got socked away at Oriental, I used to listen to baseball games on the radio. They had it on and it soothed me some, kept me calm just to know somewhere out in the world things was just goin' on the way they was supposed to. Stan Musial would double down the right field line, the crowd would be makin' noise and there wasn't nothin' to argue about. It was just a double, and that was that."

"It was the drugs kept you calm," said Lula, "more'n the baseball."

"Combination, I guess."

Lula stayed on the old highway, keeping the Mercury in the slow lane on purpose in order to take a good look at what Katrina had done to the Mississippi Gulf Coast.

"Heard the wind was so powerful it moved the casino buildin's in Biloxi back off their foundations," said Beany.

They were cruising through Pascagoula but there wasn't much to see in the way of damage. There were plenty of trucks carrying building materials on the road, however.

"People here're pretty strong," Lula said. "I don't know how I'd do if a hurricane carried off ever'thin' I owned. Wonder could I find it in myself to tough it out or just move on, start new somewheres else."

"Hard to say."

"After Sailor was killed, I kinda felt like I didn't want or need anything. Mean I didn't much care about possessions, didn't want to look at old photos, stuff like that."

"You had Pace."

Lula nodded. "'Course, I did, and he was a big help to me, but it didn't take much for me to decide to leave New Orleans and go live with Dal. Pace took most of Sailor's stuff, sold the house and made sure all the finances was in order. Dal couldn'ta been kinder, also. I had it pretty easy, a place to go and all. Nothin' like the folks down here had to face after Katrina."

"After the big hurricane in the Florida Keys in 1935?" said Beany. "They had more'n a thousand men workin' on buildin' the highway through there and didn't get 'em out in time. Weeks and months later bodies were found hangin' from trees and in the mangroves around Islamorada. Tidal wave swamped the train sent down from Miami to evacuate everyone. Eight hundred people died."

"Storm musta been the size of Katrina," said Lula.

Now on both sides of the road from Ocean Springs to Waveland were piles of debris, and behind them what was left of the houses and buildings that had lined Highway 90.

"Wonder if the old Wildrose house in Pass Christian was destroyed," said Beany.

"You mean that giant black wooden one with the fancy wraparound porch and parapets and towers and outside staircases?"

"Yeah. The one where the little girl was kidnapped from like the Lindbergh baby."

"They found her, though, right?" said Lula. "The Wildrose girl."

"Uh huh, but practically suffocated to death in a steamer trunk on a wharf in N.O. Men who took her were arrested tryin' to get on a ship to Brazil, had the ransom money on 'em. Remember seein' a picture of the kidnappers in handcuffs next to one of nine-year-old Mabel Wildrose on the front page of the *Picayune*. Two bald guys with black mustaches wearin' bush jackets."

Suddenly the sky became smoky. Sunlight penetrated the haze in narrow shafts.

"Where's all this smoke comin' from? You see all right, Lula?"

"Must be a fire nearby. Burnin' debris, maybe."

"That girl Mabel Wildrose?" said Beany. "One who was kidnapped?"

"What about her?"

"She lived to be one hundred years old. Lived all the rest of her life in the house in Pass Christian."

"She's lucky she didn't have to live to see it smashed in the hurricane."

Beany nodded, then said, "I'm glad as blazes nobody ever took me and locked me up in a steamer trunk when I was a little girl. I'll bet Miss Wildrose never got it out of her mind for the next ninety years."

As they approached the Huey P. Long Bridge on their way into New Orleans, Lula began to cry.

"What is it, baby?" asked Beany.

"It's why I made you drive this last stretch," said Lula. "This is where Sailor met his demise, on the Old Spanish Trail."

"Oh, sweetness, of course it is. You go on and sob, then. You don't mind, though, I'll cut on OZ, get us some local sounds."

Sonny Rollins' strident tenor barked at them from the radio as Beany nosed the Nightcat onto the bridge.

"Wowee! I was expectin' Mac or Irma, not this bughouse bad boy!"

Beany switched the station and settled on the 1946 Xavier Cugat Orchestra playing "Perfidia."

"Listen to them strings, Lula. Sounds like rain slidin' down windows to the soul."

They drove without talking the rest of the way across the bridge.

As they left the river behind them, Beany asked, "What's that address Pace give you? I forgot it."

Lula struggled to regain her composure and said, "Orleans Street, number 926. Close by Burgundy, I believe."

When they got to the Quarter, Beany remarked, "Ever'thin' looks so normal. Never know there'd ever been a hurricane here."

"It's mostly everywhere else got pasted, 'specially the Lower Nine. Pace says it's a ghost town over to St. Bernard."

"Yeah, saw on CNN Fats Domino's house was submerged. The shotgun, anyway, not that motel-type structure behind."

"Heard he got rescued off the roof by a helicopter."

They were surprised to find a parking place on Orleans directly across the street from 926.

"What's the woman's name owns it?" Beany asked as they got out of the car.

Lula opened her purse and found the little piece of paper on which she'd written the information Pace had given her.

"Marnie Kowalski. Pace said she's a good lookin' little blonde, about forty. Lives in the front house and rents out two rear apartments overlook the courtyard."

"Girlfriend of his?"

"Maybe, but I don't think he's keepin' special company these days."

Lula pressed the buzzer marked Kowalski. She pressed it again thirty seconds later.

"One of you gals Pace Ripley's mama?"

Lula and Beany looked up and saw a woman's head sticking out of an upstairs window. Her hair was blonde and clipped short.

"She is," said Beany.

The head disappeared for a few seconds, then reappeared.

"Catch!" the woman said, and tossed down a key, which landed on the sidewalk.

Beany picked up the key and said to the woman, "You Marnie Kowalski?"

"Marnie as in Hitchcock and Kowalski out of Tennessee Williams. Let yourselves in. I'm buildin' a gumbo up here."

Just as Beany had turned the key in the front door lock and she and Lula were about to enter the house, someone spoke to them.

"Y'all live here?"

Beany and Lula looked around and saw a short, thin, dusty bituminous-colored girl of about twelve or thirteen wearing a red dress with white polkadots standing on the sidewalk.

"Who're you?" asked Lula.

"Eclair Feu, French for fire. Used to I lived on Mystery Street, close by Esplanade. I'm almost fourteen years old. My house was destroyed in the flood and my mama and baby sister, Byzantina, livin' now in Texas, I think."

"Don't you have any other family here?" Beany asked.

Eclair wore her hair in braids and they whipped around as she shook her head. "Naw, everyone gone or drown."

"Why didn't you go to Texas with your mama and sister?" said Lula.

"Went without me. Took 'em a bus to Houston's what I hear. Ain't heard more."

Beany and Lula looked at each other, then Beany said, "Why don't you come in with us, Eclair? We'll figure out what to do for you after while. I'm Beany Thorn and my friend here is Lula Pace Fortune Ripley."

"Miz Beany?" Eclair said. "I be hoodooed."

"What's that?" asked Lula. "What you mean?"

"Hoodoo man name Cap'n Funeste spell me, lay a curse on my head, say I be dead soon. Just gon' fall down and die."

"Why would anyone put a curse on you, Eclair?" Lula asked.

"Didn't do him right, I guess," said the girl.

"Let's go in," said Beany, "sort this out."

Eclair Feu extended her long, skinny arms to the sides, her body began to vibrate and her eyes rolled back in her head. She urinated on the sidewalk, stuck out her tongue and started to whirl. The child spun around several times before she stopped. Her eyes came back into place and stared blankly straight ahead for a few moments. Eclair then turned right and began walking rapidly away in the direction of Rampart Street.

"Eclair!" Beany shouted, but the girl kept walking.

Marnie Kowalski poked her head out of the upstairs window again.

"You ladies comin' in, or what?" she said.

"We're comin'," Beany answered.

"Like you said," Lula said to Beany, "everything looks normal."

30

I have been having some mighty disturbing dreams of late. Last night I had one where someone was following me or was with me and at first I couldnt see who it was and then it turned out to be Mamas old friend and suitor Johnnie Farragut the private detective. We were in a snowy place and I met a girl who was from Czechoslovakia she said lived with her parents in a big apartment with wind blowing through cracks in the walls and windows next to railroad tracks in a northern city. She took me to her home and Johnnie followed behind. In the dream I was much younger than I am now maybe in my 20s or 30s and Johnnie was just as he always was somewhere in between not young or old just shuffling along behind the way he did after Mama so many years. The girl wanted me to meet her parents who did not speak English they wanted me to help them they were afraid to leave the apartment. I dont know how or where I met their daughter on the street I guess. The parents were dressed like country people from the forests of Eastern Europe the mother with a big black shawl over her head and shoulders and father in a shabby gray suit jacket and pants over a stained dirty long underwear shirt he had a big mustache and four day beard. Finally I understood that they wanted me and Johnnie to take them to a boat going to Egypt but it wasnt really Egypt it was an even more ancient place Mesopotamia maybe. I wouldnt take their money it was very little anyway and Johnnie tried to explain to them we couldnt get them there. The parents got angry the woman was shouting at us and the girl said nothing so Johnnie and I had to run out of there into the snowy street. This Marnie Kowalski sure is a character as Mama would say a tough talker but a hell of a good woman I believe and Beany does too. She no sooner had gotten us fixed in the upper right rear apartment on the courtyard which is nice with a little fountain water comes out of the mouths of bluebirds than here come Pace who Marnie called right after Beany buzzed her. Hes looking good losing more hair on top and in back but in shape from working construction these last few months. Marnie and he are best buddies were lovers once upon a time and somehow come out of that with good feelings towards one another a small miracle. Sat us down to a good meal of gumbo and corn-bread. Pace had to get back to the job he and his crew are doing in Gentilly Terrace for the famous Mexican Japanese artist Arturo Okazaki y Pintura rebuilding his studio Pace said the water went up eight feet wrecked forty years of the mans work. Hard to imagine losing so much in a sudden see your whole life float away like that. Beany and I are having a rest and will see Pace later tonight. Marnie Kowalski bakes cakes for a living along with renting out her apartments. She has a tattoo of a red scorpion on the back of her left hand I asked her why a red one and she said so nobody would ever mistake her for an easy woman.

31

Lula, Beany, and Pace were in Saint Wolfgang's Lounge on Iberville Street sipping snowflake rickeys, a concoction created by Saint Wolfgang's owner, Koomgang Lee, a thirty-five-year-old North Korean defector, which combined Koomgang Lee's version of white lightning with lime and Schweppes. The North Korean proprietor, who claimed to at one time have been a commander in Kim Jong-il's supreme personal service brigade, had named his establishment Saint Wolfgang's because he had opened it on Halloween, his favorite Western holiday, which also happens to be Saint Wolfgang's Day.

"I been comin' in here regular," Pace told the women, "since I run into Marnie again. She's pals with Koomgang Lee. Baked him the first birthday cake he ever had, bittersweet chocolate, Barbancourt rum, and pineapple."

Billie Holiday singing "I Didn't Know What Time It Was" lingered in the air. Koomgang Lee, Pace explained, was besotted by American culture of the 1940s and '50s, and was a jazz fanatic. He encouraged patrons to smoke, providing gratis each table in the lounge a mahogany case containing only unfiltered cigarettes: Lucky Strikes, Pall Malls, Chesterfields, and Camels. His vision of America had been formed by the movies, the viewing of which was a secret pastime of the North Korean dictator's, and one Kim Jong-il often enjoyed sharing with his closest associates, including those preferred members of his supreme personal service.

"Koomgang told me he smuggled himself out of North Korea buried under a heap of stinking fish guts used as chum on a shark trawler. Made it across the Yellow Sea to Quingdao, China, then walked a thousand miles to Shanghai. He presented himself at the US consulate there and offered information about the North Korean nutjob leader and the North Korean military in return for a visa to the United States. Two years later he settled in New Orleans."

"Heck of a story," said Beany.

"Blessed be he that fleeth from the fear," said Lula.

"Amen," said Pace, holding up his glass.

Lula and Beany raised their glasses, too, and the trio imbibed their snowflake rickeys.

"Tomorrow I'll take you on a tour of the ghost lands," Pace told them. "That's what we've taken to callin' those parts of town mostly abandoned now."

"It makes me so sad thinkin' about all those people forced to relocate and can't get back," said Beany.

"Not much to come back to in lots of cases," said Lula.

"Read where a mess of black folks were airlifted to Utah," Beany said. "Any of 'em been heard from since?"

"I know a lot of people, white and black, don't intend on comin' back," Pace said. "Most went to Texas, Houston in particular."

Lula nodded. "We met a young girl right when we arrived told us she got separated from her mama and sister who she figures got taken to Houston."

"Crime rate there's tripled, Kinky Friedman says," said Pace. "Blames it on exiles from N.O."

"He the Jewboy run for governor of Texas?" asked Beany.

"Exactly. Had a rock group called the Texas Jewboys. Writes mysteries, too. I read a few, they aren't bad."

"Talented fella," said Lula.

"Ready for another snowflake?" Pace asked.

"Not me, son. Beany, how 'bout you?"

"Seein' as how I ain't drivin' and I'm three and three-quarters past twenty-one, why not?"

Pace was about to signal for a waitress when Koomgang Lee himself came over to their table. He shook Pace's hand.

"How remarkably gracious of you to stop in this evening, Mr. Ripley," said Koomgang Lee. "Is everything to your satisfaction?"

"Absolutely, Koomgang. I'd like you to meet my mother, Lula, and her good friend, Beany. They just come in from North Carolina."

Koomgang smiled and nodded to the women. He wore his jet black hair combed straight back and was clean-shaven except for a dyed purple soul patch. His jaguar-like smile revealed even rows of very small teeth the color of balsa wood. He was wearing a gray sharkskin suit and a silver chainmail tee shirt. A Star of David hung from a gold chain around his neck.

"So pleasing to have you here in my home," he said to them. He sat down in a chair at their table.

"Pace," said Beany, "you didn't tell us Mr. Lee was such a sharp cat. Not tall but cute as hell."

"I was savin' the best for last just for your sake, Beany," Pace said. "I gave 'em the short version of your comin' to America, Koomgang."

"I have been reborn here, as you say," said the proprietor. "Now I am doing all I can to help rebuild those parts of this city that were mutilated so severely by the flood. People here have been so good to me, I am thankful for the opportunity to return the favor."

"Koomgang brought in a group of investors from Singapore to construct a new hospital," said Pace.

"You certainly are well-spoken, Mr. Lee," said Lula. "Did you know our language before you came here?"

"I knew only Korean and Mandarin until I found passage from Shanghai to Baltimore on an Israeli merchant ship. The crew of the Altalena taught me my first words in English and in Hebrew."

"Koomgang's converted to Judaism," Pace said.

Koomgang Lee laughed gently and fingered his soul patch. "Not precisely converted," he said. "Before, I was an atheist. The only belief system permitted in North Korea is the cult of the leader, Kim Jong-il. Now I am Reform Jew."

"I tried reformin' myself many times," said Beany, "but nothin' ever took for keeps. I guess I'm doomed to die apostate."

"This word you employ—apostate—" said Koomgang Lee, "is one I do not know."

"Means I got no faith. Nothin' in particular, anyway."

"To believe in yourself and in your duty to mankind is faith enough, Mrs. Beany."

"Miss Beany to you, Mr. Lee."

Koomgang Lee smiled without showing his tiny teeth, then stood up.

"It has been a most highly remarkable pleasure to have made your acquaintances and to talk with you," he said to the ladies. "Will you be in New Orleans for long?"

"Not very, I don't think," said Lula.

"But we'll be sure to come back in here before we go," said Beany.

"Please do. Good to see you, Mr. Ripley, as always."

Pace and Koomgang Lee shook hands again before the owner moved to another table to greet his customers.

Count Basie and his orchestra played as Helen Humes sang "Between the Devil and the Deep Blue Sea."

"Maybe I will have another snowflake, son," said Lula. "I'm beginnin' to feel better about bein' back in N.O."

32

It was spooky driving around today with Pace. NO definitely aint the same place as I left it eighteen years ago. Sailors and my old house in Metairie is okay there wasnt much damage in Jefferson Parish but just about every neighborhood east got hit pretty bad except for high ground like the Quarter and the Marigny and parts of Uptown. Mounds of trash no stoplights or power drug dealers cruising around in cars Pace told me in the Lower Nine and New Orleans East dead bodies are being dumped and nobody does nothing about it. Ghost lands is a accurate description of those places. The tourist area is back up plenty of people carrying on on Bourbon so youd think nothing so terrible ever happened. When I lived here I dont think I was on that street six times in the last ten years or more. Now at Marnies Im two blocks away but still cant feature going anywhere near it other than maybe if we go to Galatoires I do miss their remoulade sauce I never tasted none better. Pace and his crew are working on Arturo Okazaki y Pinturas house and when they finish it will start repairing a restaurant out on Canal across from the high school Lee Harvey Oswald went to. Pace says there is enough work for him in and around NO to last him until he decides to retire and from what we saw of the devastation I cant disagree. Most of the workers are from Mexico not many from here which is a fact that troubles me. I would think that its the local inhabitants who could use the jobs there are plenty and the money. They cant all have gone to Houston. Marnie Kowalski has invited Beany and me to have dinner with her tonight shes cooking and wants us to meet her newest beau a movie director who is shooting a picture in Shreveport so hes only in NO on weekends. Marnie says hes famous his name is Doncovay Abidjan a half African who made a movie called Death Becomes You won prizes all over the world Marnie told us but neither Beany or me heard of it. Marnie says its about a young woman from a rich Boston family who falls in love with her husbands father whos the worlds leading expert on wasps she gets pregnant by him and they run off together to a made up South American country where he falls off a cliff trying to capture a wasp. She decides to stay there and live in this mountain village and have the child though she releases all the wasps her fatherinlaw kept to study and is stung in her eyes so she goes blind but has the baby who is a boy who grows up to become the leader of a revolution and then is president of the country. Before his mother dies she tells him her last wish is for her corpse to be thrown off the same cliff his father fell from and he honors her wish and years later she is made a saint who becomes the icon of a cult that each year several of its followers jump off this cliff to prove their devotion. Her son the president tries to break up the cult but he fails when members of the cult assassinate him and they take over the government. Beany said she didnt think shed like the movie I dont think I would either but I didnt say it to Marnie.

33

"Mama, this place out here's my own special pro bono project. Man owns it lived here thirty-nine years, lost his house and all his most prized earthly possessions but one. Wanted to show you now so when it's trans-formed into what I got in my head you'll say, 'My land, Pace Roscoe, I just wish your daddy was here to witness what a marvelous thing you gone and done.' What I love about you, Mama, nobody but you ever calls me by my forenames."

Pace and Lula were rolling in Pace's red Dodge Ram east on St. Bernard Highway. He'd picked up his mother that overcast afternoon, leaving Beany and Marnie in deep discussion about the difference between clitoral and vaginal orgasms, the latter of which the eternally inquisitive Miss Thorn, even at her advanced age, remained unconvinced were anything more than an oriental myth.

"What's this man's name whose house you're gonna build for nothin'?"

"Luther Byu-Lee, Mama. Half Vietnamese, half black. His daddy was a cook on a Chinese freighter and his mama was a dancer at Big Dorothy's Shoo-Fly Club. Remember it? On Conti?"

Lula shook her head.

"Burned down, Luther told me. Anyway, he's a musician, one of N.O.'s best. Plays a dozen instruments but mostly alto sax. His horn's all he took with him when he escaped the flood."

"Sailor Ripley was partial to Charlie Parker. Said Bird took up alto 'cause Prez and Bean had a lock on tenor."

"Didn't know Daddy paid such close attention to jazz. Always thought he was more an old rock 'n' roll and R and B man."

"Sail listened to ever'thin', Pace, even classical. In his declinin' years, he got into a Hungarian composer, said his music made him feel like cen-tipedes was slitherin' through his veins."

"Probably Bela Bartok," said Pace. "Charlie Parker liked his music, too."

Pace turned off onto a road strewn with everything from fallen trees to misshapen couches and rusted water heaters.

"Mr. Byu-Lee's meetin' us, Mama. There he is."

Seated on a wooden folding chair in the middle of a clean-swept plot of land was a large, burnt orange-colored, middle-aged man wearing a white shirt and brown slacks held up by red suspenders. He was playing a golden horn that glowed under the cloudy sky. Pace stopped his truck and cut the engine.

As they sat and listened, a nail of sunlight pierced the gray. After a minute, Lula said, "Lord in heaven, no Frenchman ever painted a prettier picture."

34

"So tell us, Mr. Abidjan," said Beany, "what's it like to hobnob with all them movie stars? Lula here had her an adventure once with a director."

"Oh, who was that?" asked Doncovay Abidjan.

"Man named Phil Reál," said Lula, "but it was ages ago."

"Of course," Abidjan said, "he made *Mumblemouth*, a classic in the horror genre."

"That was him," said Lula.

"It's a pity that he died before he could make *The Cry of the Mute*," said the director. "It is a legendary project. Those who were fortunate enough to have read the screenplay said that it was certain to have been his masterpiece."

Lula, Beany, Marnie, and Doncovay Abidjan were each on their second glass of champagne prior to having dinner in Marnie's house. Abidjan was a short, stout, coffee-colored man with heavy black-rimmed glasses and a goatee. He was wearing a bright yellow dashiki, a mauve scarf and a large pendant around his neck that represented the signs of the zodiac. Marnie Kowalski had told Lula and Beany before Abidjan arrived that he was a devout believer in astrology. "He's a Libra," Marnie had said, "he'll be nice to both of you."

"Actors are still children," the director said in answer to Beany's request. He laughed, sniffled briefly and continued, "Most of them have an emotional age of not more than fourteen, so, as a director, I treat them accordingly. I make them feel as though there is no other person on the planet who could do for me what I am asking, and sometimes this is even the truth."

"Surely not all of 'em are cases of arrested development," said Lula. "There must be some exceptions."

"There are," said Abidjan, "and those few I don't have to consider, they know what to do and how to do it. It is always a pleasure to have someone who shows up on time and has prepared him or herself sufficiently."

"Give us some examples," said Beany. "What about Eddie Epps? He's my fave these days. You ever worked with him?"

"Yes, on *Way Down in Egypt Land*."

"I saw it!" Beany said. "One where Eddie Epps is disguised as a French anthropologist but he's really Prince Balkanski of Moldavia who's kidnapped and sold into slavery to a tribe of Nomads when he's explorin' the Sahara desert."

"It was the Gobi desert, actually," said Abidjan.

"He looked wicked cute in a burnoose. I loved the scene where the teenage girl with the bee lips who's also a slave really licks his wounds with her tongue. It's somethin' people always say meanin' not actually doin' it but she does it like I never seen before. Was that your idea, Mr. Abidjan, or was it in the script?"

"As the Arabs say, it was written."

"The writer never gets enough credit," said Lula. "That's what Sailor used to say."

"It's true," Marnie added. "Doncovay says the actors think they made up their lines all by themselves."

"No," said Abidjan, "what I said is that many of them believe they are spontaneously saying these words, not inventing but being."

"What's Eddie Epps really like?" asked Beany. "Is he as smart as he is cute?"

"Eddie is a delightful boy, when he wants to be. Now that he is married and a father, he seems calmer. His days of destroying hotel rooms and punching photographers are past, I think. His biggest problem now is controlling his weight. Between films he balloons up. He is addicted to *la cuisine rapide*."

"What's that?" Lula asked.

"Fast food," said Marnie.

"I will tell you a secret," said Abidjan. "Twice Eddie has had the liposuction."

"No!" Beany yelped.

"*Mais, oui*. The first time was before *Way Down in Egypt Land*, when he was only twenty-six. *C'etait necessaire* for the very scene you mentioned, Madame Beany, of the licking of the wounds."

"My land," said Lula, "who would have thought it?"

"This kinda thing is pretty common," said Marnie. "Doncovay's told me a whole hell of a lot of really nasty stuff. Some of it's downright creepy."

"Tell us somethin' creepy," said Beany, as she helped herself to another glass of champagne.

"Not before dinner," said Lula.

"Better before than after," said Beany. "Just a quickie."

"Tell 'em about Brenda du Sossé," said Marnie. "What happened with her and Federico Cazzissimo, the Italian producer."

"Brenda du Sossé, the old model?" Beany asked. "She's on those four A.M. infomercials now hawkin' Swiss face cream supposed to contain Miura bull semen. They make a big deal out of sayin' how no bulls are harmed durin' the process of obtainin' it."

"Go on, Doncovay, tell 'em," Marnie said. "Then we'll eat."

The director took a swig of champagne, then began. "Everyone in the business knows how crazy this Cazzissimo is, how he would do anything to get what he wants. He owns television stations, newspapers, ships, everything, grocery stores in Nepal, you name it. Money means everything and nothing to him. So, when Brenda du Sossé was at the height of her fame, twenty years ago, when she was often referred to as the most beautiful woman in the world, Federico Cazzissimo pursued her tirelessly. He offered to marry her many times but she refused. She told him it was not because he was so ugly—which he still is, he resembles a buzzard with two necks—but that in order for her to have a vaginal orgasm, the man's cock must, when fully erect, to measure at least nine and one-half inches. Cazzissimo's member, apparently, while of normal proportions, fell well short of her requirement."

"Marnie," said Lula, "let me have a little bit more of that champagne."

"The Italian producer," Abidjan continued, "located an Austrian surgeon who claimed that he could construct from a cadaver a super penis and transplant it onto Federico Cazzissimo's body."

"This really happened?" asked Beany. "How could he connect the nerve endin's and everything?"

"Hush, Beany," said Lula.

"The doctor—I forget his name, he's dead now—"

"Committed suicide," said Marnie, "after he was exposed as a Nazi experimented on prisoners in concentration camps durin' World War II."

"—assured Cazzissimo that the surgery would be successful, the first of its kind. Federico promised him that if the transplant worked, he would personally endorse the procedure and make the doctor wealthy beyond his wildest dreams. Cazzissimo swore that he could arrange for the doctor to be awarded the Nobel Prize for medicine.

"The operation was performed and several months later, after, as you say, the kinks had been worked out and he was completely healed, the producer made a rendezvous with Brenda du Sossé."

"Did he produce?" asked Lula. "Sorry, I just had to say it."

"He did," said Abidjan, "but Brenda du Sossé, impressed as she must have been, insisted on measuring his member. She got down on her knees and did so. According to the tape, Cazzissimo's member in full erection came—no pun intended—to precisely eight and five-eighths inches, and she declared it insufficient for her purposes. *Quel dommage*, almost but not quite. Enraged by her rejection and seized by uncontrollable desire, Federico Cazzissimo forcibly introduced his cadaver-derived organ into Brenda du Sossé's mouth."

"And she bit it off!" Beany exclaimed.

Doncovay Abidjan nodded, and said, "Only the engorged head. He was flown as soon as possible in his private jet, with the may I say, decapitated part packed in ice, from Paris, where he and Brenda du Sossé had had their rendezvous, to the mountainside clinic in Austria, so that the surgeon could reattach it."

"Could he?" Lula asked. She felt like she had as a little girl listening to *The Wolves of Willoughby Chase* on the radio.

"Evidently, yes," said Abidjan, "but in any case that was the dénouement of Cazzissimo's quest for the favors of Brenda du Sossé. One year later, he married a Sicilian barmaid."

"Did they have children?" asked Lula.

"This is the best part," said Marnie.

"Five," said Abidjan.

"No!" gasped Beany.

"Oui," Abidjan said, "but four were by artificial insemination."

"And the other one?" Beany asked.

"Who knows?"

"You ladies are gonna love this," said Marnie, as she got up and headed for the kitchen. "I got us some mighty tasty boudin sausages for supper."

35

Lula and Marnie were sitting in Marnie's kitchen having their morning coffee and Marnie had just lit up her first American Spirit of the day when they heard Beany shout in the front room. Lula got up and went in and saw her friend hang up the telephone. There was no phone in their apartment and they had come to Marnie's, at her invitation, so that Beany could call Hedy Lamarr.

"It's Melton," said Beany, "he went postal."

Marnie came in, carrying her cup and cigarette.

"Can you spare me one of them?" Beany asked.

Marnie handed her cigarette to Beany, who accepted it and took a big drag.

"What's up?" asked Marnie.

Beany puffed away. Her eyes were full of tears that refused to fall or that she refused to allow to fall. Lula had seen her this way before, "caught between brawlin' and bawlin'," as Beany described herself when in this state.

"Somethin' happened to her grandson, Melton," Lula told Marnie.

"Not 'to,'" said Beany, "it's what he done."

Beany inhaled on Marnie's American Spirit until it was almost down to the filter. Lula and Marnie waited and watched her smoke.

"He murdered Delivery," Beany said. "Shot his own daddy with a deer rifle."

"Hell's bells!" Lula cried. "You talk to Hedy?"

"Even a child is known by his doings," said Marnie, "whether his work be pure, and whether it be right."

Beany handed what was left of the cigarette back to Marnie and said, "Hedy Lamarr says Delivery was eatin' his breakfast as usual, four eggs sunnyside up, six pieces of Canadian Bacon, and five slices of raisin walnut toast, when Melton just come marchin' out of his room bare naked, carryin' the gun. Hedy Lamarr was standin' by the stove, she says. Delivery didn't even know his son had come in until he touched the barrel end against the back of his daddy's head and pulled the trigger. Delivery's brains spewed out onto his plate, turned the eggs red."

"He didn't shoot at Hedy, did he?" asked Lula.

Beany shook her head. "Melton turned right around and walked back calmly to his bedroom and closed the door. The police just come and taken him into custody. Hedy Lamarr says he didn't give 'em no trouble. Had guns drawn and bulletproof vests on like it was Scarface they was after."

"He say anything to them?"

"Not to the cops, to his mama. As he was bein' hauled away, he said, 'As long as he is a child differeth nothin' from a servant, though he be lord of all.'"

Marnie walked out of the room. Lula went over and sat down next to Beany and held her close. Marnie came back with two more cigarettes, put both between her lips, lit them, and handed one to Beany.

"I guess we'll be movin' on to Plain Dealin' sooner than expected," Lula said to Marnie. "I'm sure Hedy Lamarr's in dire need of her mama."

"He never forgave his father for bein' a midget," said Beany. "For makin' a son who was a midget, too."

Marnie looked out the front window at the sky. Fast moving clouds headed toward the Gulf of Mexico.

"We're in for some weather," she said.

36

"Really, Lula, you don't have to cut short your visit. You ain't hardly had no time with Pace."

"I'm comin', don't argue. Pace understands, he promised he'll visit real soon. I won't let you face this mess without me."

Lula and Beany had said their goodbyes to Marnie and Pace and were sitting in Lula's Mercury Nightcat, Lula at the wheel.

"Don't think I don't appreciate it," Beany said. "If I could love you any more for it than I already do, I would. I'm sure Hedy Lamarr'll want you there. Spike Jones and Tizane Naureen drove on up together last night."

Lula started the car, made certain nobody was coming and pulled out of her parking space.

"What about Elmo?"

"Tizane Naureen called the nursin' home in Ferriday, but you know he's been gaga for the last few years. Nurse there said she'd tell him but doubted he'd understand."

"Why's he in Ferriday, anyway? Isn't that where Jerry Lee Lewis is from?"

"Yes, it is, birthplace of The Killer himself, though I believe he's lived over in Hernando, Miss'ippi, for decades. Elmo's last wife, Nefertiti Larto, was from near there. She passed last year. They'd been livin' in Sicily Island until Elmo got the Alzheimer's so fierce nobody could handle him at home."

"Life just don't quit, Miss Thorn, does it?"

"You quit life, it don't quit you, is how I see it. By the way, Spike Jones says it'll be his pleasure to carry you back to Bay St. Clement, so don't worry none on that score."

"I ain't been worryin', but thanks. How's Hedy Lamarr doin' today?"

"Holdin' steady at the moment, far's I can tell. Nothin' to be done about her husband, he's gone, so her concern's for the boy. Says their lawyer thinks there won't be no trial, just a hearin' to determine Melton's mental condition. Lawyer believes he'll be declared a deranged individual and spend the rest of his days in the bin. It ain't no fun, I know, 'cause I been more'n once, but better that than Angola. Hard cases in there'd be usin' his bones for toothpicks."

They had decided to take the interstate out of N.O. to Baton Rouge, then the 190 to highway 71, which would take them almost all the way to Plain Dealing. The last stretch, from Bossier City north on highway 3, Beany said, was no more than twenty miles.

Lula reached for the radio, then asked, "You mind?"

" 'Course not, baby."

Lula cut on the dial and there was old Jimmy Reed again, singing one of Sailor's favorite tunes, "Blue, Blue Water."

"You know I never loved before," he crooned, "and I don't want to love no more."

Lula turned to tell Beany "My feelings exactly," but her friend had fallen asleep as soon as they had turned off Elysian Fields onto the 10.

"Blue, blue water, silver moon, tell me, darlin', tell me soon," Lula sang along softly. Then she stopped singing and just listened as she drove.

37

Every time I been in Baton Rouge I recall Sailor telling me about how when he was a boy his daddy would take him to visit his grandmama and theyd spend a Sunday afternoon riding the old paddlewheeled ferryboats on the Mississippi River back and forth for hours between Baton Rouge and Port Allen eating Crackerjacks and drinking Delaware Punch. Also his daddy took him to look at the bullet holes still in the Capitol walls where the famous governor of Louisiana Huey P. Long was assassinated. He said Huey was a hero of his daddys and that if he had lived he might could have been president of the USA and changed things for the ordinary working man much better but Huey was shot down in cold blood and nobody would ever know. Beany and I have stopped at the Inn of Evangeline in Ville Platte for the night its Cajun country the people are always informal but polite which I like. Beany been more quiet than normal not talking a mile a minute the way she does. This business has hit her hard like a thief in the night snuck in and taken away her energy. All day driving I done my best to make conversation but Beanys down in the rock bottoms. We ordered in to the room from a chop suey joint rice and sweet and sour pork and snow peas but Beany only picked at it she never was too eager a eater anyway. One of the coins I got in change for the Chinese was a Indian head nickel with a buffalo on the tails side. I told Beany I had not seen one of these in so many years. When I was girl in grade school they were pretty common but by the time I was in high school they was becoming rare and I wrote a report about how it was the Indian head nickel came to be I still remember some of it. I always have thought the Indian face was very sad had hard crease lines in the right cheek and forehead it is his profile of course with only a couple of feathers not a full head dress. This coin was ordered to be made by President Teddy Roosevelt the Rough Rider he was called and the government produced them for 25 years from 1913 to 1938. This one I have is from 1937. The artist who drew it was James Earle Fraser he modeled it after three Indian chiefs they were Iron Tail a Oglala Sioux who fought beside Sitting Bull beat the pants off Custer and the 7th Cavalry at Little Big Horn and Two Moons he was a Cheyenne also was at Little Big Horn and Big Tree who was a Seneca the most famous of the three he became a movie actor his real name was Isaac Johnny John. The only movies I recall now are Drums along the Mohawk and She Wore a Yellow Ribbon the first with Henry Fonda the second with John Duke Wayne in the one with John Wayne Big Trees name was Chief Pony That Walks I always liked that name. Its wild I still can remember writing about the nickel must be 65 years ago and also the buffalo used by the artist was from the Bronx Zoo in New York and its name was Black Diamond. Looking at the Indian face now he still seems sad as hell I imagine because his land and ways of life was destroyed by the coming of the white man and the black man too. In North Carolina there is the legend of the Trail of Tears with the Cherokees Johnny Cash played one in a TV movie about it. I always have thought the Indian tribes of the Great West were the most beautiful their blankets and clothes and body decorations riding paint ponies galloping into the sundown. The white man certainly did not do them no favors did they. Im going to keep this nickel and never spend it so I can look at his sad but beautiful face whenever I want to for the rest of my life it reminds me of the girl who I was when I wrote about him.

38

"Don't believe I ever told you about this, Lula, but one time I was in Shreveport, actually stayin' over in Dixie Gardens, guess it was, Elmo Pleasant had a bit of business there, prob'ly buyin' or sellin' stolen property of some kind, as usual, and I run into a gal from Mer Rouge, over by Bastrop, name of Vahida Doblez."

"Sounds like a Mexican movie star."

Beany had awakened in better spirits and insisted on driving. They had just bypassed Alexandria and Beany had been chattering practically nonstop since breakfast.

"Her daddy hailed from around Nacimiento, Mexico, she told me, part black, part Indian, and her mama was white, from El Paso, if I recall correctly. Anyway, Vahida was a real knockout, long black hair, big dark brown eyes, fabulous figure. We was both in our early thirties then. Vahida had a bad problem, though."

"Who don't?"

"She didn't have full control of her faculties. Used to she'd pass out at the drop of a hat, any time, any place. Boom! One second she'd be standin' and carryin' on normal, next she's in a heap like a pile of rags."

"What was it? Epilepsy?"

"No, just faintin' spells. Doctors couldn't figure out why she had 'em. Sometimes she'd wake up and not know who or where she was."

"Amnesia."

"Said her mem'ry'd disappear for hours, even days."

"How'd you meet her?"

"We was stayin' at the same motel, hangin' out by the pool with our kids. She had one, I already had Hedy Lamarr. Her old man was in plumbin' parts. Vahida and I hit it off and we went together one evenin' into Shreveport, left the children with their daddies. Had us a few cocktails in a nice restaurant, sittin' at the bar makin' girl talk, when a couple swingin' dicks in suits begin hittin' on us, 'specially on Vahida. I was polite and all but didn't need no more company, made that clear. Vahida Doblez, though, didn't mind the attention at all. She had on a tight-fittin', strapless, tangerine-colored dress didn't leave a whole lot to any man's imagination. Recall I tried to get her to leave but Vahida let the men buy us another round or two. She drank Maker's Mark, on the rocks, nothin' fancy. I knew if we kept on we'd be cruisin' for a bruisin' but Vahida was drivin'. Only way out of it for me was to take a cab. I didn't want to leave her there with those two guys. Said they was pharmaceutical salesmen from Wichita, someplace like that. I'd told Elmo we wouldn't be late and Vahida said for me to go on, she'd be along soon."

"Don't tell me. You left her and she passed out."

Beany nodded. "That's what Vahida said two days later when the New Orleans police contacted her husband, whose name I forget. He and their little boy were still at the motel, tryin' to find out what happened to her."

It started to rain again, so the women rolled up the windows and Lula turned on the air-conditioning.

"Them big black cumulo-nimbus clouds're guardin' heaven's gate like Nubian eunuchs blockin' the door to Cleopatra's boudoir," said Beany.

"What did happen?" Lula asked.

"Manager of the Monteleone Hotel called the cops when a maid found Vahida unconscious and naked in a bathtub half-filled with dirty water. She didn't remember nothin', of course, once the hotel doctor revived her. Vahida's purse and clothes was there but no men. Night clerk said she'd come in with a man who'd apparently given a false name and address and paid for the room with cash in advance. Her car was found right where we'd left it, in the parking lot of the restaurant in Shreveport.

"How'd you find out?"

"Had her home number in Mer Rouge. Got hold of her husband there about a week later. He had the red-ass at me for abandonin' Vahida, as he called it, but turned out she was unharmed, except for the tattoo."

"Now there's a detail," said Lula. "Vahida's husband tell you this?"

"No, she did when I spoke to her the day after I talked to him."

"What was it?"

"Three letters: A, G, and M, inside a heart."

"Man's initials, prob'ly."

"Most likely, but it weren't the tattoo so much upset her husband, it was the location."

There was a thunderclap, then Beany said, "It was smack on Vahida's butt."

Lula clucked her tongue. "How much longer their marriage last?"

"Don't know, never spoke to Vahida Doblez again. She said she'd call back but she didn't, so I let it be."

"Couldn'ta been a happy husband havin' to look at another man's initials on his wife's ass every night."

"A stranger's at that."

Rain came down harder and Beany switched the wipers to high.

"Stop up at the next exit, Beany, will you? Water streamin' down like this always makes me want to pee."

39

Tizane Naureen and Spike Jones are real good kids they been regular to see Melton in the hoosegow and the situation pretty much seems to be as Beany been told looks like a verdict of insane will keep Melton in a institution for the criminal insane the duration of his days. Hedy Lamarr wont never be entirely all right again I dont guess but she and Beany is close now its a big help they werent always on such good terms. I was sorry to have to leave Pace so sudden but Beany needed me and there werent no question about it. Maybe instead of going straight to Bay St. Clement Ill ask Spike Jones to accompany me back to NO or Ill tell Pace to come visit here so he wont have to make a long trip to North Carolina and take more time away from his construction work. I been thinking on this business of fathers and sons and why Melton felt he needed to murder his own daddy. Beany says when she visited Melton at the jail he was real calm and didnt seem sad or happy just peaceful. I asked Hedy Lamarr if her boy been drugged stupid to keep him under control and she said she didnt think so as he had not given the authorities any trouble at all since they took him away. Pace and Sailor always got along good even when Pace got into trouble I think because Sail himself had hard times coming up and then later of course so he tried to keep things together for our family and he did he took care of us. Sailor and Pace never known I found out about the time Pace hooked up with them two nasty Rattler brothers when he was sixteen and got involved in a robbery and then those boys were killed over in Mississippi and Sailor had to rescue his son while I was away in Rock Hill with the church of the three Rs when Reverend Goodin Plenty was shot to death in front of my eyes. I never have said a word to Pace in all this time and wont ever and not to Sail while he was alive that was their trial by fire not mine. As John says the father loveth the son and hath given all things into his hand. I know how very much Sailor loved Pace and did his best to keep him right. Despite its terrible what Melton done to his daddy the pain of the son hath delivered Delivery from the burden of Babylon. I remember when I was nine or ten years old hearing about a orphanage fire in a big city up north where the children were crowded on the stairs trying to get out of the building when the staircase collapsed and all of the children were crushed and burnt up. The staircase made of cement was not strong enough to support the weight of those kids it was supposed to be but wasnt built properly the construction company had cheated on the grade of cement or something to save money the result being those orphans were killed. I thought how lucky I was to not be an orphan have to get trapped in a fire like that. Jesus said suffer little children and forbid them not to come unto me for such is the kingdom of heaven. What about a forever boy like Melton not right in his brain what happens to him? I am ready for an answer why theres endless madness and suffering on the planet all I know is everything been out of control from the beginning.

40

Beany and Hedy Lamarr were on their way back to the house after visiting Melton when Hedy's cell phone rang. She was driving but took the call anyway.

"Hedy Lamarr here. Oh, hi, Spike, we're just now startin' home. What? That can't be! Oh, Lord, give us strength. Of course, Mama and I'll head there right now."

Hedy Lamarr ended the call and moved her Durango over into the far right lane, then turned right onto Confederate Highway.

"What're you doin', darlin'?" asked Beany. "You need to make a stop?"

"Yes, Mama. I got to tell you this, so be calm, okay?"

"Now that you got me nervous, I'll do my best. What is it?"

"Lula's in the hospital. She's breathin' but won't wake up. Tizane Naureen and Spike Jones are with her at Marshall Clements Memorial. We'll be there in ten minutes."

Beany sat perfectly still and stared straight ahead. She did not want to believe what her daughter had just told her. Beany wanted to go back in time fifty-seven seconds to before Spike Jones had called his mother. The thought of Lula passing away was not one for which Beany was prepared.

"Kids say doctor told 'em it's possible Lula had a stroke while she was nappin', now she's in a coma."

"Anybody call Pace?"

"I don't know, Mama. We can do it from Marshall Clements."

The image of Lula Pace Fortune at twenty popped into Beany's head. The night before Sailor Ripley was released from prison for killing Bob Ray Lemon, she and Lula had gone to the Raindrop Club in Cape Fear to talk and try to soothe Lula's nerves; Lula did not know what to expect when she picked up Sailor the next morning at Pee Dee. Lula had long, wavy, black hair then, and her big gray eyes made a person staring into them think of a midsummer's day sky just before rain. Now those cool, late afternoon eyes were closed, possibly for keeps, and the thought gave Beany the shivers.

Hedy Lamarr said, "Spike Jones told me his shrink, Ramar Rabinowitz, who's half-Jew and half-Pakistani, says Tibetans believe if a sick or hurt person lives or dies, it don't matter, they're both good."

A gigantic bug banged against the windshield, leaving a greenish-yellow squish mark directly in Beany's line of vision, but neither she nor Hedy Lamarr said another word until they arrived at the hospital.

41

Sailor took Lula's hand in his.

"Thanks for waitin', Sail," Lula said.

"Peanut," said Sailor, "don't give it another thought."

CODA

Dear Pace,

    As upsetting as it is we got no choice but to accept the fact of your Mamas passing. I am not certain she is in a better place this is only my thought not based on nothing but face it there aint nothing can be proved even by science concerning an afterlife. I heard today on the radio that astronomers have dug up a old idea of Albert Einsteins called dark energy they now believe might be true after all even though Einstein had decided it was his biggest mistake. This is a force in space he figured was a ugly form of gravity he named a cosmological constant to explain a balance between the expansion of the universe and how certain stars are yanking on everything causing all there is around us to expand and dark energy is this invisible force. Believe it or not Pace I always was interested in this type of thinking as I never have believed in God creating it all. I mean there has to be a better answer thats too easy as is the big bang. Lula was my dearest friend more than a sister for almost all our lives and I considered her a powerful force of love which is the biggest mystery after all how she could keep on the way she did being good and thoughtful of others without getting fooled too much. Now the dark energy come pulled her away from us and I dont mean Satan who is only an excuse exists in stupid peoples minds. Lulas soul is swirling in space part of the expansion of the universe which is bigger for her having been and being.

    Love you,
    Beany

It is . . . a prayer for the wild at heart.
—Tennessee Williams

ABOUT THE AUTHOR

Barry Gifford's fiction, nonfiction, and poetry have been published in twenty-eight languages. His novel *Night People* was awarded the Premio Brancati, established in Italy by Pier Paolo Pasolini and Alberto Moravia, and he has been the recipient of awards from PEN, the National Endowment for the Arts, the American Library Association, the Writers Guild of America, and the Christopher Isherwood Foundation. His books *Sailor's Holiday* and *The Phantom Father* were each named Notable Book of the Year by the *New York Times*, and his book *Wyoming* was named a Novel of the Year by the *Los Angeles Times*. He has also written librettos for operas by the composers Tōru Takemitsu, Ichiro Nodaira, and Olga Neuwirth. Gifford's work has appeared in many publications, including *The New Yorker, Punch, Esquire, La Nouvelle Revue Française, El País, La Repubblica, Rolling Stone, Brick, Film Comment, Projections,* and the *New York Times*. His film credits include *Wild at Heart, Perdita Durango, Lost Highway, City of Ghosts,* and *The Phantom Father*. He lives in the San Francisco Bay Area. For more information, visit www.BarryGifford.com.